BROTHER

BROTHER

James Fredericks

BASCOM HILL
PUBLISHING GROUP

Bascom Hill Publishing Group
212 3rd Avenue North, Suite 570
Minneapolis, MN 55401
612.455.2293
www.bascomhillpublishing.com

ISBN - 978-0-9802455-6-1
ISBN - 0-9802455-6-7
LCCN - 2008924871

BASCOM HILL
PUBLISHING GROUP

Cover design by Janet Fredericks Winters

Order Fulfilment Center:
Blu Sky Media Group, Inc.
P.O. Box 10069
Murfreesboro, TN 37129
Toll Free: 1-888-448-BSMG (2764)
Phone: 615-995-7072
Fax: 615-217-3088
E-Mail: info@bluskymediagroup.com

Printed in the United States of America

ACKNOWLEDGEMENTS

This is a work of fiction. That means I made most of this stuff up. And while the blame is all mine for any errors, factual or otherwise, I owe thanks to a number of people who contributed their expertise, offered good suggestions, or provided encouragement or support.

To the amazingly talented writer Ellen Akins, for her suggestions, encouragement, time, and so much more. Check out her work, including *Home Movie*, and *Hometown Brew*. You're in for a treat.

To my friends at Fairleigh Dickinson University, who read early drafts and contributed their comments and ideas. Thanks in particular to Martin Donoff, Tom Kennedy, Rene Steinke, and Walt Cummins. All far better writers than I can ever aspire to be.

To Ken Bell, for my money, the top trial lawyer in the country. Any errors of a legal nature in this book were made for the purposes of advancing the story, and over Ken's expressions of abject horror.

To my sister Janet, for her incredible creativity, and for always believing in me.

To Rick, Bill, Ken, Scott, Ron, and Eric, who taught me the true meaning of the word Brother.

To my amazing, and wonderfully supportive family for your continued love and encouragement.

And to my best friend, and the love of my life. You're the only reason I was able to do this. Thanks, Sweetheart.

BROTHER

PROLOGUE

Two men came into his room in the middle of the night. He heard them open the door and enter, counted steps, six, seven, eight, two sets of them, approaching his bed, heard the gurney screech across the floor, its wheels clicking rhythmically as it rolled. Though his eyes were open, the dark and the dilation of his pupils kept him from seeing more than the vague shadows of the men, but his hearing remained acute.

They picked him up, banging his head on the bed rail, laughed, and placed him on the gurney. He resumed his counting, kept his focus. Counting kept him from giving in to the pain. Breathing deeply in and out, he counted as they moved him out of the room and rolled him down the hallway. Thirty-two steps to the elevator.

The doors slid open; one of the men walked off, leaving him alone in the elevator with the other. His chest rose and fell, breaths in a deep cadence. Wriggling his fingers, he found he still retained some agility in his right hand. He kept it still, carefully testing the muscles on the rest of his body. Some feeling in his calves, the soles of his feet. His neck as well, surprisingly. Twelve deep breaths as the elevator descended, then came to a quiet halt.

"Fun in store for you tonight," the man laughed. "Wish I could stand around and watch." The same voice he'd heard for the past week, since the new doctor came. Since the new treatments began. He'd remember it. "Although I still prefer the old fashion way—pliers, a good hammer or a crow bar." The man gripped him by the arm, the spot where the IV had been, causing some pain, but minor in comparison to the constant throbbing throughout his body.

Twenty-two steps down a corridor, the echoes of the steps and the gurney reminding him of the sounds of a carnival ride he'd ridden once—what was it called, The Tower of Doom? Another set of doors opened. The big room, judging by the change in the echo. He heard another voice. The doctor. Through the course of his time in the Institute, there had been many. He thought of them all as "the doctor." This one was different, though. This one loved to talk.

"Good evening, Mr. Riordan," he said, casually as to a friend. "That will be all, Roy."

He felt the cold steel on his back, a sign of returning sensation, but a sign also of more pain to come. Bracing himself, he tried to close his eyes, but his eyelids refused to respond to the commands of his brain. A bright light appeared overhead, shining directly down on his face. Wanting to blink, he felt the burn, saw only the light. And heard the voice.

"Your muscles should all be nice and relaxed, but just in case I'm going to give you a nice shot to make sure you don't… twitch inappropriately as we continue your treatment."

He felt a sharp pinch in his left arm, thought he felt the drug enter his system, spread throughout his body to his joints. Felt a warmth come over him. He fought against it, focusing on his breathing, but he had to struggle now to breathe evenly, the drug affecting his lungs and the muscles in his chest.

"That's it, breathe in and out. That should be all you're able to do. Now tonight, we're going to try something different. Your treatment has been progressing very well, but there's always room for improvement." The lights switched off. "Sensory deprivation has proven to be a very effective technique, especially when combined with some… nuances I've added."

He felt the gurney move again, the sounds of the wheels muffled. The wheel brakes were engaged, bringing him to a sudden halt.

"You're in a chamber of my own design," the doctor said. "A kind of coffin, modified to fit the table you're lying on. When I close the doors, the chamber will be completely soundproof. But don't worry, there's sufficient air to last for the duration of our session." The voice seemed to come from a distance. "Then I'll add stimuli, as appropriate, while I monitor your vital signs from the other room. I think you'll find this quite enjoyable." The doctor barked a short laugh. "Well, perhaps not enjoyable, but definitely… interesting. You see, while pain is an effective treatment in certain cases, your ability to withstand it has interfered with our ability to move on to the next level. The chamber here allows that pain to be amplified, as there will be no other sensations to block it out. Only the pain. I think in time you'll even come to welcome it. You'll need it, need the stimulation."

The door closed, like the sound of an airplane door sealing shut. His eyes saw only darkness and his ears strained to hear the sound of his own breathing, but failed. Dampening waves of some kind? Struggling to keep counting, keep focused, he sought again to test his limbs and his muscles. Thought he might be moving his left big toe, but couldn't be sure. His back could still feel the cold, hard surface beneath him. Focusing on the sensation of cold, he recalled falling on the ice when he'd gone skating as a child. His brother had laughed, but had pulled him up, then skated off down the ice, effortlessly as he did everything else.

"Now, Mr. Riordan, we begin Phase Two of our treatment." The voice sounded from within the chamber, surrounding him. "I hope you won't mind the absence of my voice. In its place though, you'll find something far more effective." A high piercing noise sounded in the chamber, rising in pitch and intensity, piercing his ears, his brain, filling his head. Unable to hold his ears, unable to grit his teeth, he was engulfed by the sound, all thought forced from him.

After an interminable time, it stopped.

"That was all of two seconds," the doctor said. "The effectiveness of this treatment comes from the dependability of the sounds and sensations you'll experience in the chamber. Or I should say, the lack of dependability. You may try to anticipate the next sound, try to steel yourself for it, but I assure you, the sounds will be entirely at random. Both in terms of duration and frequency."

Silence again. He tried to make his own sounds, tried to scratch against the table top with his fingernails, but again, he couldn't be sure of his own senses. Did he feel anything? Did he hear anything? The next time the sound came, even though anticipated, it startled him, interrupting his attempts to feel, to count. He needed to find another focus, another control point. He was the last of his unit. He owed it to the rest of them to survive.

The sensation in his fingertips brought to mind his early days at the piano, practicing his scales and doing exercises to build agility. He'd rediscovered the use of his fingers days before, and had held off testing it in anyone's presence, scratching against the sheets under the covers at night. It had been years since he'd played a piano and the calluses he'd built up on his fingers, on the edges of his hands, made it feel unfamiliar. But muscle memory prevailed, and his fingers knew what his brain no longer did. And the fingers now somehow stirred muscles in his forearm. He heard the music in his head.

Suddenly he was on a stage, wearing a tuxedo, too small for him, but the best his mother could find. He walked out to the beautiful ebony Steinway grand and sat down. Looked out on the crowd of people who'd come to hear him play. Saw his mother sitting in the front row, her face beaming. He looked down at his hands and saw, not the hands of an eighteen-year-old boy, but the calloused and battle-scarred hands of a thirty-eight year-old man. A noise came from the back of the stage, a buzzing sound of some kind, but he focused on the crowd, his mother, and the piano in front of him. He tried a few keys, surprised at the beautiful notes they produced. An orchestra appeared behind him, the violins tuning their strings and the woodwinds blowing a few notes in response. The conductor emerged, looking at him, his baton raised.

He nodded back and the concert began. The notes came to him, flowing through his fingers. They flew across the keyboard, following the rhythmic movement of the conductor's baton. He played Brahms, Tchaikovsky, Mozart, Rachmaninoff. The music filled his head, filled the hall. He gloried in the melding of the sounds he produced on the piano with the musical harmonies of the orchestra.

The concert hall filled with light; the players and audience disappeared, the piano faded away, his tuxedo fell away from him. He lay on a steel gurney, in the middle of a large room, the doctor looming over him.

"I hope that wasn't too painful, Mr. Riordan," the doctor said, not unkindly. "Soon we'll talk. Perhaps you'll be a bit more amenable to our discussion. Your government has a lot invested in you. It would be a shame to see it all wasted." The gurney began to move again. "Roy will see you back to your room. Until tomorrow."

He felt the lurching motion as he began to move, again heard the change in pitch of the echoes as the gurney rolled to the elevator. No longer counting his breaths, or the steps, he felt his fingers, felt his arms. Felt the music. Survival was no longer his only goal; a new thought came to him, one he savored during the remaining twilight hours.

A mystic bond of brotherhood makes all men one.
~Thomas Carlyle (1795-1881)

ONE

On the opening day of the trial two men sat opposite one another in Conference Room D of the Piedmont County Courthouse.

"Death, bringing forth life," said the older of the two, former mayor Rufus Agnew. "Just look outside. You ever seen such a bustle in this city?"

Chase Riordan looked over his shoulder out the window. Media trucks bristling with antennae lined the block, traffic had come to a standstill, and the courtyard filled with people in suits, making their way like ants. He was reminded of a quote from Karl Wallenda, the tightrope walker. *Walking the tightrope was living. Everything else was just waiting.* He felt the same about trials. They connected all the other events of his life over the past fourteen years.

"It's a big trial," he said.

Agnew guffawed. "You have the gift of understatement. I'll hope for greater eloquence in the courtroom. When's the last time you saw the national television networks in Piedmont? And the newspapers? We have *The New York Times, The Washington Post,* hell, even the *Seattle Post-Intelligencer.* What's so goddamned interesting to all of them? A girl, a beautiful young woman really, dies. A tragedy, a great sadness. And from that comes this circus. Everyone within three time zones trampling down the grass of the city in their hurry to witness the drama, revel in the aftermath. They don't care about Katarina. They want blood." He spat into a coffee cup.

"They want to see a great man fall," Chase said.

Agnew unwrapped a cigar from his breast pocket, held it under his nose, took a deep breath, and put the end in his mouth. He shook his head, brow wrinkling.

"I'm seventy-two years old. My best days are long behind me. Where's the drama in that?"

"Who said I was talking about you?" Chase said.

Agnew snorted. "You know, I swear I will gain greater satisfaction seeing that man lose than I will from being found not guilty."

Chase smiled. "Somehow I suspect not going to jail might have greater long-term rewards."

"Just barely."

"Fortunately, the two aren't mutually exclusive." He looked at his watch. Already ten minutes past nine. The courts weren't prepared for such a spectacle.

"Is he here for you or me, do you think?"

"Pardon?"

"Wall," Agnew said. "He hasn't set foot in a courtroom in ten years, easy. Yet here he is, acting like the prodigal son returning. Who does he hate more, you or me?"

Chase shrugged. "No clue. But it's definitely personal for him, which should be to our advantage. He was a good trial lawyer once, though. Taught me a lot when I first started out. We shouldn't underestimate him."

"I stopped underestimating people when my first wife cleaned out my bank account and hauled away all our furniture while I was still at the office," Agnew mused. "She had spunk, Gladys did. I miss that old gal sometimes."

The two sat companionably for a few moments, more

like old friends at a bar than attorney and client. Chase remembered their first meeting, almost a year earlier.

Agnew had made headlines when the police discovered Katarina Volkova in her condo with her throat slashed. An incriminating string of threatening e-mails sent to the ex-mayor suggested a romantic relationship that had gone wrong, and made him the prime suspect in the case. Other evidence tied Agnew to the condo and to the young woman. With the discovery of a calendar entry for that night, "Katya," and no verifiable alibi, the police had been emboldened to make the arrest. Chase had been surprised when Agnew walked into his office to discuss representing him. Despite his recent successes he assumed the mayor would seek one of the heavy hitters from Raleigh. He said as much.

"Well son, I know all the locals. Hell, I know all the folks in Atlanta as well. But there's something else going on in this case. Something that doesn't smell quite right." The mayor acted the part of the old plantation owner, complete with unlit cigar, wavy white hair, and seersucker suit. But his demeanor disguised a shrewd intelligence his detractors and opponents overlooked at their peril.

Agnew stopped to chew the end of his cigar, leaned back in the cheap leather chair opposite Chase's desk, and took in the surroundings.

"Yes, son, there are plenty of lawyers out here who would love to defend old Rufus. But they'd be doing it for the wrong reasons. They'd be doing it for the attention, for the money. I've had my enemies, Chase. You can't be a politician without collecting your share. And some of the criticism I've taken, I've deserved. But I am not a murderer. During my tenure as mayor here, I ruffled some feathers. Many of them in the police department. I've also," the mayor continued, "had my run-ins with the D.A.'s Office." His mouth curled up at one corner as he looked directly at Chase.

The deck is stacked pretty strongly against me in this one. I need someone whose motivation is a bit more, shall we say, personal." The mayor sat back in the chair, stared at his cigar for a few moments, and then looked up at Chase. "Not to mention you're on a bit of a winning streak." He smiled.

The circumstances under which Chase left the D.A.'s Office hadn't been exactly hushed up. Two successful murder defenses in two years hadn't exactly improved his relationship with his former boss.

"You're not exactly a friend of our district attorney, I take it," Chase said dryly.

"Son, I wouldn't give that man a shot of bourbon if he were buried up to his neck in the desert. I know his character. He never forgave me for supporting Loren Morgan a few years back. Took every chance he could to try and stab me in the back. He set up a task force to investigate the mayor's office a number of years back. Can you imagine? Now don't get me wrong. I've followed your career. I know for a fact you're one helluva good lawyer. Saw you in court a few times. But I also saw you play ball, son, and when you played… Lord, I could swear you would die out there before you ever gave up. I watched you play against Carolina your junior year."

Not surprising, Chase supposed, since the mayor was a distinguished graduate of the University of North Carolina.

"Little Winfield College, playing the mighty Tar Heels, on our home court, no less." Agnew continued. "At the time, I believe we were ranked number four in the country. We were up twenty-four points going into the last ten minutes. Everyone in the building knew that game was over. The coaches, the fans, all the players. Except one. The way you played those last ten minutes, you'd have thought they were trying to steal away your first-born child."

Chase did not have very fond memories of that game. His team had still lost, albeit by only four points. He had scored thirty-eight points in the second half, fifty-three for the game. Not enough.

"That's the kind of mentality I want working for me," the mayor said. "Someone for whom the game is never over.

And someone who may hate Ken Wall more than I do."

The bailiff interrupted his reverie.

"It's time, Mayor, Mr. Riordan." He escorted them down the hall, through the crowds vying for a glimpse, and into the courtroom.

"THIS IS A FAIRLY SIMPLE CASE," the district attorney began, slowly getting up from his chair, "despite what my distinguished adversary will have you believe."

Chase, sitting at the defense table with his client, stifled a grin. He admired his opponent's ability to make the word "distinguished" sound like the worst kind of insult.

"You've read about cases like this before, or seen them on TV." Ken Wall crossed the courtroom to stand directly in front of the jury.

Chase recognized the grey suit. His former boss favored Zegna or Ralph Lauren, but the trusty old grey flannel three-piece suit had been his trademark when he'd first started out as a prosecutor. Made him look folksy. He'd put on a few pounds since then, though, and it looked like the suit might burst open if he ate something. His words were measured, delivered softly, forcing a hush on the crowded courtroom as they all strained to hear. An old prosecutor's trick.

"Powerful man keeps a mistress. Mistress threatens to tell his wife, wants money. Powerful man kills mistress to keep her quiet, to protect himself." He ticked off each point on his fingers. "It's as simple as that. You know the story." Walking over to the prosecutor's table, Wall picked up a photograph. "Katarina Volkova was a beautiful woman. You've all seen pictures of her in the newspapers. Of course, more recent pictures of her are a bit more gruesome, given the circumstances of her murder."

"Objection." Chase stood, glad for the opportunity to break his opponent's stride. "Argument."

Before the judge could speak, Wall held up his hand. "I apologize, your Honor. I confess to being a bit rusty. It's been a few years since I've been in the courtroom." The judge, the Honorable Helen Moody, nodded deferentially.

Slick, Chase thought. *He's been the district attorney for fifteen years, has been in the courtroom hundreds of times over his career, and manages to score sympathy points from the judge and jury.* He glanced over at his client. Rufus had his eyes fixed on the photograph, still in Wall's hand.

"Rufus Agnew is the former mayor of the City of Piedmont. He's lived in this city a long time, done a lot of good things, and has a distinguished record of service. No one denies that. He and I didn't share the same politics, but we worked together effectively and respected one another."

Bullshit, Chase thought, feeling his client bristle beside him.

"But that should not get in the way of your duty. Good men turn bad. Good men do bad things, make bad choices, commit heinous acts, even. Rufus Agnew is a man of power. A wealthy man. A former mayor, now a member of a large law firm in town. Katarina Volkova and Rufus Agnew; they are the only two players in this drama. The man of power and the mistress."

Chase rose again. "Again, your Honor, assumes facts not in evidence. Argument as well."

"Sustained," the judge said. She looked at Wall. "Ms. Volkova is the murder victim. Her relationship to the accused has yet to be proved, Mr. Wall."

"Of course, your Honor, of course. Again, my apologies. Let me keep this short. We're all going to be together for a couple weeks and I'm sure the last thing you want to do is listen to me go on and on. Katarina Volkova, the murder victim, and Rufus Agnew, the accused. Over the next few days, we're going to prove to you that Katarina Volkova had a relationship with the accused. And when she threatened to reveal the nature of that relationship, Mr. Agnew killed her. I've talked about motive. We'll also show that Mr. Agnew had both the opportunity and the means to kill Ms. Volkova. As I said, a very simple case. When we finish here, I hope you will not have found yourselves greatly inconvenienced, and I'm sure you will find the accused guilty as charged of the murder of Katarina Volkova." The district attorney thanked the jurors for their attention, bowed his head, and returned to his seat. Whispers filled the courtroom until the judge banged her gavel.

"Mr. Riordan, opening comments?"

Chase nodded at the judge, then gauged the jury. They had responded well to Wall's grandfatherly approach and now regarded him and his client with suspicion. He didn't blame them. The newspapers hadn't been kind to the ex-mayor over the past year. His own victory in the Tierney case was old news. He faced an uphill battle, but not an insurmountable one. While he still felt uncomfortable at the defense table, the courtroom itself had the feel of home. The atmosphere, the furniture, the people – all familiar. He stood.

"Mr. Wall talked about TV. We all watch crime dramas, police procedurals. They're on all the networks. As a result, you, ladies and gentlemen of the jury, may be more familiar with the process of an investigation and a trial than any jurors in history. But those are TV trials, TV investigations. No matter how realistic, they're not real. And to go back a TV generation, I'm not Perry Mason," he said. "I'm not Matlock either, although my client may bear some resemblance to him." A few smiles. "The real killer isn't sitting in this courtroom, waiting for me to reveal him or her." Chase stayed in place behind the table; he didn't want to appear threatening. He wanted to gain their trust over the course of the trial, earn the right to approach.

"I repeat. The real killer isn't sitting in this courtroom. Rufus Agnew did not kill Katarina Volkova. Of course, I'm Mayor Agnew's attorney and you'd expect me to say that. I don't expect you to take this on faith." He smiled. A woman in the back row of the jury box smiled with him. The hair on the back of his neck stood up, and he turned to face the spectators. Noticing nothing out of the ordinary, he quickly regained his composure.

"A trial in real life is very different than a trial on television. On TV, the whole trial has to be wrapped up inside of an hour. It's not enough to prove the killer didn't do it; the defense attorney needs to show everyone who the real killer is, what 'really happened.' It winds up the story nicely. This trial will not end this way. I won't be pointing a finger at someone in the courtroom, declaring, 'There's the real killer.' No one will leap out of his seat and be arrested, and the judge won't order my client released. That would be nice. But it won't happen. The only thing I can promise you is this: at the end of this trial, you will have absolutely no idea who killed Katarina Volkova. That may sound like a frustrating conclusion, especially given the time you're all taking from your lives to sit here, but it's an important conclusion for my client. It's a conclusion that will mean Mayor Agnew will be found not guilty and will be free to resume his life.

"Mr. Wall and I used to agree on many things. If you have read the newspapers you know that I used to work for him. For the City of Piedmont. Lately it seems we don't agree on much of anything." A couple of the jurors chuckled.

"But we do agree on one thing in this case. You heard Mr. Wall a few minutes ago telling you this is a simple case. He intimated I would try to make this very complicated. Throw up smokescreens, perhaps. In fact I agree with Mr. Wall completely. This is a simple case. Someone killed Katarina Volkova. At the conclusion of this trial, you will believe that someone was not Rufus Agnew. Thank you."

He sat down and looked at the note scribbled by his client. *Game on.* Nodding, he had a moment to reflect on his earlier discomfort. *The real killer is not in this courtroom,* he'd said.

The judge called a fifteen-minute recess to allow the reporters time to make their initial filings, and the silent courtroom erupted. Doors burst open, people flew from their seats, and everyone started talking at once. It startled Chase, as it always did. He looked over at the prosecutor's table, and found Wall staring coldly at him. Caught, the D.A. turned away, shuffling some papers on the table in front of him.

As he scanned the exiting crowd, Chase pondered the question Agnew had posed in the conference room. *Who's he here for?* When the mayor had first been arrested, Wall had made a big show of appearing at the arraignment, his face red, his voice rasping, vowing he'd see justice done. At the time, Chase had thought the case resurrected thoughts of his daughter Abby's death. She and Katarina had been the same age when they died and even resembled one another. He'd expected Wall to calm down after a while and assign the case to one of his top prosecutors. Yet here he stood, a year later, lead prosecutor. Patrice Vasquez, who'd once worked for Chase, sat beside Wall. She looked at him, the softness of her eyes in stark contrast to the steely squint of her boss. When Abby had died, she'd been the only one who stood by him, risking Wall's wrath. Chase nodded at her. Behind her sat Ellis Krahnert, the doughy Chief Assistant who had replaced Chase upon his departure, wearing his perpetual smirk. Avoiding risk, as always.

At that moment, Chase felt a pain in his left wrist, which surged up his arm. He jerked and gripped the table to steady himself. His client looked at him, the question in his eyes. *You all right?* Chase nodded his head, eyes focused forward. His left arm throbbed, but the pain had ebbed, leaving a residue of numbness. He tested his fingers, his wrist, clenched the muscles in his arm. The pain hadn't affected his motor control or his coordination. His mind told him his arm should be immobile, or perhaps scarred; the pain had been that severe. Yet nothing had happened. It was all in his mind. His thoughts flew to his brother. *What are they doing to you?*

TWO

Driving slowly toward the Gates of Hell, Chase felt a chill as the sun disappeared behind the pines lining the gravel road that carved through the forest leading up to the Institute. It happened every time he visited his brother.

Dark, foreboding, the tall wrought iron gates seemed freshly painted each time he saw them. He'd named them the first time he'd visited his brother two years before. They made him think he was entering a portal into another world, a dark world, far removed from the warmth of the North Carolina mountains. Chase had hiked the Smokies and the Appalachians for years, exploring the winding trails and the old growth forests, but he would never have imagined this dark scar on the land amidst the spreading green splendor.

The drive up the winding road just off the state highway gave no indication of what was to come. Four miles climbing through overgrown woodlands, sun barely peeking through, forest so thick you couldn't toss a rock more than twenty feet in any direction without hitting a trunk, a road so pocked it realistically required an all-terrain vehicle to traverse. Chase made the drive every other Sunday in his old Porsche, each time wondering whether it wasn't time to turn in the old 911 for an SUV. He viewed the drive as penance. It wasn't about comfort. It was about visiting his brother. Atoning for past wrongs. Winters made the journey a perilous one, but so far there had been only one snowfall, the previous year, which had rendered the road impassable.

Chase pulled the car into the lot, a clearing some fifty yards past the main gate, so covered with pine needles he couldn't tell whether there was pavement, grass, or gravel underneath. As always, the Porsche was the only car. In all his visits over the course of two years, no other vehicle had been parked there. Presumably, employees parked in their own private lot, although where that might be, Chase had no idea. No cars, but perhaps a heliport out back somewhere; he'd heard the distinctive whirring sounds of a helicopter in the distance on several occasions.

Getting out of the car, Chase stretched his long legs, cramped a bit from the two-hour drive from Piedmont. As he strode toward the guardhouse he surveyed the grounds, looking for some sign of change. The Institute looked as it always did: dark, ugly, misshapen. Two mountain ridges came together in the back of the property, enclosing a small valley in a natural triangle, leaving only the base, the front gates, open and accessible; if the narrow winding road leading to the Institute could be called accessible.

Stone walls rose eleven feet or so, cutting off the view of the interior property. Chase walked to the guardhouse, a stone protuberance abutting the gates, seeming to grow out of the wall itself. He knocked on the large wooden door, wondering again why the guardhouse had no windows, and why a guard was needed at all in this desolate place. Presumably there were surveillance cameras everywhere, but to date he'd never noticed one.

Thirty seconds after his knock, the door was opened by a large black man, slightly hunched at the shoulders. He held out a clipboard for a signature, and then pressed a button, opening the gates electronically.

Approximately sixty yards from the guardhouse the path came to an end, and Chase climbed the stone steps to the main, and apparently only, entrance. A white-shirted attendant met him, as usual, as soon as he opened the door. They always knew the precise moment he would walk in. The attendant was a young man in his mid twenties with a nametag that read "Roy." With his close-cropped hair, square jaw, neutral expression, deep chest, and muscular arms bulging from the short-sleeved uniform shirt, he could have served as a poster boy for the Marines. Perhaps he was one. Chase had never seen him before. The greeters, attendants—or whatever they called the people who escorted him around the complex—came and went. Anonymous people, interchangeable. Occasionally he might see the same person twice, perhaps as many as three times, but to his recollection, three times was the maximum. He didn't know where all these people came from. Was the complex so large that they could rotate staff all the time without duplicating assignments? Or did new staff members, as Chase suspected, arrive throughout the year? That made a strange kind of sense, particularly for a government-sponsored institution, in an area with no large population base nearby.

"Mr. Riordan, nice to see you today. I've been told to expect you," Roy said, nodding but not extending his hand. Standard operating procedure. "I'll be escorting you this morning. I'm afraid you'll need to meet in his room. This way please," he indicated, crisply marching down a short corridor leading toward the rear of the building, before turning down the familiar main corridor to the left.

Chase never enjoyed meeting in Jared's room. The cramped quarters and antiseptic smell gave him a claustrophobic feeling. He much preferred the larger living areas, or even the "great room," which allowed him to distance himself from his surroundings, from the pain of seeing his brother like this.

The interior of the house resembled the exterior. Plain, with an attempt at some coordinated design that just didn't come off. The hallway, for example, looked to be plaster rather than sheetrock, but the baseboard moldings had clearly been tacked on quickly, and didn't fit the contours of the walls. Paint had been applied haphazardly and there were numerous touched-up patches on the wall, with no concern for matching colors. The doors to the rooms seemed solid oak, and the knobs from room to room didn't match. As always, Chase examined the décor as he walked a few steps behind Roy. A new picture on the wall here, a new paint splotch there, a new tile on the floor. He could always count on these subtle little changes. They passed the common room, quiet as always. Someone dressed in white mopped the floor, humming to himself as he squeezed the mop into his bucket.

Past the common room and just before the corridor's end, Roy stopped in front of the last door and turned back to Chase.

"The doctor's waiting for you inside."

Chased raised his eyebrows. Roy rapped twice on the door and pushed it gently inward, remaining in the hallway. He nodded toward the room's interior. Chase held his breath and entered.

His shadow fell across the room's floor, the dim light from the hallway cast into the darkness of the room. Flimsy curtains didn't quite cover the small window criss-crossed with iron bars facing the front courtyard of the building. An overcast sky and the branches of an old pine tree conspired with the curtains to keep the room in a shroud. Two shadowy figures sat in chairs separated by a small night table beneath the window. Chase reached to flip on the overhead light switch.

"We would prefer you left the light out, if you please, Mr. Riordan," came the deep voice from the figure on the right. *Charles Laughton as Captain Bligh in Mutiny on the Bounty*, Chase thought. "And if you wouldn't mind terribly, could you close the door?"

Chase obligingly pushed the heavy wooden door shut. His shadow disappeared, and he stood just inside the door for a few moments, allowing his eyes to grow accustomed to the darkness. Over the course of his visits, Chase had met many doctors, all with their own pet theories as to why his brother's condition didn't seem to change.

"Forgive the inconvenience." The figure on the right side of the table stood up, an apparently painful exercise, accompanied by a series of grunts. "I am Doctor Brunelli," he said. He moved his considerable bulk two shuffling steps toward the door and extended a small hand. A ray of sunshine pierced the cloud bank outside, casting a glow on Chase. The doctor pulled his hand back suddenly and drew in a quick breath. He stumbled backwards, then regained his composure and stared for a few seconds.

"Remarkable," he finally murmured. "I knew, but I hadn't realized," he said. "Forgive me, please, Mr. Riordan, I suppose I should have been prepared."

Chase rescued the man from his obvious embarrassment and reached out to grasp the newly offered hand. "Not at all, doctor. It's been a while, but it's certainly something I'm used to. Even my father had trouble telling us apart. Pleased to meet you."

"I apologize again for my behavior. How rude of me. As to the light, it appears your brother prefers the dark."

The doctor had recovered his composure and punctuated his words with his small hands. It reminded Chase of a prosecutor he'd known who always spoke as if people hung on his every word. He acted as if each sentence transmitted a great secret known only to him.

"He was Special Forces," Chase said.

"Most of my patients are veterans, Mr. Riordan. I'm familiar with the typical psychoses, but here--"

"Night insertions," Chase interrupted. "My brother was trained to operate in the dark in enemy territory."

"Yes, of course."

Chase ignored him, dismissing him as another doctor who apparently hadn't even read his brother's file. He walked around the doctor to reach the window and sat down in the chair opposite Jared, feeling the pain of loss as acutely as the first time he'd come to visit. The dark eyes were dull, the face expressionless. The head lolled to the side, chin tucked to his chest. His arms lay inert on the chair's arms, his left hand clenched like a claw. Chase looked at the left arm, but the tan, long-sleeved jacket his brother wore covered it to his wrist. He looked at his own arm, his hand, remembering the feeling in the courtroom. Looked back at the doctor, busying himself by the small closet.

The doctors had told him Jared could hear him, but likely couldn't process the information. His condition wasn't much different than that of a coma patient, in spite of the open eyes and the ability to sit. Regardless, Chase talked to his brother. He knew that there had been research about how coma patients benefited from the voices of the people around him. Growing up, Jared had done all the talking; Chase had been the silent listener. Now their roles were reversed. Sometimes he read to him, books from their childhood, or novels he thought Jared might enjoy. Today he talked about the start of the trial and his feelings about being in the courtroom with his old boss, a man whose daughter had been his friend before her suicide.

Chase heard a sound, a quick pitter-patter, and thought a rat had run across the floor. It took a moment in the light before he identified the source. The fingers of Jared's right hand traced patterns on the tabletop, moving with lightning speed. Chase had not seen the hand move in the two years he had been visiting. He looked up at the doctor inquiringly.

"Nerve reflexes," the doctor said after a moment. "It's not unusual in coma patients. A good sign."

Chase looked at brother's hand. The fingers were running across the tabletop with great precision. He started. He followed the movements for a few seconds to be sure. Jared's fingers traced the opening bars to Chopin's "Minute Waltz."

He watched the fingers move, still with that amazing

dexterity. The wrist was immobile, the hand perfectly bridged, and the long fingers, which had once graced both the keys of a fine Steinway Grand in Carnegie Hall and the composite stock of an M-24 sniper rifle, continued their dance. Chase peered into his brother's eyes, searching for some sign of recognition or awareness. For a moment he thought he detected a gleam, but then realized the sun had shifted its angle to his brother's face. Still a mirror image of his own.

Jared's hand ceased its playing, settling once again on the chair arm. For the first eighteen months, Chase had arrived with high hopes that Jared would recognize him, that something he could say would spark action or memory. But those hopes were dashed each visit. After a while he'd given up. Now, Jared's fingers playing an imaginary tabletop piano led him back once again to the path of hope. He sat in the silence, peripherally aware of the doctor's continued presence. He looked at his watch and was surprised to see almost an hour had passed. Dr. Brunelli sat on the bed, staring intently not at Jared, but at Chase.

"Mr. Riordan, forgive me for saying so, but if I didn't know which chair Jared was sitting in, I'm not sure I could have told you who's the patient and who's the visitor; you have the same expression on your face."

Brunelli spoke quietly, devoid of body language. "As you can see, Mr. Riordan, some progress has been made. I hope to continue my work with Jared and have confidence that our strides will continue." He stood up and walked over to the door.

Chase followed him. He felt a twinge in his arm, a faint reminder of the earlier pain, and looked over at his brother sitting motionless by the window.

THREE

Driving home to Piedmont, Chase thought of Jared's fingers delicately, yet rapidly, executing the opening trill of Chopin's short, but perhaps most famous piece. He wondered whether he'd imagined it. Chase himself had spent an entire summer, in between basketball sessions, trying to master it. Right and left hands separately, then both together. He still occasionally sat down at his piano and played it. Or tried. Every time he made his way through the piece he couldn't help hearing Jared effortlessly flying through the music, never missing a note on the old Wurlitzer piano in the living room. Curious, the first sign of awareness on the part of his brother in years would be such a precise demonstration of manual dexterity.

"The Minute Waltz," Jared had once told him, "is one of the most exquisite pieces in all of music history. It requires deliberate, coordinated play, and a precise level of nimbleness of the fingers. When I play it precisely, my fingers are tracing virtually the exact movements of Chopin himself, and all the other masters who have played it since its composition."

Chase knew his fingers weren't tracing anyone else's movements when he played. He and Jared both had large hands with long fingers, but whereas both their hands could span almost two octaves on a piano keyboard, there the similarity ended. Jared's fingers were made to play the piano. They were long, thin and tapered, while Chase's were meant to palm a basketball. Chase always felt his fingers were too thick to play piano effectively, but when Jared played, it seemed as if his fingers and the keyboard were linked, part of the same instrument. Yet those fingers and those hands, rather than going on to play in concert halls, had proceeded to kill in support of the United States Government.

Chase had never understood his brother's decision to join the army. While Chase had been the athlete, Jared had been the studious one, the musical prodigy. And yet three months after the car crash that killed their parents, Jared dropped out of Juilliard and enlisted. After basic training, he attended jump school, and then trained with the Rangers at Fort Bragg, near Fayetteville, North Carolina. They'd written at first, then fallen out of touch, save for an occasional postcard. For their own reasons, neither had returned to New Jersey. After sophomore year, there hadn't been a home to return to. Chase would always carry around the horror of that springtime, just prior to school's end. He and Jared had yet to break down the barrier the accident had raised between them. Chase had seen him only once during training in "Fayet-nam," as it was known. He'd driven out and spent the day with his brother midway through the fall semester of his junior year. They had lunch together, wandered around the town, and talked the way they usually did—about nothing in particular. But seeing Jared with his military haircut proved unsettling, and for the first time Chase realized the big differences between them. Jared no longer looked like his mirror image and it shocked him. They'd written at first, then fallen out of touch, save for an occasional postcard. And Chase felt he'd let his brother down. Let his parents down. He was the one who'd been hardened on the playgrounds of urban New Jersey, earning his stripes as a ballplayer the hard way, while Jared sat home and practiced the piano. He was the one who was supposed to take care of his brother.

His cell phone rang. He looked for the caller. Ev.

"Hello?"

"Enjoying the drive?"

"What's up, Ev?" His friend's soft aristocratic drawl always had a calming effect. He looked at his watch. "It's late. I figured you'd be on the twelfth green by now."

"Don't I wish. At this moment, however, I'm sitting in my car, on my way to a short meeting, where I must impress a group of financial analysts as to the economic well-being of the Litchfield Group. Daddy felt having an actual Litchfield in the meeting would be helpful, so I shall endeavor to present myself in an acceptable manner."

"On a Sunday?"

An exaggerated sigh came across the line. "No rest for the wicked. Daddy's been entertaining them for the weekend, we've got the board meeting tomorrow, then something important came up and I got the call. And you know me, ever the supportive son."

Chase laughed.

"Now, now, be kind. But to the point. I'm trying to finalize the arrangements for our trip."

"I thought Peter was organizing this year."

"He set the times and booked the condo, but there are a couple of things still in the air. I know the club pro down at Harbor Town. He can get us on as a five-some, but we'll need to be the first group off the tees. That's a pretty early morning after a Saturday night."

"How early is the first tee time?"

"Six-thirty."

"Ouch."

"Indeed, but the good news is, we'll be done by lunchtime, avoid the afternoon heat, and be back sipping cold ones by 1:00 p.m."

"You heard from anyone else?"

"I left a message for Lionel. He'll grumble about getting up early, but…"

"He'll grumble about everything anyway," Chase finished.

"Peter's good to go, and Randy—that's the other reason I called. I haven't had any success reaching the man."

"I haven't heard from him for a week. I've left him messages at work and at home. Last we spoke was two weeks ago, and that's when I ran into him coming out of the courthouse."

Ev cleared his throat. "I'm not generally one to say I told you so, but I remind you of my comments at the wedding."

At the wedding reception the bride made a point of talking to everyone attending except the four of them. Ev had commented afterwards that this was the beginning of the end for Randy. "She's jealous, plain and simple. We compete for her dear husband's affections, and therefore we are not to be tolerated," he'd said.

"He sent his check, didn't he?"

"You'd have to ask Peter, he's collecting the money."

Beach Weekend was a sacrosanct event. Every year in January, the condo was booked and they all scheduled their calendars around it.

"I'll try to call him."

"Good luck. His secretary screens his calls at work and his lovely wife won't let him answer the phone at home."

"I'll figure something out. Maybe I can find a way to run into him again."

"Well, you'll be over at the courthouse enough the next month. Any chance the case runs over, interferes with our plans?"

"Possible, but I've got about a three-week buffer. Wall seems anxious to move forward, so I doubt he'll want to postpone. Judge Moody has had it on her calendar for six months now; I doubt she'll have much sympathy for any changes at this time," Chase said. "Not to mention, my client wants to get all this behind him. He's been sitting on his hands for a year waiting for his day in court."

"Just be sure he doesn't carry a gun into the courtroom. I suspect he'd put a bullet through the district attorney if he had the chance."

Chase smiled. "Maybe not a bullet, but I'm sure Rufus would be happy to thrash Wall with his cane for what he's put him through."

"He's in good hands. I've got to run, business beckons." He hung up.

Chase sighed. With the trial scheduled to take up all of his time for the next few weeks or so, he looked forward to spending at least a few days with his friends at Hilton Head. It was difficult enough trying to find the time with their increasingly busy and competing schedules, and now they had to deal with a controlling woman as well.

As he drove the last twenty miles, two images flickered through his head, over and over. His brother's hands, poised over a keyboard, playing the "Minute Waltz," and Brunelli's sharp gaze as Chase had looked up. He didn't trust the man, didn't trust the Institute, or the army, for that matter. They had yet to tell him what had happened to Jared. His last posting had been Afghanistan, so far as Chase knew. What had happened to make the army drape such a veil of secrecy over his condition and the events that brought it about? He had no physical injuries, no broken bones, no damaged organs. Yet he had retreated into himself, had shut the rest of the world out.

As he crested Monument Hill just north of the newly completed beltway, the Piedmont skyline came into view. Its jagged profile changed almost weekly, as the Litchfield Tower downtown slowly grew. The building's frame now stood taller than the nearby America's Bank tower, formerly the iconic structure in the city, and the brick and granite façade rose almost to the midpoint of the skyscraper. Ev had labeled the new headquarters Mount Everett, a monument to his father's tremendous ego. A joke, but Chase suspected Everett, Senior would approve of the characterization.

He took the Constitution Road exit, and swung into the

driveway of Ward's Flowers. The owner was on duty, recognized Chase, and had a bunch of tulips ready for him by the time he entered the shop. Nodding his thanks, he paid, and continued down the road to the cemetery, following the familiar route to a small parking lot in the southeast corner, an area full of tall elms and maples.

Walking across the trimmed green lawn, Chase passed a diverse set of inset stones and grave markers, many of them with faded plastic flowers pressed into the plots. Hard to believe it had been four years already. Abby's funeral had been a large, garish affair, full of pompous dark-suited bureaucrats making bad speeches, sobbing women, and grim expressions. She would have hated it. Chase had watched it all from the parking lot, not wanting to risk running into her father and causing a scene. He'd left early, driven to the Broyles Museum of Art and sat on a bench in front of Matisse's "L'Asie," one of Abby's favorite works. He should have hated Wall; the man had forced him out of the D.A.'s Office, kept him from the funeral, and somehow blamed him for Abby's death—but the emotions that came over him that day were of sorrow and guilt. He blamed himself. For not being there when Abby needed him; for not understanding the depth of her depression or her pain.

Wall had pushed hard for a church burial, but the Catholic Church dug in its heels. Suicide was still a sin. And so she'd been buried at Mt. Olivet, the largest memorial park in the city. Out of pique, Wall had purchased plots for himself and his wife on either side and abruptly stopped attending church services.

Reaching Abby's headstone, Chase picked up the flowers he'd left his previous visit and replaced them with the new bouquet. He got down on a knee, and brushed some loose soil off the stone. "I hope you're in a better place, Ab," he murmured, then touched the headstone and walked back to his car.

FOUR

Taking advantage of a break in the trial, Chase flew up to Washington.

With his brother, his friends, and the trial competing for his thoughts, he got off the plane, funneling along with everyone else down a narrow corridor with temporary walls, trying to avoid actually touching anyone. Most of the passengers leaving the plane were dressed in suits; business travelers who did the shuttle back and forth from D.C. to Piedmont on a regular basis.

The signs directed them up a flight of stairs, across a temporary bridge, then downstairs again. The phalanx snaked around the terminal, finally depositing the passengers at the opening of the baggage claim area.

Chase looked around, and then laughed as he spotted a beautiful black woman with a sign that read "Riordan." He walked up to her, and she reached out and grabbed his carry-on.

"Take your bag, Mr. Riordan?" she asked, deadpan.

Playing along, he handed over his satchel.

"Thank you, Miss," he said.

"This way, sir," she indicated, leading him outside toward the parking garage. "Enjoy your flight, sir?"

"It was fine, thank you."

"Come to Washington often?"

"Not often enough."

"Oh, why is that?"

"Well, the city sucks, but I love the people," he said.

"All the people?"

"No, not all the people." They walked down the escalator under the road to the parking garage.

"You here for business or pleasure?"

"Pleasure. Definitely pleasure." They approached a black BMW, and she popped the trunk and opened the doors with her electronic opener.

"How are you planning to spend your time in Washington?" she asked, putting the bag in the trunk next to her own.

"Well," Chase said, approaching her from behind. "I have some business to transact, then I'm going to take the woman I love out to a great dinner. Then, unfortunately, I'm going to catch a late flight back home." He wrapped his arms around her waist and pulled her close to him. She leaned against him, her cheek to his neck.

"In other words, wham, bam, thank you ma'am?"

"Did I not mention the great dinner?" he said.

"Oh, Chase," Reagan Thompson cried, turning around and hugging him tight. They held each other, Reagan's head coming up to Chase's shoulder. "It's been too long," she sighed.

"It's always too long," he said. "Course if you just moved to North Carolina we could solve all this." Reagan pulled away gently, and took Chase's large hands in hers, holding him at arm's length.

"You know I wish I could, Chase, don't you?" she said. "But someday. Someday." Then she slapped him on the arm. "But couldn't you at least stay overnight?"

"Can't be helped. The trial resumes day after tomorrow, and I have to prepare for the first round of witnesses."

They got into the car, and left the airport. Chase gently massaged Reagan's neck with his left hand while she drove.

"So how was he?" she asked, as they pulled onto the freeway heading north.

He told her about his most recent visit with Jared. Reagan was the only one he'd told about his brother. His friends knew of him, knew he was in the army, but that was all. For some reason he couldn't bring himself to say any more.

Chase had first met Reagan eighteen years before when she'd visited her brother Lionel at Winfield. A gangly ninth grader when Chase had finished college, she'd grown into a beautiful young woman by the time he met her again at Lionel's house one afternoon three years ago. Reagan confided she'd always had a crush on Chase growing up, and Chase couldn't get over what a change the years had wrought. He'd managed to get her number in Washington and they'd begun a phone correspondence that eventually blossomed into a full-blown love affair. Lionel still spoke of his sister as if she were a youngster in school, sweet and innocent. Chase couldn't tell him he'd fallen in love with that little girl. He had spoken at length of this conundrum with Lionel's wife Anita, who encouraged him to confide in Lionel, however much she enjoyed being in on the secret.

"At least there's some hope now," Chase told Reagan. "If Jared's able to move his fingers like that, at least we know his motor skills are intact, and there's a connection to the brain. It's not involuntary movement."

"Do you think it means something other than that?"

"What do you mean?"

"'The Minute Waltz.' Could he be trying to send you some kind of message?"

"I don't know," Chase had racked his brain trying to come up with some connection from their past, but to no avail. Maybe Jared *was* trying to tell him something, but if so, he couldn't figure out what it was. Or maybe it was just a kind of rote memory, his fingers playing a long-remembered piece.

"It has to mean something. Speaking of which, I've got something for you," she said. "Probably not what you'd hoped, but it's something, anyway." Reaching behind her seat, she pulled out a large envelope and handed it to him.

"What's this?"

"I have a few friends at the Department of Defense. One of them owes me a favor. After your last call I asked him to see what he could find out about the Pembrooke Institute. This was all he could come up with."

Intrigued, Chase withdrew two sheets of paper. Both were poor photocopies, the print barely legible. The first sheet authorized a construction project called "Project Pembrooke." Under "authorized amount," there were two words: "no limit." The signature at the bottom of the page was illegible, but printed underneath was the name of a then three-star general, known to Chase as the current Chairman of the Joint Chiefs of Staff.

The second page, a "memo to file" from a Captain Abosch, requested that individuals on an attached distribution list to go directly through him for transferees to the Institute. The memo concluded by reminding the recipients of the classified nature of the project and insisting they go through "previously established protocols" to qualify patients.

"It's not much, I know," Reagan said, "but my contact said that's all there was. I think even he was surprised. He thought he had the highest security clearance anyone could get."

Chase nodded. "Thanks. This first authorization talks about a construction project."

"Yes, and that's probably your best bet to learn more. The government is pretty paper happy. Every time funds are spent, somebody needs to sign off. I'm going to keep digging, see if I can't find the approval sheets. That information might not be as sensitive."

The forms didn't tell him a whole lot, but reinforced his perception about the peculiarity of the place. He had always presumed the security needs were based on two things: the potential danger the patients might pose and the sensitive material they might be carrying around in their heads. He wondered about the other patients, and what circumstances brought them to Pembrooke. He also wondered about the term "transferees."

"I appreciate it, love. At least you know I'm not hallucinating." Reagan had always laughed at Chase's vivid descriptions of the Institute, claiming he must have dredged it up from his memory of a childhood horror movie.

"I admit, I've had my doubts, but all this secrecy suggests something more than just a high-security rehab facility."

They drove in comfortable silence until they reached Reagan's condo.

Chase settled comfortably on the couch while Reagan got a couple of bottled waters from the refrigerator, and tossed one to him.

"How's Lionel holding up?" she asked.

"Probably wondering what the hell he's getting himself into. I think he'd make a great congressman, but I don't know why he'd want to consider living in this hell-hole."

She swiped at him with a newspaper. "Hush," she said with a smile, "it might be nice to have him around, though. We haven't spent a whole lot of time together, the past few years. I might get a chance to see my nieces a bit more. Is he going to get any big contributions from Ev?"

Chase laughed. "Tobacco money goes everywhere. Have to cover the bases." He took a swig of his drink.

Reagan raised her eyebrows. She only knew his friends through his stories, and from having seen them at Winfield as a young girl visiting her big brother. She asked, "What do you think about the trial so far?"

The newspapers had declared the opening session a victory for the prosecution, suggesting the defense would have a difficult time countering all the evidence—evidence that conveniently had found its way into the press before the trial ever started.

"Not so bad. We've got a good jury, mostly older folks who associate Rufus with the growth of the city. But it's the

South, and so far, Wall has the moral high ground, and that's a comfortable place for them. So, are you hungry?"

Reagan walked over to Chase and took his hand. "Sure, though I was thinking perhaps we'd stay in—get takeout, maybe watch a movie."

"You have one in mind?"

"In fact, I do." She walked over to the entertainment center against the wall and removed a DVD from a shelf. "I picked this up from the video store today. One of my favorite books as a child." She held up the case. To Kill a Mockingbird. "I saw it and thought of you, the trial scene and all."

"Fortunately, we have air conditioning in the courtroom. I always feel sorry for Gregory Peck, standing there in the heat, sweat dripping off him."

She cocked her head. "You do kind of look like him. A bit taller, though." Inserting the disk into the DVD player, she snuggled against Chase.

The credits came up, and he put his arm round Reagan.

"I like the music too. I mean, it's no Gone with the Wind, but it's nice, haunting."

"'Tara's Theme.'" Chase said, absentmindedly.

"Hmmm?"

"Gone with the Wind. The music. It's called 'Tara's Theme,' by Max Steiner, score by Elmer Bernstein, probably more famous for his score of The Magnificent Seven."

"Impressive," Reagan said. "The only film composer I know is John Williams."

"Hey, don't knock it. Many critics think the Star Wars theme is the best movie score ever written. Although Jared preferred Chariots—" He stopped. Couldn't be. His mind returned to his childhood bedroom, the one he'd shared with his brother.

"Chariots of Fire? Chase, what's wrong?"

"Bugs Bunny," he blurted.

Reagan put the movie on pause. She laughed. "Bugs Bunny? Chariots of Fire? What are you talking about?"

"It's all about Bugs Bunny. 'The Minute Waltz,'" he said, images flashing through his head.

"In the house where we grew up, in the room we shared, Jared kept three things on the wall above his bed. A 1958 *New York Times* article and picture of Van Cliburn, emerging victorious from the First Tchaikovsky Piano competition in Moscow, a movie poster from *Chariots of Fire*, which he considered to have the best movie score ever, and a framed cell from the Looney Tunes classic cartoon, *Hyde and Hare*."

"What's *Hyde and Hare?*"

"*Hyde and Hare* was Jared's favorite Bugs Bunny cartoon, a takeoff on Jekyll and Hyde. Bugs is adopted by a quiet old man who turns out to have a dark side—when he drinks a potion, he turns into Mr. Hyde, a hideous monster.

"In the cartoon, the moment Bugs first sees Mr. Hyde, Bugs is imitating Liberace. He sits down at the piano in the doctor's home and says, 'I wish my brother George were here.' Then Bugs commences to play what he calls 'The Min-oot Waltz, by Choppin.'"

"So you think he was trying to tell you something?"

"Even in the reduced state he was in, he was trying to communicate with me; trying to tell me something about his condition, his situation."

"You think that Jared is Bugs Bunny?"

"Yes, he's trapped in the Institute… by the Army. But who is Hyde? Or am I taking the metaphor too far?"

"No, let's keep with this. Brunelli, the doctor could be the mad scientist."

"I'm not so sure. I just met Brunelli on the last visit." Chase felt a sense of relief. Underneath the comatose exterior, his brother was still there. "My brother George," Chase said.

"What?"

"The neighborhood we grew up in, in New Jersey, was a tough place. The kids in the neighborhood teased Jared, called him a pansy for staying in and practicing the piano while we were out playing ball. 'He's a regular Liberace,' they'd say."

"So, he was reaching out to you, his brother, but there's got to be more to it," Reagan insisted. "Like drugs?"

"Drugs?"

"The potion that turns Dr. Jekyll into Mr. Hyde. Maybe he's trying to tell you he's being drugged."

Chase considered. Could it be that simple? Was Jared's condition a result of more than a battlefield injury?

"Assume it's true, that somebody's drugging him," he said. "It doesn't change anything. The army's got him, they're not letting him go, and there's nothing I can do about it."

"Chase, it changes everything," Reagan said, excitedly. "He's not a vegetable. He needs your help. Maybe he can tell you more. Who else can help him? You have me. You have my brother and your friends. All Jared has is the army."

Reagan held Chase's arm; he was suddenly reminded of the pain he'd felt in the courtroom, a brother's bond. Pain which Jared must have felt, only more intensely.

"So what will you do now?"

He thought, remembering his coach's words in college when they'd watched game film, considering the complexity of Duke's defensive scheme. Break it down. Start with the simplest things first. "Let him know I got the message," he said.

Five

The first few days of the trial were uneventful. The prosecution, under the theory that more is more, paraded a host of witnesses before the jury. The cleaning lady who'd found the body, the police officer who'd responded to the call, neighbors from the victim's condo who described her habits, her visitors. The coroner, who ascertained the time and cause of death, the mortgage company who had handled the purchase of the condo.

Chase let them talk, let Wall lead them along. He'd have been willing to stipulate to all of this. That Katarina Volkova had been murdered, her throat slashed. That the murder had likely taken place on the Friday before the cleaning lady had found the body on Monday. That Katarina had few visitors, knew the ex-mayor, and didn't socialize with the rest of the condo owners. Even that Katarina and Agnew had a relationship. But he wanted Wall to gain a false sense of security. He counted on his lack of recent trial experience and knew the overwhelming nature of the testimony would likely wear on the jury or just confuse them. So he didn't object, didn't ask many questions when it came time to cross; he sat politely and listened, pretending to take notes. He wanted the jury to view him as that polite young man sitting over next to the mayor. Until his turn came. The whole time, though, he couldn't shake the feeling that, in spite of what he'd said in his opening statement, the real killer was sitting in the back of the courtroom, enjoying every moment.

On day four, Wall called Edmond Wang to the stand. The city's computer expert, Wang had examined the victim's computer and found the damning e-mails. He walked to the front of the courtroom and took the oath. Chase knew he was a Buddhist and wondered whether the use of the Bible in this instance was entirely proper. A small man with a friendly face, Wang nodded at the jury, at the judge, at Chase, and finally at Wall, smiling all the while.

Wall began reading the man's credentials, including his work at Dell, his studies at Tech, and the papers he'd written.

Chase interrupted. "Your Honor," Chase said, "We stipulate as to Mr. Wang's impressive credentials and as to his expertise in this field."

Wall appeared flummoxed. "Your Honor, if I may continue," he said, holding up the resume in his hands.

"As you heard, there's no need, Mr. Wall," she said.

"I'd like the jury to appreciate this man's competence, your Honor. It's important to the case."

"No objections, your Honor. I was just trying to speed things along," Chase said. *Let the man drone on. Let him start reminding people of the annoying grandfather who never stopped talking, he thought.*

Wall looked at Chase, frowned, and then continued for a few minutes; he read each item on the resume before he began his examination.

"Mr. Wang, you found the computer in Ms. Volkova's apartment, is that correct?"

Wang shook his head. "No. I did not find the computer. The police found the computer."

"I'm sorry, I misspoke," Wall said. "The police found the

computer in Ms. Volkova's apartment. Did you examine the computer after they found it?"

Wang nodded his concurrence. "I examine the computer. Nice laptop. Dell Inspiron, sixty gigs."

"And what did you find?"

Chase smiled inwardly at the naïve breadth of the question.

Wang began a long recital of the programs and data found on the computer's hard drive. He was describing the operating system when Wall interrupted.

"Thank you, Mr. Wang. Let's focus on the Ms. Volkova's e-mail files, if you don't mind."

"Yes, Ms. Volkova's e-mail. Her inbox, not so full. Good file maintenance. Her Sent file, more messages."

Reaching to the prosecution table behind him, Wall retrieved a stack of papers from Patrice Vazquez.

"Yes, let's talk about the Sent file, as you call it. Who had she sent messages to?"

"Her father, her mother, companies she bought stuff from, and Mayor Agnew."

"Let's focus in on the messages to Mr. Agnew, if we might. I have here a transcript of those messages. Could you please verify if these are the same messages you found?" He handed the papers to Wang, who nodded as he read.

"Yes, same messages."

Wall moved to enter the e-mail into evidence. No objection from Chase.

"Could you please read the message I've highlighted, dated May 15th, three weeks before the murder?"

Chase laughed along with the members of the jury as Wang read down through the messages––to himself.

"Aloud, please, Mr. Wang," Wall stammered.

"Ah. Yes. Sorry. It says, 'Rufus. I'm sorry I have to do this, but you leave me no choice. I cannot continue this relationship, unless you follow through on your promise to marry me. It is time for us to tell your wife and the world that we are together, that we are a couple. Are you ashamed of me?'"

The reading took on a comic tone, as Edmond Wang's strong Chinese accent almost overwhelmed the content of the messages. Wall read aloud the four remaining notes himself, each more insistent than the last, with the most recent message, from late Thursday evening before the murder, demanding money for her silence and threatening to tell Agnew's wife and the media about the relationship. Wall kept looking up, waiting for Chase to object, daring him to contradict the evidence he presented. He asked a few more procedural questions of Wang, then passed the witness.

Chase rose. "Mr. Wang, you testified that Ms. Volkova practiced good file maintenance."

"Yes, the files were very clean. Virus protection, no spyware. Her messages did not accumulate. No excess software on her machine. Very unusual."

"Yes. The oldest message in her inbox was how old?"

"Two weeks old."

"Two weeks from the time of the murder, or from the time you examined the laptop?"

"Ah. Five days from time of murder. Sunday before."

"How about her outbox, the sent file you talked about."

"Three weeks from time of murder."

"That was the first note to Mr. Agnew?"

"Yes."

"Aside from the messages to Mayor Agnew, what was the oldest sent message?"

"Five days. Sunday before."

Chase had noticed the discrepancy the week before the trial. His own inbox had over a thousand messages in it. And he never cleaned out his sent file. The messages just accumulated over time, and so long as the computer could store them, he continued to send and receive without thinking much of it. Katarina Volkova's apartment was the most organized dwelling place he'd ever seen. The books on the shelves were not only alphabetized, their binders were perfectly aligned.

Clothes were folded neatly and stored, apparently by color. He had wondered what the cleaning lady even did, considering the condo's orderly state. Routine. And then he'd started wondering about her work on the computer.

"What was the oldest outgoing message on her laptop?" he asked.

"Victoria's Secret. Sunday before murder."

Oops. He had asked the question without thinking.

"Any messages other than to Mayor Agnew prior to that Sunday?"

"No. No other messages."

"She'd deleted all her other messages prior to Sunday, other than those to the mayor?"

Wall stood. "The witness obviously has no way of knowing whether there were any other messages prior to Sunday. Perhaps she didn't get on the computer all that frequently, or send many messages."

"Is that an objection?" the judge asked.

The district attorney sat back down, waving his hand.

Chase continued. "Is that true, is there no way of knowing whether Ms. Volkova had deleted any other messages?"

"No. Other messages deleted."

"How do you know that?"

"Ms. Volkova deleted other messages, but saved in separate file. On her hard drive."

"Ah. Some of those messages were dated prior to Sunday but after the first message to the mayor in the active file sent three weeks previously?"

"Yes."

"Any other messages to the mayor on the hard drive?"

"No. No other messages."

"Don't you find that odd?"

"Objection," Wall said. "Calls for a conclusion."

"Withdrawn," Chase said. He picked up a folder from the defense table. "You mentioned there were messages to her mother and father as well during that time period."

"Yes, one message to mother, one to father."

"Your honor, may I approach the witness?"

The judge waved him forward.

Chase handed two sheets of paper to the witness. "Are these the messages?"

Wang scanned down the first sheet, and then flipped to the second. "Yes."

"Can you please read aloud the message to her father?"

"No."

"Excuse me?"

"Can't read it. Message is in Russian."

"That's right." Chase looked at the jury. "Ms. Volkova's father lives in Russia." He handed Wang another piece of paper. "Here's a translation of the note, if you wouldn't mind reading."

"Objection, your Honor," Wall said. "We have no way of knowing whether that's an accurate translation."

"Your honor," Chase said, "The District Attorney's Office has had this e-mail in their possession over a year. I can hardly believe they haven't had the opportunity to translate it themselves. However, Professor Rudin, head of the Russian Department at UNC Piedmont is outside the courtroom. He has certified the accuracy of the translation."

The judge frowned. "Mr. Wall, you've had your opportunity. I'll allow this."

"Thank you, your Honor. Mr. Wang?"

Wang nodded, smiled, and, holding the paper in his hand, read, "Father. Thank you for the lovely music box. I remember its song; you used to sing it to me as a young girl. I hope you received by now the money I sent, or at least that your attorney has. Mr. Agnew has been trying to help with the consulate here. I feel so helpless, so far away from you. Your Katya."

Chase allowed a few moments for the message to sink in. "Mr. Wang, do you have any idea where Mr. Volkov, Katarina's father, is?"

"No. E-mail address in Russia, though."

"Yes. In Moscow, in fact. Do you need any help to read her message to her mother?"

"No. Message in English."

"If you'd please be so kind as to read it aloud, then?"

"Mother. I try to help father. My work keeps me very busy, but I have friends who help me, help father. When I can, I will visit."

"You can stop there. Thank you, Mr. Wang, I have no further questions."

Wang started to get up, but the judge stopped him as Wall stood to redirect. Wall asked a few questions about the file maintenance and got Wang to reveal that Ms. Volkova could have permanently deleted her other messages to Agnew, implying she did so for purposes of covering up the nature of her relationship with him. He avoided any mention of her mother or father. Wang was excused.

The next string of witnesses included several people who had seen Agnew and the victim together, and the officers who had executed the search at the former mayor's residence where they discovered fibers, hair, and the incriminating calendar entry. Chase concluded that in sum the testimony strengthened the prosecution's contention that Agnew and Volkova had been having an affair, and that Agnew had been at her condo (one he may have bought for her), perhaps connecting him to the crime. Circumstantial evidence to be sure, but enough of it to create a compelling case? As of yet, no murder weapon had been discovered, but Chase doubted that would get in the way of a conviction if it came to that.

The final expert called was the prosecution's star witness, the state's forensic expert, Dr. Rafael Castillo. Chase knew Castillo well; he'd used him in a number of cases. A polymath, he boasted PhD's in both molecular biology and chemistry, taught at Davidson College, and lectured extensively throughout the country on applied science with respect to criminal investigations. As he walked to the stand, he exuded authority, his posture erect, his gait determined, and his silver mane swept back from his somber face. He took the oath and sat completely still while Ken Wall read his credentials, receiving his due. Chase kept silent. He needed Castillo as much as Wall did.

The D.A. had Castillo take the jury through the murder scene, the position of the body, the location of the wound, the blood on the floor and on the body. Some information had already been covered in earlier testimony, but Chase let it go. He was as spellbound as the rest of the courtroom by the man's delivery, transporting everyone in the courtroom back to the day of the crime. Chase could see the image in his head, drawn from the man's description:

The young woman is home, alone, but expecting company. A bottle of wine is out and opened, two empty wine glasses in place on the glass coffee table in the living area. She's dressed nicely, to impress, a dress she'd bought the week before at Belk's, highlighting her shapely figure. Her dark hair hangs loose, under a red beret that matches the dress. No evidence of food; perhaps they'd planned to order in. An iPod is connected to the stereo system, and a play list is randomly playing old show tunes. Cole Porter, perhaps, or Gershwin. There's a knock on the door. She opens it to welcome her guest, closes the door behind him, and leads him through the foyer toward the living room. She's ahead of her guest, perhaps holding his hand lightly. Before they could reach the living room, her visitor must have pulled her to him from behind. He has a weapon, something flexible to serve as a garrote, a length of fishing line, perhaps. Looping it around her neck, he exerts pressure, cutting off her circulation. The garrote penetrates the skin, creating a necklace of blood. The angle of the neck wound reveals the killer to be four inches taller than Katarina Volkova, who stood five feet, three inches tall.

Castillo continued his testimony. "The victim's feet no doubt kicked out from under her, breaking a heel, and her ankle connected with a small table in the foyer, enough to cause a bruise and move the table a few inches; she died no more than three minutes later. Lowering his victim to the ground, her murderer must have straightened out her dress, and moved her legs together. She was found flat on her back, almost rigid. The blood splatter was minimal, and there was evidence the killer used paper towels to clean up the worst of it. A few drops were found on the living room rug. I was able to extract some additional blood samples from the tile, which had been wiped down."

Skillfully guided by Wall, Castillo concluded by telling the jury the killer had probably wiped down the surfaces he might have come into contact with, washed up in the bathroom, and then left, locking the door behind him. Fifteen minutes or so had likely passed since he'd entered the condo. In spite of his limited time at the scene, the murderer had lefts signs of his presence. In addition to the wiped-down tiles, there were some foreign fibers on the victim's dress. When he'd pulled her toward him from behind, his coat had left some threads on her dress. Tan colored cashmere threads, from a suit jacket or blazer. Good quality, an expensive garment. And fingerprints were found in the bathroom, which had been matched to Rufus Agnew.

Members of the jury stared at Chase and his client, accusingly. Castillo had painted a very compelling picture. The ability to evoke the actual murder itself, to present it so vividly that it created almost a video of the actual event in each juror's mind was a rare talent. And the jury now carried those images with them. They could see, Chase knew, his client doing all these things. Walking in, grabbing Katarina, strangling her, then casually cleaning up after himself and walking out. Going home to his wife.

The mayor owned a tan cashmere blazer. It hung in the closet where the police and the D.A. had found it during the execution of the search warrant. The threads matched those found on the victim's dress.

They faced an uphill battle. For Chase had little doubt the murder had happened just as Castillo had described.

SIX

"Your witness," Wall said.

"Thank you," Chase took a deep breath and released it, letting the rest of the courtroom disappear, and focused on the witness.

"Dr. Castillo, it's nice to see you again."

Castillo nodded. "You too, Mr. Riordan. Would that it were under better circumstances."

"Indeed. And thank you for coming here today. I know you're working with the District Attorney's Office, but nonetheless I appreciate you taking the time out of your busy schedule."

"Not at all, counselor," Castillo said, the corners of his mouth compressing.

"You've taken us through the murder, described it quite vividly. Is it your contention it had to happen exactly as you described?"

"I based my reconstruction not just on the forensic evidence, but on other evidence presented to me by the prosecution. The murder probably took place between six and seven p.m. on Friday. We know that due to a number of factors, not just the coroner's report on time of death. A neighbor walking toward her condo just after three o'clock had seen the victim, Ms. Volkova. Phone calls were also received by Ms. Volkova, one at 4:15 p.m., and another at 5:02 p.m."

"Who were these phone calls from?" Chase interrupted.

"I don't know," Dr. Castillo said.

"Why is that? Ms Volkova had caller ID. Surely you know the number the calls were placed from?"

"The calls were placed from an unregistered number. A pre-paid phone that had been purchased from a local phone dealer."

"But isn't the dealer required to keep records of the purchaser?"

"I am told by Mr. Wall the purchase was made with cash, and such purchases aren't registered. The phone may have been used only for a few calls and then discarded."

In fact Tony Santori, Chase's investigator, had tried to track down the phone and caller as well but had run into the same dead end. Still, he'd wanted it introduced into the record. Wall had conveniently ignored the two calls in his presentation of the case.

"So she received two phone calls from some mystery caller prior to being murdered. Don't you, as an expert in these matters, find that suspicious?"

"Objection, your Honor," Wall called out. "There's nothing to indicate any suspicious intent or mystery in a couple of phone calls."

"In which case you'll have your turn to discuss this further on redirect," the judge said.

"Dr. Castillo?"

"I don't know whether I would characterize the phone calls as mysterious. They were phone calls," Castillo said. "Perhaps from Mr. Agnew."

"Ah, but if that were the case, surely he would have gone to greater lengths to disguise his relationship with the victim. He kept the jacket in his closet, kept her name in his appointment book.

"Suppose I were to tell you, though, that Mr. Agnew can account for his time during the phone calls in question. That in fact he couldn't have made those phone calls. Would that change your assessment?"

"Objection. Facts not in evidence. It's a hypothetical that has no basis in fact," Wall said. "Not to mention it exceeds the scope of direct-examination."

"Your Honor, Dr. Castillo brought up the notion that Mr. Agnew may have made the calls. Surely I can speak to the subject, ask a question about the doctor's assumptions? So far as I can tell, the prosecution didn't bother to ascertain Mr. Agnew's whereabouts prior to the time of the murder."

Wall knocked the table standing up. "The police and the District Attorney's Office have gone to great lengths to investigate this case properly. I object to Mr. Riordan's characterization of our efforts."

"Sit down, Mr. Wall," Judge Moody said. "You invited this. It's your witness that brought up the phone calls, and if you have evidence as to Mr. Agnew's whereabouts prior to the time of the murder you've had ample opportunity to bring it forward." She turned to Chase. "And you will limit yourself to questions under the rules of cross examination. Do I make myself clear?" She looked from Chase to Wall.

"Yes, your Honor," Chase said. "I apologize."

Wall murmured something and sat down; the judge motioned for Chase to continue. "Rephrase your question."

"Dr. Castillo, does the identity of the caller matter to your reconstruction?"

The witness took his time, a thoughtful look on his face. "I'd have to say no, unless you *could* produce proof it was someone other than your client. On the other hand, if you could demonstrate someone else made the call, the mere fact that the call was made by someone who chose to disguise his or her identity would be worth considering. But no, I still stand by my reconstruction."

"Thank you. Let's get back to your reconstruction. Your

depiction of the murder itself isn't dependent upon the murderer being Mr. Agnew, is it?"

"No, of course not."

"I mean, someone other than my client could have walked in, committed the murder exactly as you described, and walked out."

Castillo's eyes twinkled. "Someone else with a tan cashmere jacket, who knew the victim, about the height of your client, who shared his fingerprints?"

"Let's talk about those last two points. You based your conclusion about the height of the assailant on the angle of the penetration of the garrote, I believe you said."

"Correct."

"That assumes the person stood directly behind her, both parties stood up, and he brought his arms up and his hands to the side of the neck."

"That is how I believe the murder took place."

"But how can you be sure? A taller person, for example, could have similarly come up from behind, crouched a bit and reached his arms over her head from above. Couldn't the angle be similar?"

The witness's brow wrinkled. "He would have lost the leverage he had. By crouching, he would have given the victim the opportunity to more easily break free."

"Granted, but if he were sufficiently strong, isn't it a possibility?"

"Perhaps," Castillo said slowly.

"And take a shorter man. If he pushed Ms. Volkova from behind, her legs might have gone out from under her, so he could catch her around the throat as she slipped. Might that not also better fit the scenario, given the broken heel, and the table?"

"Again perhaps."

"You mentioned the fingerprints. Where exactly in the bathroom were they found?"

"On the sink basin."

Chase produced a picture, and asked the judge permission to approach the witness. He handed the photo to Castillo.

"Is this a picture of the sink in Ms. Volkova's bathroom?"

"I believe it is."

"Could you show us exactly where the fingerprint was found."

The doctor held up the photo, his finger indicating a position on the left front of the sink basin. "Here. A thumbprint."

The picture was entered into evidence. "A thumbprint. On the sink basin. Not on the faucet handles, the toilet."

"No."

"The prosecution contends the killer wiped down the surfaces in the house to eliminate evidence of his presence, yet he managed to leave a thumbprint on perhaps the glossiest surface in the condo?"

"Apparently."

"Do you have any idea when the print was left?"

"Pardon?"

"Do you know for certain, that the print was left during the time of the murder, for example?" Chase had walked back to stand behind the defense table next to his client.

"I do not."

"So it could have been left there at another time, sometime during the previous week?"

"Objection," Wall said. "Asked and answered. Calls for speculation."

"Withdrawn. Could the print have been planted?"

"Planted?"

"Placed somehow on the sink by someone else, with access to Mr. Agnew's print?"

Castillo stared over at the prosecutor's table, perhaps waiting for an objection. When none came, he shrugged. "Not easily."

"But you could do it. I mean, you know how?"

The doctor's lips pursed together. "Yes."

"Did you examine the computer, Ms. Volkova's laptop?"

"I did not."

"But you did review all the forensic evidence."

"Yes."

"Do you recall whether any prints were found on the keyboard?"

"May I refresh my memory with my notes?" he asked.

"Please do."

Castillo pulled a small notebook from his breast pocket and flipped through a few page. He put the notebook away.

"There were no fingerprints on the keyboard."

Chase raised his eyebrows. "To be clear, do you mean just no fingerprints from my client, Mr. Agnew?"

His eyes hooded, the doctor kept his head lower for a few moments, and then he looked Chase in the eye. "No, Mr. Riordan, I mean no fingerprints at all."

"Not from Ms. Volkova either?"

"I said none at all, Mr. Riordan."

"Indeed you did, Dr. Castillo. Indeed you did." Chase looked at his client, sitting as he always did, respectfully, eyes on the speaker, hands folded. The polite southern gentleman, an image at odds with that the prosecution had presented. Agnew looked up briefly, caught the question in his attorney's eyes. Nodded.

"Dr. Castillo, isn't it true that your entire reconstruction today, your position on this case, is based on the premise that Rufus Agnew is the murderer?" He looked Castillo directly in the eyes, the challenge obvious.

The statement triggered a massive chain reaction. Spectators began talking, chairs moved, Wall rose to his feet, his face red, the judge's gavel pounded to restore order. Chase kept his eyes locked on the witness. It took a few minutes for a semblance of calm to return. Wall blustered about the attack on the integrity of his office and on the witness, seemingly ready to spring across the table at Chase. Chase wished the conflict between them could be settled so simply.

The judge summoned both parties to the bench.

"Mr. Riordan, I thought I cautioned you already."

"Your Honor, I apologize if I've caused offense. I merely asked the witness a question about the basis for his assumptions," Chase said, innocently.

"He attacked my office, your Honor." Wall said. "He—"

The judge held up a restraining hand. "Please let me do the talking, Mr. Wall. Mr. Riordan, I've allowed you some leeway. Can you address the issue without being so incendiary?"

"The issue, your Honor is his blatant disregard of the standards of courtroom decorum. He should not be allowed to so callously challenge my office, to challenge me." Wall turned toward Chase and poked him in the chest with a finger.

Chase looked at the finger, looked down on his former boss, expressionless. Wall pulled back the digit as if it had touched fire.

"Mr. Wall. You will refrain in my courtroom from lecturing the defense attorney or me. Do you understand?"

"Yes, your Honor," he said, recovering his composure.

"Mr. Riordan, are we clear as to the scope of your cross examination of the witness?"

"Completely, your Honor."

She bade the men return to their tables. The witness sat, his eyes now on Wall.

Chase looked at his client. Agnew gave him a sly wink, and he returned to the witness.

"Dr. Castillo," Chase began, "I apologize if my last question implied anything untoward in your behavior. You know, from previous times we've worked together, that I have nothing but the utmost respect for your work."

Slightly mollified, but with a cautious expression, the witness turned his attention back to his questioner.

"I am trying to ascertain what you were told by the prosecution when they engaged your services."

"For example?"

"For example, were you asked whether Mr. Agnew fit

the profile of the killer based on your review of the forensic evidence?"

"Yes, I was."

"And I presume you answered in the affirmative, as you have done in court today."

"Yes."

"Were you asked whether there was any evidence as to whether the perpetrator might have been someone else?" Chase said.

"No," Castillo answered, steepling his fingers.

"Mr. Agnew was in custody at the time?"

"I believe he was out on bail, but yes, he'd been arrested and charged with the crime."

"Were you aware, at that time, whether the D.A.'s office or the police were pursuing any other leads, whether there were any other suspects?" Chase asked, risking a look out of the corner of his eye at Wall. The D.A. wore a grim expression, and his arms were crossed. Patrice Vasquez had her hand on his arm, her grip apparently quite tight.

"I was not a part of the D.A.'s investigation. I have no knowledge as to whether or not there were any other suspects," Dr. Castillo sounded slightly puzzled.

"Of course. But surely you might have had some clue as to whether there were other suspects being investigated. The D.A. might have come to you and asked whether a six foot tall male, or a five foot three male could have committed the crime."

"Objection, asked and answered."

"Sustained. Counselor, please move on."

"Just to be clear, though, Dr. Castillo. Rufus Agnew was the only person you knew to be under investigation."

Castillo answered in the affirmative just as Wall rose to object again.

"Mr. Wall earlier discussed the cashmere jacket found in Mr. Agnew's closet. Did you examine the jacket?"

"I did," Castillo said.

"And the fibers, the threads, match the threads found on Ms. Volkova's dress?"

"They did. They do."

"So of course you found blood, or at least fibers from Ms. Volkova's dress on Mr. Agnew's jacket as well," Chase said.

"No, I did not."

Chase cocked his head. "I'm confused. If Mr. Agnew, wearing the jacket in question, stood close enough to the victim to shed hairs from his jacket, wouldn't there be blood spatters, or perhaps some minute fibers from the victim's dress on the jacket as well?"

"Not necessarily."

Opening his briefcase below the table, Chase pulled out a book and held it up. "Dr. Castillo, this is your book, considered by many as the bible of forensic investigation?" he said, holding it up. He opened it to a bookmarked page.

"It is my book."

"If you'll allow me, there's a passage here on page 231. It says, I quote, 'When two people come in contact with one another, whether it be for the purpose of shaking hands in greeting, or killing each other, there is always an exchange of material.'" He closed the book. "Your words?"

"Yes, although it's certainly not an original idea. Dr. Henry Fong has also—"

"Thank you, Doctor. There's no need to be modest. But whether your words or another's, do you believe them?"

"Yes, but—"

"So in this case, if Rufus Agnew is the killer, if he got so close to Katarina Volkova, held her close to him while he cut her throat, held her for at least the three minutes necessary to kill her, close enough for hairs from his jacket to attach to her dress... where's the exchange? Where is the evidence of that contact on Mr. Agnew's jacket?"

"I don't know," Castillo finally said.

"The prosecution has stated that the fibers on Ms. Volkova's dress indicate definitive evidence that Mr. Agnew was there the night of the murder. In fact, that's not true, is it?"

"I'm not sure what your question is."

"Suppose Mr. Agnew had worn this jacket, and Ms. Volkova had worn the same dress on some different date. Say a month previously. Would those fibers still be present?"

Castillo looked over at Wall, then back to Chase. "I suppose."

"Getting back to the issue of fingerprints. You testified that Mr. Agnew's thumbprint was found on the bathroom sink and that no fingerprints were found on the computer keyboard. Were there any other fingerprints found in the condo?"

"Yes, of course. The cleaning woman had opened the door to get in on Monday after the murder. Her fingerprints were found on the doorknob, the table next to the victim, and the telephone."

"Any others?" Chase asked.

"Yes. Ms. Volkova's fingerprints were found throughout the condo."

"But not on the keyboard."

"Objection," Wall called out.

"Sustained. Mr. Riordan?"

Chase held up his hand apologetically. "So that's it––Mr. Agnew, the cleaning lady, and Ms. Volkova."

"No."

"No? What other prints were found?"

"There were prints of at least three other individuals."

Chase knew he had the jury's attention. He took a moment to break his own rhythm, to allow the previous exchange to filter and settle. Clearly, the prosecution had decided early on that Rufus Agnew was their man, and ceased any investigative efforts after that. He wanted to find out how far that singular focus had extended.

"Who were these individuals?"

Again the witness pulled out his notebook. "A neighbor, a Mrs. Kay Bailey, a friend, I have her name listed as Olga Rybakova, and an individual as yet to be identified."

"Did I hear that right? There's a set of prints in the house that neither the police nor the D.A.'s Office could identify?"

"Yes."

"Any other evidence of anyone else's presence? Other than the fingerprints?"

Castillo consulted his notebook. "Some hairs that didn't match the victim or the accused. But that's to be expected. A home has some kind of record of anyone who's ever been in it."

"Hairs?"

"Yes, black hairs."

"Hairs that didn't match Ms. Bailey either."

"No."

"And you've already testified that since Mr. Agnew was the only suspect, none of these other individuals were investigated."

"Your Honor," Wall said. "Must we go over this again?"

The judge fixed her stern gaze on Chase. "Mr. Riordan, we have already addressed this issue. Dr. Castillo has already told you what he knows about this subject. No more."

"Yes, your Honor," Chase said. "Let me ask a different question then. This third set of fingerprints, where were they found?"

"It wasn't a set, Mr. Riordan. Just a slightly smudged index finger. And the forensic team found it on the victim's cell phone."

"Where was that phone, Doctor?"

"In the victim's purse. Sitting on the kitchen countertop," Castillo said.

"Thank you." Chase turned to the judge. "Your Honor, I have no further questions for this witness."

Wall shot to his feet as soon as his opponent sat down.

"Dr. Castillo, Mr. Riordan has tried to cloud the issue here a bit. Trying to create a bit of a mystery. Let's get back to the important issue at hand. Based on the evidence you've seen, the crime scene you've reconstructed, do you have any reason to believe that someone other than Rufus Agnew, the accused, committed this crime?"

Castillo looked over at Chase as he answered. "I do not."

"And that reconstruction, in fact, fits all the known evidence and facts."

"I believe it does."

"And your testimony has been that a man of Mr. Agnew's approximate size, wearing a tan cashmere blazer, who had a key to the apartment, who had motive to kill Ms. Volkova, committed this crime?"

The witness held up a hand. "I can't speak to motive."

"Excuse me?" Wall said.

"You said 'who had motive to kill the victim.' I have no knowledge, other than what I've read in the papers, about Mr. Agnew's or anyone else's motive."

Wall quickly recovered. "Of course. Let me rephrase. You believe a man of Mr. Agnew's size, and in his jacket, with a key to her apartment, killed the victim."

"Yes."

"And you confirm that the fibers from the jacket in Mr. Agnew's closet match those found on the victim's dress."

"Yes."

"The quote from your book, which Mr. Riordan read. Do you place any qualifiers on that statement?"

"Of course. There is an exchange of material. That material could be physical or biological. It may not be detectable by means known today. Ms. Volkova wore a dress made of silk. The fibers in silk are not so easily separated from the fabric. Cashmere, however, is long, fibrous. The threads easily bond to other surfaces."

"Thank you for that clarification. You also confirm that Mr. Agnew's fingerprints, more precisely, his thumbprint, was found at the scene of the crime."

"Objection," Chase said. "The sink is not the scene of the crime. Mr. Wall has mischaracterized the evidence."

"Sustained."

"Found at the condo. I stand corrected," Wall said.

"Yes."

"Thank you, Dr. Castillo." Wall turned to the judge. "I have no further questions."

Judge Moody excused the witness, who stepped down. Walking past Chase, the doctor paused briefly, before continuing out of the courtroom. The judge looked to the prosecution table. "Mr. Wall? Anything else?"

The district attorney stood and looked toward the jury.

"Your Honor, the Prosecution rests," he said. He nodded to the jury box. Chase noticed a number of jurors nodding back at him.

"It's four o'clock. We'll resume next Monday morning at 9:30," the judge said. "Court is adjourned." She banged her gavel, and amidst a hubbub of noise, the room emptied.

Chase conferred with his client for a few moments outside the courtroom before the press engulfed them both. "No comment," he said, to the reporters cries as he made his way to his car. Rufus Agnew, surrounded by a police escort, amicably waved to the press.

SEVEN

The friends met Friday evening at 4.0, a bar in the business district. In years past they'd met weekly, sometimes daily. Five of them at first, then four, as Peter Jurgens moved to Atlanta, and today three, as rising fortunes and increased pressures of job and family had whittled away at their time together.

As usual, Lionel arrived first. At the trendiest hot spot in town, a line forming out the door, he'd managed to secure a table near the window with space for his wheelchair in the corner. A pitcher of beer sat in front of him, four mugs arranged around the table, one of them half empty. He held up a beefy arm as Ev, then Chase, forced their way through the crowd, confident in their friend's ability to clear out space.

Ev glanced at the mugs, snorted, and stopped a harried waitress, somehow earning a smile as she took his order: Grey Goose vodka and tonic. He took off his blazer, carefully folded it, set it on Lionel's wheelchair back, expertly folded his sleeves up to his elbows, then dusted his seat with a napkin and sat down.

"I can't bring myself to say Grey Goose in a bar," Lionel said. "Sounds like the start of a nursery rhyme. Pitcher of beer, now that's a manly order." He poured one for Chase and topped off his own. "I keep telling myself, today's the day Ev joins the ranks of the common man."

Chase held off a smile, raising his glass. Ev's drink arrived in time for him to join the silent toast.

"I'm deeply offended," he said drolly, his eyes on the rear end of the departing waitress. "For the record, though, I did watch an insidious sitcom last evening. Two of them, to be honest. Painful, to be sure, but the company, at least, compensated." His eyes scanned the room.

Lionel and Chase shared a wry smile. Familiar territory.

"Sure, you're watching some chick sitcom while the rest of us he men are watching sports," Lionel said. "Very manly. Nice to know you're so in touch."

Ev nodded his head, as if acknowledging a compliment.

"When we first started coming here we sat by ourselves, you could hear yourself think. Now it's a meat market," Lionel said, protecting the pitcher from the elbow of a young suited man ensconced in an animated conversation with a blond in a halter-top. "What are we, the oldest people in the place?"

"Kind of nice, actually," Chase said. He appreciated the bustle, the self-absorption of the crowd, the anonymity that it afforded. For two weeks he'd had to wade through crowds of reporters scrambling for pictures and quotes as he left the courthouse. The din would grow with his defense of Mayor Agnew, which was set to begin Monday, so he enjoyed the opportunity for a bit of a breather. "At least no one here cares who the hell we are," he said.

"Who the hell are we?" Ev asked.

"Exactly," Chase said.

"The merchant of death, the sleazy ambulance chaser, and the humble preacher," Lionel intoned. "Oh Lord, protect us from the rabble that surrounds us. And protect them from my friends here," he said, finishing the last of his beer and pouring another.

"Merchant of death?" Ev said. "That's my father. I haven't

decided as yet whether to assume the mantle. What does that make me?"

"Ungrateful?" Chase tried.

Ev laughed. "Eternally grateful for the money my dear departed grandfather left me."

"And yet you still show up to work," Lionel said.

Ev sighed. "It's not so easy to get away from the family business. No matter what I do, with my name, I'm going to be tied to cigarettes and tobacco. Might as well be in a place where that's an asset, not a liability. Not to mention I can keep my eye on Daddy."

"Trust me, he thinks he's the one keeping an eye on you," Lionel retorted.

"You know what they say, keep your friends close…"

"And your enemies closer," Lionel added. "Lovely family you have."

Ev raised his glass. "Cheers. Although you'll have to explain to me how humble preachers decide to run for congress. Perhaps I'm missing something?"

Lionel grunted. "Humble preachers make humble congressmen. I figured we didn't have any of those yet. Thought I'd start a new trend." He reached down beside him and pulled out the morning newspaper.

"That artist's sketch," Lionel said. "That supposed to be you?"

Chase winced. The front page of the Friday morning paper had an artist's rendering of Chase and Ken Wall in front of the judge. Not a terrific likeness, although the one of Wall was far less flattering. Almost a caricature, with a large bulbous nose and an obvious comb over. It also exaggerated the difference in the two men's heights.

"I'm sure Chase will be happy to autograph that, if you'd like," Ev said.

Lionel swung at Ev with the folded newspaper. "Don't think just because I'm in a wheelchair I won't swat you like a fly."

"If you could catch me."

"Oh, I'm pretty fast in this thing. I sprang the extra hundred bucks for the souped-up version. But seriously, Chase, I read the paper, checked online this afternoon. Decent day?"

"I suppose. Scored some points, lost some points. Still strange sitting across from the old boss. He seems like an entirely different person."

"Showing his true colors," Lionel said.

"I don't know," Chase said. "I'm not sure anymore what his true colors are." For ten years, working side by side, Wall had treated him more like a son than a boss. He'd taken a young man fresh out of law school and taught him how to be a prosecutor. How to care about the law, about justice. Wall had promoted him through the ranks to Chief Deputy District Attorney, responsible for running the District Attorney's Office, including all major felony prosecutions. Then one day he'd taken Chase aside and told him in confidence that he had decided to step down and not run for office in the next election. He was retiring and wanted Chase to run in his stead, to "carry on the good work" the two of them had begun. He promised to line up support, working with his political contacts, and said he would "call in all his favors for this one." Chase, who wanted nothing more than to put criminals behind bars, accepted the offer, albeit reluctantly. He had a few quiet conversations with friends, gauging the waters. Then Abby died and everything changed. Wall began lashing out at everyone around him, at his secretary, his team. But he saved his most vicious attacks for Chase, who'd been ill-equipped to deal with them amidst his own grief.

Shortly after her death, Chase received a phone call from a reporter at the *Piedmont Gazette*, asking him to comment on an article that would be printed the next day, in which Ken Wall accused him of trading on his own personal successes, and "stabbing him in the back" to run for district attorney. The article included a quote from Wall: "I am shocked to learn that my chief deputy has conspired to run for district attorney, against my own stated wishes. I have made it clear to him that I intended to retire in five years, but apparently that's not soon enough for Mr. Riordan. I had hoped to groom him as an eventual successor, but apparently his ego is just too big to fit in his current office." Chase was dumbfounded, mumbled "no comment," and sat in deep thought for a long time before going to his office in the middle of the night, packing up his desk, and leaving for good. He'd opened his defense practice the next week.

And haven't looked back. That's what you were supposed to say, but it just wasn't true. Everyday he considered the direction his life had taken. Even the title, "defense lawyer," didn't sit well with him. Those words had always indicated the enemy. Now he was that enemy.

"You got any brilliant stratagems for this week?" Lionel asked.

Chase shook his head. "Just going with the truth."

"Always dangerous, in my opinion," Ev said. "You need the old razzle-dazzle. A little fancy dribbling, a few picks, come around the screen; pass the ball a few times. Confuse them, move fast so they can't keep up."

"Sometimes the best strategy is just to come down the court and spot up for the jumper. They know it's coming, but it doesn't matter," Chase said with a small smile.

"Well, give 'em hell," Lionel repositioned himself in his seat, his face in a grimace. "Damned hip. Hope the new one's as good as advertised," he said, refilling his and Chase's mugs. He stared pointedly at the empty one. Held it in the air. Shook his head disgustedly.

"Least Randy could do is be honest, tell us he can't make it because his wife cut off his balls."

"Pressure to make partner," Chase noted. "This is supposed to be his year."

"Wasn't it supposed to be his year last year," Eve said wryly.

"He wasn't married to She-Who-Must-Be-Obeyed then.

Now it's not an option," Lionel said. "I think she reads his e-mails, checks his voice-mail. I sent a joke to his home e-mail, and he sent back a request to please not send anything crude. Marinda didn't appreciate it. Marinda? If I'd wanted her to read it, I'd have sent it to her. And this is just the beginning. Mark my words: we'll get some excuse why he can't join us at the beach."

" Come on, Lionel, too soon to think that way. He's never missed a trip," Chase said, although he shared the concern. He still hadn't managed to reach Randy after Ev's call.

"He was never married to that woman before."

The rest of the evening the three friends ate onion rings and cheese poppers, caught some of the game on the big screen, and talked. About Lionel's prospects in the upcoming congressional race, Randy's change in lifestyle, Ev's succession of bimbos, how Peter's book was coming along, Chase's lack of a girlfriend. Some new subjects, some old. By ten o'clock they'd called it a night.

Instead of driving straight home, Chase detoured up East Boulevard and parked his car in front of an old abandoned high school. The site had been earmarked for demolition and conversion to a new shopping center, but there were some legal tie-ups involving zoning, so the place still stood. He popped the trunk of the car and pulled out his old Rawlings playground model ball, dribbled his way over to the single netless rim, dimly lit by a nearby streetlight, and positioned himself behind the peeling tape he'd placed marking the foul line. Then, very methodically, he began to shoot. And think. His friends offered a welcome respite from all the challenges facing him, yet he wondered why he'd left the bar feeling so alone. He'd checked his problems at the door, but walked out with them weighing heavier on him than ever. Perhaps they all approached their time together in the same way, as an escape from the stresses of their lives. Over the years they had gotten into the habit of avoiding problems when they were together, talking instead about innocuous, generally meaningless subjects.

Jared's presence loomed over him. A brother he had almost given up on showed signs of returning from the near dead. And needed his help. In high school, Jared had been the constant target of the local tough guys, who couldn't understand how someone so large couldn't run, jump, throw or shoot a ball. Chase had endured his share of bruises protecting him, standing up for him. Funny that Jared, who had avoided every fight in their childhood, had gone on to not only endure the physical rigors of the army, but to train for Special Forces, as tough a program as any in the military. Yet here he was, physically helpless again. Protected by the United States Army. But protected from what?

Then there was the trial. From day one, something had felt off. A sense of déjà vu, harkening back to his two previous murder trials. Thirty minutes later, his mind clear after having sunk one hundred free throws in a row, he tossed the ball in the trunk and drove home.

EIGHT

"Good morning," Kenneth said, entering the room. He closed the door and plopped down on the chair next to him. "I know it probably hasn't been a good morning, but I'm glad to see you survived it."

Jared sat motionless in the recovery room, settled in a chair, the IV dripping fluid into his veins. He hardly recollected the session from the night before. He still ran Mozart's "Piano Concerto No. 21" through his head. The voice of the doctor, the injections he'd received, all seemed like they had happened to someone else. His eyesight had yet to fully return, but each day he could identify more of the shapes around him, the shadows, the movements. Unable to move his head, he could only see the things that passed directly in front of him.

As if sensing his thoughts, Kenneth moved Jared's chair so they faced each other.

"How are you feeling?"

Though he couldn't answer, he considered the question. The pain of the drugs still coursed through his body, a throbbing ache, no longer the piercing sensation that had incapacitated him. His arms felt strong. His hands, his fingers; connected to his brain. He could feel gravity affecting his lower limbs. Impossibly, he felt heavy. The muscles in his neck struggled to support his head, but his abdomen kept his upper torso erect. Taking a deep breath, he could feel the muscles of his chest.

"Your strength is returning," Kenneth said. "I'm turning down the drip from the IV. It might cause you greater pain, but it should help you recover your senses."

Jared heard the sound of Kenneth's fingers moving beside him.

"Try not to breathe too deeply. Just normal, shallow breaths. Your back has been punctured. Injections directly into your spine. You may feel the wound."

His body, enveloped in numbness for so long, almost lurched with the return of sensation. Stabbing needles rippled down his legs, up his back: the feeling of trying to stand on a foot that had fallen asleep. Then came a sharp sensation in his lower back. He felt as if a railroad spike were penetrating his body. He started to focus again on the music, but returned to the pain, welcoming the sensations, the feelings. Muscles weak from lack of use cramped, spasmed, and contracted.

"It'll be okay," Kenneth said. "I'll keep some of the morphine in the IV, hold it to a more reasonable level. If you go cold turkey you'll have withdrawal. You might survive it, but everyone will notice. This way, we can keep them from knowing."

Jared mentally cocked his head. Kenneth had always been the kindest among the orderlies. He'd talked to Jared; even when Jared couldn't understand, he could identify his voice.

"My brother was Special Forces," Kenneth said. "He died in Kosovo, four years ago. He was my older brother, ten years older than me.

"He used to write me long letters. He told me about the men he fought with—how they had each other's back—when they fought, and when they didn't, too. He died trying to save one of them trapped in a building. Caught a grenade carrying him on his shoulder back to the helicopter." Kenneth's voice broke as he told the story. Jared thought he'd known people who'd served in Kosovo, although he'd never been. He wondered whether Kenneth's brother was one of them.

"I've seen some of the things they've done to you these past few months. When I joined the service I wanted to be like my brother, but I didn't have the eyesight, or the reflexes. I became a corpsman so I could help people. They told me this place was a rehab facility. But what they've done to you… I just think my brother would want me to help. I may not be able to stop it, but maybe I can help you get through it. At the rate they're going, I don't know how much there'll be left of you."

Jared wanted to reach out and comfort him, tell him things weren't so bad. Then realized the ridiculousness of the thought. His strength was returning, thank to Kenneth's help, but he couldn't move his head, and didn't know whether his legs would support him if he did stand up.

Kenneth repositioned him in his chair, trying to make him more comfortable. Jared expelled a breath, the only form of expression he could make. Then remembered he could move his hands. He made a fist. A thank you.

"They don't watch you all the time, you know. Just when you're with the doctor, and sometimes upstairs. I guess they assume the drugs will do the trick. But there's really not that much security. Just a couple of goons who mostly stay downstairs. They don't go up. Although I'm not sure about all the orderlies. They're not corpsmen, that's for sure. Marines would be my guess.

"I can help you regain your mobility, help you walk maybe, but after that, I don't know. Getting outside won't be enough. We're still miles away from anywhere, so maybe it's a foolish thought. But it's what Rick would want."

Jared shook his fist as much as his wrist would allow, trying to signal understanding.

Part of him wondered whether this was all part of the game. For months after he'd first gotten there, he couldn't tell what was real and what wasn't. As his awareness gradually returned, he could vaguely recollect a helicopter, an explosion, and a trek through the woods. Amid explosions and machine gun fire, he pictured faces, thought of names, but couldn't put them together. After Chase started coming, it all started to connect better. Chase was real, part of a remembered past. Someone he could trust. He thought he could trust Kenneth. As it stood, he had little control of his fate without some help. He didn't think he had much time left. Somehow he doubted those who'd put him here were interested in his leaving with all his faculties intact.

"I've been trying to wean you off the maintenance drugs they use. I don't think those orderlies upstairs are smart enough to recognize a change in dosage or drip speed. You should regain the use of your legs or arms soon—the muscle tone is good."

Jared heard a noise outside and instinctively turned his head toward the door. And his head responded, causing him excruciating, wonderful, pain. He felt Kenneth's hands on the sides of his face as the orderly gently turned his head back facing forward. Heard his fingers on the IV drip. Felt the returning of the numbness.

"I've got to go," he heard Kenneth say, somewhat distantly. "I don't know what you did, but it couldn't be worth this."

He heard footsteps, heard the door open, and then close. He tried to remember again what had brought him here, what he'd done. He killed some people, he knew. But that wasn't it. That's what the army had trained him to do.

NINE

Chase's head throbbed and his right hand felt arthritic. Continually flexing the fingers, he steered the car with his left hand, shifting with the heel of his right. A cardboard tube sat next to him on the seat. He had left the house first thing in the morning, two hours earlier than usual. Visiting hours didn't start until noon, but today he meant to put in an early appearance, and wait, if he had to. He needed to learn more about the Institute. Until now, lulled by his brother's condition, he'd been content to notice the oddities of the place without thinking much about them, but now he felt a sense of urgency to learn more, to notice more.

Reagan had called the day before. She'd managed to get hold of an invoice from an outside contractor.

"Excavation," she said. "The contract called for an excavation, as in underground."

"Digging a basement?" Chase suggested.

"Not at these prices. We're talking serious work, over a three-year period. There's got to be a lot more space underground than above it. With what they spent, they could have built the underground White House—a bunker in the event of a nuclear attack."

Chase meant to find out more. Was the facility really a hospital, or was it something else? A hospital might need more space, more modern facilities, which could explain the budget. But then why the need for the reconstruction—why not just build a new modern building? Unless they were trying to hide something. From experience, he knew he had a better chance of finding out if he could catch them with their pants down.

A chain blocked the entrance road up the mountain. First anomaly. Fortunately it wasn't attached to a lock; he simply removed it and continued the drive. He parked in the same space past the gate and walked over to the guardhouse, knocked on the guardhouse door but received no response. He scanned the surrounding area and finally spotted a camera, half-hidden, about forty feet up the trunk of a tall pine. Positioning himself with a view of the front gates, but in sight of the camera, he sat on a rock set back a bit from the entrance. And waited. Ten minutes passed. Then Dr. Brunelli walked out the front door, came slowly down the path, and opened the gates with a remote control.

"Nice to see you again, Mr. Riordan," said the doctor. He looked pointedly at his watch. "Although visiting hours won't begin for another hour and forty-five minutes."

"Sorry, Doc. I have some business to take care of later this afternoon, but I still wanted to see Jared. I took a chance you might relax your visiting hours. I can wait though, if need be. I'll try to reschedule my meetings."

"No, no, I'm sure that won't be necessary," said Brunelli, holding out his fleshy hand. "We know how busy you are these days. We can make an exception this once. Although your brother is still in treatment. It will be another half hour or so until he's ready for visitors."

"Thank you, Doctor, I appreciate it. Perhaps we could use the time to discuss Jared's condition. And his treatment."

"Of course. I welcome the opportunity to do so." The doctor glanced behind him. Chase looked toward the building, but saw no activity.

"Please, come this way." Brunelli led him up the path into the building and they walked together through the front door.

The whir of machinery sounded behind the walls. An elevator? Chase made a point of looking around, then looked back to his escort. "Where is everybody?"

"Ah. We had a bit of an outing this morning and most of the patients are still away."

"An outing?"

"Yes, to Asheville. For a hike, I believe."

"But not Jared."

"No. Unfortunately, our less ambulatory inmates had to remain behind."

Inmates? A slip of the tongue? But he asked, "For treatment?"

Brunelli looked at Chase sharply. Chase kept his face composed, his gaze direct but interested. "Yes. Physical therapy, counseling sessions, depending upon the needs of the patient."

Chase rubbed his temples, his head still throbbing. He could only imagine the treatment his brother was receiving. The doctor cocked his head.

"Shall we sit down?" He led Chase into the lobby area, and the two sat down. "What would you like to know?"

"Doctor, I know next to nothing about Jared's condition," Chase admitted. "He's seated in a chair every time I've come to visit, and he always looks pretty much the same. I've spent the better part of a year trying to get some answers from the army as to how Jared came to be here, and what his long-term prognosis is. And hit nothing but roadblocks. He's my brother. I want him to get the best care possible, of course, but I'd like to know what's wrong with him." He'd tried to engage other doctors during previous visits, but they'd all put him off with vague allusions to national security.

The doctor leaned forward. "Mr. Riordan, I know this is difficult for you. You must appreciate that we are providing your brother with the best possible care. The military takes care of its own, which is why they sent him to this facility. We are one of the leading treatment facilities in the country for PTSD."

"Post-Traumatic Stress Disorder?"

"Your brother's condition is properly called Post-Traumatic Stress Disorder after Traumatic Brain Injury."

"Brain injury? Could you be more specific? What's wrong with his brain?"

Brunelli sighed. "We don't really know, to be honest. Some of the functions have shut down, we believe as a result of a serious blow, perhaps in action. The brain is a complex organ, and we know very little about how it truly operates. Your brother experienced a blow to the head, and coupled with his war experience, the stress he's endured, it caused his brain to shut down, which had a ripple effect, as the brain, I'm sure you know, controls all of the other bodily functions." The doctor's fingers fumbled together as he spoke.

"So what does that mean, long term?" Chase asked.

"Sadly, we don't know. He could suddenly get better, or he could stay like this. His condition is not, I'm happy to say, degenerative––it won't get any worse."

If Jared could communicate through his fingers, demonstrating a high level of dexterity, the recollection of his past, his childhood, it was hard for Chase to believe his brain could be damaged so severely. Or had he imagined the whole thing? Was he really playing the "Minute Waltz," or had he just fluttered his fingers, twitching from some nervous reaction as the doctor had said?

"How much longer does he need to be here?" Chase asked. "Perhaps I could bring him back with me, get a nurse to stay with him at home?"

"No, no, Mr. Riordan. I don't think you realize what you'd be taking on. Jared needs constant care and attention. He needs regular therapy and treatment."

"I could get him the appropriate care. He'd be with family."

"I'm sorry, Mr. Riordan, but there are aspects of Jared's

care that remain highly confidential. I'm afraid we couldn't possibly allow physicians not cleared by the army to work with him. Aside from that, your brother signed a waiver, allowing us to provide the care needed."

"In his condition?"

"No, of course not. Some three years ago, I believe."

Chase wondered whether such a waiver would hold up in court. A year before he was admitted to the Pembrooke Institute, not upon enlistment. Randy Turner did a lot of contract law; Chase made a note to ask him. As a hypothetical.

A beep sounded, and Brunelli looked down at a pager on his waist. "Jared should be back in his room now," he said.

"Just one final question. What can I do to help his recovery?"

The doctor clapped his hands together. "I think your visits are a great help. I understand you read to him, talk to him. The more you can remind him of who he is, where he came from, the better. We have so many patients who have no family, no visitors. So sad."

Chase had never seen a single other visitor before. Sad wasn't the right word. He held up the cardboard tube.

"In that case, perhaps you'd indulge me?"

The doctor raised his eyebrows.

"Just a picture. It's similar to one that used to hang on the wall of our bedroom. I was hoping you would let me hang it in his room." He opened the tube and unrolled the poster.

The doctor bobbed his head a few times. "A wonderful movie. I much enjoyed it. With those British runners, right?"

"Yes. Jared always loved the movie. I thought if it hung in his room, it might help remind him of his childhood."

Rubbing his chin, Brunelli appeared thoughtful. "It's unusual, but I don't see why not." He stood up and led Chase down the hallway toward Jared's room.

As they proceeded down the corridor, Chase noticed all the doors, as always, were closed. He had never seen the inside of another patient's room, only his brother's. And, no stairwells. A house or a building this size would surely have a large staircase leading to the upstairs floors.

The door to Jared's room was already open. Chase saw his brother slumped in a wheelchair near the bed. He wore a robe and hospital scrubs, with a mitten of some kind on his right hand, which was strapped to the chair arm. His head tilted toward the ceiling, a bandage covering a good portion of it above his right ear.

"One of the disadvantages of acquiring some degree of movement without the appropriate brain processes in sync," Brunelli said. "He managed to harm himself with a fork. One of our attendants thoughtlessly left one on the table when we were feeding him; he managed to grab it and stab himself in the head."

Chase flexed the fingers of his right hand out of reflex, not believing a word of it. He pushed the wheelchair so it faced him and looked at his brother. He could detect nothing, no sign of intelligence or awareness. Either his condition was as severe as the doctor claimed, or he was drugged to the gills. Or both. He'd been certain that, armed with the knowledge from his discussion with Reagan and from his observation of his brother the previous week, he'd be able to know for certain that Jared still remained aware, that he could hide that fact from his doctors and attendants, but not from Chase. But the wheelchair-bound man in front of him was a stranger.

Chase took out the poster. He took a role of tape from his pocket, peeled off four small pieces, and hung the picture above the bed. "Remember *Chariots of Fire*, Jared?" he said. "You used to love that line, what was it? '"When I run, I feel God's pleasure.'" Pulling a chair over from the window, he sat down and faced Jared. Brunelli stood just outside the door, his presence still noticeable, his shadow in the room. Chase began talking to his brother, about their childhood; the time their Dad took them fishing. As he spoke, he looked around the room. The poster seemed out of place in such a sterile environment. No personal items, no colors, just a single chest of drawers, the bed, two chairs, and the small table. One of the dresser drawers was slightly askew. Keeping his eye on the door, he quietly got up and walked over, pausing in his story. He gently pulled the drawer to level it, opened it a couple inches, and then closed it flush. Brunelli remained outside his line of sight. He returned to his seat and continued talking.

After a few minutes, he got up, positioned his brother's wheelchair so it faced the poster, patted him on the shoulder, and said goodbye. As the doctor escorted him out, he considered what he'd seen in the dresser drawer. Two shoes, caked with mud.

TEN

When Garth didn't rush to the door to greet him, Chase went on alert as he entered his townhouse.

Silently, Chase eased the door shut, and walked down the hallway toward the kitchen. He snapped his fingers, calling his dog. As he did so, the hall light behind him came on. Startled, he turned.

"I would have thought you'd have better security," said the man in his doorway. "Alarm system off, key still in the flower pot out front. Even the front window was unlocked."

"I guess I thought a ninety-five pound Irish wolfhound might deter most casual visitors," Chase said. The grey stubble on his visitor's head, the U.S. flag lapel pin, his rigid posture, the way he wore the blue suit like a uniform, all conspired to label him U. S. Government or Army.

Chase backed away, picking up the kitchen phone to call 911. His visitor held up his hand.

"I apologize for the surprise entrance, but please hear me out. I didn't think it would look good if I just sat on your steps waiting for you to get home."

"Where's my dog?"

The intruder held up his hands. "That's a fine animal

you have. I used to raise wolfhounds myself." At his words Garth walked out to the hallway, allowing the man to scratch behind his ears before approaching Chase, his head down.

"Fine watchdog you are," Chase admonished, the phone still in his hand.

"Brigadier General Harold Jackson, retired. I was your brother's commanding officer at Bragg. I thought it time we talked."

"Explain to me please, why you felt it necessary to break into my house in order to meet? My number's in the book and my office is right downtown," Chase chided.

Jackson's face assumed a pained expression. "I do apologize, but phone calls leave records and I couldn't afford to be seen just showing up in your office."

"I wasn't aware the army operated with such a need for secrecy." Chase considered the phone in his hand and decided if the man had wanted to hurt him, he could have staged an ambush before Chase even knew he was there. He put down the telephone. "Might as well sit down if we're going to talk," he said. He motioned Jackson into the living room, an open area dominated by a Boesendorfer Grand Piano. Two wing-back chairs sat opposite the instrument, separated by a small table. He sat down and Jackson did the same, settling himself into the seat slowly.

"Thank you. I appreciate it. My knees appreciate it. The army has its share of secrets, to be sure, but I did say I'm retired. I'm not here in any kind of official capacity." He let his left leg stretch out and began to massage the knee.

"Even stranger then. Breaking into a private citizen's home?" Chase sat on the edge of the chair, keeping Garth close, rubbing his head. His curiosity was piqued.

"You know the Pembrooke Institute?" Jackson said in response.

"What do you know about that?"

"How'd you find out your brother was there?"

Chase narrowed his eyes, something clicked. "That was

you?" In the midst of the Tierney trial he'd received an anonymous postcard.

"Let's put that aside for the moment. But you've been to the Institute, visited your brother. That's not a question, that's a statement. You know, then, how far the army will go to keep its secrets."

"I haven't been able to find out much about the Institute yet, if that's what you mean," Chase said, hesitant to reveal what he'd learned so far.

"Or about your brother."

The statement hung in the air, the specter of Jared hovering in the room. Chase considered the man next to him. He tried to remember Jared ever mentioning a commanding officer at Fort Bragg, but couldn't recall any names.

"Why are you here?" Chase asked, staring intently at his visitor.

Jackson returned the stare. "I don't know you very well, Mr. Riordan."

"Chase."

"Chase, thank you. But I feel I do. Maybe it's just your appearance, the way you remind me of him."

"My brother and I are nothing alike," Chase said, more harshly than he intended.

"Of course. I didn't mean to imply anything other than that I feel a certain sense of familiarity, if you will. Although I know more about you than you probably realize. Jared used to talk about you all the time."

The statement surprised him.

"Oh yes, he kept a subscription to the *Piedmont Gazette*, even stationed overseas. Tried to keep track of your cases, best he could," Jackson said. "Which gets back to why I'm here. If you don't mind, I'm going to tell a bit of a story. My wife accuses me of being a bit long-winded at times, but I need to tell this in my own way. It starts about five years ago."

Chase asked him if he could use a glass of water.

"Bourbon, if you've got it. This may take a while."

He found a bottle of Jack Daniels and poured a measure for the general, thought about it, and poured himself an equal amount. Jackson took a small sip, obviously savoring the taste. He told Chase about running into Jared at Fort Benning in Georgia. Jackson had been base commander and Jared was returning from his second tour of duty in Afghanistan.

"I hardly recognized him, at first. When he first got to Bragg, he was big, but soft. A target for the other guys, especially the little guys, the scrappers. They pushed him hard, but he didn't back down. Seemed like he welcomed the attention, actually. After a while people left him alone. I think he scared some of them. When I saw him at Benning he'd put on a lot of muscle, and he had a harder look to him. I'd seen it before; war does that to a person. You see things, do things, that ordinary people can't even imagine. Afghanistan was rough duty. I served a tour there myself, and believe me, I had no desire to return. But Jared was different. He seemed to resent being back in the States, out of the action. He couldn't wait to get on the plane and get back.

"He came by my office. We talked about our time at Bragg, traded experiences. He'd made E-7 by then, Sergeant First Class. I'd heard he'd been put up for Officer Candidate School, but turned it down. I asked him about it, he told me he didn't want to push pencils. No offense, but he wanted to fight, to be among the men, not above them." The general's eyes glazed as he transported himself back in time. He sipped his bourbon. Chase might as well not have been in the room.

Jackson continued, "Jared was in Georgia waiting to be reassigned. Due to the stressful nature of the duty, two tours in Afghanistan was the limit. He'd have to either take a stateside assignment or serve a tour in a non-combat area prior to his next posting. But another option presented itself. Army Special Forces. It meant re-upping for a six-year commitment, and advanced training. He asked my opinion. "I told him what I knew. Probably not much more than he did, but I had a few buddies who'd gone that route. It was a top outfit, maybe the most elite fighting unit in the world. That appealed to him. He'd be challenged, but I knew he could handle the physical part. He'd come a long way from the skinny recruit at Bragg. Mentally, that was a different story. Those boys are pretty hardcore. But he'd become pretty hardened himself. I could tell he wanted it. We ended up grabbing dinner, drinking late into the night. I don't think your brother was much of a drinker, but he put away quite a few double vodkas. I'm sure I drank my share of bourbon.

"After a while we were sitting with a bottle between us, out near a rifle range. Don't ask me how we got there. I told some war stories from Nam; Jared talked about his time in Afghanistan. Both hellish, horrible places to serve. One particular incident stood out, something that weighed on him. On his first tour, just out of training, he was the spotter, the guy who called the target for the sniper. Their platoon was on patrol, the sniper team covered the forward area from a bluff overlooking the valley, searching for combatants, the enemy." The colonel looked at the bourbon in his glass, swished it around. "Your brother is a good storyteller. I swear I could feel the sand swirling around me, smell the cordite in the air. Anyway, they caught mortar fire, and the sniper took some shrapnel in his shoulder. Turns out later to have been friendly fire. Jared dressed the wound and picked up the rifle, using his scope to continue his scan ahead of the platoon. He spotted a small group of men, nearly invisible against a cliff face. His radio had been a casualty of the mortar fire, so he had no way of alerting his platoon they were heading into a trap."

Jackson looked over at Chase, his eyes taking a moment to refocus. "Remember, Chase, I trained your brother. So I had at least a sense of what he was capable. He'd always scored well on the range, above average, but certainly not good enough to qualify for sniper school. We trained at fifty and a hundred yards. Small targets, with M-16 rifles. And here he found himself six hundred yards from a group of Afghani rebels, with an M-21 sniper rifle, his platoon walking into an ambush and nothing he could do about it.

"He told me this story, and I didn't believe it, so I pulled up the field reports, which verified his account. Setting himself on the ground, in the same position as the sniper, he took aim. Fourteen shots later, every single rebel lay dead or dying on that cliff side. I've been at the other end of sniper fire, and let me tell you, it's an experience you'll never forget. No one around, and then suddenly one of your buddies drops, the sound so distant it doesn't register as gunfire, and the bullets arrive before the sound anyway. After the second body goes down, panic takes over, and you start scrambling for shelter, still not knowing where the bullets are coming from.

"So believe me when I tell you that Jared's feat was truly extraordinary. The first two shots may have been easy. Or would have been easy for an experienced shooter who knew the wind conditions and had a good spotter. But the next twelve he'd have been shooting at moving targets. It's not easy leading a man from six hundred yards away. I don't think there are a handful of men in the world who could do it. But your brother did. He killed fourteen men in the space of perhaps thirty seconds. From a third of a mile away."

Good God. Chase tried to reconcile this image of Jared with the brother he'd grown up with. Jared had been the calmest person Chase knew, never taking offense at anyone or anything, always the peacemaker. Despite his large size, he remained a bit timid and Chase considered him somewhat of a wimp. While Chase scrapped on the playgrounds earning his stripes against neighborhood toughs, Jared often held up his hands and pled for cooler heads to prevail. He used his wits and his humor to avoid confrontation. Chase felt the need to unburden himself, to talk about the brother he remembered. He described Jared at the piano, playing on the stage before a large crowd, his fingers flying over the keyboard and his face with a deep intensity, his eyes almost closed.

Jackson smiled kindly. "The intensity I can relate to. I

never heard him on the piano, never even knew he could play. I wish I had. When you're out in enemy territory, far from home, music is one of those things that helps you stay connected to your home." He looked over at the piano.

"You play too?"

"Not like my brother," Chase said wistfully. "Dad brought an old Wurlitzer piano home one day, found it at an estate sale. Mom made us both take lessons, but that's as much as we had in common. I can play a bit, country or old rock, at least enough for the songs to be recognizable."

"And yet you have a concert grand piano?" Jackson observed. "Not exactly a toy."

In fact, it was one of the finest pianos in the world. For years Chase had held on to the life insurance benefit he'd received after his parents' deaths. Then three years ago he had taken all of the money and bought the Boesendorfer, the same piano Jared had always preferred. He still wasn't quite sure why.

"No, not a toy," he confirmed.

The general picked up his drink, walked over and sat at the bench and played a scale.

"Still in good tune, I'm guessing?'

Chase nodded. "Every three months."

"I know you're hearing this for the first time. There's a Silver Star in his file for this action and it's just one of many decorations he received. I doubt any of them saw the light of day. Not why I'm here though. I needed to tell that part first. He told me that story, and I swear by the end of it we were both stone cold sober. When the platoon got to the cliff side where those men were, they found the bodies. Fourteen, teenage kids, armed with ancient Russian Kalashnikov rifles. That's not uncommon in Afghanistan. As soon as a kid turns eleven he's given a rifle, sent off to a camp somewhere. But I could see it had been hard on Jared. Firing at an enemy he could hardly see, which turned out to be a bunch of kids. No less dangerous for all that to the platoon, but still kids.

"I gave him a bunch of platitudes, same as I heard first time I killed someone in the war. It's a hard thing, but it's us or them. We're all combatants, they knew what they were doing, they would have killed as many of the platoon as they could. He saved a lot of lives. And so on. I told him about my first kill, how it affected me.

"I'll never forget the expression on his face when he turned to me at that point. I told you about the hard look he had about him. This went far beyond that. His eyes took on a coldness that would freeze the fluid in your joints. I was afraid at that moment, before I realized his eyes weren't focused on me, they were cocked off to the side, looking into the distance, or back in time. You know what he said? 'I'd killed before.' Just like that. Since this had been his first assignment, I wondered whether he'd been involved in a training accident. I must have said something to that effect because he shook his head and said no, not in the army. Before."

Chase was perplexed. Before. Before the Army? Before the army Jared had been studying music at Juilliard. Prior to that Chase and he had been in high school. What could that mean? Was he taking on some kind of guilt for the death of their parents? Then it hit him. He jerked his head back as if struck. Kept his face calm, trying not to reveal his thoughts.

"I didn't ask who, or the details," Jackson continued. "The army doesn't sign up fugitives, and hell, we were just a couple of drunks talking. But I thought you might have some clue, thought it might help with the answers you're looking for," Jackson said softly. "You don't need to tell me anything about it, I don't need to know. Just thought you should…"

Chase nodded. "Thanks." Jared's life had been a void to him, a fast-forward from the last time they'd seen each other in Fayetteville, during basic training, to the Institute. Now he had a few more missing pieces.

"There's more, if you'd like to hear it."

Chase motioned for him to continue.

"Jared shipped out to Special Forces training the next

week. They rushed him through sniper school as well, but he'd already proven himself. It's not as unusual as you might think, but there are some people who don't perform well until things are really on the line. Then somehow they excel. In Jared's case, he needed lives to be on the line. I know he never did terribly well in the rifle competitions. He couldn't hit a static target. But put an enemy head in his sights, and he was deadly.

"I know he went back to Afghanistan, then went to Iraq. Something happened during his last tour there. He was serving under a prick of a guy, a legend in Special Forces named Sterling. One of those guys who pissed everyone off, but since he got stuff done, took on the toughest missions, they tolerated him. The army's full of assholes like that, but Sterling took the prize. In civilian life he'd be in jail, or in a mental institution, but in the army he was the head of Special Forces in Iraq.

"Your brother got into a situation with him. It was all pretty hush-hush; I don't know all the details. I pieced some of this together just recently, called in some favors from some old friends. Seems there was a covert operation in Southern Iraq, a Sunni stronghold surrounded by Shi'ites. Something went wrong and people died. Jared came out barely alive, the only survivor of the team that had been sent in. He staggered into camp, was medevacced to a hospital in Landstuhl, and eventually sent here to North Carolina, to Pembrooke.

"That's the official story. The unofficial one had Jared making his way back to camp and confronting Sterling. They came to blows, and God help me, your brother gave that man an ass kicking he'd deserved for twenty years. Thing like that's pretty hard to keep under wraps, especially with all the people who hated Sterling. They might have cheered the action, but the army's the army, and you don't strike an officer, even if it's Sterling. MPs came in, grabbed Jared before he could do any more damage and took him into custody. Sterling must have got to him before they could get him out of camp. I'm sure if he could have, he'd have taken a limb or a finger, but Jared had been seen getting to camp," Jackson said, his voice break-ing, "so he had to work with that." He drained the last of his bourbon and poured another.

Chase's eyes watered as he listened to the account. From a great distance, his brother's career had seemed exotic. Trav-eling overseas to places he'd never been, serving his country, making a difference in the war on terror. The reality was a horror story. Filled with death, psychopaths, and torture.

"And so Pembrooke. If Sterling had left it alone they would have court-martialed Jared, given him a dishonorable discharge. But after what Sterling did, he had to create an ac-count that didn't involve him in any way. He couldn't let it be known, officially at least, that he'd got his butt kicked and that in retaliation he'd taken his revenge. So your brother became a scapegoat, responsible for the loss of his men.

"You're thinking to yourself, if I can know about this, others must know as well. I'm sorry to tell that while there may well be suspicion among the brass, Sterling's got a long record and they have no illusions about him. The only ones who know for sure what happened work for Sterling, and they'd never go against the man. The bottom line is they still need men like him. They're not going to go chase after any rumors, try to resurrect an old case. Your brother is just a ca-sualty of war. One of many."

The general got up from the piano. He picked up a small valise in the corner by the front door. "And that's the end of my story. As to the secrecy, well, the army has no interest in any more negative press about the situation in Iraq. Jared's story, if it came out, might spark some kind of investigation, might cause some heads to roll. You visit him. You're a lawyer, and they know it. They're keeping their eyes on you. But it won't matter, I suspect. So long as Jared can't talk about it, you're not much of a threat."

"Don't be so sure," Chase said softly.

Jackson looked at him. "Pardon?"

He started to tell of his visits, but thought better of

it. Shook his head instead. Walking over to the window, he looked out. Routine traffic, as far as he could tell.

Jackson laughed. "Oh, I don't mean they're watching you 24-7. They'll be listening in when you visit Jared, and I'm sure they're keeping tabs on the trial."

"The trial?" It surprised him how talk about his brother had allowed the trial to fall from his mind.

"I read the papers, Chase. You're quite the famous man around here, with your track record on murder cases. I'm sure I don't need to tell you that. Why do you think they care about you at all? It's also why I didn't come to your office. Members of the press are hanging around there like vultures."

"One of the pitfalls of success," Chase mused. He couldn't even get to his office without running the gauntlet.

"I wouldn't be surprised if they're tapping your phone, though," Jackson added.

Alarmed, Chase tried to remember his phone conversation with Reagan. She had told him about the Pembrooke Institute construction, the invoices. He wished he hadn't involved her.

Noticing his discomfort, Jackson said, "I doubt you're sharing any national secrets with anyone, so you're probably safe. You're a lawyer; they'd think it odd if you weren't curious. The government doesn't have unlimited resources, either. If they're tapping your phone, it's a passive tap. No one's sitting there listening to every word. They have computers that scan the phone traffic, looking for certain words and phrases. Still, be careful. Watch what you say and who you say it to. And watch your step."

"You know I can't leave this alone," Chase said, standing to face the general.

"You wouldn't be Jared's brother if you could," he answered. "But do be careful. These people don't play games." He opened the case and took out a small box. Chase's eyes widened at the sight of it. "Here, I thought you'd want this."

Chase looked at him quizzically and accepted the box. A

gift from their grandfather for Jared's thirteenth birthday. He looked up at Jackson.

"Jared's medals. I thought you might want to have them. They were with his effects. I managed to get hold of them before my retirement became official." He plucked the folder from the valise and pulled out a photo and handed it to Chase. "And I thought you might want this."

It looked like an army publicity photo. A man looked out at him, staring with dark, haunted eyes. His face bore a small scar just above his cheekbone. He wore a green beret, which covered short silver-black hair.

"An ugly cuss, isn't he?" Jackson said.

"Mr. Hyde," Chase said.

"Hmm?"

"Nothing. So this is Sterling?"

"That's him. I thought you might want to know the person responsible for your brother's condition. You wouldn't want to meet him in a dark alley. If you do, run."

"Thanks."

"I'd best be off. I know you have work to do and a lot to digest." He pulled a card out of his pocket. "I don't know that I can be of any further help to you, but if I can," he said, handing it to Chase.

"You need a ride anywhere?" Chase asked.

"No, I'm going to walk around the corner and catch a cab. It's how I got here." He reached out his hand.

Chase shook it, returning the strong grip. "Thank you, general. I know you didn't need to do this."

Jackson sighed. "Yes I did, Chase. Yes I did." Chase followed him to the door. Jackson opened it a crack and gave a cautious scan of the area before slipping out quietly. Chase walked over to the window to watch his departure, but he'd already disappeared.

ELEVEN

Holding the picture in his hand, he stared intently at the face. One he would remember. He carried the picture and the box to his office just off the foyer and put the picture in the top drawer of the desk, a large cherry wood antique that had been his grandfather's. Then he took the box in his hands, opened it, and took out the medals inside; quite a collection. He turned the box over, examining the inlaid patterns of different woods. Setting it down, Chase reached into the closet and pulled out a cardboard box from the back of a shelf and set it on the desk. He sat down in the chair and opened it.

The box held a half-dozen large photo albums, the only remaining record of Chase and Jared's childhood. He sat these aside and pulled out what he was looking for. A set of old yellowed newspaper articles. They were in chronological order. The first in the series was a clipping from the day after the accident. John and Claire Riordan, dead after being struck by a car that careened across the median and smashed into them head on. The driver of the other car had sustained lacerations and bruises and was hospitalized. Not many details, just the bare facts. Struck on their way home from a concert. Jared's performance, Chase remembered, although he had been away at school. Twin sons, Chase and Jared, age nineteen, survived them. He skipped over the obituary and the glowing tribute to John Riordan written by his students.

The next piece came a few weeks after the funeral. The driver who'd caused the crash had been drunk. He'd come from a party, had a .12 blood alcohol level. Negligent homicide charges might be filed. The case was under review.

He remembered receiving the articles in the mail from Jared after the funeral. The last one had a note attached. The driver, Leonardo Cardenas, had been in another accident a month and a half after the accident that had killed their parents. This time he hadn't been so lucky. Jared's note still stuck to the article. "Sometimes there is justice." A week later Jared joined the army.

Looking at the note, Chase knew. His own troubles with Ken Wall seemed insignificant in comparison to what his brother had gone through. Jared was the one who'd gotten the call from the police, who had to identify the bodies at the morgue and share the news with his brother. Jared had always been close to their mom in particular and Chase knew that her sudden death affected him deeply. When he read the article about the driver of the other car, he remembered a rage coming over him. How could this man be walking around after what he did? But he contained his feelings, never even contemplated doing anything, relying on the courts to redress the wrong. He, the physical man of action, had done nothing, while Jared, the academic and musician, had taken revenge. So he had killed before the army. Had given up his dream to do so, and then escaped into a physical world, far beyond the reach of music, perhaps as a form of self-punishment.

The death had been ruled an accident. It had happened years ago and Chase doubted anyone was losing any sleep wondering whether it had been anything but that. And in the interim, Jared had more than served his time. He'd suffered and paid for his crime with his life, or at least a large part of it. It was not the judgment of the law, but rather the judgment of a brother. Chase needed to help him. With the knowledge he'd gained from General Jackson, he should be better positioned to do so.

He knew a lot more than he had just a few short weeks ago. He knew the army's interests and Jared's were not one and the same. He wasn't sure how that helped just yet, but it was an important fact. Know your enemy; know your opponent. In college he could watch game film of opposing teams, preparing for the type of players they had, the types of defenses they'd employ, their offensive schemes. Preparation was always the key to effective execution. The enemies in this case: a man and an institution. A man who used Jared to cover up his own crimes, and an institution that protected him in the process. *Covered up his crime.* Something nagged at the back of his mind. He sat for a few moments, trying to sort it all out, gain a better mental foothold. Lost it. Picking up the phone, he called Reagan, reaching her voicemail. He tried her cell, still no luck. He left an urgent message for her to call him.

He was still sitting at his desk two hours later when the phone rang. Chase jumped to answer it.

"What's up?"

"Reagan—where have you been?" he asked, relieved to hear the sound of her voice.

"We're setting up a task force to support our counter-terrorist efforts. A few of us had dinner to discuss inter-agency cooperation, lines of authority, wildly exciting stuff like that. Why? What's so important?"

"Nothing important, "he said, Jackson's words still in his mind. "I just wanted to talk to you before bed. It's been a long day. Say, do you remember your friend George Epstein?"

There was a few seconds pause. "Oh sure, George. Sorry, I dropped the phone."

"How's he doing?"

"Oh, same old, same old. I don't see him as much as I used to."

Chase pulled out his laptop and plugged in his ethernet

cable, connecting to the Internet. "If you see him, would you tell him I said hello?" He logged in, keying in a website address.

"I'll be sure to do that," Reagan said. In the background he could hear her fingers typing away on a keyboard. *Good.* He hoped she'd gotten the message.

They continued to exchange pleasantries, talking about friends, and innocuous events from their past, as he waited to log in to the new website. George Epstein was a polymath who had attended law school with Chase. In addition to his JD, he also had an MBA, PhDs in physics and math, and had been applying to medical schools the last time Chase had seen him. He'd also just sold an application to the federal government, which had netted him millions––a web-based communication tool that allowed federal employees to chat in a completely secure way. Unlike many online sites, including Yahoo, Google, AOL, and MySpace, which had minimal security, Epstein's application was protected by an encryption system that, according to George, would require all of the Cray super computers in the world working simultaneously for two hundred years to crack. Knowing George, Chase didn't doubt it. During a demonstration, he'd acquired a login name and account. He knew Reagan had one as a federal employee, as the system had recently been installed at the FBI.

As they talked on the phone, Chase received an invitation on his computer to join a chat room with "hotblackchick." He laughed. His own screen name was "Straitman," after his favorite country performer. Accepting, he found himself on a black screen with dragons flying around across the top. Epstein had a dragon fetish and incorporated them into everything he did. He didn't know whether he believed Jackson's assertion that the army listened in to his phone conversations, but he thought it best to take what precautions he could. He communicated to Reagan about his visit from Jackson, what he'd learned about Jared's military career, leaving out the part about the man Jared had killed before joining the army, and downplaying the extent of the torture he'd suffered at his own commanding officer's hands, whom he didn't identify by name.

"Oh my God," she keyed.

He told her how, when they were young boys, although they shared a room, their schedules kept them from seeing a lot of each other. Chase might be coming home from basketball practice while Jared was leaving for a piano competition. Their father had a temper, and on any given day could be looking for a chance to vent his anger. As a means of letting each other know when he might be on the warpath, they'd adopted a simple means of communicating. One of them would leave the third drawer of the dresser open a crack. That was their signal that said, "Avoid Dad at all costs, it's one of those days." Then he told her about the drawer in Jared's room, including the muddy shoes.

"He can walk?"

"If he can move his hand, I suppose there's no reason he can't move his feet. They've said all along there's nothing wrong with him physically. For all the lies I've heard, I've no reason to doubt that one. Especially now."

Jared wanted him to know he was more mobile than he appeared. Perhaps, though, only at certain times. When the drugs wore off, late at night? Regardless, there was hope where there had been none. But there was a danger in the game Jared was playing. If the army, represented by Brunelli or anyone else, learned of his attempts to communicate with Chase, they might take more severe action. Was it coincidence Jared's hand had been bound his last visit?

"I'm going to go to bed, Reagan," Chase said over the phone. "It's getting late, and I'm pretty wiped."

"You've earned the rest. Talk to you soon."

"Love you."

"Love you, too."

They hung up but continued keying in messages for a few more minutes. Chase thought to set up a regular time when they could communicate on-line if need be. Reagan urged him to be careful. Finally, both reluctant to break the contact, they typed their goodbyes. Chase logged out, closed down the website, and got up to give his dog, scratching at the door, some much needed attention.

TWELVE

The board meeting had been going on for over three hours. The twelve board members seated at an imposing mahogany table were tired, sweaty, and irritated. There had been the usual litany of committee reports. One agenda item remained: Miscellaneous Business.

Near the head of the table stood Ev's father, Chairman and CEO of the Litchfield Group. Everett Litchfield, III, presided, his head encircled by the smoke from his ever-present cigarette, three-packs worth of butts filling a large black ceramic ashtray in front of him. Only his son knew it was all a pretense. His father was a fitness nut, who jogged daily, swam laps in his pool, and ate only organic vegetarian produce. "Image is important," he'd told Ev. "Your grandfather died at a young age because he didn't take care of himself."

"He died of lung cancer, I believe. Brought on by smoking the wonderful products this company produces," Ev said.

"He died because he was weak and couldn't control his urges. He let them control him. Every company sells products that could hurt people if used irresponsibly," his father replied. "People have free will. If they want to kill themselves by overeating or by putting too much junk in their bodies, that's their right."

Ev smiled thinly. "Which is why you carry around those cigarettes you so conspicuously don't smoke?"

"As I said, image is important. I represent this company. You do the same. It wouldn't hurt you to support the business that allows you to live the way you do." The most recent exchange, merely the last in a long-running conversation, had taken place in the exercise room at his father's estate, while Everett, Senior huffed and puffed on the treadmill and Ev fiddled with the remote control on the big-screen television.

"I shall remember that, father. But you and I already agree on the subject."

"What's that?"

"The importance of image."

Today, as on that day, his father's physical condition was belied by his red face, this time from the anger vented as he began to pace back and forth. Around the table sat the other eleven members of the board, all but Ev looking uncomfortable, but making no moves to leave or say a word. Most of the members were professional board sitters; retired executives making a living off their board fees.

"Let me try to summarize the issue, if I may." Ev waited for his father to acknowledge him with a vague wave, then continued, in a calm southern drawl.

"The *Piedmont Gazette* has been publishing a series of articles on the tobacco industry. Nothing shocking there, we all know the drill."

Sporting an Italian blue blazer, tan linen slacks, and an elegantly tailored cream-colored shirt, Ev was the only person not wearing a suit, although he had by far the most expensive wardrobe. He looked up, inquiring whether he should continue.

His father, still breathing heavily, still angry, carefully put his cigarette out. He looked as if he were about to make some violent retort, but waved his hand and said, "Go ahead."

"Thank you, sir. We all understand the justifiable concern of our board chairman regarding the irresponsibility of the press. However, I wonder whether we're not putting the cart before the horse, so to speak. All we've seen so far is just a rehash of the same things reporters have been carping about for years. They want to paint us as the devil incarnate, enticing young children to put our cancer sticks in their mouths, robbing them of both their innocence and their lives."

To a person, everyone around the table visibly cringed at the description, rarely spoken so bluntly.

"So what's different now? The public can only read so many of these so-called exposés. They become desensitized to the issue. Besides, many of these readers' livelihoods are tied up with the tobacco industry. Who's going to worry about what one crusading journalist says? And the man's probably taken his best shot by now. Where's the rest of the story coming from?"

Ten pairs of black wing-tipped shoes shuffled restlessly under the table.

"Ev, I appreciate your sentiments," his father said in a measured tone. "But I'm not sure you quite understand the reason behind my, um, how did you characterize it, my *concern.*

"Now you're a bit new to the board, and I can appreciate that. I invited you to participate as a member because I thought we could use some new blood up here among us old fogies."

And because I control a good bit of grandfather's stock, Ev thought.

"And I do thank you for your concise, uh, summary. My *concern,* as you put it, is not so much over the articles themselves, but rather, the writer's apparent knowledge of events and information known until now only by a privileged few people at our small company." His father enjoyed characterizing the firm as "just a small tobacco company," even though its most recent annual revenues, if publicly reported, would place it in the upper half of the S&P 500. "And I am 'concerned' that more such information will be revealed." His voice rose in intensity. "So on the one hand, Ev, you are certainly correct. These articles have received relatively little attention. And I hope it remains that way." His voice rose. "But someone had better damn well find out who in God's name is leaking information to that reporter."

A coughing fit struck the chief legal counsel, very actively smoking next to the chairman. Ev sat calmly at the opposite end of the table, legs crossed, examining his manicured fingernails. Taking advantage of his father's momentary silence, he leaned forward on the table and again spoke quietly. "Thank you, sir. I do indeed appreciate the gravity of the situation facing us. I propose we set up a board-sponsored investigation of the matter. And I volunteer to take personal charge of the investigation. I will be sure to alert you, as well as the rest of the board, as to my findings. Now I'm sure everyone here is tired from a long meeting, so I move that we adjourn." He looked at his father and added, "With your permission, sir."

His father stared back, held his gaze for a moment, then finally nodded; the motion was quickly seconded, approved, and the meeting adjourned.

AS EV STROLLED down the corridor back to his office, a strong grip on his shoulder halted his progress. Ev didn't flinch. "What, attending a board meeting, then staying to actually work in the office? How nice of you to grace us with your presence."

Ev removed the hand on his shoulder, and turned around and faced his father, standing almost nose to nose. "Why father, I'm an officer and shareholder of this company. Whatever do you mean?"

"Don't play games with me, boy. I could write my name in the dust on your office furniture."

Ev smiled. "You know I have my office dusted every evening."

The older man sighed. Scorn showed on his face, the massive eyebrows coming together. "Would it hurt you to at least make a pretense of showing up on a regular basis? You're my goddamned son, for Christ's sake."

"Quite likely, father." Ev laughed at the characterization. "In fact, quite likely."

His father squinted. "You've learned something from the old man after all. Fine. You handle that investigation, son. But you report back to me and me alone. I want to nail that bastard, you hear me?"

Ev looked his father in the eye. "I understand," he said.

As Ev approached his office, his secretary stopped him. "Ev? A Randall Turner keeps calling. He's called like five times already. I told him I didn't know where you were, although when he called the last time you were with your father so I did know where you were."

Ev smiled patiently. "Thank you, Savannah. Why don't you go ahead and take your lunch break now."

Savannah cocked her head. "But I already ate lunch!"

"That's fine. Take another one. Buy yourself something." He peeled a few hundred-dollar bills from his money clip and handed them to her.

"Gee thanks, Everett!"

For a moment Ev's face clouded over. "Don't call me that. Ever."

A look of alarm crossed her face. "I'm sorry, Ev, what did I do?"

The cloud across Ev's face remained. "Never mind, Savannah. I'm sorry. Have a nice lunch. And if you're good, I'll take you to dinner someplace expensive."

Savannah brightened up, grabbed her purse, and bounced out of her chair. Ev enjoyed the view as she shimmied to the elevator.

Ev walked back to his desk, saluting the photograph of E. M. Litchfield, II on his desk. He punched in Randy's number. A woman answered the phone, then put the call through when he mentioned his name.

"Randall Turner."

Randall. And picking up his phone today. "Randy, Ev. How's the legal battle today?"

"Fine Ev, I was wondering if we could get together. I have a few things I'd like to discuss."

"How about over racquetball? We could resume our regular game. I don't think we've played since the wedding."

"Racquetball? No I... that is, what I meant was, could we get together at the office? For a business meeting."

"Lunch perhaps, tomorrow?" Ev suggested. "Twelve-thirty? Why don't you just come by the office? I'll have the chef whip something up."

"That would be great. I'll look forward to seeing you then. And thanks."

"I've been trying to reach you about Beach Weekend, just a few details to clear up."

"Well... uh, I haven't cleared that with Marinda yet."

"Okay, we can talk over lunch then. Regards to your lovely wife." Marinda Faye Turner, née Grady. The southern belle Randy had married six months before, who had then begun her major reclamation projection. First, the new house on Providence Road, clearly beyond their means, then the matching Lexus sedans. Randy's wardrobe had gotten a major overhaul as well, his off the rack suits and shirts from JoS. A. Bank replaced with custom suits, monogrammed shirts, accessorized with designer silk ties, and Ferragamo and Cole Haan footwear. And now his name. What was next? Ev wondered.

Ev looked at his watch, wondering what to do to kill the time. He found himself wishing he hadn't sent Savannah off quite so quickly.

THIRTEEN

Chase arrived at the courthouse at eight, hoping to beat the crowds. The news trucks were parked out front, still in the process of setting up, so he managed to make his way inside unimpeded. The routine business of the courts proceeded, and the administrative staff arrived with him, allowing entry to the building without a challenge from the media. He passed through the security gates, found the conference room on his own, and opened his briefcase on the table.

The case against his client had never been ironclad. Driven more by emotion and, in Chase's mind, a rush to judgment, the investigation into Katarina Volkova's death had been less than stellar. Had Chase been the prosecutor, he would not have been comfortable bringing the case before a jury. That wasn't to say it didn't present problems for him as defense attorney. The biggest in his mind was Wall's presence at the table. Not his skill as a prosecutor, but his stature and position. The mere fact that the District Attorney for the City of Piedmont considered this case important enough to take the seat, for the first time in years, would stick in the minds of the jury. They would grant the case credence it might not otherwise deserve. Chase had given Wall some rope, and he hadn't hung himself;

in fact, he'd acquitted himself well. On a few occasions he'd allowed Chase to rile him, but otherwise he'd stuck to the facts of the case. This lead to the second problem for the defense, the physical evidence placing Rufus, or at least his jacket, at the crime scene, and his client's lack of an alibi.

Prosecutors always hammered on alibi for one simple reason: Juries get it. If the accused can't prove he wasn't at the crime scene, the inference is he might have been there.

Rarely is an alibi perfect, Chase knew, especially given the time between the trial and the actual crime. *Where were you seventeen months ago on Friday? Can you prove it?* And while Rufus Agnew was fishing on the day of the murder, the prosecution wanted to know: Who saw him? How many fish did he catch? What time did he return home?

The fact that Rufus went fishing every Friday afternoon didn't matter. No one might have seen him on any of his previous fishing trips, but it was this particular one that was relevant to the case. The prosecution had shown that Rufus hadn't stopped at a gas station, hadn't purchased a soda, hadn't stopped at the bait shop, wasn't seen by another motorist, and implied that surely, had he really been fishing, someone would have seen him. Things like that stuck with juries. They found the behavior suspicious: if the accused wasn't doing something stealthy then surely he would've been seen. In fact, Chase thought, it was unfortunate.

When Rufus had first approached him, Chase had no illusions about the case. He didn't know whether the mayor had murdered Katarina Volkova or not, but he'd been surprised he had been arrested on such flimsy evidence. He presumed either the D.A. had held something back, or Agnew would be exonerated before the case went too far. As time wore on, Chase kept expecting a smoking gun of some kind, or a glimpse into the psyche of his client. When neither appeared, Chase began to believe he had that rarest of things in a murder case ––an innocent client. And after two other murder trials, this was starting to feel too familiar.

Innocent or not, Rufus Agnew still could be convicted. Certainly no one else had shown up as a better candidate for the crime. Not that the police investigated any further. In addition to his own investigator, Chase had spent a lot of his client's money on a private firm, but they'd been unable to find out any more than he had, specifically relating to two vital pieces of information: who'd called Katarina in the hours prior to her murder, and whose fingerprints were in the condo other than Agnew's. He hadn't expected success on the second front—the police had better access to fingerprint databases—but he'd hoped to gain at least some insight into the caller. The phone that made the calls had been purchased at a certain wireless store on the outskirts of town. The purchase had been on a Saturday, two weeks before the murder, during a busy time at the store. Store employees interviewed could not identify the purchaser. The buyer had paid in cash and later activated the phone with sixty minutes of time at another store, also paid for with cash.

Rufus showed up at 8:45, nattily dressed in a cream-colored linen suit, adorned with a gold watch and fob. "Shall we?" Chase said.

"I thought I'd welcome this day, to be honest. But I have to tell you, I'm scared shitless," Agnew said. "I've put my neck on the line a whole lot of times during my career, but in this case it really is my neck on the line. Believe me, there's a world of difference, son."

"I won't say I know how you feel. I don't. But here we are, here you are, and we're going to get through this together."

Agnew gave a nod. "All right."

Chase noticed his client's trembling hands, the sagging skin, the prominent veins. He'd thought of Rufus Agnew as an iconic figure, a lion of a man who'd dominated city politics for years, who made things happen. The mayor appeared before him as a scared old man. Chase realized he'd allowed his earlier impressions of Agnew, his vitality, and his presence, to color his perceptions. Perhaps the jury needed to see him in this light as well.

The bailiff appeared at the door. "Five minutes."

Chase gathered up his things, the two men stood, and they walked into the courtroom.

After the jury had taken their seats, the district attorney walked down the aisle. Making an entrance. Sill wearing his grey suit. Chase had deliberately chosen a new Hugo Boss suit, blue, with a crisp white shirt, and a maroon silk tie with a muted pattern. All with Ev's help and advice.

"When I'm interviewing someone, I expect them to dress to impress me," Ev had explained. "Which, granted, is difficult to do. They're there for one reason. To try to get me to hire them. Therefore, they should put on their best suit, and present their best case to me as to why I should do that."

The logic made sense to Chase. Let Wall wear his ratty old grey suit. The jury knew he could afford to dress better. As for himself, he wanted the jury to think of him as young, honest, respectful of his elders. Dressing nice enough to impress without overdoing it. New versus old.

The judge called the court to order. Chase gathered himself and stood: "The defense calls Rufus Agnew."

He couldn't have chosen an opening statement more calculated to send the court into an uproar. The media had long speculated as to whether the ex-mayor would take the stand in his own defense. Most experts had predicted he would not. It would provide the district attorney the opportunity to destroy his credibility, to diminish his *star power*. Keeping him off the stand would at least preserve the image people had of him. The greater reason for the clamor in the courtroom, Chase knew, was the fact he hadn't called any other witnesses. It would end here, and everyone in the courtroom could feel it.

When order was restored, Rufus Agnew stood up with dignity, his cane gripped hard in his left hand. The sound of his cane and feet hitting the floor reverberated through the room. He settled in the witness box, leaned his cane against the back railing, and faced the bailiff, who held out the Bible. The oath administered, Chase walked around the table to a position halfway between the defense table and the witness. He wanted to make this seem conversational, but he also needed to make sure his client could hear his questions.

"Mr. Mayor," Chase began.

"Objection," Wall said, "This man is not the mayor of this town. He is an accused killer."

Chase raised his eyebrows at the judge. "Your Honor?"

The judge sighed. "Mr. Wall, it has long been the practice of decorum to address ex-politicians by their former titles. I hardly think the jury has been prejudiced by this practice. However, I understand your objection. Mr. Riordan, perhaps you could find another form of address? Mr. Agnew will suffice."

Chase bowed his head deferentially, grateful for the objection. "Of course. Mr. Agnew, you've heard a lot of speculation and innuendo about your relationship with the accused. If you please, what was your relationship with Katarina Volkova?"

Might as well hit the toughest nail first. Wall had made the case about their relationship, the powerful man and his mistress. He'd made a lot of assumptions, but hadn't taken the time to verify all of them.

"Katarina Volkova was my niece."

Chase wished he could have been focusing on Ken Wall's expression when Agnew answered his question. The judge had to silence the spectators.

"Can you clarify?'

"Yes. You mentioned earlier that Katarina's mother lives in Florida. She and her husband divorced four years ago, but have stayed on good terms. Galina's been in this country a few years now. Three years ago she married my cousin, James Hogan."

"Beyond your family relationship, in what capacity did you deal with Ms. Volkova?"

"Ms. Volkova was a client of mine, of the firm."

"And how did that come about?"

"Ms. Volkova approached me to try and help with her father."

"Help in what way?"

"It's a bit of a long story."

"I think you have the time," Chase said, drawing laughs, including from the jury.

"Quite. Ms. Volkova's father is Vladimir Volkov, the former CEO of a large conglomerate headquartered in St. Petersburg, Russia. He'd built the firm out of the ashes of the former Soviet Union, buying up smaller companies, and invested a lot in new technology. His firm had a large number of drilling platforms out in the Black Sea and in Siberia. Along the way, he acquired his share of enemies, including the State. The current regime in Russia was less than enamored by his economic wealth, his power. They decided to make a lesson out of him. Two years ago, they began to methodically strip him of his assets, all in the interests of national security.

"Accidents began to occur at some of the larger drilling sites. Fires, equipment malfunctions, that sort of thing. Volkov knew the source of his difficulties, and did his best to contain the damage. But his opponents were ultimately too powerful. Two years ago he was arrested on trumped-up charges, and his company placed effectively in State hands. He's been under house arrest ever since," Agnew said. He pulled out a handkerchief from his breast pocket, wiped his brow, and asked for a glass of water.

As he drank, Ken Wall stood. With an air of forbearance he said, "Your Honor, I'm sure we all appreciate, even sympathize with, the plight of Ms. Volkova's father, but I fail to see what relevance this has toward the issues at hand. Are we next to hear about Ms. Volkova's poor destitute mother, struggling to make ends meet with her millionaire husband's assets frozen?"

"Mr. Riordan?" the judge asked.

"Judge Moody, the district attorney has gone to great lengths to portray my client as a lecherous old man and the victim as his young mistress. Her relationship with her father is critical to the defense's case in establishing the true connection between the Mayor, excuse me, Mr. Agnew and Ms. Volkova."

"I'll allow it, but please get to the point," the judge said.

"Yes, your Honor," Chase said, and half-turned toward the still standing district attorney, adding, "and for the record, Mr. Wall, Mr. Volkov was a billionaire, and his former wife Galina is a film star, of some international repute, currently living in Miami, Florida."

Wall murmured something under his breath and sat down.

Chase turned back to face his client.

"To get back to your relationship with the victim, Ms. Volkova. You've described the situation with her father. You said you had been approached to help Ms. Volkova with that situation. How could you have helped?"

"Our firm does a lot of work internationally, for one thing. We represent clients who do business in Russia. The business community over there is a relatively tight one. We hope to exert some influence, through those clients, to apply some pressure on the government."

"Why did Ms. Volkova approach you, specifically?"

"A number of years ago, when I was still mayor, I took a trip to Moscow, along with a number of other city and state officials. Part of a cultural exchange program. While there, I met Konstantin Makharovsky, then mayor of Moscow. We struck up a friendship. Makharovsky is today the Vice Premier of Economic Development. In that role, he's responsible for trade, and relationships with trading partners. Ms. Volkova hoped I would be able to prevail upon him to help free her father."

Chase walked slowly back to the table and picked up some papers. They weren't relevant to his line of inquiry, but he could tell his client needed a bit of a breather. He shuffled through the papers, pulled one to the front of the pack, taking his time.

"Thank you. I have only one final question. Did you kill Katarina Volkova?"

Agnew sat up straighter, raised his head, and looked toward the jury. "I did not," he said, his voice trembling with emotion.

Chase thanked the witness and sat down. He knew he was taking a gamble, cutting his questions short, but he could sense Wall champing at the bit. A more experienced prosecutor, or one without an axe to grind, might have simply passed the witness, betting on the fact the witness hadn't contradicted any of the presented evidence. That would entail some risk, though, as the last thing the jury would have heard was his emotional denial, and they would wonder why the prosecution, faced with an opportunity to confront the man accused of murder, passed on the opportunity. And Chase knew that was the kind of risk Wall wouldn't be willing to take.

Fourteen

"Mr. Agnew. That was a wonderful, heart-warming version of your relationship with Ms. Volkova. And we all feel for her poor father. But the fact is, you have no blood relationship with the victim. Isn't that correct?"

Unruffled, Agnew sipped his water and cleaned his glasses.

"No. She's my cousin's stepdaughter. But she calls me Uncle Rufus. Called, rather," he said, the last part in a soft voice.

"Fine. You're not related by blood. I don't know, what does that make you, her third cousin, twice removed?"

Agnew cocked his head.

"Is that a question?" Chase asked.

"Never mind," Wall said. "Do you deny you had a relationship with the victim, Ms. Volkova?"

"No."

"You admit you had a relationship with her?"

"She was my client, and also my niece," Rufus said.

"Your Honor, move to strike. Per his own admission, Ms. Volkova had no blood relationship to Mr. Agnew."

Chase stood. "Your Honor, Mr. Agnew was answering

the question asked by the district attorney. He considered Ms. Volkova to be his niece."

The judge sustained Chase's objection, this time with a bit of a smile.

Wall walked over to the table and picked up a file. "You received these e-mails from the victim?" he said, waving the file in the air.

"I did not," Rufus said forcefully.

"We pulled these e-mails off of Ms. Volkova's own computer, addressed to you. You deny receiving them?"

"I do."

"The e-mail address Ms. Volkova used to send messages to you was RAgnew34@gmail.com, was it not?" Wall said.

"No. We never communicated via e-mail. And my e-mail address is Rufus.Agnew@williams.com."

"You were born in 1934?"

"Yes."

"You didn't establish a gmail account two months prior to the death of Ms. Volkova?"

"I did not."

"You didn't read the messages from the victim?"

"We talked by phone. We met in person."

Wall picked up another file. "Speaking of meeting in person, I have here the receipt for a hotel room in Baltimore, Maryland. You attended a conference there in March of 2005?"

"I did. The Legal Trade Association annual conference."

"Did Ms. Volkova accompany you on that trip?"

"She did."

"You stayed in Room 434 with Ms. Volkova?"

"I stayed in Room 434. Ms. Volkova stayed in another room. On the third floor, I believe."

Wall frowned. "We have your receipt for the conference, Mr. Agnew. We also have the guest list. Ms. Volkova's name is not on the hotel registry."

"No, it's not. The conference had representatives from

Eastern Europe, including Russia. I felt we should protect Katarina's identity, given the status of her father. You'll find her registered under the name Katy Hogan."

Agitated, Wall scanned the list in front of him, and looked up after a while.

"How do we know she actually stayed in the room?" he said.

"Objection," Chase said. "Mr. Agnew answered the question. Now Mr. Wall is badgering the witness. How do we know anyone stayed in the rooms assigned to them?"

"Mr. Wall, please move on," the judge said.

"Yes, your Honor," the D.A. said stiffly. "Let's turn to the day of the murder. Friday, June 19th. In the statement you gave the police you said you were fishing."

"Yes, I was."

"Did anyone see you?"

"Apparently not, or I wouldn't be sitting here today," Agnew said softly.

"You fish at Lake Luray?"

"Yes, along with a few friends, we lease some property up there, and keep a few boats. I try to get up there every Friday."

"You fish by yourself?"

"As a rule. Occasionally a few of us will go out together in one of the bigger boats, but usually I go up and take one of the smaller craft out and try to catch some bass."

"You catch any that Friday?" Wall asked.

"You a fisherman?" Agnew asked.

"I'll ask the questions, if you don't mind," Wall retorted.

"Yes sir, I apologize. I've been fishing for years, ever since my daddy, God rest his soul, took me out on the dock and handed me a rod. Point is, fishing's not really about catching fish."

Chase could see a few heads nodding in agreement among the jury. He had suspected during selection that the middle-aged hardware store owner and the young elementary school principal might do a little angling occasionally.

"So you didn't catch any fish, no one saw you and you

have no way of proving you were out fishing on that Friday?" Wall said.

"Now I didn't say I didn't catch any fish. Just that it didn't matter. As to the rest of it, when I set out that day I had no idea I'd need to be seen by anyone. I've lived a large part of my life in the public eye. I take advantage of those times I can stay out of it."

"So you have no alibi for the time of the murder," Wall pressed.

"Mr. Wall, it's a two-hour drive from Lake Luray back to Piedmont. I put up the boat, got in my car around seven o'clock, and drove straight home."

"Was your wife at home?" Wall asked, already knowing the answer.

"No sir, she was not. She spent the night with her sister in Dobson."

"How convenient. So she didn't see you arrive home, didn't see what you were wearing when you returned."

Agnew smiled wearily. "I'd say it was decidedly inconvenient, given the circumstances."

"Again, so you have no alibi for the time of the murder."

"Objection," Chase said. "Asked and answered."

"Sustained."

Wall shifted tactics. He pulled out luncheon receipts, accounts from people who had seen the ex-mayor with the victim, asked about details of meetings. Throughout, the witness continued to answer the questions put to him, retaining his cool. Yes, they had lunch together on numerous occasions. No, not everyone he met knew the nature of his relationship with the victim. Yes, she'd held his arm when they walked together. It helped him avoid the use of his cane. Their meetings were covered by attorney-client privilege, and he couldn't share the details, but he confirmed the times and locations. Wall tried returning to the e-mail messages, but made no headway. To Chase's mind, Wall was losing the battle of elder statesmen, appearing peevish and impatient. Agnew, by contrast, answered the questions calmly, remained respectful of his interrogator, and held an air of dignity about him. As the noon hour approached, however, Rufus Agnew began to show signs of wear. The sweat on his brow extended to his cheeks, and he frequently had to pat his face with his handkerchief. His voice began to sound more strained. He had to make a visible effort to keep his posture erect.

Chase interrupted the flow of Wall's questions to suggest a break. The judge looked to the district attorney.

"How much more do you have, Mr. Wall?"

Wall glanced at the jury, and perhaps sensing their sympathies shifting, said, "I only have a couple more questions, your Honor. I'm almost through here."

"I'll hold you to that," the judge said. "I think we're all ready for a break."

"Yes, of course. As I said, I only have a few more questions. Mr. Agnew, do you own a tan cashmere blazer?'

"I do," he said.

"The blazer found in your closet during the search of your premises?"

"Yes."

"The same blazer we matched against the fibers from the victim's dress?"

"Objection," Chase called. "The witness is not an expert on fiber evidence."

"I'm merely trying to show the connection between the jacket we found in Mr. Agnew's closet, and the forensic tests we did from the scene of the crime, your Honor," Wall said.

"I believe you demonstrated that connection with your experts, Mr. Wall. Objection sustained."

"All right, so let's summarize, Mr. Agnew, if I may. The jacket was yours?"

"As I said."

"Yes, as you said. Your jacket, matched to fibers at the crime scene. On Ms. Volkova's dress. You have no alibi for the time of the murder. Your fingerprints were found in the victim's condo. You acknowledge you had a relationship with the victim. She threatened to reveal the nature of that relationship to your wife, and you killed her in cold blood."

"No!" It was the first time Agnew had raised his voice.

Wall smiled. "You killed her and now you make up a story about a business relationship with the victim. A relationship no one at your firm can confirm."

A true statement as far as it went. Katarina Volkova did have a billing file and account with the firm, but Rufus Agnew had been her sole contact. It didn't help that Rufus had never sent an invoice to his client, that he had effectively represented her on a pro bono basis.

"You killed her, strangled her." Wall pulled a photo from a file and waved it at the jury. "Then you left her. This is how she looked when they found her."

"No," Rufus Agnew said again, this time with a cracking voice.

"I have no further questions for this witness," Wall declared, and walked back to his seat.

The judge banged her gavel and called the lunch break.

There were key moments in every trial, Chase found, when the world came into better focus. It had been the same on the basketball court. A moment came when the world stopped and the texture of the basketball, the lines in the floor, the colors in the crowd, the coordinated movements of his teammates and the opponents, all could be perceived as part of an elaborate mosaic. In court it sometimes came during the questioning of a witness, or after opening arguments. Today it came as the crowd filed out of the courtroom. All of a sudden he could hear every sound clearly—the fabrics moving against skin, the low whispers, the pressing of cell phone buttons, the rubber and leather of footwear padding along the floor. He smelled the tobacco, the perfumes, the aftershaves. He noticed the patterns in the wood grain of the table. Rufus came and sat next to him. Chase could swear he could smell the fear, the anger, the weariness.

"You enjoy this, don't you," Agnew said.

Chase looked up, noticing the bloodshot eyes, the liver spots on the hands, the translucence of the skin, and felt a strange chagrin.

Agnew held up a hand. "Don't worry, I don't mean me, my part in this. You'd have to be a masochist to enjoy that. But you, I don't know the right words, this fuels you, somehow, doesn't it?"

Chase considered—how to explain it?

"Actually, I hate it sometimes," he said. "All the preparation, the adversarial nature of the process, the cold-heartedness of the law. But I love it as well. It's life-enhancing somehow. Does that make any sense?"

Rufus smiled kindly. "I'm all in favor of life-enhancing," he said. "In fact, I hope the verdict will be exactly that."

Chase smiled back. "You holding up okay?"

"Oh, don't worry about me. I'm tired, but I've been tired the last twenty years. Sorry I snapped at the end there. I could only take so much of that sanctimonious prick. Taking up air the rest of us could be breathing."

The two shared a laugh.

A HALF-HOUR LATER, Rufus Agnew reclaimed his seat at the front of the courtroom. The bailiff reminded him he was still under oath, and Chase stood.

"Just a few follow-up questions, Mr. Agnew. You told the district attorney you were fishing on the Friday of the murder, is that correct?"

"Yes."

"You also said you often go fishing on Fridays. Is it rare not to see anyone when you're up at the lake?"

Rufus considered. "No, in fact it's rare that I see anyone at all. Especially in June. There are six of us who lease the acreage with a few hundred yards of shoreline. The other partners travel a lot more than I do. Two of them live in Virginia, one's in South Carolina, and two are in Raleigh. I live the closest; so

I kind of keep an eye on the place, spend the most time there. We have a private lot, and our own dock."

"Thank you. We've heard about the fiber evidence, the jacket in your closet. When's the last time you wore that jacket, if you can recall?"

Agnew poured another glass of water, and looked to the side as if trying to recall. The two men had covered this issue in great detail during their preparations.

"Well, cashmere tends to be something I wear in the winter, when it's cold. Summer I tend to stick to breathable fabrics like cotton, or lightweight seersucker. Light colors. I'd have to say I might have worn it in January, sometime last year."

When Chase considered all the elements of the case against his client, the jacket stood out as the strongest evidence in favor of Agnew's innocence. Agnew had a certain style, one founded in his folksy demeanor, and in his wardrobe.

"Can you imagine me wearing cashmere in the summertime?" he'd said to Chase. "God forbid. And how stupid do they imagine I am, picking out the one garment in my closet that would shed the most to commit a murder? I might as well shed some skin and comb my hair out at the scene of the crime while I'm at it."

He'd cautioned Agnew not to put it quite that way when asked, but he wanted the point raised. During the course of the trial, his client had worn cotton or seersucker, light colors, every single day. Three-piece suits, occasionally, but always stylish, in an old-fashioned way. Chase wanted the jurors to have a hard time imagining him wearing a tan cashmere blazer at any time.

"Your fingerprints were found in the bathroom at Ms. Volkova's condo. How do you explain that?"

"I can't. I've never set foot inside of her condo."

"Never?"

"Never."

There was no way around the fingerprint. In the jury's mind, it placed Rufus at the condo, at the murder scene. On the other hand, they'd placed his coat there, and all the other evidence pointed to his presence there as well. You have to play the hand you're dealt. Which in this case meant one strategy, to which Chase had alluded in opening arguments. SOGDI. Some other guy did it. And in this case AFMC. And framed my client.

"Do you have an e-mail account through gmail, RAgnew34?"

"No."

"Did you ever sleep with Katarina Volkova?"

"Of course not."

"Did you buy her condo?"

Rufus snorted. "No. She had more money than I do."

"How's that?"

"Trust fund from her father, I think."

"Did you kill Katarina Volkova?"

"No. I did not." He said this firmly, with vigor.

Chase looked toward the jury box, watched them watch Rufus Agnew. He turned back to his client. "Thank you, Mr. Agnew."

Agnew used his cane to get up, then walked slowly back to his chair. Silence enveloped the courtroom, as all eyes followed his short journey. All eyes save for the district attorney's, gazing forward, expression fixed. Chase allowed the moment to linger, allowed time for the ex-mayor to settle himself into his seat. He nodded to him, and then faced forward.

"Your Honor, and ladies and gentlemen of the jury, the defense rests."

His original strategy had been to bring in his own forensics experts, challenge the findings from the murder scene. They could have called into question the collection of the evidence, the chain of custody, and the competence of the individuals involved. Confuse the jury; make them question the competence of the police, the crime scene specialists. But in the end, the evidence hadn't seemed compelling enough to convict. Besides, he knew these people—the police, the criminologists. He'd worked with them, relied on them, trusted them. They did good work and he couldn't bring himself to challenge it. The case had to boil down to whether the jury trusted his client, believed him. And whether they felt the evidence as presented by the district attorney overcame the weaknesses of the prosecution's case.

The judge looked at the clock, asked each party how long they expected closing arguments to take, and how soon they'd be ready.

"I don't expect to take more than an hour, your Honor," Chase said. "I can be ready to go tomorrow morning."

Wall was squirming. Clearly he hadn't expected the case to end on the first day of defense testimony. "Your Honor, I believe Friday will be a good day to begin. Or perhaps Monday."

The judge frowned. "Mr. Wall, I understand the defense presented its case with, shall I say, great efficiency. But I know your calendar is cleared for the entire week, and surely you can present your arguments to the jury before Friday. We'll hear closing arguments Wednesday morning, at 10 a.m. Court adjourned."

FIFTEEN

Peter Jurgens sat in front of a blank computer screen staring at the coeds of the Atlantic Coast Conference calendar on the wall over his desk. The red circle around June 22nd seemed to flash at him like a traffic light. He hated Miss June, a long-legged brunette cheerleader from Duke University. Misses January through April had been evil temptresses, taunting him from their respective campuses, leering at him, daring him to actually write something. Miss May, a perky blonde from Virginia, had a knowing smirk, intimating their time together would soon be over. Miss June, though, knew his excuses were coming to an end.

With less than three weeks to go until his deadline, he avoided the telephone. For two reasons: his agent had already called a half-dozen times and would soon be followed by his publisher; and his bank account held exactly $314.56, not enough to pay his pending rent or his past-due utility bills. Utility companies were almost as incessant as agents, he'd found. That meant floating another month on his credit cards. He had maxed-out two of them, but had received another in the mail the previous week. The more he spent, the more the banks were interested in loosening his noose.

He knew he'd have to break down and answer the phone eventually, particularly when Mac Seaver from Doubleday called. After all, he had taken $80,000 of their money and owed them a manuscript in return. Back when Miss January was still a friend, he'd assured them the novel was moving along steadily, words flowing out of him like an uncapped fire hydrant. His deadline had been pushed back twice already but there would be no more extensions. With no manuscript to show, he wondered whether they'd go after his advance, or just wash their hands of him entirely.

Looking around the small apartment, he tried to figure out how he'd managed to blow through so much money in six months' time. Other than the MacBook Pro laptop, he was down to a couple tattered chairs, his kitchen table, and the twin bed. And the liquor cabinet. Once it had held a collection of some of the finest single malt Scotches in the world, along with some premium vodkas and Pinot Noirs. The only liquor in the apartment now sat in the refrigerator, the remains of a case of cheap beer. He walked over and got one out, popped the top, and took a long swig.

He considered his options. He could get a loan, but from whom? He had kept his friends in the dark along with his agent and publisher; he wasn't ready to face them. He couldn't write, he couldn't speak the truth, and he couldn't reach out to the only people who could help him.

The whole time he sat, the blank computer screen stared back at him. While he pondered his situation, the phone rang. He stared at it. After the fifth ring, he looked at the caller ID: Unknown. After the twelfth ring he cursed himself for throwing out his answering machine. Finally, he picked up.

"Hello?"

"Mr. Jurgens?" A raspy whisper, not a voice he recognized.

"Yes, who's this?"

"It doesn't matter who this is," the voice continued. "I just need you to listen carefully."

"Look, what's this about? I'm busy right now, so if you could get to the point?"

"You are *not* busy right now. You are sitting, same as you do every day, doing very little, in fact," the voice said in a dry monotone.

Peter looked around the room, panicked. He walked over to the window, peered through the blind: nothing, just the street, the traffic.

"Who are you? Did Mac Seaver put you up to this?" Was this some way for the publisher to light a fire under his ass, try to get him to finish the manuscript? He'd never heard of such tactics.

"Mr. Jurgens, Peter, I need you to listen carefully, so please refrain from any further outbursts. I have a simple message for you. We have your son."

"My son? I don't have a son."

"Please don't insult me, Mr. Jurgens. We have your son, and if you'd like him to stay healthy, you need to do exactly what we tell you."

His thoughts raced. Tried to imagine who could be on the other line. Could they have him mixed up with someone else?

"What do you want?"

"Nothing at the moment."

"Nothing? You call me like this, tell me you have my son, which I don't have, by the way, threaten me, all to tell me you want nothing? What kind of a sick joke is this?" He started to wonder whether Ev or Randy were playing some kind of sick prank on him.

"Mr. Jurgens, this is no joke. Let me clarify. We have your son. He is perfectly safe at the moment. You need do nothing at the moment. However, in a short while you will receive another phone call. The caller will tell you a friend suggested he contact you. You are to do exactly as he asks. This in return for you son's continued safety."

This was crazy. "Look, I don't have a son, I don't have any money, are you sure you don't have the wrong guy?"

"Peter Jurgens, formerly with *Time*, currently working on the great American novel, graduate of Winfield College, Atlanta resident since 1998," the caller recited, continuing with additional biographical facts, including his parents' address, his social security number, and the numbers of his Visa and American Express cards.

"In the meantime," the voice continued, "feel free to do whatever you like. Oh, and as a gesture of good faith, we've taken care of Mr. Seaver. He won't be bothering you any more.

"And one more thing. Should you attempt to tell anyone about this phone call, we can no longer guarantee the safety of the boy. Goodbye."

The caller hung up. Peter found himself staring at the handset. A son. There were two people in the world who knew, and that had been eighteen years ago. It couldn't be. And yet.... He made a note to cancel the credit cards the caller had cited and to let his parents know to be watchful, just in case.

SIXTEEN

There were two pairs of shoes in his closet. Also garments, neatly hung, as if he could change whenever he wanted. Army fatigues, a pair of jeans, even a dress shirt of some kind. Show for his visitors. Or visitor. But how convenient for him. They never expected him to walk into the closet, put on a pair of shoes, and venture outside, navigating his way through the dark zones of camera coverage. They never expected him even to open the door. Their intent was to keep him an invalid, helpless, as they plied their skills, trying to break his will, while they controlled his body. At first they'd asked him questions. Where is it? Over and over. He didn't know what they were talking about. And just when things started clearing up, as Chase began to visit, they'd moved to a different approach. To induce vocal cord paralysis, and drug him up. They no longer wanted him to speak or communicate.

During the past few weeks, he'd become more aware of time. The deprivation chamber had become his friend, shielding him, allowing him to retreat into his past, into his music. It had helped him mark the days as well, as the visits became more regular. He also had Kenneth, who, true to his word, had helped him regain the use of his limbs.

He braced himself on the doorknob of the closet and looked around the room. He'd had most of the day to prepare for his excursion. Under the schedule he'd been following, he wouldn't see the doctor until Monday morning. Tomorrow they'd leave him in the room, or bring him down below for observation, which meant leaving him alone in a room with no furniture other then the chair he sat in, occasionally with electrodes monitoring his vital signs. He worried they'd discover how far he'd progressed. Surely they'd be able to tell how his muscles, skin, and nerves reacted to stimuli. He couldn't fake that. Time was pressing. He wasn't strong enough yet, but his window of opportunity might be closing, forcing him into action before his body had fully recovered. Most alarming had been the discussion he'd overhead two days before, lying on the gurney outside the chamber. The doctor had been talking with someone on the phone. "We'll see you next week, Colonel Sterling," he'd said, hanging up.

Sterling. The name had triggered an avalanche of memories. The images in his head, of men, explosions, and woods, began to connect. For two days he had reassembled the pieces of his lost life. He remembered a man looking down upon him, face bloody and scarred. And he remembered what the man had done.

According to Colonel Sterling, allied forces had uncovered the location of a terrorist cell operating in Southern Iraq. Raed Al-Tariq, the leader of the cell, a local Sunni tribal chief but working with Al Qaida, operating out of a deserted warehouse outside of Amara, a Shi'ite stronghold. Jared had seen satellite footage showing trucks and jeeps moving in and out of the warehouse, delivering weapons, which were being used against both U.S. and Sunni forces. Weapons, he'd been told, that came from Syria and Iran. The team's mission had been to kill Al-Tariq and his men then wait for allied forces to move in and seize the warehouse. The weapons housed in the warehouse would either be destroyed or reapportioned to allied troops.

When Jared and his team positioned themselves strategically, they settled in to observe the routines of the facility. On the second day, one of the scouts, Davies, spotted Al-Tariq in conversation with one of the drivers, just inside the perimeter fencing. Sensing an opportunity to take the Al Qaida leader alive, Jared deployed his men to cover the gate and the exit points from the warehouse, and personally fired the shot that felled Al-Tariq. A tranquilizer bullet, designed to incapacitate, not kill. So long as the bullet didn't damage any internal organs or sever an artery. Jared placed the bullet perfectly, hitting the left shoulder. His men immediately rushed in and surrounded the warehouse, two of them taking out the drivers of three trucks that had yet to unload.

Cautiously approaching the downed man, Jared compared his face with the picture from surveillance photos. Satisfied, he radioed back to headquarters, described what had happened, and awaited further orders. Told to remain in place until troops could arrive with a helicopter to transport the terrorist to an interrogation facility, he wasn't alarmed when he heard the distinctive sounds of the whirring blades. Even when he identified the pair of AH-64 Apache attack helicopters approaching, he assumed it was their support. But then the first air-to-ground missile tore into the warehouse entrance, its explosive power sending the men covering the entrance flying, helpless. The second and third missiles from the second copter took out the trucks and the men covering them. Knowing only that something had gone terribly wrong, he hoisted Al-Tariq over his shoulder and squeezed through the hole they'd cut in the fence to get in. As the helicopters swooped around for a second pass, he ran to the cover of the trees where they'd camped and dumped his load. He watched as the warehouse, all its inhabitants, and all his men, were efficiently reduced to rubble. Picking up his radio, he pressed down the button to call, but then lifted his thumb. It was too late anyway. He resumed his burden and continued back along the path to Amara.

Two hours later, sun-blistered and dripping with sweat, he set Al-Tariq down against a tree, drawing his handgun. He'd sensed the man's recovery, his legs jerking as he began to regain consciousness. The terrorist didn't look so terrible as he coughed, then retched on the ground beside him. He had a scraggly beard, short dark hair, and an aquiline nose that appeared to have been broken. Blue eyes looked up at his captor and Jared realized the man couldn't be more than twenty-five years old. The frightened look on his face seemed greatly at odds with the image from the intelligence photograph. Then, inexplicably, he smiled, relieved, it seemed.

"I thought you were a Shi'ite," he said. "Your black hair, the markings on your face." He nodded to the U.S. flag insignia on his shoulder. "Thought they'd come to kill me." His English was flawless, accented, if anything, with a touch of New England.

"You're Al-Tariq?" Jared challenged.

"Yes. Please call me Ray, though. I've come to prefer the less formal means of address you Americans adopt. Quite… friendly."

"You lived in the States?"

"Harvard Law, class of '05," he said.

That didn't accord with the terrorist's history, as related by Sterling. According to it, he'd trained in Syria, spent some time in Afghanistan, and moved back to Iraq to build operations in the southern theater.

Jared kept his gun trained on his captive, trying to assess what had happened. The man sitting before him didn't appear to be who he thought he was, and it called his assumptions into question. After over an hour's talk with Al-Tariq, he was even more confused. The man claimed to have been working with the Coalition, passing on information and serving as a broker for weapons he and his men managed to procure.

"Didn't you notice the markings on the crates in that truck? U.S. Army—a shipment of M-4s, with replacement cartridges." According to Al-Tariq, he'd confiscated the shipment from a Shi'ite group, who'd waylaid an American convoy. His business involved selling the weapons back to the U.S. Army, then using the money to feed and clothe the people from his village.

"You sell the weapons back to us?"

Al-Tariq looked somewhat wary. He squinted at Jared. "Why are you here? Why am I here?"

Jared described the attack on the facility, leaving out the affiliation of the helicopters, or his mission.

"So they are—all dead, gone?" At Jared's nod, he heaved a sigh, then propped himself up with his right hand and rubbed his bandaged left shoulder. "You?" he questioned.

Jared nodded.

"You didn't come alone," he said. A statement, not a question.

"No."

"So, your men too? Not just my men?"

"Not just your men."

Nodding, Al-Tariq winced with pain as his fingers explored his shoulder. His eyes looked into Jared's.

"You didn't come to rescue me."

"No."

"And they weren't Shi'ite helicopters, were they."

"No."

Slumping back against the tree, Al-Tariq closed his eyes for a few moments, a wry smile on his lips. Jared watched him, his gun lowered by now to his side.

"Your boss hasn't been happy with me, I take it?" he said, his eyes still closed.

"My boss?"

"The colonel."

"Colonel?"

"Sterling."

Jared sat down on the ground beside Al-Tariq, his gun still at the ready.

"I guess not," he said.

"Ah," the Iraqi sighed. "I tried to tell him, I had to reduce his cut in order to make my profit—I have to feed my
people."

Jared let him talk, occasionally nodding, prodding him
to continue. It was a fairly simple operation. At least it had
started out simply. Al-Tariq came across a cache of weapons,
Army grenades and landmines. He'd contacted someone with
the army, who'd contacted Sterling, who then arranged for the
deal by which the army purchased the weapons back, Sterling
taking a cut. After a while, Sterling had taken a more active
role. Truck convoys were misdirected, shipping containers
were mislaid, or drops were made in the middle of the desert.
In each case, Sterling would let them know where the weapons would be and they'd get hold of what they could and sell
them back to the army. As best as he could determine, the
deals added up to millions of dollars, a hefty percentage of
that making its way into Sterling's pocket.

"You can prove this?"

Al-Tariq had looked at him, a small smile on his face.

HIS MIND FAST-FORWARDED through his return to camp
and subsequent confrontation with the colonel. The last thing
he remembered, was Sterling face. Then came the MPs at the
door, and… nothing. Until the Pembrooke Institute.

He thought back to the phone conversation.

He knew he needed to plan his escape. And soon. Re-
gaining his bearings, he catalogued the contents of the closet,
and returned to his chair to save his strength while he considered his options. If Sterling were coming to the Institute,
it couldn't be good news. It was a long way from Iraq. Jared
might be able to fool the doctors and the orderlies here, but
he wouldn't fool Sterling.

Listening carefully, ear to the door, he eased it open.
Not a soul to be seen, or heard. He wondered about the other
patients. What were their crimes? What did they know? His
eyes now adjusted to the darkness, he was able to see the con-

tours of the hallway, the doors, the ceiling, the light fixtures. His focus remained limited, but his vision had improved immensely in the past two weeks. His biggest challenge had been maintaining the dull, listless look they expected, not reacting to sudden noises or changes in light. Fortunately, he'd had enough practice, and the drugs they pumped through his body the rest of the week helped.

Padding softly down the corridor, he was surprised at the lack of security. Kenneth had mentioned it, yet he hadn't believed they would leave him on the floor by himself without any supervision. The other prisoners, as he'd come to think of them, must be equally drugged or incapacitated.

Keeping to the walls to avoid the cameras, he paused, listening for the sound of elevators or footsteps. All he heard was the incessant whine of the generators.

Unused to supporting his weight, his leg muscles were still weak from lack of use. His exercise routines were painful, but necessary. He stopped to massage his calves and his quads, wincing from the movement in his back. The front door was heavy and locked. The mechanism, though, was old and didn't present a problem. Peering through the window, he could see nothing. Just the darkness. No lights of any kind outside, not even motion-activated ones. His last trip around the perimeter had confirmed that. Popping the lock, he opened the door, let himself outside, and slowly began his routine.

Within half an hour, he was back in his room, exhausted. Facing the bed, he saw the poster his brother had left on the wall. He couldn't read the words, but he knew what they said. He'd stared at the poster at night in his bed as a child, imagining the athletes running in slow motion along the beach, the wonderful Vangelis score playing. Curious, he walked over to the wall and delicately removed the poster, careful not to damage it in any way. Flipping it over, he laid it on his bed. The flat blank back of the poster confronted him, even in the limited natural light. Curious, he took the poster into the closet and closed the door, then reached for the light switch.

Stretching his arms, he held the poster high over his head against the light bulb from the ceiling. Lines and words jumped out at him, illuminated, not by the light, but by the heat it cast. He smiled, remembering how he and Chase used to send notes to each other in invisible ink, their own special concoction of lemon juice and vinegar. His eyes couldn't quite make out the words. Yet. Examining the lines more closely, he saw a single square in the middle of the page. He laughed. It was a map, with the Pembrooke Institute at the center. Turning off the light, he blinked to recover from the unaccustomed brightness. Then he left the closet and reattached the poster to the wall. He'd read it when his eyesight had recovered more fully.

Stretching his arms and legs, he began a series of isometric exercises. He needed his strength and agility if he had any hopes of eluding Sterling. And of beating him.

SEVENTEEN

In the time since Ken Wall's last court case, media tools had become easy for everyone to use, even the technologically-challenged. The district attorney accordingly made use of every conceivable medium to present his closing argument.

He began with a PowerPoint presentation that summarized all the testimony from his key witnesses. He then showed digital video clips of the crime scene and the ex-mayor's residence, making sure to show its opulence, and taking the jury on a tour leading to the closet that held the incriminating jacket. A timeline came up on the screen, accompanied by a number of still photographs, showing all the times Agnew and Ms. Volkova had been seen in public. She appeared holding his arm, smiling broadly for the cameras. Then came the day of the murder, broken down into fifteen-minute increments, accounting for both Katarina Volkova's movements during that day, and Agnew's, in accordance with the prosecution's theory and eyewitness accounts. A mockup of the victim's computer flashed the incriminating e-mail messages, with relevant passages highlighted. Finally, embedded photos reminded the jury of the forensic evidence, the fibers, the fingerprint, and the blood.

Two hours into the presentation, Wall concluded his argument.

"Ladies and gentlemen of the jury, I remind you of my comments at the beginning of this trial. This is a simple case and I think the facts and the evidence point to only one conclusion. Rufus Agnew had a relationship with the victim. He's acknowledged this in court. The two of them attended a number of social functions together, even traveled east and stayed in a hotel together. Agnew wanted to have his cake and eat it too. He wanted to remain married to his wife, Emily, but also wanted to enjoy his relationship with his young mistress, Ms. Volkova. But Ms. Volkova forced him to choose. And indeed, Mr. Agnew chose. He chose to kill Katarina Volkova in cold blood, to shut her up.

"Hard evidence places Mr. Agnew at the scene of the crime, despite his denials. He has no explanation for the presence of his fingerprints, or the presence of his jacket, which he obviously wore on the night of the murder. He has no alibi, in spite of the thousands of cars that drove back and forth on the interstate highways between Piedmont and Lake Luray, and in fact, the number of other fishermen out on the lake on the day of the murder. That's motive, and that's opportunity, ladies and gentlemen. The means, as our experts have indicated, was a simple piece of fishing line, or something similar. That's right, fishing line. Mr. Agnew has acknowledged his passion for fishing. All it took was a short length of line, pulled tight around the victim's throat.

"Motive, means, and opportunity. Mr. Agnew may have been a respected politician at one time, but on that day, that Friday, he became a murderer. In the courtroom, Mr. Agnew came across as a charming old man. Well, I think you know appearances can be deceiving. And you must not let your feelings for the ex-mayor get in the way of doing your duty. Murderers come in all shapes and sizes. Some are easy to spot and some look just like the people sitting next to you in this courtroom. Or over at the defense table with Mr. Riordan, the defense attorney.

"I told you at the start Mr. Riordan would try to cloud the issues, make the simple seem complex. He would have you believe that someone else committed this crime and framed Mr. Agnew in the process. Some super-criminal, perhaps, so adept at killing that he can leave no traces of his own presence, and selectively leave evidence to implicate Rufus Agnew.

"You may have heard of something called Occam's Razor. It states that the simplest explanation of the facts is usually the best. Why complicate things here? The evidence points to Rufus Agnew as the killer. In this case, the simplest explanation is the logical one. The right one. Rufus Agnew killed Katarina Volkova. You've seen a lot of drama in the courtroom during this trial, but now it's time for the conclusion, the verdict. I have great confidence in your abilities to judge the merits of this case on the evidence, and the evidence alone, and I know you will find the defendant, Rufus Agnew, guilty of murder in the first degree. Thank you."

The district attorney sat down. His words lingered in Chase's mind, connections forming. His client nudged him, forcing his attention to the judge, who called his name.

"Mr. Riordan, are you all right?"

He recovered quickly. "Yes, your Honor, thank you. Just taking some mental notes from Mr. Wall's presentation."

"It's one o'clock, we'll take an hour for lunch, and reconvene at two o'clock," she said, adjourning court.

STANDING DIRECTLY in front of the jury for the first time in the trial, Chase greeted each one, nodding as he acknowledged and thanked them for their efforts during the trial.

"You have taken time out of your busy lives. Serving on a jury is an important civic duty. You and I know a lot of people shirk this duty, but your presence here shows your commitment to our judicial process. I add my thanks to those of the district attorney. No matter the verdict, both he and I are appreciative of your efforts.

"Mr. Wall gave an impressive presentation this morning.

I'm sure the images are still flashing through your minds. I can see them as well." Chase held up his index cards. "I chose a low-tech approach today. No computer graphics, no video, no timelines." A few of the jurors smiled good-naturedly.

"And I'm not going to use these," he said, tossing them onto the defense table. "I've been working on this case for a year now, along with other associates from my office. If I can't talk to you about this case, if I don't know it frontward and backwards, and if I need notes to talk about it, well then I wouldn't be much of a lawyer, now would I? They'd be props, and I think you've had enough props for the day." He allowed himself a smile.

"The district attorney told you a story, which he backed up with pictures. He implied that because he had the pictures, the story was true. A lot of investigation went into this case, on the part of the police and the District Attorney's Office. But the investigation was very one-sided. It focused from the very beginning on Rufus Agnew and never strayed from that focus. I'm going to go over this case at a very high level and show you all the things the district attorney and the police missed, things they didn't investigate, either because they were so convinced from the start that my client was guilty, or perhaps because they didn't have the manpower.

"They do have a few pieces of evidence that are crucial to their case, and I'm not going to insult your intelligence by ignoring them, or glossing over them. Mr. Wall contends that the fingerprint and the fibers from the jacket place Mr. Agnew at the scene of the crime. But is that really true? Mr. Agnew claims he's never set foot in Ms. Volkova's apartment. In fact, in spite of their best efforts, there are no other facts that support Mr. Agnew's presence in the apartment, not on the day of the murder, or on any other day prior to that. Think about that. That means there are no witnesses who saw the mayor, excuse me ex-mayor, at the condo complex where Ms. Volkova lived. Hundreds of people come and go there, you saw the pictures. Ms. Volkova's condo is set back, so in order to get to the door, you'd have to pass at least four other condo units. But let's put that aside for the moment.

"Let's talk about the jacket. Fibers from the jacket in the mayor's closet were found on the victim. We don't question that evidence. We believe the expert testimony. But ask yourself this. If Mr. Agnew killed Ms. Volkova and covered up the crime, why did he just hang the jacket in his closet? Why didn't he dispose of it, somehow? And where's the blood? If he were wearing the jacket, surely some blood would have spattered on it. Similarly, why does the one fingerprint show up, on the glossiest surface in the entire residence and nowhere else? Either the killer wore gloves, or he didn't and he wiped down the surfaces. Maybe he wore them and took them off to wash his hands in the bathroom, leaving the fingerprint. A possibility, I suppose, but then his hands would have been wet and the print wouldn't have shown up as clearly. The towels were hanging, drying in the bathroom, remember. Mr. Agnew, as I'm sure you've seen, is not a stupid man. Yet Mr. Wall would have you believe he was foolish enough to A: leave a fingerprint behind in an obvious location and B: hang onto a jacket that no doubt contained trace evidence of the crime.

"Let me list for you the items that the police failed to investigate: the phone calls from the mysterious caller, just prior to the murder. We don't know who made the calls, only that they were made from a pre-paid cellular phone—which I've demonstrated was purchased at a time during which Mr. Agnew had an ironclad alibi. So he didn't purchase the phone or make the phone calls. Who did? Isn't it reasonable to assume the murderer did? Perhaps someone known to the victim was setting up the meeting, which led to her death?

"And how about the computer? The incriminating messages. There has been no proof, either that Ms. Volkova wrote the messages or that Mr. Agnew ever received them. There were no fingerprints on the computer keyboard. That's suspicious, don't you think? If Ms. Volkova had typed the messages, her fingerprints should be all over the keyboard. If Mr.

Agnew accessed the keyboard and then wiped off the keys, why didn't he delete the incriminating messages? The answer is, someone else typed those messages, planted them on Ms. Volkova's computer, and then wiped the keyboard to eliminate the evidence of his presence. Yet the police didn't ever look for another suspect.

"Let me show you something." He walked over to his briefcase and pulled out his laptop. "Here's my computer. Bear with me for a moment." The laptop was already booted up; he clicked to access his e-mail file. "Here. These are my e-mail files. My inbox, my outbox, some saved files with specific labels." He clicked on outbox. "These are messages which have been sent by me. You'll notice there are a lot of messages to colleagues in my office, to a few friends, so let me organize by recipient. Here, you'll notice a large number of messages sent by me to one specific individual." He held up his computer, and walked along the jury box, showing his files. A few smiles broke out among the jurors.

The district attorney stood up. "Your Honor, Mr. Riordan may be enjoying his theatrics, but the rest of us fail to see the humor. Perhaps he can share with the rest of the court?"

The judge, in front of whom Chase now stood, his computer open, restrained a smile.

"I apologize," Chase said, walking over and plugging his computer into the projector Wall had set up. "I'm showing the jurors messages sent by me, during each day of this trial, to Ken Wall, the district attorney." The big screen in front of the courtroom flashed his Sent file.

Wall looked up, and Chase could swear he almost smiled. "Of course Mr. Riordan knows that is not my e-mail account."

Chase looked back toward the jury. "Of course not, that's the point. I sent these messages to kwall42@gmail.com. Mr. Wall didn't set it up. I did. I used his first initial, his last name, and the year of his birth, the same formulation used to set up an account for Rufus Agnew. An account anyone could have set up, and an account that was not found on Mr. Agnew's home computer or the computer at his office. No investigation was done as to who might have opened this account other than the defendant.

"Moving along, Mr. Wall chose not to consider the true nature of Mr. Agnew's relationship with Ms. Volkova. He made an assumption, and stuck with it. He didn't know, or didn't care, that Ms. Volkova's father is under indictment in Russia for crimes against the State. That he has many enemies. He didn't know, or didn't care to find out, that Ms. Volkova has money of her own, rather choosing to imply that the victim needed money from my client to buy her condo and also sought money for blackmail purposes.

"This is a case that has been built, from the very beginning, on the thinnest of pretexts. There is no proof whatsoever that Rufus Agnew and Katarina Volkova were having an affair. There is proof that they are related and that Ms. Volkova had retained Mr. Agnew's services as an attorney. There is no proof whatsoever, that Rufus Agnew called Ms. Volkova on the day of the murder, although someone obviously did. There is no proof Mr. Agnew received any e-mails from Ms. Volkova, and no proof that Mr. Agnew was not fishing, as he said he was. This last is critical. The fingerprint and even the fibers on the dress do not constitute proof that Mr. Agnew was in Ms. Volkova's condo on the day of the murder.

"So what are we left with? A lot of holes. Holes that should have been filled before the D.A. ever brought this case to this court. And what do we know? We know, of course, that someone killed Ms. Volkova. But who? Was it some Russian thug, sent to silence her, to prevent her from helping her father? Was it a jealous lover? A former enemy? Someone out to discredit and perhaps frame Mr. Agnew? I don't know. Surely, though, someone wanted people to think Rufus Agnew was connected to this crime.

"I told you at the beginning that you wouldn't know by the end of this trial who killed Katarina Volkova. The district attorney doesn't know either. He wants to believe the killer is Mr. Agnew, and he wanted to believe this so much he didn't look for any other suspects, in spite of the fact that all the evidence cried for further investigation. He also referenced Occam's Razor, although he misrepresented it. What William of Occam actually said was, don't multiply things *unnecessarily*. It's that word 'unnecessarily' that gets in the way for me. Given all the things the prosecution failed to notice, to investigate, I believe it's absolutely necessary to look further."

Chase took a breath; surprised he was still holding his laptop, using it for emphasis. He smiled sheepishly and returned it to his briefcase. Turning back to face the jury, he folded his hands in front of him, aware he had their complete attention.

"Mr. Agnew did not kill Ms. Volkova. She was his niece. She wanted to help her father and she needed Mr. Agnew's help. He knew her father's plight, knew some of the players involved, and was in a unique position to help, and he tried to help her. She was his client, not his mistress. So how then, to explain those e-mails? Simple. She didn't send them. How could she have? She was not in a romantic relationship with Mr. Agnew. There was therefore no threat to his relationship with his wife. If there was no blackmail, there could be no ultimatum. If you get rid of those two pieces, the case falls apart. The logical conclusion is that someone else found a way to enter those e-mail messages on Ms. Volkova's computer. Why else would there be no fingerprints on the keyboard? If Mr. Agnew had wiped the keyboard of fingerprints, isn't it likely he would have erased the incriminating evidence? Isn't it more likely the killer wiped his prints, precisely *because* he had used the computer?

"I submit that Mr. Wall, on behalf of the state, has not met the burden of proof. As a prosecutor, I lived by the maxim 'leave no stone unturned.' Mr. Wall left a lot of stones unturned. When you examine all the evidence submitted, and all the evidence *not* presented, I think you will come to the same conclusion I've stated here. We still don't know who killed Ms. Volkova. That's what reasonable doubt is. Thank you."

As Chase took his chair, Rufus Agnew gripped his forearm. He'd meant to refrain from challenging Wall personally in his argument, but the emotions of the past four years had overtaken him. He kept his composure by recalling the D.A.'s final words in closing.

Judge Moody charged the jury and excused them. They filed out, many looking over their shoulders, glancing back and forth between Chase and Ken Wall.

WHEN THE JURY returned its verdict three days later, bedlam broke loose in the courtroom. Expecting a disappointed Wall to poll the jury, Chase was surprised to see what appeared to be a tight smile on the face of the district attorney. Wall gave him a slight nod of the head, before leaving the courtroom, trailed by Patrice Vasquez, who took the time to congratulate Chase and his client. He and Rufus shook hands warmly, the silver-haired old mayor saying "Chase, my friend––" then halting, at a rare loss for words. Finally he simply said, "anything, anything at all, you ever need, you call me, hear?"

Chase barely had time to nod before the crowd, mostly local pundits and reporters, engulfed Agnew. Chase gathered up his stuff into the old battered Atlas briefcase that had been a gift from Ken Wall himself. Sensing someone behind him, he looked up and recognized the trial bailiff, an old veteran he'd seen many times over the years.

"Come this way, Mr. Riordan." The guard gestured with his arm for Chase to follow. Surprised, he did so. The bailiff led him to the back of the courtroom, where he indicated a seat. Chase was touched. As a prosecutor, he'd developed a habit of remaining in the courtroom for a while after the conclusion of a trial. Trials were such intense affairs and Chase found he enjoyed the silence afterwards, the empty courtroom, the chance to reflect on what had just taken place there. He loved to breathe it all in and relax once the people had cleared out.

"Please sit down, sir. I'll see to it the rest of these folks get out okay. You stay as long as you like." The old bailiff then departed, ushering the remaining spectators and reporters out of the courtroom. Rufus Agnew, with the press corps hanging on his every word as they walked out with him, spied Chase quietly seated in the back, winked, and continued whatever story he was telling.

After a while, when everyone had gone, Chase got up and left the room.

EIGHTEEN

Sitting in his study, sipping from a neat glass of twelve-year-old Highland Park single malt, his one per-trial allotment, Chase heard Wall's line of thought again, and through it the echo of Jackson talking about the cover-up of Sterling's crime. The prosecution had asserted the defense theory was that the killer must be *someone so adept at killing that he left no traces of his own presence, but selectively left evidence implicating Rufus Agnew.* He reached into the file cabinet next to his desk, and pulled out two files. *Lewis* and *Tierney,* his two previous murder cases. Opening his briefcase, he set his papers from the Agnew case next to them. How could he have been so blind? The phone rang.

"Chase, I just heard!" Reagan's excited voice jogged him. He'd forgotten to call her immediately after the verdict as he had promised.

"It just came across the wires, I've been keeping an eye on the Internet."

With an effort, still distracted, he related the day's events.

"I'm just glad that man can get back to his life. Old man like that, had to be hard on him."

"He'd been so strong through all this, it took the trial for me to realize how old Rufus is. Maybe he's thinking a little more seriously about retirement now."

He continued to stare at the files, not really listening. "Chase?"

"Sorry. What were you saying?"

"I can see you have a lot on your mind. I'll let you go. Be sure to get some sleep, and call me tomorrow, okay?"

He had a thought. "Sounds good. I'll give you a call on your mobile." They hung up, and he got out his laptop. "Mobile" was the codeword they'd agreed upon.

Within a few minutes, they were in a chat room together. "I'm going to send you some files via FedEx," he said.

"What files?"

"My case files. Rufus Agnew, Ray Lewis, and John Tierney. Abbreviated versions—trial transcripts, client interviews, pleadings." The papers for each case filled up an entire file cabinet.

"Why?"

So adept at killing he can leave no traces of his own presence. But of course, there was other evidence. Other traces. In the Tierney case, there had been drops of blood from an unidentified person at the scene of the crime. In the case of Ray Lewis, Jr., a footprint outside the boy's bedroom. And in the Agnew case, hairs and an unidentified fingerprint. The police hadn't been able to identify the sources, had passed over them in favor of the obvious suspects.

"They're all connected." They had to be. When he'd started the Agnew case, something had felt off to him, and he couldn't figure out what it was. Then after Jackson's visit, the feeling had returned. And with Wall's closing argument, it had all come together. Agnew marked his third murder trial as a defense attorney. That in itself was unusual, three murder trials for a new defense attorney, even with as much experience as he had. Wall asserted a miscarriage of justice. Once, maybe. Twice, unlikely. But three times?

"If John Tierney, Ray Lewis, Sr., and Rufus Agnew are

all innocent, as I believe they are, and as three juries have found, then there are three killers out there. And no one's looking for them."

"Or just one," Reagan said.

He smiled, gratified. "One person, who's used these men as scapegoats. Who killed three people, and covered up his crimes by framing my clients. That's where I need your help. Your contacts at the FBI."

His clients to date had all been high-profile, well-off men: two politicians, and a business executive. He could see no connection among the victims: Katarina Volkova, Ray Lewis, Jr., and Winston Reese. A beautiful Russian woman, a young boy, and a middle-aged gay executive. Different walks of life, different ages, all from different parts of town. But there had to be a connection.

All three clients were the obvious suspects in murder cases, with compelling, albeit circumstantial evidence, tying each to the respective crimes. The politician and his young paramour in the middle of a hushed up affair, soon to be made public; a supposedly abusive father and his young son; a top executive passed over for a promotion and his gay rival. And yet, they were all innocent.

Chase explained his logic.

"I need you to talk to one of your profilers," he said. "Maybe I'm way off base here. Three murderers, all unrelated. But what are the odds?"

"I'm not sure which thought scares me more, that there are three murderers walking free, or one serial killer. Maybe with you in his headlights. We don't close our books until there's a conviction. Why isn't Wall pursuing these cases, or the police?"

The same thought had occurred to Chase. "I don't know," he typed. "Wall may have it in for me, but I never knew him to let personal feelings interfere with a case. He's not incompetent, whatever Lionel might tell you."

"Why don't you hand the file over to someone on the

police force in Piedmont? You must still know some people. Light a fire under them."

"All I have are my own suspicions. They have bigger files than I have on the same cases, and they know the result. I'm sure they're all still listed as open cases, but unless I can bring them something they don't have already, I doubt there'll be any action taken. On an individual case basis, I have nothing. But—"

"But, if you can bring corroborating opinion that one single person may have committed these crimes, they'd have to act."

"Coming from the FBI?" Chase keyed. "They'd feel pressure to move forward. Not to mention it would change the way they thought about the crimes. They might not have any leads for the crimes individually, but if you lump all the cases together as the work of a single person, they could start looking for patterns, connections between the crimes.

"I've worked with a lot of criminals, but never one like this. Serial killings are federal territory." He'd prosecuted many people; criminals who'd killed, stolen, destroyed, vandalized or just plain did stupid things, but he'd never had to deal with the psychological side of criminal behavior. Commit a crime, do the time.

Reagan typed back after a moment. "That's not a side of the Firm I've had dealings with. Mostly I've been working bank fraud, money laundering. But there's a guy over at Georgetown. He teaches a few classes, but works with us on a consulting basis. I've heard him lecture a few times, said hello. He'll have some questions though."

"Such as?"

"Such as why isn't this request coming through channels, through the Piedmont police force. He's a paid consultant, and has to account for his time."

"And this can't show up anywhere on his time sheets."

"Exactly. However, there is one thing that might get his interest."

"Your feminine charms?"

";) With this guy I could show up in a see-through negligee and I don't think he'd notice. This guy is a mystery nut. Loves to solve problems. If I can show him a compelling enough puzzle, I might be able to hook him. Get his help."

"All I can do is ask. I'll send the files out tomorrow."

"You did a good thing, today. Congratulations."

They said good night. He signed off and closed the laptop.

The files still in front of him, he thought of some of the implications if it were true—that a single killer had killed all these people, and framed his clients. He knew he was a good lawyer, but with all the time and effort he'd put into the cases, he'd only defended innocent people framed by the real killer or killers. At least he hadn't screwed it up, and had perhaps thwarted the efforts of a murderer. Or had the killer meant for him to succeed?

He'd thought the case behind him. Perhaps it was just beginning. He had an enemy with a face, Sterling, but he'd added another without one.

As he stacked the files, his eyes were drawn to the wooden box sitting on his desk. A memory stirred. The box had been a gift to Jared during his magic phase, when he was learning sleight-of-hand and studying the illusions of Houdini and the card magic of Marlo. Made of four different woods, it had a number of intricate designs that used the patterns of the grain to aesthetic effect. Flipping it upside down, he found the panel, and keeping his thumb on the mahogany seal, pushed it against the wood grain. Turning the box around, he opened it the ordinary way and lifted out the bottom. To his surprise, a CD popped out. He popped open the CD-ROM drive on his computer and slid the disk inside.

A bunch of letters and numbers scrolled down the page. Perhaps digital music files in a format with which Chase wasn't familiar? He set it on top of the files, wondering why his brother had felt the need to hide the disk in a box with his service medals.

NINETEEN

"Help me understand this, Chase. We're sitting in traffic, in a car with no air conditioning, driving four hours to Hilton Head, while Ev flew down in the company jet." Lionel Thompson honked at the caddie that had just pulled into the left lane then continued at forty miles an hour.

"Jesus, forgive me Lord," Lionel raised his face to the heavens. "But if God had meant for old people to drive, He'd surely have granted them the wisdom to understand the concept of a speed limit. Not to mention the whole notion of a passing lane."

Chase looked over at his friend and smiled patiently. Life for Lionel Thompson was always annotated and captioned for the hearing impaired.

"Relax. Sure, Ev's sitting out by the pool with a Boodles martini, surrounded by a veritable phalanx of bodacious women. But he didn't get to spend the last three hours in the company of his buddies, engaging in witty repartee, catching up on old times." Chase sat back in his seat, his knees scrunched up around his chin, his arms pulled in to his side uncomfortably. "At least he could have fit in this car. But I have to admit, I thought we'd be viewing the scenery from the Lexus."

"I told you. Anita needed the Lexus. She's showing hous-es this week, and the new minivan we bought hasn't arrived at the dealer yet."

"Minivan. Nice."

"Well it's not like we could even fit in your Porsche. When are you going to get a real car anyway?"

"Yeah, but the Datsun? They don't even make these things anymore. And if I had known you didn't have air con-ditioning in this stupid car..."

"Don't you be complaining. It was *your* brilliant idea to drive down to the beach this year. I'd have been more than happy to ride in the corporate jet with Ev. And since when are you worried about catching up with me? We see each other all the damn time! Hell, my wife is starting to wonder about me. I tell her you're still saving yourself for the priesthood." His last remark brought Lionel out of his funk. He grinned and threw back his broad shoulders, practically shoving Chase out the passenger door.

"Don't you start," Chase sighed, with a hint of exag-geration, the comment bringing up an old argument. "I get enough of that all week long. From everyone I meet who has a nice young lady who would be perfect for me. And I'm sure as soon as we pull up to the bar, Ev will have some beach bimbo for me to meet."

"And that would be a bad thing because..." Lionel prompted.

"You can be a real horse's ass sometimes, you know that?"

"Aw, you're jealous of my incredible charm," Lionel joked. "And my beautiful wife."

"Enough about me. You're the one not seeing straight. You'd rather fly in Ev's jet? You think that makes sense? You've about got the democratic nomination within the grasp of your massive hands, hands so large I can't imagine how you could possibly have dropped the football against ECU in the fourth quarter—" Chase ducked in anticipation of Lionel's response.

"How would it look for you to be seen accepting a free ride from a jet owned by the Litchfield Group?"

Lionel considered then sighed. "Unfortunately, my constituency might see that as a good thing. More than half the district are either smokers, or highly dependent on the tobacco industry, and are somewhat, shall we say, disturbed by my unwillingness to embrace said industry." He shrugged, and abruptly laughed out loud. "I can see it now. We take the jet; I leak it to the papers. Picture the story: 'Congressional Candidate Lionel Thompson departs for a weekend of merriment under the sponsorship of tobacco magnate and heir to the Litchfield fortune, Everett Montfort Litchfield, IV.' I could be puffing on a big old stogie—might be enough to swing the election."

"It might at that," Chase admitted soberly, hoping it would be his last sober thought of the week. "Come on, big guy. Let's dust these old folks. There's a margarita with my name on it up the road here." He sat back and relaxed as much as the cramped quarters allowed, enjoying the respite from recent events.

Despite his best intentions, he'd been unable to take time off the past two weeks. Staying home while Kasey organized the move to the new office suite on North Bryan, he'd continued to be inundated by interview and speaking engagement requests, as well as by calls from the television networks to appear as a guest commentator. He'd accommodated some, and put off others, overwhelmed by all the attention when he preferred, and needed, solitude. He had other clients to tend to, clients he'd had to put on hold during the Agnew trial; he couldn't turn his phone off.

He'd visited Jared once more, sat with him and talked, about the outcome of the case and his suppositions, and about the New York Yankees. A one-sided conversation to placate Brunelli who was hovering inside the door, affecting an air of nonchalance. As he got up to leave he leaned down to tie his shoes and quickly snuck an envelope under the mattress. He hoped he'd read the muddy shoes correctly.

All in all, a frustrating time. Time at the beach was just what he needed. He was glad when Reagan had told him she had a field assignment somewhere in Colorado, and would be gone for a few weeks. Maybe in the company of his friends he could share what he knew, seek their advice. For all their closeness, they'd all built up a shell around themselves, trying to preserve an image from earlier days, perhaps afraid of revealing their vulnerabilities. Chase wondered what thoughts they kept in reserve, or whether he was the only one who shielded parts of his life. They used to have no secrets from each other, but then, the secrets they'd shared tended to involve girls, or school, or job-related stuff.

"Well, Chase, looks like the Datsun got us here safe and sound," Lionel said as he pulled into Sea Pines Plantation and parked in front of the lobby of the hotel.

"Safe, sound, but hot as hell and ready to get out," Chase finally replied, opening the passenger door before the car had come to a stop. He hopped out gingerly, massaging his right knee out of habit, then stretched out, enjoying the smell of the salt air and the cool breeze drifting from the ocean. The beach could be glimpsed from the north end of the building, the water a brilliant gray-blue reflecting the rays of the sun.

Lionel got out as well, pulled the crutches out of the back, and leaned against the car for a few moments. "I'll sure be glad when I don't have to carry these around," he said, looking at them with disgust.

"Better than the wheelchair at least. You know, after my third knee surgery, I don't recall needing a wheelchair," he said.

Lionel snorted. "Cartilage tear. What the hell is that? Seems to me I played the Furman game with my ACL about gone. And scored two touchdowns."

"Ah yes, the good old days. Now when I was a lad, I once scored forty points in a game with both my arms broken and in splints."

"Damn straight," Lionel smiled. "So why is it I'm hobbling around on crutches now?"

"It's called getting older, Lionel. You put a lot of wear and tear into your hip when you were young, and now it's time to pay for it. Same with my knee. Hell, I can tell when a storm front is coming by the degree of throbbing. I'll bet by Sunday those crutches will be sitting in the car."

"Well I sure as hell am not going to bring these things out onto the beach, I can tell you that."

Chase grabbed the keys from his friend, and pulled their duffel bags out of the trunk. A porter came out and grabbed the golf bags from the back seat, and handed him a claim check.

"Playing the Resort course, sir?" the porter asked, both bags over his shoulder.

Chase looked over at Lionel, then back at the porter. "I think we'll be giving Harbor Town a try this time around," he answered, "assuming our friend Ev has made all the arrangements."

The porter, a young college-age kid with a buzz haircut, safari shorts, and a Hawaiian shirt with a nametag that read "Jeff," lugged their bags over to a golf stand just off the lobby entrance. "Would that be Mr. Litchfield, sir?"

"Yes, that would indeed be Mr. Litchfield," Chase said.

The young man grinned. "He asked me to look out for you. Gave me a hundred dollar bill to make sure I took you straight out to the pool bar, got your bags into the room, and gave you a couple drinks to get you started. Although he said you'd be driving a Lexus." He looked at the battered Datsun dubiously.

Lionel laughed and shook his head. "I should have known. Well, I have to give the boy credit. He takes care of his friends." He turned. "So lead away, Jeff. And where are those drinks, by the way?"

Still smiling, the porter reached over to a cooler behind the valet stand. After a few moments he stood holding a tray. "Corona with a twist of lime for Mr. Thompson, and a margarita on the rocks with salt for Mr. Riordan."

Chase took a long sip of his ice-cold drink. "Well, Lionel, so far so good." He licked the salt from the side of his glass. "Not bad. Herradura?" he asked the porter.

"Yes, sir. Mr. Litchfield said you knew your tequila."

"And I'm guessing this is a Corona," Lionel said facetiously.

"Wow, you're good, Lionel. That's the kind of mind we want working for us in Washington."

The big man grinned, pushed the lime wedge into the bottle, deftly stuck his thumb in the bottle and turned it upside down, allowing the lime to float to the bottom. Then he took a big swig, and held his beer in Chase's direction. "Escaping life," he toasted.

Chase returned the toast, wishing it were that simple. But Beach Weekends were about escape and nostalgia, comparing the girls they'd dated in college, girls they'd wanted to date, professors they'd had, parties they'd attended. They'd laugh about how Ev got so drunk at a frat party that he'd shown up wearing nothing but a Speedo and a coonskin cap. How Lionel had one time on a dare ripped the stair railing off the sidewalk next to Wilson Hall, how Chase had been with Celeste Harding, the captain of the cheerleading squad, back in his room, when Peter walked into the room and got sick. They would evaluate film actresses, women they knew in town, the Winfield Badgers chances for the coming year, either in football or basketball. The same conversations every year. Past exploits, past conquests, past regrets. Anything except their present circumstances.

Maybe this time, though, Chase thought, *it might be different.*

At the pool bar, they found Peter and Ev talking to a couple of beautiful young coeds. Chase hadn't seen Peter in a few months, and the appearance of his friend surprised him. He'd lost weight, his face appeared gaunt, and he had a nervous look to him. A half dozen empty beer bottles sat in front of him.

"Ladies, if you'll excuse us, we have some important business to discuss," Ev said. "But I'm sure we'd love to share your company a bit later. The girls made disappointed noises and moved away from the table over to the pool. The men's eyes followed their disappearing figures.

"Must have a bunch of rich daddies, paying for them to come down here and soak up the rays after school let out," Lionel said. "Sound familiar guys?" he asked.

"Sure, everything except the rich daddies part," Chase answered. "Present company excepted," he added, looking at Ev. "And what was that about 'later'? Are you serious? They're what, twenty years old?"

Ev smiled, pushed up his sunglasses, and leaned his head back.

"Speaking of which," Lionel said, turning to Ev, "where was your rich daddy when we were down at Myrtle in college? I don't recall him offering to put us up in some ritzy condo down at Hilton Head. Hell, we crammed eight of us into a place the size of a couple of dorm rooms at Winfield."

"Ah yes, the good old days," Ev replied, leaning back in his chair, never relinquishing the grip on his drink, now down to the ice. "Living among the hoi polloi, sharing meals with the commoners, attending actual sporting events and sitting among the crowd. My daddy wanted to make sure I had a, shall we say, normal college experience. Although hanging out with you low-life's wasn't likely what he had in mind." He smiled, revealing perfectly capped teeth. "I didn't come in to any money until I turned twenty-one, the trust fund from my dear departed grandfather, God rest his soul."

The day grew hotter as the sun rose higher in the sky. After a while a group of young men began to play volleyball in front of them on the sand court. The game attracted some attention from the women around the beach, encouraging Peter to suggest the four of them get out and play some.

"You're forgetting my hip," Lionel noted sadly.

"Right," Peter said, disappointed. He'd been an All Conference volleyball player at Winfield. "So when's Randy coming down?"

Chase and Lionel looked at each other. "I called his office before we left. I had a premonition he'd be working, for some reason. They told me he'd be in meetings all day."

"In meetings?" Lionel said. "Meetings with whom?"

Ev smiled. "Not to fear. He'll be here by dinner time."

Chase raised an eyebrow.

"I had an interesting visit this past week," Ev said. "A 'business lunch'"

"A business lunch? The two of you?" Chase asked.

"Not only that, he insisted on paying—for a lunch prepared by my personal chef."

According to Ev, during lunch, they'd exchanged pleasantries, talked Winfield football and lamented the fall of the basketball team. They talked around a lot of things, while avoiding any discussion of Randy's wife or his increasing absence from their get-togethers.

"Finally, over scones, he proceeded to deliver a business pitch. He actually took out a bound PowerPoint presentation. Extolled the virtues of March Maples, the preeminent law firm in North Carolina. Wants us to hire them for our corporate legal work." His voice rose as the background music increased in volume. "I felt as if the poor man were selling me insurance."

"How did you leave it?" Lionel asked.

"He treated me like a prospect; I treated him like a solicitor. I told him I would be happy to take up his proposal with the Governance Committee of our Board of Directors, and that I would be sure to put in a kind word on his behalf." Ev screwed his face in evident distaste. "Had he approached me somewhat differently, perhaps as a friend of twenty years, I might have had a different reaction.

"He was selling me. I figured I'd use my leverage. So I told him to tell Marinda we'd get the chance to talk more during Beach Weekend. Perhaps about March Maples doing our trust and agency work."

"Great, so now we have to blackmail him into coming?" Lionel grimaced as a volleyball smashed into his Corona, knocking it over and splashing him with beer.

"You guys ready to play?" Four kids were down on the court laughing. They were shirtless in baggy shorts down around their knees that showed off their whippet-thin physiques,

Peter deftly grabbed the ball, turned his Atlanta Falcons cap backwards, put on his Oakleys, and kicked off his Docksiders. Chase and Ev smiled at each other, recognizing Peter's game face. Lionel glowered down at the court and a small smile came to his face as well.

"I think the young fellows need a lesson," he said quietly.

BY NINE THAT EVENING they sat around the kitchen table of the condo, where cards and poker chips competed for space with an array of drinks, snacks, and Advil. Ice bags covered shoulders, knees, and ankles, and groans could be heard anytime one of them reached into the middle of the table to sweep a pot toward himself. Most of the poker chips sat in front of Randy Turner, the only sober one among them.

"The name of the game is seven card stud, high-low splits the pot," he said, dealing out a hand.

"I think the name of the game is, take a damn drink," Lionel said, puffing on a cigar. "It's going to be a long night if we're going to have to watch you drink Diet Cokes the whole time."

"I have to call Marinda soon. I don't want her to think I'm down here drinking."

"I'll bet five," Ev said, tossing some chips in the middle. "No, we couldn't have that. She might think we're a bad influence."

"It's not that. It's just that we don't drink unless we're together."

"Call," said Peter. "I get it. We're not good enough to drink with anymore?"

Randy had the decency to look embarrassed. "Come on,

guys, it's not like that. It's different now, being married. We try to do stuff together."

"I'm out," Chase said, standing up gingerly, taking the ice bags off his knees. He walked over to the counter and poured tequila in a tumbler, then brought back beers for Peter and Lionel.

"I call," Randy said. "We've only been married a short while. It's going to take a bit of time to figure all this stuff out. She let me come down—I mean when I decided to come down, I told her I wouldn't. Drink, that is."

"You want to see how this works?" Lionel said, tossing his chips in the pot. He picked up his cell phone and punched in a number. "Anita? Hey sweetheart, how's it going? Good, good. I'm drunk, hanging with the guys. Say hi, guys." He held up the phone so they could shout their hellos. "She says hi back. Okay honey, I love you too. Kiss the girls for me. Talk to you in a few days." He held the phone out to Randy. "Your turn."

"No, thanks. I told her I'd call at ten, before she goes to bed. It's different for you, Lionel. You two have been married since college. Marinda's still a little insecure."

Chase ambled over to the balcony and tuned out the banter. The moon cast a glow on the breakers. Randy had shown up by six, as Ev had promised. He might not be drinking, but he was there. Diminished somehow, but he'd made the drive, played cards with them, and absorbed the ribbing. Maybe a positive sign.

He looked inside and saw his friends in the familiar setting. He realized he couldn't say anything to them—about Jared, Reagan, his suspicions. He pulled his cell phone out and called Reagan. She answered on the second ring.

"Hey. I thought you'd be two sheets to the wind in the midst of a big hand."

He laughed. "Just one sheet, so far. And no big hands for me tonight. How's Colorado?"

"How the hell should I know? I spend all my time in a hotel room with a stack of spreadsheets."

"Sounds like fun. Any progress?"

"Some. You'd be amazed how sophisticated terrorists are financially. They know more about our banking laws than we do."

With the phone to his ear, Chase sat down in a lounge chair, and closed his eyes.

TWENTY

Jared opened his eyes, careful not to move until he could be sure of his privacy. Still in his room, in his bed. No restraints. He flexed his muscles in sequence, from his feet, to his calves, his quadriceps, his stomach, his arms, his neck––all in working order. Strong, even. His exercises were paying off. Tonight had to be the night. Sterling would be there shortly. Their confrontation would have to wait until they were a bit more evenly matched. And on more favorable turf.

His arms were sore; he remembered his treatment from two nights before. Rolling up his sleeves, he could see a series of small welts running from his wrists to his shoulder. His back ached, and he reached around and felt the bandage at the base of his spine. The room lay in darkness, but he saw everything with great clarity. Not just shapes, or shadows. Using his legs, he pulled his blankets down.

Slipping out of bed, he quietly stretched, allowing himself to become accustomed again to the weight on his legs. Arms still sore, but less numb, he slowly padded over to the small closet, passing the poster his brother had taped on the wall. He removed it again, and rolled it up. In the back of the closet, pushing aside the shirts and two jumpsuits, he felt his way along the wall panel. He found the seam, pulled the panel off, and exposed a space between the closet and the adjoining room. It had taken him all of an evening of awareness to remove the panel, his strength being still considerable despite his condition. He felt around and removed all of the items from the space, laying them on the closet floor. Closing the door, he turned on the closet light to expose his hoard. It was a paltry set of items, things he'd managed to procure during the past week. A table fork and knife from the cafeteria, a box of matches taken out of the coat pocket of an orderly, the muddy shoes he'd replaced, and his most prized item, a pass card left lying on a table by one of the staff doctors.

He gathered up the items, including the poster, in a satchel he made of an old tee shirt and left the closet. Feeling under the mattress, he removed the envelope left there by his brother and added it to his pack.

The building was quiet and cold. He slipped on the shoes, a clean tee shirt, the fatigue pants, and slipped out into the hallway, listening for sounds from any of the other inmates.

A garbage can near the main entrance hadn't been emptied. He rummaged through it, discovering a scrap of biscuit, which he ate, some napkins, which he tucked into his pack, and an old newspaper, which he kept. He'd planned for this moment, as much as anyone could plan anything while maintaining lucidity a few days at a time. He had hoped to enlist Chase in his efforts, had hoped to walk out the front door in the light of day, but he was out of time. He knew in his heart Sterling would never let him leave. He was only surprised he'd let him live. Wondered why he had. It was a mistake that was going to come back to haunt him.

Using the pass card, he opened the door to the main hall next to the entrance, a simple room containing a desk and chair, a phone, a bulletin board and a lamp. A phone directory was posted on the bulletin board. Noting the extension for Administration, Jared dialed the number. As he'd hoped, he got voicemail. "Tell Sterling I have what he's looking for," he whispered, and hung up. His voice was weak; the drugs affecting his vocal cords still kept him from speaking in anything resembling a normal voice.

Taking out the matches and a wadded handful of newspaper, Jared carefully walked around the floor until he found a room filled with file cabinets. He pulled out all the files from the cabinets and positioned them around the floor. His own name jumped out at him, stenciled at the top of a red folder. Another acquisition for his satchel. Then he reached up, popped out a ceiling tile, and used a chair to poke his head up though to check out the insulation and ductwork. Somehow he doubted the building had met the local fire codes. An hour of work lay ahead of him, and then he'd be on his way.

MOST OF THE STAFF and inmates were outside by the time the fire started. An alarm had sounded at two a.m. Administrative staff, what few doctors there were, and those patients who were ambulatory and not locked down, made it to the exits, most through the front door. They arrived outside in time to see flames shooting from an upstairs window. Any thoughts of reentering the building to unlock and unfetter the remaining inmates evaporated with a loud explosion, followed by a burst of heat through the open door. The fire spread quickly.

Fires were a frequent hazard in the forests of the Appalachians in summer. The Parks Department operated around the clock trying to prevent and contain any conflagrations from spreading. Fortunately for the Parks Department, whose helicopters arrived within the hour, the stone wall and bare grounds surrounding the building acted as a buffer, preventing the fire from reaching the tree line. Unfortunately, it was too late to do anything to save the building. It took only three hours to reduce the structure to a smoking shell. Smoke from the fire could be seen for miles.

Remarkably, when the staff gathered to count heads and assess the damage, they found three inmates who had been under restraints in their rooms on the back grounds, bruised and burned, but otherwise unharmed. Perhaps thrown clear somehow. That left one inmate unaccounted for: an apparent victim of the fire.

TWENTY-ONE

The Sunday after returning from Hilton Head, Chase dutifully awoke to visit Jared. Having felt nothing all week
other than the effects of too much alcohol, he drove with an
odd sense of anticipation. Turning off Highway 64 to Fletcher,
he pulled into the gravel turnoff for the Institute two miles up
the road. About two hundred yards in, the path was blocked
by a large pine tree across the road. Chase stopped the car, got
out, and examined the trunk. At first it appeared to have just
fallen across the road, but further examination revealed the
cut marks of a chainsaw at the base. Leaving the car parked
directly in front of the tree, Chase set off on foot.

The same sense of anticipation had prompted him to
wear clothing that served him now: a pair of walking shorts
and an old pair of Nike Air Mada hiking shoes. It took him
approximately ninety minutes to cover the winding pathway
to the top. He considered walking off the path to avoid the
view of the cameras, but decided the going was tough enough
without trying to negotiate the thick pines and scrub.

Approaching the top, panting from the steep climb and
sweating heavily, he smelled the faint aroma of smoke. On
reaching the gates he saw the reason why no one had met him.

Blackened stone walls, with the remains of a slate roof at their base, were all that remained of the building. Smoke rose from the ruins like steam off the road after a summer shower. The exterior walls stood intact, still encircling the property, and the grounds looked more scorched than usual. *Jared.* Somehow he knew this was his brother's work. The connection between them was so strong, that if anything had happened to him, he'd have known. He supposed he should have considered possible victims, but all he could think was, *he got out.* He looked around. The guard shack, not surprisingly, stood empty. Peeking in through the side window, Chase could make out the small desk and two chairs. The door remained locked, as did the gate to the Institute itself. Chase looked around, surprised to see the one obvious camera, positioned to observe the gateway in a tall pine outside the gate, broken. Completely smashed, in fact. He considered whether he could hit the camera with a rock so precisely.

Taking advantage of the opportunity afforded him with no one around, Chase set out to walk the perimeter. He noticed cameras positioned at thirty-foot intervals along the wall, and occasionally detected others in the trees outside the wall. When he had walked a hundred yards or so to the southwest corner of the property, he climbed the slope of the mountain away from the Institute to see beyond the stone wall. The stumps had been cleared from the back of the property, creating a large flat area that ran from the house all the way to the wall. There was a defined cement area of a helipad. He could also see the other entrance to the property: a gondola station, with cables running straight down the mountain over the wall. The place had clearly been a private ski resort at one time. Chase could make out the remains of the runs now that he knew what to look for. Scrub growth had taken over where the trails had not been maintained. The gondola station was set about two hundred yards from the back of the house. It was a small station, but well maintained, freshly painted a deep forest green.

Chase searched for a possible entrance through the stone

wall, but the walls were well kept; some showed signs of recent repair. He found a spot directly in back of the property where the diagonal walls came together and an old growth pine tree grew at a slight angle from the mountain slope toward the wall. If he could climb the tree, he could possibly jump from the tree to the top of the wall, and slide down to the other side, assuming he could avoid the glass shards he could see bristling from the top of the stone. While considering this, he noticed a small scrap of white about seven feet up the same trunk. It turned out to be a piece of material, about two inches by two inches. The bark of the tree was sharp, and had snagged the material, probably doing some damage to the wearer. There was even a small dark spot on the material—blood? Chase put the swatch in his pocket and scanned the surrounding area. The forest took off in every direction with no clearly defined path. The only two clearings he could see were the one he had come up himself, and the swath cut down the mountain under the gondola cables. Both risked exposure to the outside cameras, although the cameras in the immediate vicinity of the angled tree were smashed. Ruling out the tree climb, Chase continued his journey around the perimeter wall. He paused below the gondola cable. The trees were cut back from the gondola route fifty yards on either side. He looked down the slope, but saw nothing. A person heading down that route would be clearly visible to passengers on the gondola cars, or to the cameras positioned on the gondola pylons.

Another fifteen minutes of exploration took him back at the front gate. During his entire trip, he'd seen no signs of life within the walls. The site had been abandoned. He wondered about the other inmates, but only in passing. His real concern: what had happened to Jared. Where was he? No one from the Institute had called to alert him of any change of status. Had the confusion and chaos of the fire overwhelmed every other consideration?

Chase reached his car, surprised to find that four hours had passed. His thoughts were for his brother's safety. On the drive home, he pulled a small cell phone from his glove compartment and set it on the seat beside him. Now all he could do was wait.

HE AWOKE TO THE SOUND of the phone. Glancing at the caller ID, he groaned and reluctantly picked up the receiver.

"Didn't we see enough of each other this past week?" he said.

"I try to be the kind of friend who is on call 24-7. Full service," Ev replied.

"Lucky me. And what service are you providing so bright and early this morning?"

"Not five minutes ago, I received a call from an acquaintance of mine, Miss Kate Wagner. The police had come to her apartment Friday night and asked her to accompany them down to the station to answer a few questions. She called me and asked if I could arrange an introduction."

"With me?"

"Who else could this young damsel in distress possibly depend upon to defend her against the evil Piedmont police state?"

A bell rang in the back of Chase's mind. "Wagner?" he said. "And why do they want to question her?"

"Oh, did I neglect to mention that?" Ev asked. "She is, or was, the fiancée of Josh Samuels. The young gentleman who drowned in the triathlon a couple weekends ago?"

"Young couple doing their first triathlon together? Isn't she world class or something?"

"In more ways than one," Ev said. "The police, or more accurately the District Attorney's Office, are of the mind that Mr. Samuels' untimely demise may not have been a mere act of fate. They believe that he was, shall we say, helped to his end by Ms. Wagner. You may wish to read your local newspaper. Saturday's edition contained some speculation on the case."

"I'm not sure I'm ready to jump into another case at the moment, Ev."

"I'm sorry, I was under the impression this is what you do for a living. Anyway, I already told Kate you'd contact her. She's quite anxious to make your acquaintance. She was reluctant to believe she needed an attorney at all, other than to deal with the paperwork. Spending the night in a holding cell, however, has made her a bit more of a believer."

"The police held her overnight?" It was unusual to hold a suspect without charges, even in a murder investigation. "Wait a minute. Is this the same Kate Wagner who beat you in squash a couple of months ago?"

"The same. And come now, Chase. So I let her win a game. I am a gentleman, after all."

"And where is she now?"

"At the moment, so far as I know, she's at home awaiting your phone call. Much as how half the women at Winfield spent their Friday nights," Ev said. He sighed audibly. "Although alas, all of them waited in vain. You know, Chase, you really should get out more. This doesn't help your reputation any, and even I, as your—"

"Why don't you ask her to come by my office mid morning, say eleven," Chase said, "And why don't you come by as well? You can help with introductions. That is, if you can manage to get away from work."

"I might somehow find the time. Ten-thirty work?"

"See you then."

"I doubt you'll have to spend much time on this. I'm sure you'll be able to straighten things out quickly."

Chase sighed and hung up. With luck, it would be a simple matter. Maybe the police were just covering their bases before ruling on the accidental drowning.

TWENTY-TWO

C hase walked into his new offices a few minutes before ten, earning a frown of disapproval from his office assistant Kasey when he strolled in. He'd been told to stay away until Wednesday. He expected boxes everywhere, but the only things out of place were the pictures lined up at the base of the walls, waiting to be hung.

"Sorry, Kase, couldn't be helped. New client. Kate Wagner. She should be here at eleven, and I'm expecting Ev shortly. See if you can round up Ernesto, I'll need him for this."

She raised her eyebrows at the mention of Kate Wagner's name, nodded, and handed him a blank legal pad and some pens.

"Ernie's still over at the old office packing the legal books." She halted his objection. "I know, but he insisted. I'll send him in when the truck gets here." She walked back to her desk, set in a large, immaculate reception area.

"Oh and Chase, Steve Riveira called, wants you to call him back."

"Thanks. Hey, could you see if you could track down some back issues of the *Piedmont Gazette*, going back the last three weekends?" Chase walked into his new office for the first time. He stopped and stared. His diplomas were neatly displayed on the far wall, alongside a number of letters or appreciation from his time in the D.A.'s Office. The wall opposite his desk held a collection of memorabilia from his basketball-playing days: a signed basketball from the Winfield Final Four team; his All America plaques; a few trophies displayed on a wide-based pedestal; and some photos of him with the governor, with his teammates, with Larry Bird, and with Ev, Peter, Randall, and Lionel. He didn't even know where she found that one. Chase didn't know he owned any pictures of the five of them together. His old office had held a Government Issue desk, a couple of cheap bookcases, and a folding chair. Kasey walked up behind him carrying a stack of newspapers.

"You like it?" she asked.

"It's unbelievable, Kase. I don't know what to say." He just stood there, staring. "Thanks."

"You're welcome. Now that you're here, you might as well get back to work." She deposited the papers on his desk. "We keep 30 days." She pulled one paper out of the pile. "This is the first mention of Josh Samuels' death," she said, indicating the Sunday paper the day after the triathlon.

"Remind me to give you a raise. I sure wouldn't want you going back to work for the other side."

She smiled at him. "You gave me a nice raise last month. And if I ever tell you I'm going back to the District Attorney's Office without you in it, you can take a gun to my head and shoot me, because I'll have gone crazy."

"Thanks. I'm surprised you haven't cut out all the articles already. But I'll forgive you this time."

"I'll be at my desk. Let me know if you need anything else."

Chase took a few moments to look through the newspapers Kasey had brought him. The Latta Plantation Triathlon, an annual event north of Piedmont, had taken place two Sundays before. Josh Samuels, participating in his first triathlon, never made it past the swim leg. As the winners crossed the finish line, a few college students out for a sail and enjoying the race found his body. Apparently in the sea of arms and legs thrashing about in the dark waters, he was struck in the head, got tangled up in some fishing line, and drowned. On the Wednesday following the race, an editorial appeared about the danger of the event, calling for, at the very least, a group of observers out on the water to prevent such needless tragedies. There was no coverage for almost a week then he spotted a small article in Thursday's paper. "Murder by Drowning?" read the tagline on page four of the front section. The article quoted police sources saying they were looking into the possibility of murder in the death of Josh Samuels. There were indications of foul play. All sources were "unnamed," and no specific evidence indicated murder.

Chase stood up to stretch. At that moment Ev Litchfield walked in, an armful of flowers in his hands.

"Well, I do declare, Chase, you are moving up in the world. I didn't need to bring along any bug spray. Now where is that marvelous assistant of yours? Ah, there she is," he said, as Kasey appeared at the door. "Beautiful lady, these are for you. You have done wonders with this place. Of course, you'll have your work cut out for you, keeping up with the slovenly habits of your degenerate boss." Bowing, he handed the beaming Kasey the bouquet of flowers.

"Thank you, Ev. These are beautiful. Let me just set the coffee down and then I'll put them in a vase. They'll look nice on that table in the corner."

Ev watched her, waiting until she had closed the door behind her.

"Things still okay in Litchfield land?"

Ev sighed. "The things I do for the company. The public may not like us, but the gentlemen from Wall Street sure do. I suppose they're enamored of our ability to poison the lungs of the great unwashed masses in Asia. They appreciate our stellar earnings growth and don't care much about the ancillary issues."

Chase laughed. "Yeah, those ancillary issues. Who could care about lung cancer? As long as the bottom line continues to be positive, right?"

"You have hit the nail on the head. We're doing our part, though. Just think how much money the tobacco settlement is taking out of yours truly's pocket. I ask you, is that fair?" He looked at his watch. "I can stay for a few minutes, but have to get back to the office."

"Good thing they're not paying you by the hour."

"Indeed."

"So tell me about Kate Wagner."

Ev had met Kate Wagner at The Show, an exclusive health club that took up the top three floors of the Founder's Bank Tower. He held memberships at almost every club in town, but went to The Show because they had the only squash courts in Piedmont. Kate swam there; in fact, her picture adorned the wall in the club, identifying her as a former World bronze medalist in the one-hundred-meter butterfly. She also participated in the squash ladder. The men's. Ev held the top ranking in the club, and a year earlier Wagner had challenged him. He'd beaten her, but she'd offered the most competition he'd had so far, and they'd begun to play on a regular basis.

Wagner had been a swimmer in college, had, as advertised at the club, been on the U.S team at the World Championships ten years earlier, and had been a strong favorite for a medal at the last Olympic Games. Unfortunately, she had done poorly in the trials, and hadn't made the team. Still a top athlete, she began competing in triathlons, where her swimming ability proved a real plus. She had trained hard for the past few years in the hope of getting back to the Olympics as a triathlete. Ev believed she got free club privileges and that she worked at a local advertising agency to pay her bills.

"She's a fitness nut, in superb condition. And that's about all I know about her," Ev concluded. "Other than that she and this Josh Samuels had been dating for a short while. We don't generally talk a whole lot while we're playing. I'm sure it takes all of her energy to stay on the court with me. Not that I wouldn't have minded if she spent some of that energy elsewhere."

Chase raised his eyebrows. "No off the court action?"

Ev raised his hand and fluttered his fingers, sighing. "Scout's honor. I always meant to introduce her to you, in fact. This Samuels just got there sooner. Besides, she's not really my type." Generally his type was a blonde with what he called "Las Vegas potential."

Kasey poked her head in. "Ms. Wagner is here."

"Bring her in."

He had pictured a muscular, broad-shouldered, short-haired athlete. Not the red-haired beauty in front of him. Standing perhaps a shade under six-feet tall, she wore a short skirt and an embroidered tee shirt. Her legs were nearly as long as Chase's, with orange-painted toenails visible through her Teva sandals. Her shoulder-length hair was pulled back in a ponytail. Her face glistened with moisture, as if she'd come in from a run, which Chase suspected she had. He was mildly annoyed at her appearance; not exactly the behavior he hoped for in a potential client about to be accused of murder. He caught himself, remembering he didn't need any new clients.

"Please sit down, Ms. Wagner," he said, offering his hand. "I'm Chase Riordan." She gave the proffered hand a quick squeeze.

"Pleased to meet you, Mr. Riordan." she said. She nodded at Ev.

"Call me Chase. You know Ev. A colleague of mine may be joining us shortly."

"Thank you Chase," she said, looking at him directly with those crystal blue eyes. As she sat, a sudden nervous smile came across her face, which highlighted her perfect nose and lips.

"Relax, Kate," he said, taking a deep breath to help himself do the same. "Okay if I call you Kate?" She nodded. Ev sat back observing the two, smiling like the Cheshire cat. "Kate, I wanted to meet with you first—I don't know yet what's going on here, other than what's been in the paper—but it's to your benefit for us to meet before we go see the police."

At the mention of the word 'police' Kate flinched.

"I didn't do anything," she blurted.

"At this point, all that matters is that the police want to speak to you. Apparently, they believe Josh Samuels' death wasn't accidental, and it's only natural they would want to talk to you. We want to control, as much as possible, the circumstances of that conversation."

Chase raised his eyebrows in Ev's direction, nodding his head in the direction of the door.

"I need to get going, Chase," Ev said. "Kate, you're in good hands. Mr. Riordan here may not be the best-looking attorney in town, but you won't find a better lawyer." Ev gave Chase a wink and left the room, closing the door behind him.

"He said you went to school together," she said.

"We've been friends a long time, if that's what you're wondering. Although I need to work for a living." Chase pulled over a legal pad and pen Kasey had left. "Why don't you start by telling me about your relationship with Josh Samuels? How it started, how the two of you got along, up until the day of the triathlon."

For the next hour Kate Wagner talked. At first she spoke with some reluctance, and her words came slowly, measured, but after a while she began to talk more freely. She and Josh had been introduced by friends and had dated for about three months. They shared a love of working out, and Josh, at Kate's urging, trained with her to participate in a triathlon. They ran together, biked together, and trained at the gym.

As Kate talked, Chase observed her: a reserved woman, emotions held close, words restrained. When she spoke about Josh, Chase could sense a certain distance, as if she were talking about her remote past, not someone with whom she'd had a recent serious relationship. He probed gently, asking a few questions to help the narrative move along. She had just finished discussing training and dinner the day before the race when the conference room door opened and a Chase's associate, a handsome young Hispanic, walked in.

"Hey boss, sorry, I've been running back and forth to the old place. I tell you, I'm not going to miss it. The view we got from this place." He closed the door behind him, and bent over Wagner, extending a hand, "Ernie Perez. Nice to meet you," he said, and sat down in the chair between her and Chase.

"Ernie is my associate. He'll be helping out if we get involved in your case," Chase explained.

"Mr. Riordan, honest, I didn't do anything. I just want to continue training, what with the Olympics coming up and all." *No expression of grief about Josh's death,* Chase noticed.

"We'll certainly do the best we can. Maybe we can clear this up when we see the police. I'd like to set up the meeting with them for Wednesday. That will give us another day together to prepare." They spent the next few minutes discussing schedules and fees. After confirming the time to meet in the morning, Kasey came in and escorted Kate out of the office.

"So fill me in, boss. Kasey mentioned this gal might be connected with the triathlon death a couple weeks ago?"

Chase gave him a quick outline of the day, starting with the call from Ev, and finishing up with Kate's account of her relationship with Josh Samuels.

Ernie snapped his fingers. "I thought I'd heard his name before. He wrote the series in the *Gazette* about the tobacco industry." He laughed. "I'm sure Mr. Litchfield has heard of him. He's been all over their asses."

Curious. Ev hadn't mentioned anything about it.

"I'll run down some of his recent articles. Should make for interesting reading. And I'll have Tony round up some of the race officials, see if I can get anything from them," Ernie said.

"Check the coroner's report. And ask Tony to get some background, find anyone who knew the two of them."

"Will do."

"Steve Riveira called. I'll talk to him and we'll set a time for us to meet with Wagner and the police. We have our library intact?"

"One more trip. But the computers are all hooked up, we've got LexisNexis, WestLaw, and Internet access, so we're okay on resources for now." Ernesto left the office.

A few minutes later Kasey stuck her head in the door. "I have Steve on the line for you."

"Put him through, thanks." He punched two buttons on his phone before getting it right. "Steve?"

"We're not talking."

"Excuse me?"

"You and I, we're not having this conversation. I'm just strolling along the street chatting with an old girlfriend." Traffic sounds and voices dominate the background. "After we hang up, I will reach my office, call you back and we can talk and set a time to meet."

"Ah. So who is this old girlfriend?"

"Since this is a conversation we are not having, let's call her Muffy. Let's say she was the captain of my high school cheerleading squad, with a killer body, who suddenly had the urge to call up the second string guard on the basketball team. We so seldom had the chance to talk when we were in school."

Chase laughed. He and Steve played pickup basketball at the Y on Thursday nights, and had known each other since Chase's days in the D.A.'s Office.

"I think I remember this girl myself."

"Yeah, I'm sure she had plenty of time for you."

"You'd be surprised. So, what's up?"

"Josh Samuels. Kate Wagner. The victim and the accused. You're on offense; we're on defense. We both know the drill." Steve Riveira had testified in a number of cases Chase had prosecuted. He made a good witness. A professional cop, on top of his facts. Chase also knew him as a straight shooter who wanted to get things right, not just clear a case. When on opposite sides of the fence, they kept their relationship to basketball. "I wouldn't think you'd have much to say. You're not the investigating officer, are you?"

"I've been nowhere near this one. Odd that you ask my opinion. A reason you and I need to meet. Alone. But none of this should be any great secret. I am, in fact, authorized to share this much with you by my boss, Captain Knowles. Strictly off the record."

A face flashed through Chase's mind. Gray sideburns, slicked-back black hair. "Peterson case? Took a bullet in the foot or something?"

"Shot off one of his own toes. The same. Not a very personable fellow, but he doesn't take shit from anyone. Something about this case doesn't sit well with him. Obviously I can't tell you anything confidential, but the arrest warrant will state all this anyway.

"Josh Samuels. Definitely murdered. The fishing line found around his body didn't come from the lake. Don't know how they know that. He didn't just swim into it and get caught. At least that's what the coroner claims. Traces of some drugs I can't pronounce in his system as well. Kate Wagner. The obvious suspect. Emphasis on that. She and Josh had taken out insurance policies on each other just the week before the race. A bit odd for a couple that had been dating for only a few months."

"That it?"

"What more do you want? A million bucks makes for a pretty good motive."

Chase whistled. The size of the insurance benefit hadn't been in the paper.

"Exactly. That and the fact Wagner can't account for her whereabouts during the time of the murder."

"Her whereabouts? She swam, biked, and ran past a thousand spectators, along with a few hundred competitors. Plenty of people saw her."

"Ah, but that's the interesting part. No one can recollect seeing her during the swim." His next few words were drowned out by a car horn.

Chase pictured a few hundred bodies splashing their way through the dark waters of Lake Norman. Not difficult to imagine no one could distinguish who was who until they emerged on the other side of the lake for the bike leg.

"She finished the race, so she got on the bike and ran the last ten kilometers in front of a lot of folks."

"True. But Kate won this race last year. This year she finished tenth in the elite class. Her lowest finish of the season. Attributed by many to her slow swim. Her strongest event."

"Go back a minute. Did you say he was killed with fishing line?"

"Yep. Wrapped around Samuels' neck, and his arms. We got lucky—the killer probably meant the line to loosen and fall to the bottom. Why?"

"Nothing. I was just taking some notes."

The police case was clear. They had motive and potentially opportunity. As to means, Kate was a big girl, strong and athletic. A jury could easily be convinced she had the strength to kill someone in the water, especially if the victim were drugged. An obvious suspect and a reasonable motive. Too convenient.

"That's all I have on the case. On the other subject, we should get together soon."

"Place we hung out after the first game of the playoffs last year? Five-thirty?"

"Sounds good, and Muffy, thanks for the call. I appreciate your tracking me down after all these years. Why don't we get together when you're in town? I'd love to see some of those splits you were so famous for."

Chase laughed. "Talk to you soon."

He hung up the phone, curious. He scribbled on his pad for a few minutes, then called Ev and got his voicemail. "Call me if you get a minute. Couple things I'd like to ask you about."

Next he called Riveira back officially, and set up the meeting between his new client and the police for the Wednesday afternoon. He needed to read the *Gazette* series Samuels had written and check that out with Ev. He also had a lot more questions for Kate Wagner before meeting with the police.

TWENTY-THREE

Joggers and bikers lined the cinder pathways of Bryan Park, a new addition to the city of Piedmont. The Litchfield family had donated the land when they'd decided to relocate their headquarters to the new downtown project, and the city had carved out an urban park complete with fountains, trails, and picnic areas. Standing near the statue of Jesse Helms, Chase greeted Steve as he crossed the lawn.

"Esteban," he said, clasping his hand firmly.

"Ola, Chase."

"You have any trouble getting away?" He led him to a bench set back from the path.

"Nah, I'm never in the office anyway. If I'm there too much, captain figures I don't have enough work to do so I get assigned another case."

Chase smiled with his friend. Esteban "Steve" Riveira stood about five foot nine, had wiry, close-cropped hair that was dark on the sides, and dyed blond on top. He wore a pair of black jeans and a long-sleeved rugby shirt with black military-style boots. A blue-collar worker just off his shift in the plant. Twice decorated for bravery, he carried a scar across his left arm that ran almost from his bicep to his wrist, from an altercation during an arrest.

"So what's going on, Steve? Everything okay with the department?"

"Can't complain. Captain's a bit of a dick, but he's generally a straight shooter. He runs a pretty good department." He looked around to see who was nearby. A young woman jogger, stretching ten yards away was the only one remotely within earshot. He leaned across the bench, speaking softly. "I knew you were defending Wagner," he said.

Chase raised an eyebrow. "That's no secret. I filed my papers with the judge's clerk first thing this morning."

Riveira shook his head. "Not what I meant. What would you say if I told you I knew last week you were defending Wagner?"

"I'd say you couldn't have. I didn't meet Kate Wagner until this morning."

"I wondered." He nodded. "About what I figured though. So let me tell you a little story." Riveira looked around again, scanning the area. He turned back to Chase.

"We were investigating the murder, not me personally, but it was our precinct that caught the case. Anyway, we were asked to keep a close eye on this one and next thing I know the captain is on the phone with the D.A.'s Office, and your name came up."

"Not surprising. The D.A.'s Office always pays attention to the filings. I always wanted to know who I was up against when I was on a case."

Steve shook his head. "The phone call occurred at around 4:00 p.m. Last Thursday." He paused to let that sink in.

"How's that possible?"

"I didn't think a whole lot of it at the time, since I wasn't following the case myself. And for all I knew, Wagner had hired you already. But I heard Knowles mention your name, and I perked up a bit. When they brought Wagner in Friday, I looked at the sheets. No attorney-of-record. Then when you showed up this week, I connected the dots. I started wondering what they had been talking about Thursday afternoon."

"So they're talking about the case, getting ready to talk to Kate Wagner, wondering who might defend her, and my name came up?"

"That's what I thought at first," Steve nodded. "But I don't think so now. I heard bits and pieces of the conversation, and it was heated. Knowles was yelling and I could hear Wall almost like he sat at the next desk. The captain is a bit hard of hearing, so he keeps the volume on his phone turned way up."

"How'd you know it was Wall?" Chase asked.

"Captain's secretary took the call. Patched it into him. 'D.A.'s Office on one.' So the captain's yelling, and Wall's yelling, and I'm hearing words like 'nail the bastard' from Wall, and the captain's yelling at Wall to follow procedure or something like that. Didn't sound like they were talking about a woman. That's why I didn't make the connection until Friday. When they arrested Wagner, that was the first I knew the murderer—"

"Accused," Chase interrupted by force of habit.

"Sorry, but you know what I mean. Then I started thinking back on the phone call. I thought they'd been talking about some guy you were defending."

"And now you think they were talking about me," Chase finished.

Steve nodded. A group of bikers stopped near them, parking their bikes to drink some water. "Let's walk," he said.

The two men stood up. Neither said much of anything on their way to the side street where Steve had parked. As they arrived at the detective's car, an old, nondescript gray Honda Accord, they stopped.

"So maybe they were just talking. Maybe they thought Kate Wagner might approach me. As the D.A., or anyone from the D.A.'s Office, you always want to win your case. If they want to try to nail me in court, let them have at it. No big deal. I admit the timing sounds a bit odd, but not an un-reasonable assumption. That I'd get the case, I guess."

Steve chuckled. "No surprise Wagner would choose you, Chase. I had a problem, you'd be the first I'd call too. Though I doubt I could afford you." He sobered. "But this seemed a bit different. Maybe it's nothing, but I'd be careful. They're paying a bit more attention to this one and something doesn't smell quite right. And the other funny thing? Yesterday the Wagner case was passed off to the D.A."

"That's how it's supposed to work."

"Yeah sure, but when you were in the D.A.'s Office, did you ever stop the investigation entirely once you'd made an arrest?" he asked.

He got into his car, waved, and drove off, leaving Chase to ponder his last comment.

Standard procedure would be to continue to take depo-sitions from witnesses, to firm up the case, pull employment records of the accused, and continue to keep on top of every-thing while the defense began its own investigation. It was important to track who the defense talked to and verify the physical evidence. Usually there were DNA tests, hair and fiber analyses, and in this case, there were over a thousand potential witnesses. All the participants in the Latta Park Triathlon. It was unthinkable the investigation could be complete.

He put together the pieces he knew. Wall knew he would be Wagner's attorney. Or maybe he just assumed it. Fair enough. Perhaps from Wall's point of view it was a worst-case scenario. What if Chase Riordan gets the case? Add to that, though, the halting of the investigation before the police ar-rested the suspect. And then there was the fishing line. All these pieces had to add up to something. He felt as if he were in a chess game where the only pieces he could see were his own. Wall was a political animal who rarely spoke up about his office's activities, save to take credit for victories after the fact, and distance himself from losses. Oddly though, in spite of his courtroom demeanor, after the jury had exonerated Agnew, Wall had thanked Chase publicly for proving the city wrong in its prosecution of the well-loved ex-mayor. He'd practically taken credit for the acquittal himself, glossing over the incident that had led to Chase's departure, and the obvious animosity between them.

Still, Wall would no doubt love to knock him down a peg. If that was all that was going on, he could deal with it. But he sensed something deeper. The hand of another: the faceless killer, perhaps? A case he'd had no interest in might be the means to flush him out.

TWENTY-FOUR

"Peter? Peter Jurgens?"

The voice on the phone sounded vaguely familiar. Tempted to hang up, he grunted an acknowledgement, setting down his beer.

"Paul Givens. Where've you been keeping yourself?"

Paul Givens. Assistant Editor for *The Journal and Constitution,* innocuous little guy, prematurely bald and middle-aged.

"Hey Paul, nice to hear from you." They exchanged pleasantries; Peter dredged up the wife's name from somewhere in the recesses of his mind.

"I understand you might be expecting my call. A friend might have mentioned it?"

The caller will tell you a friend suggested he contact you. You are to do exactly as he asks. That in return for your son's continued safety.

"Oh?" he managed.

"I know you're not a newspaper guy anymore, but you did some pretty good work for *Time,* and I thought if you were done with the book you might be interested in a new project. A friend suggested you'd be very interested. It seemed right up your alley, what with you knowing Chase Riordan and all."

He'd been only half listening. "Did something happen to Chase?"

There was a pause, and then Givens came back on the line. "Something happen—oh no, nothing like that. But I remember you mentioning when we spoke a while back that you and he were old friends. Went to college together, I think?"

"Uh, yeah," he said, not remembering talking with Givens about his friends, and wondering where this was going.

"Look Paul, it's nice talking with you and all, but could you get to the point? I really do need to get back to work on the book."

"Okay. Let me start over. Couple weeks ago a guy was killed at a triathlon up in Piedmont. You hear about it?"

He hadn't looked at a newspaper or turned on the TV in weeks.

"Well, there was this guy who was killed. His first triathlon, and he drowns on the swim leg. Except the police think it was murder."

"Murder? I thought you said the guy drowned."

"Oh, no. It wasn't an accident at all. I thought I was making myself clear."

"And what does this have to do with Chase?" Peter asked.

"The murderer, or I should say, the alleged murderess, is being defended by Chase Riordan. And that's where you come in," he said.

"Where I come in."

"Uh, yes. You see, when Mr. Riordan defended Mayor Agnew, he became quite the celebrity in these parts. Even drew some national attention, I suspect."

Peter snorted. Suspect hell, Greta van Susteren and Marcia Clark were talking about the Agnew case on *Larry King Live.*

"So when I found out that Riordan would be defending Kate Wagner—she's the murderess—I thought: beautiful woman, handsome young defense attorney, high profile case. And it came to me."

"What came to you?"

"The idea for a series! Covering a murder trial from an insider's perspective. I mean, if this one goes national, everyone will be coming to us. And we'll have been there from the beginning."

"We, meaning me?"

"Well, yes of course, you, we—us. The bottom line is I'd like you to consider doing a series of pieces for us. Cover all the proceedings up to the trial, the trial itself, the lives of the participants. The prosecutor, the defendant, the victim, and of course, the defense attorney. It's never been done before! Or at least not since the Simpson trial, and we only saw what they wanted us to see. This time we'll be in on it."

"Won't that take a long time? Like a year or so. And you know that conversations between the accused and her defense attorney are privileged? You're not asking me to try and––"

"No, no, no! We just want the sense of things—the atmosphere, what Chase and Ms. Wagner are willing to tell you. Nothing funny. And we'll pay you well; you won't need to be in Piedmont the whole time. You can commute for the important things. Although you would need to be there this week, to make sure we catch the beginning of all this."

So what was the catch? Peter wondered? He needed money, needed work, he needed Mac Seaver off his back; it didn't make sense. Someone calls him, tells him they have his son and threatens to hurt him unless he complies with their demands, which turn out to be a job offer? And they get his publisher off his back all at the same time?

Parched men in the middle of the desert don't ask where the water came from, or what they have to do to earn it. They drink. He'd followed the Agnew case as much as anyone, and talked to Chase plenty throughout the trial. This didn't have to be much different, except he'd be in Piedmont, in an "official" capacity. Close to his friends. The conversation with Chase— that might be the difficult part. Convincing him this was a natural progression from his work, perhaps even connected to his book. He could sell him on the publicity angle, perhaps. Chase knew the value of the right kind of PR. He'd been roasted in the press for months, when everyone thought Agnew was guilty. Then he emerged a hero. *I can tell his side. I can humanize the accused. And if he happens to get her off, we'll all come off looking good.*

He stopped for a moment, realized he'd rationalized a lot in a short time. Something else was at play here, but he didn't know what.

"How about if I messenger you over some details: expense account, fees. We'll put you on a contract basis, pay you top rate…"

They finalized the general terms of the contract, with details to follow. Employed again, with even an expense advance on its way. *At what price*, he wondered.

As he was grabbing a beer, from the refrigerator, the phone rang.

"So, you're employed again." The Voice.

"This is what you want me to do? You kidnapped a kid so I'd go up to Piedmont and write a few stupid articles?"

A chuckle. "Ah, but then I wouldn't have your complete attention, would I? Go to Piedmont. Check into the Hilton, and wait until you hear from me. Talk to no one."

"Aside from Chase?"

"I repeat, talk to no one. I'll be in touch." He hung up.

After the call, he wanted to phone Randy or Ev. They were the only ones he'd ever told about the boy. But he didn't want to drag them into this. It had been his fault, after all. And the caller had said talk to no one.

He began to pack.

TWENTY-FIVE

"We're scheduled to meet with the police tomorrow morning at 10:30," Chase said. "I want to make sure both of us are as well prepared as possible, Ms. Wagner."

"This is all so crazy," she said. "I loved Josh, and would never do anything to hurt him."

"Why don't we start there. Did you?"

"Did I what?"

"Love Josh."

"Well of course I… Josh and I were… we… what kind of question is that?"

"The prosecution will push hard on that kind of question. You loved Josh. Were you engaged? Were you in a long-term committed relationship? These are the types of things you'll need to be prepared to address." He spoke calmly, observing Kate's reactions.

She composed herself, and took a deep breath. "Josh had asked me to marry him. He'd bought the ring and everything. I hadn't said yes. We talked about it a bit, but I wanted to wait until after the Olympic trials. He pressed me and told me if I loved him I wouldn't insist on waiting."

"What made you take out a life insurance policy on Josh?"

She flushed. "I had nothing to do with that," she said. "Josh did that entirely on his own."

"But you did know about it, didn't you?"

"After the fact! We were working out together one day last month and he casually mentioned it. He said that's the kind of thing people who love each other do. He wanted to show me how he felt about me."

Roses might have sufficed, Chase thought. The insurance policy represented the strongest piece of the prosecution's case against his client.

"Your time?"

Kate glanced at her watch. "My time?"

"In the race."

Kate swiveled her chair, avoiding Chase's eyes. She murmured something.

"You finished the race twenty minutes slower than the previous year. You finished out of contention for the first time in the past three. The simple question is, why? If you can't answer that, we're going to have some problems." He looked at her, smiled to take the edge off the comment.

"I don't know."

"You don't know what?"

She stared directly at him, then turned away. Her eyes blinked rapidly. "I don't know," she said. "I was in the best shape of my life. I planned to win the event this year. Sally O'Neill and I have been going back and forth in the points standing, and I knew she'd entered this year. I wanted to show her she couldn't beat me head-to-head."

Danskin sponsored the women's triathlon series, Chase had learned. Similar to NASCAR, they maintained a points list for the top competitors, with a $100,000 fund established to share among the top three finishers at the end of the year. An S. O'Neill had won the race.

"You finished strong in the 10k, your bike ride was decent, but your swim, your strongest event, fell far short of even an average effort for you." Chase had in front of him a copy of all the split times for the top finishers.

"I don't know," she repeated. "I felt a bit sluggish to start, but Josh and I had… stayed up late the night before, so I attributed it to lack of sleep. But I've traveled halfway across the world and showed up at a race jetlagged and still did well, so…"

"Sluggish? Enough to slow you down fifteen minutes in the swim?" He allowed skepticism to show on his face.

"I know. Look," she held up her wrist. "I wear a state-of-art Nike Triathlon watch. They send them to me to test. I track my intervals throughout the race with it. I had it on that morning too. I couldn't believe it when I got out of the water and saw my split. Thought it had broken down, but then I saw a few other women getting on their bikes before I even got to the staging area—women I'd never seen before. I don't know what happened."

Chase stood up. He could detect truth and genuine frustration.

"Tell you what, Kate. Let's stop here. When the police ask the question, tell them the truth. If they're intent on arresting you, they're going to do so anyway, so we'll have to wait and see. Take some time, compose yourself, and you'll be fine. Why don't you come by here tomorrow at ten and we'll go over together."

Kate nodded. She packed up her notebook and attaché and left with Kasey after shaking Chase's hand.

Here it was again. Obvious suspect, obvious motive, circumstantial evidence. Motive: the million-dollar insurance policy. Opportunity: a chaotic race, with Kate and Josh had been in the water at the same time, Kate starting only ten minutes or so ahead of Josh in the lead women's flight. And there was the issue of the missing twenty minutes. That left no alibi either, although perhaps they could find someone in the race who had seen Kate in or leaving the water. No one had come forward yet, however, in spite of all the press coverage.

It was still very early, and the case likely wouldn't be set on the trial agenda for several months, but he could already see the beginnings of a defense. He could weave a story about the tobacco industry, threatened by the articles young Samuels had written. Maybe not their style; they weren't the Russian Mafia, just an industry under fire for promoting products that killed thousands of people a year. They fought their battles the way all good Americans fought their battles these days: in the courtroom. Still, it might play well to a jury.

He'd had a brief conversation with Ev over lunch the previous day on the subject.

"Those fluff pieces?" he laughed. "I must admit I read them with great amusement. After all, they offered a scathing indictment of my dear old daddy. In fact, I'm currently on a fact-finding mission authorized by our esteemed Board of Directors. I'm to find the person leaking such scandalous information, and bring that person to the attention of the board. Observe my investigative technique," Ev said, sipping his iced tea.

"So your father took it pretty seriously," Chased commented.

"What does my father *not* take seriously? Daddy worries any time the word Litchfield appears in print. He has a staff of twelve people who do nothing but scan all the newspapers, websites, and television broadcasts that mention Litchfield to keep track of our sacred name. But this particular series had the great one's personal attention." Ev munched happily on a celery stick. He rarely allowed anything non-organic, processed, fried, or cholesterol-laden into his mouth.

"What got him so riled up over these particular articles?" Chase inquired. "There didn't seem to be much that would cause any great concern, other than the promise of more to come."

"Ah yes, the ubiquitous 'be sure to read next week's installment, where we learn intimate details proving tobacco industry knowledge of the danger of cigarettes.'" Ev smiled, his perfectly spaced and whitened teeth flashing briefly. Then he wrinkled his mouth. "It's not so much that the articles were damaging, but more that the allegations contained therein were actually true, not just speculation. Daddy's paranoid under the best of circumstances, but when he saw actual statements made in an executive meeting in print, it really set him off. And if the material in the articles so far was true, however innocuous, who knew what might show up in the next installment." Ev shrugged. "A moot point now. Whatever secrets or sources Josh had, they died with him. Daddy would call that fortuitous, not truly perceiving the tragic nature of this affair. But it doesn't obviate his concern."

Chase had held on to his friend's expression. Fortuitous indeed. Perhaps motive for murder. In the end, though, if no one had seen Josh go under or struggle in the lake, and if there were no additional pieces of physical evidence, the prosecution would have a hard time gaining a conviction. Hard, but not impossible. Still, Chase would only have to prove reasonable doubt. He stopped himself, again realizing he was thinking like Kate's attorney in a case going to trial.

It all fit a bit too neatly. A suspect with an apparent motive but no alibi. Just like all the others. The difference this time was his awareness, or at least suspicion, that Kate might be a pawn in bigger game. And Chase at last was a knowing player in the game. Turn the case on its head; Kate was innocent, and someone, perhaps the same person who framed his other clients, killed Josh Samuels, but wanted the police to think she did it. Why go to the trouble of framing someone else? Was the purpose simply to divert suspicion, or were there darker motives in play? And what tied Ray Lewis, Katarina Volkova, Winston Reese, and now Josh Samuels together? He couldn't see the connection. The victims, his clients, how did they all fit?

TWENTY-SIX

Two hours before Kate Wagner was due to arrive Wednesday morning, Chase, Ernesto, Tony, and Kasey sat around the conference table, reviewing what they knew so far. Chase recounted his meeting with Kate, as well as the phone call and subsequent conversation with Steve Riveira.

"I also talked with Rolly Northwood at the *Gazette*. He passed on some gossip that's been making the rounds at the paper. Word is that Ken Wall personally called a number of media folks in Washington, New York, Chicago, Atlanta, and Raleigh. He suggested they might want to get down to Piedmont."

"And?"

"And they're coming."

"Why the hell would he do that?" Ernie asked. "The trial date won't be set for another month. Hell, we haven't even had the arraignment yet."

"That's my question too," Chase said. "Wall had to give them something. They wouldn't jump and spend the money to send someone this way just on his say so. He told them it was in connection with the Samuels murder. Another arrest was forthcoming." He let that sink in.

"A co-conspirator or something?"

"No idea. But it would have to be something big to get the interest of the out-of-town media this early."

"You've made him look bad three times now," Kasey organized the papers in front of her. "It would be out of character for him to stick his neck out like this unless it was something pretty big." Chase sometimes forgot how well Kasey knew Wall. She had been his secretary before she was Chase's.

"I agree," Chase said. "Tony?"

"Samuels had a source at Litchfield. Billerette, the publisher, implied he's got another segment in the bag, waiting for the right moment to release it."

"Either that or some Litchfield lawyers have filed papers against him," Chase observed.

Tony continued, "People at the paper liked Samuels, even Billerette, and he doesn't seem to like very many people. So far, the pieces were just background. Billerette must have felt confident the heavier stuff was coming or he wouldn't have published the first few. He's not the kind of guy to just take something on faith. I'd say Samuels had some kind of source document or else he introduced Billerette to the source personally."

Chase said. "We should keep tabs on Billerette. We might be too late, but it would be nice to know who meets with him. He won't like holding off on a story like this. Maybe he'll push for a meeting with the source, or else whoever's putting the pressure on him."

Tony nodded.

"I reviewed the coroner's report," Ernesto said. "Best I can tell, the report backs up the cause of death in the police report. Death by drowning, ligature marks from the fishing line, signs of struggle, probably would have been some scratch marks on the killer."

"Unless he or she were wearing a full wetsuit," Chase said. "Speaking of which, we should probably have an expert go over Kate and Josh's wetsuits. A long shot, but we might find something. Also, the warrant was legally executed, and the search of Kate Wagner's apartment turned up a copy of the insurance policy in her bureau drawer, as well as her own wetsuit, which matched that of the victim."

"Matching wetsuits?" Kasey laughed.

Chase held up his hands. "It might be cute, but it's one of the stronger pieces of the prosecution's case. In the lake, with all those other swimmers thrashing around, it would be hard to distinguish one from the other. These wetsuits practically glow in the dark with the big yellow stripe down the side and the fluorescent color. Make a note to check out what color wetsuit Kate wore in her previous races. Might be good to find out if she wore the same one each time, and got a free one for Josh."

Kasey nodded, and flipped open her pad.

Ernie began to talk about his interviews with the neighbors. As he spoke, Chase reflected on the confluence of events. Wall had known Chase would be involved in the case, he'd personally called outside media to alert them to an arrest and a forthcoming announcement, and he'd taken over the investigation of Kate Wagner from the police. It made no sense.

His left shoulder stiffened, and he felt a momentary sense of guilt for not worrying about Jared. He tried to picture the map, wondered where his brother might be now. The phone rang. A moment later Kasey announced to the room that Kate Wagner wasn' t coming.

"Did she call?"

"No, Howard Metzler did."

"He still on the line?"

"Couldn't get off quickly enough."

So. Chase looked around the room quizzically, inviting comments.

"Skipping out?" Kasey suggested.

"Why let us know? We've still got time to alert the police, get them to pick her up," Ernie said.

"The police already have her." Chase looked over at Tony, standing behind Kasey, surprised he'd reached the same conclusion.

"I agree. But why?"

"Ask them," he shrugged.

Chase made the call from his office, and was surprised to hear Steve Riveira's voice after the first ring.

"Figured you might be calling."

"I guess you know why I am, then."

"She's here. Someone from Wall's office is talking to her now. Her lawyer, um, her other lawyer is with her."

"Metzler?"

"Short emaciated guy with a bad toupee?"

"That's him."

"Is he handling the questioning?"

A long pause. "There's not going to be any questioning."

"So Kate Wagner is no longer a suspect?"

"To that, I'm afraid I have to say, 'no comment.'" Then, in a hushed tone, "Chase, I can't talk. This place is crawling with media people. They're all waiting for some big announcement. People are breathing down my neck, and they know I'm talking to you."

"I read you," Chase said. This had to be connected with Wall's work behind the scenes. But he'd spoken with Kate the day before; what did Howard Metzler have to do with this? And if she was no longer a suspect, why was she at police headquarters?

"Hey Chase, I've got to go. Only advice I have is, keep your eyes open. They know we're friends, so I'm a bit out of the loop. But all of this adds up to nothing good."

"Thanks Steve. Talk to you later."

He turned on the television. Flicking through the channels, he found a local station, the camera showing the painted brick façade of Piedmont Police Headquarters. A local reporter stood in front of the building, microphone in hand, reporting live from the scene.

"—we're anxiously waiting to hear from District Attorney Ken Wall. According to sources in the police department, he'll be issuing an announcement shortly. As we understand it, Kate Wagner, the leading suspect in the triathlon murder of Josh Samuels, has been with police since early this morning. A spokesperson for the department has told us she is no longer a suspect, and is cooperating fully with the investigation."

A commotion on the screen caught his attention. The reporter had to shout to be heard among all the people suddenly racing around him. He seemed to be listening to his earpiece, while he raced to talk.

"I understand there's been a development," the reporter said. "A number of police cars have left headquarters."

The screen cut back to the gray-haired anchor in the studio, asking whether an arrest was about to be made.

"I don't know," answered the field reporter, still shouting. "We're going to follow, and report back to you shortly."

Chase could hear the sirens outside. He walked over to the window, pushed aside the blinds, and tried to identify the direction they were heading. The sirens grew louder, but he couldn't see any flashing lights. The television was still on, and for a few moments he watched the feed from one of the reporter's vans, maneuvering through traffic, then coming to a stop. A few minutes later, Chase heard Kasey outside talking to someone, and the door opened. "I'm sorry, Chase, they wouldn't—"

It seemed to happen in slow motion. Two men in suits shouldered in behind her. Chase looked outside and saw the news vans parked on the street in front of his building. Reporters with cameras emerged, followed by others, all scrambling to get in through the revolving doors of the entranceway. Shutters snapped behind him and he turned toward the door. Four uniformed police officers walked into his office, hands on their weapons, and encircled him.

He didn't recognize any of the men, didn't even recognize their uniforms. He wasn't surprised though, when Ken Wall strolled casually through the door, holding a folded piece of paper in his hand. This time dressed for the media in a new suit. Wall wore a serious expression on his face as the cameras clicked again, and he walked casually up to the officer in charge.

"Thanks, Sergeant, nicely done. I'll take it from here." The officer nodded to the other three policemen facing Chase and they backed off a few yards. Wall turned to Chase.

Chase was about to say something, but seeing the suppressed excitement in Wall's eyes made him close his mouth. He returned Wall's stare. After a moment the D.A. broke off his gaze, and turned to the paper in his hands.

"Chase Riordan, you are under arrest for the murder of Josh Samuels."

Chase blinked. He should have paid more attention to Steve Riveira's warning. With all the scenarios playing out in his head, he hadn't seen this coming. And suddenly now it was blindingly obvious. Ray Lewis, John Tierney, Rufus Agnew. *The connection wasn't to the victim; it was to his clients.* Because of course there was a common thread tying all these people together. Him.

"Sergeant, would you read this man his rights?"

As the officer behind him began reciting, Chase faced his doorway. Wall stood aside to allow the photographers to take his picture. The television in his office displayed the scene, the feed coming from a handheld camera pointed over Wall's shoulder. He saw himself, surrounded by uniformed officers, two of them with hands still held on their weapons, as if they were about to draw. Startled, he looked over his left shoulder where the officers stood, poised. Young men; they couldn't have been long on the force. The look on their faces though, was not anger, as he had thought from the television, but rather, fear.

Chase tuned out the Sergeant, saw Wall, preening for the cameras, and scanned the faces outside his office door. He recognized some of the local media, some of the same reporters who had competed for his time after the conclusion of the Agnew case. He picked out Kasey, angry tears on her face, trying to avoid being swept aside by the crush of reporters vying for space. And in the front, a hand half-covering his face, he saw Peter Jurgens, who quickly turned away as Chase's gaze met his.

TWENTY-SEVEN

The call had come at six-thirty that morning. He'd let the phone ring at least a dozen times, hoping it was a ringing in his head that would stop, then he finally opened his eyes, surprised to find himself in a hotel room. Last thing he remembered from the night before had been this woman at the bar wanting him to check out her new implants. Alarmed, he looked at the other side of the bed. Empty. He reached for the phone.

"Remember me?" rasped the voice.

"Yeah. What do you want?"

A dry chuckle sounded in his ear. "Those room service charges will add up pretty fast."

He looked anxiously around the room.

As if this too, had been observed, the caller laughed. "We're keeping track. We want to make sure you're doing exactly as you're told. And so far, I'm pleased to say, you're meeting expectations."

"Great." He rubbed his temples, trying to fend off the pounding in his head. The hangover gave him courage. "So let's talk about this kid you say you have. If you know all you say you do about me, you know I don't have any ties to him;

I don't know his name, where he lives, or what he looks like. Why pick on him?"

"Let's just say we needed you know how serious we are. Anyone could find your parents, or your sister. You could warn them, or try to protect them in some way. But how can you protect someone if you don't even know where he is?"

"Sure, but why would you think I'd even care about him?"

"Because we know you, Peter. And because you're in Piedmont, doing exactly what we asked."

Or what Paul Givens asked, but it amounted to the same thing.

"You'll be happy to know, by the way, that the boy favors his father."

Asshole. "Fine, so I'm here. What now?"

"Why it's simple. You need to do the job you're getting paid to do. Cover the case. I expect you'll be pretty busy." Then the caller proceeded to tell Peter precisely what was required of him.

Peter wondered at the explicit instructions, which suggested an inside source with the police, and tried to imagine why he had to be there. What was about to happen? Were the police going to arrest Kate Wagner? Why was that such a big story? She'd been the lead suspect now for almost a week, and hadn't skipped town.

"Oh, and one last thing," the voice said. "You are not to call Mr. Riordan today for any reason. We'll be watching." The call ended.

He hung up the phone, curious at the last words. Didn't they want him here precisely because of his relationship with Chase, his ability to connect with one of the lead figures in the case? Perplexed, he walked over to his suitcase and pulled out a bottle of aspirin. Maybe when his head cleared, this would all make a bit more sense.

An hour later, per instructions, he was at police head-quarters, along with a dozen or so other reporters who were awaiting news. He wasn't the only one who'd gotten an early morning call. Kate Wagner wasn't going to be charged, he heard people saying. She had been spotted arriving through a side entrance a half hour earlier, accompanied by some other lawyer––not Chase. Later, when the police wagons left the station, he followed along with the other reporters, hitching a ride with a guy who'd recognized him from his days at *Time*. The cars had traveled a few blocks to a downtown high-rise. He rode the elevators along with everyone else, following the phalanx of people who all seemed to know exactly what floor to press.

In the crowd trailing the uniformed police officers, he didn't notice the name on the doors as they entered a suite of offices. But he recognized the pert blond woman trying to hold back the police and the crowd, and a sickening feeling settled on him.

"Get the story," the caller had said. "When the police make the arrest, you be there, front and center. Make sure you see the suspect, make sure he sees you. Then write the story, and don't pull any punches." He wanted to slink away, disappear into the crowd, and make his way back to the bar.

Chase looked over and saw him. Turning his head guiltily, Peter wished he were still in Atlanta. Two of the officers started pushing Chase forward, while the others tried to push back the crowd. One of the men in suits, familiar to him, faced the cameras. Microphones from the network stations thrust into his face, and the cameras all pointed in his direction.

"Ladies and gentlemen of the press, you'll understand that we'll want to process Mr. Riordan quickly, and I ask your cooperation in clearing a path for our city's finest to escort him to the station. I plan to hold a press conference at one this afternoon to address any questions you might have. Thank you." He nodded at the uniformed officers, who prodded Chase forward, the crowd clearing a path.

Peter watched Chase try to walk as the officers kept pushing him along. Wall followed behind. A few questions were shouted out as he left the office suites. The district attorney turned back to face them.

"Someone asked whether there's anything personal about this. And yes, I take it personally whenever anyone subverts justice in my city, let alone commits murder. I look forward to answering all of your questions this afternoon," Wall said and left the offices.

Rather than following the procession down to the street, Peter lingered in Chase's office, in the new office suite he'd just moved into. He spotted Kasey, working hard to get the crowd through the doors, picking up the garbage some had left behind. He debated whether he should talk with her, but decided it wasn't the time. Looking around the room, he spotted a picture of himself on the wall, along with Lionel, Chase, Randy, and Ev. It was from their trip to Jamaica a few years before, at the base of Dunn's River Falls. They were all wet, smiling, with arms around each other. Peter remembered dunking Lionel in the river as soon as the photo was snapped.

The district attorney's words came back to him. Or rather the question that had preceded them. Peter knew some of Wall's history with Chase, but that didn't explain anything. As the last of the reporters filed out, Peter caught up with them and left the offices, not wanting to face Kasey. It wasn't until he arrived back at the street that he realized what had just happened. His friend had been arrested for murder, treated like a career criminal. He knew if they'd arrested Kate Wagner, they would have given her a chance to turn herself in. Yet with Chase, they'd surprised him in his office and filmed the whole spectacle.

He pulled out his cell phone to call one of the guys, then put it back in his pocket, not wanting to have to explain how he happened to be at the scene. With all the media present, they had to have heard the news by now, anyway. Peter grimaced with distaste at the thought of the work ahead of him. Write and then file the story. Then sit through a press conference.

Twenty-Eight

The dog crossed the street, following its nose into the culvert. A solitary figure sat huddled there, gnawing on a piece of chicken. Nose to the ground, the dog, perhaps a cross between a German Shepherd and a Lab, bone-thin and dirty, approached cautiously. The man and dog considered each other. A truck passed, and the two shrank almost as one. The man pulled a piece of stringy chicken off the bone and tossed it toward the dog.

"I'm Jared," he rasped. "You got a name?"

It took a full five minutes for the dog to walk over to the chicken, but he finally did so, and wolfed it down, then licked the ground where it had been. There were only a few small morsels left on the bone, but the man split them with the dog.

"Guess not."

When there was no more, Jared put the chicken bone in the bag, crumpled it into a ball, and stuck it in a large pocket of his overcoat, an acquisition from the front seat of a car the previous evening. A like-new tan London Fog men's overcoat, it had served as a nice blanket and offered protection from the elements. Large as it was, his hands extended from the sleeves several inches. Beneath the overcoat he wore a white tee shirt and a pair of blue hospital scrub pants, now stiff from wear. His Nikes were old and muddy from his journey, perhaps thirty miles or so, a difficult slog in his condition.

Some of the drugs they'd given him must have been addictive. He felt the hunger for—something. In spite of how little he'd eaten, he had a hard time keeping food down, and he'd stopped frequently to retch. He felt feverish and knew he needed to get hold of some aspirin. He hadn't realized how far removed from civilization the Institute was. Without the map Chase had invisibly placed on the back of the poster, he might not have found his way.

Just past dawn, there was a nip in the air. The mountains to the west were sheathed in a morning fog, the direction of the highway, the direction he needed to go. The early morning light illuminated the road. Peering at street level and noticing no traffic, human or vehicular, Jared climbed up the bank of the culvert and stood on the side of the road. Thus far he'd been traveling under cool of night. He'd originally walked in a circular pattern to try to throw off any pursuers, but with no sign of anyone in two days, he'd decided either he'd thrown them off or they weren't looking for him. He hoped the latter. If Sterling were involved, though, he knew he needed to remain vigilant.

Still not trusting the daylight, he crossed a field and entered the now familiar forest and began walking, paralleling the road. Maintaining a distance of about fifty yards behind him, the dog followed. Aware of his presence, Jared smiled for the first time in ages.

An occasional truck or car passed by on the road, a rural state-maintained highway that followed the path of the interstate. The last town had been ten miles back. When it had closed down at two in the morning, he'd crept in, searched for food and clothing, emerging with the coat and some food scraps.

The past few days had taxed his skills and his muscles,

both weakened from lack of use. Despite the lack of nourishment, though, he could feel his strength returning, along
with his clarity, long dimmed by a daily regimen of drugs. The
walking helped to build up his leg muscles, although the lack
of sufficient food and vitamins was becoming something of a
problem. He had no money, and he was still reluctant to show
his face. He was reluctant to use the credit card Chase had left
in the envelope under his bed—he didn't want to leave such
an obvious trail. Sterling was resourceful.

As he walked, the dog continued to shadow him, easily
following his scent and his sound, quiet as he was. Jared welcomed the companionship, albeit of the canine variety, and
fifty yards behind. He'd been alone for a very long time. Alone
mostly in his mind, where the cobwebs were still shaking
away. Since leaving the Institute he'd survived almost entirely
on instinct. There were some large gaps in his memory, but
his self-awareness grew and his survival senses, once impec-
cable, were sharpening again.

The sign on the highway off to his left indicated twenty
miles until the town of Mill River. When night fell, he'd quietly enter the city and steal a car.

TWENTY-NINE

"L adies and gentlemen, the District Attorney for the Great City of Piedmont, Kenneth Wall."

The lobby of the Bryan Building, which housed many of the city's municipal offices, had been set up as a theater, with a makeshift stage. Ken Wall strode up the risers to the podium, accommodating microphones from the major networks. Onlookers and members of the press crowded the lobby, surrounding the stage, both standing and sitting.

"Thank you. With me today are the Chief of Police, the Honorable Richard S. Burroughs," Wall nodded to his left, "and the Deputy Chief in charge of Public Affairs, Ms. Catherine Wolcott." From either side of him, the two nodded.

"The purpose of this press conference is to explain the events of earlier today. I will give a statement, then accept questions from the press.

"First, the facts. This morning, we arrested Chase Patrick Riordan and charged him with the murder of Josh Samuels. The police department, keeping in mind the need to protect the safety of the public, handled the arrest effectively. The arrest proceeded without incident and Mr. Riordan is safely behind bars, awaiting due process.

Wall opened a water bottle and took a long drink. "The arrest of Mr. Riordan was the culmination of an investigation that was a cooperative effort between our offices and the offices of the police department of the City of Piedmont. In short, we believe, and expect to prove in court, that on the day of the Latta Park Plantation Triathlon, Chase Riordan swam out into the waters of Lake Norman, caught up with Josh Samuels, and held on to him until he drowned." He looked out on the crowd, apparently enjoying the buzz his statement generated. "If you've seen Mr. Riordan, you know he is a physically imposing person, blessed with exceptional athletic ability, and the strength to commit this heinous act. After killing Mr. Samuels, Mr. Riordan simply joined up with the rest of the racers, blending into the pack.

"An hour after we arrested the suspect, we executed a search warrant on his premises. That search produced evidence that, together with the forensic evidence we've already gathered, ties him to the crime. Mr. Riordan is being held in the City Jail, awaiting a bail hearing, which will be scheduled later in the week. You can rest assured we will follow the letter of the law in dealing with this… kil… ah… suspect, according him the due process he denied Josh Samuels. I'll take questions now." He acknowledged a woman in the front row who had shot to her feet. "Nancy."

"*Piedmont Gazette*. Thank you, Mr. Wall. What motive did Mr. Riordan have to kill Josh Samuels? Did he even know him?"

"Thanks for the question, Nancy. Obviously, I can't speak to all the details of the city's case. Mr. Riordan will no doubt hire an attorney and we don't want to reveal our entire hand just yet." He smiled conspiratorially. "But I will say this. We believe Mr. Riordan had a strong motive, the details of which I'm not willing to get into at this point. Our investigation is still ongoing and we're still dotting all the i's and crossing all the t's. I feel quite certain we will be able to prove the strongest possible motive. I hope to be able to address that issue next week in further detail. Next question."

"Mr. Wall, what led you to suspect Mr. Riordan?"

"Cliff, the arrest followed a very thorough police investigation. During the course of it we uncovered a number of leads, all of which we followed up on. One of those led us to Mr. Riordan and we built the case from there."

PETER SAT IN THE THIRD ROW, taking notes along with all the others. He'd hoped he might get insight into what was happening. Instead, just a lot of doublespeak. Chase had been arrested, suspected of murdering Josh Samuels, and now sat in a jail cell. "Why did he do it?" "We'll tell you later." The sad thing was the reaction of his fellow journalists. They lapped it all up, salivating over the story to come: a respected attorney, accused of murder by his former boss. Wall spoke with such conviction that Peter had to wonder what evidence he was sitting on. He had filed his story a few hours before, and it had been posted, in edited form, on the paper's Internet site. They would post his follow-up piece after the press conference, and the complete article in the newspaper the following morning. Nice to see his name in print after all these months, but the circumstances could have been better.

He craned his neck and spotted Ev, Lionel, and Randy standing off to the side. Lionel stood with his big arms crossed, a scowl plastered across his face. Ev had his usual air of amused detachment, and Randy looked around nervously. Peter hadn't yet felt up to calling them; they still didn't know he was in town. Slipping out of the chair, he quietly walked toward them.

"Enjoying the show?"

Ev looked over. "One of the paparazzi again, Peter?" he said softly, acting as if it were the most natural thing in the world to run into him.

"What are you doing here?" Lionel said.

"Nice to see you too. Randy." He held up his pad. "On assignment. Just found out about it last night, or I would have called. Until this morning, I thought I was covering the arrest of Kate Wagner."

Lionel grunted. "Surprise."

"Exactly. What do you make of all this?" he said, glad they didn't press him for any further explanation.

"It's fucked up," Lionel said.

"What our eloquent friend means, I believe, is that we are stunned. Perhaps Wall believes he had only made a partial ass of himself and needs to complete the process," Ev offered.

Randy chimed in, "This is serious shit. You don't charge murder on a whim, no matter who you are. This is a serious charge and Chase is in deep."

"What are you talking about?" Lionel asked.

"Randy's right," Ev said. "This is serious. I don't know what's going on here, but you don't charge murder just because you're pissed off. You know any more than the rest of us, Pete?"

"No. I saw the arrest. Wall did his best to make him look as bad as he could. He sandbagged him in his own office. Chase took it pretty well, though, considering."

Randy excused himself, and quickly walked over to join another group at the periphery of the lobby.

"Partners?" Lionel asked.

"Indeed," Ev said. "So, Peter, you're covering this?"

"For the *Journal and Constitution*."

"Let us know if you hear anything."

"Well?" Lionel said.

"Well what?" Peter said.

"What are we going to do?"

"What can we do?" said Peter. "You heard Wall. Chase is in jail, and he'll get a lawyer and fight this."

"The question, I believe," said Ev, "was not what Chase will do, but what *we* will do. We aren't exactly helpless here. You're a member of the Fourth Estate and have the ability to sway public opinion. Lionel has a political platform, Randy is well positioned within the Piedmont legal community, and I—"

"Have more money than God," Lionel said.

"I was about to say, am not without resources. However, given all that, perhaps we should wait to see what shakes out here? I don't believe there's anything we can do at the moment; the toothpaste, so to speak, is out of the tube. But we should stand by, ready to do what we can."

Lionel glowered. "This ain't right."

"No," Peter said. "But Ev's right. Chase will get out on bail and then we can all get together and figure out what to do."

"I know he's right, but that doesn't mean I like the idea of sitting here doing nothing."

"Chase is a big boy," Ev said. "He can take care of himself." He indicated toward the podium, where Wall still stood talking. "I think that's the man we need to worry about."

"Speaking of which," Peter said, "I need to get back to make sure I don't miss any true words of wisdom."

"Later."

Peter made his way back to his chair. Wall droned on about the dedication of the police force, then finally closed, vowing to keep the press informed throughout the process. As he walked away from the podium, he looked directly at Peter—only briefly, but Peter would've sworn to it.

THIRTY

Randy Turner had been Chase's first phone call. He wanted someone he could trust to represent him in the early stages, but his friend had not been able to convince the partnership. Or so he said.

"We don't do much in the way of criminal law," he told Chase. "If we do, it's incidental; corporate clients who have need of our services for personal issues."

Now three days later, Chase languished in jail. And unless things changed dramatically, he was going to be tried for murder. The arraignment was three weeks out, and the city would attempt to prove it had sufficient evidence to hold him on charges of aggravated First Degree Murder. Chase had no doubt as to the outcome of that hearing. Allowed to read the papers in jail, he had a pretty good sense of the evidence the D.A. planned on presenting. He had thought he was a player in a grand game, opposing the faceless killer. Instead, he had been relegated to the status of a pawn.

Sitting at the table waiting for his lawyer, he decided the view from the other side as much better. For one thing, this chair turned away from the window, facing door and the wall, with its peeling, faded pale green paint. He'd never noticed the paint before, couldn't have identified the color of the room. He made a mental note to appreciate more the point of view of his clients. He had never stopped to consider how long his clients had sat at this table, or how it felt. Still, he welcomed the warmth of the sun on his back. The jail cell was cold, and bare, the mattress far too small for his large frame, and the sole tattered blanket barely covered his body from his neck to his feet. At least he had his own cell.

At the moment, his chances of going home anytime soon looked decidedly dim.

"Your Honor, this man didn't just kill a man," Wall had told the judge at the bail hearing. "He abused the public trust. He was an officer of the court, charged with protecting and upholding the best and most noble traditions of our legal system. Now that he has been exposed for what he is, he knows he can't return to his former life. He's a flight risk, and I suggest, a danger to society."

Chase could tell from the way the judge stared at him that the outcome was predetermined. It figured he'd get Judge Hoppin at the bail hearing. No love lost there. Chase had appealed one of the judge's rulings to the State Supreme Court and won, which didn't make him exactly welcome in the courtroom. Probably not a coincidence, although judge selection was supposed to be an arbitrary process. Had Chase been defending himself, he'd have launched into a passionate attack against the prosecutor's statements, which presumed his guilt from the start. Ernesto had done his best, but couldn't stand up to the challenge, Chase knew, and he put his hand on his friend's arm and shook his head when he stood up.

"Let it go," he said.

He'd been surprised, though, when the judge, at Wall's request, had set visitor guidelines that only included relatives and his lawyer.

Ernesto pulled up the chair opposite him, while the guard retreated to stand with his back to the door. He was wearing the pinstriped suit Chase had purchased for him the day he'd passed the bar: "Now you look like a lawyer," he'd said. Depositing his briefcase on the table, Ernesto opened it, took out a yellow legal pad, and pulled a pen from his inside jacket pocket. "You doing all right, man?"

Chase nodded. "Looking sharp, Ernie."

"My wife told me if I was going to be in the newspaper…" Ernesto loosened his tie, and unbuttoned the top button of his shirt. "So, you ready to bring in the big guns yet?"

"We'll get to that in a moment," Chase said. "I have an idea. But first, tell me what you know. What's the case so far?"

Perez outlined the basis of the charges as outlined in the D.A.'s brief. First, Josh Samuels had been killed with fishing line, or at least a length of fishing line had been used to incapacitate him in the water. The same make and weight of fishing line had been found in Chase's storage space in his townhouse when the police searched the place.

"The fact that I occasionally fish doesn't mean anything, I suppose?" Chase asked rhetorically.

Ernie snorted his agreement. "The D.A. maintains the ends match the two pieces of line. The cut marks match."

"Interesting."

"Second, the coroner discovered that at least some of the blood on the body of the victim wasn't the victim's own, and therefore likely came from the killer. Type O. Same as yours."

"And half the population of Piedmont," Chase said.

"They're going to test for DNA," Ernesto added.

"And third?"

Ernesto sighed. "Third, you have no alibi. You as much as admitted that yourself."

Chase smiled wryly. He wondered how many people in the city could prove their whereabouts at seven in the morning on a given weekend. Then wondered who would have known he took his dog to Hickory for a hike that morning.

"They also found a jet-black wetsuit in your closet, which they claim will prove you were swimming in Lake Norman. Something to do with the water quality, silt levels, or something. They've sent the suit off for tests."

Chase had bought the wetsuit for a scuba diving trip he and the guys had taken off the coast of Puerto Rico a few years back.

"All pretty circumstantial, but not inconsequential. And if they match the DNA…" Ernesto let the word linger.

"Is that a question?"

"I'm sorry, I didn't mean to suggest—"

Chase waved him off. "You're my attorney, Ernesto. You don't have to pass judgment on my guilt or innocence. I thought I taught you that."

Ernesto was embarrassed. "You know I don't think you're guilty, boss. It's more, I, uh, don't trust what's going on."

"I know what you mean. It's a little too neat." The DNA results would make or break the case. He only wished he had confidence in the results.

"Finally, they found a vial of a drug called botulinum toxin in your medicine cabinet."

"Let me guess. The same drug found in the victim's body."

Ernesto pulled out a sheet of paper from his briefcase.

"Here's a list of attorneys Randall Turner put together and faxed to the office. They're all top-notch people. You'll recognize most of the names." He slid the paper across the table to Chase. The guard by the door moved a bit closer to make sure nothing inappropriate had been passed.

Chase scanned the list. Some big names, including a few national players he'd seen on CNN, and a local guy he respected. He slid the list back to Ernie.

"Tell Randy thanks, I appreciate his efforts. He did a nice job."

"So which ones would you like me to approach?"

"None of them," Chase replied.

"But you said—"

"I said I had an idea on that subject."

Ernie held up the sheet of paper. "Chase, these are the best guys out there. Present company excepted, of course."

Chase stretched his arms, causing the guard to once again spring to alertness. "Relax, Ern. I know I need a new lawyer. You've done a great job for me, but this is getting heavy. Wall's laying it on and it doesn't look like he's planning on letting up the pressure. I'm going to need someone with a lot of experience with this kind of thing."

"Then who, if not one of these guys?"

Chase turned over the piece of paper, and, with a wary look at the guard, delicately took the pen and wrote down a name.

THIRTY-ONE

"Rufus Agnew? That old coot hasn't seen the inside of a courtroom, except as a defendant, since the Nixon administration."

"That 'old coot' has more experience in the courtroom and politics here in Piedmont than anyone on that list. And make no mistake about it, this case has something to do with politics. This is an election year, and Wall is grandstanding, looking to extend his term yet again. Rufus knows this town like the back of his weathered, liver-spotted hands. He knows the ins and outs of the system like no one else. Folks will think twice before messing with him, knowing he's still got a lot of clout with the party and the city."

It was true. Rufus had proven himself extremely resilient, already resuming a leadership position after his recent exoneration in court. He'd been asked to chair the city's efforts to bring the Olympics to North Carolina and appeared frequently as a guest on the morning show, *Wake Up, Piedmont*, lending his Southern drawling commentary to a wide range of local issues, from the economy to the state song.

"You know, you might have something there," Ernesto rubbed his chin. "But when it comes to the trial…"

"I'm not sure how far this will go, but if it comes to it, I know a little something about trial preparation and strategy. Don't worry, Ern. Trust me—I need someone like Rufus. He'll have the sympathy of the jury and the judge from the beginning, something I'd have a hard time gaining at the moment with all that wonderful publicity circling about." At Chase's request, Ernesto had reluctantly shown Chase news from the past few days. He'd been gratified to see that Rolly Northwood hadn't jumped on the bandwagon, despite being *The Observer's* crime beat reporter. His column had been remarkably subdued, and had been relegated to the inside pages of the local section; it just reported on the facts: the charges, the arrest, and next steps.

"Do you think he'll do it? I mean, he's pretty busy these days, and hasn't exactly been brushing up on his courtroom etiquette."

"Oh, he'll do it. Think of all the attention it will bring. And Rufus is the one guy who probably hates Ken Wall more than Wall apparently hates me," Chase said, echoing the statement Rufus had when he'd hired him. "Besides, he kind of owes me a favor."

Ernesto smiled. "He does at that."

The guard indicated time was up and Ernesto locked up his briefcase and stood up. "By the way, you'll be pleased to learn the local cops aren't entirely supporting this, uh, thing. Those were out-of-town cops from Raleigh that Wall deputized to make the arrest. The locals wouldn't go for the show of force when they heard it was you."

That explained why Chase hadn't recognized any of them.

"Seems there's a bit of a feud going on between the D.A. and the cops. He conducted his own investigation here—didn't even involve any of the local detectives. Just thought you should know."

Chase nodded appreciatively. "Oh, Ernesto—another piece of paper?" He looked at the guard with the question, and the guard waved his okay. Chase scribbled a moment then handed the paper and pen back.

"Do me a favor. Call this number for me and leave this message. Tell her I love her, I'm thinking of her, and I'm all right."

Ernesto nodded dumbly, then was escorted out the door by the guard. As the guard returned and brought Chase back to his cell, he broke his stony glare for a moment and nodded.

A jail cell is generally thought of as a solitary place, cut off from the rest of the world, no TV, no radio, no choice of books, no Internet. But, in an odd way, Chase found his cell strangely comforting. He missed his freedoms—the freedom to go for a run when he wanted, to walk Garth, now languishing in a canine version of Chase's own jail cell. He missed his friends. And he missed Reagan. He could only imagine what she must be going through, hearing the news second-hand out in Colorado. But for all its drawbacks, he at least had the time to think.

All his life he'd been a man of action. Now with an entire day stretched out before him, he looked forward to uninterrupted contemplation of his current situation. He accepted his arrest, originally a shock, as a piece of the puzzle shifting into place.

Denial of bail in his case was highly unusual. Wall had to have something more. Ernesto had suggested early on that Kate Wagner had been part of a plot to ensnare him, set up either by Wall or the local police, but Chase didn't think so. Kate had been genuinely rattled. And the local police had believed she was the killer. Perhaps still did. All this talk about her cooperating with the police—Chase suspected that had more to do with the power struggle between the District Attorney's Office and the local cops.

The comments of Steve Riveira and Ernesto had stuck with him. Wall had conducted his own investigation, hadn't involved the locals. Then he'd made the arrest on his own, using officers from another precinct. The problem with all that was the D.A.'s Office didn't have an investigatory arm. The police for the City of Piedmont were supposed to provide that service. And Wall had no experience with investigation. That meant another source with ample credence to prompt a high-profile arrest. The real killer perhaps? That would make the most sense.

The obvious suspect would be Wall himself, but Chase didn't buy it. If Wall were the killer, if he had set Chase up, he wouldn't have taken all those blows in the courtroom with his previous three cases. Wall wasn't that devious, that clever, or that patient. The killer here had to be someone playing a deep game. Who would benefit by sending Chase to prison?

Lying on his cot, knees contorted, elbows tucked into his side, his back aching, he wondered how Jared was doing, and where he was. Their situations had been reversed. Now it was Chase in a cell, put there by someone with an agenda. The parallels were almost eerie. At least he had his faculties, and for all the feelings he had about Wall, he stood a fair shot of proving his innocence, provided he could uncover some answers. Answers that might be difficult to come by so long as stayed locked up.

THIRTY-TWO

Ev Litchfield maintained residences in two of Piedmont's premier locations. The first was a swanky, bachelor pad in the penthouse of the new Titanium Towers, a sleek, sharply decorated place with all the modern comforts: a six-person Jacuzzi, exercise room, golf simulator, a modern stainless steel kitchen, with three thousand square feet of living space and the city's best view; the place where he brought his women.

Today, the friends met in his home, an old Georgian brick mansion that reminded Peter of Stately Wayne Manor from the *Batman* TV series. The house was filled with a wide-ranging array of antiques, including a half-dozen carousel horses, in a sumptuous setting complete with old plank floors he'd removed from a barn in Hickory, topped with old Persian rugs, and an expansive collection of impressionist artwork.

The four men sat outside by the pool on a stone veranda. Lionel's flock wouldn't have recognized him, off the campaign trail, wearing old gray sweatpants and a Winfield U. tee shirt. Randy wore a suit and looked ready to leave for the office at any moment. Ev looked the part of Baron of the Manor in a green silk-patterned shirt, a well-pressed pair of ivory chinos, and Ferragamo loafers with no socks. At ten in the morning, he sipped a Glen Morangie single malt from a Waterford crystal tumbler. Lionel held a beer, but hadn't taken a drink yet. Randy tossed an unopened Evian bottle back and forth in his hands. Peter stood off to one side, eyes focused on the ground.

"He wants who?" Lionel thundered at Randy. "Didn't you put together a list of lawyers for him?" he accused Randy.

"I faxed it over to his office first thing Monday morning. Ernesto Perez assured me he reviewed the list with Chase."

"Then why the hell would he want that old geezer? He was old when we were still in school!"

"Maybe it was the money," Peter suggested. "Those guys command a couple hundred grand just to walk in the door."

"Now I'm hu-urt," Ev drawled, making "hurt" a two-syllable word. "You know I'd write a check in an instant. But Chase still has the first dollar he ever earned. Besides, I'm quite certain any of these gentlemen would have been happy to take Chase on as a client, with all that free publicity. There are more paparazzi here than in all of Italy right now."

"You got that right," Lionel grunted.

"Maybe we should trust Chase," Peter said. "He's the guy who's on the line this time. He knows Agnew better than any of us."

Grudging nods of assent. The judge's order had precluded any of them from visiting and they'd had to rely on communicating through Ernesto.

"All right, at least Chase has a lawyer now, and he's ready to fight," Lionel said. "He's still going to need to hire an investigator."

"What about Tony?" Peter asked. Randy and Ev exchanged a look.

"What? What am I missing here?"

Ev spoke first. "Randy and I are of the belief that someone close to Chase has been, shall we say, feeding information to the enemy camp."

This came as a surprise to Peter. Although it made some

sense. The police seemed to know exactly where to look for things, according to Ernesto. That this insider might be Chase's investigator came as a bit of a shock, but he hadn't been with Chase all that long. It probably wouldn't have taken much to get him on the D.A.'s side.

Peter nodded slowly. "Maybe. Maybe. But I still haven't figured out what's in this for Wall. What's the real purpose of all this?"

"I get the jealousy thing," Lionel said. "Wall couldn't carry Chase's gym bag, but this goes further than that. It's one thing to kick Chase out on his ass and try to discredit him in the process. But to wait four years, and then accuse him of murder? There's definitely something we're missing." Lionel continued to ruminate. "What makes this guy tick? He likes the spotlight, likes his job, but for some reason he hates Chase Riordan so bad steam practically comes out of his ears and he's frothing at the mouth. Why?"

No one could answer the question. Peter wondered how this all connected with The Voice. Why was he here?

"Unless," Randy said slowly, then stopped.

"Unless what?" Lionel asked impatiently.

"Unless," he repeated, not looking anyone in the eye. "Well, I mean what if..." They waited, but he was struggling with himself now, swallowing audibly. "Well, Marinda thinks..."

"Marinda thinks what?" Ev asked coolly.

Randy opened the water bottle and took a long swig. "Never mind."

"No, seriously. I'd like to know."

"Forget it," Randy said, looking at the ground.

Peter started to say something, but Lionel grabbed his arm and shook his head. He nodded toward Ev, who was staring at Randy with a look they both recognized: a look that had backed off people twice his size. A look that said, I might do anything— don't test me. "Shall we play twenty questions?" Ev said.

Randy looked up.

"I'll start. Chase being in prison only confirms what Marinda has thought all along, about him, and the rest of us, right?"

"No! That's not true."

"Marinda suggests hanging around with us can only be damaging to your career at this point."

Randy shook his head.

"Although she'd be worried you'd say anything to me, and risk the Litchfield account."

"You can't imagine that—"

"She thinks we should consider the possibility that Chase might be guilty, and act accordingly."

"That's not what she—"

"But of course you can't possibly believe that Chase could be guilty, right?"

"Of course not," Randy said softly.

"I'm sorry, I didn't hear that. You couldn't possibly think Chase had anything to do with this, could you? Because Chase is one of us, right? We've been looking out for each other for, what, twenty years now? That's what friends do, isn't that right? We're all trying to do our part. Pete's working on an article to tell the other side of this for the *Journal and Constitution,* Lionel's been consorting with the great unwashed among the party faithful."

"Anita's already working with my campaign manager to set up meetings with the party leaders. Wall's running for re-election; maybe we could turn up the heat a bit," Lionel said.

"I have some small influence in the area of political contributions in this state," Ev said. "As in who gets them and who doesn't. Even you, 'Randall,' have done your part, compiling that list of attorneys. You did compile that list, didn't you?"

His comment unnerved Randy further. Randy sweated visibly, paling at the same time under the onslaught. Lionel fumed, but seemed content to let Ev handle this his way.

"I, um, got it from a newspaper article on the top defense attorneys in the Southeast."

Ev frowned.

Randy finally looked Ev in the eyes. "Look, guys. Of course I don't think Chase is guilty. And Marinda—she just suggested we be careful, and not get in the crossfire of some war between Wall and Chase."

Peter didn't buy the shift in gears; none of them did, but they'd been friends together too long. They knew each other's strengths, and each other's weaknesses; the gold ring he wore on his left hand signified Randy's weakness.

Lionel grunted. Ev looked back into his house, letting the rage that had built in him subside.

"I really need to be getting to the office," Randy said, looking at his watch. "Look, I've got a major issue at work, otherwise I'd stay and we could talk more. I'll call you, or you can call me when you need something or if I can do anything more to help." Without another word he left through the sliding glass door into the house. A few moments later they heard his car drive off.

"I doubt I've ever seen him so glad to leave us," Lionel said. He shook his head sadly. "What's become of our boy?"

"No doubt his lovely wife has convinced him that associating with a known murderer might have negative consequences to his career, not to mention her social life."

"And his sex life," Lionel added.

Of course, they were both right, Peter thought. *Marinda Turner says jump and Randy asks permission before letting gravity assert itself.* His cell phone rang. He looked over at his friends. Ev waved his hand in assent, sipping his drink.

"Hello," he answered, not recognizing the local number.

"Mr. Jurgens, Ken Wall with the D.A.'s Office. I believe we've met?"

They had, several years before when Peter had been in the midst of his arson series. Wall had introduced himself at a charity function he attended with Chase.

"I remember," he said. Lionel looked at him, and he mouthed "Wall" with raised eyebrows. Lionel made to grab the phone from Peter's hand. Ev signaled for him to stop.

"I wonder if you'd care to get together," Wall said. "I've

got some information I'm sure you and perhaps your readers would be interested in."

The *Piedmont Gazette* had reported that morning, in bold print just below the headline, that the D.A. had been "on the killer's trail" from the beginning, intimating that the arrest of Kate Wagner had been a charade, part of a setup to nail the real murderer. Why such a ploy would be necessary wasn't explained. There were holes in the story big enough to drive Ev's 600 series Mercedes through, but no one had raised any questions. The press believed the public liked to read about fallen heroes, so they created one.

He told Wall to name a place and time. Wall suggested his office later that afternoon. After he hung up he faced Lionel's angry, inquisitive glare.

"So?" he raised an eyebrow.

Peter related Wall's end of the conversation. Lionel picked up a rock about the size of a baseball from Ev's garden and tossed it up and down in his meaty right hand. He turned toward the back of the property, open to a thatch of trees, and with a grunt threw the rock high into the air. A loud thud sounded as the rock struck a tree trunk. The muscles of his arms stood out like the contours of a topographical map, his short-sleeved polo shirt barely containing the massive biceps. Peter knew if the world were a simpler place, without all the rules and laws, he would surely single-handedly storm the jail cell and free Chase, pulling down the walls of the cell brick by brick if he had to. Then he'd seek out Ken Wall and challenge him to mortal combat. The outcome of that contest would not be in doubt. But Lionel, a civilized man, living in a civilized world, couldn't do that.

Ev continued smiling, looking off into the distance. "So meet with the man, find out what he wants."

Peter nodded. He wanted to tell them about the caller. And his demands. So far, he'd been asked to report the truth, but he knew a piece in support of Chase would somehow run counter to the interests of his blackmailer.

"He's still up to something." Lionel walked over to one of the Greek statues by the pool. "Play along with him. He wants something from you, but he also wants to gloat. Let him. Listen to what he has to say, let him think you're willing to roll over on your friend, whatever it takes to get him to reveal what he's got. He wants to talk, hell he's talking to anyone who'll listen. The bastard is enjoying the hell out of this. But there's something more, and we need to know what it is." Shaking his head in disgust, he walked over to the immaculate garden, a full thirty by thirty patch of earth filled with dozens of varieties of rose bushes.

Ev just smiled, now lost in his own thoughts. He got up and walked them through the house to the front door, pausing to adjust his hair as he passed the hall mirror.

Lionel and Peter left together, walking down the path toward their cars. Ev stood watching at his front door.

"Is it my imagination or is that man acting a bit odd?" Peter asked Lionel.

Lionel laughed, getting in his car. "I've got news for you, Pete. Ev's always been a bit odd."

WHEN PETER GOT BACK to his hotel room, the message light was blinking. He sighed, and hit the button. A woman's voice came on, throaty and emotional.

"Peter Jurgens? This is Reagan Thompson. Lionel's sister? We met, um, seventeen years ago I think? You might remember me. Would you please give me a call?" She left a number, which he wrote down. He had forgotten Lionel even had a little sister. He'd always been chided by his ex-wife when he got together with the guys and she asked how their families were and he had no answer. It just wasn't the kind of stuff they talked about. He punched the number Reagan had left into his cell phone, a 202 area code. Washington, D.C.

"Hello," answered a tremulous voice.

"Reagan Thompson?"

"Yes, that's me."

"This is Peter Jurgens. You called—"

"Oh, thank God, you returned my call!" She sounded nearly hysterical. "I didn't know what to do, who to call. I saw your name in the paper yesterday and called all the local hotels."

He slowed her down. "Do you have some information about the case?"

"Information? I have something for Chase, but I think… I needed to talk with someone."

There was a pause at the other end of the line. When Reagan spoke again she seemed more in control of herself, and suddenly sounded a lot older.

"Peter, I'm sorry. Let me start over. I just feel like I know you so well. I've heard so much about you."

"It's nice that Lionel speaks so well of me—"

She interrupted him with a sigh. "I'm doing it again. I apologize. No, I've heard your name from Lionel, of course. I've heard all your names. But Lionel's not exactly a repository of information about any of you guys. I feel I know you from all I've heard from Chase."

"Chase?"

Another pause. "We wanted to tell all of you, but…"

"Tell us what?"

A quick stifled laugh. "That Chase and I are… together."

"In jail?" Now Peter was the one all flustered and confused. It took him another moment. Chase and Reagan Thompson? When all of them had been kidding him about his dating habits? He laughed out loud.

"Excuse me?" she said.

"No, excuse me, Reagan, it's just that we were starting to think Chase was a monk or something."

"Believe me, he's no monk." They shared a laugh, quickly comfortable with each other.

"I just had no idea, Reagan. If you don't mind my asking, how long has this been going on?"

"Over a year. It's just been terrible not being able to tell anyone. But with all this, I've just felt so helpless. I can't talk to anyone, and I just have to do something!"

"Of course, we all feel the same way. Lionel, Randy, Ev, and I were just meeting, talking about that very thing."

"I wonder if we could meet. I'd feel so much better if I could talk to somebody."

"Well, that would be fine, although I don't have any plans to come up your way."

"Up my way? Oh no, I'm in town. This is my cell phone," she said.

"Of course. I'd be happy to meet with you. I have a two o'clock appointment. We could meet up afterwards for a drink, if that's okay with you." He proposed a place, and gave her directions, suggesting they meet at five, and hung up, smiling. All this time, Chase, and Lionel's sister. He glanced at the clock. Just enough time to grab a burger, then go dance with the devil.

Thirty-Three

Following the instructions from the poster Chase had left, Jared drove the Honda he'd stolen to the town of Jonesborough, Tennessee. By the time they got there it was night. He and the dog slept in the car on a side street lined with others just like it, then drove carefully to the post office in the morning, circling the block a few times. Convinced there were no lurking observers, he drove to the bus station and parked, leaving the dog in the backseat. Then he walked toward the post office, stopping several blocks away by a bus stop, and waited for the doors to open.

"Package for Chase Riordan," he whispered, greeting the postal clerk, an indifferent middle-aged man, reading a tattered copy of *Fahrenheit 451*. Sighing, the clerk got up, walked over to a shelf, and scanned the brown paper packages stacked there. He settled on one the size of a small shoebox, and brought it back. Jared could see the address, scrawled in black marker: Chase Riordan, General Delivery, Jonesborough, TN 37659.

"Identification," the clerk said flatly.

Jared pulled out the driver's license Chase had left under his mattress with the credit card. He tried to relax his face in the casual look his brother wore on the photo, but he might as well have been Ray Charles for all the man paid any attention. Sliding the package across, he went back to his novel. Later, if asked, he might remember the tall whispering man, but perhaps not.

Once outside, Jared found a secluded park bench and opened the package. He laughed, as the contents spilled out into his lap. Ten thousand dollars cash, a cell phone with a piece of paper taped to the back with two phone numbers, one that said "your phone," and the other, "my phone," and a Flash comic book, with another note taped to it, "for your collection." He pocketed the cash and the comic book, glad his brother still retained his sense of humor. The Flash had been Jared's favorite comic book superhero growing up, and he kept a stash of first editions in a storage facility back in Fayetteville, still in the original sleeves. He stared at the phone and finally keyed in the numbers, but the phone rang twenty times with no answer. He'd try again later.

He drove the car to Asheville, parked in the long-term parking lot, and stole another from the same lot. With luck, the car wouldn't be noticed missing for at least a week. With ten thousand dollars in his pocket, he could have bought a used car, but he wanted to limit his exposure. His trip to the post office had been as much public scrutiny as he wanted to endure for the moment. Keeping his speed just above the posted limit, he drove back toward the mountains of Eastern Tennessee, constantly checking in his rearview mirror for pursuers, and listening for helicopters. *Better to be paranoid then caught.*

Stopping for gas at an old convenience station, he bought a stack of newspapers, an area map, and some personal items: a razor, a pair of scissors, toothbrush and toothpaste, and a pair of sunglasses. At a rest stop along the highway he parked, and waited for two other cars to leave. He entered the men's room and shaved, first his head, then the growth of beard, leaving a goatee and a moustache. With the sunglasses, he no longer resembled the face on the driver's license. More importantly, though, he might escape scrutiny if the army posted his picture in the area. He could do little to disguise his height. Wearing his last new tee shirt and pants, he found a Wal-Mart and purchased a cheap backpack, a sleeping bag, and as much food as he could carry. In the parking lot he swapped license plates with an old Chevy Impala, then consulted his map, which highlighted the various mountain trailheads along the Cumberland Trail. He drove down a small state highway through a town called Crab Orchard, found one of the entrances, parked the car, and packed his gear on his back and shoulders. Leaving the car created some risk, but its discovery would only alert his pursuers as to where he'd been, not which direction he'd headed into the mountains. He'd offered the dog numerous opportunities to leave him, but he'd stayed with him. Together, they entered the Cumberland Mountains.

THIRTY-FOUR

The Office of the District Attorney of the City of Piedmont was on Union Street, in the old Independence Center, an imposing granite-faced building, and one of the oldest in Uptown, just across the street from the city courthouse.

Peter took the elevator to the fourth floor and entered the offices through the glass door embossed with Ken Wall's name and title. Peter's image stared back at him from an array of glossy surfaces as he entered and approached the small neatly put-together woman who perched behind the reception desk. He told her his name; she nodded, and repeated it over the phone, then directed him to sit down. He took a seat in one of the high leather wingback chairs in front of a steel and glass coffee table covered with newspapers opened to pages featuring the district attorney, including *The Raleigh Sentinel*, *The New York Times*, and his own *Journal and Constitution*. After waiting for almost a half hour, a young woman stepped in front of him and said, "District Attorney Wall will see you now. This way please, Mr. Jurgens."

Following her down the hall, Peter admired the gentle swaying of her hips, the soft swishing sound of her skirt. They passed a number of offices, with open doors and suited occupants seated at their desks in front of computer screens, either typing away or on the phone. Quiet, more like a library than an actual workplace.

They walked around a corner and traversed the entire back wall before arriving at Wall's private office. The woman announced Peter, then stood by the door and waved him past. Wall leaned back in his chair, talking on the phone. Full of largesse, he waved at a small wooden chair on the far side of the office. Peter opted for the overstuffed chair next to his desk.

Wall spoke bombastically on the phone, apparently energized by the presence of a guest.

"No, that's right, Mr. Mayor. My office is all over it. I've got the CNN team scheduled in here tomorrow afternoon—we're going to do the shoot right here in my office. Of course you're welcome to attend—in fact, we could probably even get you some airtime. No, I understand. I was just offering. Okay, I'll keep you posted. Yes, thank you very much, I appreciate your confidence in me. Good day to you too." He hung up, moved some papers on his desk, then seemed to remember his visitor. He stood up.

"Mr. Jurgens," he said, standing. They shook hands. "Thanks for coming."

Peter sank back into the chair and Wall pulled his desk chair opposite, maintaining the advantage of height. With a smile he offered something to drink, indicating a refrigerator behind the desk.

"No thanks," Peter said. "Nice office."

Wall waved his hand around the place. "This? Thanks, it's a little large for my taste, but we have so many people come through here I guess we need the space.

"You're probably wondering why I invited you up here today. I'll get right to the point. I know Chase is your friend and I'm sorry you had to witness the indignity of his arrest. I appreciate your loyalty, I really do. I see far too little of it today, you know. Loyalty, that is. It's a trait I admire. In spite of what you think you know or may have heard, I loved that boy too—like my own son. Thought I'd pass the torch, so to speak, but—"

Peter started to rise. *Fuck this*, he thought. His face showed his obvious distaste at Wall's words. Wall put up his hand to stop him.

"No, please hear me out. Trust me, you're going to want to hear this."

"I came here at your invitation, Wall," Peter said tightly. "I'm not going to sit and listen to you give me a line of your bullshit. It might work on the other flunkies you're feeding stories to, but don't try it on me."

Wall reddened, and moved back behind his desk, putting some distance between them.

"How dare you suggest that this office would have anything to do with these so-called leaks to the media," he said, then stopped. His face was a study in attempted composure.

"Save it, Wall. I'm not buying," Peter said. He stood and headed toward the door. He had his hand on the doorknob when the D.A. finally spoke again.

"Fine, we'll play it your way. I had hoped this might be a civilized conversation among civilized men, but I can see that was a forlorn hope. No skin off my back—it will be a lot more fun this way."

Peter hesitated. "Ten minutes."

Rather than stand at eye level, Wall sank into his desk chair. "Fine. You want to deal straight; we'll deal straight. Your friend is going down. He's going down so far the devil will have to dig a well to find him. He's fooled you all for years, and it's going to cost you. All of you. He even fooled me, but just for a short while. Then I caught on, but it's taken me a long time to nail him. And trust me, he is nailed. To a fucking tree. And I'm holding the hammer."

Peter rolled his eyes and started to wonder whether Wall was truly insane.

"You think I'm funny? You think I don't have the evidence to back it up?" He lowered his voice. "I'll let you in on a little secret. The papers don't know the half of it. If the papers knew what I know, there'd be a lynch mob out after your friend."

His vehemence set Peter back. He'd had no idea of the true depth of the man's obsessive hatred for Chase.

"All off the record, of course," Wall said. "That's not why I invited you here. There's more. Riordan will be convicted. You can take that to the bank."

"Where's the motive, Wall," Peter asked. "Why the hell would he want to kill Josh Samuels? He didn't even know the guy."

Wall leaned back in his chair, hands folded behind his head. "This isn't about Josh Samuels. Early next week this office will announce that we will be trying Chase Riordan as a multiple murderer. And that's on the record. You're the first to hear it. I wanted to give you the chance to cut your losses. Pick sides, if you will. You have the chance for an exclusive story that will blow this city sky high. If you take what you're offered." He pulled a cigar from an inside pocket and rolled it between his hands.

Peter was reminded of Red Auerbach, the old President of the Celtics, sitting courtside and lighting his victory cigar when his team had finally salted away another win. His face must have shown the emotions he felt. Fear, hatred, shock, all competing. His stomach sank.

"Multiple murders?" he tried to say calmly, but it came out as a choking sound. Wall took his time now, a gleam in his eyes. His secretary came through the door with a message in her hand, but he waved her away.

"Multiple murders," Wall said, clearly savoring the words. "Not only will this office try him for the murder of Josh Samuels, but also for the murder of Katarina Volkova. And we're looking into charging him for Winston Reed, and Ray Lewis, Jr."

All victims in cases Chase had handled.

"Chase won those cases," he said. "Agnew and Tierney were found not guilty. Ray Lewis, Sr., too."

"Yes, and I'm of course now thankful, because they were in fact not guilty. Much as it pains me to say it in the case of our former mayor. And your friend knew it at the time because he had committed the murder himself. Kind of helps as a defense attorney when you can have absolute certainty of the innocence of your clients, don't you think? And clients who can afford to pay? Not to mention the evidence trail. He left it, so he knew exactly how to leave clues that incriminated his clients, but also contained ambiguous elements pointing to another killer and to their innocence. Quite ingenious, I must admit. But then, I never said he was stupid."

Peter stood speechless. Searching Wall's eyes for a trace of this insanity, he saw instead only conviction.

"I don't expect you to take my word for it. Facts are facts, and when all the facts come out your friend will join an infamous list of serial killers, and I will take great personal satisfaction in putting him away."

Serial killer. The term had become almost commonplace. Usually, it was reserved for evil, distorted men fighting personal demons, carrying out some bizarre agenda, or acting out satanic rituals. Not a distinguished, decent man like Chase Riordan. Peter came to his senses. Of course, all of this was not true. It had to be part of some greater scheme.

"Nice try, Wall," he said. "Just because you couldn't convict the people you put on trial for those murders, you think you can tar Chase with your ridiculous brush. Because that would make it not your fault, wouldn't it? You want to try him in the press, ruin his reputation, then it won't matter later that he turns up innocent."

Wall smiled calmly. "Innocent? Oh, I assure you, Mr. Jurgens. Your friend is far from innocent. I can and will prove everything I told you today. But I don't really care whether you believe me now. I promise you, when this is all over, even you will be convinced." Peter must have still looked skeptical, because Wall pointed the cigar. "DNA doesn't lie. We've already got the results from the Samuels case, and we'll have them back soon on the hairs from Katarina Volkova's condo. You didn't hear that from me. But if you report it from an unnamed source I won't deny it." Now Wall stood up.

"So there's your choice, Jurgens. You've heard the story before anyone else. By tomorrow afternoon it becomes national news. What you do with this *exclusive*," he said, "is up to you. You report this and my office says 'no comment.' Then next week we release and you've scooped the field. Take care how you handle this. Opportunities such as this don't come along often in this lifetime, I imagine."

At that moment, Peter couldn't hold on to a single coherent thought. Somebody was off his rocker, and all of a sudden he wasn't sure who. Then he felt shamed for thinking it.

"Why would he do it?" he blurted out. "What reason could Chase possibly have for killing those people? He didn't even know them."

Wall pulled a gold lighter out of his pants pocket and lit the cigar. He'd been waiting for this question. He took a few puffs to get the cigar started, squinted, and blew a cloud of smoke in Peter's direction.

"Why, for the basest of all motives: greed," he said quietly. "The goddamned bastard killed a bunch of people he didn't even know, just so he could have clients."

THIRTY-FIVE

When he left Wall's office, Peter's head was spinning. In possession of knowledge most newsmen would kill to have, with the rights to an exclusive story; one he'd have to sell out his friend to write. A scoop of this magnitude would enhance his reputation, and keep him on the payroll, if not for the *Journal and Constitution*, then for another publication. Not to take advantage of this information would be professional suicide, especially if his editor found out after the fact that he knew but didn't do anything about it. But to take advantage would be betrayal of the highest order. Betrayal of his friendship with Chase, betrayal of his personal loyalties, and betrayal of himself.

Did it matter whether Wall's comments were true or not? He grappled with the thought, trying to justify writing the article by convincing himself that Chase's innocence would trump everything.

He walked the streets of Uptown Piedmont, heading toward his rendezvous with Reagan Thompson. A secret Chase had kept. What if there were other secrets, far worse? Could he be a murderer, a serial killer? If so, then he obviously wasn't the person Peter thought he was. In that case, would it be betrayal to write the story Wall had presented him with? After all, in that case Chase would have been the one who'd betrayed him—betrayed all of them. He'd have to have a psychopathic personality if his motive was simply to make a name for himself as a defense attorney, as Wall implied. But if he were a psychopath, surely there'd have been some signs over all the years they'd known each other.

Peter racked his brain trying to come up with examples of behaviors from their collective past, anything odd at all. He thought of the mad intensity in Chase's eyes on the basketball court, the focus on winning, and the killer instinct. He recalled the weekend at Hilton Head, Chase going up to spike a volleyball, all business, pounding the ball into the face of a young college kid. Had it been intentional? He remembered numerous other incidences where, if he were so inclined, he could interpret signs of aberrant behavior.

If Chase wasn't guilty, then there were some nefarious forces at work here. Wall mentioned DNA evidence. Either this was one big mistake or it was part of some massive frame. If that were so, Chase would need his friends more than ever to help clear his name and expose the truth. Which was the more likely scenario? That Chase committed these crimes or that it was part of something bigger? Did Wall have it in him to concoct something so evil? Was he even physically and mentally capable of such a thing? He sure hated Chase enough. But hating someone and arresting and trying them for multiple murders you knew they didn't commit were two vastly different things.

He had no real answers. Upon reaching that conclusion, he discovered he'd overshot his destination by several blocks. He found the restaurant and settled into a table, doodling on his pad, sketching out the outlines of the article, if he decided to submit it. His cell phone rang.

"Peter, Paul Givens.

"Hey Paul, everything okay?"

"Sure—loved what you've submitted so far. Nice eyewitness account of the arrest. I might have preferred a bit more of a personal angle, as you know the guy, but I think we'll have some opportunities over the next few months."

Peter had written "just the facts," allowing the drama of the scene, an arrest in Chase's own office, to drive the piece. "Thanks. Obviously it wasn't what I thought I was up here for…"

"Believe me, me neither, but what a lucky break for us!"

Lucky. Right.

"But now that you're there, we're obviously in great position to get a scoop that no one else has."

"How so," Peter asked cautiously.

"Why, taking advantage of your relationship with the accused! Everyone's going to want to know what was going through his head, what kind of person commits this kind of crime."

"He didn't do it."

Pause. "You know, I can be a real horse's ass sometimes. I apologize. I know Mr. Riordan's your friend. If he's innocent, great. Maybe even better. Regardless, it's a great story."

"Right." He couldn't even begin to imagine trying to interview Chase in the jail cell, assuming he were allowed visitors.

"But on another subject. I heard you had a private meeting with the district attorney. Anything come out of that?"

He'd "heard?" Was Givens as much a pawn in this as he was, or did he have another agenda? "We'd met a while back. I think he knew a lot of the local guys, but he wanted to renew acquaintances," he tried.

"Interesting. Well, that's all to the good. If you're on good terms with both the D.A. and the accused, that will make for some compelling copy."

"Sure."

"Hey, I just wanted to check in. Keep it coming. It might not hurt to include in your next piece that you met with the district attorney to discuss his views on the case. Something like that."

And if he did that, and the new charges came out in a news release, everyone would know Peter had passed on the exclusive and his career would be finished. "Will do, Paul. I've got to run."

He was into his second mug of St. Pauli Girl when a beautiful black woman entered the place, the eyes of half the guys in the joint following her as she walked over to the bar. Just as Peter got up to wave, she spotted him, and came over to his table, taking the booth seat opposite. She introduced herself, then removed her sunglasses. Her eyes were red and puffy.

"I'd recognize you anywhere," she said. "I've seen Chase's pictures from your guy weekends."

She caught a waiter's attention and ordered a double Baileys on the rocks. The same guys who had followed her progress to his table whispered among themselves, heads nodding in their direction.

"Don't worry about them," she said, aware of Peter's wandering attention. "If you'd like I'll fold my hands nicely and we can act like you're conducting a job interview."

"Maybe I should have suggested another place."

She laughed, a beautiful, throaty laugh that rose to her eyes. "We could really give them something to talk about." Her drink arrived and she took a big swig before speaking.

"I know this is probably a bit of a surprise to you, but I honestly didn't know what else to do. I probably should come clean with Lionel, but Chase and I wanted to do that together, when we were sure…" She lost her composure momentarily, her voice faltering, but recovered after another sip. "When we were sure we wanted to be together. Besides, it's probably not the best timing for his campaign."

Peter assured her he was happy for both of them.

"Thanks. I needed to talk to someone. It's tough enough to have that secret, but now with Chase in jail, and I can't even see him…"

"We all feel the same way—helpless. But we've been trying to help, each in our own way." He told her of their meeting, the article he'd been writing—before the meeting with Wall—and Lionel and Ev's efforts. He was still reeling from his meeting with Wall, although the beer helped.

"So I'm trying to decide whether that makes sense," she interrupted his thoughts, and he realized he hadn't heard a word she'd said.

"Excuse me?"

She looked at him and a soft expression came over her face. "Are you all right?" she asked. "Here I am going on about me and my problems and emotions, and I haven't once thought about how this must be affecting you. You've been one of Chase's best friends for years—far longer than I've known him. This must be terrible for you."

The waiter replaced his beer with another he didn't recall ordering.

"I'm so sorry," she said, "I know, I'm sure that Chase will be out soon. He didn't even know that Josh Samuels, but I keep asking myself 'why is all this happening? Why must he go through this, and all alone too?'"

With her words, tears welled in Peter's eyes and he felt powerless to stop them.

"It's okay," she said. "It will all work out. It's just a matter of time. The truth will tell in the end."

Each word brought a new pang. She considered his face. "What is it? What's bothering you? Do you know something?"

He told her about his meeting with Wall, about his announcement to come. When he got to Wall's comments about DNA, she stared pensively. He didn't stop there. He told her about his difficulties with his book and the second chance he had with the newspaper. As he spoke, she sat and listened, never interrupting, attentively following every word. When he finally finished, drained from the experience, he felt surprisingly relieved. With a person he had revealed more than he'd ever told one of his friends. Guys never really talked. Not about how they felt.

Reagan sat calmly, looking at him, her face a study in

composure. He'd just told her that her boyfriend might be a killer. A sociopath. That was the label. But she sat calmer now and in more control then when she walked in the door.

"What's your impression of Wall?" she finally asked.

He considered. He told her that he hated Chase with great passion, but he couldn't picture him going to such great lengths just because of that.

She nodded, accepting his opinion. "I've heard about him from Chase. He doesn't like to talk about him. But I've always found it odd. He's the only guy I've ever heard that actively doesn't like Chase. I'd never been able to figure out why and I know it bothered Chase too. He likes people, and he likes to be liked. Plus he used to admire the guy."

Peter hadn't thought of it in quite those terms before, but it was true. People just liked Chase. They couldn't help themselves. Chase's basketball opponents genuinely respected and liked him, even after he'd roasted them for forty points. Hell, they wanted to have their picture taken with him, tell their friends that Chase had "only" scored that many on them. He was that kind of guy. Of course, sociopaths could be likeable too. As if sensing his thoughts again, Reagan grabbed his hands and squeezed hard.

"Peter. You *know* he's not guilty, don't you?"

He looked away, unable to hold her gaze. "I want to believe, Reagan. I love the guy like a brother. But the evidence…

"Is fabricated! What do we really know? What Wall has told us? I wouldn't believe a word that man said if Jesus Christ put his arms around him and blessed him." She was practically yelling, "Peter, this is Chase! This is not some guy you're reading about in the newspapers, wondering whether he did it or not! This is a guy you've known half your life! The man I love." There were tears in her eyes, but she didn't shift her gaze. The conviction in her voice was compelling, making Peter feel ashamed of his doubts. She continued, relentless.

"And besides. Chase saw this coming."

"Huh?"

"Not his arrest, but the connections of these murders. He believed they were committed by the same person."

"He did? What made him think that?"

"A bunch of things: his intuition, some things didn't fit. He felt strongly enough about it to ask me to look into it. Or find someone who would."

"Why you?"

Reagan smiled. "I guess I forgot to mention I work for the FBI."

He sat still for a moment.

"And did you? Find someone?"

Reagan pulled out a large envelope from her purse. "I brought it to give to Chase. But I can't get in to see him."

"What's it say?"

"It confirms what he suspected."

Peter considered what she'd said. Chase had seen the hands of a single individual connected to the murders. So Wall's theory about some kind of serial killer might not be too far off. Maybe he just had the wrong man. He corrected himself. He had the wrong man.

"You might want to find Rufus Agnew, then. Chase has hired him as his lawyer. If you can get the file to him, he'll make sure Chase gets it."

"I know. I wanted to visit with you first. I thought you might be more understanding than my brother, or your other friends."

"Thanks, though I'm not sure I deserve your confidence in me. I'm not exactly at my best these days."

Reagan laughed. "Chase always said you were hard on yourself. He said you had the most empathy of any of the guys. So I took a chance."

He smiled wanly. "Yeah, well, it's not exactly a high bar." He looked at his beer. "I still have an article to write, one way or another."

"Wall is counting on you to give in and accept what he's telling you. But none of it is true—you'd be writing lies!"

Actually it wouldn't be lies, Peter thought. In fact, quite the opposite. If the D.A.'s Office planned to file multiple murder charges and he reported it, there wouldn't be anything untruthful in that, but he didn't correct her.

Reagan continued. "Chase needs us Peter. He needs us on his side. I don't know exactly what we can do, but we can sure do something!"

He smiled at this reiteration of her brother's comments. He nodded, accepting her words. "You're right. I'm sorry for acting like such an idiot."

She waved this away. "Sometimes it's hard to keep your head above the clouds and see what's really going on. I've been living in Washington for ten years. Believe me, I know it's not easy."

They pushed their glasses aside at the same time and laughed. Clear heads were needed.

"What are you going to do?" he asked.

"Go meet Rufus Agnew. Then come clean with big brother." She sounded like a young girl with the last statement.

They exchanged cell phone numbers and Reagan threw thirty dollars on the table, waving off Peter's attempts to pay. They shook hands and parted at the bar, the guys behind him now commiserating with him, as they left separately. He gave them a wan smile and held up his hands. Can't blame a guy for trying.

Back in the hotel, he booted up his laptop and stared at the screen. In the restaurant it had been easy to get caught up in Reagan's enthusiasm for his friend's innocence. Now, sitting by himself, he still faced a difficult decision. His belief alone wouldn't make much difference in the case. That Chase had previously considered the multiple murder scenario added an interesting wrinkle, but it didn't change what Wall planned, that he'd be charging Chase. He would have liked to have seen the file Reagan had brought with her. Sighing, he put his hands on the keyboard and began to type.

THIRTY-SIX

Rufus Agnew held court outside his home, a modest down-stairs apartment in perhaps the only brownstone in all of Piedmont, about three blocks from City Hall.

"Mister Mayor, is it true you're going to represent Chase Riordan?" the reporter asked.

"Thank you, young man, but I haven't been mayor of this fine city for twenty years. I'm a private citizen like the rest of you," he responded, standing in the midst of a gaggle of reporters who had descended upon him as he casually exited his house on his way to his customary afternoon lunch at the Hyatt.

The reporters laughed good-naturedly. Rufus Agnew had been Mister Mayor in the City of Piedmont for as long as most of them could remember and almost as long as some of them had been alive. The headlines had trumpeted "Mayor Agnew NOT GUILTY" at the conclusion of his trial. It was unthinkable to refer to him as anything else.

"Are you representing Riordan?" the reporter persisted.

"Are you even a practicing attorney?" another asked.

Rufus squinted to identify his questioner, undoubtedly a newcomer to the city, or one of those 'out of town' reporters.

"Son, I've been a member of the bar in good standing in the state of North Carolina since before you were born," he answered. "Now if y'all will excuse me, I have a lunch date." Using a cane of beautiful ebony, topped with a carved ivory ram's head in honor of his alma mater, the former mayor started up Church Street. The reporters cleared the way, following at a short distance. The group made for a comical sight, one old man with a cane followed by a group of young reporters moving at barely a crawl so as to avoid overtaking him. One of them, a smaller older man himself, separated himself from the group and walked side by side with the cane wielder.

"Rufus, you will be taking the case, yes?"

"Rollie, it's nice to see you. Things okay down at the paper? I see your colleagues are getting a lot more column space than you lately."

The small man nodded amiably. "No real story yet, don't you think? Just an arrest and lots of idle gossip?"

"That's right, Rollie, that's all it's been so far."

The two strolled companionably, not saying much, the other reporters still close behind. As they turned from Church Street onto Trade, Rufus finally acknowledged the other's question.

"You know, Rollie, the only time I've been in a courtroom these past twelve years was for my own trial. Not a terribly pleasant experience. And the last time before that as executor of my dear mother's will. But if Chase Riordan asks me to be his attorney, I'm his attorney."

Rollie nodded, as the other reporters suddenly scrambled away, talking rapidly on their cell phones. They'd gotten the story they'd been after. "You've met with him then?" he asked, and the older man nodded.

"I know first hand what it's like to sit in a jail cell, Rollie, although I had the advantage of being out on bail during my trial. It pains me to see that man locked up. I swear, he's lost ten pounds already." Another block took them to Fourth Street, where they turned again and continued their stroll.

The ex-mayor reflected on his first visit with Chase, after his initial contact by Ernesto Perez.

The meeting had gone well enough. Rufus had expressed surprise at Chase's request of him, but had accepted his explanation as to why he needed someone like himself. He thought Chase looked pretty good considering, and was in better spirits than he had been when he'd been under indictment.

"I don't know whether I'll be able to reopen the issue of bail," Rufus said. "The judge seemed pretty strong on that subject. I'm not sure I want to start off my representation by pissing him off."

Chase shrugged. "Wall met with him behind closed doors—he's got something else, I'm guessing. I'd like to be out, but I'd really like to see my friends."

"Now there, I may be a bit more helpful. The judge and I are old fishing buddies. I'll file an order this afternoon requesting visitors other than your legal staff. Shall we talk about the case?"

Chase explained his working theory for a defense, the same theory he'd begun when he was working for Kate Wagner. Josh Samuels had been doing an exposé of the tobacco industry, with expectations of incendiary information to follow. Chase recounted the results of Tony Santori's investigations. Rufus questioned how much Chase trusted the investigator, after a local reporter had snapped a picture of him leaving the District Attorney's Office. He hadn't shown up for work since.

"He's a good man, Rufus. I don't know what Wall has on him, but it's not his fault." He detailed his investigator's interview with Billerette, the *Gazette* editor, as well as the suspicions he'd raised.

"Bottom line, someone wanted Samuels to stop and chose to stop him permanently."

"Someone at Litchfield?"

Chase shrugged. "Not really their style. They've had

people after them for years, worse than this. I don't recall any
dead bodies turning up as a result."

"What about Kate Wagner?" Agnew asked.

"What about her?"

"Seems to me she was the first person the police looked
at. Same things still apply, I should imagine. She encouraged
Josh to participate in the race, and I've never heard any explanation for her slow finish. Still a logical candidate if you ask
me."

Chase shook his head. "She didn't do it, Rufus. I didn't
spend a whole lot of time with her, but I'm convinced she's
innocent. She's a pawn here, as much as I am."

His new attorney looked at him, his bushy eyebrows
curling in surprise. "Why, I'm surprised at you, Chase. I may
not have practiced law for a good many years, but I was under
the impression the job of a defense counsel is to raise reasonable doubt. It doesn't matter, surely, whether the woman is
guilty or not, only what we can get the jury to believe."

"I won't do it, Rufus. She's been through enough already,
with her fiancé dead. The papers were hard enough on her at
the onset of all this. She doesn't need to be dragged through
this more than she already has." The look in his eyes, along
with his forceful delivery, reminiscent of a closing argument,
told Agnew it wasn't worth pursuing for the moment.

"Fine, fine, I just hope your sentimentality doesn't get
in the way of an acquittal. So tell me more about the tobacco
story."

Chase told him Ev's account of his father's view of the
exposé.

"And there's something else," he added, after a pause.

"Hmm?"

"Just that there's something going on here that isn't quite
right. I need some time to organize my thoughts around it.
Then we'll talk some more."

"Connected with Wall's closed-door meeting with the
judge, I imagine? Fine. You know Chase, I'm going to need

some help on this case. An old man like me, I don't get around like I used to."

Chase nodded. "Ernesto will help. So will Kasey. And if you need an investigator, hire one. I'm sure you know some good folks."

"I do at that," Rufus said. "I should also let you know I've already received a retainer for my services, from a Mr. Everett Litchfield."

Chase laughed. "You send that check right back to him, Rufus. I'll pay my own way."

It was his lawyer's turn to smile. "I already did. I didn't spend six months with you without getting to know you a little bit." The guard tapped his wrist and Rufus prepared to leave.

"By the way, Rufus, you never asked me if I was guilty or not," Chase said seriously.

Rufus took a moment, straightening out the wrinkles in his suit as he stood up.

"Why, I believe my earlier statement still applies," he said. "And besides, I don't recall you ever asking me that question, either." He winked at Chase as he left.

"ROLLIE, YOU HAVE ANY PLANS for lunch?" he asked. "Funny thing happened to me on the way out of the jail."

He told the reporter how he'd been walking for a block, not paying much attention to his surroundings, when a grizzled man in an old leather jacket had bumped into him. He checked for his wallet, found it still there, and raised the cane to ward off the possible attacker. He was surprised, then, to recognize Tony Santori, Chase's former investigator.

"His head darted around furtively, constantly looking over his shoulder. He told me he knew some things. Things I needed to know. He told me he wanted to help Chase. I told him he'd already helped quite enough. At that he grew quite agitated, and insisted he'd been set up. It appears our unkempt friend had a conviction on his record, which he'd covered up. He'd been forced off the police force, and Wall found out about it and threatened him. He claimed he had no idea anything he did might harm Chase in any way, but once his boss was arrested, he realized he was being used.

"I didn't know what to say to that, other than to reassure him I'd do all I could to help his boss. He told me he could help, to make up for what he'd done. We walked a half block over to a park bench by the courtyard in front of the county office building. Very cloak and dagger. Making sure we weren't being watched, he withdrew an envelope from inside his jacket and slid it across the bench to me. Told me to look at it when I left and was sure that I was alone. Then he ran off through the grass. I'm still not sure what he was afraid of."

"And this envelope? What did it contain?" Rollie asked, when they'd been seated at the Hyatt.

"Why, nothing but two photographs. One of two men, and the other a close-up shot of one of those same men." He reached into his coat pocket and tossed the photos across the table, face up.

The photo on top was slightly blurred, but showed a man Rollie recognized giving something to another man, whose back faced the camera. The photo on the bottom showed the second man, looking over his shoulder in the direction of the camera. Rollie looked up at Rufus Agnew, appreciating the significance of the find, but now also confused. Rufus picked up the photos and returned them to his pocket.

"It didn't make a lot of sense to me either, Rollie. Why would Ev Litchfield be meeting with the editor of the *Gazette*? Why would he be the source for Samuel's articles against his own company?"

And, Rufus thought, *what significance did the photos have to the case at hand?*

"One thing is certain, my friend," said the ex-mayor. "There's more to this case than meets the eye."

THIRTY-SEVEN

Colonel Sterling. The man's image brought Jared lurching awake in the middle of the night. When he opened his eyes he saw the stars peering through the branches of the tree he'd camped under. The dog looked up from its place at his side. Pulling himself from the sleeping bag, he listened to the sounds around him, but could hear nothing unusual: no branches snapping, no intake of breath, no sounds of movement that shouldn't be there. He'd camped deep in the forest, at least a half-mile from the old Cumberland Trail. Old growth pines enclosed him and the fire he'd allowed himself the night before had long since burned out. Sliding out from the sleeping bag, he crept on all fours to an opening in the branches, low to the ground, and scanned the forest around him. The dog followed. The silence of the forest became a symphony as he tuned his ears to its cadence. An owl hooted in the distance. Insects chirped in the trees and in the leaves and scrub grass. A pair of squirrels scampered along a branch above him. A rabbit sat still twenty yards away in a small clearing, almost invisible save for the pale glow cast upon it from the moon. He considered killing it for breakfast, but he still had a pack full of dry food. He'd strung fishing line a few inches above ground-level around the campsite, attached to a collection of loose tin cans, but they wouldn't trip up a man like Sterling, a man with the same training he'd had. The feeling that had woken him lingered, despite the natural sounds around him.

The forest remained as before. Alive. But only with the natural sounds and smells of its inhabitants. No predators of the human variety. The anxious feeling that had awakened him lingered and he realized with a start the feeling didn't have to do with Sterling. It had been so long since he'd felt the connection that he hadn't recognized it. Chase. He and his brother had always shared a special bond. On the one hand, they were as different as twins could be. But for all their differences in personality and outlook, in temperament and interests, he and his twin brother retained a connection both emotional and physical. They knew what each other felt.

When Jared had broken his leg falling off a swing at age nine, Chase had been playing basketball in the adjoining playground. As Jared yelled with the impact, Chase stumbled to the ground while going up for a jump shot. Rarely was the connection quite so acute as that, but ever since that day, Jared and Chase had become more and more accustomed to the daily twinges and emotional swings their connection entailed. Over time, the two learned to shield themselves from the effects and only the more severe feelings got through: the pains of body and soul. Jared knew, for example, exactly when Chase blew out his knee. It had occurred on March 29, seventeen years before, and had caused him to miss training for two whole days. During his time in the service, he could still feel the link to his brother, but he learned to ignore it and in time forgot about it entirely, as he shut out his former life.

When they'd pumped him with drugs at the Institute, he'd shut off most of his physical and mental senses to survive. As he gained strength now, and his physical senses returned, so did the link to his brother. He tried to analyze the feeling. Not physical, this time. Emotional. He could sense despair, anger, perhaps betrayal. Feelings that mirrored his own. He wondered if they were merely his own emotions, surfacing more strongly after a few days in the mountains. No, he could isolate those. He'd long ago learned to contain those feelings, to keep them compartmentalized, away from his conscious thoughts. It was the only way he could function in the army. Killing people, even from a distance, came with a price. Each kill, each face in his scope, carried with it a residue of the life he'd extinguished. His collection now exceeded sixty; sixty-plus lives his trigger finger had removed by a subtle squeeze.

No, these weren't his feelings. They were his brother's. As he opened himself up to them more fully, for the first time in years, they overwhelmed him. The depth of the emotions accompanying them was so... foreign. His brother had his moments of doubt, of worry. Everyone did. When he'd been forced to give up his dream of playing basketball, for example. But this was more.

Chase was in trouble. Of that he had no doubt. Had he gotten caught up in the consequences of Jared's escape? Was the army after him? Something else? He had no way of knowing, at least in his current location. He knew only one thing. His camping days were over.

Thirty-Eight

Rather than the stooped form of his lawyer, the man who walked into the visitor's room was tall, almost his own height, tan, with a ramrod straight posture, and the uniform of a full colonel in the U.S. Army. Chase had wondered whether the army would acknowledge his brother's situation. He stood up and the man did a double-take—then quickly recovered and held out his hand.

"William Lamp," he said. "You look just like him," he added unnecessarily.

Chase sat down without a word and examined the man's uniform. It appeared new and contained none of the insignia he expected to see adorning its sleeves or pockets. A few ribbons, the name "Lamp," and the silver eagle epaulets were the only distinguishing features.

"Mr. Riordan—"

"Chase."

"Chase. I'm here on behalf of the U.S. Army. Our visit is probably overdue, and for that I apologize. As well as for your current circumstances."

"Where is he?"

The colonel blinked, obviously not used to being interrupted. "I'll get to that, if you don't mind. I thought perhaps you might like to hear some background." He obviously had a script he intended to follow. "It might help you to understand how we got to this point."

Chase considered, then nodded. Might as well hear the man out; see what he could learn. Compare his story to what General Jackson had told him after breaking into his home.

The colonel continued. "What I'm about to tell you is classified. There were a number of us who argued you shouldn't hear this, especially with the, um, charges pending, but I believe you need to know, and I'm pleased to say that point of view won the day.

"Your brother was part of an elite unit that I created. I trained him, and others like him, although God knows, there were very few like him. It was a team put together for one purpose. To operate behind enemy lines. The guys who made it into that unit were all very carefully screened, both physically and psychologically. Your brother had the smarts and the raw physical skills, but he was, quite frankly, borderline on the psych eval. Borderline, I say, but within parameters. He was accepted into the program on the basis of his prior military experience and he excelled from the outset. Not just as a shooter—the army has plenty of people who know how to fire a weapon—but as a leader. Jared took to the physical training like he'd been looking for it all his life. His first few missions went flawlessly: well-executed, well-coordinated, and all achieved stated objectives. I'm afraid I can't tell you just what those missions were. I was the commanding officer of the unit, and over the course of several years, Jared became our go-to guy. The guy we trusted with the tough assignments, the ones others didn't really want, but were critical to the success of our missions. He reveled in this work. Perhaps a bit too much, but no one paid much attention to that so long as he did the job.

"We were in Iraq a few years back, with a pretty straightforward assignment. A rescue detail. A level below our typical work; pretty much a cakewalk. Your brother's assignment was to take a team and rescue a guy, a political leader held by the rebels at a warehouse somewhere in the south. The insertion went well, the intel was good. But something went wrong. The stories that came back were confused, but we later reconstructed what happened. As best we could determine, the guy he was sent to rescue wasn't alone. He was being held with his entire family, a wife, and two small children. Instead of trying to rescue the man and his family, your brother grabbed the man, pulled him outside the perimeter of the facility, and called in an air strike on the entire facility.

"Assuming he had identified an enemy stronghold, helicopters came in, fired their missiles, and left. They killed everyone in the warehouse, including the man's family, and the rest of Jared's team. After the missile attack, he dragged the man along to a river, which bordered the nearby town. Our men, the rescue team, were just on the other side. When he saw them, your brother went berserk, firing indiscriminately at everyone in his path." He stopped, assessing the impact on his listener. A cigarette appeared in his right hand, which he lit with a lighter in his left. A lighter with a "Ranger" imprint.

Chase compared the story Lamp told with the one he'd heard from Jackson. The two stories were consistent in certain respects, which was to be expected. When Lamp had described himself as Jared's commanding officer, he paid closer attention. To his face and to his hair. Instead of a tan, and dark hair, he saw makeup and a bad color job.

"They had to tranquilize Jared to take him down. When the tranquilizer wore off, your brother remained in a catatonic state, unable perhaps to accept what he had done."

Chase observed the man carefully, his lawyer's "truth sense" engaged. The colonel was good. He'd be convincing on a witness stand.

"The army takes care of its own," the colonel continued. "We created him and we took responsibility. Rather than court-martial him, we tried to treat him. Had him evaluated by our top docs. As a result or their evaluation, we've revised our screening techniques. A guy like him wouldn't make it to the next level any more. I doubt that gives you any great comfort, but I thought it worth mentioning. We put him in an experimental facility and kept a close eye on him. The alternative would have been to send him to Leavenworth on charges of murder.

"Bottom line, your brother is a sociopath. That's what the docs say. He's a danger to himself and others."

"Where is he?" Chase asked again. He considered the irony of both Jared and him being considered murderers. *Wouldn't mom be proud*. He waited for the colonel to answer his question, letting the time pass. A valuable prison lesson.

"I came here to see if I could help," he finally said. "I can have our doctors talk to your defense counsel. They'll testify on your behalf. They say there's a genetic link to this—"

Chase stopped him. "Wait a minute, Colonel. I thought you came here to tell me what happened to my brother. And I appreciate what you've told me. But do you mean to say you came down here to help convince a jury that it runs in the family? That my brother's a psycho, and I am too, and to please show pity on this poor family? That I'm not responsible for my actions?"

The colonel narrowed his eyes, causing a small line to appear on his face below his ear. *True colors indeed*, Chase thought. Well, at least he had another theory for the defense to offer Rufus. *Sure, I did it. But look at my brother. He's crazy—what possible chance did I have, genetically predisposed as we both obviously are.* The funny thing was, it might work. Of course he'd end up spending a good bit of time in a psych ward or hospital someplace, but it would no doubt be better than prison.

"Colonel, I'm going to assume your intentions were honorable in coming here. I've learned some things, assuming what you've told me is true." The colonel moved to speak but Chase overrode him. "The only thing I really want to hear is where my brother is. The last I saw him was in your precious 'experimental' facility, which is now a smoking ruin."

The colonel now regarded him with open hostility. His jaw stiffened and Chase felt he wanted to reach across the table and grab him. He actually hoped for a little personal contact. And he felt a pang of sympathy for his brother, being "molded" by this man.

"Mr. Riordan," the colonel said tightly. "You're an accused murderer. You have no right to demand anything of anyone. I came here to offer my help. And to find out what you knew. You're right. I don't know where your brother is. I hoped you might. And I hoped by sharing the facts and circumstances of his predicament, you might realize he'd be better served being in our care than on the loose. I can see my time has been wasted, although maybe I should have my conversation with the prosecution."

Ah, finally, the other shoe drops. Now Chase was in more familiar territory. The colonel had confirmed all the preconceived notions he had about the military. Finally he smiled.

"You're afraid, aren't you" he said softly. The colonel maintained a rigid expression. "You don't know where he is and you're afraid of what he might do." Chase nodded at the man's expression, confirming his speculation. "I'm sure you have good reasons for your fear, given the terms on which the two of you last met." For a moment the colonel's carefully guarded look disappeared and he saw the true face that lay beneath.

"Well, if you're afraid of Jared, and you're sure of your genetic link, I suggest you be doubly afraid." He couldn't help adding the last and enjoyed the expression that flickered over the colonel's face.

Colonel Lamp pointed a stiff finger at Chase. "You have no idea who you're dealing with. And I should point out you're in a prison cell, and from what I hear, you'll stay in one a long, long time."

"Bold words from someone uncomfortable wearing his own face or using his own name."

The colonel rose abruptly. His hands gripped the table and he rose to his feet. At that moment, when Chase felt his visitor about to erupt, the guard reentered the room, shutting the door loudly behind him. Chase leaned back in his chair, lazily observing the tightly wound man opposite him.

"Regardless of what you think you know, if you have any clue as to your brother's whereabouts, you should tell me. He's a danger to people around him and to himself."

"And to you, perhaps?"

The colonel stood, fixing Chase with a stare that no doubt intimidated his trainees. "Do they still have the death penalty in this state?"

Chase allowed him the last word as he walked out the door. Not a good enemy to have, but that die had been cast long ago. Sterling, or Lamp, or whatever the man called himself, had put his brother in the Pembrooke Institute. Unspeakable things had had been done to Jared at this man's instigation. Not exactly someone he could sit and break bread with.

He considered a meeting between Sterling and Wall. A match made in heaven. At least the colonel had confirmed what Chase had already assumed. That his brother was free. He hoped he'd at least gotten the money and the phone and was far away by now.

A few minutes after the colonel left, a guard escorted Rufus Agnew to the table.

"Chase," he greeted him.

"Rufus." They shook hands. "I see my visitor policy has been relaxed."

Agnew's brow wrinkled. "Not as of yet. The judge said he'd consider the request. Why?"

Chase told him about his previous visitor and brought him up to date on his brother's situation.

"Must have a lot of pull," he mused. "Although I don't know what he thought he'd accomplish by seeing you. Seems to me you got more out of the meeting than he did."

"I'm guessing he wanted to gauge what I knew. And I'm afraid I revealed more than I intended."

"No harm done, there, I imagine. Sometimes you have

to fire a shotgun into the tree, see what shakes out. Sounds like he has good reasons to fear your brother."

Chase shared the colonel's comments on his genetic heritage.

"A novel defense," Agnew chuckled, then quickly assumed a more serious expression. "Unfortunately, the latest news only supports the notion." He withdrew two items from his briefcase and set them on the table.

"First things first. This morning's newspaper. Read." He slid the paper to his client.

Chase read. By now, he was beyond shock, and the story, unfortunately, only confirmed what he had suspected. The murder of Josh Samuels was only a piece of a much larger investigation. The city would have a difficult time proving motive for that murder alone. Add Katarina Volkova, and perhaps Winston Reese, or Ray Lewis, Jr., and his motive became clear. Greed. He realized now what the D.A. had likely presented to the judge behind closed doors: "evidentiary" indications that the defendant might be charged subsequently with additional violent crimes that the prosecution was not as yet prepared to file. Chase had used the tactic himself in the past. The newspaper report confirmed his suspicions, but he was surprised and disheartened by the byline: Peter Jurgens, special reporter to the *Gazette*.

The article certainly didn't represent Peter's best work. Chase had read almost everything his friend had ever filed, appreciated the fluidity of his friend's prose, and the personal perspective he brought to each article. The story in the paper had a more formal tone to it, and Chase could detect nothing of his friend's personality. It confirmed, though, all of his previous suspicions. That the murders had been the act of a single individual. He got to the reference to DNA evidence and flashed back to Sterling's visit. Were he and Wall already in league with one another?

"So I killed Katarina, too," he said, wondering how his attorney would deal with this particular accusation.

Agnew smiled grimly. "Unfortunately, the prosecution

will use all your arguments from my trial in their favor."

He thought back to the case and realized the truth of his attorney's statement. He'd argued the killer could have been a tall, stronger man. Then remembered the black hairs found at the scene.

"Gives us a wedge, though," Agnew said, "to reopen the case. Wall may not be looking for Katarina's real killer, but we may have to."

"I always wondered about that 'older man' seen with her at the condo," Chase said. "I wish we could have found out more about the phones."

"I've given that some thought in the time since. Katarina never came out and told me she was seeing someone, but there were some signs. She showed me a new watch one time—a Raymond Weill—I didn't think much of it at the time, but it's not the kind of thing you buy yourself. And a diamond bracelet. Maybe the prosecution's theory was right—her lover killer her—they just got his identity wrong."

"Maybe," Chase said, doubting it could be quite so simple. "Let's follow up on that. Maybe we can find out where the jewelry came from."

"Good idea." Agnew slid over the second file. "On another subject, I had the pleasure of receiving a visit from a certain young lady who shares the name of one of our great presidents."

Reagan was in Piedmont? He looked up and saw Agnew's eyes twinkling.

"I can honestly tell you, Chase, that if I had a woman like that, I wouldn't be keeping her a secret. Oh, I might keep her under lock and key, but I'd be bragging all over town.

"As I said, she came to see me, very agitated. She insisted she had information you just had to have. Something you'd asked her to look into. So, being the faithful messenger boy, I came over as soon as I could."

Chase looked down at the file in front of him. It had a Georgetown University imprint.

"I hope you don't mind, but as your lawyer, I have an obligation to review all materials I might share with you. Or at least that's how I interpret my obligation. I take it this might be in support of the theory you started to mention the other day?"

"Sorry, Rufus, but at the time I thought that's all it was—maybe some kind of harebrained idea. After this article though..."

"No need to apologize. I admit, after reading it, it still sounded crazy to me. But it fits, somehow. Shall I summarize?"

Chase nodded, opening the envelope.

"According to this fellow here, the odds that all these murders were the work of separate individuals are less than twenty percent. He claims the circumstances of the cases support the theory that one individual killed all four victims. He began to look for patterns and found them in the way each of the murders had been organized. That's the word he used. Organized. According to him, all of the murders had a highly organized approach. All the murders were 'hands on.' Meaning no guns, no knives. But also all from behind, or from a position of concealment. He also claimed to see patterns in the type of evidence left implicating the suspects. Circumstantial, yet highly incriminating. A demonstrated knowledge of criminal investigative technique and basic forensics. The fact that all the victims and suspects were well-off upper middle-class individuals also played into his conclusion. Bottom line, one killer."

While the conclusion supported his own, it had already effectively been borne out by his arrest and the article in front of him. If Wall had evidence to charge him with Katarina Volkova's murder and others, that evidence had to have come from a single source, not multiple killers conspiring to frame him. Occam's Razor, the adage Wall had referred to in the Agnew case, led now to an easy conclusion. One person committed all four murders, and framed Rufus Agnew, Ray Lewis, John Tierney, and Kate Wagner. And Chase.

Chase scanned the materials, covering the arguments Rufus had summarized. The report covered seventy-plus pages, with footnotes referencing various criminal behavior studies, citations from the author's own previous work, and a few pages of numbers. Statistical calculations, perhaps. He pointed to a section.

"Any conclusions as to what kind of person might have done this?"

"Now that's the million dollar question, isn't it? Who dunnit? Colonel Mustard with a wrench, in the study?" Agnew sighed. "Unfortunately, that's were it gets a bit fuzzy. White male, well-off, age thirty-five to sixty-five. Strong ego, intelligent, successful in his field."

"Guess it won't help to give this to Wall, eh?"

"Afraid not. You fit the profile like a glove. He'd nail your coffin shut if he could share that document with a jury.

"Interesting point, though. Look at page twenty-two, halfway down the page."

Chase flipped forward, to a section headed "motivation." According to the doctor, motivation was difficult to determine. However, and Rufus had underlined the indicated sentence, "...the killer no doubt had clear and compelling motivations for each murder." He looked up.

"Not just random victims," he said.

"No. They're connected somehow, at least to the killer. The killer had motive to kill each of these people. He didn't just randomly pick his victims, or the people he framed. And he didn't do it just to get you. So if we can figure out what those motives were, we might identify the killer."

"Maybe we don't need to figure out all the motives," Chase said.

"What do you mean?"

"Katarina," Chase said shortly. "That one was personal."

Agnew nodded, his mouth grimly set. "And we know something the author of this study didn't know."

"What's that?" Chase asked.

"You hadn't been arrested yet." Agnew let the statement linger.

Right. The killer had motive for each of the murders. And had framed Chase. So logically…

"It's someone you know, Chase. Someone who knows you well. And has access to you."

A conclusion he'd sadly already reached.

After Rufus left, Chase sat in his cell considering the implications of what he'd learned. Someone highly successful, intelligent, with a large ego, and who had motive to do this to him. Someone he knew, someone close to him. A profile that fit too many people close to him. He remembered Castillo's reconstruction of the murder of Katarina Volkova, and tried to match the profile from the report with Castillo's conclusions.

What would Wall do with the information? Perhaps he already had it. If the professor followed the news, he might have felt obligated to share his findings with the prosecutor. Wall's reaction would be simple: why assume yet another killer, framing Chase on top of the initial frames? Why not assume Chase was the killer all along? It eliminated a whole layer of complexity. And they could ascribe a motive to him, greed, not to mention revenge against Wall. Whereas Chase had no clue as to the motive of his hypothetical killer. If he were Wall he might approach the case exactly the same way. Focus on the individual already in custody, rather than some mystical, unknown master criminal.

The thought made him think more kindly of his former boss. Perhaps Wall was as much a pawn in this case as Chase. And what of Jared? How could all this happen at a time his brother might need him most? Could Sterling be involved in some way? The mention of DNA evidence raised the question. The cases went back almost four years, before Jared's troubles began; still, he couldn't dismiss the notion. Perhaps Wall would only be able to connect Volkova and Samuelson, which would put the timeframe well in the midst of Jared's time at Pembrooke, and his involvement with Sterling.

One thought comforted him. If Sterling was in Piedmont, then he was probably hundreds of miles from Jared.

THIRTY-NINE

The Toyota Camry was the third car he'd stolen since he left the mountains. A roomy car, it accommodated his long legs, ran smoothly, and most importantly, blended in. He'd already passed two others just like it on the road. Pearl gray, clean lines, innocuous. He felt relatively safe with this one, as he'd swapped plates with an old Cadillac parked on a side street in Kinston. The Caddie had a thick layer of grime on it from the trees spreading above it, indicating it hadn't been moved for quite some time. Some retired person who didn't drive anymore. He'd debated driving straight through to Piedmont, but his survival instincts convinced him to take the more cautious approach. Despite having noticed no signs of pursuit, he knew Sterling wouldn't give up. He'd likely convinced the army that Jared represented a threat to national security, which meant local authorities throughout the area would be looking for him.

The dog in the back seat barked as if to remind Jared of his presence. Both man and dog looked a lot better than when they had first met. Their sojourn in the mountains had been good for them. They'd eaten well and had washed. Jared had shaved again after returning to the road, still sporting the goatee and moustache. He adhered to the philosophy, "hide in plain sight." With his mirrored Maui Jim sunglasses from the Sunglass Hut in Boone, he hoped he looked like a celebrity you just couldn't quite place. He still had most of the money Chase had sent and carried his weapons and gear in the trunk of the car. The former he'd obtained from a gun shop in Blowing Rock, which he had broken into early the previous the morning. He wanted to have a few specialty items, items he couldn't buy without showing ID and registering. He'd taken two deer rifles with ammunition, a 9mm Glock, and some camouflage gear. In his search he had also uncovered a crate of very illegal weapons, including land mines, and an array of specialty electronics, some of which he'd even used in Iraq. He'd taken as much as would fit in his trunk. With luck, the owner wouldn't even report the theft. The dog had proven a useful ally, serving as lookout. When he came out of the store, the dog was waiting for him, looking alertly around, taking his lookout job seriously. From then on that had been the dog's name: Lookout.

His circuitous route to Piedmont kept him off the interstates. He kept his eyes on the mirrors, making sure no one was following him. He wasn't one hundred percent yet, but close, and he hoped that was enough.

A newspaper lay open on the seat next to him. On the front page the picture of his brother stared out, a shot of him in his office, surrounded by police, his face a mask. The headline over the picture read "Killing for Clients?" with a lengthy article below under the byline Peter Jurgens, special to the *Gazette*.

Accompanying the article was an autobiographical sketch of Chase. A good boy gone bad. An interior spread of pictures chronicled his career, from a shot of him on the basketball court, obviously selected for the focused expression on his face, scraping for a rebound, to his recent appearance as Kate Wagner's defense counsel. The last picture was his mug shot. Another photo on a facing page caught Jared's attention, a photo of a group of men in front of the courthouse. He read the caption under the photo and identified Ken Wall, quoted prominently in the article; he committed the face to memory. Another face caught his eye. Chase's lawyer. A couple of places to start.

FORTY

"We need to talk about your future."

"My future? My immediate future includes getting nine holes in this afternoon, then dinner at La Strada. Perhaps a nice soak in the hot tub afterwards, if the company is right. Are you offering?"

Everett Litchfield, III calmly looked across the room at his son, who flipped through a *Playboy* magazine by the window. He tapped his cigarette into an ashtray on his son's desk. Ev kept removing the ashtray, but every time he did so, another identical one would show up in its place.

"I'm talking about your future with the company."

"Haven't I been a dutiful enough son, father? I beg your humble forgiveness."

"Don't be such a smartass. It doesn't become you. Perhaps I've been too soft. Let you run off to New York, play around with your grandfather's money."

"My money, father. My money. And I don't recall needing your permission to live my life," Ev said blandly, meeting his father's stare.

"Fine, your money. Money, I shouldn't have to remind you, which came from the blood and sweat of three generations of Litchfields. And I'd rather you not squander that inheritance to indulge your whims. It's time for you to take a more serious look at your future. With the company."

Ev put down the magazine. "I come to work, I sit on your executive committees, and I've even met with some outside investors. I smile, dress nice, and put on a good show. Isn't that good enough for you, father?"

"You damn well know it isn't."

"What more do you want, father?"

"I want you to take this all seriously. I want you to represent this company, represent our family. And I want you to go to Berlin and run our Eastern European operations."

Ev smiled. "You can't be serious."

"I'm dead serious," his father said. "After the merger with ARG Tobacco, we'll be the biggest player in one of the highest growth markets in the world. The ARG President will be stepping down and I have the opportunity to appoint his successor, reporting directly to me. I choose you."

"You know I have no interest in running anything. I came back from New York to be closer to my friends. I've participated in the company out of respect for my grandfather, along with other shareholders that want to see some changes. I've kept an eye on my investment. But that's as far as it goes. Those were my terms when I returned, and they haven't changed."

Everett walked over to the couch and sat down. "I'm afraid they're going to have to."

Ev sighed. "Father, empty threats don't become you."

His father smiled. "No empty threats, Ev. You *will* take this job."

"What about my investigation?" Ev asked with a smirk.

"You know damned well that whole investigation is moot," his father said, placing his hands on the desk and leaning toward Ev. "Or should I say dead." A corner of his mouth rose.

"Yes, and thank you so much for your concern about my friend being arrested for his murder," Ev responded, coldly.

"I'm sorry to hear about Chase," he said. "You know I always liked him. Or at least he was tolerable."

Ev smiled. "Spare me, father. Admit it. You're glad young Samuels is dead. And if Chase happened to kill him, good riddance, at least he took your problem off your hands. Why, I should think you'd be grateful. Pay him a bonus or something.

"As it is," he continued, "Samuels' death, fortunate as it might be for you, doesn't end the problem. I was tasked with finding out who might be leaking the information published in *The Gazette*. I don't believe a murder solves that. Unless you'd rather presume the individual doing the leaking is dead as well?"

Litchfield Senior considered his hands. "I've grown used to ignoring your attitude." He paused. "You feel the need to rebel against the family. I understand that. Even admire it to an extent. Believe it or not, there was a time I didn't want this either."

Ev raised an eyebrow.

"That's right. I wanted to start my own business. Your grandfather disabused me of that notion. I know you view the man as a saint, but he was a difficult father.

"So I do understand your feelings. A family business is a heavy responsibility to bear. But I've borne it, and you might want to reconsider your approach. It's one thing to talk and challenge your father. It's another to air our dirty laundry outside the family. That's serious business, Ev."

Ev considered his father. This was the first serious conversation they'd had in a long time. "So you know," he said.

Everett sighed. "I suspected from the beginning. I'd hoped it wasn't you, but I'm not stupid, whatever else you might think of me. I wanted you to make the decision to stop on your own. And I even think you would have. Nothing that Samuels printed caused any great harm. But you led him on and would have had to give him something more. Had to promise him, I suspect."

"And now he's dead. How convenient."

"Ev, sometimes the world shits on you and sometimes it hands you a gift. Samuels is dead. Does that solve the problem? Hypothetically speaking, whoever's leaking the information could find someone else to tell his information."

"Hypothetically?"

"Let's talk turkey, Ev. I want you to take this job in Europe. Take over the business there, grow it, show me, and show the company, what you can do."

"And if I don't?"

Everett stood up and walked over to the window. "You've built up some support in the company, son. People who share some of your concern for the health of our customers. But I'm sure you'd lose that support if they were to learn you were trying to sabotage the company, leaking information to the press. Come to think of it, I wonder what Rufus Agnew and your friend Chase would think if they knew you were Samuels' source."

"Probably that it was in character."

"Perhaps," Everett said calmly. "But I do have one more lever."

"What's that?" Ev said warily.

"While you've been gallivanting around town, hanging out with your friends, the details of the merger with ARG might have escaped your notice."

"Anyone who reads the paper is aware of it," Ev said woodenly.

"Yes, aware. But probably not familiar with the terms of the deal. Allow me to instruct you. First, the Litchfield Family Trust, of which I am the head, controls sixty-one percent of the shares of the company. Various private equity firms and investors control the rest.

"Second, ARG is publicly traded on the Frankfurt exchange. In order to do the deal, we have to swap shares of Litchfield for shares of ARG, effectively diluting our overall ownership stake. You might have missed the meeting where we discussed this. I persuaded the board we had to have this merger to survive. At the conclusion of the deal, the trust will control forty percent of the shares, ARG shareholders will control thirty, and private investors the rest."

"We're giving up majority control?"

"Majority control, yes, but we'll still be the single biggest shareholder. Your small stake might still be sufficient to retain a board seat, but your voting rights will be diminished. But that's not the issue at hand. In this stock swap, we are all bound by the securities laws of our country not to trade in our shares for the next twelve months." He paused to let the last statement sink in.

Ev stared at his desk, considering. "And dividends?"

"Ah yes, I can see you've reached the appropriate conclusions. We all had to agree to forgo dividends for the time being. I, as the CEO, will control whether and when we offer a dividend again."

"So you're blackmailing me? If I don't take the job, you'll cut me off? I have assets."

"Please," his father said with disdain. "What you have in your accounts won't support your lifestyle for another year. Of course, you could mortgage your house; I can't prevent you from doing that. Or that monstrosity you call a penthouse downtown."

"Chase needs me," Ev protested.

"I need you," his father said forcefully. "This company needs you. The hell with your friend."

Ev regarded his father coolly. "You may get me to do what you want. But never say that again."

"Fine. But I'm sure your friend Chase can fend for himself. Perhaps I'll pin a medal on his chest for taking care of our little problem. At least with Samuels dead, there's no one else who knows who his source is." He walked over to the door. As he exited, he turned one last time to his son. "Look on the bright side. You do a good job, you can come back to Piedmont and kick me out of the executive offices."

FORTY-ONE

Jared sat in the coffee shop on the first floor of the Piedmont Bank Building, sipping his black coffee and holding a newspaper. Behind his sunglasses he scanned the people entering and leaving. He'd thought he'd have to move after a while so as not to be conspicuous, but there were at least ten other people who'd been there longer than he had, sitting with their laptops, holding business meetings, reading. Rufus Agnew, supported by his cane and carrying a large briefcase, entered the building at nine sharp.

The law offices of Harrison Williams occupied the top two floors of the building. Accordingly, Jared had positioned himself to watch the elevators to floors twenty-six to thirty-two. Of the hundred-plus people who'd entered the building, only twenty-two had taken them. None looked like cops, either civilian or military. He tucked the newspaper under his arm and got up to go, just as an attractive black woman got off the elevator. He had noticed her earlier when she had come in the door shortly after Agnew, taking the same elevator. As she made her way to the exit, two men appeared out of nowhere. Trim, short-haired men, dressed in matching blue suits. With a start, he realized he knew one of them. The men hustled in her direction, one of them bumping into her just as she was about to enter the revolving door. Apologizing profusely, he distracted the woman sufficiently to allow the other man to catch up, a rat-faced man with short dark hair. Russo. He stood behind the woman, appearing to whisper something in her ear. Nodding, she left with the two men, one of them holding her arm as they walked.

Tracking their progress to the street, he noticed a white van parked with the engine running. Casually, he put his ball cap on his head, and walked out of the cafe. Keys in hand, he reached his own car, parked in a handicapped spot, and started the engine just as the van pulled away. Lookout barked behind him.

"Sorry, boy. Hope you didn't mind the wait." He pulled the car out of its space, keeping his eyes on the van. It kept to the speed limit and made few turns. He stayed a few cars behind, keeping his eyes open for any other vehicles: a trailer, or a lead. The van took a right, a turn leading to the freeway. Debating, he decided to continue the pursuit. He didn't know what the connection might be to Agnew or to Chase, but military goons in civilian suits abducting a young woman raised a clear red flag. Especially goons connected to Sterling.

On the freeway, the driver seemed intent on getting to his destination, and took none of the precautions that would have been second nature to Jared. He kept to the center lane, drove a few miles over the speed limit, and signaled a switch to the right lane, and the subsequent exit. Jared followed, now two cars behind, and tailed the van into a residential neighborhood with large wooded lots. There were houses still under construction, houses for sale, and empty lots. He dropped back to stay hidden on the straight road then drove past, looking down the side streets. He spotted the van pulling into a long driveway that led to a house set well back from the road, drove around the block, and stopped in front of a house with a for sale sign. He got out of the car, looked at the house, then walked carefully around the block. The van had disappeared, presumably into the garage at the end of the driveway.

Jared walked back to his car, then drove past the house where the van had pulled in. It was a ranch-style white house surrounded on three sides by heavy vegetation and trees: the only completed house on the street so far. With a driveway that led to a large attached garage. The shades were all drawn, but Jared continued past, in case anyone was watching from inside.

Making a note of the address, he drove back to town, and cruised past the city jailhouse, stopping at a distant spot in the parking lot. He wondered what his brother thought, sitting in a jail cell, charged with murder. The military man in him wanted to charge into the facility, free his brother, and drive off. He had no doubts about his ability to do so, given sufficient time and resources. But once they got into the car, then what? Pursued by a combination of civil and military law enforcement personnel, they wouldn't be safe anywhere in the country. No, they needed a more permanent solution.

He wanted to go back to Agnew's office; he needed to meet with the man, but he doubted the direct approach would work. For all the care he'd taken, he hadn't spotted the blue suits until the woman came out of the elevator. He couldn't risk being seen returning to the building. Well, there was one more person on his list.

The district attorney didn't keep a listed address, but it hadn't taken much to find out where he lived. A little time in the public library at an internet terminal and he knew what church Wall belonged to, what pre-school his children attended, and what charities he supported. He'd phoned the school and told them he hadn't received a copy of the latest school bulletin. They confirmed the address, told him they'd send another copy, and he'd hung up.

"You hungry, Lookout?" he said.

The dog barked.

"Me too. What say we go get a bite to eat and take a little drive?"

FORTY-TWO

Getting inside Wall's house caused Jared little more trouble than walking in through the front door with a key. He entered through a rear window after disabling the electronic system, routed through an exterior phone box. *Ridiculous.* The man didn't even own a dog. Dressed in a black sweatshirt and slacks with a pair of running shoes on his feet, he wandered through the downstairs, sticking to the carpeted areas to avoid hitting a loose floorboard. The family bedrooms were all upstairs; he'd watched as the shades were drawn, and the lights turned out hours before. Now all was still.

The ground floor consisted of a large kitchen and dining room, a formal living room, a TV room, and an office. The furniture and décor were relatively Spartan; more important to have the big house in the nice neighborhood, less important how it looked inside. In the kitchen, he opened the refrigerator and helped himself to a can of Coke as he looked around. Pictures of children covered the room; posed school portraits, as well as holiday shots including the whole family. Wall's wife appeared at least twenty years younger than he, the young children supporting the notion that this was a second marriage. The living room had contained a few photos of a much older girl, a daughter from an earlier marriage, perhaps.

Pausing to listen at the base of the stairs, he quietly crossed the foyer and entered the office, obviously a man's sanctum, with the heavy mahogany desk, twin leather wingback chairs, and a built-in humidor. The floor to ceiling bookcase took up an entire wall, although it contained only a few books. Instead, it displayed a collection of photographs. Wall with the Governor, Wall in the Oval Office, Wall with the winner of the Piedmont 600. A monument to himself. Some of the framed displays were letters and certifications. Jared was tempted to remove all of them, toss them into the fireplace, start a fire, and leave the way he'd come. He wondered what message Wall would take from that.

The desktop was pristine, containing only a computer, and a pen and pencil set. Not a speck of dust; he could see his face in the polished surface. The drawers were all locked, but yielded to his screwdriver. A few files, nothing of great importance. Personal correspondence, a few trade magazines, and a handful of bills. In the back of one of the drawers he found an old photo album, well worn. He sat down at the desk and leafed through it. Wall's current life might be on display throughout his house, but his old life was hidden here. Jared found more pictures of the young woman from the living room photos. As a baby, a young girl, celebrating birthdays, mom, dad, and daughter together—the mom a woman around Wall's age, grim faced and petite—graduation from high school, from college. Her diplomas were included in the book. Abigail Lynn Wall.

Toward the back of the book photos were missing; he could see the imprints where they had been. One photo in particular caught his eye: a barbecue at an outdoor park. He wasn't sure, but he thought he could pick out his brother at the end of one of the tables, his face smiling toward Abigail, who was making a face at the picture-taker.

Returning the album, he noticed a small envelope, the

size of a credit card. It bore the name of a storage facility, and contained a key and a pass code. Jared stuck it in his pocket and closed the desk drawers. Since the desk contained so little, Wall must keep most of his files in at work. Or in a safe. It didn't take long to discover its location; it was poorly hidden in the back of the closet. A recent model, it likely wouldn't take Jared too much effort to open, presuming he had the time and the tools. Today he had neither.

The clock on the desk said three-fifteen. He gave himself another fifteen minutes to look around. A door in the kitchen led to a basement, a large, unfinished space that held a few boxes, and a couple of tricycles. The garage contained Wall's Lexus, and his wife's Mercedes. Both leased, judging by the bills he'd seen in the desk. No yard tools, no lawn mower. Barren as the rest of the house.

He climbed out the window, closing it behind him, re-engaged the security system, and left the property. The neighborhood lay still and quiet; the lone sounds those of a sprinkler system watering a lawn a few houses down. Picking up the leash he'd left by a tree, he whistled. A few moments later Lookout rushed over from the yard next door. Jared clipped on the leash and continued down the sidewalk, a neighbor taking his dog for a late night walk. A few blocks later they reached his car, parked on a side street beneath a broken streetlight. Driving away from the neighborhood, he couldn't help wondering what a man with a four thousand square foot home and a near-empty basement needed with a storage unit.

FORTY-THREE

"Let's start again, Ms. Thompson. Why are you here in Piedmont?"

Reagan faced her questioner with barely concealed fury. "I've told you, Colonel Lamp. My brother lives here."

Lamp smiled. "Yes, you've been saying that. Although I continue to wonder at the family emergency that forced you to take such a sudden leave of absence. Your employer is most concerned." He poured a glass of water from a pitcher on the table between them and slid it over to her.

"You are not my employer. And I fail to see why my personal life is any business of yours. I am an agent of the FBI, not a member of the United States Army. You abducted me off the street, and I demand to be released."

The colonel pulled back the water glass and drank it himself. "Really, Ms. Thompson. We've been through all this. Abducted you? My men asked you to accompany them. A simple request."

A simple request, backed up by the name of Morris Stevens, the Director of the FBI.

"You'll be allowed to leave once you've cooperated fully. We are in the midst of an investigation that has national security implications. The FBI and Director Stevens have been informed of its scope, and have directed me to compel your cooperation."

In fact, Lamp had shown her a letter from Stevens, asking for her cooperation and telling her to consider herself under Colonel Lamp's authority for the time being. Cooperating was one thing, but he'd confiscated her watch, her cell phone, and had yet to let her make a phone call or leave the house. Two thugs guarded her at all times, even when she went to the bathroom.

"And I have cooperated," she said. "I told you I came to Piedmont to see my brother. He's running for Congress and needs my help. His wife contacted me and asked me if I could get away. It's fundraising season and they need help with the kids so they can both campaign."

"So you've said. And yet we found you at the Piedmont Bank building. Your brother lives in Gastonia."

Reagan sighed. "Must we go over this again? I flew into the airport here and had a few people to meet with in Piedmont before I drove to Lionel's house. Some loose ends from an investigation I've been working on."

Lamp opened a folder in front of him. "You're a government employee, Ms. Thompson. A good one, I understand. So I felt I owed you the courtesy of checking out your story. First, your brother has no idea you're in the area, or had any plans to come here." He held up his hands at her protest. "A simple phone call from an old college classmate did the trick. She's in town, trying to hook up, blah, blah, blah. Your brother informed her you were still in D.C. You'll be happy to know that even though the caller pressed, he didn't give her your phone number. Told her instead he'd be happy to take her number and pass it on to you.

"Second, I spoke personally with Assistant Director O'Keefe. So far as he knows, the only reasons you have to be in Piedmont are personal. No cases involving locals, no leads that he's aware of. So let's cut the crap, shall we?"

For the first twenty-four hours in the house, Reagan had

been willing to give the colonel the benefit of the doubt. In her ten years with the Bureau, she'd been involved in her share of investigations and with the new Department of Homeland Security, all the intelligence-gathering agencies were rolled into one and cooperation was the new name of the game. Lamp had introduced himself as a member of Army Intelligence, working with local law enforcement and federal agents to trap a Hamas cell operating in the area. Since Reagan had spent a good portion of the past year working on a similar case involving Hezbollah operating out of Denver, it made sense they'd seek her out. When they'd taken her phone, she'd protested, not quite believing the answer that they couldn't afford any leaks getting out as to their whereabouts. She'd written it off to army paranoia. Lamp had provided her with information on the Hamas operation and asked questions about the Hezbollah sting.

On the second day, however, the questions about terrorist operations in the U.S. gave way to questions about her personal life. Her suspicions turned to hostility and her thoughts turned to escape. Lamp wanted something from her. She didn't yet know what it was, but knew this was personal. It connected somehow to Chase.

"Colonel Lamp, I've worked dozens of cases during my tenure with the FBI. Obviously you've read my file, so you know that's true. I've specialized in money laundering and domestic funding of terrorist operations. Piedmont Bank is one of the largest financial institutions in the South. I've worked with officials there on a couple of my cases. You can check that out. Just because Assistant Director O'Keefe is not aware of any current work I'm doing with the bank, does not mean I don't have reason to be there. Does your boss know every single thing you do in your investigation?" She let the word linger.

Lamp smiled. "You're good, Ms. Thompson. Very good. And I've no doubt you can come up with a convincing account of your meetings at the bank. Maybe even give me a name of someone who might back up your story."

"It's no story, Colonel. And you've still failed to tell me

what connection my personal life has to do with Hamas operations in North Carolina. Or am I now under suspicion for funding terrorist operations?"

One of the men who'd brought her to the house came up and whispered in the colonel's ear. He shook his head. "My colleague suggests there might be other ways to get you to cooperate. I'm sure he doesn't appreciate, as I do, the strength of your character. You're a civilized woman, a black woman who got where you are by your own hard work and efforts. Mostly. I admire that."

"And I so much appreciate your admiration, Colonel. On behalf of my people, thank you. But you've yet to tell me what I'm supposed to be cooperating with?"

His hand came out of nowhere, a backhand slap across her face that nearly knocked her off the chair. She put her fingers to her mouth, feeling the blood trickle. Sitting up in her chair, she folded her arms and stared at her captor, allowing herself a small smile.

"Well, at least one of us is civilized. Shall we drop the pretense, Colonel? You don't care a lick about Hamas or terrorists. You're probably not with Army Intelligence. Care to tell me what you really want? Why you kidnapped an agent of the FBI?"

Recovering from his outburst from a moment before, Lamp stood up and walked over to a window, facing the front of the house. He pulled back the shade and looked out for a few moments. Then he gave an indication to the other man in the room, who left through the front door.

"You want me to be frank? Fine. I'll be frank. You think I'm playing some kind of a game here? I'm not. I am involved in an investigation. An investigation that involves you."

Reagan continued to sit with her arms folded, waiting.

"You've been meddling in something that doesn't concern you. Something that touches on national security. And the powers that be in Washington take these kinds of things very seriously."

"I work every day in the interests of this country, Colonel Lamp. Please tell me how that could possibly damage national security"

Lamp pointed his finger at her. "You've been looking at files. Top secret files that have nothing to do with any case you've been involved in."

He'd finally confirmed her suspicions as to why she was here. "Colonel, I've done no such thing. I have looked at nothing that's exceeded my security clearance. How could I? I can only access files my personal password or clearance will allow me to access."

"Don't be cute, Agent Thompson. You've been nosing around in army territory, looking for information. Did you think we wouldn't find out?"

Reagan stood up from her chair and walked around the table to face Lamp. He was tall, but only topped her by a few inches. "Oh, I'm not the one being cute here, Colonel. You want to be frank, fine. I have a friend who has a relative in one of your facilities. Only it's not supposed to be one of your facilities, is it? He asked me to find out more information about it. Not such an odd request, is it? You folks in the army sure haven't told him much, so naturally, he's curious. So what? I looked through a few files. I may be a better researcher than most, but I didn't find anything any other government employee couldn't have found. If you didn't want that information found, you should have done a better job hiding it.

"I have violated no law, have done nothing against the interests of the United States. I wonder if you could say the same. Now I demand you release me and let me get back to my own business."

Lamp looked at her, lifted his hands, formed a fist, and then dropped them, fingers still clenched. "Sit back down, Ms. Thompson," he said tightly. "You're not going anywhere. I don't care whether or not you think you broke any laws. And since we're being honest, let's acknowledge that your reasons for being here have to do with your friend's arrest on murder charges."

Reagan held the colonel's gaze.

"But let's put that aside. Your activities in support of your friend, the murderer, have brought you under suspicion by the Department of Homeland Security. Your so-called research brought you to my attention and I intend to fully investigate your motives and your access. Until I am comfortable with your answers, you will remain here."

"Under suspicion? For looking into the construction of a mental health hospital?" she said.

"Come now, Ms. Thompson. You've been digging into this for over a month now. By your own admission you're a good researcher. Surely you realize by now that Pembrooke's where we shipped all the prisoners from Guantanamo."

Guantanamo. "You mean…"

Lamp laughed. "You live in D.C. You've seen all the Committees, all the pressure to close down Git-mo. Fortunately, we've been planning this one for years. We built a facility up in the mountains, started moving prisoners there. Along with their… doctors. By the end of the year, there won't be any more poor souls being tortured in Guantanamo. Problem solved."

"So Pembrooke is a facility for terrorists?"

"You hadn't figured that out yet? Oh, not the hardcore operatives—the behind-the-scenes guys. The ones who know stuff. It's a win-win situation. The President does the humanitarian thing, closes down a hot spot and we move it someplace where we can get better access to medical facilities. You'd be amazed what we've learned already, the new techniques we're developing."

"Poor Jared," Reagan murmured.

"Now we're finally getting someplace. Jared. That should tell you something about the people you're helping. Jared Riordan was not at Pembrooke to recover. He has information we need, information involving a terrorist organization operating in the Middle East. And you've been helping his brother, and indirectly, him. Which is why I have the authority to keep you here as long as I need to."

"What do you want?" Reagan asked weakly. She felt a tremendous sense of sympathy for Jared, locked up with these people. Fortunately Lamp didn't seem to know about her online conversation with Chase about Jackson's visit, or her knowledge of what had really happened to Jared. That, at least, was something.

"Your help. Jared Riordan is an escaped convict, a threat to the security of this country. He is a danger to anyone he comes into contact with and I will do anything and everything I can to make sure he is safely recaptured."

"How can I help?"

"You told me you were contacted by a friend to find out more about Pembrooke. I want you to make sure your friend cooperates with us."

FORTY-FOUR

In contrast to his very public arrest, Chase Riordan's arraignment was almost a private affair. Expecting another media frenzy, he'd been surprised when the guards escorted him into the courtroom. Rufus Agnew, Ken Wall, the court reporter, and a bailiff were the only people present. Chase looked around, expecting the doors to open and the hoards to descend.

"No one here but us chickens," his lawyer said.

Chase raised an eyebrow as the guards uncuffed him and sat him in the chair next to Agnew. "Not exactly Wall's style," he whispered.

"I believe our distinguished opponent is a bit off his stride this morning."

"Oh?"

The bailiff announced the entrance of the judge and they all stood. The judge gaveled court into session.

"The purpose of this arraignment is to provide an opportunity for the defendant to enter a plea. Mr. Agnew, have you had the opportunity to review the complaint with your client?"

"Yes, your Honor."

"Do you waive reading of the full complaint?"

"We do."

"Mr. Riordan is charged with one count of murder, in the case of Josh Samuels. Is that correct, Mr. Wall?"

"It is."

"Mr. Agnew, how does your client plead? Guilty, not guilty, or nolo contendere?"

"Not guilty."

"Mr. Wall, in the preliminary hearing, you addressed the issue of special circumstances. I failed to note your addressing any of those items in the grand jury?"

Wall rose, shoulders slumped. "Your Honor, I believed at the time the original indictment would be amended, as I discussed with you, to include additional charges. Unfortunately, we were not able to fully satisfy the evidentiary requirements to bring the additional charges before the grand jury."

Rufus Agnew got to his feet. "I don't need to remind the judge it was the special circumstances that influenced the court's decision to exclude bail in this case."

Judge Grady Hoppin frowned. "Mr. Wall, you understand the position you've put me in. You informed this court, and apparently the news media as well, that you'd be charging Mr. Riordan with multiple counts of murder. Am I to understand you will not be filing those additional charges?"

"No, your Honor," Wall said. "We fully expect to file those charges at a future date. In fact, we're now working with the United States Government—"

The judge held up his hand. "This is not the time or place to discuss your strategy for the future, Mr. Wall. Although I'll be curious to learn what interest the government has in this case. What's before this court is the issue of the complaint as it relates to this case and the matter of bail. Mr. Agnew, do you have a motion?"

"Yes your Honor, I move that Mr. Riordan be released on his own recognizance, or at least with a reasonable bail."

"Your Honor, I object," Wall said.

"Your objection is noted. However, given the circumstances of the case, and the promises made to this court, I feel obligated to set bail in the amount of $750,000. Any objections?"

"No, your Honor," Agnew said.

"Now, as to the matter of trial, does the defendant waive speedy trial?"

"Your Honor, Mr. Riordan would like to proceed as quickly as possible in order to clear his name."

"Fine." The judge consulted his calendar. "As it happens, I have a block starting August 15 for two weeks. That should be sufficient. Trial is set for nine a.m. on that date."

Wall stood up. "Your Honor, with the work we're doing to assess the additional charges, that won't be sufficient time to prepare. I request a date later in the fall."

The judge smiled. "Mr. Wall, I'm sure you know the Speedy Trial Act better than I do. I don't have a great degree of latitude with respect to this matter. The defendant is required by law to have a trial set no earlier than forty days from arraignment, and no later than seventy days from that time. Today's the arraignment. The clock starts ticking.

"Now if you come back with additional charges you want to file, you can take them to the grand jury and we can meet back in court and go from there."

"Yes, your Honor."

The judge adjourned court, allowing Chase to sit a bit longer with his lawyer. Wall left quickly without a glance at either Chase or Agnew.

"Not a happy camper," Chase said.

"It's what happens when your mouth writes checks the state crime lab can't cash."

In spite of all his brash announcements in the media, the case against Chase for killing Katarina Volkova came down to the unidentified hairs and fibers at the crime scene. Without verification from a laboratory, Wall couldn't place him at the crime scene.

"Why the rush, though?" Agnew wondered. "And why

the sour face? He can always file the charges when he gets the results back. Consolidate the cases. No great loss from his perspective."

"Oh, it's a great loss, all right. He made such a big show with the serial killer angle and now all he has to show for it is a single charge of murder." Chase smiled wryly. "Listen to me. Only a single charge of murder."

"It might make our job easier, though."

"How's that?"

"The case Wall is arguing is strung together by a single motive. That you killed these people to gain clients. Individually, though, it's more difficult to prove that motive. If he can't bring in the other cases, he'll have a much harder time proving you murdered Josh Samuels. If we're only defending the one case, I'd say we have a pretty good chance. Although I admit your friend being the source for Samuels' articles presents a bit of a problem. Harder to argue the tobacco company did it if one of their own provided the information."

Chase nodded thoughtfully. He hadn't been entirely shocked when Rufus told him about Ev's involvement. It sounded like something he'd do––stick a finger in daddy's eye once again—but he had been surprised he'd lied to him about it. "True. But that presumes he can't pull any of the previous cases together in pretty quick order. DNA results should be back soon, he'll go back to the grand jury and we'll be back to square one."

"Maybe so. Might as well enjoy your freedom for the moment then."

"Hmmm?"

"Did you not hear that you've been granted bail? I've already made arrangements with a bail bondsman. He's waiting outside. Don't you want to see the sunshine?"

"I don't know about the sunshine, but much as I enjoy our time together, Rufus, I wouldn't mind seeing someone else's face. No offense to you, Sergeant," he added, turning to the guard at the door.

"None taken, Mr. Riordan," he answered good-naturedly.

"I see you're making friends," Rufus Agnew said. "That's always important in a new town."

"Stuff it," Chase said with a grin. "So why the grim face?"

"After the bill came back from the grand jury, I thought it a reasonable assumption you'd get out today. I tried to get in touch with a certain young lady. I couldn't find her."

Chase frowned. "Reagan?"

"After she dropped off the file, we had another meeting—she wanted to know how you were doing, whether the file she'd given me had been of any help. She left me a card with some numbers, and told me she'd be back in touch. I haven't heard from her since. I tried her, but nothing."

Reagan's absence troubled him. According to Agnew, she had come to Piedmont to be near Chase, to help if she could. *Besides, it's not like her not to answer her cell phone.*

"Odd. I'll try her when I get home after rescuing Garth from his own prison cell."

"Um, I hesitate to mention this, but as your lawyer, and as your friend, I'm afraid I must."

"What's that?"

"Surely it has occurred to you that the profile of the killer here fits your friends? I mean, they're all successful, athletic, they all have healthy egos, and of course, they're sufficiently close to you to know your comings and goings. And with none of them around at the moment, well, I've no idea of any possible motives, but—"

Chase held up his hand. "I know," he said softly.

"Just be careful. Keep an open mind. You've got a couple days, at least, make the most of them."

"I will. And thanks."

"Of course. I do know someone who's interested in seeing you."

"Who's that?"

"Esteban Riviera, with the Piedmont Police force. Friend of yours?"

Chase nodded.

"You going to need your lawyer present?"

"Steve's one of the good guys. He tried to help me before this all went down." Chase explained about Steve's warning to him. "At the time I didn't know what to make of it. Now it seems a bit more conspiratorial."

"That's the word for it, all right."

"But there are different elements here. I think we need to separate out the arrest and prosecution from the actual crimes. Much as I'd love to include Wall in a grand scheme here, I don't think that's what's going on. I get the sense he's being manipulated as well."

"I do admit, it's hard to buy him as the puppet master. Especially after his performance of late."

"Exactly. It's like he's been handed a gift that he really wanted, but can't quite take advantage of. Someone's pulling his strings. Someone who knows exactly which ones to pull and when."

"But even the string puller couldn't get the state crime lab to move any faster."

"True. So it's unlikely to be someone with the city. It's an outsider who knows how things work, who can affect things to an extent. Someone with access to my townhouse, to my calendar."

"You're forgetting one very important characteristic," Agnew said softly.

"What's that?"

"You've got a killer who's murdered at least four people that we know of. But take it a step further. He wants you to go down for his crimes. Maybe his intent all along. We're looking for a psychopath who has no qualms about killing, including young children. Yet rather than putting a bullet through your head, he chose to set you up. This is someone who wants you to suffer both personally and professionally. He wants to ruin you."

FORTY-FIVE

"Give you a ride?"

Chase looked over his shoulder and saw Steve Riveira leaning against a column.

"Better than calling a cab. Especially since I wasn't carrying much cash when they arrested me."

"I thought you might need some help navigating the crowds outside."

Chase could already see the cameras and reporters, held outside the building by a line of officers. "Any side exits?"

Riveira nodded toward a stairwell. "My car's at the bottom in the fire zone. There are some advantages to being a cop."

Reaching the car without incident, they hit the road unnoticed.

"Home?"

Chase rubbed his ankle. "Only place I'm allowed to go for now. Courtesy of the Probation Department." He looked at the back seat. "You think you could fit an Irish Wolfhound back there?"

"Long as he lies down. There's a blanket under the seat."

"Thanks."

"You know, those ankle bracelets are pretty easy to gimmick. I could show you if you want."

Chase laughed. "That's all I need my first day out. Thanks for rescuing me back there. You sure you should be associating with a serial killer?"

"I think I'll take my chances. You should know I'm armed though. Just in case."

"Wouldn't stop a mastermind like me."

Riveira turned to look at him. "Chase, if you did choose to kill someone, I'm pretty sure you wouldn't get caught."

"I suppose there's a compliment in there someplace."

"I mean, wetsuit in the garage, hairs, fibers, what have you all over the place. Really, quite messy."

"Don't forget the vial of drugs with my fingerprints on them found at Kate Wagner's place."

"In the vitamin jar? Yeah, that was kind of amateur hour, if you ask me."

"Let me ask you something?" Chase said. "You don't have to answer, I don't want to compromise you or anything."

"Fair enough."

"What brought me to the attention of the police? I can't imagine I'd be high on a list of suspects in a case like this."

"So far as I know, an anonymous tip."

Thought so. "What about Reese and Lewis? I'm not asking about me here. I'm wondering what the police did after Tierney and Ray were acquitted. What happened to the cases?"

He didn't answer immediately. Pursing his lips, he glanced over again at Chase. "Officially? Open cases. Unofficially? Tierney and Agnew committed the crimes, so why look any further. Prosecutorial error, you might say."

"But didn't you think it kind of odd? Didn't anyone consider the possibility that my clients were not guilty? Think about what that meant?"

"Hey, don't look at me. I don't decide this kind of stuff. Wall pushed hard for those convictions and he and the chief were in lockstep the whole way."

For some reason Chase believed the answer. Not a conspiracy, just general bureaucratic ineptitude. Why make problems? Better to sweep it all under the rug.

They were almost to the kennel when a phone rang. Chase looked at Riveira.

"Not my phone," he said, catching the look.

Surprised, he realized the sound came from his pocket. He'd forgotten he'd been carrying it when he'd been arrested.

"Hello?"

"Enjoy the open air while you can. Your free time isn't likely to last too long."

"Sterling?"

Steve looked over at him, a question in his eyes. Chase shook his head.

"Colonel Lamp, if you please. Listen carefully and keep your mouth shut. The only thing I want to hear from your mouth is 'sounds good.' Are we clear?"

"Why the hell would I—"

"Reagan Thompson."

He stopped short.

"You want her to be safe, you do what I tell you. I'll ask again. Are we clear?"

"Sounds good," he said.

"Better. You need to know I'm serious. About finding your brother. And before you get all high and mighty, making threats, you should know I'm holding her entirely legally. She's officially under suspicion for aiding in the escape of a threat to national security. And she's safe, for now. So long as you cooperate. Say, 'Sure, I appreciate that.'"

"Sure, I appreciate that," Chase repeated.

"Fine. Now we're going to meet. And you're going to tell me what you know. I'll be in touch. Oh, and sorry about your place." He hung up.

Chase put the phone back in his pocket, stunned. Sterling had Reagan. His mind raced as he tried to consider what options he had.

"News?" Steve asked.

He shook his head. "Ernesto, from the office. They're going to shut the office down for now, save money on utilities."

"Makes sense, I guess. Well, here we are."

They picked up the dog, happy to be reunited with his master. The ride back to his townhouse was spent in silence. Riveira occasionally tried to reopen the conversation, but Chase just stared at the road and mumbled responses.

"At least someone's cut your lawn," he said, as they pulled into the driveway.

"Neighbor kid," Chase said absently.

"You need any help getting inside? You seem a bit under the weather."

"Just tired." He grabbed the leash, let Garth out of the back seat, then stuck his head back in the front door.

"Thanks, Steve, I really do appreciate it. Sorry I'm not better company."

He laughed. "I think I'd be a little out of sorts if I just got out on probation. You're entitled." He grew serious. "Not sure what I can do, but if there's anything…"

Chase waved. "Thanks, Amigo. See you."

Entering the townhouse, Chase found out what Sterling had meant. The place was in a shambles. Books on the floor, pillows slashed open, the kitchen totally ransacked. He looked into the office. Files were on the floor; all the boxes from the closet had been emptied out. Sterling or his men had done a thorough job.

He sighed, picking up the picture frames, broken on the floor; the picture of his mother and father, and the picture of Reagan, which he kept in a desk drawer when friends were over. He slumped in his chair. Garth came up to him and put his head in his lap, begging for attention.

"Well boy, we have some cleaning up to do," he said. His thoughts were of Reagan, held by the same monster who had put his brother in Pembrooke. He felt out of his depth; wearing an ankle bracelet to monitor his movements, out on probation until the DNA results came back from the lab, his girlfriend held hostage to force cooperation from him, cooperation that might result in his brother's recapture. The phone rang again.

"What do you want," he answered in a tight voice.

There was a pause at the other end of the line. "Not exactly the warm welcome I might have hoped for."

"Jared?" It had been a long time since he'd heard his brother's voice.

"Better. I'll cut you some slack since you just got out of prison. I know from personal experience that's not the easiest transition to make."

He realized belatedly Sterling might be monitoring the call.

"How did you know—"

"I read the papers."

"Sterling's here."

"I know."

"He wants you. Bad. He's holding my girlfriend hostage, to give you up."

A pause. "Ah."

"You need to be far away from here. He might be listening to this call."

"Sounds like him."

"Just run and keep running. If I don't know where you are, I can't tell him anything."

"I ran once," Jared said after a moment.

"Jared, listen to me. I… know what happened to you. What really happened? I know what Sterling did. You can't let him get you again."

Another pause. "He won't."

"Good, so we're agreed. Get out of the country, or something. I can manage here. It's trial stuff. It's what I know."

"I'm not running away this time. "

His eyes welled unexpectedly. This was the most conversation he'd had with Jared since he'd left basic training. "I didn't kill anyone," he thought to say.

"I know that, too," Jared said, "I've got to go. Something I need to do." He hung up.

Chase stared at the phone in his hand. While he'd hoped Jared had disappeared, gotten far away from North Carolina, he felt comforted by his brother's words. He wasn't alone. He had family.

FORTY-SIX

There'd been no more calls since Peter left Piedmont. Which meant the caller had gotten what he wanted: Peter's name on the article branding Chase a serial killer. But he'd had to leave. He needed to look for answers. He decided to start with his son.

Myrtle Beach, South Carolina. Junior year. During their Beach Weekend following exams that year he'd met Gloria McMinn at Crazy Zacks. A local girl, she'd been fun, enjoyed dancing, and, at the end of a long evening, the two of them found their way to a secluded spot on the beach. He doubt he'd have remembered her last name if he hadn't received a letter from her, almost six months later. She'd obviously remembered his name. He remembered the shock he'd felt upon opening the envelope and reading its contents. Gloria was pregnant. According to her, she'd managed to shield her pregnancy from her parents; she hadn't gained too much weight and they never paid much attention to her anyway.

She'd arranged with a local attorney for a private adoption. The family would take care of all medical expenses and was making sure she had the best possible care. Her doctor had told her the child was a boy. The only purpose of the letter had been to request Peter's signature on a form consenting to the adoption. Numbly, he'd signed it and sent it back to her. And that had been the last contact they'd had.

He'd kept it to himself for five years. Five years during which he beat himself up over his inaction. Should he have gone down to Myrtle Beach, offered to marry her, kept the child? Or should he have offered to take the boy himself, and raise him? Finally, he'd shared his story with Randy and Ev during a late night out. They'd helped him come to terms with his decision. And rationally, eighteen years later, he knew he'd made the right one. If Gloria had wanted him in her life, she'd have offered him a choice long before the letter she sent. She'd been pregnant for six months and had chosen not to involve him that entire time. And, at age twenty, he hadn't been in any position to raise a child or take care of a wife. So adoption had been the right choice for everyone: for Gloria, for the baby, and for him. He knew the grief he continued to feel wasn't rational. He'd never even seen the boy.

There were two major hospitals in Myrtle Beach. In the second, Baptist Hospital, he got lucky. He was able to get a copy of the birth certificate. The name read "Baby Boy Mc-Minn, five pounds, eight ounces. Born February 17th, 1990." Holding the certificate in his hand, he imagined himself playing ball, going to the playground, doing things his dad did with him. Then the nurse at the hospital had asked him the question.

"Would you like the death certificate as well?"

Stunned, he reached across the counter, and picked up the second sheet of paper. "Baby Boy McMinn. Died February 19th, 1990." The nurse was sympathetic. The cause of death wasn't listed on the form, but it had been clear the baby had been born prematurely. Perhaps his lungs or his heart weren't fully formed. He grieved for a boy who had never known his mother, or his father, or a day in the park. It wasn't until he'd made his way back to the hotel that he did the math. If the baby had been born prematurely in February, he couldn't have been the father. He tried to understand what had happened, but knew he couldn't know the truth without tracking down Gloria. Perhaps she'd had a boyfriend, got pregnant, didn't want to marry him and didn't think he'd give up a baby for adoption.

For eighteen years he'd felt guilty for something that didn't have anything to do with him. And the caller had taken advantage. He'd achieved two objectives: he'd gotten Peter to write the article accusing Chase, and he'd made him suspicious of two of his best friends. Ev and Randy were the only ones who knew the impact Gloria's letter had had on him, how it haunted his dreams and waking hours. And of course, they were two people connected, as he was, to Chase. His best friends.

Now that Peter knew the truth, he doubted he'd hear from the caller again. And besides, there was nothing to hold over him anymore. Somehow he suspected the caller knew that he knew. It probably suited his purposes to get him out of town.

With Chase in prison, he knew he should call Lionel, but he couldn't bring himself to do it. Oddly, the only person he felt he could trust was Reagan Thompson. And she wasn't answering her phone. She probably felt betrayed by the article. He didn't blame her.

Who could benefit from all this? He stayed in Myrtle Beach, hanging out in the bars, walking along the beach, trying to puzzle it all out. Unfortunately, he hadn't come to any clear conclusions. Someone wanted people to think he'd turned on his friend. Who would care so much? Certainly not Chase. Being arrested for a series of murders had to be a bit more hurtful than any article in the paper. And all he'd written were the facts; the district attorney planned to bring additional charges against Chase, which in fact he had announced a few days later. He'd just done his job. And, he rationalized, he had extenuating circumstances.

He tried Reagan again and her voicemail picked up on

the first ring. He left a message for her to call him. Again. He checked his own voicemail. Paul Givens hadn't forgotten him. He'd called a few times, wondering when to expect the follow-up article. Peter put him off, telling him there'd be nothing new in the case until the arraignment.

The arraignment. He looked at his watch, checking the date. *Shit.* Had so much time gone by? Staring at the beer in his hand, he realized he couldn't remember the last time he wasn't holding one. Disgusted with himself, he hurled it far out into the ocean, earning comments and stares from the group of young men boogey-boarding nearby.

He walked back to the hotel, his body sluggish from his weeklong consumption and lack of exercise. Stuffing his clothes in his bag, he left the hotel without bothering to check out. Whoever the caller was, whatever role he wanted Peter to play, the answers were back in Piedmont.

FORTY-SEVEN

J ared lay perched in the branches of a giant oak, ten feet above the ground, obscured by the foliage and the night, watching the front of the house. He put the binoculars to his eyes, scanning the property. It was almost time for the security sweep.

Four hours of scrutiny had confirmed his earlier assessment. There were only two men in the house. Sterling's men. Jared couldn't fault the security arrangements. They could have no idea he saw them take the woman; it had been luck on his part. Given the location of the house, two men should have provided more than enough security.

Every thirty minutes, one of them exited the rear of the house and did a sweep, walking around the front, pistol in hand. The property was well-lit, and the expanse of lawn on all sides left little room for a full-on assault. He considered taking the man out, an easy shot. If the man inside, however, followed protocol, he'd hunker down and call in reinforcements. Jared preferred to remain anonymous for the moment. Sterling might or might not know he was in town, but he didn't want to so overtly advertise his presence. Yet.

He'd spotted the colonel for the first time an hour after

settling into the tree. A dark-colored Yukon had driven down the long driveway, parked directly opposite the front door, and a man had gotten out. He couldn't see him from his vantage point, but he knew who it was. Taking his usual paranoid precautions. He'd smiled, glad of the notion he might be in the colonel's head, and watched him leave an hour later. The car had driven almost directly under his position and sped away.

Russo came around the corner right on schedule, acting as if he hadn't a care in the world. Arrogant. Just how Jared remembered him. Acting as if he had the colonel's power and authority. He hadn't liked him in Iraq, but he was happy to see him here in Piedmont. Sterling had always favored men like him, loyal, but with no moral compass. They did the things that needed to be done, no questions asked. Without the benefit of the skills Jared and his men had acquired.

Such as patience. As soon as Russo turned the far corner, he climbed to the ground, leaving the deer rifle and the binoculars in the tree. He withdrew a gun from his backpack, a 9mm Glock, and screwed on a silencer. Cinching the backpack tighter, he began crawling on his belly toward the house, staying six feet off the driveway in the undergrowth. His green camouflage outfit, and the paint on his face helped him blend into the vegetation.

At the bottom of the driveway he saw a shade peel back and a head peek out. He stayed low, face down. He waited another ten minutes, listening for the sound of a door or a window opening. He heard neither. He continued around the back, framed by a dense growth of kudzu and weeds. Keeping under the level of the windows, he crawled across the flower-beds, overgrown with weeds, and reached the door, where he stopped and waited.

It had taken him twenty-two minutes to crawl from his concealed position near the road to this position. Eight minutes to go. At three-thirty a.m., the men inside would be feeling overconfident, bored, and tired. The one who stayed inside might be sleeping.

On schedule, the door opened and Russo stepped outside. He turned left, coming out the door. Jared sprang up behind him and grabbed him around the neck. He coldcocked him, and, as the man slumped to the ground, caught the screen door before it closed. He stepped inside, weapon at the ready. The house was silent, save for the hum of the air conditioner. A mistake. The sound from the cooling system would keep them from hearing noises from the outside. He stood just inside the kitchen and took a moment to allow his eyes to adjust to the light. Gaining his bearings, he saw a short corridor leading to his left. Probably where the bedrooms were. To his right he could see a dining room and the adjoining living area. Staying low, he crept along the kitchen floor toward the corridor. When he reached it, he carefully placed his left foot on the hardwoods, then the right. As his foot hit the board it gave off a loud creaking groan.

"Joe?"

The voice came from his right, just around the corner, near the front foyer.

Deciding he had no more time for subterfuge, he sprang from his position in the direction of the voice. He could make out the shape of a man standing near the door, hand on his hip. With no time to think, he barreled into the shape, knocking him to the floor. Jared used his bulk to pin him to the ground, grabbing at the man's arms, trying to get a hold of a weapon. A shot fired, but neither man changed position. Finally he was able to throw the man over on his stomach, pinning his arms behind him.

"You got handcuffs?" he whispered, pulling the arms tight.

"Yeah. In my bag."

"Where."

"Dining room, on the floor."

He jerked the man to his feet, pulled the gun out of its holster, and tossed it on the floor. Training his weapon on the man's back, he pushed him in the direction of the dining room.

"Let's go get them. You make a move, I shoot. Understand?"

The man nodded. Jared hadn't recognized him earlier, but if he worked for Sterling, he had to be dangerous, however inept he had just been.

They found the bag and the cuffs. He looked around, spotting a supporting column.

"One on your left wrist, the other around the column to your right." He secured the man with the cuffs, and then stood back.

"You," the man said, a venomous look on his face.

"Me." He bowed.

"You're a fucking killer."

"All evidence to the contrary notwithstanding?" he said wryly. "I'm sure if you wait here long enough, your partner will wake up and free you. Or your boss will when he gets back. Although I wouldn't want to be you when he finds out you let his prisoner go."

The man sneered. "I told him no way you'd be anywhere near here. He must know you better than you know yourself—said he knew you'd be around someplace nearby."

"Yes, well, he's had a long time to get to know me. Pass on my regards please?"

"You enjoy killing your own men?"

Jared stared the man into silence. He set off down the corridor, pausing for a moment to check that Russo was still out cold.

"Hello? Anybody out there?" A woman's voice.

He walked deliberately toward it, senses still on alert, checking for booby traps.

"I'm a federal agent!" the voice called again.

He smiled. Brother, you sure know how to pick 'em.

"I'm being held prisoner!"

Reaching the door, he called softly. "You might want to step clear of the door, if you're anywhere close." Counting to three, he brought his foot up, and broke the door in.

Inside the room, wrist chained to the bedpost, lay the same woman he'd seen abducted days before. Fully clothed, she looked haggard, but defiant.

"I'm FBI agent Reagan Thompson," she said. "I've been held here for three days, against my will."

"I know."

Her eyes wild, she looked up at him and focused. Scrutinized his face.

"Why you're—"

"In the flesh." He glanced down at the floor and spotted a pair of black pumps.

"I wish you had a better pair of shoes."

"Why?"

"We've got a bit of a hike through the woods."

She laughed. "Hell, when I was growing up I hardly ever even wore shoes. A little walk through the forest sounds pretty good about now." She reached down, grabbed her shoes, and broke off both heels.

He smiled, admiring her spirit. "Wish I could offer more in the way of transportation, but I had to park a bit up the road to avoid being spotted."

"You have to kill the guards?"

He cocked an eyebrow. "Why would I want to do that?"

"No offense, or anything, I just heard you were a—"

"Killer? Why does everyone keep saying that?" He helped her up from the bed, snapping off the bedpost with a kick to release her hand. He looked her in the eyes. "I've killed people. But I'm no killer. There's a difference."

"Sorry, I didn't mean—"

He held up a hand. "No apologies necessary. I can understand the confusion. We need to get out of here." He reached out an arm to help her up, but she shrugged him off.

"I'm okay. Let's go."

They retreated through the house the way he'd come in, stepping over the slumped figure of Russo. The other man continued his ranting from inside the house. He pulled a roll of duct tape out of his pack, and held it out.

"Care to help? I need to do a few things inside first."

"With pleasure."

As she starting pulling the tape, Jared slipped back inside the house. A few minutes later he was back. He did a double take.

"You use the whole roll?" Russo was bound mouth to ankles, hardly an inch of clothing showing.

"He wasn't terribly nice to me," she said grimly.

"Remind me not to get on your bad side. I hear you say your name is Reagan?"

"Yes. Wait. Didn't you know that?"

"As in Ronald?"

She sighed. "I had to have the only conservative black father in North Carolina. He served a tour in California when Reagan was Governor."

"Cute."

They made their way across the lawn toward the woods adjoining the property.

"Why'd you go back inside?"

He tapped the backpack. "Cell phones. I also disabled the phone system. I suppose I could have found out when the next scheduled contact was with their boss, but I didn't want to make it easy for them."

"Ten a.m."

"Hmm?"

"That's when Colonel Lamp said he'd be back. To see if I'd cooperate. You should know he might have the legal authority to hold me. At least he said he did, and it's possible he's right."

Jared snorted. "Lamp? That's what he called himself? You can be pretty sure if he's involved, there's little legal about it. He might cloak himself in righteousness, but he's a true son of Satan."

"You know him?"

"I know him," he said in a low voice.

"So how'd you end up rescuing me if you didn't know my name?"

"It's a bit of a story."

Panic washed across her face. "Is Chase all right?"

He helped her across a thick bush. "Last I talked to him," he said.

"He's out?"

"Arraignment was this morning. Yesterday, rather. D.A. filed charges on just the one count of murder, for now. He made bail."

She calmed. "Where to?"

"Someplace safe." he laughed.

"And where might that be? We're a couple of fugitives from justice, in case you hadn't noticed."

"I've been in that category a bit longer than you. Don't worry. I found a place."

FORTY-EIGHT

They pulled around a long circular driveway and swung to the back toward a multistory eight-car garage. Jared clicked a remote clipped to the car's visor and pulled smoothly into a space in the fourth stall. They were greeted by three vintage cars upon exiting.

"You're staying here?"

"Not up to your usual standards?"

Reagan looked around, her eyes wide. "Isn't that the Batmobile?" she asked.

He turned around. "One of them."

"Yours?"

He laughed. "Sure, I'm secretly a multimillionaire, I joined the army for kicks." Grabbing his backpack, he escorted her out of the garage.

"You have his sense of humor," she said shortly.

"Chase has a sense of humor? I hadn't noticed."

"You're doing it again."

He sobered. "Sorry. It's just I haven't seen that side of him in quite a while." Reaching into his backpack, he removed a key and inserted it into the lock. A security beep sounded.

Reagan looked at him.

"No worries," he said, walking over to a console on the wall. He punched in a few numbers and the beeping ceased. "Always helps to have good security." He draped his jacket over a large ceramic horse.

He saw the question in her eyes. "Friend's house. Well, not a friend of mine, but same thing. Owner's out of town." Tossing the backpack onto a chair, he led them into the living room, a cavernous room that resembled the lobby of a five star hotel. Removing a large box from a long leather couch and setting it on the floor, he flopped down into the cushions.

"Take your pick of bedrooms. I haven't checked them all out." He nodded toward the grand staircase that arose from the middle of the room. "Might be good to get some sleep."

As he said that, Reagan yawned. "I am tired. But shouldn't we call someone?"

"It's after four in the morning. Chase is asleep. Well, maybe not, but his phone is bugged. And as you reminded me, you're a fugitive. How loudly do you want to announce your freedom?" He saw the look in her eyes.

"Maybe we should drive over and wake him up."

"At least four people are watching his townhouse. Wouldn't be easy, with the two of us."

"Army people, or Wall's?"

A good question. "I don't know," he said kindly. "Best thing we can do right now is get some sleep. We can think with clear heads in the morning."

"You have a plan?" she said, the hope in her voice evident.

He cocked his head and returned the yawn. "I have a few ideas. You really a federal agent?"

"FBI."

"You any good?"

She looked down at him, narrowing her eyes. "Well, I think I'm—"

"No false modesty. You any good?"

"Damn straight."

"You know some people you can trust?"

She nodded.

"Good," he said. "Now, if you're not going to bed, why don't you tell me what went on in that house."

For the next few minutes, Reagan told him about the past few days, from the moment she'd been approached. She related the conversations with Lamp, the threats, and the charges.

"Lamp said you were a traitor, a threat to national security."

A cold smile crossed his face. "More like a threat to his personal security."

"I didn't believe him. Chase told me something about what really happened," she said softly.

"No way he could know what really happened. Only one other person knows that and I doubt Sterling's found him yet."

"What makes you say that?"

He shrugged. "He wouldn't still need me if he had."

Reagan sat down in a large wingback chair against the wall under a large portrait. "I think I know that guy," she said, glancing up.

"He's got one of those faces," he said absently.

"What did happen? If you don't mind asking."

Considering, he put his hands behind his head. Looked at the portrait of Everett Litchfield, II.

"I don't mind," he surprised himself by saying.

He'd never had the chance to tell the story to anyone. He told of events in Iraq from the beginning. When he finished, he sat back, surprisingly relieved at the opportunity to speak with someone. He realized it had been a long time since he'd even had a conversation with a sympathetic individual.

"That's why you were at Pembrooke?" she asked, compassion in her voice. "Why didn't he just kill you?"

"Two reasons. I suspect too many people knew I'd returned alive, and he needed a fall guy."

"How'd he get the doctors to go along with it?"

"Doctors?" he snorted. "I doubt it took much. Sterling's a pretty powerful guy. He has friends all over the place."

"Wait a minute. Lamp—"

"Is Sterling."

"Right." She'd just made the connection.

"Sterling doesn't just want me just because I know what he did, though."

He looked over at Reagan, who raised her eyebrows. "I guess he didn't like you beating the crap out of him either."

"No, it's not that," he said, "although that was fun. He thinks I can help him find Al-Tariq."

"And can you?"

"If I could go back to Iraq, and if Al-Tariq is still alive, perhaps I could find him."

"It's a Catch-22," she said, frustrated. "Unless we can prove he's the bad guy, he's the good guy."

"But I don't need to find Al-Tariq."

"Why's that?"

"Al-Tariq gave me all his files."

"Well get them! Give them to me, we'll nail the son-of-a-bitch."

"I wish it were that simple. I don't know where they are."

"So why not go to the press, or the Judge Advocate General?"

"I'm an escaped felon. An ally of terrorists. Probably certifiably crazy. Without proof, I couldn't get an audience with a busboy, let along a JAG lawyer."

"I could."

Jared smiled thinly. "Your credibility isn't much better than mine, I'm afraid. If what you said was true."

"Damn."

The grandfather's clock in the hallway chimed five o'clock, reminding Jared how long he had been awake. How tired he was. He wished he had another few months to recuperate, to rebuild his strength. His reflexes were good, but his joints ached, his muscles were tired, and his energy felt sapped from the events of the day.

He turned to Reagan, who was blinking her eyes, struggling to stay awake in the chair. She smiled sleepily.

"Thanks," he said.

"For what?" she said, yawning.

"For worrying about me, about my problems. I know you have other things on your mind."

"It's not just your problem. He kind of inserted himself into my life as well. Quite forcefully."

He nodded. "I know. But all the same…"

Lookout barked twice and ran into the room, looking over at Jared before settling on a Persian carpet in front of the massive fireplace at the end of the room.

"You dog-sitting?"

"I'm not sure who's watching whom," he said. "But he's been good company." He stood up. "We'd both better get some rest. I'm going to sleep in the downstairs bedroom. You need anything, let me know. I think the bathrooms are all pretty well-equipped."

Reagan nodded and started to unfold herself from the chair.

Jared picked up the box on the floor and walked toward the downstairs master bedroom.

"What's in the box?"

A tired smile came over his lips. "Some pretty interesting shit."

FORTY-NINE

Restlessly stirring in bed, Chase heard Garth barking downstairs. He peered through the shades and spotted two photographers snapping photos, perhaps waiting for him to emerge in the morning. They had a long wait ahead. Stretching, he went downstairs into the kitchen, pulled a beer out of the refrigerator, the only thing that hadn't spoiled, then sat down on the floor of the living room against what remained of the couch. He petted his dog, surveying his earlier efforts at cleanup.

In a corner of the living room, he'd stacked the broken, irreparable items. Picture frames, torn clothing, the remains of the coffee table, books with torn spines. The D.A. had executed a search warrant the day he'd been arrested. Chase hadn't been able to return to the house since, so he had no clue how much of the damage had been done by Wall and how much by Sterling. If the district attorney took everything that might be evidence, what else remained? What was Sterling looking for?

His mind had been muddled by his time in jail. Smacking himself on the head, he went into his office. Earlier he had gone through his files spread out all over the office floor, but had noticed nothing obvious missing. His photo albums and books had been ripped, but the purpose seemed to be wanton destruction, rather than careful scrutiny.

He opened the top desk drawer. The photo of Sterling was missing. Colonel "Lamp" covering his tracks. Chase realized he now had no proof Sterling even existed. Who would believe him if he reported the incident? Steve Riveira, certainly. But what would be the point? It would just create another excuse for the police and the district attorney to return to his house. They might wonder the same thing he did; what was the perpetrator looking for? What could Chase be hiding? Wall had mentioned working with the government at the arraignment. That meant he'd met with Sterling. How closely were the two allied? Concerned about Reagan, he took some comfort from the fact Sterling wanted something from Chase and would lose what leverage he had if anything happened to her. Still, it pained him to think of his girlfriend in the hands of a man like Sterling.

Garth barked again. He walked over to the window and looked outside. This time he didn't see anyone. The photographers must have grown tired of waiting for him to come outside. His dog paced back and forth in front of the door, growling. On alert, Chase went into the kitchen to get his gun. He reached up into the cupboard. Found nothing. They'd taken it as well.

He looked over to the front door and saw his dog settled down, ears pricked. Of course he knew what they were after. Back in the office, he looked to the shelf where he'd placed his brother's box. The one with Jared's medals. He moved his hands around to be sure, then stood on a chair to get a clear view. Gone.

They'd taken all the things Jackson had given him. The only connection to his brother in the army. They were looking for the disk.

It occurred to him there might be another reason they'd gone through his house. A careful search of his office yielded two small black buttons, one affixed to the underside of his lamp and the other to the back of his fax machine. He had some experience working with electronic surveillance devices from his time as a prosecutor. One of his cases had involved an undercover cop who had infiltrated a local drug ring. He'd had to explain the workings of the various bugs involved to the jury. These were smaller than the ones he had worked with, but resembled the passive listening devices they'd planted in the gang leader's house. Bugs that broadcast when someone spoke but were dormant otherwise, making them difficult to detect via electronic means.

A search of the living room, both bedrooms, and the kitchen revealed four more, two identical to the ones found in the office and two others that resembled watch batteries. Six bugs. Along with whatever else might be better hidden. He considered looking further, but decided there'd be no point. If Sterling wanted to listen, he'd listen. So far all he could have heard would be his end of the voicemails he'd left for his friends. And Jared's call. About to grind the bugs under his heel, he changed his mind and replaced them. Perhaps he could use them to his advantage.

He laughed, realizing the ludicrousness of the thought. His advantage? The bleakness of his situation overwhelmed him. Confined to his neighborhood, stalked by paparazzi waiting for him to leave the house, accused of multiple murders, his friends not around, his brother and girlfriend's lives at risk from a homicidal maniac, and he had no weapon. Not to mention he'd probably return to jail as soon as the lab results came back.

Look on the bright side. His brother hadn't been captured. Yet. Even in the hands of Sterling, Reagan was probably all right. For now. He had his health. It was a short list. The phone rang. He looked at his watch, 9:00 a.m.

"Hello?"

"You have a good night?"

Sterling. "Where's Reagan?"

"In time. Your lady is fine, for the moment, and she'll stay that way, so long as you cooperate."

"You know, kidnapping is a federal offense. It doesn't matter whether you're in the army or not," Chase said coldly.

"Kidnapping? Reagan Thompson is in my custody, with the support of her superiors. Impeding an investigation, and aiding and abetting in the escape of a dangerous criminal. Those are serious crimes."

Chase snorted. "You don't know the law, do you Sterling? Jared wasn't convicted of anything. You never held a court-martial. Aiding and abetting doesn't exactly apply here."

Sterling laughed. "I forgot you're a lawyer. No matter. The FBI didn't question it."

Because they don't know the truth, Chase thought. *Why would they assume a Special Forces colonel would lie to them?* All Sterling had to do was say the word terrorist and the agency would jump to help. "I'm not the FBI. You're holding her illegally. I don't care what paperwork you have. You can't prove your case and the government won't take it lightly when they learn what you did."

The jocular voice at the other end of the line turned cold. "The operative words here, Riordan, are 'holding her.' You don't need to give a shit about the legal niceties of all this. Cooperate and I'll release her. You can go back to your cell, I'll leave town, and you can cry all you want. I'll be long gone. But I doubt the words of an accused murderer will carry much weight."

That much might be true, but Reagan could make a lot of trouble for Sterling. Which caused him to worry for her safety. Could Sterling afford to let her go?

As if reading his thoughts, Sterling said, "And don't worry about your girlfriend. When this is all over, I'll report back that this was all a mistake, that Ms. Thompson cooperated in our investigation, which helped us nab the real culprit. With her safe and sound, there won't be much of a case to make. And of course, we'll have your brother to ensure your continued cooperation."

There was the crux of the matter. He couldn't give up his brother. But he couldn't leave Reagan in Sterling's hands either. He had to stall for time.

"So what do you want?"

"The whereabouts of Jared Riordan, of course."

"And what if I don't know where he is?"

"I'd be surprised if you did know. But he'll come to you. You can make him come to you. All I need is a little advance warning. We'll be waiting for him. And as soon as we have him in custody, we'll give you back your girlfriend."

"That's not good enough," Chase said. "How do I know she's okay? Let me talk to her."

"I'm afraid that's not possible at the moment. However, I'll be seeing her shortly. I can arrange to have her talk with you. Briefly. As a token of my good intent."

A burst of static came over the line and Chase had to hold the phone away from his ear for a moment. When the burst died out, he returned the receiver to his ear.

"Hello?" Sterling said. "Are you still there, Riordan?"

"I'm here," said a voice that sounded like Chase, before Chase could say a word.

"Are we clear on the next steps?"

Chase was about to answer, but was interrupted again. "Not entirely. So you're to call me shortly to let me speak with Reagan?"

Static intermittently interrupted the call. "If you're trying to trace this call, you won't have any luck," said Sterling after a moment. "You can keep me on the line all you want, you'll never find me."

"I sort of figured I'd let you come find me," came the voice. "Isn't that the whole idea?"

"Who is this?"

"Come now, Colonel. After all the time we spent together, you don't recognize my voice?"

"I don't know what kind of game you're playing, Riordan. If your brother is there, my team will be on you in minutes. You're putting Reagan Thompson's life at risk here."

"Jared?" Chase said.

"No worries, Bro." Then to the colonel, "I have to say, though, your threats are a bit hollow."

"I'm warning you, Sergeant. You're still under my command. You turn yourself in or—"

"Or what, you capture me, court-martial me, send me back to what's left of the Institute, or to Leavenworth? We both know that will never happen. As I said, your threats are somewhat hollow."

"Jared, he's got my girlfriend."

"Colonel, is that true? Did you capture my brother's girlfriend to try and get to me? Shame, shame."

"You should know me well enough to know I don't make threats." The colonel's voice was tight.

Chase worried that his brother's baiting might make the colonel mad, or at least madder than he already was.

"Does 126 Lake Drive ring a bell?"

Silence.

"That is the address of the safe house, isn't it Colonel? What's the matter, cat got your tongue?"

He heard a click.

"Colonel Sterling? Jared?"

"I'm still here."

"Jared, what's going on?" Chase said.

"I'm sorry. I got a bit caught up renewing acquaintances with my old boss. Reagan is fine. She's with me. I'd explain more but I don't have Sterling's sophisticated equipment. He's probably trying to trace my end of this call as we speak. Suffice it to say she's sound asleep right now, unharmed. Angry, more than anything else. I can see why you like her."

Relief swept over him. Reagan was safe.

"I've got to go. I'll be in touch. And don't worry, she'll be safe."

He hung up.

An interesting turn of events. Jared had stolen Reagan

out from under Sterling's nose. Eliminating whatever leverage he had over Chase. But only increasing the colonel's desire to find Jared. And when he found Jared, he'd find Reagan.

Fifty

J ared replaced the headset and unplugged it from the receiver. Amazing what you could buy at a Radio Shack these days. He stretched, still tired. Three hours of sleep didn't quite cut it. He knew the colonel would make the call—he just wasn't sure whether it would be before or after he saw Reagan at the safe house. Sterling had been overconfident.

But now he faced the problem of not knowing Sterling's location. While the colonel would be looking for him, along with whatever men he could add to the task, Jared could leave or lead him on a chase. But that wouldn't help his brother.

The box sat next to the bed. He pulled out the papers he'd found in Wall's storage facility. An interesting place. Rather than the attic-like profusion of boxes and garage sale items he'd expected, he'd found a bizarre tableau: a bed made up with a multi-colored pastel comforter; a bookcase, full of children's books; dolls arranged on a bureau; pictures on the wall, some juvenile, some quite good, all signed "Abby." His daughter's bedroom, recreated in a self-storage facility. Two chests of drawers held girls clothing: sweaters, blouses, most for a young girl, but some for a teenager. One of the drawers, though, held the contents of the box now beside him. Papers, including newspaper clippings, and a death certificate. Obviously wife number two didn't want any reminders of Wall's life before they'd met. Or of his daughter who had killed herself.

Abigail Lynn Wall. Died, September 23rd, almost five years ago. Cause of death? Well, it could have been the fall onto the highway, or the dozens of cars that struck her after she hit the pavement. Or it could have been the bottle of sleeping pills she'd taken before taking a header off the bridge over the interstate. Jared, used to death, still cringed when he read the account of her suicide in the newspaper. Her jump off the bridge had created a traffic jam that backed up the highway for over two hours. Her body had no doubt been a pulpy mess when the ambulance and the coroner finally arrived. No wonder Wall had come unhinged. Jared remembered his own grief, his own breakdown when the police arrived at his apartment in the city and told him of the accident that had taken his mother and father's life. He'd followed them zombie-like to the morgue where he identified the bodies.

Wall no doubt performed a similarly horrible function. His only daughter, the apple of his eye, crushed, lying on a slab in the morgue. How had he reacted? That was the time Chase had left the office and set up his own practice. He remembered the brief postcard he'd received from him at the time. "Leaving the D.A's Office. Picture me as a defense attorney?" He'd wondered what had happened. Now he understood. Particularly when he found the letter.

He pulled out the letter he'd read the day before, when it had spilled out of the pile of papers he gathered. It was addressed to Abby, on Chase's stationery.

"Abigail:

I know this is a difficult time for you. This isn't what either of us wanted, what we expected to happen. But it doesn't have to be the end of the world. We both have our lives ahead of us, and, I think you know in your heart, there's only one real solution here. You know I'll help you with this. I know, in spite of what you've told me, that you don't really want this baby. Neither of us is ready for this. We've had some good times together, but we both know that's all it was.

I've identified a clinic. They're reputable, they work with a lot of young women, and they'll take good care of you. Of course I'll pay for everything, don't worry about that. Keep your spirits up, and we'll get through this together.

Love,
Chase

The date on the letter was September 22nd, the day before Abby's death. The fact the letter was in Wall's possession spoke volumes. It explained Chase's career change, and it explained why Wall had held him responsible. Had it been enough to ultimately drive him to frame his brother for murder? Jared knew what he had done when he'd discovered the truth behind his parents' death. Had Wall instead bided his time, creating a more torturous scenario to not just kill Chase, but make him suffer to ruin him completely?

Chimes sounded throughout the house. It took him a moment to place the melody, and he laughed, remembering the car in the garage. The Batman theme. He cracked the shades in the master bedroom, but didn't have a view of the front. The chimes rang again.

Reagan came running down the stairs calling his name. "Jared, is everything all right?"

"Just the doorbell," he said, walking out of the master bedroom.

"That's a doorbell?" She looked over at the front door, then back at Jared. "You expecting anyone?"

He shook his head, went back to the bedroom, and returned with a gun, sliding in a magazine.

"Anyone know you're here?"

Again he shook his head. "Not even the owner," he said.

Motioning her to stand back, he walked over to the door.

"Maybe they'll go away if we don't answer it," she said. As she spoke, the dog barked.

He peered through the peephole, and saw a medium-sized guy with sandy hair.

"Ev, you in there?"

Reagan walked over to stand behind Jared. "I recognize that voice," she whispered.

"Peter, is that you?"

A pause, then, "Reagan?"

Shaking his head, Jared opened the door, admitting their caller. As he walked in, Jared had a recollection of a crowd of guys around Chase in college. *Ah. Peter. The journalist.* He'd read his article. Keeping the gun behind his back, and standing behind the door, he allowed Reagan to greet him.

"What are you doing here?" he asked, "I've been trying to reach you." He must have noticed her eyes, because he turned around. A puzzled look came over his face.

"You're—"

"Peter, this is Jared, Chase's brother."

He snapped his fingers. "Right. I thought you were in Afghanistan."

Jared looked at Reagan with a curled eyebrow.

"He didn't tell many people about your—change in assignment," she explained.

"Nice to meet you," Jared said, holding out his hand.

They shook then moved into the living room. Peter was obviously familiar with the place and flopped down on a chair in the corner.

"Where's Ev?"

Reagan looked at Jared. He shrugged.

"He's out of town," she said, still staring at him.

Jared sat down next to Peter and Reagan took the couch.

"If he's out of town, what are you two doing here?" He looked at Reagan. "I've been trying to get in touch with you."

"I've been a bit indisposed," she said. "Apparently Ev is letting Jared have the use of the place while he's away." Jared avoided her eyes.

"I didn't know you two knew each other," he said. "You and Ev, that is."

"We don't."

Peter looked back and forth between Jared and Reagan, clearly confused. Reagan smiled at him.

"Jared's in town to help Chase. He needed someplace quiet to stay, and with Ev out of town…"

"Makes sense," Peter said. He turned to Jared. "Are you on leave?"

"In a manner of speaking," Jared said with smile.

"You wrote the article," she said to Peter.

"Hmm?"

"The article. The one we were talking about after you met with Wall. I thought you'd decided not to write it?" Her tone was accusatory.

Peter didn't meet her eyes. Reagan waited him out. "Okay, I wrote the article. I thought about what you said, but I had other pressures to deal with. And I only told the truth. Wall *did* tell me those things. He planned to charge Chase with the crimes. I reported that. I didn't make any judgments. That's what news is," he said.

"But you had to know Chase would see the article, would see your name on it. How do you think he felt when he saw that? Accused by his own friend?" Her tone had softened somewhat, but she wasn't letting him off the hook.

"I know," he said, hanging his head. "But as I said, I had other things to deal with." He looked up at her, meeting her eyes. "I left town. I've been away for over a week. But I came back, to help. That's why I'm here. I went to Randy's, but he's away, Lionel's on the campaign trail, so I came here."

Reagan's eyes softened. "I'm glad you came back. I know Chase will appreciate it."

"If he's still talking to me," Peter said.

Jared followed the exchange. He turned to Peter.

"Tell us about this other 'pressure,' I think you said."

Peter sat still, eyes lowered. He sighed, and turned to Jared.

"It all started with a phone call."

He told his story, starting with the first call and then the threat.

"When I got the call about the trial, I was relieved. But when Chase was arrested, it was too much of a coincidence. So I drove down to Myrtle Beach." He described his trip, what he'd discovered.

"It still doesn't make sense. I thought I had a son. But apparently, I never did."

Reagan looked at him with sympathy.

"So why would the caller insist he had your son?" Jared asked.

"Don't you think I've asked myself that? I don't know," he practically shouted. "But he didn't. That's the point. He didn't, but knew that I would worry about it. So much so I'd do what he told me to do." He paused. "And I did. I'm sorry, but I did."

Reagan walked over to him and took his hand. "I don't blame you, Peter. Chase wouldn't blame you either. This is not your fault. Someone played you."

"Someone who knew enough about you and about the baby to make it work," Jared said. He walked into the bedroom and returned with a piece of paper in his hand. He handed it to Reagan. She read down, her brow furrowed, eyes narrowing as she got to the bottom.

"But Chase wasn't the father," she said to Jared angrily, when she finished.

He considered her. "Are you sure of that?"

Reagan handed him back the letter. "Of course I'm sure. Does that look like something Chase would write? A typed letter? To his girlfriend? And look at that signature at the bottom. Does that look like Chase's?"

Jared looked at the signature line. "I think so."

"Look at the ink. It's black ink. Chase always uses blue ink. Thinks black is unprofessional. And look at the C. See how it curls a bit to the left, then the rest of the letters are a bit smudged after that?"

He looked, realizing she was right. Someone had forged Chase's name. And the letter too. Had tried to set him up as the fall guy for Abby's suicide. If it was a suicide.

"What are you guys talking about?" Peter said.

Jared handed him the letter and sat back down in the chair.

"Wow," Peter said, when he finished it. "So that's why Wall's been so pissed at him."

"You're not the only who's been manipulated," Jared said.

FIFTY-ONE

A thud at the door startled him awake. He'd fallen asleep on the living room floor, head against his dog. Garth padded over to the door, Chase close behind. Peering through the curtains, he couldn't see anyone outside. He opened the door. A rolled newspaper with a rubber band lay on the mat. Picking it up, he retreated inside.

Pulling the rubber band off, he opened the paper, revealing a small envelope. He opened it and read the note inside. "*Wall has the lab results back. He's reconvened the grand jury for Friday morning.*" No signature, but he assumed it came from Steve Riveira. Three more days until he'd be back in jail. No way Wall would call the grand jury back to session if the DNA results were negative. Three more days of relative freedom. He realized something else. Sterling had caused the holdup in the lab results. He'd wanted Chase to be free so he could use Reagan to force a meeting, where he could capture Jared.

Garth nuzzled him and he realized how desperate he must be for a walk. His dog had been cooped up as long as he had. The terms of his probation allowed him a radius of two miles around his house, to allow him to buy groceries, run errands, and such. He looked down at the ankle bracelet, chafing a bit under his jeans.

"Might as well test this, eh boy?" he said, grabbing the leash from the closet.

As he crossed the street, he heard someone call his name. Without looking back, he waved, then continued around the stadium grounds. Keeping to a brisk pace, he tried to identify any tails. Had Sterling called them off now that he no longer had Reagan? Or were they hidden among the construction workers, busy working on the framing for the new stadium? What about the lady sitting on the bench, eating her lunch? Or the postal truck parked across the street? Any one of them could be working for Sterling. Or Wall. Perhaps the D.A. had detectives keeping an eye on him, worried he'd flee somehow.

Cutting across the park grounds, he turned up Demarest Street, which paralleled the stadium grounds on the other side of his townhouse. He reached Gino's, an independent convenience store whose owner had been holding out for years, despite offers from 7-11. He tied Garth up on the bike rack outside and went in.

The owner was behind the counter, an old Iranian who'd changed his name to Gino after buying the place ten years before.

"Business okay?" Chase asked, as he set his items on the checkout counter.

"Mostly all the construction workers these days," he answered, looking down at his newspaper. "Not that it's not good business, but the neighborhood crowd don't come back here much, with all the work on the stadium." He looked up and recognized Chase, looked like he had something to say, then lowered his head and bagged his items.

"Twenty-two ninety-three," he said woodenly, now averting his face.

Chase paid him, took his change, and left, not wanting to further embarrass the man. Typically he and Gino exchanged stories, talked sports. *A bit more uncomfortable when your customer is an accused murder.* He sighed, unwrapped Garth's leash, and started back the way he'd come. He nearly bumped into a man running in his direction.

"Mr. Riordan," the man said, panting. "Chase."

He recognized the cap from the bearded photographer who'd camped in front of his house all evening. Steering around him, he grunted a hello, and continued on his way, keeping his head down.

The man followed behind him. Chase picked up his pace.

"Mr. Riordan, it's me, Tony."

He stopped and turned around.

"Tony?" Underneath the cap and the beard he could see the face of his old investigator. The man who had taken the picture of Ev and Billerette.

"I just want you to know I didn't do what they said I did," Tony said. "Rat you out, I mean. Wall made me tell him some stuff, but I didn't tell him anything real, if you know what I mean."

"It's okay, Tony. Mr. Agnew told me about your conversation. I don't hold you responsible for any of this." In fact, he felt sorry for the man, another casualty of Ken Wall's vendetta against him. "I'd say let me know if I can do anything for you, but I'm not really in much of a position to help, if you know what I mean." He offered him a tired smile.

"I'm sorry I never told you about the way I left the force. I should have told you. It's just, I wanted the job, and I was afraid––"

Chase held up his hand. "I understand. I have some things in my past I don't exactly like to share with everybody." He nodded at the camera. "You working? I thought I saw you taking pictures outside my house last night."

Santori laughed. "Yeah, there was a photographer from the *Gazette*. I convinced him it would be in his best interests to leave the picture taking to me." He held up the camera, an expensive-looking Nikon. "It's always been a hobby of mine. I figured I should look the part." He walked up closer to Chase, then backed away after a growl from Garth.

"It's okay, Garth. He's a friend." He clicked his fingers once. The dog sat down, ears up. "So you were in disguise? As a photographer?"

"I knew you were getting out. I've driven by here a few times the past couple days. Lot of coming and going. Suspicious-looking people. I thought you could use someone to watch your back, first night home and all."

Touched, Chase reached out and gripped the man's shoulder. "You should be careful, Tony. These people are serious. I wouldn't want you to get hurt."

He laughed. "Hey, I can take care of myself. Remember, I served five years with NYPD." He patted his left shoulder. "I still have a license to carry." He looked around, then steered Chase behind a tree. "I know what you mean, though. The other night this van pulled up in front of your house. The guys that got out, they wore coveralls and carried toolboxes, but they looked like some badass dudes. Ex-military, maybe."

Chase smiled to himself. There actually had been a photographer outside when the men broke in.

"Then after the guys went inside, this older guy gets out. He stands there, like he owns the block. Fifteen minutes later the two guys come out, talk to the older dude, and he goes back inside for a couple minutes. When he comes out, he's mad. Yells something at the other guys and they all get back into the van and pull away."

"You saw them enter my house?"

Tony reached into his shirt and pulled out a folder. "Saw 'em, took their pictures." He handed the folder to Chase, who moved the grocery bag to the hand holding the leash to accept it.

"Don't know if it helps any, but––"

"Did they see you?"

"Nah, I used my telephoto lens. These were tough guys, but not necessarily smart guys, if you know what I mean."

Not knowing what to say, he managed a thanks. They shook hands.

"Least I can do. You got enough troubles." He fumbled with his shirt buttons, reached under his left armpit and pulled out a revolver.

"As I said, I don't know if it helps much, but I always figure, know your enemies. I think you can use this more than I can." He pressed the gun on Chase.

"I can't take this."

"You need it more than I do. Besides, I'm leaving town; this is goodbye, Mr. Riordan. Got a buddy down in Florida who owns a bar; he's been asking me join him for years. I kept resisting, wanting to stay in the game. But all this, I think it's time for me to pack it in." He held the folder while Chase put the gun in a pocket, and then returned it. Pulling his cap down low over his head, he tucked his camera under his shoulder. He started to walk off, then turned around.

"Best of luck, Mr. Riordan. I hope you find your way through all this. You're a good guy. Not too many of those." He pulled his collar up, stuck his hands in his pockets, and strolled away.

"Good luck, Tony. And thanks again."

Chase watched as he cut across the stadium grounds, losing sight of him behind a dumpster. Tucking the folder in the shirt, and conscious of the gun in his pocket, he tugged on the leash and walked his dog back to his house.

Sterling might no longer have Reagan, but Chase remained his only connection to Jared. If the colonel had heard Jared's last comments on the phone, he'd keep a close eye on Chase, hoping a contact would lead him to his brother. If Sterling's men were still watching the house, though, they were invisible. Even the lady on the bench was gone. The construction workers were all on their lunch break. He wondered what kind of resources Sterling might have at his disposal.

Back in the house, he cleared some space out on the floor, sat down on the couch, and spread out the photos Tony had taken. There were four of them. The first showed a white van parked in front of Chase's home. It had tinted windows, and a sign on the side that read "A&R Pest Control." *Cute.* The picture was taken with the van facing the camera from an angle and the resolution was good enough to read the license plate. Grabbing a pen and paper from his office, he wrote it down. The second picture showed two men in blue coveralls, the A&R logo on their backs, holding red toolboxes. One of the men stood at the front door, no doubt picking the lock, or maybe using a key. By this point Chase assumed he had no privacy or protection, other than the dog sitting beside him. In the third picture, the men were seen leaving the house and Chase could see the back of a man's head on the other side of the van facing the house. The men were looking at him as they exited, anxious expressions on their faces. Guess they hadn't found what they were looking for.

The last shot showed the other man leaving the house. The grim set of his lips and the furrowed eyebrows that made his eyes disappear revealed his displeasure. Sterling. Not hiding behind makeup and hair dye this time.

Something caught Chase's eye in the last picture. He searched around in his office until he found a magnifying glass and held it over the picture. There was a red placard on the driver's side dashboard the size of a paperback novel. The letters on it were blurred, but with the magnifying glass he could make out an H, the first letter, and the mathematical symbol pi. He squinted and realized it was not pi, but rather two T's. TT. H, something, then TT. Recalling Tony's perspective on the perpetrators, Chase laughed. They had left the parking pass for the Hyatt Hotel on the front dashboard. An easy mistake to make; with the flatness of the dashboard it wouldn't be easily visible to the driver or passenger of the vehicle.

Sterling and his men were staying at the Piedmont Hyatt. *Nice to know our taxpayers' dollars are supporting stays in first class hotels.* Not a bad choice, though. The hotel, in the middle of downtown, had underground parking and elevators from the parking garage that led to the rooms upstairs. From a security standpoint, they couldn't do better. Close to everything, including Chase's town home. In fact, he realized, within the radius of his ankle monitor.

The doorbell rang. Through the shades he saw the bright cheery face of his assistant Kasey, hands full.

He opened the door and followed her as she walked straight into the kitchen.

"I wanted to give you a night's sleep, but I knew you wouldn't have anything in the refrigerator," she said. She set down a shoulder satchel and a pan covered with foil. Noticing his grocery bags still sitting on the countertop, she pulled out the boxes and made a face of disgust.

"Honestly, you were going to eat this stuff?" Peeling back the foil from the pan, she revealed homemade lasagna. "Heat at 350 degrees for thirty minutes or so." She put the boxes in one of the cupboards. "Save these for when you're really desperate."

Looking around the townhouse, she noticed the disarray.

"Look what happens when you don't have a housekeeper for a few weeks. The place goes to hell."

Chase couldn't help laughing. "Nice to see you, too."

Kasey smiled. "You don't call, you don't write, what am I going to do with you?"

"Rufus been treating you all right?"

She waved her hands up in the air. "He's afraid to ask me to do anything except make coffee. I had to practically force him to let me help him with all the motions."

"I can imagine."

Opening the refrigerator, she set the lasagna on a shelf, and took out another foil-wrapped item from the satchel. "Garlic bread," she explained, setting it beside the lasagna. When she had finished in the kitchen, she turned to him.

"So. Ready?"

"You have everything I asked for?"

She smiled.

"Right." Remembering the bugs still in place, he took a piece of paper from Kasey, scribbled a note, and folded it, writing a phone number on the outside.

"Call that number, read him that information."

She took the paper, and stuck it in her purse, nodding.

"You might not want to call from the office phone. Mine or Rufus's," he whispered.

She gave him an annoyed look.

"My friends?"

"Lionel's campaigning. Fundraisers, speeches, that sort of thing. Randy is in the Bahamas with his wife, on vacation, apparently. Ev is, let me see..." She rummaged through her purse and found a newspaper article. "He's been appointed as the new head of European operations for the newly-formed Litchfield-ARG Tobacco. Headquartered in Berlin. He started last week." She handed him the article. "I haven't been able to reach Peter." She looked up with a smile. "Easier for administrative assistants to talk to other administrative assistants. We share. Sometimes way too much."

"Oh?"

"You have no idea. I was on the phone for a half hour with Ev's assistant, Savannah. I got flights, times, where he's staying, and then she wanted my advice."

"On what?"

"Girl stuff. I guess she and Ev are an item, no big surprise there. She wanted to buy him a present, wanted my advice on what to get him. He wanted her to get a tattoo but she wasn't sure she wanted to put one on her ankle—her butt, sure, but her ankle? And she wanted to get a dolphin or something, and Ev wanted her to get a bird. She wanted to know what I thought. Stuff like that."

Chase could picture Ev's latest, probably doing her nails as she spoke. "You win the award for patience. And thanks. Hard to believe Ev left without letting Rufus know. Randy I can understand, but..."

"And he's not just in the Bahamas. They're staying at Atlantis, that big fancy one with the bridge between the towers? Celebrating something. That from Randy's secretary, who was clearly envious."

"I'm jealous."

"Me too. Closest I've ever gotten was Miami."

"Any luck on the jewelry?"

"You were right. Volkova had a jewelry box on her nightstand. That's in police custody. The pieces she wore when she was killed included a bracelet from Cartier, a watch, and a necklace, a costume piece from Nordstrom. The D.A. has those."

"Do we know which Cartier store?"

"Far as we can tell, only the New York store carried it. Ernesto's tracking down the receipt."

Chase nodded pensively. It fit.

"I know that look."

"What look?"

"You know something."

"Just an idea."

Kasey smiled, indulgently.

"Did the toxicology reports ever get back to Rufus on Josh Samuels?"

"I don't think so, but I'll check."

"We'll need to line up a DNA expert. I used a guy at Chapel Hill for a trial a number of years back."

She nodded. "Marvin Rutherford. Mr. Wall has already retained him. Mr. Agnew knows someone up in Maryland, he's going to call him." She looked up at him. "So how do you think your hairs came to be at the crime scene—Katarina Volkova's that is?"

He considered whether she was accusing him, and realized she was just asking the obvious question. If someone was framing him, they'd gotten his hairs from someplace.

"I don't know," he admitted. "But I've been thinking about it. Unfortunately, there are a lot of answers. My cleaning lady, my barber, anyone who's been in my house."

"What about blood, though? Not just anyone would have access to your blood."

No, indeed. He'd had a physical exam two years before, but other than a rare cut, there weren't a lot of opportunities for someone to draw his blood and use it at a crime scene.

"That's a puzzler. Check with Dr. Machos. See if he can account for the blood samples he took at my last exam. At least eliminate the obvious. Any luck tracking down Ray Lewis?"

After the trial three years back, after his divorce, Ray left town. A nervous man, Chase always had the feeling he hadn't told him the whole truth. He was certain Ray hadn't killed his son, but his anxiety had been the most difficult thing he had to overcome at the trial. He *looked* guilty. Chase had always wondered what Ray had been hiding. Lewis had also been his first client; he'd walked in the door within weeks of the opening of his office. Somehow, it had all started with him.

"Last bill I sent went to Newport News, Virginia. He has a sister there. I left a message for him to call." She tucked her memo pad back in her purse and got up. On her way out she handed him the satchel. "Here. A few items you left in the office."

"Thanks. Oh, and ask Rufus to bring that file with him when he comes to meet with me later. The one from D.C. He'll know which one I mean." He hugged her, and saw her out the door.

The satchel contained a few innocuous personal items from his desk: pens, a picture of his parents, his memo pad with his scribblings after his meeting with Kate Wagner, his calendars, and a cell phone. A phone he'd forgotten; the twin of the one he'd bought for Jared. His first impulse was to run outside and make the call, talk to both Jared and Reagan. Unfortunately he'd left the phone on, and it wouldn't power up. He found the phone charger and plugged it in. Now he could use it, but only if he stayed in the house. He wasn't willing to risk that. The call would have to wait.

He pulled out the calendars from his office, surprised

Wall hadn't taken them. May 22nd, the morning Josh Samuels
was killed. A Saturday. And the day Chase had gone hiking in
the mountains. He paged back. June 19th, the day Katarina
Volkova had been killed. A Friday. The calendar entry showed
a court date in the morning, then blocked out the afternoon
after two p.m. Nothing came to him. June 21st was a Saturday
as well.

April 14th; that date was etched indelibly in his brain.
It was the date his parents had been killed. Not the year, but
the anniversary. Each year, he took two days off to drive up to
New Jersey and visit the gravesite. How convenient, then, that
Ray Lewis, Jr. was killed on that date. He'd been six hundred
miles away, by himself, sitting in front of two flat stones on
the ground. With no proof he'd been there.

Although… gas receipts. He'd stopped along the way to
fill up the tank. Surely the credit card company kept records
that long. He could prove he'd driven his car to and from New
Jersey. As quickly as he got excited, his prosecutor's brain de-
flated him.

"Mr. Riordan, your tank holds how many gallons of
gas?"

"Fourteen gallons."

"And how many miles to the gallon to you get on the
highway?"

"Thirty-two."

"You left Piedmont with a full tank of gas. You say you
drove to New Jersey. Yet your credit card receipts show gas purchases in Maryland, the day prior to the murder, and in Northern Virginia. Two gas purchases, two days apart, correct?"

"Yes."

"Ray Lewis, Jr. was killed at approximately ten in the
morning on day two of your 'trip.' You have a hotel receipt?"

"No."

"And why is that?"

"I stay in my parents' old house."

"Who owns that house?"

"I do."

"You make any phone calls from the house?"

"No, it doesn't have a working phone."

"You could drive to Maryland and back in a day. You could have driven there, come back, killed Ray Lewis, Jr. the next morning, then driven to Northern Virginia. Those times still work?'

"Uh, yes."

Not exactly an ironclad alibi. And of course, Wall hadn't gone that far back, yet. Chase wasn't charged with killing Ray Lewis, Jr. The indictment would likely only charge him with the murders of Josh Samuels and Katarina Volkova. Only, he thought grimly. But the message was clear: the killer knew his schedule. Intimately.

He played it back to the beginning. Four years ago, Abby had just died, Chase had been forced out of his job, and Ray Lewis, Jr. was found in a dumpster around the corner from his parents' house. What else had happened in Piedmont at that time? After Chase left the D.A.'s Office, Wall promoted Ellis Krahnert to Chief Assistant D.A., a position he'd held ever since. He'd likely be the next district attorney when Wall left the office. There'd been talk of a Senate run; Wallace Thorne turned 80 this year, and Wall might be a good candidate to replace him.

In terms of his friends, Lionel was pastor at a small church outside of Gastonia and Peter was with *Time* in Atlanta. Randy had left the Public Defenders Office and joined March Maples six months earlier, about the time Ev returned to town from New York.

He'd told Kasey he had an idea. Again, he asked himself, who benefited from the deaths of all these people, and from Chase in jail? He remembered what the report had said: the killer had a motive for each murder, and no doubt had a motive for what he was doing to Chase. At the moment, he was only concerned with the murder of Katarina Volkova's murder. Castillo's testimony lingered in Chase's mind, his recreation of the murder.

The other question Chase had to address was, why now? If the killer had set things up going back four to five years ago to frame Chase, why wait until now to spring the trap? His phone rang.

"Hello?"

"Chase Riordan." The voice of an old man, thin and gravely. He didn't recognize it.

"Speaking."

"I've heard about what's happening to you. I don't read the news much anymore, but it's a hard story to avoid, these days. Figured it's about time we talked."

"Who is this?"

"After all the time we spent together?" A painful sounding cackle. "Your secretary called, said you wanted to talk. I wondered whether I'd hear from you. I've thought about calling you over the years, somehow never got around to it. I guess that makes me a coward. But I'm here now. Long overdue, but maybe I can help."

"Ray?"

"I know, trust me, I know I've changed. When I look in the mirror these days I hardly recognize myself. Had cancer, a while back. Went through all the treatments, chemo, radiation, what have you. It's in remission now, though."

"Glad to hear it."

"Enough about me, though, you've got your own troubles. Maybe I can help, a little. Let me tell you a story."

FIFTY-TWO

Jared smiled as he hung up the phone. He'd expected to have to make Sterling come to him. Now the tables were turned.

"What's up?" Reagan asked. Her hair was wrapped in a towel after a long shower.

He passed on the details from the phone call.

"He's staying at the Hyatt? Boy, we always stay at Best Western or Motel 6. Must be on a different expense account." Her eyes narrowed. "Now what. So we know where he's staying. What are we going to do, go knock on his door?"

"It's a thought," Jared said, walking over to the couch where he resumed cleaning his rifle. "He'd certainly never expect it. We'd have the element of surprise going for us."

"You're not serious."

He thought for a moment. "No, he's got at least a couple of men with him. Bodyguards, henchmen, whatever. We don't know his room number, just that he's probably staying there. You know anything about the hotel?"

"Just that it's in the middle of town. It's across the street from the new Litchfield Tower."

"The one that's under construction?"

"What are y'all talking about," Peter asked, as he came in from the kitchen, a sandwich in hand.

Reagan told him what they'd just learned.

"So why don't you go over there and find out what room he's in? Aren't you with the FBI?"

Reagan shrugged.

"I guess I am tired," she said.

"It's worth a shot. Hard to imagine a desk clerk wouldn't give up the room numbers if you flash your credentials at him."

"Play his own game back at him," Jared said. "Tell them he's under investigation for aiding and abetting terrorists. Which isn't far from the truth."

"Okay, so we get his room number. Then what?"

Jared threw the bolt on his rifle. "Well…"

She gave him a hard look. "We are not going in there to shoot the man! Although Lord knows, he deserves it. And you just said he's got men with him. We don't want a shootout in the middle of a hotel corridor. Innocent people could get hurt. Besides, you'd go to jail. Is that what you want? Isn't it bad enough that one Riordan brother is accused of murder?"

He flinched as the remark hit home.

Her tone softened. "I'm sorry. I'm worried about Chase. I know you are too. But we have to do this the right way. If only we had that proof." She looked at Peter. "You make any more sandwiches?"

"Two more on the counter," he said. "What proof?"

"The colonel's got his own black market going. He's been profiting off of thefts of allied weapons," Reagan said, walking into the kitchen.

"Not just profiting. He told them where to find them—helped them steal the weapons to begin with," Jared added, his lips tight.

"So what kind of proof did you have? Witness statements?"

"Files on a computer disk."

"Wait a second," Reagan said, coming back from the kitchen with half a sandwich. "What did the disk look like?"

"Small, round, shiny…"

"It's a CD?"

He looked at Reagan curiously. "Yes."

She slammed her hand down on the coffee table. "Damn!" She started laughing.

"What is it?" Peter asked.

"What did you do with the disk?"

Jared told her how he'd gone back to the village with Al-Tariq, who had given him the computer disk. "For your own protection and mine," he'd said. He'd gone back to the barracks, and before confronting Sterling, slipped the disk into the box where he kept his medals.

"I've no idea what happened to it after that. I figured if Sterling didn't find it, it's sitting in storage somewhere."

Reagan sat down and took a few bites of her sandwich, nodding her head as she ate. "And let me guess. The disk contains dates, wire transfer amounts, bank accounts."

Jared nodded. "How do you know that?"

"Because I'm an idiot," she said. "Chase must have got your medals somehow. From General Jackson, I'm guessing. He didn't say anything about it, but he sent me a bunch of case files. Ones he wanted me to have someone take a look at—he thought there was something funny about his cases." She noticed Peter's curious look. "I'll come back to that. He sent me the files and stuck the disk in with them. I thought it was connected to the files he sent, and I gave them to a guy at Georgetown to look at."

"You gave the disk to someone else?" Jared demanded.

"It's okay. He must've thought the same, so he printed out copies of the information and added it to the profile he did. I should've realized what they were. I thought they must be statistical analyses or something. But I can see it now in my head. They were a record of all the transactions."

"With dates corresponding to the weapons thefts in Iraq.

And the passwords to access the accounts," Jared said.

Reagan turned to Jared. "How did you get hold of this information?"

"Al-Tariq had been making transfers into accounts Sterling had set up in the Caymans. There was a master account, which Al-Tariq maintained, and a subsidiary account for Sterling. Al-Tariq set up the accounts to begin with. Sterling thought he was the only one with access to the subsidiary account. What he didn't know was that Al-Tariq had set them so the master account holder could still control the subsidiary accounts. So when Ray found out Sterling was after him, the first thing he did was transfer the money back into another account, whose password only he knew. He gave me the disk."

"Why didn't he just keep it for himself?"

"He didn't want it. He was a businessman, not a terrorist, remember. The records show he paid Sterling; he wanted proof of that in case everything went sour. This way he maintained some leverage."

"And we have all that information?" Peter asked.

"Rufus Agnew has it. I gave him the entire file." Reagan looked at Jared. "We have the proof. It's not just your word against his."

He looked doubtful. "It would still take an expert to look at all that data, figure out whether the accounts were real, when the transfers occurred."

Reagan smiled and finished the last bite of her sandwich. "Did I ever tell you what it is I do?" she said.

A phone rang and Jared, startled, pulled a cell phone out of his pocket.

"I wondered if you'd ever get around to using this phone. Hold on, there's someone here who'd like to talk to you." He held up the phone for Reagan, who looked at him with eyebrows raised. He just smiled and passed her the phone.

FIFTY-THREE

Jared got up, and tipped his head at Peter, who followed him as he left the room.

"Chase?" Peter asked, when they reached the game room at the back of the house.

He nodded. The room held every conceivable kind of video game, from Space Invaders and Asteroids to a cockpit-style virtual reality spaceship. Jared pressed a button and started up a game of Pac Man.

"This guy sure likes his games," he commented.

Peter sat in front of a tabletop version of Pong. "You have no idea."

"He's a good friend to Chase?"

Peter looked over at him, seemingly intent at his game. "He practically worships him, if you want to know the truth."

"Friend of yours, too?'

"Yeah, for twenty years."

"He worship you, too?"

Peter frowned. "We're all friends."

"Ev's relationship with Chase any different than yours?" He looked over to gauge Peter's reaction.

"Ev has always been a bit of the odd-man out," Peter said after a brief pause. "He was Chase's freshman-year roommate. They were a strange pair, a real Mutt and Jeff. Chase tall, easy around everyone; Ev short, awkward around people. Chase really helped Ev fit in. He was a snobby rich kid, but around Chase, people accepted him." Peter sat back from the game, hand to his chin. "It's not that we didn't like Ev or anything. Just that without Chase, I doubt we'd have all become friends. Chase was kind of the glue, if you know what I mean."

Jared laughed softly. "I grew up with him, remember? I was the geeky brother who played piano, who hung out with the theater kids. Chase was the jock, but also a good guy. We helped each other, but he always had a way about him. People wanted to be around him."

"Exactly. Chase was a good influence on Ev. He helped him make other friends, made him one of the gang. Our gang, as it turned out."

"Ev realize this?"

"You know, I'm pretty sure he did. Ev's changed over the years; he's mellowed, knows how to get along with people. He may choose not to get along with some, mind you, but he knows how to play the game. A lot of that he learned by being around Chase."

"Back to games."

Peter turned to Jared. "Life is a game to Ev. All this… " he waved his hand around the room, "is nothing. Ev doesn't take anything very seriously. Sure he has money, and he always has women, but none of it matters much to him."

"Your friendship matter to him?" Jared asked.

"Yeah, I'd have to say it does," Peter answered finally. "Maybe the only thing that matters."

"What about the rest of this gang of yours. Lionel and Randy. They feel the same way as Ev?"

Peter laughed. "No one feels the same way as Ev about anything."

"Explain."

"I don't mean anything by it. Just that things are always different with Ev. I don't think he'd ever had a friend until he came to Winfield. Although I'm sure growing up with his money he was never short of hangers-on, but until he hooked up with Chase, I don't think he knew anyone who liked him— just liked him.

"I grew up with Randy. Our families knew each other; we started playing together when we were six years old. I never had a brother, but Randy's as close as it gets for me. We're probably each other's harshest critics, we've fought a lot over the years, but we love each other. When we met Ev and Chase, we were kind of a package deal."

"What about Lionel?"

"He came along a year later; he's the baby of the bunch. All of us but Chase grew up in the South. We'd never known a black man, save by watching them on TV. We lived on different sides of town, went to different schools. Private schools, in our case. Becoming friends with Lionel was a bit of an experiment. He had a great sense of humor, was loyal, and could poke fun at himself. Chase got all that day one. It just took us longer."

"And how did Ev take Lionel?' Jared asked, fascinated by the discussion. He'd never had many friends outside the army. The bonds he understood came from sharing a common experience, from risking death and counting on the guy next to you to watch your back. Maybe it wasn't all that different.

"Funny you should ask. I think Ev was jealous of Lionel at first. He and Chase understood each other, where for Ev it was work. It didn't come to him naturally. Still, after a while, something clicked with all of us. We became almost this independent entity. Us against the world." He appeared wistful.

Jared stood up and walked over to the window, holding his arms on either side of the frame. "So where's your gang now?" He turned around and stared at Peter.

Seeming to sink into himself, he crossed his arms, then rubbed his eyes. Looked away.

"It's different now. In school, nothing could touch us," he said quietly. "We had opportunities everyday to stick up for each other. Got in a few fights, helped each other out with schoolwork, with girls. But after a while, after we left school, it changed. We changed.

"Life is complicated, you know. I mean, I guess you know that as well as anyone. For a while after school it became competitive. At least that's the way it seemed to me. Who got a job quicker, who made the most money. We all pretended it didn't matter, but it did to me, and I could see it did to them, too. We still saw each other, but less all the time. For a while we all lived in different states.

"Relationships changed things for us, too." He looked at Jared, who returned a sympathetic. "Girls can do that. We were always at different stages of relationships. Lionel got married early. Then we all wanted what he had, but none of us could find it.

"We'd get together every year; we still do. Pretended nothing was different, tried to relive our past glories. As if college was the highlight of our lives. And in a way, maybe it was. I remember thinking, oh, six years ago, that this was it. Our friendship was going to fade away and die. We didn't have things in common anymore, we were all moving in different directions.

"But Chase wouldn't let it happen. He was the one among us who didn't take our friendship for granted; he worked at it. Called people all the time, connected us at different opportunities. Kept our trips going."

Observing the emotions that passed over Peter's face, Jared was suddenly uncomfortable. He felt like an outsider, intruding upon someone else's grief, but was at the same time fascinated.

"And now?" he prodded.

"A few years ago," Peter said, acting like he hadn't heard Jared. "I think we all finally rediscovered how important our friendships were. After years in the workplace and the dating scene, we realized that what we had was special. A rare thing

other people didn't share. Ev moved back to Piedmont, Lionel
took a job at a church close by. We started treating our friendship with the respect it deserved. But…"

"But?" Jared prompted, when Peter didn't say anything
more.

"But it was different," he said. A funny look came over
Peter; he stood up now and faced Jared. The defensive look
was gone; the furtiveness was gone. In their place was a kind
of resignation.

Jared saw Reagan standing at the doorway holding the
phone up, but he shook his head slightly, telling her to wait.

"It may be just an expression, but I told you Randy and I
were like brothers. I can't pretend to know what having a real
brother is like. But Randy, Ev, Chase, Lionel and I––we're all
brothers. As close as it gets outside of blood, anyway. It's not
easy being a brother, though. Brothers turn on each other–
–they leave."

Jared flinched from the comment, but kept his eyes
locked on Peter.

"The last couple years we've all made the effort. We have
our friendship. It's just not the most important thing. How
can it be? We don't have the things in common we used to."
He sighed. "It's the nature of things; they change, evolve. Our
friendship has evolved. We don't live together, we don't date
the same girls, and life has hit some of us harder than others."

"You trust them?"

"Before all this…" He couldn't finish the sentence. The
despair in Peter's eyes as he returned Jared's gaze was painful
to look at. Sparing him an answer, Jared nodded, which Reagan took as her cue to walk into the room with the phone, her
eyes and skin glowing. She held the phone out to Jared, giving
Peter a look of sympathy.

"He needs to talk with you."

He crossed the room, put his hand on Peter's shoulders,
gripped them hard, and then took the phone from Reagan.
He walked out of the room.

When he returned fifteen minutes later, Reagan and Peter were sitting across from each other at the Pong console. He looked at Peter and held out a phone. A different phone.

"Call Chase at the house. Tell him you're trying to get in touch with your other friends. He'll ask for the fax number. Give it to him, then tell him you've got to run, someone's coming by to pick you up. You'll talk to him later."

Peter looked at him oddly. He took the phone, made the call, and hung up.

Jared left the room. A few minutes later he came back and handed Reagan two sheets of paper.

"You can work with this?" he said.

Excitedly, she scanned the pages. Her eyes gave him his answer.

Peter looked quizzically at Jared.

"Fax. Wonders of modern science."

"I'm going to need to bring in some other people. I think with this," she held up the papers. "It won't matter what Sterling is telling people. Time to come in from the cold."

"Use the office. Off the master bedroom. It's got every conceivable electronic gadget. But be quick; we need to be out of here soon."

"How soon?"

"Fifteen minutes."

She raised her eyebrows, then nodded.

"Why's that?" Peter asked, as Reagan rushed out of the room. "Why do we have to be out of here?"

"The fax was the only way to get the information we needed quickly. But Chase's phones are bugged. The fax transmission only lasted a second or two, but Sterling might still be able to trace the outgoing call to this number. Come on." He motioned for Peter to follow him.

Back in the master bedroom, Jared noticed Peter's eyes go wide at the collection of hardware on the bed. Jared opened a large duffel on the floor and started packing the items into the bag. He spoke as he worked.

"Two problems. Reagan's working on one of them. The other is a bit more complicated."

"Chase, you mean?"

"Right. We have, let's say, a window of opportunity." He could tell Peter wasn't following him.

"I don't like Chase being in jail any more than you do. But there's a process—he'll have the chance to prove his innocence in court."

"Sure, months from now. In the meantime he'll be sitting in jail and the real killer will have more time to maneuver, to cover his tracks. We have a chance, if we do this right, to maybe clear Chase's name before he goes back to jail. Before a trial. But we'll need your help."

"Anything."

Jared weighed his next words carefully. "We need all of you together. Can you help?"

"All of us?"

"Lionel, you, Ev, Randy. You need to all be here. In Piedmont. By Thursday."

"But I don't even know where they all are," Peter said.

Jared threw down a sheet of paper on the bed. "Here's all the numbers, locations. You need to make sure every one of them shows up."

Peter looked at the numbers. "Germany? Ev's in Germany?" He laughed. "North Carolina's got a better chance of landing the Olympics than I do of getting Randy out of the Bahamas. His wife would kill him."

Jared looked at him patiently. "You told me you were like brothers. Here's your chance to be there for each other. For Chase."

Peter looked dubious. "I don't know…"

"You told me you don't know what it's like to be a brother, but you call yourselves that. I've never known what it's like to have friends. But I've been in combat situations where I had to trust the guys standing on either side of me. We had to watch each other's backs, and we had to do our jobs, because if we didn't, we could die." He stared at Peter, waiting for him to raise his eyes.

"Randy's not good at standing up to Marinda."

Jared zipped up the bag, slung it over his shoulders, and nodded toward the box on the floor. Peter picked it up and they left the room.

"I know you have some trust issues now. Look at it this way. You've been manipulated, you feel used. You wonder whether one of your friends is involved. Here's your chance to find out."

"What if they won't come?" Peter said.

"That'll tell you something, won't it?" Jared replied.

Peter shuddered. "What should I tell them? Why do they need to come back to Piedmont right now?"

"Tell them the truth. Chase is going back to prison Friday. You talked to Wall and it doesn't look good. It might be his last day of freedom. That good enough?" He smacked his hand on the door of the office. "Let's go." He looked back to Peter.

He nodded. "Okay. But where to next?"

"Drop you off at a hotel somewhere. Let you do your thing."

"What are you going to do?"

Reagan caught up with them, gave a thumbs up, and they headed out the back door.

"Got some other people we need to get to. After that, we'll try and catch two birds with two stones."

As they walked toward the garage, Peter stopped.

"What about my car?"

"Leave it," Reagan said. "If Sterling does make it here, maybe he'll think Chase was communicating just with you."

Peter shrugged. "Makes sense, I guess. What are you doing?" he said to Jared.

Jared had opened the back of the trunk. Now he set the duffel bag in, took the box from Peter, then started back to the house.

"Getting my dog."

A few minutes later he returned, followed by Lookout. They all got in the car, Peter in the back seat with the dog, and pulled out of the driveway.

Jared kept his eyes on the road and maneuvered the car expertly around the streets leading away from the neighborhood. He glanced briefly at Reagan.

"Well?"

"I was able to reach O'Keefe. My boss's boss. After the yelling and the screaming stopped, he listened to what I had to say. It's a bit of a delicate matter; we all report to Homeland Security now and Sterling has a lot of friends. He's not sure who to trust. But I think he smells promotion."

Jared snorted. "Enlightened self interest."

"Way Washington works."

"What's he going to do?"

"He's already doing it. He's sending someone over to Georgetown to secure the disk. I gave him the account numbers, the transfer amounts. I've worked with this particular bank before. In fact, I know the director personally."

"Will they help?" he asked dubiously.

"They'll help," she said. "Banks in the Caymans are secure, but when it comes to accounts we suspect are affiliated with terrorists, they tend to bend over backwards. Bad for tourism."

"How long will all that take?"

"Not too long." She looked at her watch. "Unfortunately, it's after banking hours. I left a message for the director. Someone else is trying to wake him up. I also placed a call to the Minister of Finance. An old friend."

"So tomorrow morning."

"Right. In the meantime, O'Keefe is assembling a team to come down here, make the arrest. They'll be on a plane first thing tomorrow. They plan to be here at eight tomorrow morning." Reagan leaned her head back in the seat. "Turn right here," she directed. "You think Sterling will just sit in the hotel?"

"If we could get him at three in the morning, maybe,

although we'd put the guests at risk. Better to get him out in the open." Jared said.

"What I figured. Any ideas?"

"Already covered." Before she could ask him what he meant, he added, "But you'll want to have someone cover the hotel just the same. Never know what you might find."

"You care where you stay?" Jared asked Peter, as they approached uptown.

"Given that my suitcase is still in the car with all my stuff, I don't have a car, my credit cards are maxed out, and I have to make a few international phone calls..."

"The Hilton it is," said Jared. A few minutes later, they pulled into the front courtyard of the Uptown Hilton. At Peter's inquisitive glance, he reached into his pocket and pulled out a wad of cash. "This cover what you need?'

Peter nodded, looking a bit stunned. "What about you two? Where will you stay?"

Jared looked at Reagan. "You could stay here, too, but on the off chance someone saw you, reported back to Sterling..."

"You have a better idea? Someplace safer?"

He nodded.

Peter said, "How will I get in touch with you?"

"Check in under your own name. Either Reagan or I will call you tomorrow at five." Jared extended his hand. "Good luck. Chase is counting on you. I'm counting on you."

Peter returned the handshake, the look in his eyes somber, his mouth set. Reagan got out of the car with him, and gave him a hug. He walked into the hotel.

Getting back into the front seat, Reagan turned to Jared. "You going to share your brilliant plan for getting Sterling out in the open?"

"It's simple. We just need to use the right bait."

Her eyes widened as he pulled away from the hotel. "You're not going to give yourself up."

He kept silent for a few moments. "No. Although it was

my first thought. But it wouldn't work. If I told him to meet me, told him where I was, he'd have his scouts out and they'd grab me before he ever showed his face. It's what I would do."

"Then what… oh, no."

He turned toward her. "It was Chase's idea." At her glare he said, "He should be safe. Sterling knows he'll be going back to prison. He practically orchestrated his release from jail so he could put pressure on him. He's got no reason to harm him."

She continued to stare at him.

He returned her gaze. "Don't worry. I'll be watching him. I didn't come here to let Chase fall into Sterling's hands." Pulling into a quiet side street in the downtown area, he parked the car and got out. Popping the trunk, he turned toward her as she got out of the car, a curious look on her face. He tossed her the keys. "Here."

"I thought we were going someplace together."

He shook his head. "Nope."

"But where will I stay?"

He pulled a card and a small key out of his pocket and handed it to her.

Reading the card, she gave him a look of indignation. "This is a storage unit."

"Climate controlled, private." He smiled. "Trust me. It's as safe as could be."

"Fine," she said. "So what are you going to do?"

"I've got a few loose ends to take care of." He opened the back door and rubbed the dog's neck. "Sorry, but you're going to have to take the dog. Dog food and a leash are in the trunk." Taking the duffel bag in one arm, he gripped her hand with the other. "Call me when everything's set up at your end."

Her eyes welled up, but she just nodded and walked around to the driver's door. Jared zipped the bag open six inches and pulled out a handgun. He tossed it to her.

"You said you knew how to use one of these?"

In answer, she pulled back the slide, checked the magazine, and slammed it home. She smiled in answer, gave a small wave, got in the car, and drove off.

With the duffel bag over his shoulder, Jared walked back in the direction of town.

As soon as Reagan was out of sight, he pulled out the pre-paid cell phone and punched in a number.

"We should be set for eight o'clock tomorrow. You'll need to keep Sterling there for fifteen minutes or so." He listened for a few minutes. "She's fine. Safe. Okay bro, it's your show. See you tomorrow." He continued into town, staying in the shadows.

FIFTY-FOUR

Chase sat at his desk, the killer's profile in front of him. The problem was, knowing who the killer might be and proving it were two different things. Knowledge was not evidence. The evidence still pointed to his own involvement. The only way he could see to make this work would be to elicit a confession. Play to the killer's weakness.

The conversation with Ray Lewis had provided some clues, but it had been the revelations from Jared on the pre-paid phone while walking his dog that had yielded the final pieces of the puzzle. So far as he knew, Sterling didn't know about the phone. Now he had to hope their plan would work.

First things first, though. Sterling. He went to his office and spoke into the lamp.

"Colonel. We need to talk. I think we might be able to come to some kind of accommodation." He hoped that the bugs were still operational.

He didn't have to wait long to find out. A few minutes later the phone rang.

"Well?"

"Nice to hear from you, too, Colonel."

"I don't have time for games, Riordan, and neither do

you. I'm sure you've heard by now the DNA evidence has come back. Enjoy your few remaining moments of freedom."

Just hearing the man's voice was grating. Imagining his brother smashing his fists into that face helped him continue.

"No games, Sterling. I have something you want. You have something I want."

Sterling laughed. "The only thing you have that I want is your brother."

"Actually, I think you're wrong. Why else did you trash my house so thoroughly?"

A pause. "Go on."

"Let's say I have what you were looking for. What would that be worth to you?"

"If you have what you say you have, why haven't you gone to the authorities?"

"In case you haven't been paying attention, I've been in jail. No one's listening to me about anything. Plus, you have something I want. My brother's freedom."

Silence. Before the colonel could say anything else, Chase continued. "You and I both know without evidence, any testimony by my brother would be worthless. He's been in a mental hospital for two years, he's experienced trauma in the war. If you have the evidence, my brother is no longer a threat to you.

"Here's the deal; I give it to you, in exchange for an honorable discharge for Jared. Leave him alone. I want to be able to see him before I go back to jail, without worrying about your men taking him."

"How touching," Sterling said. "And how is this supposed to work?"

He'd been counting on the colonel's greed to make this work. "Simple. I give you the information, you can verify that all the funds are still there; you can close them out, move the money wherever. After that, you'll have no reason to pursue Jared. You'll have your money, Jared gets his honorable discharge, everyone's happy."

"What's the evidence look like?"

He bought it. "It's a CD." Jared hadn't been sure whether Sterling knew what storage format Al-Tariq had used.

"So, do we have a deal?"

He heard Sterling conferring with someone else in the background. "I'll come by to pick it up."

"No way," he said. "You've worn out your welcome at my house." He and Jared had considered Chase's townhouse as a possible meeting site, but had rejected it as too confined a space. And Sterling's men would see the FBI coming from a mile away. Literally.

"Here's the way it will work. There's a secluded area on the east side of Stadium Park. A patch of grass about fifty yards in from the fence, surrounded by a stand of trees, and a stack of building materials. Meet me there at eight tomorrow morning. Alone. I see anyone else and the deal is off."

"What's to stop me from just taking the disk from you? Not, of course, that I would do something like that." The menace in Sterling's voice came through the receiver like a needle in Chase's ear.

Almost there. "Two things. One, my dog, Garth. He doesn't take kindly to someone assaulting me."

"And the second," Sterling prompted.

"I'd like to say your word, but we both know how much that's worth. The second is, anything happens to me, or I tell my brother you double-crossed me, you think Jared will rest until he tracks you down?"

He could tell by the silence that the threat had hit home. It confirmed his suspicions. Sterling was afraid of Jared. He had been for the past two years, even locked away in an institution.

"Eight o'clock," Sterling said, and disconnected.

When he got off the phone, he walked around the house and pulled out all of the bugs he'd found earlier. Throwing them into the sink, he ran some water and turned on the garbage disposal. He hoped whoever was listening on the other end got a splitting headache. He called Jared on the pre-paid phone from the bathroom with the shower running, confirming the time and location. Counting on the FBI to pull this off caused him concern; he didn't relish the prospect of standing in front of Sterling with nothing. Fortunately, Reagan would be involved, although part of him wished she were back in Washington, away from the colonel who had abducted her.

With Sterling out of the way he could concentrate on his own frame-up. He returned to his conversation with Ray Lewis. Even after all these years, the case still shook him.

The first big case taken on by C. P. Riordan and Associates had been a whopper. State Senator Raymond P. Lewis accused of murdering his eight-year-old son Ray Jr. The boy's body had been found in a garbage dumpster, in an apartment complex not far from Ray Sr.'s house in Fourth Ward, one of Piedmont's oldest neighborhoods. For three days prior to the discovery of the body, it had been thought to be a kidnapping. Ray Lewis and his wife Charlene had contacted police about the missing child after he didn't make it home on the school bus. No call or note was forthcoming, the neighborhood was canvassed, and by the next day, all of Piedmont knew of the missing boy. His face was plastered all over the city and the police began an exhaustive search. They weren't going to have a JonBenet Ramsey case, where the trail to the killer got cold through police inaction and the parents' refusal to cooperate.

Unfortunately, in the end, the outcome was the same. An apartment owner had a large bag of garbage to dump, couldn't toss it over the fence surrounding the dumpster, so he opened the gate, climbed the stairs, and discovered Ray Jr.'s body, encased in a clear plastic bag. As in the Ramsey case, the parents were the immediate suspects. Only this time they didn't flee the city or refuse to cooperate. They allowed a complete search of their property and spent hours closeted with investigators, revealing what they knew. Meanwhile, the police compiled scraps of evidence that ultimately added up to a compelling case against Ray Sr.

The most damning indictment of Ray Sr., however, came

from Charlene Lewis. In the JonBenet Ramsey case, although the parents were suspected of some involvement in their daughter's death, they stuck together afterwards, and kept to their stories. Charlene Lewis, upon learning of the evidence pointing toward her husband, immediately filed for divorce and came out in the press claiming he had abused the child, and was jealous of the time she and Ray Jr. spent together. The D.A.'s Office filed charges against Ray Sr.: murder one.

Ray Lewis had been one of Ken Wall's biggest supporters when he first ran for D.A. Wall had been his hand-picked successor to the legendary Jesse Fowler, holder of the office for over a decade, and he made it known to the powers that be that they should get behind Wall or else. Now, with Wall pressing murder charges against him, he felt betrayed: by his wife, by Wall, and by the media, all of whom turned on him as soon as they saw which way the wind was blowing.

When approached by Lewis, his office had only been open for two months. The case made regional headlines, with the police and prosecutors rushing to show that Piedmont was not the kind of town where authorities let this kind of thing happen without swift punishment. Zealous as they were, however, their case was built on a foundation of sand. In court, Chase was able to tear apart the circumstantial evidence connecting Lewis to the crime, painting a consistent picture of a loving parent who attended Little League games, volunteered at the school, and never missed an important function, even during his term as mayor. Charlene Lewis, for all her accusations, never testified in court and the case that had seemed rock solid at the onset became a collection of speculative thinking.

The jury had taken just six hours to come back with a verdict of not guilty, and Chase and Lewis hugging outside the courtroom made the front pages of papers up and down the Eastern seaboard. The case had cemented Chase's reputation, but more importantly it had made him feel like a lawyer again.

Something had never felt right about the case. While it made sense for Lewis to leave the city after the case concluded, looking to start anew, it had roused Chase's suspicions. After the phone call, he knew he'd been right.

"It was never a kidnapping," Lewis started off. "It was a message." His ravaged vocal cords forced him to speak slowly in order to be understood, as he told his story.

The senate election was a year off. Everyone knew Wallace Thorne would win; he'd served four successive terms, and in spite of his cantankerous behavior, he was a beloved figure in the state of North Carolina. He'd run unopposed in the primary, the Republicans would put up their usual sacrificial lamb in the general election and it would be back to Washington for the senior senator.

Ray Lewis organized the fundraising efforts. In spite of the fact that the election was effectively in the bag, the senator always raised huge sums of money, building his war chest. By the time the primaries rolled around, he already had over $12 million, with promises of much more to come.

Then Lewis discovered an irregularity in the allocation of the senator's funds. It seemed money was coming in, and was going out again, but not for the purpose of financing the senator's campaign. Rather, it appeared money was being disbursed to major party leaders in the state, including state representatives and a number of party officials. Lewis had discovered the deception quite by accident and was determined to learn how long the practice had been going on. With no hard evidence, he took his information to a friend in the State Attorney General's Office, who promised to look into it.

A few weeks later, he received a phone call. An anonymous voice, artificial, perhaps, told him to stop what he was doing; to contact the A.G. and tell him it was all a mistake, that in fact the funds had been disbursed properly. But Lewis stood firm and hung up on the caller. A week later the call came again.

"I heard the voice and I knew this wouldn't be the end

of it. It said that if I didn't stop my investigation, if I didn't call my friend, I'd be sorry. That I would suffer," Lewis told Chase. "Of course I didn't take it seriously. I should have, but I'd had my share of threats over the years. Well, two days later," Chase could hear the already ravaged voice crack. "They took my son. Called me on my cell phone and asked me if I needed any further demonstration."

Fearful for his wife's safety, Lewis had destroyed all the notes he'd made, and called his friend, who was glad to learn he wouldn't have to involve himself in what could potentially become a huge scandal for the senator and for the state.

"I never knew who made the call. I didn't suspect it at the time, but I've come to believe my friend was involved in this. We talked a little before the trial, but after the verdict was announced, I didn't hear from him again. When he died, I knew my suspicions had been right. But I was done. They'd killed my son and I wasn't about to risk losing Charlene. Although in the end I lost her anyway. At least she's still alive."

Chase tried to take it all in. The story accounted for Lewis' behavior during the trial. It made sense. Someone had killed his son to prevent him from breaking the biggest political scandal in state history, and had set him up as the killer as a message to others who might want to reveal their own participation. Had the killer planted the seeds that far back for his own demise?

"Your friend," he asked slowly, knowing the answer. "It was Winston Reese."

He thanked Lewis for calling, feeling hopelessly inadequate. The man had lost everything: his family, his home, and his health. He may not have gone to prison, but he might as well have. Chase considered the implications of what he'd heard. A statewide conspiracy that included murdering a young boy.

By the time Rufus Agnew showed up later that afternoon, his head was still spinning. One of the toughest aspects of this ordeal had been the elusiveness of the killer and Chase's inability to see anyone but a mysterious, nebulous mastermind lurking in the background, pulling everyone's strings. Now he knew him as a man, motivated to behave like everyone else--according to his own self-interest. Now that Chase knew the killer's motive in the Lewis case, and perhaps in the Tierney case as well, his eyes were opened to other possibilities. By the time he finished meeting with Rufus, and after spending time on the phone with his brother, he had a more complete picture of the killer.

FIFTY-FIVE

Holding a pair of 10X30 Brunton binoculars to his eyes, Jared looked in the direction of the hotel from his perch twenty stories high in the unfinished Litchfield Tower. The hotel garage exited onto a one-way street that ran in his direction. He'd spent the night opposite the hotel, watching cars coming and going. At eleven, a white van had entered. A few moments later, an SUV, similar to the one he'd seen at the safe house, followed. He continued his vigil for another three hours, saw one more white van enter the garage, and started scanning the hotel windows. All reflective glass. A pity.

At 5:00 a.m. he took the worker's elevator down to ground level and left the Tower. Stadium Park was a mile walk west. The half-completed stadium dominated the skyline as he identified the meeting spot. It wasn't perfect; but it was easily visible from a number of vantage points. He scanned the area, considering where he would place men, then looked up at the stadium, gauging the line of site. Best to have the high ground.

Upon reaching the construction site, he cut a hole in the fence surrounding it. Moving quietly, he looked for an entrance to the stadium, couldn't find one, and ended up climbing the scaffolding, a difficult ascent with the heavy bag on his back. He reached the framing of what would be the upper deck, found a spot shielded from view by steel girders, and settled in.

His senses went on alert. Looking in the direction of the street, he saw why. A white van coming in his direction. It turned left down the street paralleling the meeting place, passed it, and turned into a side street. He looked for the SUV or another van to follow, but none did. His watch said 5:30 a.m. Sterling was getting an early start, trying to get the jump on Chase. He'd almost gotten the jump on Jared.

Using his binoculars, he again scanned the area. He wondered what time the construction workers would start to arrive. The phone in his hip pocket buzzed. He flipped it open.

"They're in the air. They'll be here in two hours, tops."

"Roger that. Everything go okay?"

"We reached the Minister. He was very accommodating."

He spotted two men approaching the park from the street in back of the hotel. "I've got to go. Make sure the team is here by 8:10." He hung up. He watched the men trying to appear to be casual morning strollers, their erect posture and alert appearance belying their performance. They put their heads together when they stood directly opposite the meeting place then scanned the area as Jared had. For a moment he feared one would head in his direction, but he'd correctly judged they weren't prepared for long-range work. The men split up momentarily and he tracked their progress till they disappeared from view.

By seven o'clock, he judged that everyone was in position. He did another scan, picked out three men. He knew there'd be a fourth, in the building opposite no doubt, but behind the glass where Jared couldn't see him. He identified the window with the best view of the park, hoped he was right. Unfortunately, in an operation, the best planning couldn't account for every detail.

At 7:50, he saw Chase emerge from the far side of the park, walking with his wolfhound. He put the binoculars down, picked up the rifle, and tracked his brother's progress through the scene. It had been two years since he'd fired a shot, but the motion of setting the stock against his shoulder, putting his eye to the viewfinder, his finger to the trigger guard, felt as natural as if he were sitting at a piano again. He watched his brother's path take him within twenty feet of one of the men, hidden behind a tree. He took aim.

Chase continued past, but the man took no action. Perhaps Sterling meant to honor the bargain after all. Too bad he'd be disappointed. He swung the barrel of the rifle ahead of his brother, spotted movement, and focused in on the source. Sterling. He was coming from a different direction than Jared had expected. The van must have dropped him off a few blocks south, allowing him to walk toward the park at a ninety-degree angle to the path Chase took. Jared watched him pause, obviously waiting for Chase to pass in front of him and reach the meeting place. Five targets: the four men, and Sterling. The FBI needed to arrive shortly, and quietly. He had discussed the best approach with Reagan. On foot, from behind the stadium, a hundred eighty degrees opposite. Any cars pulling up would be noticed by Sterling and his men, and would put his brother at risk.

CHASE REACHED the meeting place. He stopped, signaling Garth to be on alert.

Hands low at his sides, he was conscious of the handgun in his pocket. The park seemed unusually quiet for this time of the morning. He'd counted on a bit more activity for safety. He heard Sterling before he saw him, his footsteps measured as he came up the same pathway Chase had followed. Chase stood with his back to a small tree, conscious of his vulnerability. Tempted to look for the FBI agents he'd been assured were coming, he kept his head still, careful not to betray himself as Sterling approached.

The colonel got to within fifteen feet and stopped, as Garth emitted a low growl. Chase scratched the top of his head.

"So," the colonel said in greeting. He wore a pair of loose-fitting black pants, and an olive tee shirt, covered by a red flannel shirt that hung loose. He carried a computer case over his shoulder.

Chase nodded, certain the colonel's garb concealed a variety of weapons. Even carrying his own gun, he felt helpless before the military man. He reached into his shirt pocket and held up a silver disk.

"I brought what I told you I would. Do you have the papers?"

The colonel made a motion forward with his hand extended. Garth growled ominously and Chase put the disk back in his pocket. Sterling glowered, but reached into an outside pocket of the computer case and withdrew a single sheet of paper.

"Put it on the ground and step back."

Sterling complied, smirking as he did so.

Chase picked the paper off the ground. The words were right, honorably discharging Jared Riordan from the service of the army, signed by William A. Sterling, Colonel, United States Army.

"No seal?" he said, holding it up, trying to buy some time. *Where were they?*

"What did you expect in an evening," Sterling said. "I assure you it's perfectly legal. As his commanding officer, I have the authority to authorize and sign the discharge. Your turn." He walked two steps forward again and held out his hand.

With no other choice, Chase folded the paper and tucked it in his left pants pocket. He reached a hand out with the disk, restraining his dog as he did so. Sterling took the disk in his right hand and examined it. He reached down and unzipped his computer case. "You won't mind if I verify the contents, I presume."

The colonel knelt on the ground, opened the case, pulled out a small laptop computer, and booted it up. Chase took the opportunity to look around, but could see only a jogger running along the perimeter of the park and routine traffic along Stadium Drive. No doubt sensing his anxiety, Garth growled again, his head pulling at the leash.

"Keep that mutt in check," Sterling said. He pulled a gun out from under this arm and pointed it at Chase. "There's another gun trained on your dog. You make a move and the dog gets it first."

"I said to come alone," Chase said with as much bravado as he could muster.

"You didn't think I'd let you walk away from here," he said. "Not when I can use you as bait to catch your brother." He popped the disk into the computer. As he did so, Chase heard a small popping sound in the distance. The colonel's head looked up for an instant, then returned to the computer. He punched in a few keys with one hand, still holding the gun on Chase.

"You can't think you'll get away with this," Chase said loudly. "Wall's not going to be happy if you take away his prisoner." He heard more pops and kept talking to distract Sterling.

"I cut off your ankle bracelet, Wall will think you escaped. Then you're a fugitive in addition to being a murderer. I simply wait for your brother to come to your rescue. Or to give himself up in exchange for you; he believes all that noble selfless crap."

Music suddenly came out of the computer, startling the colonel. The Eagles "Hotel California." Chase had been alerted. As the music started, he pulled out his gun and pointed it at the colonel.

Sterling looked up at Chase. He saw the gun, snarled, and held up his left hand. He seemed to expect something to happen. When nothing did, he stood up and leveled his own gun at Chase's face. "You…"

Before he could get out anything further, there was a cacophony of activity. A window shattered in a distance. A shot rang out. Then another. The gun flew from Sterling's hand. Three men burst from behind Chase, yelling "FBI! Freeze!"

Garth broke free and leaped on Sterling. Two more men came from the direction behind Sterling, surrounding the colonel, now locked in combat with the wolfhound, fangs buried in the arm that had held the gun.

"Get this damn dog off me," he managed to yell, as the FBI agents moved in.

Chase suddenly felt weak. He looked down and saw blood oozing from his left shoulder. He dropped the gun and held his right hand up to the wound. As he did so, he heard a voice, and a few minutes later Reagan was by his side, holding him up as he slumped. She waved to someone who approached them with a first aid kit.

Through the medic's ministrations, Chase managed to call off his dog. Garth dutifully came back to his side but sat facing the colonel, who was muttering obscenities as he was lifted to his feet.

AN AGENT PULLED the colonel's hands behind him and cuffed him.

"You've got nothing on me. I'm an officer in the United States Army. You have no power to arrest me."

The agent-in-charge reached inside his flak jacket and pulled out a piece of paper. "Assistant Director O'Keefe. We spoke on the phone, I believe. This says that I do. It's signed by the Head of Homeland Security. But we can sort all this out later. In the meantime you're coming with us."

Sterling's eyes locked on Chase's, who held his gaze as the medic worked on his shoulder.

"I am Colonel William Lamp. I've been working with the district attorney here on a case involving this man. I agreed to meet with him, hoping to elicit some information from him that would help the city's case. He pulled a gun on me and I simply tried to defend myself."

Sterling looked down. "Mr. Riordan knows I'm working with Wall. He didn't believe he'd get a fair shake with his former boss. I was trying to—"

"My pocket," Chase managed. "Discharge papers.

Reagan pulled the paper out of his pocket and handed it to her boss.

A walkie-talkie squawked, alerting the agent in charge. "Go ahead."

"Sir, we've secured the hotel room. Or rooms… there were three of them. Found a lot of electronic equipment, surveillance, by the look of it. Wiretaps, recording stuff, that kind of thing.".

"Also a large cache of weapons. Semi-automatics."

"Thank you, agent. Secure the premises. We have the prisoner."

Sterling blustered, his eyes still blazing, as he was led off toward Stadium Drive, where a brown SUV waited. By now, a group of people had surrounded the site, held back by local police, who must have been alerted by the FBI. O'Keefe picked up the computer left on the ground by Colonel Sterling and handed it to Reagan.

"You might find some interesting stuff on here, Agent Thompson," he said, "Monday okay to get started on it?"

She nodded in appreciation.

Chase looked down at his arm, bandaged heavily. The bleeding had stopped, and he could feel a dull ache.

"You're lucky," the paramedic said. "Bullet passed straight through. You should see a doctor, but you'll live.

Chase nodded his thanks, and took a moment to rub his dog's head.

"Good boy, Garth. Good boy."

Reagan remained by his side and he looked down. She was holding his hand. He raised his eyebrows, but she just smiled. As the men began to clear the site, her boss turned to him.

"This the same Jared Riordan you told me about?" he asked Reagan, nodding toward the discharge papers.

She nodded.

"Where the hell is he?"

"Here I am," came a voice from behind Chase. Chase turned and saw his brother walking toward them. Empty handed, he favored his left shoulder, giving his brother a wan smile.

"I guess this is yours, then, soldier," the man said, and handed him the discharge papers. At Jared's skeptical look, he added, "It's good. Colonel Sterling may be going to Leavenworth, but he did have the authority to sign it." He offered his hand, which Jared shook.

"A moment, sir?" Jared asked.

He and O'Keefe walked over to the side and talked softly. After a moment O'Keefe nodded, then returned. Motioning to his team, he called, "Come on boys, let's give these people some privacy." When Reagan hesitated, he looked at her. "You too, Agent Thompson."

She smiled at Chase, squeezed his hand, and nodded at Jared.

"Thanks," she mouthed, as she followed her boss.

O'Keefe looked over to the two brothers. "Join us when you're ready."

Within minutes, the FBI team had retreated, leaving Chase and Jared alone.

"Hey, bro," Jared said.

"Good to see you, too."

"Ah, hell," he said. They embraced, both of them wincing at the contact, their shoulders protesting. They stepped back from each other, assessing.

"Nice look," Chase said. "It works for you."

Jared stroked his goatee. "I might keep it. But I'm not sure I'm ready to be bald."

Chase laughed, noticing how good it felt to do so in his brother's presence. He'd imagined this moment over two years of seeing him helpless at the Institute.

"Thanks," he said simply.

"You too," Jared answered.

"You take out his whole team?"

"Three of them should live; I hit them in their shoulders. The fourth, I don't know. I had to wait until I heard the window break and saw the muzzle flash. Him, I'm not so sure about."

He could see FBI agents swarming around two different locations just across the street from the park.

"You shoot the gun out of his hand?"

Jared nodded.

"I'm surprised that's the only thing you hit."

Jared took a moment to answer. "I'd like to say I spared him so he'd face justice, answer for all the things he's done, but the truth is I swung my rifle around toward him, had him in my sites, and suddenly felt this great pain in my shoulder."

They shared a smile.

"Managed to get his gun, though. But by that time, though, this beast here looked like he had everything under control." He knelt down. Garth allowed him to scratch under his chin. "That's a fine animal you have."

"I know." Chase tried to read his brother. "You're a free man now. The FBI may need you to make a statement, but then you can pretty much go wherever you want."

"I haven't thought much about it yet. Think I'll stick around here for a while, see how this show ends." He put his hand on Chase's good shoulder. "Come on, let's go join the boys in black. And the girl."

Stadium Drive had been blocked off by the police, but was by now full of onlookers. The teams of agents were gathered around one of the SUVs parked there.

"Smile," Jared said. Chase noticed all the photographers gathered around. "Looks like you're going to be in the news again."

Chase looked for Tony Santori, but knew he wouldn't see him. The elation he'd felt at gaining Jared's freedom and putting Sterling away dissipated before the cameras, a stark reminder of his own predicament. Jared steered him away from the scene, sensing his change of mood. The brothers, wearing identical grim faces, walked together toward the street.

FIFTY-SIX

Sterling was taken care off, but there was still the matter of the murders. Shortly after 7:00 a.m., he got the word from Peter that his friends were all in town. Or were on their way. Surprisingly, Randy had been the first to return to Piedmont. Ev's plane was due to land within the hour. He and Chase had had a long conversation the evening before.

Chase put down the papers, from Jared, from Kasey, from Rufus, trying to piece them all together. So many secrets. He could see the whole picture now, and was surprised to find himself overwhelmed not with anger, but with sadness. At what was to come. At the tough choice that would have to be made; testing the bond of friendship against that of family. He tried to think if there was any other way through this, without the pain this would cause. But the killings had to stop.

Individual notes sounded from the piano in the next room. Tentative, at first, a simple melody, and then growing in complexity, the music filling the house. Quietly, he stood up from his desk, walked out of his office, and stood in the hallway, transfixed by the image of his brother sitting at the piano. Garth had settled himself under the instrument, his eyes closed, enjoying the music.

Chase sat down on the couch, and leaned back, taking it all in. It had been years since he'd heard his brother play, years in which the image of him at the piano had been replaced in his mind by images of him in soldier's gear, or in a hospital bed. He watched his fingers move, watched his brother's head moving with the changes in the melody, eyes closed, saw the way the music lifted him up. The song built to a crescendo, then slowly wound down, until the same simple melody from the beginning emerged; the same yet different, he noticed. Now it seemed more complete.

As he played the last note, Jared bowed his head, the index finger from his right hand still holding the key. Noticing his brother sitting at the couch, he smiled a wistful smile.

"Brahms?" Chase asked.

Jared smiled. "Thanks, but no." He got up from the piano, stretched his arms his fingers, and gently closed the keyboard, caressing the wood as he did so. "Something I've had in my head for a while. Never had a chance to play it."

"It's nice," was all Chase could come up with, still moved by the piece.

"Needs a little work. And I'm a bit rusty, but…" He shrugged.

"You sleep well?"

Jared nodded.

By the time they had finished meeting with the FBI the day before, giving their statements, and helping sort through the events of the previous week, it had been later afternoon. Still a member of the bar, Chase acted in the role of his brother's attorney, knowing he might have to face charges at some point, possibly in connection with the dead body found behind a window of a building bordering Stadium Drive. Fortunately, ballistics matched the bullet that had passed through Chase's shoulder with the gun in the dead man's hands.

In the end, O'Keefe had been kind and allowed them to leave, with the assurance Jared would stay in the area and make himself available as needed. The two of them had returned to Chase's townhouse and talked through the day and early evening, trying in some small measure to make up for the years apart. Jared, with only four hours sleep in the past two days, retired to the guest room at eight. Unable to sleep, his mind still racing, Chase stayed up in his office, going over the details once again. He'd been interrupted by a phone call.

Rufus Agnew had met with Ken Wall for two hours the previous evening. The meeting had been behind closed doors, with no one else present. Wall had scheduled a press conference for Friday morning at eleven.

"You ready for this?" Jared asked.

Chase gave a tentative nod.

"You know, when you're in a war zone and get your orders, you know the next morning you have to wake up to what might be your last day on earth. And still you have to get up, get dressed, get your gear, and go out there and do your job. Because if you don't, you'll be court-martialed," he smiled.

"Just kidding. But that's not why you do it. You do it because you made a commitment, to your country, and to your fellow troops. Even if you don't believe in what you're doing."

Chase frowned. "I'm not sure I see the relevance."

Jared shrugged. "There isn't any. I've just been waiting for years to give you that speech. Sounds very big-brotherly, doesn't it?"

In spite of himself, Chase laughed.

Jared stood up, walked over to the couch, reached out a hand, and pulled him up.

"I guess the point is, we all have to do things that are distasteful. But unless you want to go to jail, which I don't recommend, you're going to have to do this. And trust your friends."

"But forcing him to make that choice."

"It's his decision. Not yours."

He knew Jared was right, but it didn't make his task any easier.

"You're going to pick up our friend?"

"It will be my great pleasure," Jared said with a wicked grin. "I'll give you boys a little time to get reacquainted first."

"Thanks. I guess I'll see you in a bit," Chase said.

"You sure you don't want to use a more neutral location?"

"Nah, I've always wanted to see Ev's penthouse. Should be a more comfortable environment."

"Good friends, are you?"

Chase laughed. "You saw his house, where he lives. You think he brings women there? He says he likes to keep things separate."

"The Bat Cave, you mean? Didn't exactly look like it had a woman's touch, now that you mention it."

Chase reached down and scratched Garth's ears. He looked at his watch. Nine o'clock.

Almost exactly on cue, he heard a knock at the door. Walking over to answer it, he kicked a large duffel bag on the floor. Jared must have retrieved it sometime in the night.

"Anything in there I need to know about?"

Jared said, "Are you asking as an officer of the court?"

"Never mind. The keys to the Porsche are in the kitchen." He opened the door to Steve Riveira and stepped outside quickly.

"I appreciate the ride."

"No problem." He held up an odd shaped key. "Feel like shaving your legs today?"

Chase rolled up his pants leg and allowed Riveira to remove the ankle bracelet. He rubbed the chafed skin. "Thanks."

"Temporary, but you're welcome."

Ev's penthouse was at the other end of downtown, about a fifteen-minute drive.

"Interesting goings-on yesterday?"

"Yep." The morning papers had it all wrong, which didn't bother Chase in the least.

"A drug bust? Want to tell me why you were in the midst of a drug bust?"

That was the FBI's spin. O'Keefe had managed to keep

Chase away from the press, steering them in the direction of his press officer.

"Wrong place at the wrong time, I guess," Chase said. "Garth was trained as a drug dog, must have got a whiff of something when we were out on our morning walk. Next thing I knew there were shots and the FBI is everywhere."

Riveira looked over at him. "Right. Maybe someday you'll give me the real story."

Chase said nothing.

"I've been thinking about what you asked earlier."

"Oh?"

"About how you came to be a suspect. The informant."

When Chase again didn't say anything, Riveira continued.

"So you're this big mastermind. You've killed, what, four people without getting caught? Got the police running around in circles, the D.A. prosecuting other people. But somewhere along the way you slipped up, maybe told someone about all this. How else would an informant know so much?"

"You tell me," Chase said after a moment.

"Either you're seeing a shrink, you had an accomplice with a guilty conscience, which I seriously doubt, or…"

Chase looked at him. "Or?"

"Or the informant's the killer."

Or someone paid by the killer, but he didn't say anything. Riveira was likely correct. This was all part of an elaborate scheme, and Chase could only conclude the killer took pleasure in involving himself in everything, in addressing every detail. He doubted he'd leave something as important as a phone call to Wall to someone else.

"No one else talk to this informant except Wall?" Chase asked.

"So far as I know. The captain's in a knot about this one. He doesn't like being a gopher: open this evidence bag, go to this address. Not detective work, more like fulfilling a grocery order. Wall's playing him, trying to convict you."

"It won't be easy."

"What?"

"Getting a conviction." He felt he owed his friend at least a version of the truth. "Think about it, Steve. The only motive Wall's offered is greed and self-promotion. I wanted clients, so I created them. In order to prove motive, he'll have to go back to the Lewis case. Unless he can go back and prove I killed Ray Lewis, Jr., the rest of it falls apart. What, I tried to drum up a little more business after already establishing my reputation? It won't hold water."

"So what's Wall doing here, he playing some kind of game?"

"No, I think he honestly believes he can win. He's blinded by his emotions."

"He's playing the captain, and someone's playing Wall," he said.

"Exactly.

"I guess I'd put my money on you, if you put it that way." He brightened. "So you won't be going to prison."

They had reached their destination. The car pulled in front of One Titanium Tower.

Chase hesitated before he opened the door.

"I wish it were that simple. Just because he can't convict me for murder, doesn't mean I won't go to jail." He could see the puzzlement on his friend's face.

"What if he makes me an offer I can't refuse?"

Sorry to leave it that, he thanked Riveira and got out of the car.

AN OVERWEIGHT, middle-aged man wearing a faded gray uniform sat behind a desk guarding the entrance to the building. He looked up as Chase came in, pushed a logbook in his direction, took his picture, his information, and directed him to the elevator.

"Mr. Litchfield's on the top floor."

The elevator doors opened, not to a hallway, but to a residence. A large residence.

So this was the famous, or infamous, "Litchfield Lair" as Lionel had named it. The contrast with "Wayne Manor" was stark. Always amazingly shallow when it came to women, Ev went out of his way to impress them, either with his style, his money, or both. He always seemed to be putting on a big show complete with props, and himself as both leading man and director. The props in this case included garish artwork in pastel colors, a multitude of electronic gadgetry, a Jacuzzi in the corner, three big screen TVs, and speakers all over the place. Chase could only imagine what the bedroom must look like.

The tableau that greeted him was an odd one. Three men he'd known his entire adult life, looking like they've been watching a collection of weepy chick flicks. They were teary eyed and, most definitely, drunk. At least two of them were. Ev's plane had arrived recently, making it unlikely he'd had the time to get too tanked up. Chase waved a casual hello with his left hand, then winced at the effort. For a moment they all froze, as if they were friends who hadn't seen each other for years and weren't sure where they stood. Then Ev smiled, and hugged him; Randy came over, then Lionel.

Chase looked at the three of them. "I appreciate you all coming. It means a lot to me." And it did.

Lionel shook him off. "No big deal to me, I was on my way back anyway. But iron balls over here left the ice princess by herself." He put a large hand on Randy's shoulder.

Embarrassed, Randy shrugged. "Marinda's still in the Bahamas," he said. "When I told her I had to come, she stopped talking to me. Which made it easier to get on the plane." He looked at Chase. "You really going back to prison tomorrow?"

"That's Wall's plan. Grand jury meets first thing in the morning."

As Chase turned to Ev, the elevator opened again, and Peter and Reagan entered the penthouse. For a moment everyone looked from Reagan to Lionel to Chase, then Lionel laughed and grabbed his sister. He introduced her and they all laughed, recalling her as a middle-school teen. Peter stood off to the side, looking nervous and uncomfortable. Chase walked over to him and hugged him. Ev ushered them into the living room, a huge room with windows overlooking the city, dominated by a large black circular couch. Settling into seats around the room, the others shunning Peter, they settled in as Reagan took a seat next to Chase. She kept checking out of the corner of her eye for Lionel's reaction. Surprisingly, he was beaming, laughing, and slapping Randy on the back. Chase was glad for Reagan's sake. He had tried to tell her that Lionel would be the happiest among them to learn his little sister and his best friend were together, but it hadn't allayed her anxiety.

Ev stood at a large bar, poured himself a drink, and took orders from the others. Chase took a Diet Coke.

Ev raised his eyebrows, and said, "Prison food must agree with you. Lord knows it has to be better than your own cooking."

Chase examined his friend in a new light after all he'd learned, feeling, among other things, great sympathy. So much between them. The conversation between them the previous evening had been difficult for both of them.

"To think I've wasted all those young ladies on you, trying to steer them in your direction. I could have saved myself the trouble and kept them for myself."

Chase had no doubt he'd done that anyway. "Well, apparently we've all had our secrets," he said.

Ev tipped his head, then brought drinks to the group on a tray.

After a few minutes the talk became awkward and flattened.

Lionel finally said to Peter, "Where the hell have you been?"

"Myrtle Beach."

"Myrtle Beach? You down there taking a vacation, celebrating your big scoop?"

Chase held up a hand. "Let him talk."

Peter started slowly, relating the events that had brought him to Piedmont. When he mentioned the caller and the reference to his son, Chase noticed Randy and Ev exchanging a look. As he continued, telling the story of his visit to the hospital and what he learned there, Peter teared up.

"I should have told you guys about the call. For years I've worried about what might have happened to the child. I never meant to write anything that would hurt Chase."

"But I still don't understand one thing. Who was this caller?" Lionel said.

"One of the things we need to talk about," Chase said.

"Somehow I knew this wasn't just a reunion." Lionel shook his head, smiling.

Here goes, Chase thought.

"The call that Peter got hasn't been the only odd thing that's happened. Aside from my arrest. Obviously, that was a pretty odd thing to me, although not as odd as you might think."

He told them of his early suspicions of a serial killer in Piedmont. Gave them his rationale, inviting them to challenge him. No one did. Reagan picked up and talked about passing along his case files to a professor at Georgetown, a profiler, who'd agreed with Chase's conclusions.

"By that time, Wall had arrested me, which struck me as a pretty big coincidence. It meant he agreed with my conclusion—that a single killer was responsible for all the murders. Only he believed it to be me. On the basis of a call from a confidential informant and a few key pieces of evidence that conveniently showed up.

"Of course I wondered who could be setting me up. They seemed to be doing a pretty thorough job of it. Wall had a compelling motive, he had evidence that placed me at the scene of the crime, and tomorrow he'll present DNA evidence to the grand jury, which places me at Katarina Volkova's condo. My hairs."

Chase took a moment to look around the room. Lionel

and Randy paid rapt attention, brows furrowed. Peter nodded, no doubt because he'd heard pretty much the same thing from Wall himself. Ev sat staring at his drink, swirling ice cubes around. Sensing Chase's gaze, he looked up. "You were set up. We all knew that from the beginning," he said, staring down Randy, who flinched from the look.

"I appreciate that. But why?"

Puzzled looks.

"At first, I couldn't figure it out either. I was stumped. It had to be someone who hated me, or else someone who was terribly jealous. I've made some enemies, but––"

"Wall?" Randy asked. "I think he hates you enough."

"Maybe. And I'll come back to that." He needed their next guest for that one.

Right on cue, the elevator door opened again, revealing a pale, heavy-set, bespectacled man with curly brown hair in a blue pinstriped suit. He wore a scowl on his face.

Chase could see that Randy recognized him.

"Ellis, nice to see you. Thanks for joining us." Chase said, waving him toward the couch.

Squinting at Chase, he stumbled into the room. "I wasn't given much choice," he mumbled.

Chase said, "Let me introduce Ellis Krahnert, Chief Assistant D.A. for the City of Piedmont."

"And why exactly is *he* here?" Lionel asked menacingly.

"I'm sorry, Ellis, we were just talking about some personal matters. If you don't mind, I'll finish up, and we'll get to you." He stood up and offered his seat. Krahnert sat down; Reagan inched away.

"When I heard about Peter's caller and the pressure that had been put on him, I thought about who might do such a thing, and the answer seemed obvious to me."

"The real killer," Randy chimed in.

Krahnert snorted.

"Setting a false trail," Chase agreed. "But again, why?" He looked at Randy.

"Why were you in the Bahamas?"

Startled, he answered, "We're celebrating. I made partner."

"Congratulations. I thought, though, they announced the partners lists in the Fall."

Looking uncomfortable, Randy answered, "Well, sure, but when I got the Litchfield account…"

Chase noticed Ev twitch.

"Lionel, you were approached to run for Congress last year, is that right?"

He nodded, "Yes, by Gerald Roach."

"Wallace Thorne's former campaign manager?"

"Yes, what's all this got to do with anything? My campaign manager, Randy making partner, Peter's mysterious caller?"

"I'm getting there, "Chase said. "Ev, you're kind of quiet. How much money have you contributed to the Democratic Party over the last, say, six years?"

If he was offended by the question, he didn't show it. His eyes rose to the ceiling as he calculated. He looked at Chase, and said drolly, "Two point three million, give or take a hundred thousand."

"Shit," Lionel said. "That's more than I make in a month."

Nobody laughed.

"Randy, when I said I thought it had to be someone who hated me, you said Wall. Why?"

Randy laughed. "Everyone knows the answer to that one. You've whipped his ass in court a bunch of times."

Chase shook his head. "Before that."

Lionel answered. "The man went psycho on you. He railroaded you out of his office."

"Correct, but again, why? This whole case has been confusing because none of the motives have been clear. And in fact, my assumptions turned out to all be wrong. You've all heard the story from me. How Wall somehow blamed me for what happened to Abby."

Krahnert, sitting on the edge of the couch, arms folded, shrank back.

"Yesterday I found out why."

Ev raised his eyebrows.

"It's not well known, but Abby was pregnant when she died. I learned that Wall thought I was the father of her baby and had encouraged her to have an abortion."

Ev leaned forward, staring at Chase.

"Why did he think that?" Ev asked.

Chase returned his look, held it for a moment, and continued.

"Because he intercepted a letter he thought was from me that said those exact things."

"Any idea who wrote it?"

"Oh, I have a pretty good idea," Chase said, and glanced at Ellis Krahnert, who was looking increasingly uncomfortable.

"Hey, don't look at me," he said. And all eyes in the room turned to him.

"I thought to myself: who would stand the most to gain from all this? You became Chief Assistant almost the minute I walked out the door. You're next in line to be the District Attorney of Piedmont. I'd say that's a pretty strong motive."

Krahnert jumped to his feet and started to walk out. Lionel grabbed him with one arm and swung him back to his seat. "Sit," he ordered.

"You can't prove any of this."

"No, I can't," Chase said sadly. "But someone who had access to my letterhead and was familiar with my handwriting..."

"Who was left-handed," Reagan said, looking at the wristwatch on Krahnert's right wrist.

"Why left handed?" Peter asked.

"The signature smeared across the page. The hand following the pen across the page," Reagan explained.

"That doesn't prove anything. It was your letterhead, printed on your computer."

Chase smiled. "I never said it was a typed letter, Ellis. Just that is was on my letterhead."

Lionel made a move to grab Krahnert, but Chase held him back.

"It doesn't matter. I was glad to learn it wasn't something I'd actually done to Ken, or to Abby. I could understood why the D.A. felt the way he did about me. He had reason to believe I'd harmed his daughter, perhaps induced her to commit suicide. But as Ellis said, I can't prove it." *Now to sell it,* he thought.

"All this manipulation. I thought it would help me, seeing these different instances of the killer's hand at work, but in the end, it's taken me nowhere. It's like the letter. I can't prove anything."

Randy's said, "So, what, you're giving up?"

Chase shook his head sadly. "Not giving up, but I'm going to accept a plea."

"A plea?" Lionel exclaimed in disbelief.

"Ellis is the Chief Assistant. He'll confirm that Wall has offered me a plea agreement."

Krahnert smirked and said, "If it were up to me, we'd take you to the mat on this one. But Wall authorized a plea to the charge of manslaughter."

Chase looked only at Ev. "I have to take the deal."

Ev knocked over his glass, spilling its contents on the floor.

"Twelve to fifteen years if I plead to manslaughter two on Josh Samuels. He'll drop the charges on the others. Or rather, they'll never get filed to begin with. I think he realizes it would be a long shot to try those anyway. The juries in the two cases had already seen a lot of the evidence. It would be awfully difficult to come forward claiming someone else did the crimes after they'd already tried other people for them."

"But why?" Ev blurted out, almost at the same time as Randy and Lionel reacted. "You're innocent!"

Chase looked around the room. "If this case goes to trial and Wall even touches on the other charges, which he'll undoubtedly do, regardless of whether he can win those cases or not, I'll be lucky not to get life in prison. This way I could be out in six to eight years. I'll never practice law again, but at least I'll be young enough to still have a life."

Randy said, "Why should you go to prison for a crime you didn't commit?"

Chase ignored the question. "Rufus spent some time with Wall yesterday. Wall was pretty forthcoming about the evidence. According to Rufus, it's pretty compelling. If I were the prosecutor here, I wouldn't be offering any deal. I'd take it to the jury and be pretty confident of a favorable outcome, at least on the Samuels case." His delivery was very matter-of-fact. Lionel looked like he wanted to punch someone.

Only Ev sat completely still. "But there must be some other explanation," he said. "I'll spare no expense. We'll hire the best investigators out there. You'll get off and Wall will have egg on his face again! You'll be more famous than ever!"

Chase regarded his friend, his eyes sad. "Unfortunately, there are two other explanations for the evidence, one of which is why I need to take the plea. My brother." He paused to allow his words to sink in. O'Keefe had made sure to keep Jared out of the story. The pictures in the paper had all been of Chase, walking away from the scene with his dog. One of the captions read: "Accused murderer Chase Riordan seen leaving the site of an FBI drug bust." No one had any interest in the bald guy with glasses next to him.

"I know I haven't spoken of him much, but you all know I have a twin brother, Jared. For the past few years, he's been in a mental health institution in western North Carolina." No sense yet getting into any of the details. "He's not well. Wall has threatened to bring Jared into this. It could explain the DNA the prosecution has attributed to me. Hair and skin cells apparently, somehow discovered at the scene of the crimes."

"Exactly!" Ev cried. "It had to be him. The DNA, the killings—he's a trained killer! Everything fits. "

Everyone else looked stunned. Chase sighed. "That's the problem, Ev. It does fit. The institute where they kept Jared doesn't seem to be around anymore, so there won't be anyone to attest that Jared was locked up during that time. Wall knows all this. He knows all about Jared, about his war record, his incarceration––all thanks to a certain colonel who dropped in to visit. And he's left me with no choice.

"He told Rufus he'd prosecute my brother. I can't let him do that, Ev. The only way to stop that is to confess."

"But that's exactly what he wants. He's trying to coerce you into doing the noble thing—to protect him by pleading guilty yourself."

"I know that, Ev," Chase said quietly. "But unfortunately it doesn't change anything. Knowing doesn't change the course of action I have to take here. Jared's the only family I have left. If Wall gets hold of him, he'll never see the light of day, and he won't get the help he needs. At least if I do this, there's a chance the army, much as I mistrust them, will take care of him. Trust me, this is the best thing for everybody. At least when I get out I'll still have a brother. And you guys." Only Peter knew the truth about Jared. He kept silent.

Chase saw Ev twitching, his eyes moving wildly. He suppressed a smile. "But if he did it, you can't plead guilty. He should be the one to go to jail, not you."

"I never said he did it," he said quietly. "But regardless, I can't let him go to jail. My mother and father are both dead. I have no other relatives. You, Lionel, Peter and Randy have always been like family to me, but Jared's my blood. I know you can understand that. Much as you might despise your dad, you still have been loyal to your family. I admire that." He nodded to Krahnert.

"I have to do this, Ev."

Krahnert stood up. "So is that it? Are you accepting the plea?" Chase took a sip from his Diet Coke and walked toward Krahnert.

"You can't do this," Ev pleaded.

Chase stopped.

"You can still win this." Ev looked around the room frantically. He focused back on Chase. "Look, you can use Jared in your defense. Make it a 'one of us did, it, but prove which one.' They have DNA, but they can't prove it's yours or his. The jury will have to acquit. There'll be reasonable doubt about which one of you did it. I think I saw that in a movie once."

Chase shook his head. "It would ruin both of us. Make it seem like we were both in on it. They'd end up convicting us both, one as an accessory. Even if it could be a successful defense, what kind of life could either of us have after it's all over? We'd be the killers that got away. We'd be O. J.

"No, this is the only way. It offers a chance for Jared to get the help he needs and minimizes the time I spend in jail. With luck I'll be joining you guys at the beach again before you know it. Wall will announce our deal at a press conference tomorrow morning. It was part of the arrangement we made that he could grandstand one more day so I'd get to see all of you before I had to go away."

Krahnert now threw up his hands. "All right, enough with this crap. I don't have all day. You going to accept the plea?"

Chase stared at him for a moment.

"You said there were a couple explanations for the evidence," Randy said.

"Yes."

"What's the other?"

"That's up to Ev," Chase said slowly.

Lionel sat up straight on the couch, his eyes squinting. "What do you mean, it's up to Ev?"

Chase turned to Ev. Along with the nervous look on his friend's face, Chase thought he could detect a hint of amusement. He wondered whether anyone else noticed.

"What I said."

Silence.

Chase said to Lionel, "This isn't college anymore, Lionel. It's not some juvenile prank, like stealing the other team's mascot. This is murder, and my life."

Ev sat immobile, then his hands started to shake.

Chase watched the light dawn in Lionel's eyes, then Randy's. He held out his hands to Krahnert. "I don't think you need to cuff me, Ellis. If you'd just give me a few moments to say my goodbyes?"

Krahnert smirked and ran his fingers through his hair. "Sure, I'll just go use the head." He walked around the back of the couch.

"Wait," Ev blurted out.

Krahnert stopped.

"Look, it wasn't supposed to happen this way. This was supposed to help Chase." He said to Chase, "You beat Wall again, he'll be laughed out of town."

"What are you saying?" Randy asked.

Confusion replaced the smirk on Krahnert's face. He said to Ev, "If this is some kind of weird trick…"

Ev sat with his head in his hands for a moment, then stood up and scanned the faces of his friends.

"You know how much Wall hated Chase. He needed to be taught a lesson. I thought this might be a way to get it right."

"Are you saying you killed all those people?" Lionel said loudly.

Ev walked over to the bar and with unsteady hands poured himself another Scotch. His back to the rest of the room, he said, "They were bad people. You don't know…"

As he faced them again, his eyes had a colder look. Blinking rapidly, he said to Chase, "I never meant to hurt you. You have to know that."

Chase kept Krahnert in his view. "I'd like to believe that," he said. To the rest of the room, "I said before I had the motive all wrong. Remember, I assumed the motive to be hate or jealousy. What if there was a different motive?"

Krahnert had moved closer to Ev, stopped an arm's length away.

"I finally realized Wall had the motive right all along. He said the motive was to advance my career, to gain fame and fortune, to get even with him. Turns out he was right. Only he had the wrong guy." He looked at Ev, who had his head lowered, his eyes shielded. He wondered what was going through his head. He imagined he was enjoying this, strange as it might seem.

Krahnert pulled his cell phone out of his pocket. "I think you might need a police escort," he said blandly.

Chase thought to protest, but stopped at a movement of Ev's head. Maybe for the best.

Krahnert made the call. Then they all watched as he read Ev his Miranda rights.

"You knew," Ellis said to Chase.

"I said I couldn't prove it, Ellis, not that I didn't know who did it." He saw other questions in his friends' eyes, but he shook his head. *Another time.* "Guess you might have another story to write, Peter."

Peter looked thoughtful.

After a few moments they could hear a siren approaching.

"That's our cue," Krahnert said. "You know, Riordan, you should probably come, too. Might help to clear some things up." He grabbed Ev by the arm and led him to the elevator. Looking back, Chase gave a small wave. Reagan ran over to hug him, whispering into his ear. He nodded.

The elevator opened and the three men entered.

FIFTY-SEVEN

The story had first broken in the *Atlanta Journal* and *Constitution*, outlining the specifics of the government's case and offering an inside perspective on the sting operation that nabbed Sterling. Chase had smiled upon reading it, thankful that his friend had kept Jared's name out of the story, as promised.

In Piedmont the previous Friday, District Attorney Ken Wall had held the press conference as scheduled on the steps of the county courthouse. It went off without a hitch, although not as expected. The courthouse was ringed with reporters, everyone anxious to hear the latest news. The events of the day before were not yet widely understood. The papers had reported Ev Litchfield entering police headquarters with his longtime friend Chase Riordan. The police had released no information other than the fact that Litchfield was being questioned, presumably in connection with the Samuels murder. Everyone was poised to hear the perhaps anticlimactic announcement that Chase Riordan would be charged with multiple murders.

Chase knew from Peter that many of the news outlets had brought in psychologists to help explain to their readers how such a thing could happen—how a seemingly normal man could turn cold calculated killer. They ended up earning their pay.

Watching on television, Chase took no pleasure in the dance. He thought of Ev, going through what he'd been through himself. He wished there had been another way. But in the end, he'd allowed Ev the choice.

Wall did his bit, the cameras flashed, and the reporters asked their questions. The mad scramble began, everyone rushing off to meet deadlines. No matter. Peter would still scoop them all. Forgotten were stories about the young lawyer gone bad. Now the new spin began. The tobacco heir helping his friend, and then stabbing him in the back. That, at least, was how the story would play.

He hadn't known if the public would buy the rest of it, as it had unfolded in Ev's penthouse; that Ev's intent all along had been for Chase to get off and take down Wall in the process. It made a warped kind of sense, but only for those who knew Ev well. Peter had written it that way, at Chase's request, but the other papers hadn't followed, focusing instead on the family pressures involved in growing up as the fourth generation of a global family business. Chase had smiled thinly at that characterization, knowing the truth of it. Ev himself would no doubt agree.

Not ready to face the media, Chase had taken refuge in a hotel room in Gastonia, but he'd not spent much time there, choosing instead to spend his days with his brother and friends. Randy had returned to the Bahamas to try and soothe the hurt feelings of his wife. Meanwhile Peter was much in demand for his insider's perspective on the case, first with Chase and now Ev.

THE CALL HE'D BEEN waiting for came on Tuesday, at noon. An hour and a half later Chase pulled through an open gate into a long driveway lined with tall trees. Years before, the trees had been elm, but had fallen victim to Dutch Elm Disease. Full-grown maples had been planted in their place, no doubt at tremendous expense. Aside from the trees, the house looked much as Chase remembered it; imposing, with its Georgian architecture and multistory windows. The grounds were well maintained; in fact, a gardener was at work trimming bushes. Parking the car directly opposite the open front door, he got out, thought of knocking but continued inside.

He compared the décor with the last time he'd been to the house, noting that the inside had been totally redone, the leather and chrome furniture of the interior standing out in stark contrast to the classic brick façade. On that day he'd been greeted at the door by a butler, escorted into the kitchen, where the cook and two assistants prepared the meal he was there to enjoy, and then another servant had appeared to offer him a drink. This time, the gate had been unmanned, and aside from the gardener, there was no one else present.

Looking around, he noticed the open French doors at the rear of the salon. An invitation? He walked past the modern sculptures, the sleek leather furniture, the bookshelves lined with old volumes, and through the doors.

His host sat in an Adirondack chair by the pool, dressed incongruously in a dark business suit. Chase was conscious of the sun beating down on his skin as he returned a wave.

"Have a seat, Chase. So nice to see you. It's been too long." He indicated another chair at a forty-five degree angle to his. "Care for a drink? I've got gin and tonic." Nodding at a pitcher on the small table between the chairs, he held up his own drink.

Chase allowed him to pour another glass. He took a small sip.

"Thanks for coming."

Chase waited. He took a moment to examine the man sitting opposite him. Still an imposing figure, he was trim and physically fit, looking easily ten years younger than his age. His hair was an iron gray, his face had added a few wrinkles, and the gaze he fixed on Chase had an odd mixture of arrogance and vulnerability. Under ordinary circumstances, he might have felt some pity for the man.

"I'm not sure how to begin," Everett Litchfield, III said. "Obviously the events of this past week were quite unexpected. They've shaken me quite a bit." He sipped his drink.

"You're not alone," Chase said neutrally.

"Of course," he waved his hand. "I don't mean to minimize what you've gone through. I'm sure it must have been horrible. For that reason I'm sure you'll grant my special concerns."

"He's my friend."

"Yes, but he's my son, damn it!" he snapped, a small vein in his forehead bulging.

Chase kept his face still, not wanting to reveal anything. "Have you been to visit him?"

"He wouldn't see me."

Can you blame him, Chase wanted to say. Instead he took another sip from his drink and pulled out a pair of sunglasses. His chair had been positioned to catch the sun.

After a while, Everett Litchfield, III sighed. "His absence leaves a large hole in our European operation. He'd actually gotten off to a good start over there."

And how nice of his father to worry first about the company.

"You know of course, he didn't do this," Litchfield added, almost conversationally.

"Oh? I heard his confession. As did five other people. It seemed rather heartfelt."

"That boy could never hurt a fly. He's got no backbone, no balls. You think he could plan all this?"

"Ev's always been smart," Chase said.

"Maybe so, but something like this takes a lot more than just smarts. It takes a willingness to carry it out, to plan for the long-term. The ability to do whatever it takes."

"Qualities that the district attorney was willing to attribute to me."

The senior Litchfield chuckled. "Quite so. But you're an attorney, you've been in the courtroom, you've had to unravel schemes, solve crimes. And let's face it, you've always had that competitive instinct, that go-for-the-jugular attitude."

"Have you ever played your son in tennis," Chase said dryly.

"But he's good at that. There's a difference."

And you don't know your son nearly as well as I thought.

"Surely he's got an alibi. For at least one of the killings."

It sounded like a casual comment, but Chase could tell he was fishing. He decided to oblige him.

"From what I understand, he's been very cooperative. He may have had an accomplice."

"An accomplice? How could you trust another person with that kind of detail? I mean, it's difficult enough to commit murder. Not just anyone can do that. But to leave the right kinds of clues––that takes a special talent. I wouldn't think you could trust that kind of effort to someone else."

"Oh, I don't know," Chase said casually. "I don't know what kind of special talent it takes to kill a nine-year-old boy."

Litchfield's face darkened, his legendary temper briefly on display. He finished his drink. Set it down. Took a few measured breaths and regained control of himself.

"The boy was just a pawn," he said distantly.

"No one likes to think another person is capable of such things. Especially someone they know well."

"Like your brother," Litchfield said coldly.

So. He knew about Jared. As he'd suspected. Chase locked eyes with his friend's father. "A little different, don't you think. The work of a soldier, and the work of a butcher."

"Semantics," he said. "Killing is about gaining advantage. About will. Whether you do it as a civilian or cloak it under a uniform is irrelevant."

"Do you really think so? Do you believe that killing terrorists who are trying to kill us, individually and as a nation, is the same thing as strangling an innocent young woman?"

Drawing a cigar out of his inner coat pocket, Litchfield regarded it, then placed it in a corner of his mouth.

"I doubt she was innocent. To answer your question, though, I do think it's the same thing. We label a group terrorist, and everyone in America is willing to stick their hands up in the air and yell, 'kill them!' But in their country, they're fighting for their freedom; they have wives and children, just like the U.S. soldiers who oppose them. Soldiers who haven't a clue why they're there, following the knee-jerk reactions of a bunch of pompous politicians."

"The soldiers, as you say, have their excuse. They're sent somewhere by their government, told to do their duty. But in the civilian world, what gives one person the right? There would be anarchy if everyone thought the way you do."

"Not everyone. There are causes––just as right, just as justified––that require actions to be taken. Actions by a few who can see the big picture. Who can do what needs to be done. What *needs* to be done."

He really believes this. Everett Litchfield, he knew, was an exacting and demanding father, and a ruthless businessman, but he had never seen a glimpse of the fanaticism that lurked beneath his poised exterior.

"And is Ev one of those people?"

Settling back into his chair after his outburst, Litchfield chewed on his cigar.

"I wanted him to be," he said softly. He turned to Chase his eyes hooded. "But you got in the way."

Chase stared back at him.

"I raised that boy to run this company, to take his responsibilities seriously. Instead he had to join up with you and your merry group of men. You made him soft, you made him want to be like…like *you*," he spat out the last word.

"He came back. From New York," Chase prompted. "Took a role in the company."

"Yes, he came back. But not for the company or for me. He wanted to be closer to you, his friends," he snarled. "He spat on my efforts keeping this company together. Didn't want to have anything to do with me or with the business his great-grandfather built. He played at it. He never realized the work that went into running a company like this, keeping it strong."

"Like dealing with pawns."

"Exactly," he said shortly.

Sensing he wanted to talk about this, wanted to brag to someone, Chase said to him, "And reporters?"

"He thought he was being cute, talking to that Samuels guy. Wanted to rub my nose in it. Did he think I didn't know it was him? I couldn't let it continue; he was hurting the family. I had to teach him a lesson."

"So Ev didn't kill Samuels?"

Litchfield looked at Chase with disdain. "I told you. You made him soft. Made him think he should be like you, instead of like me. He didn't have what it takes. He chose his friends over his family." *The real motive*, Chase thought. *Finally.*

"The lesson you taught him. It wasn't just Samuels."

Looking into the air as if talking to himself, Litchfield said, "I had to teach him who he could really count on."

"So you set me up."

Litchfield poured himself another drink. He looked at his glass. "Child's play," he said finally.

When Chase had read the killer's profile, there had been a line in it that had caught his attention. "The killer will be someone who believes he can get away with anything. He will have a strong personal motive that won't be obvious to others." Perhaps, though, it should have been. He hadn't suspected Ev's father until he learned of the pressure brought to bear on Peter and saw the letter to Abby, intercepted by Wall.

"You tried to push us all away. From each other."

"Tried? I succeeded," he said. "Where were all your friends when you got out of prison? They all abandoned you. Who was there for you? Surely Ev had to see if they wouldn't be there for you, they wouldn't be there for him." He looked coldly at Chase. "And you wouldn't be there at all."

Chase returned the look. The man sitting with him had killed at least four people, all to teach his son a lesson. Ironically, to teach him the importance of family. Litchfield figured Ev would have to return to the company, to his father, when he saw his friends fall by the wayside.

"Katarina Volkova? Was she a pawn too? Didn't she like the jewelry you bought her?" He wanted to get it all.

For a moment, Litchfield looked diminished, his eyes sinking into his head. "She was… necessary. She wanted more than I could give her. Consorting with that old coot Agnew, she practically rubbed my nose in it. Trying to make me jealous. She tried to manipulate me."

People who manipulate others, in Chase's experience, never took kindly to others doing it to them. Ev had discovered something else about Katarina Volkova while he was in Berlin. Before he'd gone to prison, Katarina's father had been the head of a far-reaching conglomerate, headquartered in St. Petersburg. After he'd been imprisoned, control of the individual companies had fallen into a state of flux, with ownership contested among shareholders, family, and the government. One of those companies had been ARG Tobacco.

"All this work? And for what? Your son's in prison," he said.

"He made a choice! Even after all I did, he chose you over me. He's willing to go to prison to protect you. His friend. And you're willing to let him do it."

"Actually, he's not," came another voice from behind him.

Chase watched Litchfield, as he registered the presence of others behind them. Saw his head sink, his eyes squint, his stare shift back to Chase.

Ken Wall, District Attorney for the City of Piedmont stood side by side with Everett Litchfield, IV, flanked by two uniformed police officers.

"You…" he started. His face reddened and his left eye twitched.

Standing up, Chase nodded to the D.A. "All yours." Before he walked away, he leaned down and whispered in Litchfield's ear. "And maybe you're wrong. How do you know he didn't do it to protect you?"

Leaving him, he walked to meet his friend, as the D.A. and police officers stepped down to the pool.

Ev stood watching his father, and laughed as the old man huffed up and became indignant as Wall read him his rights.

"I'm sorry," Chase said, clasping his friend's shoulder.

"I know," Ev said. "But I heard all that."

Together, they walked into the house.

"You gave quite a performance, back at your penthouse," Chase said.

Ev smiled. "I did, didn't I? It's been a long time since I've been on stage."

"I particularly enjoyed the comment about the twins movie. Clever."

"I did actually see a movie like that. Back in high school or something. I worried that I might be overplaying it a bit."

"No, overplaying it was when you started shaking your hands and blinking your eyes. I thought for a moment I'd lose it."

"Worked with Krahnert."

That had been the point. "I think you were starting to convince Lionel and Randy as well."

Chase and Ev had cooked up the idea after their long telephone conversation the night before. He'd laid out his suspicions, told him what he knew. Ev related he conversation he'd had with his father about Josh Samuels. Apparently he'd had his own suspicions. He didn't take much convincing. Peter and Reagan had known. They knew Jared had spent time with him and wouldn't believe the lie Chase had to tell. Neither Lionel nor Randy could know. The performance had to feel real; they had to react naturally. Up to a point.

"Thanks for bringing up the mascot. I didn't really want to leave the room with Randy and Lionel thinking I was a killer."

In college, the male captain of the cheerleading squad had stolen the rival Westfield College's boar, the team mascot.

The honor council had brought a number of suspects together, demanding to know who was responsible. When at first no one stepped forward, Ev Litchfield raised his hand and said he had done it. He was suspended from school for the semester, until the real culprit, shamed, came forward.

"You almost had me going," Chase said.

They sat down in the study, filled with advertising posters extolling the virtues of smoking.

"That one's my favorite," Ev said, pointing to a framed poster in the corner. In it, a beautiful buxom blonde pursed her lips at the camera as a smoke ring drifted to the top. "Almost made me want to smoke. Or be with a woman who did."

"I need to thank you," Chase said. "You didn't have to do this. Put yourself through it."

"Hey Chase, my old man tried to frame you as a serial killer. It's the least I can do. Besides in this town it can only help my reputation." He winked.

They sat in companionable silence, then Ev said, "You really think Krahnert is my dad's man?"

Chase shrugged. "I don't know if he still is, but he was once, at least." One reason the performance had to look real.

"But if he did report back, my father would know I was lying. That it was all an act."

"He'd know it was an act, but Ellis believed it, and your father couldn't correct him. Krahnert might be your father's man, but I can't believe your dad would share the truth with someone from the D.A.'s Office. You heard him; he believed you did it to save my skin. Which of course, you did, but not for the reasons your father thought."

"The last few years he's become paranoid. He got rid of all the staff here because he was convinced they were spying on him. I doubt he trusts anyone anymore, including me."

"Killing that many people will do that to you." Litchfield Senior's own words had validated that. His belief in his own inherent superiority kept him from relating to or trusting others. They weren't worthy.

"Did he really make Krahnert send that note?'

"I doubt he had to work too hard to convince him." He looked sympathetically at his friend.

"How long have you known?" Ev asked after a few moments.

"About Abby? Not long. Kasey was talking to your new secretary, Savannah is it?"

Ev nodded.

"Something about a tattoo of a bird. I remembered Abby had a tattoo on her left ankle. Not just a bird, I realized, but a robin."

"She was special to me, Chase. You have to know that. All these other girls since… it wasn't like that with her."

He nodded. "I know, Ev. Because I knew her. And I know you."

"We both wanted to tell you, but I think she was a little ashamed of me at first, because of my reputation. I didn't want to make it seem like I was bragging or anything, I wanted to respect her."

Having had a year-long relationship with Lionel's sister without telling anyone about it, Chase could well understand. He smiled, thinking of Abby,

"She got pregnant. We weren't trying or anything, it just happened. We talked about it; I told her I'd marry her." His eyes filled with tears. "I could never understand it. We were going to—" He couldn't finish the sentence.

Chase realized that Ev had been wrong before when he'd said he hadn't been on stage in a long time. He'd had to act for the past four years, hiding the love he'd felt for a woman, and the tremendous grief he must have felt. He thought carefully, wondering whether he should tell his friend about his suspicions about his father's involvement in Abby's suicide. Decided he didn't deserve to have his faith in his father so completely shattered on a single day.

"I'm sorry," he said instead.

As he said that, they heard the procession outside in the

hall as the police officers prodded Litchfield Senior toward the front door.

"You'll never convict me," he said. "Call my lawyer, Ev."

Ev started to get up, but Chase put a hand out to restrain him. Ev tugged his arm away, then shrugged, and sat down. "Let him call his own damn lawyer."

Looking out the front window, they saw the policemen putting him into a squad car. *A more dignified arrest than I had*, Chase thought.

Ken Wall stuck his head in the office. "You've got a ride home, I assume, Mr. Litchfield?"

"I'm good. Thanks."

Looking to Chase, Wall seemed uncertain what to do. Chase made it easy for him, getting up from his chair and meeting him at the door, holding out his hand.

Wall gratefully grabbed the hand. "I'm not quite sure what to say."

Rufus Agnew had performed masterfully when he'd met with Wall the week before. The ex-mayor had been hesitant to approach it this way, preferring to save their ammunition for trial. Revealing their hand bore a lot of risk. It forewarned Wall about defense strategy, and if he didn't buy it, would give him information that would help him solidify his case. Chase, however, had been adamant. He believed Wall, for all his actions, to be a man of integrity, blinded by a misguided desire for revenge. Agnew had found a more receptive audience than he had expected. In the package Wall sent to the lab to compare Chase's DNA with that found at the crime scene, he'd included a sample from the fetal tissue from his daughter's autopsy. Once he realized Chase was not the father and the letter he'd intercepted was a fake, he'd begun to consider the possibility this was all a setup.

Presented only with Chase's suppositions, receipts from a New York jewelry store, a press release showing Ev's father in town at that time for an investor's conference, Rufus' persuasiveness, and the story from Ray Lewis, he'd agreed to participate in the sting operation to set up Everett Litchfield, III by having Ellis Krahnert sit in on the meeting among friends. The biggest challenge they faced was Wall's fear that Chase had set Ev up to make the statements in order to create reasonable doubt for his own case.

"I've not been myself. For four years. Can you ever forgive me?" Wall said.

"We were all victims here, Ken."

"Thanks," he said after a while. He looked for a moment as if he wanted to say more, then nodded at Chase, then Ev, and left.

Ev said, "I doubt that I'd be so charitable to a man who made my life hell the past several weeks."

"He could have told Rufus, thank you, I'll consider it, but he realized the truth of all this and actually dropped the charges. That took a big man, Ev. To acknowledge a mistake that large. He put himself out there on this case."

In fact, he had taken a huge risk. While they hoped that the plan for Ev to confess would force his father to come forward, there were no guarantees. How could anyone predict the actions of someone who had done the things he'd done. If he didn't confess, Wall would be stuck with no suspects for the Samuels murder, and would have to explain himself to the police, the public, and his boss, the mayor. And might have been out of a job.

"So, to sum it up," Ev said, his voice back to something approaching normal, "My father fakes a note so my best friend would take the blame for my girlfriend's suicide and lose his job. Then he kills four more people, setting you up to take the fall. At the same time he tries to push all our other friends away through unscrupulous means, all in an effort to convince me that it's all about family and the company business. Am I missing anything?"

Chase shrugged. "You know, I sure hope not." They both laughed, a release.

FIFTY-EIGHT

The five sat around a table in the corner of the bar at Hilton Head Island. They enjoyed the Labor Day weekend scenery, largely consisting of bikini-clad women drinking a variety of frozen concoctions.

"To traditions," Lionel said, raising his glass.

"Traditions," they echoed.

The past two months had seen big changes in all their lives. Peter had made the decision to move back to Piedmont the previous month. After his work on the Litchfield case, he'd received a number of offers from newspapers throughout the south and accepted an offer from the *Piedmont Gazette* as a features writer. Lionel had withdrawn from the congressional race, returned to his place as pastor of Gastonia Baptist Church, and was involved in building a new youth center in South Piedmont. Ev was serving on an advisory committee overseeing the family trust.

"I have an announcement," Chase said, looking at Randy. "I have decided, after much consideration and deliberation, to take on a partner."

"About time," Ev said. "And who's the unlucky bastard?"

"Effective October 1ˢᵗ, we will do business as Riordan, Turner and Associates."

The news called for another round, and they all clapped Randy on the back.

"What's Marinda up to these days?" Peter asked.

"I still see her all the time," Randy answered. "She's dating Mike Maples, Jr."

"The managing partner's son?" Peter groaned.

"Hey, it works for me. Might make for a more equitable divorce settlement."

"They deserve each other," Lionel grunted.

Chase shared news of his brother, enrolled at UNC-Chapel Hill. Jared was studying music theory and composition, hoping to make his mark someday as a composer and conductor. Working with a therapist, he was struggling to piece his life back together.

"I've killed a lot of people," Jared said, after Chase had been cleared of the charges against him.

"You were a soldier," Chase said.

"I didn't even see their faces. They were just targets. You shouldn't be allowed to kill someone without seeing their face. Look them in the eye, at least."

He'd talked about his experiences in the military, some of the good people he'd met, along with the bad. Told of the places he'd seen: Bosnia, Afghanistan, Iraq. Of the people in those countries and how they lived.

"For the first ten years, I was a robot. It felt good. I wanted someone to tell me; go here, do this. I didn't want to think. Then later, it took me over. I was a soldier. It became my identity. After a while, though, maybe three, four years ago, I started to think about all the things I was missing. Things I'd run away from. You, my music, what I did."

Chase hadn't revealed his knowledge of his brother's confession to General Jackson. He'd hoped Jared would eventually be able to talk about it.

"You didn't need to run away," he said.

Jared looked down.

"There was this guy," he began, "He'd been at a bar with his buddies, celebrating a promotion, I later learned. After a few too many, he got into his car to drive home. Only a few short blocks away. He might have made it, but it was raining, the visibility was poor, and he ran a stoplight.

"A Volvo came through the intersection from his left. He broadsided it, killing the passenger instantly. The driver died in the emergency room." They were sitting in Chase's hotel room in Gastonia the Sunday after Chase had been released.

"You remember that car? Remember how dad was so proud when he bought it, said it was the safest car on the road? Steel construction? You should have seen it. It might as well have been made of wood.

"I had to identify the bodies. Dad had some bruises on his face, they kept his body covered with a towel. But when I saw Mom... I only knew it was her because she was wearing the earrings I'd bought her for her birthday. One of them was embedded in the side of her head."

Chase could only listen; he knew the story, but had never heard it from Jared.

"This guy had killed our mother and father. And he'd gotten away with a broken arm and a cracked rib. From the airbag," he laughed, almost a sob. "I found out where he lived, and I started to follow him around. Going to work, coming home. One day he was coming home from a bar. The same bar he'd been to that night. Anyway I parked a few blocks down, sat on a bench and waited for him to come out. He got in his car and started up the road. Going the speed limit, thirty miles an hour or so.

"I saw his car coming toward me. Without thinking, I walked into the middle of the road and stood there facing him. It was dark, but he must have seen me in his headlights. I don't know even now what I wanted to happen. Whether I wanted him to kill me too. But at the last minute he must have seen me, and he swerved out of the way. His car hit a streetlight and rolled over. I ran back to my car. I sat there for two hours, while the ambulance and police came."

Mesmerized, Chase said, "You didn't kill him."

"I might as well have. When I found out he'd died in the hospital, I was glad. But I saw in his obituary he had a wife and two small daughters. After a couple weeks I started having nightmares. I withdrew from school. You know the rest." He paused and wiped his eyes. "I still see his face in my dreams."

"JARED AND I HAD DINNER together last week," Chase said to his friends. "I'm going to go up to Chapel Hill to help him get settled, look for an apartment."

After years of avoiding the topic, it felt good to talk about his brother.

"You and Reagan set a date yet?" Lionel asked innocently. "I have a right to know if you plan to make an honest woman of my sister."

Now that their secret was out, everyone assumed they would be married. There remained, however, the obstacle of location.

"I think we're going to have to have a commuter relationship for a while, although we do have a trip to Bermuda planned for next month. The advantage of having a partner. How's the story coming, Peter?" he asked, changing the subject.

"Like peeling back the layers of an onion. I've had three anonymous death threats and an offer to meet with His Highness, Wallace Thorne himself. We had lunch last week. I think someone figured after I met with the great man, I wouldn't have any interest in exposing his campaign finance irregularities."

"Is he involved?" Randy asked.

Peter looked thoughtful. "Funny, but I really don't think he is. He seemed to genuinely want to get to the bottom of this. Gave me his personal number, said to call him if I needed his help for anything."

The first article in his series had appeared two weeks before, detailing corruption throughout the State Democratic

Party. The rats were all scampering for high ground. One of Chase's questions had been answered when he learned that, seven years before, Winston Reese had been Treasurer of the Party and had been involved in the scheme. Perhaps he had tried to blackmail Litchfield, or else had taken money that wasn't his. Regardless, the connection was there.

"I have to say," Peter said, "I couldn't have made the progress I've made without your dad's financial records. Funny how they showed up in my mailbox."

"Funny," Ev agreed. "Just goes to show you, never leave your records sitting in a locked desk. You never know what might happen."

"You might want to think twice before you commit any more money to the Party. At least in the short run."

"I shall be sure to contribute funds to those who are deserving. Maybe those running for City Parks Commissioner."

"Speaking of your father," Lionel said. "What's the latest?"

Everett Senior had retained a team of high-powered attorneys from both coasts—Dream Team II, as he referred to them. He'd made bail and talked to anyone in the media who would listen.

"Maintaining his innocence," Ev said woodenly. "Living large. No longer head of the company, thank God, but he's still the largest shareholder. Sends memos all the time. Half my job is doing damage control with our other investors."

It would be a difficult conviction, Chase knew. The D.A. was behind the eight ball, on record as having already accused four other people with the same crimes. Litchfield's arrogant assertion in the press might well be right; in the end, he'd probably walk. Millionaire's justice.

Randy stood up to change the somber mood. "I've got another toast, y'all. We've made it through twenty years together. We've discovered a lot about ourselves and each other this past year, and one thing I learned is, I need you guys. I've been a real horse's ass, I know, but I need you in my life. Nothing's going to allow that to change."

They all raised their cups in agreement.

"I think there's only one thing that can really get in the way, and that's another Marinda."

They all laughed.

"All kidding aside," He raised his glass, "To friendship."

To brothers, Chase amended mentally, holding up his glass with the others.

EPILOGUE

Pushing the hair out of his eyes, he strode into the study. The master of the house, sitting in a high-backed chair under an antique reading light, looked up from his newspaper and smiled.

"How nice to see you again, Chase. No wire this time, I trust?"

He held his arms out to his side, offering to be searched.

"Forgive me. I'm sure you can't blame a person in my position for being careful. Looks like you tanned a bit at the beach."

"My voice is a little hoarse. Too much drinking."

The old man chuckled. "I'm not so old that I don't remember hanging out with the guys and having one too many. Please, have a seat," Litchfield indicated the couch to his left.

"So. I'm sure you're at least a little surprised at the turn of events over the past couple weeks."

"Win some, lose some."

"How magnanimous of you." He set the newspaper down beside him and walked over to a wet bar against the wall, picking up a crystal decanter. Raising his eyebrows at his guest, he poured two glasses.

"Enjoy," he said, proffering the brandy snifter to his guest.

"Napoleon Brandy. One of the finest in the world. Salut."

They clinked glasses.

"I must admit, when you came here three months ago, I underestimated you. You came into my house, and you beat me."

"You confessed to killing at least four people."

Litchfield sat back down in his chair. "The word 'confess' implies an admission of guilt. I made no such admission. In fact, as I'm sure you know, my lawyers have moved to dismiss my so-called confession. I have every expectation that it will be suppressed. And then what will the city have, I ask you? Nothing. Ashes in the wind, if you'll allow me the metaphor."

"There's still the matter of evidence."

He waved his hand. "What do they have, a few jewelry receipts? It's a long way from buying a watch for a girl to killing her."

"Your financial documents will probably be of some interest to the D.A. Some interesting accounts, and bank deposits."

"Obtained fraudulently. And even if they subpoena the records, my attorneys advise me they've been tainted."

"You seem pretty confident."

"It's no coincidence that I've won at each step of the way. Mr. Wall tried to deny bail; the judge disagreed. How could he not? I'm one of this city's biggest benefactors, and I have a flawless record. We moved to have the charges dismissed for the Lewis murder and the Reese murder. They've been dismissed."

"But not the Samuels or Volkova murders."

"Just a matter of time."

"You've lost your company."

"Ev's just a caretaker," Litchfield said. "As soon as I'm cleared of all charges, our investors will beg me to resume command."

"So justice will be denied."

"Justice. What does that mean: 'fairness'? Life isn't fair. Get over it."

"Do you have your next victim picked out?"

He laughed. "What kind of man do you think I am?"

"I know exactly what kind of man you are. Your actions have made it abundantly clear."

Litchfield said, "If I were the person you think I am, you wouldn't have walked in that door."

"I should be afraid of you?" He took a sip of the brandy. Smooth.

"Aren't you?"

"You didn't exactly give your victims much of a chance: Katarina Volkova, killed from behind, a piece of fishing line pulled around her throat, Josh Samuels, drugged, then attacked from behind. Ray Lewis, Jr., a nine-year-old boy. Winston Reese, pushed off a ledge. Face to face, I think I'm safe."

Litchfield's brows curled like caterpillars. "And sent you to prison. Allegedly."

"Always behind the scenes. Making phone calls, threats. Never willing to face, either your victims or the people you've threatened?"

"You're trying to rile me, and it won't work."

He scratched his head. "You're probably right."

"And what difference would it make? This is going to be settled in the courts, and Wall and his team will be completely out of their element. Did you happen to catch your former boss's performance in court this past week?"

"No, I try and stay away."

"Pathetic. My lawyers had him whimpering like a whipped dog. Now if you were still in the office, it might be another story."

"Perhaps. Although maybe you shouldn't underestimate the district attorney."

"I don't underestimate anyone; I do my homework, I find their weaknesses, their strengths and I exploit them. It's how I've always operated. Why I'm successful."

Silence.

"You and I, we're a lot alike," Litchfield said.

"How's that?"

"You operate the same way. Know your enemy. Remember, I watched you play ball, I watched you in the courtroom."

"You watched all of us."

"You stole my son from me. Of course I watched you. I've been watching you all for twenty years."

"Makes it easier to pull the strings."

"Of course." He winced. "Oh, you're very clever, Mr. Riordan. In the end, though, all it will get you is a world of disappointment."

"Oh, I don't know. I'm happy so far. You've lost your job, you're under indictment for two murders, your son isn't talking to you, your investors mistrust you, and most of all, you don't have any friends. You're a lonely old man, sitting alone in his home."

Litchfield held his brandy snifter up to the light, a small Tiffany lamp, swirling the liquid around. "Are you a student of history? That's a rhetorical question. I know every course you ever took in college, and in law school. You're familiar with Winston Churchill, I presume?"

He indicated a number of volumes on the bookshelf behind him. "His *History of the English Speaking People*. Still considered one of the definitive works on the subject. A man who led a nation in and out of war, a man who did whatever it took."

"The same could be said of Adolph Hitler," he responded dryly.

A frown, and then a small smile. "I forget your droll sense of humor. Churchill had a sense of humor. I'm sure you're familiar with this story. A woman once said to him at a dinner party, "Mr. Churchill, you're drunk," to which Churchill famously replied—",

"Madame, you're ugly. But in the morning I will be sober."

Litchfield frowned at the interruption.

"Your point?"

"When I'm cleared, my investors, and my friends, will like me again. Even Ev might begin to wonder."

He laughed. "Such good friends you have. You do know what that word means, don't you?"

"What?"

"Friend. It means someone who sticks by you. Even during hard times."

Litchfield stood up, a dark expression on his face. "I think you've outworn your welcome. As always."

"I'm just getting comfortable. Would you mind pouring me another drink?"

"Such ill manners. You've always been a bad influence on my son."

"And that's the crux of the matter, isn't it? Must be my New Jersey upbringing." He stood up and walked over to the portrait of Everett Litchfield, II above the fireplace, identical to the one hanging in Ev's mansion.

"Do you own a gun?" he waved a hand. "That's another rhetorical question. Of course I know every gun you've ever owned. In fact, you keep a 9mm Browning Renaissance in your safe. A bit of a collector's item." He swung the portrait on its hinges to reveal a wall safe. "Kind of cliché," he said.

"I don't know what kind of game you're playing, Chase. But I really must ask you to leave."

"You think justice is just a word. But it's so much more than that. Your friend Winston Churchill once said 'All the great things are simple, and many can be expressed in a single word; freedom, justice, honor, duty, mercy, hope.' I believe in justice. Churchill apparently did too."

"How wonderful for you," Litchfield said, clearly annoyed. "If it means so much to you, come to the courtroom and you'll witness justice administered when I walk out a free man."

"I believe in justice," he repeated, "but I also believe in retribution. Would you mind opening the safe?"

Litchfield stared at him. "Enough. Get…out…of…my…house."

Ignoring his host, he said, "You know, I agree with you."

"Excuse me?"

"I think you're right. Your case will never even go to trial. But justice must be served." He opened a drawer, and pulled out a piece of paper and a Mont Blanc pen.

Litchfield laughed. "'Justice must be served.' What crap. That might work on one of your juries, but it means nothing to me. What do you want me to do, sign a confession? It's not going to happen. And what would it be worth? How much did that farce you engaged in the last time gain you? They threw out the tape. Face it, Chase, you've been beaten. You won a battle, but you've lost the war."

"Funny you used that analogy." He walked over, grabbed Litchfield by the arm, and steered him in front of the safe. "Open it."

Smiling, Litchfield said, "You forget, Chase, I know you. Better perhaps than you know yourself. I know what you're capable of. You believe in the law, and you believe in the system. And in fighting fair, although I admit your little escapade last time you were here pushed the boundary a bit."

"Sometimes it's not enough. Sometimes you have to take justice into your own hands."

"What do you expect me to do? You want me to take the gun out of the safe, so you can call the police and claim I threatened you? Please," he scoffed.

"No, I just want to be sure you don't take the easy way out," he said quietly.

"It won't work, Chase. I know you; I call your bluff. Do your worst." He stood holding his hands out, palms up, a grin on his face.

A sigh. "You told me you've made a study of all of Ev's friends and contacts. You know Peter, you know Lionel, you know Randy, and you know Chase. And you're right. Chase couldn't take the law into his own hands; he believes in justice.

"But you made a mistake. You left one thing out of the equation."

"Oh, and what's that?" Litchfield said indulgently.

"Me." He dialed a combination and casually opened the safe to reveal the gun. "Beautiful weapon." He tucked it into his pants. "Though I'm more of a rifle man myself."

Jared peeled the wig from his scalp. "You put my brother in prison. You would have been happy for him to go to jail for the rest of his life. That doesn't sit well with me."

Litchfield sat in his chair, seemingly unable to move. His bravado was gone, and the hand holding his glass trembled slightly.

"What do you want?" he managed.

"You have a choice."

Litchfield shrank back from him. "You wouldn't—not in my house."

"I told you. I'm better with the rifle; you'd never see it coming." He allowed the implication to sink in, and then steered the cowering man to a chair at the desk. He indicated the pen and paper on the desk.

"Write it out. Deliver it to the D.A. Include some details only the killer would know. Tell the world you decided to spare everyone the expense of a trial. Be magnanimous. However you'd like to handle it."

"Or?" The word came out almost as a whisper.

"Or, you look over your shoulder for the rest of your life. However long, or short it may be, waiting for that bullet to arrive." Jared walked to the door. As he opened it, he turned toward the old man one last time. The quivering figure sitting in the chair little resembled the pompous man who had greeted him just a few minutes earlier.

"Trust that I'll choose my moment well," he said, eliciting a coughing spasm from Litchfield. For the first time, Jared found himself grateful for the reputation that followed him.

As he walked away from the house, Jared was reminded of a quotation from the great chess grandmaster Emanuel Lasker; sometimes the threat is more powerful than the execution.

The End.

FREEMASONRY
AND ITS ETIQUETTE

FREEMASONRY
AND ITS ETIQUETTE

BY

WILLIAM PRESTON
CAMPBELL-EVERDEN

PM, 19; PZ, 19; LR.

WITH WHICH IS INCORPORATED
"THE ETIQUETTE OF FREEMASONRY"
BY "AN OLD PAST MASTER"
REVISED AND ENLARGED

WITH A NEW FOREWORD BY
ALLAN BOUDREAU, PH.D.
GRAND LODGE LIBRARIAN

WEATHERVANE BOOKS
NEW YORK

This 1978 edition is published by Weathervane Books, distributed
by Crown Publishers, Inc., 225 Park Avenue South, New York,
New York 10003

Printed and Bound in the United States of America

Library of Congress Cataloging in Publication Data

Campbell-Everden, William Preston.
  Freemasonry and its etiquette.

  1. Freemasons. 2. Freemasons—Handbooks, manuals,
etc. I. An old past master. II. Title.   III. Title:
The etiquette of freemasonry.

HS395.C25   1978   366'.1   78-15432

ISBN 0-517-25914-1

n m l k j i

CONTENTS

Contents

FOREWORD

MASONRY, or Freemasonry, is a 600-year-old fraternity with a 3,000-year-old tradition. The oldest, largest, and most widely known fraternal organization in the world, it is the prototype of most modern fraternal societies and service organizations.

Modern Freemasonry dates from the year 1717 when four very old Lodges met together in London to form the first Grand Lodge. Today there are over six million Masons in the world, and over half of these in the United States. The unit of organization is the Lodge, which may consist of a few dozen or several hundred members, and each Lodge belongs to a Grand Lodge. There are over 30,000 Lodges in the world, and more than 100 Grand Lodges. There is no central author-

vii

ity, and world recognition is maintained by a system of mutual fraternal recognition among Grand Lodges.

Freemasonry and Its Etiquette has long been the standard ready reference book for the individual Mason desirous of improving his knowledge of the fraternity, both the early history and the actual work that takes place within every regular and well-governed Lodge. Written by a member of a London Lodge, the Mother Grand Lodge of all Masonry, its carefully detailed and explicit suggestions are applicable to all English-speaking Lodges throughout the world.

Among the many facets of the fraternity covered are:
- Who are fit and proper persons to be made Masons?
- What is a Lodge of Freemasons?
- Ritual
- The Ceremonies
- The Lodge Officers and their duties
- Concordant Bodies.

Unlike the earlier exposés of the early Eighteenth Century, *Freemasonry and Its Etiquette* is a well-documented account of the details essential to the workings of the business of the Masonic Lodge.

Well written, in a lively and very readable manner, it is a valuable and necessary addition to the working library of anyone interested in the actual happenings within a Lodge.

ALLAN BOUDREAU, Ph.D.
Grand Lodge Librarian
Grand Lodge Free and
Accepted Masons
of the State of New York
May 1978

FREEMASONRY

AND

ITS ETIQUETTE

INTRODUCTION

In introducing this treatise on Freemasonry and its Etiquette to the attention of the members of the Craft, it is desirable that a brief explanation should be given of the title selected for the work.

Obviously the word 'Freemasonry' conveys its own meaning and scope; but 'Etiquette' is intended to be understood, not only in its somewhat restricted signification —namely, 'The social observances required by good-breeding'—but also in its wider and more comprehensive meaning, as 'Regulations as to behaviour, dress, etc., to be observed by particular persons upon particular occasions; forms which are observed in particular places.'

In accordance with this wider interpretation of the word 'Etiquette,' many duties and details not provided for in the Book of Constitutions, or in the Ritual, will be fully considered; and, where necessary, will be discussed and explained in this work. It is also intended that the means and appliances, the technicalities and ceremonial observances (as distinct from the verbal portions of the Ceremonies), which are indispensably necessary for the decorous and harmonious working of the business of the Lodge, shall be detailed; and, where it may be needful, they will be fully explained.

It will readily be conceded that, in addition to the words of the several Ceremonies, there is need for instruction in the manner in which the Officers of the Lodge should perform certain portions of their respective duties. The Ritual contains directions here and there; but they are necessarily brief, and in some cases they may be misunderstood or wrongly interpreted. The saying is trite, but strictly true, that the Master of a Lodge—however perfect he may be himself—cannot achieve his best unless he be well supported and assisted by his Officers: whereas, if he be intelligently and zealously assisted by them, and the Ceremonies be well rendered by all concerned, the resultant effect upon the Candidate—almost to a certainty—will be, that he will form so favour-

Introduction

able an opinion of the Institution, as to inspire him with a lasting love of the Craft, such as will cause him to become—in fact, and not in name only—'a true and faithful brother among us.'

On the other hand, if the duties of the subordinate Officers be performed in a perfunctory or slovenly manner, the beauty and the impressiveness of the several Ceremonies will be materially marred or altogether lost, so far as their effect upon the Candidate is concerned.

The experience of every thoughtful and intelligent Freemason, who attends his own Lodge with tolerable regularity, and who occasionally visits other Lodges, will fully confirm this assertion. He must have known instances wherein the want of attention to details, on the part of certain of the Officers, and the absence of the necessary preparation for the business to be transacted, have led to confusion and delay; and have in a great measure marred the effect of the Ceremonies. At a critical moment, in some important part of the Ceremony, which may have been led up to by a serious address, something—indispensable to the continuity of the work—was not at hand; perhaps the alms-dish, or the badge with which the Candidate in either degree was to be invested;

or the heavy M. in the Third Degree; or some other equally important detail.

In cases such as those mentioned, a certain degree of confusion was inevitable; whisperings, and hurried messages, and dartings hither and thither, to the great annoyance of all concerned, and to the certain distraction of the attention of the Candidate.

This work is commended to the attention of Officers of Lodges, of aspirants to office, and of all Freemasons who are lovers of order, in the earnest hope that the irregularities and inconveniences hereinbefore mentioned may, as far as is possible, be guarded against in their several Lodges.

*   *   *   *

One of the objects of this work is to discuss 'the minor jurisprudence of the Craft.'

Jurisprudence is defined as 'the knowledge of the laws, customs, and rights of men in a state or a community.'

As far as we, as a community, are concerned, the Book of Constitutions may be taken as containing the major jurisprudence of the Order; but there are numberless small but far from unimportant matters not considered in the Constitutions, which form part of our System, and to which it is desir-

Introduction

able to call attention in a work of this character, dealing, as it is intended to do, with all the details, great and small, in any way connected with the Lodge, the Ceremonies, and the general business of the Craft, as far as private Lodges are concerned.

There is in every state and community the 'lex non scripta,' which, from precedent and immemorial usage, is held to be of equal force with statute law. Of this character are many of our ancient customs, upon which our Constitutions are silent, and upon which 'Freemasonry and its Etiquette' is expected to be an illuminating guide.

Some—probably many—of the subjects will be discussed, with more or less of elaboration of detail. It is hoped that the criticisms may not be considered to be unnecessary because they treat of things in constant use in every Lodge, or that more has been said than there is a positive necessity to say. If the thought should arise in the minds of any reader of these pages, 'All these requisites for a Lodge, and the mode of arrangement, etc., are to be found continually in the Lodge of which I am a member, and in the majority of those which I occasionally visit; then why this long repetition of detail of things with which I am perfectly familiar?' let such a Brother remember that there are many hundreds of Lodges lying beyond the sphere of his observation, and which, from various causes, are very far indeed from coming up to the standard of perfect equipment such as the proper performance of our Rites and Ceremonies demands.

Want of carefulness in details and in arrangement, and a deficiency in certain necessary things, ought not to occur in any Lodge of Freemasons; such a state of incompleteness is incompatible with the dignity of the Worshipful Master. It is the duty of the Director of Ceremonies, and, indeed, the duty of every Officer of the Lodge, to see 'that everything be done decently and in order.'

To sum up briefly, it may be said with entire truthfulness that a want of acquaintance with, or a great degree of disregard of, the 'Etiquette of Freemasonry' exists in too many of our Lodges; and that both in 'the forms which are observed in particular places' and in 'regulations as to behaviour, dress, etc., to be observed by particular persons upon particular occasions,' many of our Lodges and their members are more or less open to improvement.

It is with the view and in the hope of effecting corrections where they may be

Introduction

proved to be necessary that these pages
have been written; not in any censorious or
captious spirit, nor with any desire to promulgate fads or crotchets; nor, above all,
'to make innovation in the body of Freemasonry'; but in perfect singleness of mind
and heart to give the results in plain language of the experience gained during a
protracted and varied Masonic career, in the
hope and trust that some instruction may
be imparted, and possibly some improvements may be effected, where the need of
improvement may be felt to exist.

So mote it be.

CHAPTER I

WHAT IS FREEMASONRY?

SPEAKING generally, Freemasonry is a Science which comprehends the principles, practices, and institutions of a secret brotherhood existing in all parts of the world, and known universally by the generic name of Freemasons.

The Fraternity is composed of a series of groups or communities known as Lodges, and these Private Lodges respectively own allegiance to one or other of the Grand Lodges or Grand Orients, according to the country in which they carry on their operations or according to the fundamental principles they profess.

Originally the one basic principle of them all, without exception, was an emphasized belief in the existence of a Supreme Being or Creator, in whose Name every Lodge was conducted; and subject to the confession of that belief, the follower of any theistic religion was, in that respect, acceptable as a member. In comparatively recent time

What is Freemasonry?

the Grand Orient of France, in the development of what it considered liberty of conscience, discontinued its acknowledgment of the existence of a Supreme Being; and as a consequence, in 1878, relations were ruptured between the Grand Orient of France and Grand Lodge, which remained true to its original principle and reaffirmed that a belief in TGAOTU is the first and most important of the Ancient Landmarks (see Chapter II).

In 1898, for the same reason, Grand Lodge withdrew its recognition from the Grand Lodge of Peru, and again took occasion to reaffirm the Landmark.

This volume, 'Freemasonry and its Etiquette,' is specifically addressed to those Freemasons, wherever dispersed over the face of earth and water, who own allegiance to The United Grand Lodge of Ancient Free and Accepted Masons of England, which is hereinafter referred to as THE GRAND LODGE.

By the solemn Act of Union between the two Grand Lodges of Freemasons of England in December, 1813, it was 'declared and pronounced that pure Ancient Masonry consists of three degrees and no more—viz., those of the Entered Apprentice, the Fellow Craft, and the Master Mason, including the Supreme

Order of the Holy Royal Arch' (Chapter XXX).

Very early in our Masonic career we are taught that Freemasonry is a system of morality the peculiarities of which are veiled from the uninstructed and popular world by allegorical treaching and symbolical illustration.

Most of this teaching and illustration being oral, it is natural that diversities, small though numerous in their origin, should arise, and unless there exists some standard by which present practice may be brought continually into conformity with original precept, slight diversities beget other and larger diversities, and the result is sometimes interesting and sometimes disastrous, producing 'confusion worse confounded.'

The object of 'Freemasonry and its Etiquette' is to supply that standard, and the enable the Brethren to apply the Square and Compasses of certain duly recognized but often forgotten Principles to the incidents of their own everyday Masonic life, and with their aid to produce a Perfect Ashlar which may in turn be of service to less experienced Craftsmen as a faithful and reliable guide and model.

Freemasonry claims to have existed in

some form or other from the earliest period of time; but is more immediately derived from and based upon the secret organizations of the Operative Masons of the Middle Ages; and to distinguish it therefrom it is now termed Free and Accepted or Speculative Masonry.

The Masonic Lectures (see Chapter XXVII) thus refer to the two classes:—

'Masonry, according to the general acceptation of the term, is an Art founded on the principles of Geometry, and directed to the service and convenience of mankind. But Freemasonry, embracing a wider range, and having a more noble object in view—namely, the cultivation and improvement of the human mind—may with more, propriety be called a Science, although its lessons for the most part are veiled in allegory and illustrated by symbols.'

The following sentences are taken from a brief sketch, entitled, 'Freemasonry: its Origin, History, and Design':

'The descendants of the Roman colleges of artificers established schools of architecture, and taught and practised the art of building among the newly enfranchised people. . . . From this school of Lombardian builders proceeded that society of architects who were known at that time by the appellation of Free Masons, and who from the tenth to the sixteenth century traversed the Continent of Europe, engaged almost exclusively in the construction of religious edifices, such as cathedrals, churches, and monasteries. The monastic orders formed an alliance with them, so that the convents frequently became their domiciles, and they instructed the monks in the secret principles of their art. The Popes took them under their protection, granted them charters of monopoly as ecclesiastical architects, and invested them with many important and exclusive privileges. Dissevering the ties which bound them to the monks, these Free Masons (so called to distinguish them from the rough masons, who were of an inferior grade, and not members of the corporation) subsequently established the guilds of stonemasons, which existed until the end of the seventeenth century in Germany, France, England, and Scotland.

'These stonemasons, or, as they continued to call themselves, Free Masons, had one peculiarity in their organization which is necessary to be considered if we would comprehend the relation that exists between them and the Freemasons of the present day, The society was necessarily an operative one, whose members were actually engaged in the manual labour of building, as well as in the more intellectual occupation of architectural designing. This, with the fact of their previous connection with the monks, who probably projected the plans which the Masons carried into execution, led to the admission among them of persons who were not operative Masons. These were high ecclesiastics, wealthy nobles, and men of science who were encouragers and patrons of the art. These, not competent to engage in the labour of building, were supposed to confine themselves to philosophic speculations on the principles of the art, and to symbolizing or spiritualizing its labour and its implements. Hence there resulted a division of the membership of the brotherhood into two classes, the practical and theoretical, or, as they are more commonly called, the operative and speculative, or "domatic" and "geomatic." The operative Masons always held the ascendancy in numbers until the seventeenth century, but the speculative Masons exerted a greater influence by their higher culture, their wealth, and their social position.

'In time there came a total and permanent disseverance of the two elements. At the beginning of the eighteenth century there were several Lodges in England, but for a long time there had been no meeting of a great assembly. In the year 1717, Freemasonry was revived,* and the Grand Lodge of England was established by four of the Lodges which then existed in London. This revival* took place through the influence and by the exertions of non-operative or speculative Masons, and the Institution has ever since mainly preserved that character. ...

'Freemasonry of the present day is a philosophic or speculative science, derived from, and issuing out of, an operative art. It is a science of symbolism.'

Freemasonry is founded on the purest principles of piety and virtue; and the Grand Principles on which the Order is founded are Brotherly Love, Relief, and Truth.

It is natural, therefore, to find that upon such foundations have been erected many lasting monuments; and among the foremost of these may be mentioned the three great Masonic Institutions, to which Chapter XXVI is devoted.

But it may be as well to add here a few words indicating what Freemasonry is NOT. Freemasonry is *not*, and is not intended to be, a benefit Society, from which in return for certain calculated subscriptions, certain

* See Operative Masonry, Chapter XXXII.

calculated benefits are received by the subscriber; in other words, any person intending to be initiated should be solemnly warned
against entertaining or being influenced by
any mercenary or other unworthy motive
as regards his own advantage in joining
such an altruistic Society as Freemasonry
claims to be. Its aims are to help others;
and its noble gifts are intended for the benefit
of others; and those who join it ought to be
in such a position as will permit them, without detriment to themselves or their connections, to give freely of their substance for
the maintenance of those truly masonic
ornaments, Benevolence and Charity.

Freemasonry may be said to be the highest
expression of those noble watchwords,
'Liberty, Equality, Fraternity,' and its
true meaning has been happily described
as 'the building of every part of a man
into a spiritual house fit for the habitation
of God.'

CHAPTER II

GRAND LODGES AND GRAND ORIENTS

THE Grand Lodge of England (1717) recognizes and is in fraternal relation with—
 The Grand Lodge of Ireland (1730),
 The Grand Lodge of Scotland (1736),
 14 Foreign Grand Lodges and Grand Orients in the Eastern Hemisphere,
 7 Colonial Grand Lodges,
 9 Grand Lodges in the Dominion of Canada,
 50 Grand Lodges in the United States of America, and about 12 other Grand Lodges and Grand Orients in the West Indies, Mexico, Central America and South America; and besides these there are
 656 District and other Lodges abroad; so that the claim of Freemasonry to be 'Universal' would seem to be well supported.

The Grand Orient of France is not included in the above list, but on December 3, 1913, the Grand Secretary read to Grand Lodge the following message from the M.W. Grand Master:

Grand Lodges and Grand Orients

'It is with deep satisfaction that I find myself able to signalize the auspicious occasion of the Centenary of the Union by an announcement which will, I am convinced, cause true rejoicing throughout the Craft.

'A body of Freemasons in France, confronted by a positive prohibition on the part of the Grand Orient to work in the name of the Great Architect of the Universe have, in fidelity to their Masonic pledges, resolved to uphold the true principles and tenets of the Craft, and have united several Lodges as the INDEPENDENT AND REGULAR NATIONAL GRAND LODGE OF FRANCE AND OF THE FRENCH COLONIES.

'This new body has approached me with the request that it may be recognized by the Grand Lodge of England, and, having received full assurance that it is pledged to adhere to those principles of Freemasonry which we regard as fundamental and essential, I have joyfully assented to the establishment of fraternal relations and the exchange of representatives.

'We are thus enabled to celebrate the hundredth anniversary of that Union which was the foundation of our solidarity and world-wide influence, by the consummation of a wish which has been ardently cherished by English Freemasons for many years past, and we are once more in the happy position of being able to enjoy Masonic intercourse with men of the great French nation.

'I trust that the bond thus established will strengthen and promote the good understanding which exists outside of the sphere of Freemasonry.'

It will be interesting to add that the obligations which will be imposed on all Lodges under this French Constitution are the following:

1. While the Lodge is at work the Bible will always be open.

2. The ceremonies will be conducted in strict conformity with the Ritual of the 'Régime Rectifié' which is followed by these Lodges, a Ritual which was drawn up in 1778 and sanctioned in 1782, and with which the Duke of Kent was initiated in 1792.

3. The Lodge will always be opened and closed with the invocation and in the name of the Great Architect of the Universe. All the summonses of the Order and of the Lodges will be printed with the symbols of the Great Architect of the Universe.

4. No religious or political discussion will be permitted in the Lodge.

5. The Lodge as such will never take part

officially in any political affair, but every individual Brother will preserve complete liberty of opinion and action.

6. Only those Brethren who are recognized as true Brethren by the Grand Lodge of England will be received in Lodge.

CHAPTER III

GRAND LODGES OF ENGLAND

[The history contained in this chapter was published in the *Freemason* on December 27, 1913, on the occasion of the Centenary of the Union (vol. liii, No. 2,338).

The historical account of the proceedings which took place on December 27, 1813, is based upon a report in William Preston's 'Illustrations of Masonry,' which has been amended by references to the late Brother W. J. Hughan's 'Memorials of the Masonic Union, 1813.']

FORMERLY England had four Grand Lodges. The oldest, and much the strongest, was founded at the Apple Tree Tavern, Charles Street, Covent Garden, London, in 1717. Members of it traced their origin to an assemblage of Freemasons by King Athelstan at York, in 926 A.D. The Scotch Lodges did not go back nearly so far. They were content to claim descent from those foreign Masons who came to their country in the twelfth century to build the abbeys of Melrose, Holyrood, and Kilwinning, and there is abundant evidence that the Lodges of York and Kilwinning were the parents of many Lodges founded in various parts of Great Britain. The Brethren of York, conscious that their city was the Mecca of Freemasonry, and believing that their Time Immemorial Lodge was a direct descendant of that which was existing in the fourteenth century, determined that they would not be behind those of London, and in 1725 formed the Grand Lodge of All England. Despite its ambitious title, it had a very chequered career down to the last decade of the eighteenth century. About 1740 it, as did also the private York Lodge, became dormant. Both were revived in 1761, but there is no evidence of their existence after 1792. That Grand Lodge confined its activities within a limited area of 'All England.' Under its banner were two Lodges in the City of York, one each in Scarborough, Ripon, Knaresborough, Hovingham, Swainton, and Rotherham, in Yorkshire; one in Macclesfield, Cheshire; and one in Hollingwood, Lancashire. The Grand Lodge of All England also chartered at York the Grand Lodge of England south of the River Trent in 1799. It consisted of discontented members of the Time Immemorial Lodge of Antiquity, of the Premier Grand Lodge (of which Sir Christopher Wren* in his day was the Grand Master), and it granted warrants to only two Lodges, both in London. One was named Perfect Observance, the other Perseverance and Triumph. The career of this 'Mushroom Grand Lodge,' as the late Brother W. J. Hughan described it, was as inglorious as that of its parent.

The fourth Grand Lodge was the only real rival of the Premier Grand Lodge. It was constituted, on July 17, 1751, at the Turk's Head Tavern, Greek Street, Soho, London, as 'The Grand Lodge of England, according to the Old Institutions.' Its members were designated 'Ancients,' while those of the body from which it had seceded were known as 'Moderns.' The 'Ancients' were also spoken of as 'Athol Masons,' they having elected the third Duke of Athol as their first Grand Master in 1772, his son succeeding to the office at his death. Two reasons are offered for the founding of the new Grand Lodge. One is that the Regular Grand Lodge adopted severe measures against recalcitrant and impecunious Lodges.

---

* There is no real proof that Sir Christopher Wren was ever a Speculative Mason. The Minutes of the Worshipful Society of Free Masons (Operative) are said to show that their Grand Master, Sir Christopher Wren, was interred in St. Paul's with the proper ceremony of that Society.

Grand Lodges of England

The other is that it introduced innovations in the customs of the Craft which were particularly objected to by the operative section. 'The new body,' wrote the late Brother W. J. Hughan, 'became very popular, and in a few years was no mean competitor; its prototype and senior, but less pretentious organization, having also to contend against the introduction of the "Royal Arch," which was warmly supported, though not originated, by the "Ancients," who became known as the Grand Lodge of "Four Degrees," thus (for a time only) placing the parent society at a disadvantage.'

The 'Ancients' having established many Lodges and Provincial Lodges in England and in foreign countries, particularly in America, and having obtained the recognition of the Grand Lodges of Ireland and Scotland, and side almost unanimous support of the Grand Lodges of America, were eager to maintain their independence, and rejected all overtures tendered by the 'Moderns' for reunion; and in 1757 unanimously ordered:

'That if any Master, Wardens, or presiding officer, or any other person whose business it may be to admit members or visitors, shall admit or entertain in his or their Lodge during

23

Lodge hours or the time of transacting the proper business of Freemasonry, any Brother or visitor not strictly an Ancient Mason conformable to the Grand Lodge rules and order, such Lodge so transgressing shall forfeit its warrant, and the same may be disposed of by Grand Lodge.'

In 1801 the older Grand Lodge issued a counterblast. Some of its members were convicted of having patronized and acted as principal officers in 'an irregular society calling themselves Ancient Masons, in open violation of the laws of the Grand Lodge'; and it was determined that the laws should be enforced against these offending Brethren, unless they immediately abandoned such irregular meetings. These Brethren solicited the indulgence of the Grand Lodge for three months, hoping that during the interval they might be able to effect a union between the two societies. The indulgence was granted, and 'that no impediment might pervert so desirable an object, the charge against the offending Brethren was withdrawn, and a committee, consisting of Lord Moira and several other eminent characters, was appointed to pave the way for the intended union, and every means ordered to be used to bring the erring Brethren to a sense of their duty and allegiance.' Nothing came of this, for two years later the Grand Lodge was informed 'that the irregular Masons still continued refractory, and that so far from soliciting readmission among the Craft, they had not taken any steps to effect a union.' Their conduct was deemed highly censurable, and the laws of the Grand Lodge were ordered to be enforced against them. It was also unanimously resolved:

'That whenever it shall appear that any Masons under the English Constitution shall in future attend or countenance any Lodge or meeting of persons calling themselves Ancient Masons, under the sanction of any person claiming the title of Grand Master of England, who shall not have been duly elected in the Grand Lodge, the laws of the society shall not only be strictly enforced against them, but their names shall be erased from the list, and transmitted to all the regular Lodges under the Constitution of England.'

In 1806 Lord Moira reported to Grand Lodge that he had visited the Grand Lodge of Scotland and explained the position relating to the 'Modern' and 'Ancient' Masons in England, and that the Socttish Brethren had declared that they had been always led to think that the 'Moderns' were of very recent date and of no magnitude; and being convinced of their error, were desirous that the strictest union should subsist between the Grand Lodge of England and Scotland, and in proof thereof elected the Prince of Wales Grand Master of Scotland. Lord Moira further stated that, when the Scottish Brethren expressed a hope that the differences between the English Masons would be speedily settled, he replied that, after the rejection of the propositions of the Grand Lodge by the 'Ancients' three years before, it could not now, consistently with its honour, make any further advances; but would always be open to accept the mediation of the Grand Lodge of Scotland if it should think proper to interfere. Two years afterwards the Grand Lodge of Ireland approved the declaration of their Scottish Brethren, and pledged itself 'not to countenance or receive as a Brother any person standing under the interdict of the Grand Lodge of England for Masonic transgression.'

In April, 1809, the Grand Lodge agreed in opinion with the Committee of Charity that 'it is not necessary any longer for to continue in force those measures which were resorted to in or about the year 1789 respecting irregular Masons, and do therefore enjoin the several Lodges to revert to the ancient landmarks of the Society.' This was accepted as a step towards the much desired union. Still, more than four years elapsed before it was achieved; and then it came about as the result of the tactful intervention of three of the sons of George III. The Prince of Wales, who was initiated in 1787 at the Star and Garter Tavern, in Pall Mall, became Grand Master of the Premier Grand Lodge of England in 1790. When he accepted the Regency he vacated the office, and his brother, the Duke of Sussex, was elected to succeed him. The venerable and worthy head of the 'Ancients,' the Duke of Athol, was, says a contemporary record, 'soon convinced by the Royal Duke's arguments, strengthened by his own good sense and benevolent mind, how desirable must be an actual and cordial relation of the two societies under one head; for to pave the way for the Masons, his Grace in the handsomest measure resigned his seat of Grand Master.' He recommended as his successor the Duke of Kent, father of Queen Victoria, he having been initiated under the 'Ancient'

constitution in the Union Lodge of Geneva.
The Duke of Kent was acclaimed Grand
Master in 1813. The two Royal Dukes,
taking into counsel three distinguished
Brethren belonging to each society, arranged
Articles of Union between the two Grand
Lodges of England (see Chapter IV), and
these were ratified, confirmed, and sealed
in each of those Lodges on December 1,
1813.

The same day a joint meeting of the Grand
Lodges received the articles 'with Masonic
acclamation,' and to carry them into effect
constituted a Lodge of Reconciliation, consisting of equal members of the Old Institutions and the Constitution of England.
Every care was taken that the parties to
the union should be on a level of equality.
As to the precedence of the Lodges, it was
arranged that the two first Lodges under
each Grand Lodge should draw lots for
priority. The draw favoured the 'Ancients,'
whose Grand Master's Lodge became No. 1
on the revised roll, the Lodge of Antiquity
of the Regular Grand Lodge taking the
second position, No. 2 of the 'Ancients' in
the same order taking No. 3, and the second
of the Time-Immemorial Lodges becoming
No. 4. 'For two such old Lodges to accept
lower positions in the united roll than their

age entitled them to says much for the truly Masonic spirit of their members, who, to promote peace and harmony, consented to their juniors taking precedence of Lodges in existence prior to the formation of the Premier Grand Lodge.' Up to the time of the union 'Modern' Lodges placed on the roll numbered 1,085, while 'Ancient' Lodges warranted between 1751 and 1813 were 521.

The reunion of the two Grand Lodges of England was consummated with great solemnity on St. John's Day, December 27, 1813, in the Freemasons' Hall, London. The platform on the east was reserved for the Grand Masters, Grand Officers, and visitors. Masters, Wardens, and Past Masters, all dressed in black (except regimentals), with their respective insignia, and with white gloves, occupied the sides of the hall—the Masters in front, the Wardens behind, and the Past Masters on rising benches behind them. Care was taken that the Lodges were ranked so that the two Fraternities were completely intermixed. The two Fraternities had previously assembled in two adjoining rooms, and having opened two Grand Lodges, each according to its peculiar solemnities, they passed to the Assembly Hall in the following order:

Freemasonry and its Etiquette

Grand Usher, with his Staff.   Grand Usher, with his Staff.

The Duke of Kent's Band of Music, fifteen in number, all Masons, three and three.

Two Grand Stewards.   Two Grand Stewards.

A Cornucopia borne by a Master Mason.   A Cornucopia borne by a Master Mason.

Two Grand Stewards.   Two Grand Stewards.

Two Golden Ewers by Master Masons.   Two Golden Ewers by Master Masons.

The nine worthy and expert Masons, forming the Lodge of Reconciliation, in single file, rank to rank, with the emblems of Masonry.   The nine worthy and expert Masons, forming the Lodge of Reconciliation, in single file, rank to rank, with the emblems of Masonry.

The Grand Secretary, bearing the Book of Constitutions and Great Seal.   The Grand Secretary, bearing the Book of Constitutions and Great Seal.

The Grand Treasurer, with the Golden Key.   The Grand Treasurer, with the Golden Key.

The Corinthian Light.   The Corinthian Light.

The pillar of the Junior Grand Warden on a pedestal.   The pillar of the Junior Grand Warden on a pedestal.

The Junior Grand Warden, with his gavel.   The Junior Grand Warden, with his gavel.

The Deputy Grand Chaplain, with the Holy Bible.   The Grand Chaplain, with the Holy Bible.

The Grand Chaplain.   Past Grand Wardens.

Past Grand Wardens.   Provincial Grand Masters.

The Doric Light.   The Doric Light.

Grand Lodges of England

The pillar of the Senior Grand Warden on a pedestal.

The pillar of the Senior Grand Warden on a pedestal.

The Senior Grand Warden, with his gavel.

The Senior Grand Warden, with his gavel.

Two Past Grand Masters.

The Deputy Grand Master.

Acting Deputy Grand Master.

His Excellency the Count de Lagardje,the Swedish Ambassador, Grand Master of the first Lodge of the North, visitor.

The Royal Banner.

The Ionic Light.

The Ionic Light.

The Grand Sword Bearer.

The Grand Sword Bearer.

THE GRAND MASTER OF ENGLAND, THE DUKE OF KENT, WITH THE ACT OF UNION IN DUPLICATE.

THE GRAND MASTER OF ENGLAND, THE DUKE OF SUSSEX, WITH THE ACT OF UNION IN DUPLICATE.

Two Grand Stewards.

Two Grand Stewards.

Grand Tyler.

Grand Tyler.

Sir George Nayler, the Director of Ceremonies, having proclaimed silence, the Rev. Dr. Barry, Grand Chaplain to the Fraternity under the Duke of Kent, offered solemn prayer, and Sir George read the Act of Union. Then the Rev. Dr. Goghlan, after the sound of trumpet, proclaimed aloud: 'Hear ye: This is the Act of Union, engrossed, in confirmation of articles solemnly concluded between the two Grand Lodges of

31

Freemasonry and its Etiquette

Free and Accepted Masons of England, signed, sealed, and ratified by the two Grand Lodges respectively, by which they are to be hereafter and for ever known and acknowledged by the style and title of The United Grand Lodge of Ancient Freemasons of England. How say you, Brothers, representatives of the two Fraternities? Do you accept of, ratify, and confirm the same?' To which the assembly answered: 'We do accept, ratify, and confirm the same.' The Grand Chaplain then said: 'And may the Great Architect of the Universe make the Union perpetual.' To which all assembled replied: 'So mote it be.' Thereupon the two Grand Masters and the six Commissioners signed the deeds, and the Grand Masters affixed the great seals of their respective Grand Lodges to them. The trumpet again sounded, and the Rev. Dr. Barry, stepping forth, proclaimed: 'Be it known to all men that the Act of Union between the two Grand Lodges of Free and Accepted Masons of England is solemnly signed, sealed, ratified, and confirmed, and the two Fraternities are one, to be from henceforth known and acknowledged by the style and title of the United Grand Lodge of Ancient Freemasons of England, and may the Great Architect of the Universe make their union perpetual.' And the assembly said 'Amen.'

This was followed by a deeply impressive scene. 'The two Grand Masters, with their respective Deputies and Wardens,' says a contemporary record, 'advanced to the Ark of the Masonic Covenant, prepared under the direction of Brother John Soane, R.A., Grand Superintendent of Works, for the edifice of the Union, and in all time to come to be placed before the Throne. The Grand Masters standing in the East, with their Deputies on the right and left; the Grand Wardens in the West and South; the Square, the Plumb, the Level, and the Mallet were successively delivered to the Deputy Grand Masters, and by them presented to the two Grand Masters, who severally applied the Square to that part of the Ark which is square, the Plumb to the sides of the same, and the Level above it in three positions; and, lastly, they gave three knocks with the Mallet, saying, "May the Great Architect of the Universe enable us to uphold the Grand Edifice of Union, of which the Ark of the Covenant is the symbol, which shall contain within it the instrument of our brotherly love, and bear upon it the Holy Bible, Square, and Compass, as the light of our faith and the rule of our works. May

He dispose our hearts to make it perpetual."
And the Brethren said: "So mote it be."
The two Grand Masters placed the said Act
of Union in the interior of the said Ark.
The cornucopia, the wine, and oil were in
like manner presented to the Grand Masters,
who, according to ancient rite, poured forth
corn, wine, and oil on this said Ark, saying,
"As we pour forth corn, wine, and oil on
this Ark of the Masonic Covenant, may the
bountiful hand of heaven ever supply this
United Kingdom with abundance of corn,
wine, and oil, with all the necessaries and
comforts of life; and may He dispose our
hearts to be grateful for all His Gifts." And
the assembly said, "Amen." '

It having been found impracticable, from
the shortness of notice, for the sister Grand
Lodges of Scotland and Ireland to send
deputations to the assembly according to
the urgent request of the two Fraternities,
conferences had been held with the most
distinguished Grand Officers and enlightened
Masons resident in and near London, in order
to establish perfect agreement upon all the
essential points of Masonry, according to the
ancient traditions and general practice of
the Craft. The members of the Lodge of
Reconciliation, accompanied by Count de
Lagardje and Brother Dr. Van Hess, and

other distinguished Masons, withdrew to an adjoining room, where, being congregated and tyled, the result of all the previous conferences was made known. Returning to the Temple, Count de Lagardje declared that the forms agreed on and settled by the Lodge of Reconciliation were pure and correct. These forms were recognized as those 'to be alone observed and practised in the United Grand Lodge and all the Lodges dependent thereon until Time shall be no more.' Then, the Holy Bible spread open, with the Square and Compasses thereon, was laid on the Ark of the Covenant, and the two Grand Chaplains approached. The recognized obligation was then pronounced aloud by the Rev. Dr. Hemming, one of the Masters of the Lodge of Reconciliation, the whole of the Brethren repeating it after him, with joined hands, and declaring, 'By this solemn obligation we vow to abide, and the regulations of Ancient Freemasonry now recognized strictly to observe.'

The assembly next proceeded to constitute one Grand Lodge. All the Grand Officers of the two Fraternities having divested themselves of their insignia, and Past Grand Officers having taken the chairs, the Duke of Kent stated that when he took upon himself the important office of Grand Master of the Ancient Fraternity, his idea, as declared at the time, was to facilitate the important object of the Union, which had that day been so happily concluded. And he now proposed that his illustrious and dear relative, the Duke of Sussex, should be the Grand Master of the United Grand Lodge of Ancient Freemasons of England for the year ensuing. This having been seconded by the Hon. Washington Shirley, and carried unanimously and with Masonic honours, His Royal ·Highness was placed on the Throne by the Duke of Kent and Count de Lagardje, and solemnly obligated. The Grand Master then nominated his officers: Rev. S. Hemming, D.D., Senior Grand. Warden; Isaac Lindo, Junior Grand Warden; John Dent, Grand Treasurer; William Meyrick, Grand Registrar; William Henry White and Edward Harper, Grand Secretaries; Rev. Edward Barry, D.D., and Rev. Lucius Coghland, Grand Chaplains; Rev. Isaac Knapp, Deputy Grand Chaplain; John Soane, Grand Superintendent of Works; Sir G. Nayler, Grand Director of Ceremonies; Captain Jonathan Parker, Grand Sword Bearer; Samuel Wesley, Grand Organist; B. Aldhouse, Grand Usher; and W. V. Salmon, Grand Tyler. It was then

solemnly proclaimed that the two Grand
Lodges were incorporated and consolidated
into one, and the Grand Master declared it
to be open in due form according to ancient
usage. The Grand Lodge was then called
to refreshment, and from the cup of brotherly
love the Grand Master drank to the Brethren,
'Peace, Goodwill, and Brotherly Love all
over the World,' and then passed the cup.
As it was going round, a choir sang a piece
of music specially composed for the occasion
(which is reproduced on another page of the
same issue of the *Freemason*).

The Grand Lodge was recalled to labour,
and as the first act of the United Fraternity,
the Duke of Sussex moved:

'That an humble address be presented
to H.R.H. the Prince Regent respectfully to acquaint him with the happy
event of the reunion of the two great
Grand Lodges of the Ancient Freemasons
of England, an event which cannot fail
to afford lively satisfaction to their
Illustrious Patron, who presided for so
many years over one of the Fraternities,
and under whose auspices Freemasonry
has risen to its present flourishing condition. That the unchangeable principles of the Institution are well known

37

to His Royal Highness, and the great benefits and end of this reunion are to promote the influence and operation of these principles by more extensively inculcating loyalty and affection of their Sovereign, obedience to the laws and magistrates of their country, and the practice of all the religious and moral duties of life, objects which must be ever dear to His Royal Highness in the government of His Majesty's United Kingdom. That they humbly hope and pray for the continuance of the sanction of His Royal Highness's fraternal patronage; and that they beg leave to express their fervent gratitude for the many blessings which, in common with all their fellow-subjects, they derive from his benignant sway. That the Great Architect of the Universe may long secure these blessings to them and to their country by the preservation of His Royal Highness, their Illustrious Patron!'

Resolutions thanking the Dukes of Kent and Sussex for 'yielding to the prayer of the United Fraternities to take upon themselves the personal conduct of the negotiations for a reunion, which is this day, through their zeal, conciliation, and fraternal example so happily completed'; and commending the proceedings of the day to Grand Lodges of Scotland and Ireland, were also passed before the Lodge was closed 'in ample form and with solemn prayer.'

CHAPTER IV

ARTICLES OF UNION
BETWEEN THE TWO GRAND LODGES OF FREEMASONS OF ENGLAND

IN THE NAME OF THE
GREAT ARCHITECT OF THE UNIVERSE—

The Most Worshipful His Royal Highness Prince Edward, Duke of Kent and Strathearn, Earl of Dublin, Knight Companion of the Most Noble Order of the Garter and of the Most Illustrious Order of Saint Patrick, Field-Marshal of His Majesty's Forces, Governor of Gibraltar, Colonel of the First or Royal Scots Regiment of Foot, and Grand Master of Free and Accepted Masons of England according to the Old Institutions; the Right Worshipful Thomas Harper, Deputy Grand Master; the Right Worshipful James Perry, Past Deputy

The Most Worshipful His Royal Highness Prince Augustus Frederick, Duke of Sussex, Earl of Inverness, Baron Arkton, Knight Companion of the Most Noble Order of the Garter, and Grand Master of the Society of Free and Accepted Masons under the Constitution of England; the Right Worshipful Waller Rodwell Wright, Provincial Grand Master of Masons in the Ionian Isles; the Right Worshipful Arthur Tegart, Past Grand Warden, and the Right Worshipful James Deans, Past Grand Warden; of the same

Articles of Union

Grand Master; and the Right Worshipful James Agar, Past Deputy Grand Master; of the same Fraternity: for themselves and on behalf of the Grand Lodge of Freemasons of England, according to the Old Institutions: being thereto duly constituted and empowered: —on the one part,

Fraternity: for themselves and on behalf of the Grand Lodge of the Society of Freemasons under the Constitution of England: being thereto duly constituted and empowered:—on the other part,

HAVE AGREED AS FOLLOWS—

I. There shall be, from and after the day of the Festival of Saint John the Evangelist next ensuing, a full, perfect, and perpetual union of and between the two Fraternities of Free and Accepted Masons of England above described; so as that in all time hereafter they shall form and constitute but one Brotherhood, and that the said community shall be represented in one Grand Lodge, to be solemnly formed, constituted, and held, on the said day of the Festival of Saint John the Evangelist next ensuing, and from thenceforward for ever.

II. It is declared and pronounced, that pure Antient Masonry consists of three degrees, and no more; vizt. those of the Entered Apprentice, the Fellow Craft, and the Master Mason, including the Supreme

41

Order of the Holy Royal Arch. But this article is not intended to prevent any Lodge or Chapter from holding a meeting in any of the degrees of the Orders of Chivalry, according to the constitutions of the said Orders.

III. There shall be the most perfect unity of obligation, of discipline, of working the Lodges, of making, passing and raising, instructing and clothing Brothers; so that but one pure unsullied system, according to the genuine landmarks, laws, and traditions of the Craft, shall be maintained, upheld and practised, throughout the Masonic World, from the day and date of the said union until time shall be no more.

IV. To prevent all controversy or dispute as to the genuine and pure obligations, forms, rules and antient traditions of Masonry, and further to unite and bind the whole Fraternity of Masons in one indissoluble bond it is agreed that the obligations and forms that have, from time immemorial, been established, used, and practised, in the Craft, shall be recognized, accepted, and taken, by the members of both Fraternities, as the pure and genuine obligations and forms by which the incorporated Grand Lodge of England, and its dependent Lodges in every part of the World, shall be bound: and for the purpose of receiving and communicating due light and settling this uniformity of regulation and instruction (and particularly on matters which can neither be expressed nor described in writing), it is further agreed that brotherly application be made to the Grand Lodges of Scotland and Ireland to authorize, delegate and appoint, any two or more of their enlightened members to be present at the Grand Assembly on the solemn occasion of uniting the said Fraternities; and that the respective Grand Masters, Grand Officers, Masters, Past Masters, Wardens and Brothers, then and there present, shall solemnly engage to abide by the true forms and obligations (particularly in matters which can neither be described nor written), in the presence of the said Members of the Grand Lodges of Scotland and Ireland, that it may be declared, recognized, and known, that they all are bound by the same solemn pledge, and work under the same law.

V. For the purpose of establishing and securing this perfect uniformity in all the warranted Lodges, and also to prepare for this Grand Assembly, and to place all the Members of both Fraternities on the level of equality on the day of Re-union, it is agreed that as soon as these presents shall have received the sanction of the respective Grand Lodges, the two Grand Masters shall appoint each nine worthy and expert Master Masons, or Past Masters, of their respective Fraternities, with Warrant and instructions to meet together at some convenient central place in London, when each party having opened in a separate apartment a just and perfect Lodge, agreeably to their peculiar regulations they shall give and receive mutually and reciprocally the obligations of both Fraternities, deciding by lot which shall take priority in giving and receiving the same; and being thus all duly and equally enlightened in both forms, they shall be empowered and directed, either to hold a Lodge under the warrant or dispensation to be entrusted to them, and to be entitled the Lodge of Reconciliation, or to visit the several Lodges holding under both the Grand Lodges for the purpose of obligating, instructing and perfecting the Master, Past Masters, Wardens, and Members, in both the forms, and to make a return to the Grand Secretaries of both the Grand Lodges of the names of those whom they shall have thus enlightened. And the said Grand Secretaries shall be empowered to enrol the names of all the Members thus remade in the Register of both the Grand Lodges, without fee or reward: it being ordered that no person shall be thus obligated and registered whom the Master and Wardens of his Lodge shall not certify by writing under their hands, that he is free on the books of his particular Lodge. Thus on the day of the Assembly of both Fraternities, the Grand Officers, Masters, Past Masters, and Wardens, who are alone to be present, shall all have taken the obligation by which each is bound, and be prepared, to make their solemn engagement, that they will thereafter abide by that which shall be recognized and declared to be the true and universally accepted obligation of the Master Mason.

VI. As soon as the Grand Masters, Grand Officers, and Members of the two present Grand Lodges, shall on the day of their Re-union have made the solemn declaration in the presence of the deputation of Grand or enlightened Masons from Scotland and Ireland, to abide and act by the universally recognized obligation of Master Mason, the Members shall forthwith proceed to the election of a Grand Master for the year ensuing; and to prevent delay, the Brother so elected shall forthwith be obligated, *pro tempore*, that the Grand Lodge may be formed. The said Grand Master shall then nominate and appoint his Deputy Grand Master, together with a Senior and Junior Grand Warden, Grand Secretary, or Secretaries, Grand Treasurer, Grand Chaplain, Grand Sword Bearer, Grand Usher, and Grand Tyler, who shall all be duly obligated and placed, and the Grand Incorporated Lodge shall then be opened, in due form, under the stile and title of the UNITED GRAND LODGE OF ANTIENT FREEMASONS OF ENGLAND.

The Grand Officers who held the several Offices before (unless such of them as may be re-appointed) shall take their places, as Past Grand Officers, in the respective degrees which they held before; and in case either, or both of the present Grand Secretaries, Ushers, and Tylers, should not be reappointed to their former situations, then annuities shall be paid to them during their respective lives out of the Grand Fund.

VII. THE UNITED GRAND LODGE OF ANTIENT FREEMASONS OF ENGLAND shall be composed, except on days of Festival, in the following manner, as a just and perfect representative of the whole Masonic Fraternity of England; that is to say, of—

Articles of Union

The Grand Master,

Past Grand Masters,

Deputy Grand Master,

Past Deputy Grand Masters,

Grand Wardens,

Provincial Grand Masters,

Past Grand Wardens,

Past Provincial Grand Masters,

Grand Chaplain,

Grand Treasurer,

Joint Grand Secretary, or Grand Secretary if there be only one,

Grand Sword Bearer,

Twelve Grand Stewards, to be delegated by the Steward's Lodge from among their Members existing at the Union; it being understood and agreed that, from and after the Union, an annual appointment shall be made of the Stewards if necessary.

The actual Masters and Wardens of all Warranted Lodges,

Past Masters of Lodges, who have regularly served and passed the Chair before the day of Union, and who have continued without secession regular contributing Members of a Warranted Lodge. It being understood that of all Masters who, from and after the day of the said Union, shall regularly pass the

47

chair of their respective Lodges, but one at a time, to be delegated by his Lodge, shall have a right to sit and vote in the said Grand Lodge; so that after the decease of all the regular Past Masters of any regular Lodge, who had attained that distinction at the time of the Union, the representation of such Lodge shall be by its actual Master, Wardens, and one Past Master only.

And all Grand Officers in the said respective Grand Lodges shall retain and hold their rank and privileges in the United Grand Lodge, as Past Grand Officers, including the present Provincial Grand Masters, the Grand Treasurers, Grand Secretaries, and Grand Chaplains, in their several degrees, according to the seniority of their respective appointments; and where such appointment shall have been contemporaneous, the seniority shall be determined by lot. In all other respects and above shall be the general order of Precedence in all time to come, with this express provision, that no Provincial Grand Master, hereafter to be appointed, shall be entitled to a seat in the Grand Lodge after he shall have retired from such situation, unless he shall have discharged the duties thereof for full five years.

VIII. The Representatives of the several Lodges shall sit under their respective banners according to seniority. The two first Lodges under each Grand Lodge to draw a lot in the first place for priority; and to which of the two the lot No. 1 shall fall, the other to rank as No. 2; and all the other Lodges shall fall in alternately, that is, the Lodge which is No. 2, of the Fraternity whose lot it shall be to draw No. 1, shall rank as No. 3, in the United Grand Lodge, and the other No. 2, shall rank as No. 4, and so on alternately through all the numbers respectively. And this shall for ever after be the order and rank of the Lodges in the Grand Lodge, and in Grand Processions, for which a plan and drawing shall be prepared previous to the Union. On the renewal of any of the Lodges now dormant, they shall take rank after all the Lodges existing at the Union, notwithstanding the numbers in which they may now stand on the respective rolls.

IX. The United Grand Lodge being now constituted, the first proceeding after solemn prayer shall be to read and proclaim the Act of Union, as previously executed and sealed with the great seals of the two Grand Lodges; after which the same shall be solemnly accepted by the Members present. A day shall then be appointed for the installation of the Grand Master and other Grand Officers with due solemnity; upon which occasion the Grand Master shall in open Lodge, with his own hand, affix the new great seal to the said instrument, which shall be deposited in the archives of the United Grand Lodge, and be the bond of union among the Masons of the Grand Lodge of England, and the Lodges dependant thereon, until time shall be no more. The said new great seal shall be made for the occasion, and shall be composed out of both the great seals now in use; after which the present two great seals shall be broken and defaced; and the new seal shall be alone used in all warrants, certificates, and other documents to be issued thereafter.

X. The regalia of the Grand Officers shall be, in addition to the white Gloves and apron, and the respective Jewels or emblems of distinction, garter blue and gold; and these shall alone belong to the Grand Officers present and past.

XI. Four Grand Lodges, representing the Craft, shall be held for quarterly communication in each year, on the first Wednesday in the Months of March, June, September, and December, on each of which occasions the Masters and Wardens of all the warranted Lodges shall deliver into the hands of the Grand Secretary and Grand Treasurer, a faithful list of all their contributing Members; and the warranted Lodges in and adjacent to London shall pay towards the grand fund one shilling per quarter for each Member, over and above the sum of half a guinea for each new-made Member, for the registry of his name, together with the sum of one shilling to the Grand Secretary as his fee for the same, and that this contribution of one shilling for each Member shall be made quarterly, and each quarter, in all time to come.

XII. It shall be in the power of the Grand Master, or in his absence of the Past Grand Masters, or in their absence of the Deputy Grand Master, or in his absence of the Past Deputy Grand Masters, or in their absence of the Grand Wardens, to summon and hold Grand Lodges of Emergency whenever the good of the Craft shall, in their judgment, require the same.

XIII. At the Grand Lodge to be held annually on the first Wednesday in September, the Grand Lodge shall elect a Grand Master for the year ensuing, (who shall nominate and appoint his own Deputy Grand Master, Grand Wardens, and Secretary), and they shall also nominate three fit and proper persons for each of the offices of Treasurer, Chaplain, and Sword Bearer, out of which the Grand Master shall, on the first Wednesday in the month of December, chuse and appoint one for each of the said offices; and on the Festival of St. John the Evangelist, then next ensuing, or on such other day as the said Grand Master shall appoint, there shall be held a Grand Lodge for the solemn installation of all the said Grand Officers, according to antient custom.

XIV. There may also be a Masonic Festival, annually, on the Anniversary of the Feast of St. John the Baptist, or of St. George, or such other day as the Grand Master shall appoint, which shall be dedicated alone to brotherly love and refreshment, and to which all regular Master Masons may have access, on providing themselves with tickets from the Grand Stewards appointed to conduct the same.

XV. After the day of the Re-union, as aforesaid, and when it shall be ascertained what are the obligations, forms, regulations, working, and instruction to be universally established, speedy and effectual steps shall be taken to obligate all the Members of each Lodge in all the degrees, according to the form taken and recognized by the Grand Master, Past Grand Masters, Grand Officers, and Representatives of Lodges, on the day of Re-union; and for this purpose the worthy and expert Master Masons appointed, as aforesaid, shall visit and attend the several Lodges, within the Bills of Mortality, in rotation, dividing themselves into quorums of not less than three each, for the greater expedition, and they shall assist the Master and Wardens to promulgate and enjoin the pure and unsullied system, that perfect reconciliation, unity of obligation, law, working, language, and dress, may be happily restored to the English Craft.

XVI. When the Master and Wardens of a warranted Lodge shall report to the Grand Master, to his satisfaction, that the Members of such Lodge have taken the proper enjoined obligation, and have conformed to the uniform working, cloathing, &c., then the Most Worshipful Grand Master shall direct the new Great Seal, to be affixed to their warrant, and the Lodge shall be adjudged to be regular, and entitled to all the privileges of the Craft: a certain term shall be allowed (to be fixed by the Grand Lodge) for establishing this uniformity; and all constitutional proceedings of any regular Lodge, which shall take place between the date of the union and the term so appointed, shall be deemed valid, on condition that such Lodge shall conform to the regulations of the Union within the time appointed, and means shall be taken to ascertain the regularity, and establish the uniformity of the Provincial Grand Lodges, Military Lodges, and Lodges holding of the two present Grand Lodges in distant parts, and it shall be in the power of the Grand Lodge to take the most effectual measures for the establishment of this unity of doctrine throughout the whole community of Masons, and to declare the Warrants to be forfeited, if the measures proposed shall be resisted or neglected.

XVII. The property of the said two Fraternities, whether freehold, leasehold, funded, real or personal, shall remain sacredly appropriate to the purposes for which it was created; it shall constitute one grand fund, by which the blessed object of Masonic benevolence may be more exten-

sively obtained. It shall either continue
under the trusts on which, whether freehold,
leasehold, or funded, the separate parts
thereof now stand; or it shall be in the
power of the said United Grand Lodge, at
any time hereafter, to add other names to
the said trusts; or, in case of the death of
any one Trustee, to nominate and appoint,
others for perpetuating the security of the
same; and in no event, and for no purpose,
shall the said united property be diverted
from its original purpose. It being understood and declared that, at any time after
the Union, it shall be in the power of the
Grand Lodge to incorporate the whole of
the said property and funds in one and the
same set of Trustees, who shall give bond
to hold the same in the name and on the
behalf of the United Fraternity. And it
is further agreed, that the Freemasons' Hall
shall be the place in which the United
Grand Lodge shall be held, with such additions made thereto as the increased numbers
of the Fraternity, thus to be united, may
require. And it is understood between the
parties, that, as there are now in the Hall
several whole length portraits of Past Grand
Masters, a portrait of the Most Worshipful
His Grace the Duke of Atholl, Past Grand
Master of Masons, according to the old

Institutions, shall be placed there in the same conspicuous manner.

XVIII. The fund, appropriate to the objects of Masonic benevolence, shall not be infringed on for any purpose, but shall be kept strictly and solely devoted to charity, and pains shall be taken to increase the same.

XIX. The distribution and application of this Charitable Fund shall be monthly, for which purpose a Committee, or Lodge of Benevolence, shall be held on the third Wednesday of every month, which Lodge shall consist of twelve Masters of Lodges (within the Bills of Mortality); and three Grand Officers, one of whom only (if more are present) shall act as President, and be entitled to vote. The said twelve Masters to be summoned by the choice and direction of the Grand Master, or his Deputy, not by any rule or rotation, but by discretion; so as that the Members, who are to judge of the cases that may come before them, shall not be subject to canvass, or to previous application, but shall have their minds free from prejudice, to decide on the merits of each case with the impartiality and purity of Masonic feeling: to which end it is declared that no Brother, being a Member of such Committee or Lodge, shall vote, upon the petition of any person to whom he is in any way related, or who is a Member of any Lodge or Masonic Society, to which he himself actually belongs, but such Brother may ask leave to be heard on the merits of such petition, and shall afterwards, during the discussion and voting thereon, withdraw.

XX. A plan, with rules and regulations, for the solemnity of the Union, shall be prepared by the Subscribers hereto, previous to the Festival of St. John, which shall be the form to be observed on that occasion.

XXI. A revision shall be made of the rules and regulations now established and in force in the two Fraternities, and a code of laws for the holding of the Grand Lodge, and of private Lodges; and, generally, for the whole conduct of the Craft, shall be forthwith prepared, and a new Book of Constitutions be composed and printed, under the superintendence of the Grand Officers, and with the sanction of the Grand Lodge.

Done at the Palace of Kensington, this 25th Day of November, in the Year of our Lord, 1813, and of Masonry, 5813.

EDWARD, G.M.
THOS. HARPER, D.G.M.
JA. PERRY, P.D.G.M.
JAS. AGAR, P.D.G.M.

In Grand Lodge, this first day of December, A.D. 1813, Ratified and Confirmed, and the Seal of the Grand Lodge affixed.

EDWARD, G.M.
ROBT. LESLIE, G.S.

In Grand Lodge, this first day of December, A.D. 1813, Ratified and Confirmed, and the Seal of the Grand Lodge affixed.

AUGUSTUS FREDERICK, G.M.
W. SHIRLEY, D.G.M., V.T.
WILLIAM H. WHITE, G.S.

In the presence of

JANO, PONTRISSON DE LAGARDJE, G.M. of the Lodge of the North.

CHAPTER V

UNITED GRAND LODGE

THE United Grand Lodge of Antient Freemasons of England, or, as it is now styled in
the Book of Constitutions, the United Grand
Lodge of Antient Free and Accepted Masons
of England, came into existence, as narrated
in Chapter III, on St. John's Day, in
winter—viz., December 27, 1813—and now*
consists of the Masters, Past Masters, and
Wardens of all private Lodges on record,
together with the Grand Stewards of the
year and the present and past Grand
Officers, and the Grand Master at their head.

The Grand Lodge possesses the supreme
superintending authority, and alone has the
inherent power of enacting laws and regulations for the government of the Craft, and
of altering, repealing, and abrogating them,
always taking care that the antient Landmarks of the Order be preserved.

The Grand Lodge has also the power of
investigating, regulating, and deciding all
matters relative to the Craft, or to particular

* See Article VII.: Articles of Union.

Lodges, or to individual Brothers, which it may exercise either of itself or by such delegated authority as, in its wisdom and discretion, it may appoint; but the Grand Lodge alone has the power of erasing Lodges and expelling Brethren from the Craft, a power which it does not delegate to any subordinate authority in England.

Every Brother regularly elected and installed as Master of a Lodge, under the constitution of the Grand Lodge of England, who has filled that office for one year, so long as he continues a subscribing member of any such Lodge, is a member of the Grand Lodge; but having for twelve months ceased to be a subscribing member of any English Lodge, he no longer continues a member of the Grand Lodge, nor can he retain the right of membership of the Grand Lodge, as a Past Master, until he has again duly served the office of Master of such a Lodge.

Four Grand Lodges are held in London, for quarterly communication, in each year —viz., on the first Wednesday in the months of March, June, September, and December.

There is a Grand Masonic Festival annually, on the Wednesday next following St. George's Day, to which all regular Masons who provide themselves with tickets from the Grand Stewards of the year are admitted.

United Grand Lodge

The Grand Master, according to antient usage, is nominated at the Grand Lodge in December in every year, and at the ensuing Grand Lodge in March the election takes place. The Grand Master, so elected, is regularly installed on the day of the Grand Masonic Festival.

No Brother can be a Grand Master unless he has been a Fellow Craft before his election, who is also to be nobly born, or a gentleman of the best fashion, or some eminent scholar, or other artist, descended of honest parents, and who is of singularly great merit in the opinion of the Lodges.

The Grand Master, if a Prince of the Blood Royal, appoints a Pro Grand Master, who must be a Peer of the Realm.

And for the better, and easier, and more honourable discharge of his office, the Grand Master has a power to choose his own Deputy Grand Master, who must then be, or have formerly been, the Master of a particular Lodge, and who has the privilege of acting whatever the Grand Master, his principal, should act, unless the said principal be present, or interpose his authority by letter.

These rulers and governors supreme and subordinate, of the antient Lodge, are to be obeyed in their respective stations by all the brethren, according to the old charges and regulations, with all humility, reverence, love, and alacrity.

* * * *

Nineteen Grand Stewards are annually appointed, for the regulation of the Grand Festival, under the directions of the Grand Master. They assist in conducting the arrangements made for the quarterly communications and other meetings of the Grand Lodge.

The Grand Stewards are appointed from nineteen different Lodges, each of which recommends one of its subscribing members, who must be a Master Mason, and presented by the former Grand Steward of that Lodge, for the approbation and appointment of the Grand Master; when so approved and appointed, he is entitled to wear the clothing of a Grand Steward (see p. 343).

* * * *

All members of the Grand Lodge may have papers of business and notices of special Grand Lodge meetings, together with all reports of the quarterly communications forwarded to them by post on registering their addresses and paying a fee of five shillings per annum in advance.

* * * *

United Grand Lodge

The Grand Lodge is declared to be opened in ample form when the Grand Master or Pro Grand Master is present; in due form when a Past Grand Master or the Deputy presides; at all other times, only in form, yet with the same authority (as prescribed by Rule 51 of the Book of Constitutions).

Grand Lodge is always considered to be opened for Master Masons only, and the correct Sn., when addressing the Chair, appears, by custom, to be that of the E.A.; and the correct method of employing it is explained on p. 178.

The Ceremonies of Opening and Closing Grand Lodge form the basis of, and are similar to, the Ceremonies, *mutatis mutandis*, of Opening and Closing Provincial or District Grand Lodges (see pp. 270 to 275).

(see pp. 270 to 275)

*   *   *   *

There will be found in the Book of Constitutions, in Grand Lodge Transactions, in the Ritual, and in Masonic writings and conversations generally frequent references to the Antient Landmarks of the Order.

The powers of Grand Lodge are circumscribed by these alone; and every Master Elect solemnly pledges himself to preserve them, and not to permit or suffer any deviation from them.

It will be well, therefore, for the reader to have some clear and accurate impression of the term.

The word Landmark in its ordinary sense is quite well understood to mean a conspicuous and immovable object (such as a mountain), or an object not easily moved or likely to be moved (such as a church), and so on, in descending scale, until we come down to pillars and posts of a more temporary and easily movable character.

A Land mark may thus be itself a boundary or a mark by which a boundary may be calculated and fixed, or by which a ship's course may be determined.

This is the expressive word which has been appropriated by our ancestors to indicate, metaphorically, the immutable character of the fundamental principles and customs of our Institution.

But while it is quite easy to understand what is meant by a Landmark, our difficulties commence when we attempt to apply the term in detail.

No official list of Landmarks has ever been complied. Writers of importance have prepared various enumerations of them; but these enumerations command more or less assent according to the individual judgment of the reader.

United Grand Lodge

There is one, however, about which there is no question in the mind of any Free Mason, and Grand Lodge has on more than one occasion affirmed and reaffirmed it—viz., that "a belief in T.G.A.O.T.U. is the first and most important of the Antient Landmarks."

The relation of this Landmark to Freemasonry is as unalterable and undebatable as the relationship of the sun to the earth.

All the rest are dependent upon it and comprehended within it. In some of the others may be detected possibilities of change, gradual, involuntary, or deliberate.

The claim of a Landmark to be so regarded, must be tested, therefore, by its antiquity and by the degree in which it has resisted whatever mutability may be inherent therein.

By this gauge the reader may consider and determine for himself the respective rights and the relative importance of the following claimant which have been suggested and discussed by Dr. Mackey as additional Antient Landmarks of the Order:

> Modes of recognition.
> Division of Symbolic Masonry into three
> Degrees.
> The Legend of the third Degree.
> Government of Craft by a Grand Master.

Prerogative of Grand Master to preside; to grant Dispensations; to make Masons at sight.

Necessity of Lodge meetings.

Government of Lodge by a Master and two Wardens.

Necessity of Lodge being duly Tyled.

Right of every Mason to be represented in General Assembly; to appeal to Grand Lodge; to visit any regular Lodge without invitation.

Examination of visitors.

Equality and independence of Lodges, *inter se*.

Subjection of every Mason to Masonic Jurisdiction.

Qualifications and disqualifications of Candidates.

Obligation on appropriate V.S.L.

Equality of all Masons.

Secrecy of the Institution.

Speculative Science founded on Operative Art.

Immutability of the Landmarks.

To the above may very fairly be added:

Uniformity of the Ritual,

as practised in each Jurisdiction.

(Art. XV of the Articles of Union, 1813.)

CHAPTER VI

PROVINCIAL AND DISTRICT GRAND LODGES

PROVINCIAL Grand Lodges emanate from the Provincial Grand Masters by virtue of the authority vested in them by their patents of appointment from the Grand Master. It therefore follows that Provincial Grand Lodges possess no other powers than those specified in the laws and regulations contained in the Book of Constitutions, and cannot meet but by the sanction of the Provincial Grand Master or his Deputy.

In Colonies and foreign parts the terms District Grand Master and District Grand Lodge are used to distinguish such Officers and Lodges from Provincial Grand Masters and Provincial Grand Lodges in England.

A Provincial or District Grand Lodge consists of the Provincial or District Grand Master, the present and past Provincial or District Grand Officers, the Provincial or District Grand Stewards for the year, the Master, Past Masters, and Wardens of all Lodges in the Province or District, and Past

Masters of any Lodge under the English Constitution, if members of Grand Lodge; but no Brother can be a member of a Provincial or District Grand Lodge unless he is a subscribing member of a Lodge within such Province or District.

Provincial and District Grand Officers must all be resident within the Province or District, unless by Dispensation from the Grand Master.

District Grand Lodges fix stated times for their regular meetings, not exceeding four times in the year; but the District Grand Master may summon and hold a special District Grand Lodge, whenever, in his judgment, it may be necessary.

Provincial and District Grand Officers do not take any rank out of their Province or District, but are entitled to wear the clothing at all Masonic meetings.

Provincial or District Grand Stewards do not take any rank out of their Province or District, and when out of Office are no longer members of the Provincial or District Grand Lodge unless otherwise qualified, but are entitled to wear the clothing at all Masonic meetings.

When the Provincial or District Grand Master presides, the Provincial or District Grand Lodge is to be declared open in *due form.* If the Deputy or any other Brother preside, in *form* only. (B. of C., 79.)

In many Provinces and Districts the Provincial or District Grand Lodge is invited by the different Lodges to hold its meetings one year in one locality and another year in another. In some Provinces two meetings are held in the year. The Lodge which is honoured by a visit is expected to make— under the direction of the Provincial Grand Secretary, assisted by the Prov. G. Director of Ceremonies—all arrangements for the proper reception and accommodation of the Provincial or District Grand Lodge, and for the members of the various Lodges.

The meetings being as a rule larger than could be accommodated in an ordinary Lodge-room, a room is engaged in some large building, sufficiently capacious for the general meeting, and some other rooms (preferably in the same building); one for the reception of the Provincial or District Grand Master (who requires a room for his exclusive use); another for Provincial or District Grand Officers; and a third for the Brethren generally.

The Brethren, not having present or past Provincial or District rank, enter the Lodge-room. The Worshipful Master and the Wardens of the Lodge visited occupy the three chairs, and open the Lodge in the three Degrees.

The Provincial Grand Director of Ceremonies marshals the Provincial or District Grand Officers in processional order, the Provincial or District Grand Master at the rear. Arrived at the door of the Lodge the report is given, the Provincial or District Grand Officers open out right and left, the Provincial or District Grand Master walks up the centre, the Senior Officers closing in; the others do the same, and in that inverted order they enter the Lodge. The Brethren all rise, and the Organist plays a march, or some appropriate composition, while the Provincial or District Grand Master and the Officers take their seats.

The Master of the Lodge and the Wardens back out of their respective places and hand in their Provincial or District successors.

*   *   *   *

The Provincial or District Grand Lodge is then opened in due form, or in form according to No. 79 of the Book of Constitutions. The ceremonies of opening and closing Provincial or District Grand Lodge will be found on pp. 273-274.

*   *   *   *

Provincial and District Grand Lodges

All Lodges held at a greater distance than ten miles from Freemasons' Hall, London, are Provincial or District Lodges, and are under the immediate superintendence of the Provincial or District Grand Master within whose jurisdiction they meet.

The Provincial or District Grand Master may preside in any Lodge he visits within his Province or District, his Deputy being placed on his right, and the Master of the Lodge on his left hand; his Wardens, if present, shall act as Wardens of the Lodge during the time he presides; but if they be absent, the Provincial or District Grand Master may direct the Wardens of the Lodge, or any Master Masons, to act as his Wardens *pro tempore*.

Unless the Provincial or District Grand Master be present, his Deputy may preside in any Lodge he may visit within his Province or District, the Master of the Lodge being placed on his right hand. The Provincial or District Grand Wardens, if present, are to act as Wardens of the Lodge during the time he presides.

*   *   *   *

The reader's attention is invited to the remarks on the subject of the Charity Representative on pp. 359 and 362.

*   *   *   *

Calendars are now published in many Provinces, containing the day, the hour, and the place of meeting of every Lodge within the Province; and many Lodges year by year send a copy to every subscribing member. The convenience of possessing such a Calendar is very great in many ways. A Brother is enabled on reference to his Calendar to make his engagements so that he may be free to attend his own Lodge, or to visit any other to which inclination or duty may lead him. The word 'duty' is used advisedly, because it is highly desirable that a kind and fraternal feeling should exist between neighbouring Lodges; and nothing tends so much to create and to foster this feeling as the interchange of visits between the several members of the Lodges in a district. The Principal Officers, especially, should consider it a part of their duty to set a good example in this respect. Something may be, and often is, gained in Masonic Knowledge by the interchange of such visits.

CHAPTER VII

GENERAL COMMITTEE

THE General Committee consists of the President of the Board of Benevolence, who, if present, acts as Chairman, the Present and Past Grand Officers, and the Master of every regular Lodge. It meets on the fourteenth day immediately preceding each quarterly communication.

Notices of such meetings are from time to time sent to the Secretaries of Lodges; the packet is marked 'to be forwarded,' and should be transmitted to the Worshipful Master without delay.

If the Master of any Lodge cannot attend the General Committee, the Immediate Past Master may supply his place; should that Brother be unable to attend, any other Past Master of such Lodge may act for him, but in every case the Past Master must be a subscribing member of that Lodge.

At this meeting all reports and representations from the Grand Master, or the Board of General Purposes, or any Board or Committee appointed by the Grand Lodge, are read.

In normal times the work of the General Committee is of a very perfunctory character; indeed, its very existence seems to be forgotten by most, except the *ex-officia* members of it, certain habitual attendants, and the permanent officials, whose duty it is to conduct its proceedings. From time to time, however, matters of importance are to be debated in Grand Lodge, and then the proceedings of the General Committee become more animated, as any member of the Grand Lodge intending to make motion therein, or to submit any matter to its consideration, must, at such General Committee, or by notice previously given or sent to the Grand Secretary, state, in writing, the nature of such intended motion or matter, that notice thereof may be printed on the paper of business.

No motion, or other matter, may be brought into discussion in the Grand Lodge, unless it shall have been previously communicated to the General Committee.

The General Committee may direct that any notice of motion which, in its judgment, is not within the cognizance of the Grand Lodge, shall be omitted from the list of business to be brought before the Grand Lodge.

All nominations for Boards or Committees must be given to the General Committee in writing, signed by a member of the Grand Lodge.

CHAPTER VIII

BOARD OF BENEVOLENCE

THE Board of Benevolence consists of a President, appointed by the Grand Master, two Vice-Presidents, elected at the Grand Lodge in December, and of all the present and past Grand Officers, and all actual Masters of Lodges, and twelve Past Masters of Lodges nominated at the General Committee annually in November, and elected by the Grand Lodge in December, in the same manner as the elected members of the Board of General Purposes.

No Past Master is eligible to be re-elected who neglects to attend the Board of Benevolence at six meetings.

If the actual Master of the year of any Lodge cannot attend, the Immediate Past Master may supply his place: should that Brother be unable to attend, any other Past Master of such Lodge may act for him; but in every case the Past Master must be a subscribing member of the Lodge.

The Board meets on the last Wednesday but one of every month, to administer the

Fund of Benevolence. This Fund was established in 1727, and is applied to relieving Masons and their families.

Article XVIII of the Act of Union provides: The Fund, appropriate to the objects of Masonic benevolence, shall not be infringed on for any purpose, but shall be kept strictly and solely devoted to charity, and pains shall be taken to increase the same.

The Fund is at present derived partly from Interest on Investments, partly from Fees of Honour, partly from Dispensation Fees, and partly from a capitation fee from each member of the private Lodges (4s. per head in London, 2s. in country), known as Quarterage.

The sum so produced is considerable, totalling £22,000 in the year 1913; and the grants made are generous, especially in any exceptionally deserving case, or in cases where the Brother in question is shown to have been active in charitable affairs when in a position to have been so.

Members who are to judge of the cases that may come before them may not be subject to canvass, or to previous application; but must have their minds free from prejudice, to decide on the merits of each case with the impartiality and purity of Masonic feeling: to which end it is declared

Board of Benevolence

that no Brother, being a Member of such Committee or Lodge, may vote, upon the petition of any person to whom he is in any way related, or who is a Member of any Lodge or Masonic Society, to which he himself actually belongs; but such Brother may ask leave to be heard on the merits of such petition, and must afterwards, during the discussion and voting thereon, withdraw.

No Brother can claim relief 'as of right.' The fund of Benevolence is not a Benefit Society.

No Mason registered under the constitution of the Grand Lodge of England can receive the benefit of the Fund of Benevolence unless he has paid the full Initiation or Joining fee, continued a subscribing member to a contributing Lodge for at least five years, and during that period paid his quarterly dues to the Fund of Benevolence. The limitation of five years, however, does not apply to the cases of shipwreck, capture at sea, loss by fire, or blindness, or serious accident, fully attested and proved. Any Brother who has ceased subscribing for the immediate past twenty years is not eligible to petition the Board unless he has previously subscribed to his Lodge for fifteen years or upwards.

A Brother who has been relieved cannot petition a second time within one year. A widow who has been relieved cannot petition again.

It is a matter of considerable thought to the Board that claims are arising in greater numbers from Masons of short standing, thus indicating that not enough care is taken to see that Initiates are in sufficiently assured circumstances to warrant their admission to a Society of which the basis is assistance to others (see p. 15).

CHAPTER IX

BOARD OF GENERAL PURPOSES

THE Board of General Purposes consists of the Grand Master, Pro Grand Master, Deputy Grand Master, the Grand Wardens of the year, the Grand Treasurer, the Grand Registrar, the Deputy Grand Registrar, a President, Past Presidents, the President of the Board of Benevolence, the Grand Director of Ceremonies, and twenty-four other members.

The President and six of such 'other members' are annually appointed by the Grand Master, at the quarterly Grand Lodge in June; and the Grand Lodge, on the same day, elects by ballot from among the actual Masters and Past Masters of Lodges as many as may be required to make up the remaining eighteen members. A Master and Past Master or more than one Past Master of the same Lodge cannot be elected as such on the same Board; but this does not disqualify any Past Master, being a subscribing member and Master of another Lodge, from being elected for and representing such other Lodge as Master.

One-third at least of the members must

go out of office annually, but are eligible for re-election.

The Board meets on the third Tuesday in every month at four o'clock precisely. It may also be convened at other times by command of the Grand Master, or by the authority of the President.

Five members constitute a Board and proceed to business, except in the decision of Masonic complaints, for which purpose at least seven members must be present.

The Board has full power to inspect all books and papers relating to the accounts of the Grand Lodge, and to give orders for the correct arrangement of them; and to summon the Grand Treasurer, Grand Registrar, Grand Secretary, or other Brother having possession of any books, papers, documents, or accounts belonging to the Grand Lodge, and to give such directions as may be necessary.

Except when otherwise specially directed by resolution of the Grand Lodge, the Board has the direction of everything relating to the buildings and furniture of the Grand Lodge.

The Board may recommend to the Grand Lodge whatever it shall deem necessary or advantageous to the welfare and good government of the Craft, and may originate plans for the better regulation of the Grand

Board of General Purposes

Lodge and the arrangement of its general transactions, but no recommendations or reports of the Board or of any Committee appointed by the Board may be issued for the consideration of or be voted upon by the Craft until they have been discussed by the Members of Grand Lodge in regular or especial meeting assembled.

The Board has likewise the care and regulation of all the concerns of the Grand Lodge, and conducts the correspondence between the Grand Lodge and its subordinate Lodges and Brethren, and communications with sister Grand Lodges and Brethren of eminence and distinction throughout the world.

The Board has authority to hear and determine all subjects of Masonic complaint or irregularity respecting Lodges or individual Masons, when regularly brought before it, and generally to take cognizance of all matters relating to the Craft.

The Board may proceed to admonition, fine, or suspension, according to the laws; and its decision is final, unless an appeal be made to the Grand Lodge.

The Board may summon the Officers of any Lodge to attend it and to produce the warrant, books, papers, and accounts of the Lodge, or may summon any Brother to attend it and produce his certificate.

CHAPTER X

WHO ARE FIT AND PROPER PERSONS TO BE MADE MASONS?

THIS is a most important question, and one which lies at the foundation of the Masonic edifice. It should be carefully considered *before* the initiation of a Candidate, as it is too late to discuss it afterwards. Indeed, it should be carefully considered before the Candidate is proposed in Lodge, and great responsibility attaches to those who seek to introduce members from the uninstructed and popular world.

One excellent test to be applied is this: Is the proposed Candidate one whom we would unhesitatingly admit to our own home, and introduce to our own family circle with confidence?

The Book of Constitutions warns us against the great discredit and injury likely to be brought upon our antient and honourable Fraternity by the admission of undesirable members, and enjoins strict inquiry into the characters and qualifications of persons wishful to become members; and in order that this injunction may be properly obeyed there should be a written proposal and recommendation from both proposer and seconder. It is an excellent custom in many Lodges to refer to a Standing Committee every such notice of intention to propose a person for initiation. That Standing Committee is responsible to the Lodge for a personal interview with and a proper inquiry into, and report upon, the merits of the Candidate; who must be of good report (see Proposition Form, Appendix (D), p. 429). There is no ambiguity about the necessary qualifications. The answer to the question above propounded is authoritatively stated to be—just, upright, and free men of mature age, sound judgment, and strict morals; and at the time of initiation every Candidate should be in reputable circumstances (see pp. 15 and 101) and of sufficient education (see p. 101).

He ought to be free born, but it is conceded under the present Constitution [1847] that if a man be free, although he may not have been free born, he is eligible to be made a Mason.

He must profess, and should earnestly hold, a sincere belief in the Great Creator and Ruler of the Universe.

The Antient Charges instruct us that a Mason is obliged, by his tenure, to obey the moral law; and if he rightly understand the art, he will never be a stupid atheist nor an irreligious libertine. He, of all men, should best understand that God seeth not as man seeth; for man looketh at the outward appearance, but God looketh to the heart. A Mason is, therefore, particularly bound never to act against the dictates of his conscience. Let a man's religion or mode of worship be what it may, he is not excluded from the Order, provided he believe in the glorious Architect of heaven and earth, and practise the sacred duties of morality. Masons unite with the virtuous of every persuasion in the firm and pleasing bond of fraternal love: they are taught to view the errors of mankind with compassion, and to strive, by the purity of their own conduct, to demonstrate the superior excellence of the faith they may profess. Thus Masonry is the centre of union between good men and true, and the happy means of conciliating friendship amongst those who must otherwise have remained at a perpetual distance.

A Mason is a peaceable subject to the civil powers, wherever he resides or works, and is never to be concerned in plots and conspiracies against the peace and welfare of the nation, nor to behave himself undutifully to inferior magistrates. He is cheerfully to conform to every lawful authority; to uphold, on every occasion, the interest of the community, and zealously promote the prosperity of his own country. Masonry has ever flourished in times of peace, and been always injured by war, bloodshed, and confusion; so that kings and princes in every age have been much disposed to encourage the Craftsmen on account of their peaceableness and loyalty, whereby they practically answer the cavils of their adversaries and promote the honour of the fraternity. Craftsmen are bound by peculiar ties to promote peace, cultivate harmony, and live in concord and brotherly love.

The persons made Masons or admitted members of a Lodge must be good and true men, free born, and of mature and discreet age and sound judgment; no bondmen, no women, no immoral or scandalous men, but of good report.

Candidates may, nevertheless, know that no master should take an apprentice, unless he has sufficient employment for him; and, unless he be a perfect youth, having no maim or defect* in his body that may render

* In 1875, the Board of General Purposes issued a circular intimating that so long as physical deformity did not prevent a candidate from exercising Masonic functions—presumably from making the signs—it is not a disqualification.

him incapable of learning the art, of serving his master's lord, and of being made a Brother, and then a Fellow Craft in due time, after he has served such a term of years as the custom of the country directs; and that he should be descended of honest parents; that so, when otherwise qualified, he may arrive to the honour of being the Warden, and then the Master of the Lodge, the Grand Warden, and at length the Grand Master of all the Lodges according to his merit.

*   *   *   *

It may be convenient to state here that for all practical purposes the terms Free Masonry, Freemasonry, and Masonry; Free-Mason, Freemason, and Mason are synonymous and interchangeable—that is to say, that the words Masonry and Mason in the mouth of a Freemason mean Freemasonry and Freemason.

In ancient documents persons are recorded as Free Man and Free Mason; this gradually shortened into Free Man and Mason; and finally Free Mason.

About 1717 period, Dr. Anderson appears to have made the two words into one, Freemason.

No confusion is likely to arise in these

days by employing either, whether at will or by accident. The correct style of a Freemason is equally a Free and Accepted Mason, or an Ancient Freemason. Masonry in its operative sense is the parent of Masonry in its speculative sense. The greater includes the lesser, and the true Mason will see nothing but Honour, Grace, and Dignity in the beautiful mechanical Art of Masonry which gave birth to the Speculative Craft now called Free Masonry.

The Articles of Union, than which there can be no better guide or authority, speak (Article I) of the two Fraternities of Free and Accepted Masons, to be hereafter and for ever known and acknowledged by the style and title of Ancient Freemasons; Article II defines pure Antient Masonry; Articles VI and VII speak of Freemasons; and throughout there seems to be no attempt to establish any distinction of differentiation in the terms.

CHAPTER XI

WHAT IS A LODGE OF FREEMASONS?

A LODGE is an assemblage of Brethren met to expatiate on the mysteries of the Craft, or, in the language of the Antient Charge, a Lodge is a place where Freemasons assemble to work and to instruct and improve themselves in the mysteries of the antient science. In an extended sense it applies to persons as well as to place; hence every regular assembly or duly organized meeting of Masons is called a 'Lodge.'

Every brother ought to belong to some Lodge, and be subject to its by-laws and the General Regulations of the Craft.

A Lodge may be either general or particular, as will be best understood by attending it, and there a knowledge of the established usages and customs of the Craft is alone to be acquired.

From antient times no Master or Fellow could be absent from his Lodge, especially when warned to appear at it, without incurring a severe censure, unless it appeared to the Master and Wardens that pure necessity hindered him.

What is a Lodge of Freemasons?

'In the Lodge while constituted you are not to hold private committees, or separate conversation, without leave from the Master, nor to talk of anything impertinently or unseemly, nor interrupt the Master or Wardens, or any Brother speaking to the Master; nor behave yourself ludicrously or jestingly while the Lodge is engaged in what is serious and solemn, nor use any unbecoming language upon any pretence whatsoever; but to pay due reverence to your Master, Wardens, and Fellows, and put them to worship.'

No private piques or quarrels must be brought within the door of the Lodge, far less any quarrels about religion, or nations, or State policy, we being only, as Masons, of the universal religion above mentioned; we are also of all nations, tongues, kindreds, and languages, and are resolved against all politics, as what never yet conduced to the welfare of the Lodge, nor ever will.

CHAPTER XII

'PARTICULAR' OR PRIVATE LODGES

No Lodge may be held without a Charter or Warrant of constitution from the Grand Master. Every Lodge must be regularly constituted and consecrated; and no countenance ought to be given to any irregular Lodge.

Lodges rank in precedence in the order of their numbers as registered in the books of the Grand Lodge.

The Grand Steward's Lodge does not have a number, but is registered in the books of the Grand Lodge; and placed in the printed list, at the head of all other Lodges, and ranks accordingly.

The Warrant of the Lodge is specially entrusted to the Master for the time being at his installation. He is responsible for its safe custody, and must produce it at every meeting of the Lodge. The Lodge of Antiquity, No. 2, and the Royal Somerset House and Inverness Lodge, No. 4, act under immemorial constitutions.

If a warrant be lost, the Lodge must

suspend its meetings until a warrant of confirmation has been applied for and granted by the Grand Master.

Every Lodge is distinguished by a name or title, as well as a number.

The regular Officers of a Lodge consist of the Master and his two Wardens, a Treasurer, a Secretary, two Deacons, an Inner Guard, and a Tyler.

The Master may also appoint a Chaplain, a Director of Ceremonies, an Assistant Director of Ceremonies, an Almoner, an Organist, an Assistant Secretary, and Stewards.

No Brother can hold more than one *regular* office in the Lodge at one and the same time.

In cases where Officers other than Regular Officers are appointed, the order of appointment is as follows: Worshipful Master, Senior Warden, Junior Warden, Chaplain, Treasurer, Secretary, Senior Deacon, Junior Deacon, Director of Ceremonies, Assistant Director of Ceremonies, Almoner, Organist, Assistant Secretary, Inner Guard, Stewards, Tyler.

As 'all preferment among Masons is grounded upon real worth and personal merit only,' the foregoing order of appointment and investiture give no Brother the right to claim advancement by rotation, 'that so the lords may be well served, the brethren not put to shame, nor the Royal Craft despised.' The appointment of all Officers except the Treasurer and Tyler is in the sole discretion and power of the Worshipful Master.

Every Lodge must, annually, on the day named by its by-laws for that purpose, elect its Master by ballot.

'Mo Master is chosen by seniority, but for his merit.'

At the next regular meeting, immediately after the confirmation of the Minutes, he is duly installed.

No Master Elect may assume the Chair until he has been regularly installed.

No Warden can be installed as Master of a Lodge (except by Dispensation from the Grand Master) unless he has served the office as an Invested Warden for a full year—that is to say, from one regular Installation Meeting until the next regular Installation Meeting. (See p. 320.)

No Installing Master may proceed unless satisfied of such service or Dispensation.

Every Master Elect, before being placed in the chair, must solemnly pledge himself to preserve the Landmarks* of the Order; to

* See pp. 63, 64, 65, 66, 67.

observe its ancient usages and established customs; and strictly to enforce them within his own Lodge.

The Master is responsible for the due observance of the laws by the Lodge over which he presides.

No Brother may be Master of more than one Lodge at the same time, without a Dispensation.

No Brother may continue Master for more than two years in succession, unless by a Dispensation.

No Brother can be a Grand Warden until he has been Master of a Lodge.

N.B.—In antient times no Brother, however skilled in the Craft, was called a Master-Mason until he had been elected into the Chair of a Lodge.

Upon his installation the Master appoints and invests his Wardens and other Officers, and invests the Treasurer.

No Brother can be a Warden until he has passed the part of a Fellow Craft.

No Warden is chosen by seniority, but for his merit.

The Treasurer is annually elected by ballot on the regular day of election of Master.

The Tyler is to be chosen by show of hands.

No proprietor or manager of the tavern or house at which the Lodge meets may hold any office in the Lodge without a Dispensation from the Grand Master or the Provincial or District Grand Master.

Should the Master be dissatisfied with the conduct of any of the Officers, he may lay the cause of complaint before the Lodge at a regular meeting (seven days' notice thereof in writing having been previously sent to the Brother complained of), and if it appears to the majority of the Brethren present that the complaint is well founded, the Master has power to displace such Officer, and to appoint another.

If a vacancy occurs in any office other than that of Treasurer or Tyler, the Master appoints a Brother to serve such office for the remainder of the year; and if the vacancy be in the office of Treasurer or Tyler the Lodge may, after due notice in the summons, elect a successor for the remainder of the year.

If the Master dies, is removed, or is rendered incapable of discharging the duties of his office, the Senior Warden, and in the absence of the Senior Warden, the Junior Warden, and in the absence of both Wardens, the Immediate Past Master, or in his absence the Senior Past Master, acts as

Master in summoning the Lodge, until the next installation of Master.

In the Master's absence, the Immediate Past Master, or, if he be absent, the Senior Past Master of the Lodge present, or if no Past Master of the Lodge be present, then the Senior Past Master who is a subscribing member of the Lodge takes the chair. And if no Past Master who is a member of the Lodge be present, then the Senior Warden, or in his absence the Junior Warden, rules the Lodge. When a Warden rules the Lodge, he may not occupy the Master's chair; nor can initiations take place or degrees be conferred unless the chair be occupied by a Brother who is a Master or Past Master in the Craft.

The Master and Wardens of a Lodge are enjoined to visit other Lodges as often as they conveniently can, in order that the same usages and customs may be observed throughout the Craft, and a good understanding cultivated amongst Freemasons.

No visitor may be admitted into a Lodge unless he be personally known to, or well vouched for, after due examination, by one of the Brethren present, or until he has produced the certificate of the Grand Lodge to which he claims to belong, and has given satisfactory proof that he is the Brother named in the certificate, or other proper vouchers of his having been initiated in a regular Lodge. Every visitor during his presence in the Lodge is subject to its by-laws. (See p. 308.)

No Brother who has ceased to be a subscribing member of a Lodge is permitted to visit any one Lodge more than once until he again becomes a subscribing member of some Lodge, but this does not apply to the visits of a Brother to any Lodge of which he has been elected a non-subscribing or honorary member.

All Lodges held within ten miles of Freemasons' Hall, London, are London Lodges.

Every Lodge has the power of framing by-laws for its government, provided they are not inconsistent with the regulations of the Grand Lodge. The by-laws must be submitted to the Grand Secretary for the approval of the Grand Master. When finally approved, a printed copy must be sent to the Grand Secretary; and when any alteration is made, such alteration must, in like manner, be submitted. No law or alteration is valid until so submitted and approved. The by-laws of the Lodge must be printed, and a copy delivered to the Master on his installation, who by his acceptance thereof is deemed to solemnly pledge himself to observe and enforce them.

Every Brother must be supplied with a printed copy of the by-laws of the Lodge when he becomes a member, and his acceptance thereof is deemed to be declaration of his submission to them.

The regular days of meeting of the Lodge and its place of meeting are specified in the by-laws, and no meeting of the Lodge may be held elsewhere, except by Dispensation. The by-laws also specify the regular meeting for the election of the Master, Treasurer, and Tyler.

A Lodge of Emergency may at any time be called by the authority of the Master, or in his absence, of the Senior Warden, or, in his absence, of the Junior Warden, but on no pretence without such authority. The business to be transacted at such Lodge of Emergency must be expressed in the summons, and no other business may be entered upon.

The jewels and furniture of every Lodge belong to, and are the property of, the Master and Wardens for the time being, in trust for the members of the Lodge.

Every Lodge must keep a minute-book, in which the Master, or the Brother appointed by him as Secretary, must regularly enter from time to time—

First—The names of all persons initiated, passed, or raised in the Lodge, or who shall become members thereof, with the dates of their proposal, initiation, passing, and raising or admission respectively, together with their ages, addresses, titles, professions, or occupations.

Secondly—The names of all members present at each meeting of the Lodge, together with those of all visiting Brethren, with their Lodges and Masonic rank.

Thirdly—Minutes of all such transactions of the Lodge as are proper to be written.

The minutes can only be confirmed at a subsequent regular meeting of the Lodge.

Secretaries who, by the by-laws of their Lodges, are exempted from the payment of subscription, shall be considered in all respects as regular subscribing members of their Lodges, their services being equivalent to subscription, provided their dues to the Grand Lodge have been paid.

All money received, or paid for, or on account of a Lodge, must be from time to time regularly entered in proper books, which are the property of the Lodge. The accounts of the Lodge must be audited, at least once in every year, by a committee appointed by the Lodge.

The majority of the members present at

'Particular' or Private Lodges

any Lodge duly summoned have an undoubted right to regulate their own proceedings, provided that they are consistent with
the general laws and regulations of the Craft;
no member, therefore, is permitted to enter
in the minute-book of his Lodge a protest
against any resolution or proceeding which
may have taken place, except on the ground
of its being contrary to the laws and usages
of the Craft, and for the purpose of complaining or appealing to a higher Masonic
authority.

Whenever it happens that the votes are
equal upon any question to be decided by a
majority, either by ballot or otherwise, the
Master in the chair is entitled to give a
second or casting vote.

Great discredit and injury having been
brought upon our antient and honourable
Fraternity from admitting members and
receiving candidates without due notice
being given or inquiry made into their
characters and qualifications, and from
passing and raising Masons without due
instruction* in the respective degrees, it is
declared to be specially incumbent on all
members of Lodges to see that particular
attention be paid to these several points.

No person may be made a Mason without

* See Lodges of Instruction, Chapter XIII.

having been proposed and seconded at one regular Lodge, and balloted for at the next regular Lodge.

No person may be made a Mason under the age of twenty-one years, unless by Dispensation.

A Lewis is entitled to the 'privilege' of being made a Freemason *in precedence* of his fellow Candidates. Thus, his name stands first upon the Summons, and is the first mentioned at the door of the Lodge, and he is the foremost in the perambulation. The privilege of a Lewis has this extent—no more.

On the occasion of the Initiation of one of the sons of H.R.H. the Grand Master, a short account of the event was given in one of the London daily papers. The writer of that description, evidently a Freemason, added: 'The young Prince had not availed himself of the privilege which, as a Lewis (*i.e.*, the eldest son of a Freemason), he might have claimed, that of being made a Freemason before he had attained the full age of twenty-one years.'

This is a wrong idea altogether: no Lewis, be he Prince or peasant, can successfully claim such a privilege. Rule 157 in the Book of Constitutions is clear and emphatic upon the subject. Only by dispensation can any person be made a Freemason under the age of twenty-one years. The whole extent of the 'privilege' of a Lewis is, that it gives him precedence at his Initiation 'over any other person, however dignified by rank or fortune.'

Every candidate must be a free man, and at the time of initiation in reputable circumstances.

Previously to his initiation, every candidate must subscribe his name at full length to a declaration. (See p. 430.)

N.B.—A person who cannot write is consequently ineligible to be admitted into the Order.

No Brother may be admitted a joining member of a Lodge without being proposed and seconded in open Lodge at a regular meeting. (See p. 333.)

No person may be made a Mason in, or admitted a member of, a Lodge, if, on the ballot, three black balls appear against him.

No Lodge may initiate into Masonry more than two persons on the same day, unless by a Dispensation.

No person may be made a Mason for less than five guineas, in England.

No Lodge may confer a higher degree on any Brother at a less interval than four weeks from his receiving a previous degree, nor until he has passed an examination* in open Lodge in that degree.

No Brother may appear clothed in any of the jewels, collars, or badges of the Craft, in any procession, or at any funeral, ball, theatre, public assembly, or meeting, or at any place of public resort, unless the Grand Master, Provincial Grand Master, or District Grand Master, as the case may be, shall have previously given a dispensation for Brethren to be there present in Masonic clothing.

Should a Lodge fail to meet for one year it is liable to be erased.

When a Lodge can prove an uninterrupted working existence of one hundred years, it may, by Petition, and on payment of the prescribed Fee, obtain from the M.W. Grand Master a Centenary Warrant. (See p. 189.)

* See Lodges of Instruction, Chapter XIII.

CHAPTER XIII

LODGES OF INSTRUCTION

'A YOUNGER Brother shall be instructed in working, to prevent spoiling the materials for want of judgment; and for increasing and continuing of brotherly love.'

No Lodge of Instruction may be holden unless under the sanction of a regular warranted Lodge, or by the special licence and authority of the Grand Master.

This special licence has never been granted. There is only one instance of its having been applied for, and it was then refused (1830), on the ground that the licence ought to be given only in cases of a very special nature where the application of an extraordinary remedy had become requisite.

The Lodge giving its sanction, and the Brethren to whom such licence is granted, must be answerable for the proceedings, and responsible that the mode of working adopted has received the sanction of the Grand Lodge.

The object of this Law is that Grand

Lodge may have a known responsible party in the event of irregularity; and the refusal of the special licence mentioned above was based on this important principle.

If a Lodge which has given its sanction for a Lodge of Instruction being held under its warrant shall see fit, it may at any regular meeting withdraw that sanction by a resolution of the Lodge, to be communicated to the Lodge of Instruction; provided notice of the intention to withdraw the sanction be inserted in the summons for that meeting.

Lodges of Instruction should be constituted as formally as Regular Lodges, and should meet with as much regularity, but more frequently.

Notice of the times and places of meeting of Lodges of Instruction within the London district must be submitted for approval to the Grand Secretary, otherwise to the Provincial or District Grand Secretaries respectively.

Lodges of Instruction should, for continuity of management and policy, be governed by a Committee, including one or more competent Preceptors; and all the Officers, permanent and rotational, should be elected and appointed, with as much regularity and formality as in Regular Lodges.

Lodges of Instruction

Lodges of Instruction must keep minutes recording the names of all Brethren present at each meeting and of Brethren appointed to hold office, and such minutes must be produced when called for by the Grand Master, the Provincial or District Grand Master, Board of General Purposes, or the Lodge granting the sanction.

The Furniture, Working Tools, and Appointments should be as complete as possible.

'All the tools used in working shall be approved by the Grand Lodge.'

The Officers should all wear Masonic clothing during the performance of their duties.

All the 'proceedings' should be carried out in such a methodical way as to be a careful, elaborate, and complete education, not only in the ceremonies, but in all those matters which the Mason will encounter in Regular Lodges; in fact, all the proceedings should be object-lessons in Masonic Etiquette.

Everything should be watched with much more strictness than in Regular Lodges, as a mistake uncorrected in a Lodge of Instruction is more likely to create a precedent of evil, than the same error in a Regular Lodge.

In Lodges of Instruction the Preceptor's word is Law; and there must be no questioning of his ruling or discussion about the Ritual while Lodges of Instruction are open for Masonic business.

Prompt obedience to all 'signs' is the motto for workers in Lodges of Instruction.

It is quite permissible, and, indeed, desirable, that from time to time, in addition to the ordinary routine work of Ceremonies and Lectures, miscellaneous instruction should be afforded to members upon all matters which interest them, care being taken to distinguish between those points which are matters of Law and those which are matters of individual taste and discretion.

Needless to say, there should be complete unanimity and uniformity among the Preceptors as to the mode of working.

Brethren, able and willing to conform to these conditions, are not too numerous. Those who are capable are often unwilling, and those who are willing are often unable.

Educational enthusiasm, however, is spreading, and educational facilities are increasing. The true standard is becoming more and more widely recognized. The desirability—indeed, the necessity—for conformity is more readily accepted.

Lodges of Instruction

Brethren nowadays are more desirous of 'doing the work,' and in doing it the desire of doing it well is engendered and fostered.

The Masonic Year Book gives a list of 221 Lodges of Instruction meeting under sanction in London, and 345 Lodges of Instruction meeting under sanction in the Provinces.

No doubt there are others which have not complied with the prescribed rules, and are therefore not mentioned in the Year Book; while there are, of course, various unauthorized clubs meeting on Sundays the existence of which is officially ignored.

In June, 1874, certain Brethren were summoned to Grand Lodge and reprimanded for holding a 'Club of Instruction,' without due authority, in an Inn, and advertising the same in the public journals.

A great responsibility is cast by Grand Lodge upon those 'answerable for the proceedings' of Lodges of Instruction; and it is to be feared that this responsibility is insufficiently realized in many quarters.

Many Lodges of Instruction meet by force of circumstances, on Licensed Premises, where the use of a room is granted for a nominal sum in the expectation of further

profit resulting from the sale of drinks
and smokes to be consumed in the Lodge
Room!

Nothing more derogatory to the dignity
of the proceedings can well be conceived,
and the repetition of the beautiful phrases
of the Ritual in such an atmosphere amounts
to a desecration of it. On the practical side
of the question, nothing could be more con-
ducive to an imperfect rehearsal than the
petty interruptions caused (say) by lighting
a pipe in the middle of a ceremony. Very
little self-denial would be needed to dispense
with these indulgences until the 'call off,'
while the profit of 'the house' would not be
less—it might even be more—by postponing
the slaking of thirst for a brief season.

What says the 'Antient Charge' on this
point? 'After the Lodge is over you may
enjoy yourselves with innocent mirth, treating one another according to ability.'

But, apart from and above 'the proceedings' of the Lodge of Instruction, there is
the far more important responsibility 'that
the mode of working adopted has received
the sanction of the Grand Lodge'; and this
is a matter about which much argument
often arises, argument which for the most
part arises from want of knowledge of cer-

tain cardinal facts. Indeed, it may often be said with truth, the more vehement the argument, the less the foundation for it.

It is an excellent rule in cases of doubt to go to the fountain-head in search of knowledge; and, to apply this rule to the case in point, if a Preceptor of a Lodge of Instruction wishes to discharge his responsibility, and wishes to be sure that 'the mode of working adopted has received the sanction of the Grand Lodge,' the surest and most direct method for him is obviously to ascertain 'whether Grand Lodge sanctions any particular "mode of working" or form of Ritual, and, if so, what it is, and where it can be obtained.'

This is the course recently followed by the writer, who is a Preceptor of a Lodge of Instruction, and the important and convincing reply of the Grand Secretary will be found on pp. 118-119.

The subject of 'mode of working' or Ritual is so important that it will be treated at length in the next chapter.

CHAPTER XIV

RITUAL

NEXT in importance to 'the foundation on which Freemasonry rests—the practice of every moral and social virtue'—the solemn ceremonies by which every Mason is made acquainted with 'the mysteries and privileges of Freemasonry' undoubtedly must take a prominent position in the thoughts of every earnest member of our great Fraternity.

Every Mason remembers the deep impression made upon his mind by the first touching experiences of his novitiate, and in after-years it becomes his valued and responsible privilege to assist in creating those sacred impressions upon the minds of his Brethren in the early stages of their Masonic education.

These ceremonies are comprehensively described as 'Ritual.'

Our ancient Brethren viewed the question of 'Ritual' very seriously, and almost the first act of the United Grand Lodge in 1813 was to constitute the Lodge of Reconciliation, composed (in conformity with the Articles of Union) of an equal number of representatives of the two previous Grand Lodges, for the express purpose of *settling the Ritual once and for all*; and Grand Lodge approved, sanctioned, and confirmed that Ritual on June 5, 1816.

Article XV of the Act of Union (*q.v.*) provides:—

'For this purpose the worthy and expert Master Masons, appointed as aforesaid, shall visit and attend the several Lodges, . . . and they shall assist the Master and Wardens to promulgate and enjoin *the pure and unsullied system*, that perfect reconciliation, unity of obligation, law, working, language and dress, may be happily restored to the English Craft.'

Article XVI reads:

'It shall be in the power of the Grand Lodge to take the most effectual measures for the establishment of this *unity of doctrine* throughout the whole community of Masons, and to declare the Warrants to be forfeited, if the measures proposed shall be resisted.'

Ignorance of these cardinal facts breeds in the minds of some an idea that the Ritual can follow the deviations of personal idiosyncrasies, individual and collective.

It is not so. *No Mason has a right to*

tamper with a comma of it. Only Grand Lodge could do that (*vide* Article 4 of Book of Constitutions).

'The Grand Lodge possesses the supreme superintending authority, and alone has the inherent power of enacting laws and regulations for the government of the Craft; and of altering, repealing, and abrogating them; always taking care that the antient Landmarks of the Order be preserved.'

'It is not in the power of any man or body of men to make innovation in the body of Masonry,' and any attempt to introduce or perpetuate *any deviation* is a breach of that Law of Obedience to which a Mason's attention has been 'peculiarly and forcibly directed.'

It may be freely, if sorrowfully, admitted that there are, unfortunately, many errors and discrepancies, and even misstatements of fact, in the Ritual submitted by the Lodge of Reconciliation and approved by Grand Lodge in 1816; but it is difficult to conceive with what *authority* any subordinate Mason or body of Masons, can imagine himself or themselves to be clothed, which would warrant him or them in even deliberating upon the subject of the Ritual with a view to alter it after it has once been sanctioned and confirmed by the United Grand Lodge.

Ritual

Every Worshipful Master is under a special obligation 'not to permit or suffer *any deviation* from the established Land-marks of the Order.'

If Grand Lodge in 1813 treated the question of Ritual as of such primary importance, there can be no excuse for us to treat it lightly or irreverently in these days; and as in civil matters, *ignorantia legis neminem excusat*, so in Masonic matters it is inexcusable to blunder as a consequence of failure 'to make a daily advancement in Masonic knowledge,' and it becomes our bounden duty to assure ourselves that we are rightly discharging our responsibility in this connection.

This, however, is a busy world, and many causes conspire to make us treat our Masonry more as a social relaxation than an earnest probing of 'the hidden mysteries of Nature and Science'; and we are, often perforce, more content to remain in the category of those whose duty it is to 'submit and obey' than to qualify ourselves by study and research to occupy fitly the position of those whose function it becomes to 'rule and teach.'

The subject, however, is of primary importance, and the following collated facts will enable the reader to arrive at a sound conclusion upon a serious and vexed question:

The constant desire of Grand Lodge to insure Uniformity of Working is evidenced by the measures it has taken from time to time for the purpose of supervising and co-ordinating the 'Working' of subordinate Lodges.

That this desire is by no means of modern growth may be learned from official records of the ancient régime. So far back as September 2, 1752, it was resolved: 'That this Grand Committee shall be formed immediately into a working Lodge of Master Masons, in order to hear a Lecture from the Grand Secretary. The Lodge was opened in antient form, and every part of real Freemasonry was traced and explained, except the Royal Arch.'

In the year 1792 the Nine Excellent Masters, familiarly known as 'The Nine Worthies,' were instituted by the Grand Committee. These Brethren were elected annually to assist Grand officers in visiting Lodges, in order 'that the general uniformity of Ancient Masonry may be preserved and handed down unchanged to posterity.'

The Lodge of Promulgation was instituted by Warrant, dated October 28, 1809, from the Grand Master of the Grand Lodge of

England, *'authorizing certain distinguished Brethren to hold a special Lodge for the purpose of ascertaining and promulgating the Ancient Land-Marks of the Craft.'*

In the case of the Lodge of Promulgation, '. . . the object to be attained was to make the Lodges of the Moderns fall into line with those of the Antients as regards their Land-Marks and esoteric practices.'

'There can be no possible doubt that the Grand Lodge of the Moderns gave in on all points where their Ceremonies differed from those of the Antients.'

The Articles of Union, November 25, 1813, themselves lay especial stress on the point of Uniformity.

Articles III, IV, and V refer to '. . . the purpose of establishing and securing Uniformity of Working.'

Article XV provides '. . . that perfect reconciliation, Unity of obligation, law, working, language, and dress, may be happily restored to the English Craft.'

Article XVI enacts that ' . . . Grand Lodge may declare the Warrants to be forfeited if the measures proposed shall be resisted.'

The Lodge of Reconciliation was constituted December 7, 1813, '. . . with power to meet, unite, and incorporate themselves with a Lodge of equal numbers . . . according to the Old Institutions contained and set forth in Articles 4 and 15 of a certain instrument bearing date November 25 last entitled "Articles of Union" between the two Grand Lodges of England. . . .'

The Lodge of Reconciliation worked for over two years at its important task.

On May 20, 1816, the Ceremonies of the three degrees were rehearsed for the approval of the United Grand Lodge.

On June 5, 1816, alterations on two points* in the Third Degree having been resolved upon, the several Ceremonies recommended were approved, sanctioned, and confirmed.

On August 6, 1818, the Grand Secretary (E. Harper), in reply to an inquiry concerning the correct Ritual, wrote that 'Bro. Peter W. Gilkes would instruct "in the *correct* method adopted since the Union."

'Bro. Peter W. Gilkes was officially acknowledged as the most perfect exponent of the Ceremonies and Ritual of the Craft.

'He was in a manner something Johnsonian in regard to Masonry. No advantage could be taken of him in Lodge; *he would not allow the slightest deviation in word, or manner, or matter. . . .*'

In 1823 Emulation Lodge of Improvement was formed to teach this approved

* See Appendix: Master's Light.

'Mode of Working,' and did so under the leadership of Bro. Peter W. Gilkes from 1825 until his death in 1833.

The Board of Installed Masters was Warranted February 6, 1827, in these words: '. . . And feeling how important it is that all Rites and Ceremonies in the Craft should be conducted with Uniformity and correctness, and with a view, therefore, to produce such Uniformity, we have thought it proper to appoint, and do accordingly nominate and appoint . . . to make known to all who may be entitled to participate in such knowledge, the Rites and Ceremonies of Installation as the same have already been approved by us. . . .'

In 1827 this Board of Installed Masters held three meetings at Freemasons' Hall, which were very numerously attended by Masters and Past Masters, who 'expressed themselves highly satisfied with the ceremonies and explanations which were then afforded them.'

In 1833 Bro. Stephen Barton Wilson (afterwards P.G.D.) succeeded Bro. Peter W. Gilkes as Leading Member of the Emulation Lodge of Improvement.

On September 6, 1843, the Grand Secretary (W. H. White) wrote, in reply to an inquiry whether any alteration had been made in the Ceremonies, that no alteration had 'been made since the Grand Lodge formally approved and decided on them in the year 1816. Bro. Gilkes was fully Master of all the Ceremonies, and, I believe, most strictly observed them.'

Bro. S. B. Wilson remained in command until his death, April 25, 1866.

Bro. Thomas Fenn (afterwards P.B.G.P.) succeeded Bro. S. B. Wilson, and remained in charge until 1894, when

Bro. R. Clay Sudlow (afterwards P.G.D.) took up that position, and retained it until his death in 1914.

There has thus been an uninterrupted chain of communication from the Lodge of Reconciliation down to the present day, and at this point the following letter finds an appropriate place:

'UNITED GRAND LODGE OF ENGLAND,
'FREEMASONS' HALL
'GREAT QUEEN STREET,
LONDON, W.C.
'*November* 22, 1912.

'DEAR SIR AND BROTHER,

'I am in receipt of your letter of the 20th instant, and am pleased to learn that a correct rendering of the Ritual is a subject of concern to the members of your Lodge.

'While it is true that no *edict* has ever

118

Ritual

been issued by Grand Lodge as to any particular working being accepted, nor is it considered compulsory that Lodges should conform to what is termed the "Emulation" system of ritual, on the other hand it is an historical fact that Grand Lodge in 1816 definitely adopted and gave its approval to the system of working submitted to it by the Lodge of Reconciliation, and it is also a fact that this is the system which the "Emulation" Lodge of Improvement was founded in 1823 to teach, and which is taught by that Lodge to-day.

'The late Bro. Thomas Fenn, who was considered the most able exponent of Masonic Ritual of his day, always held the opinion that the "Emulation" working was authorized, and that opinion is also held by Bro. Sudlow, his successor in the teaching of that system. Certainly no other system or ritual has received at any time the official approval of Grand Lodge.

'I am,

Yours fraternally,

'E. LETCHWORTH, G.S.

'W. Bro. W. P. Cambell-Everden, L.R.,
Lodge No. 19, London.'

It must be admitted by all unbiased minds that, having regard to the great and extraordinary care which Emulation Lodge of Improvement has, fortunately, always taken to preserve its own rigid and absolute conformity with the original 'Mode of Working' adopted by the Lodge of Reconciliation in 1816, while no other Lodge has had the inclination or the means to take such measures, it would redound to the credit of Freemasonry in general if every Lodge were now to revert to, and in the future adhere to, that standard of accuracy and strict conformity with—

1. The 'Mode of Working' and Ancient Ceremonies of Initiation, Passing, and Raising, as approved, sanctioned, and confirmed by the United Grand Lodge on June 5, 1816; and

2. The Ceremony of Installation as agreed by the Board of Installed Masters and sanctioned and approved by the Grand Master in 1827; and

3. The Lectures corresponding with the said Ceremonies and the ancient usages and established customs of the Order.

Ne Varientur.

CHAPTER XV

No work embracing Lodges of Instruction and Ritual would be complete without a reference to the Emulation Lodge of Improvement.

Those who wish to know all about it cannot do better than read Bro. Sadler's 'Illustrated History of the Emulation Lodge of Improvement' (published by Spencer and Co.); and their 'desire of knowledge' may be gently stimulated by a perusal of a pleasant little pamphlet by Bro. F. Bebbington Goodacre (published by Hutton and Co., Ormskirk, Lancs.).

'Emulation Lodge of Improvement,' which meets every Friday evening at six o'clock at Freemasons' Hall from October to June inclusive (Good Friday excepted), was founded in 1823 to work the precise form of Ritual settled by the Lodge of Reconciliation, as approved, sanctioned, and confirmed by the Grand Lodge on June 5, 1816, and as recorded on the Minutes of Grand Lodge.

The fundamental principle of 'Emulation,' its absolute *raison d'être*, is the conviction that *no one has any right to alter one word* of that Ritual, or to tamper with it in any way.

Its claim is that it works now, always has worked, and always will work (without variation, and even without the possibility of variation, of a letter, character, or figure), that Ritual and that alone.

It takes its stand upon the simple idea that whatever the Ritual was settled to be by Grand Lodge in 1816, so it must remain, word for word and letter for letter, until (if ever) Grand Lodge should see fit to alter it.

It is unable to conceive with what authority any subordinate Mason, or body of Masons, can imagine himself or themselves to be clothed, which would warrant him or them in even deliberating upon the subject of Ritual, with a view to alter it, after it has once been sanctioned and confirmed by United Grand Lodge.

Consequently it has no sympathy with those who desire to 'correct' or 'improve' the Ritual, or to render it more 'consistent,' 'harmonious,' or 'logical,' or more 'historically accurate,' to introduce words into it, or to round off phrases, or to make it 'more grammatical,' 'more dignified,' or to 'bring it up to date'—in other words, to 'tinker' with it.

It is from the erroneous idea that any neophyte may exercise his prancing fancy upon the sacred ground of our ancient and honourable institution, and rush in where angels fear to tread, that the existing diversities of practice have unfortunately emanated.

Many causes have contributed to this idea, and among them may be mentioned:

1. Apathy of Masons generally on the subject.

2. Want of knowledge or remembrance of past history.

3. Failure to instruct incomers.

4. Bad advice on the subject.

5. Modesty on the part of 'Emulation.'

By the wonderful expansion of Freemasonry, thousands and thousands of Masons have been brought into being; and, as during the last eighty years there has been unfortunately no Official, no Authorized Preceptor* charged with the duty of keeping

* Several attempts have, from time to time, been made to induce Grand Lodge to appoint a Committee for the purpose of securing and insuring Uniformity of Ritual. On December 1, 1869, a motion for the appointment of such a Committee was carried unanimously in Grand Lodge, but on June 1, 1870, it was agreed to postpone the appointment *sine die*.

Masons within due bounds as to Ritual, many Lodges, from want of knowledge, or from indifference, have, in the most haphazard fashion, dropped into a little system of their own or followed local ideas.

Some 'Clubs,' indeed, have started with the *avowed* object of constructing a Ritual of their own, not perceiving that *ipso facto* they are transgressing their elementary vows of Obedience.

The consequence has been that many variations of the Ritual have arisen; and, not having been officially stamped out, they have flourished like weeds, become numerically considerable, and have audaciously developed themselves into 'Workings.'

These 'Workings' are, of course, utterly unauthorized.

The only Ritual which has ever been authorized is the Ritual which was settled once and for all by the Lodge of Reconciliation in 1813 to 1816.

The Grand Secretary writes on the subject:

'This is the system which the Emulation Lodge of Improvement was founded in 1823 to teach, and which is taught by that Lodge to-day' (see Letter, *in extenso*, pp. 118 and 119).

The corroborative evidence of this invariability is manifold.

In the first place there is the uninterrupted

descent of the Emulation Ritual from Peter William Gilkes, who was officially acknowledged by Grand Lodge as the exponent of the Ritual of the Lodge of Reconciliation.

Peter William Gilkes personally taught that Ritual to Stephen Barton Wilson, who personally taught it to Thomas Fenn, who personally taught it to R. Clay Sudlow.

Then there is the evidence on which they all base themselves as to the extraordinary care which has always been taken to safeguard its accuracy, amounting to an impossibility of alteration, all of which will be found in Bro. Sadler's 'History.'

The reverent spirit in which this care is exercised is apparent in the following extract from a speech by Bro. R. Clay Sudlow (February 23, 1894):

'. . . We look upon the Trust delivered to us by those Brethren as very important indeed—a very sacred one—and speaking for myself, and I am sure speaking in the name of my colleagues, I may say that that Trust shall be most faithfully, most honourably, and most religiously preserved.'

Finally, there is one most convincing test which is available to-day, and that is: Let anyone working there try to make a tiny little variation in the course of his work and see what happens!

Every Mason should visit the Emulation Lodge of Improvement, even if only to see what it is like.

No one can judge without facts in evidence.

The beauty of the work as it is performed there, the absolute accuracy, the unvarying system, the attention to detail, will enable the observant Mason to realize that here, at any rate, is a wonderful model.

But when to that admiration is added the conviction that it is the only authorized version, the intending student must come to the conclusion that he ought not to learn any other. It is simply waste of time to do so.

But Emulation Lodge of Improvement is not in the ordinary sense a Lodge of Instruction. It is rather a Lodge of Demonstration to which Masons, from all parts of the world, come with the object of seeing how the work ought to be done.

Therefore anyone undertaking to work there is expected to be a qualified exponent of the work of the office he undertakes.

To meet this difficulty and to permit the gradual development of the system, Emulation Lodge of Improvement has of late years recognized a series of Emulation-Working Lodges of Instruction, in which the Emulation system is strictly adhered to, and in

Emulation Lodge of Improvement

which the earnest Mason may thoroughly learn the various Ceremonies, and so qualify himself to work at Headquarters. Obviously he can the more readily do this if he has not already filled his mind with the vagaries of various unrecognized 'Workings.'

Every Mason, therefore, should join one or more of these Emulation-Working Lodges of Instruction* in order to learn, and perfect himself in, the one and only Ritual ever authorized by Grand Lodge.

He should make a practice also of attending Emulation Lodge of Improvement on Friday nights to familiarize himself with every detail.

Then when his turn comes to take up regular Office in his own Lodge, he will not only have confidence that he will be able to do the right thing in the right way, but he will doubtless feel it to be his privilege and duty to assist the good work by leading the footsteps of his younger brethren in the straight and narrow path he himself has trodden.

*   *   *   *

A few words are added, by request, with reference to that which is sometimes accus-

* A List of Lodges of Instruction recognized by the Committee of the Emulation Lodge of Improvement may be had by application to the Secretary direct.

127

ingly spoken of as the Intolerance of Emulation.

The form of the answer greatly depends upon the spirit in which the accusation is made; but, assuming it to be made *academically*, let us freely admit—nay, *claim*—that Emulation is, and always will be, intolerant to the last degree of—wilful error, or intentional deviation from the Ritual of the Lodge of Reconciliation which, and which alone, Emulation recognizes and teaches.

Let us also admit and claim that, in its moments of teaching and demonstration, Emulation is also intolerant of the slightest accidental error, or unintentional deviation from the absolute accuracy which is its basic and fundamental principle.

The I.P.M., assisted by brother committeemen, sits earnestly watchful for the slightest lapse, so that it may be corrected on the instant.

This *educational intolerance of error in the Emulation Lodge of Improvement* is the greatest—indeed, the only possible—safeguard for the pure and unsullied transmission of the Ritual of the Lodge of Reconciliation from generation to generation; and, in the minds of the thinking Masons who support the Emulation Lodge of Improvement, constitutes one of the principal claims to their gratitude and praise.

But the *intolerance of Emulation is limited to its educational aspect*, and any suggestion of intolerance, in any other than an educational sense, can only emanate from some among those (and unfortunately they are many) who do not know Emulation as it really is, and are not on visiting terms with it.

Obviously the primary object of Emulation is that the only Ritual ever authorized should, in consequence of previous instruction, be worked in the Regular Lodges with ease and accuracy and uniformity, but Emulation does not claim that its *authority* should penetrate into the Regular Lodge, and overshadow the functions of the Master.

In the Regular Lodge the Worshipful Master is supreme, and the principal object of solicitude is the Candidate; and all Forms, Ceremonies, and Ritual are, uninterruptedly, subservient to that object, and in that spirit.

In the Lodge of Instruction the Preceptor as I.P.M. is, *de facto*, supreme, and the principal object of solicitude is the absolute accuracy of every detail; and all Forms, Ceremonies, and Ritual are, interruptedly, subservient to that object.

The occasions being unlike, the circumstances do not admit of comparison.

Emulationists recognize to the full that purity of Ritual is not the *sum total* of Freemasonry—that it is not even of the *essence* of Freemasonry.

It is the beautiful goblet from which the good wine of Freemasonry is poured; but if the *quality* of the Nectar offered to the Candidate be inferior, in vain will be the artistic *beauty* of the vessel.

Emulationists fully recognize that the Mysteries and Privileges of Freemasonry may be taught, and often are taught, in phrases which do not correspond with any known form of Ritual; they recognize also that Brethren who give proof in their conduct from day to day that the Grand Principles on which the Order is founded are in their *hearts* are better exemplars of Masonry than those who possess merely the literal and verbal accuracy of its teachings.

But Emulationists also recognize that it is possible to have *both sincerity and accuracy*, and they desire to have both.

Hence the self-sacrificing labours of those who have devoted their time and energy, and practically their lives, to the achievement of the high object they have in view.

CHAPTER XVI

A LODGE AND ITS FURNITURE

It may not be unprofitable for us to consider in some detail the Lodge and its Ornaments, Furniture, and Jewels.

The jewels and furniture of every Lodge belong to, and are the property of, the Master and Wardens for the time being, in trust for the members of the Lodge.

With regard to the Furniture, we shall discuss it, not only in the technical and restricted sense of the word, as it is described in the Explanation of the Tracing Board, and in the Lectures (that is, as consisting of the Volume of the Sacred Law, the Compasses, and the Square), but also in the more general acceptation of the term, including everything that is necessary for the decorous performance of the Ceremonies, and for the reasonable comfort and convenience of the Officers and the Brethren.

When 'the good man of the house' calls together 'his friends and his neighbours,' he makes all necessary arrangements for their reception, in order that they may derive the fullest enjoyment from his hospitality. This is the etiquette of private life. It should be with us also a matter of etiquette that our Lodge should be fitly arranged; that nothing be wanting; that all the means and appliances should be good of their kind; not mean or sordid, and, so far, unworthy of our Order; and especially that we should fulfil the conditions of the old adage, 'A place for everything, and everything in its place'; because, without a proper arrangement of everything that may be used, or to which attention may be directed, in the course of the several Ceremonies, the solemnity and the impressiveness of those Ceremonies may be considerably lessened, or altogether destroyed.

Unless the established order be strictly observed in the arrangement of the Lodge, and its Ornaments, Furniture, and Jewels, the Lodge cannot be said to be properly prepared; or to be 'just, perfect, and regular,' in the ordinary acceptation of the term; and the 'etiquette of Freemasonry' cannot be strictly maintained.

We will discuss these subjects consecutively, in the order in which they stand in the Explanation of the Tracing Board of the First Degree and in the First Lecture.

The form of the Lodge is said to be a parallelopipedon; and its situation is described as being 'due east and west.' For the latter proposition full and sufficient reasons are given in the Explanation.

It is highly desirable that these two conditions should be literally fulfilled whenever and wherever it may be possible. Too often, however, from circumstances which are beyond the control of the members of a Lodge, a literal fulfilment of the prescribed form and situation is impossible.

Very many Lodges are compelled to hold their meetings in hotels or public rooms, the shape or the position, and often both, of which do not agree with the model or ideal Lodge. Frequently there is no alternative room in the locality, and nothing can be done but to make the best of existing circumstances, and to hold, in practice, that the Master's chair denotes the East, and the Senior Warden's the West, of the Lodge.

It is very desirable, indeed necessary, that the door of entrance should be in the west, or quasi-west, and on the left of the Senior Warden's chair. In this position there are several advantages. The Junior Deacon on the one side of the Senior Warden and the Inner Guard on the other, balance each other, as it were. The Junior Warden and the Inner Guard are within clear view of each other; and members of the Lodge and visitors are, immediately on their entrance into the Lodge, brought under the direct notice of the Junior Warden. This is highly necessary, because he is responsible for all who enter, notwithstanding that all announcements of the names of both members and visitors are made by the Inner Guard to the Worshipful Master, who directs their admission. If the Candidate be admitted on the left of the Senior Warden, he is at once in the proper position for all that is to follow; from that starting-point he is enabled to make the complete perambulation of the Lodge, and on his return to the same place he is presented.

On the other hand, if he must enter on the right he must pass behind the Senior Warden's chair.

In cases where the door is on the right hand of the Senior Warden, and no change is possible, the tact of the Deacons and of the Director of Ceremonies must be exercised in order to minimize the awkwardness of the position.

The Ornaments of the Lodge are the Mosaic Pavement, the Indented or Tessellated Border, and the Blazing Star or Glory in the centre. One sometimes sees in a Lodge a carpet of some conventional pattern upon the floor; this is highly objectionable, and forms a direct contradiction to the description given in the Explanation of the Tracing Board previously quoted. It is happily becoming more and more rare in practice.

A carpet woven in the pattern of the Mosaic Pavement in black and white, or printed on felted drugget, is easily procurable—the latter at a small cost. A carpet the full size of the room, with a wide border, both of the prescribed pattern and colours, is highly desirable. In any case, 'the Blazing Star or Glory in the centre' should not be omitted.

'The furniture of the Lodge' comprises 'the Volume of the Sacred Law, the Compasses, and Square.' It is sad to find in some Lodges (probably few in number) that these indispensable furnishings of the Lodge are more or less mean and sordid in character—the Bible small, old, and dilapidated, and the Compasses and Square an ill-assorted couple: the Square of some common wood, the Compasses of brass, cheap and objectionable.

These things should not be. They show, first, a want of proper and becoming respect to the Volume of the Sacred Law, 'which is given as the rule and guide of our faith';

secondly, to the Compasses, the distinguishing Jewel of the Grand Master of our Order; and thirdly, to the Square, the time-honoured emblem and cognizance of the Craft, which teaches us to regulate our lives and actions.

A handsomely-bound Bible of moderate size, and the Square and Compasses *in silver*, will scarcely be beyond the means of any Lodge. They are often presented by zealous and liberal Brethren to their respective Lodges, and in such cases the gifts are almost invariably worthy of the givers and of the recipients.

The Jewels comprise 'three movable and three immovable.' 'The movable jewels are the Square, Level, and Plumb-rule.' 'They are called movable jewels, because they are worn by the Master, and his Wardens' (during the period of their tenure of their several offices), 'and are transferable to their successors on nights of installation.' The collars bearing these several jewels should be placed upon the chairs, respectively, of the Master and his Wardens, previously to the opening of the Lodge.

The Jewels of the Officers of private Lodges are prescribed as follow:

Masters: The square.

Past Masters: The square and the diagram of the 47th prop. First Book of

A Lodge and its Furniture

Euclid engraven on a silver plate, pendent within it.

Senior Warden: The level.

Junior Warden: The plumb rule.

Chaplain: A book within a triangle surmounting a glory.

Treasurer: A key.

Secretary: Two pens in saltire, tied by a ribbon.

Deacons: Dove and olive branch (p. 338).

Director of Ceremonies: Two rods in saltire, tied by a ribbon.

Assistant Director of Ceremonies: Two rods in saltire, tied by a ribbon, surmounted by a bar, bearing the word 'Assistant.'

Almoner: A Scrip Purse, upon which is a heart.

Organist: A lyre.

Assistant Secretary: Two pens in saltire, tied by a ribbon, surmounted by a bar bearing the word 'Assistant.'

Inner Guard: Two swords in saltire.

Stewards: A cornucopia between the legs of a pair of compasses extended.

Tyler: A sword.

The above jewels to be in silver, except those of the Officers of the Lodge of Antiquity, No. 2, and of the British Lodge, No. 8, which are golden or gilt.

'The immovable jewels are the Tracing

Board, and the Rough and Perfect Ashlars.'
'They are called immovable jewels because
they lie open and immovable in the Lodge,
for the Brethren to moralize on.'

Tracing Boards are doubtless derived from
the Operative Free Masons' Trestle Boards
which are placed in each stoneyard (or
degree), and upon which the actual tools and
other requisites are placed.

With regard to the position of the Tracing
Boards, there is much difference in practice
in different Lodges. In some old Lodges
they are simply the canvases not framed;
this is objectionable chiefly in consequence
of the difficulty experienced by the Junior
Deacon in handling them rapidly, and the
consequent damage and defacement likely
to ensue, as he lays and relays them upon
the floor according to the Degree in which
the Lodge is working.

In other Lodges the three Tracing Boards
are framed and are hung upon the walls of
the Lodge room. By this arrangement they
are better secured from damage; but it is
objectionable because it not infrequently
happens that the whole of the three are left
upon the walls, irrespective of the Ceremony
which is being performed. Clearly, during
an Initiation the Tracing Boards of the
Second and Third Degrees should not be

exposed to view, and similarly during the Ceremony of Passing the Tracing Boards of the First and Third Degree should be kept concealed.

Probably the best plan is to have the Tracing Boards painted on wooden panels and laid, according to the degree in which the Lodge is open, either upon the floor of the Lodge or against the Junior Warden's Pedestal, so that all may be reminded (and especially incoming Brethren) of the degree in which the Lodge is at that moment working. It is the duty of the Junior Deacon to attend to these changes.

A regards Biblical, and even traditional, accuracy, the present Tracing Boards leave much to be desired, especially the Second and the Third. A criticism of their inconsistencies and anachronisms will be found in the Appendix.

The proper place for the Rough Ashlar is on the Junior Warden's pedestal; it is there in full view. The stone should not be quite 'rough-hewn, as taken from the quarry' by the Quarrymen, Rough Masons, or Cowans. This is intended 'for the Entered Apprentice to work, mark, and indent on.' It should show evidence of having been so worked, marked, and indented; it should be as though a succession of E. As. had tried their ' 'prentice hand' upon it; had indeed *rough-dressed* it with the Gavel, and had knocked off some at least of the 'superfluous knobs and excrescences.'

Indications might also be shown of some rudimentary work with the Chisel, this working tool being presented to the Entered Apprentice in order that he may with it 'further smooth and prepare the stone and render it fit for the hands of the more expert Workman.'

After the stone has been 'rough-dressed' by First Degree men, and made one-sixteenth of an inch larger than the required size in each direction, it is passed on to the second stoneyard, where the Fellows of the Craft bring it to the exact size required, and polish it if so ordered. It is then a Perfect Ashlar.

The Perfect Ashlar is 'a stone of a true die or square.' The severest test to which the skill of an operative Mason can be submitted is the production of a perfect cube. It has even been asserted that a *perfect* cube has never yet been produced.

Its position should be on the Senior Warden's pedestal, properly suspended, with the Lewis inserted in the centre. The explanation of the Lewis, as it is given in the 'Explanation of the First Tracing Board,' runs thus: 'It is depicted by certain pieces of metal, dovetailed into a stone forming a cramp; and when in combination with some of the mechanical powers, such as a system of pulleys, it enables the Operative Mason to raise great weights to certain heights with little encumbrance, and to fix them on their proper bases.'

This may be seen in operation during the erection of any edifice which is being built wholly or partially of stone, and notably in the case of the laying of a foundation or chief corner-stone, at which some Masonic or other ceremony of a public character is observed.

It will readily be seen that a chain or rope passed *round* the stone, and especially the keystone of an arch, would prevent its being properly bedded in its place. Nothing could answer the purpose more effectually than the Lewis, which, with slight—if, indeed, any— modification in its form, has been for many centuries an indispensable implement in Operative Masonry; while in Speculative Masonry it has from time immemorial been one of the most interesting and expressive of the Symbols of our Order.

In some old Lodges one may sometimes see a curious and complicated structure, consisting of a crane with a windlass, on a platform (a cumbrous affair, generally broken or otherwise out of order), for the purpose of suspending the Perfect Ashlar. It may be interesting from its age, but it takes up too much room, and is altogether inconvenient wherever it may be placed in the Lodge.

A very simple plan of construction is to have three quasi-scaffold-poles, with their bases fixed to a flat triangle, and with a 'tackle and fall,' and a 'cleet' to which the end of the cord is made fast; the poles are tapered, and, of course, are brought together at the top. This plan is neat, inexpensive, and efficient, and at the same time it has the merit of being a model, in miniature, of that which is in constant use in Operative Masonry in laying foundation-stones, etc.

The three great Pillars which support a Freemasons' Lodge are called Wisdom, Strength, and Beauty, and find expression in the Ionic, Doric, and Corinthian Columns which are respectively attributed to Solomon, King of Israel; Hiram, King of Tyre; and Hiram Abiph, and are now assigned to the Worshipful Master and the Senior and Junior Wardens.

The Columns of the Senior and Junior Wardens are symbolically brought into service in the ceremonies of opening and closing the Lodge. The Master's Column is always stationary.

142

A Lodge and its Furniture

The three lesser Lights, which represent the Sun, Moon, and Master of the Lodge, are placed in candlesticks, which correspond, as regards Orders of Architecture, with the respective columns above mentioned.

The pedestals of the Worshipful Master, and of the Senior and Junior Warden, should be of sufficient size to accord with the rank of those Officers. Each should bear on the front the Working Tool by which each Officer is specially distinguished—namely, the Square for the Master, the Level for the Senior Warden, and the Plumb-rule for the Junior Warden. These may be really working tools, of the size and make of those in use in the Second Degree, securely fixed in the centre of the front of the pedestal. The effect of this is bolder and better than when the emblem is merely painted or gilt on the pedestal.

The top of each pedestal and the plinth should be in the usual form—a rectangular oblong.

The three chairs should be large and grandiose in character, made each in strict accordance with the Order in Architecture assigned to each of the three principal Officers. They should be spacious, well proportioned, and very handsome. The pedestals should also correspond to the three

Orders—that is, they should have each two columns, the bases, the shafts, and the capitals of each pair of columns being perfectly true to each of the three Orders.

Each of the Wardens' chairs should stand upon a platform (7 to 8 inches high). All the three pedestals should stand upon the floor; consequently, they should be of sufficient height to allow for the elevation of the platform, and in the case of the Master's pedestal for the platform and the daïs combined. It is by no means uncommon *in outlying districts* to see tall pedestals and the Wardens' chairs standing on the floor—that is, without a platform—the result being that those officers partially disappear when they sit down.

Of the Working Tools of the Entered Apprentice Degree little mention need be made of the 24-inch Gauge or the Chisel. The most important is the Gavel. This is presented to the Worshipful Master when he is installed into the Chair, as the Gavel is an emblem of power; yet one sees occasionally in the Lodge the Master and the Wardens each with, not a Gavel, but a light Mall (a miniature copy of the heavy Mall of the Third Degree)—that is, a small mallet with a turned head—whereas the Gavel has a slightly elongated head, with one end *flat-*

faced like a hammer, the other end having a blunt axe-edge.

This shape is admirably adapted to the work which it is represented as being designed to perform—namely, 'to knock off all superfluous knobs and excrescences.' An actual working tool of the operative mason of the present day is really a Gavel, with the head longer than that which we use. It is called a 'Walling Hammer.'

It is highly desirable that the regulation Gavels should be used in every Lodge. They are supplied in sets of three, bearing respectively the emblem of the Master, and of the Senior and the Junior Warden. They can be procured at a small cost from those who supply Lodge furniture.

Incidentally, it may be mentioned that some provision should be made for the protection of the tops of the Pedestals from the result of the strokes of the Gavel, and the Wardens should understand that heavy gavelling is unnecessary, and painful to nerves.

In the First Degree there are other and indispensable requisites, among which may be mentioned in their proper sequence the Bfd. and C.T. required by the T. before the admission of the Candidate; the Pd. required by the Inner Guard on the entrance of the

Candidate; the K.S. in the W. for his use immediately after his entrance; the K.S. at the Master's Pedestal for use during the Ob.; the Cs. during the Ob.; the C.T. during the Address; the Lambskin for the investiture of the Candidate by the Senior Warden; the Almsdish, or Charity Box, which should be the real thing and suitable, not a part of the Ballot Box; the Charter or Warrant, for the inspection of the Candidate; a Book of Constitutions, and a copy of the By-laws of the Lodge, both of which latter should be presented to the Candidate, to remain in his own possession for his future serious perusal. This is an essential custom. The newly-admitted Brother naturally is desirous to gain all the knowledge that is possible to him of the nature and the Constitution of the Fraternity of which he has become a member. He can take them to his home, and at his ease he can read them with the attention and carefulness which have been recommended to him by the Worshipful Master; and the zeal, born of his recent Initiation, will lead him to follow literally, and with profit to himself, the way of 'Masonic knowledge,' in which, in the Charge, he is told that he is to make 'daily advancement.' The desirability of every member of the Craft possessing a copy of

A Lodge and its Furniture

the Book of Constitutions led to its being produced in the first instance at the low price of one shilling and sixpence, and the Constitutions require (Section 138) that every member of a Lodge shall be supplied with a printed copy of its By-laws, as his acceptance thereof is deemed to be a declaration of his submission to them.

In addition to the Working Tools of the Second Degree, two additional Ss. will be required; one by the Inner Guard on the entrance of the Candidate, and one by the Junior Deacon at the Master's Pedestal.

The P.R. is to try and adjust uprights while fixing them upon their proper bases.

In erecting stone great care must be taken that each stone must be placed upon its 'proper basis'; that is, upon its 'natural bed,' and to prevent error every ashlar stone must be marked with the 'proper basis' or 'bed-mark.'

In addition to the Working Tools of the Third Degree, an extra pair of Cs. will be needed by the Inner Guard on the entrance of the Candidate.

Among the requisites indispensable in the furnishing of a Lodge in the Third Degree are the heavy M., the Sheet, and the Emblems of Mortality.

All sorts of devices are resorted to, to represent *that* over which the Candidate has to pass, in advancing from West to East. In one Lodge, the Tyler was brought in, and was made to take the necessary position, and was covered up. In a very great number of Lodges at the present time, a canvas painted to represent a C. of the modern shape is used. This utterly fails to represent the thing signified, which is an O. G.; besides being at variance with the custom of the East.

A Tracing Board for the Third Degree giving a representation of an O. G., with *something*, dim and indistinct, lying in it, would be the beau-ideal of a Third Tracing Board; an accurate presentment of the event commemorated, as distinguished from the picture, which does duty for a Tracing Board in the vast majority of Lodges— a travesty of the scene which is the central object of the Third Degree.

Inexpensive substitutes may easily be found; the least costly, perhaps, is a piece of black cloth or linen (a parallelogram, of course, as a G. would be) about six feet by two; a white or light-grey border round it, in order to define its limits, is desirable, considering the state of the Lodge at the time.

A Lodge and its Furniture

The Working Tools of the various Degrees are nowadays, with rare exceptions, generally appropriate, and in order. In newly-formed Lodges it may be said that they are invariably so, having been generally purchased in sets complete; but in some old Lodges we find notable exceptions, such as a nondescript Level or Compasses, and far too often a common *lead pencil* instead of the port-crayon.

A criticism of the Third Tracing Board will be found in the Appendix.

*　　*　　*　　*

An organ or harmonium is happily now considered to be an indispensable item in the furniture of a Lodge.

*　　*　　*　　*

See Masonic Mourning, p. 268.

CHAPTER XVII

ETIQUETTE WITHIN THE LODGE

PROCESSIONAL ENTRY

IT is customary in some Lodges for the Worshipful Master, Past Masters, and Wardens to make a formal entry into the Lodge Room. If this be intended, the Brethren should assemble in the Lodge Room, and the Procession should be formed up in the Ante-Room, and when ready the Organist should perform a suitable accompaniment, and the Procession should enter in the following order:

The Tyler, with drawn sword; and I. G.
The Dir. of Ceremonies (with A.D.C.).
The Deacons.
The Wardens.
The Worshipful Master.
The Past Masters.

On arriving near the Master's Pedestal, the Brethren preceding him open out to right and left, and the Worshipful Master passes through to his Chair. The Senior Deacon remains with him, at, or near to, his right.

The procession passes on, leaving the Past

Etiquette within the Lodge

Masters when they arrive at their appointed place in the S.E. on the left of the Master's Chair.

On arriving near the Junior Warden's Chair, the preceding Brethren again open out as before, and the Junior Warden passes through to his seat.

Similarly, on arriving near the Senior Warden's Chair, where the Junior Deacon remains.

The Tyler, I. G., and D. C. pass on.

The I. G. takes his place on the left of the S. W.; the Tyler passes out of the Lodge, and closes the door, which the I. G. locks, and the D. C. or D. Cs. take their places.

In taking their places in their respective chairs, the Worshipful Master and the Wardens should invariably follow the course of the Sun—that is, the Master should enter on the North side. The Senior Warden should enter on the South side, and the Junior Warden should enter on the East side.

ARRANGEMENT OF SEATS

On the RIGHT of the W.M.

The Prov. G.M. and/or Dep. Prov. G.M.
Grand Officers next to Dep. Prov. G.M.
Prov. G. Officers (or London Rank).

Distinguished Visitors.
Senior Deacon.
Ordinary Visitors.

On the LEFT of the W.M.
Immediate Past Master.
Chaplain.
Past Masters in Rank and Seniority.
Brethren generally.

Every visiting Brother who is a Master of a Lodge or a Past Master should, immediately upon his entrance into the Lodge, be conducted by the Director of Ceremonies (or, in his absence, should be invited by the Worshipful Master) to the daïs or to a seat on the right of the Worshipful Master. (The daïs is out of date nowadays in most London Lodges.) If all the seats there are occupied, it will be in accordance with etiquette—and, indeed, with ordinary politeness—that a member of the Lodge shall give place in favour of the visiting Brother. (See p. 319.)

Opening Ode

When the formal entry has been completed, as above, or (in cases where there is no formal entry) when the Brethren are assembled, the opening Ode may be sung.

Etiquette within the Lodge

This is a well-known Ode, commencing, 'Hail Eternal!' (see p. 238).

In the third verse there is a reference to the Badge and mystic Sign. Certain ingenious Brethren make certain motions when these words are sung, but it is quite improper to do so—as, for one reason, the Lodge is not yet open; and no masonic Sign should ever be given except in open Lodge.

The opening Ode should always be sung *before* the Lodge is opened, and *not after* (see p. 294).

Warrant

'No Lodge can meet without a Warrant'; and the Worshipful Master is responsible for its safe custody and for its production at every meeting of the Lodge.

Care should therefore be taken to see that the Warrant is in evidence before proceedings are commenced.

Opening, First Degree

The Lodge is then opened in the First Degree.

When the W. M. addresses the J. W., the J. W. should not make any Sn. When directed to do so by the J. W., the I. G. 'sees' that the L. is P. T. by giving the E. A. Ks. He does not open the door to do so.

These Ks. being answered by the T., and reported by the I. G. to the J. W., the J. W. gives ━▐ and reports to the W. M. (Ks. only; no Sn.).

In doing this, the J. W. should not turn his body towards the W. M., only his head.

When the W. M. addresses the S. W., the S. W. should not make any Sn.

When the Brethren are called to order, they should all simultaneously take Sp., and then give Sn. of E. A., looking (not turning) to the E., so that they may presently keep time accurately with the W. M.

All Sps. and Sns. should be silently done.

Care should be taken that the Sn. should be perfect and uniform and square. There is much slovenliness with regard to this.

The Sn. should commence where it rests. There should not be a preliminary motion, or point.

One point connected with the opening (and closing) of the Lodge arises in this place—namely, Is it etiquette for one or more or the whole of the Brethren present to pronounce the words 'So mote it be' at the conclusion of the prayer by the Worshipful Master? Opinions and practice differ upon the subject. It is held in Emulation Working Lodges that the Immediate Past Master *alone* should use the words; in others, that the right belongs to all the Past Masters, and to none below that rank. The practice in many Lodges is for all the Brethren to join in the repetition of the words; and in many Lodges the words are sung to the accompaniment of the organ.

There is no authoritative pronouncement upon the subject, therefore we must expect to find differences in practice in different Lodges.

The Sn. should be maintained until the word 'open' is pronounced by the W. M., when the Sn. should be dis. with perfect uniformity, hand remaining open.

W. M. ◀ S. W. ◀; and Col.

J. W. ◀ and Col.

I. G. ks., and T. replies.

J. D. adjusts T. B.—I. P. M. opens V. S. I. (2 Chron. vi), and adjusts S. and C.

All sit when W. M. sits—not before.

MINUTES

By direction of the W. M. (no ◀), the Secretary reads all unconfirmed Minutes of all preceding Meetings; Regular and Emergency. The Minutes should always be read in the First Degree, as every Initiate is entitled to hear them and vote on them.

The W. M. then puts the Minutes—

separately, if of more than one Meeting.
(No ━▐.)

The Confirmation of the Minutes is usually
a perfunctory proceeding, and in ordinary
circumstances can only relate to the accuracy of the record or the propriety of recording the item.

The single exception is in relation to the
election of Master, who is not deemed to
be elected until the Minutes, so far at least
as relates to his election, have been confirmed (Const. 105). (See note on p. 318.)

Votes at one meeting which, by their
nature or according to the By-laws, require confirmation at a subsequent meeting
—*e.g.*, votes relating to grants of money—
cannot be properly dealt with on the motion
for confirming the Minutes.

They should be the subject of a separate
motion, on due notice printed on the summons, "that . . . . be confirmed."

In other words, if in the interval between
one meeting and another other counsels
prevail and that which was done at the
previous meeting does not meet with the
approval of those assembled at the next
meeting, then, if the vote in question is one
which requires confirmation, the alteration
must be effected by voting against the
motion to confirm the previous resolution

as mentioned in the preceding paragraph. But if the matter complained of is already complete (*i.e.*, does not require a confirmatory vote), then in that case any alteration can only be effected by a substantive motion, on due notice given, to rescind the previous resolution.

In June, 1905, Grand Lodge decided that due notice must be given of any intended motion for non-confirmation of Minutes, so that it may appear on the printed Agenda.

In September, 1911, Grand Lodge upheld the ruling of a District Grand Master that a proposition of non-confirmation could not be made for the purpose of a revision of opinion, nor for the purpose of allowing second thoughts to prevail; the only question involved being accuracy of record.

Further, a motion to rescind a previous resolution would, if carried, have more force than an inoperative refusal to confirm the Minutes of the previous meeting.

On the other hand, the confirmation of the Minutes does not legalize that which was illegal *ab initio*.

As to signing Minutes, see p. 339.

ADMISSIONS AFTER OPENING

The correct manner of saluting the Worshipful Master by Brethren who enter or leave the Lodge after it has been opened follows well-defined rules according to the circumstances of the moment—*i.e.*, whether the Lodge is in the First, the Second, or the Third Degree.

There is no law upon the subject, but the custom is sufficiently established to enable us to dogmatize upon it.

On Entering

1. If the Lodge is in the First Degree, the entering Brother should take Sp. and give Sn. of E. A.

2. If the Lodge is in the Second Degree, the entrant should take Sp. and give Sn. of E. A.; then take Sp. and give the three Sns. of F. C. in consecutive order.

3. If the Lodge is in the Third Degree, the entrant should take Sp. and give Sn. of E. A.; then take Sp. and give the first two Sns. of F. C.; and (instead of giving third Sn. of F. C.) he should take Sp. and convert F. C. position into Sn. of H.; then give S. of S., and P. S. of third.

On Leaving

4. In whatever degree the Lodge is open, the exeant should take Sp. and give the P. S. of that degree.

Etiquette within the Lodge

On Re-entering

5. Exactly the same as 4. (See p. 340.)

The only exception to these rules is in relation to the Candidate, who salutes according to the special instructions given to him at the time by the Deacon.

The body should be erect while Sns. are given. Even in the S. of S. it is only the head which is bent. There should be no ceremonial bowing to the W. M. On the contrary, there should rather be a military stiffening.

The Worshipful Master, upon the admission of a visitor from another Lodge, may say: 'I greet you well, Brother A.B.' This form of greeting would appear to be of ancient date; it has a good old Masonic flavour about it; it is courteous to a visitor as distinguished from a Member of the Lodge. It is a form of welcome quite distinct from anything one hears in the outer world. This, or some other equally courteous greeting to visitors, is worthy of observance in Lodges generally.

When a Member of the Lodge enters or leaves the Lodge, and salutes according to the then Degree, it is a simple act of courtesy for the Worshipful Master to bow an acknowledgment. It is unnecessary for the Master to utter any words of welcome to a member of the Lodge; that form of greeting being reserved for visitors only.

It is, perhaps, unnecessary to mention that in the case of a Brother of Grand Rank, or Provincial or District Grand Rank or London Rank, visiting a Lodge other than his own, the Brethren should all rise, and remain standing until their visitor has taken his seat.

The correct salutes to Grand Officers within the Lodge are as follow:

M.W.G.M. and M. W. Pro. G.M. 11
R.W.D.G.M. 9
R.W. Brethren 7
V.W. Brethren 5
Other Grand Officers 3

Provincial Grand Officers:
R. W. Prov. G.M. 7
W. Dep. Prov. G.M. (in their own Province) 5
W.Asst. Prov. G.M. (in their own Province) 5
Other Prov. Grand Officers (in their own Province) 3
Prov. Grand Officers (on investment) 3
G. or R.Sns. (given only in 3rd Deg.)

Etiquette within the Lodge

On the occasion of a report after the Lodge is opened, the Inner Guard announces it to the Junior Warden, who by a single knock directs the I.G. to ascertain who wants admission. The I.G. then announces the claimant for admission to the Worshipful Master, who directs the I.G. to admit him.

This authority of the J.W. relates to ordinary *reports* only. When a Candidate is announced in either Degree, the Junior Warden, after receiving notice thereof from the Inner Guard, conveys the announcement to the Worshipful Master in the proper form, who replies as prescribed in the Ritual.

The difference of procedure pointed out in the two preceding paragraphs will show the indispensable necessity of the Tyler and of the Inner Guard being thoroughly conversant with the proper knocks in each Degree, because any mistake or confusion between the two must inevitably lead to confusion in the Lodge (see pp. 305-307).

In some Country Lodges there is a distinction made between a 'Report' and an 'Alarm.' There is considerable force in the argument which supports this course of procedure, but the fact remains that the only recognized ks. are those detailed on pp. 306-307.

Freemasonry and its Etiquette

When two or more Brethren are announced it is not necessary to give the names of all; on the other hand, it is not right to omit the mention of any name, as one too often hears, in this way: 'Several Brethren seek admission.' The correct form is for the Tyler to say to the Inner Guard: 'Brother A. B. and other Brethren'; and the Inner Guard will say: 'Worshipful Master, Brother A. B. and other Brethren.' If a visitor or visitors happen to be of the group, he or they should be allowed to go first, and, as a matter of course, his name or their names would be announced. In the case of a visitor it is customary for the Tyler and Inner Guard to add: 'Vouched for by Brother . . . .' (the member inviting him). (See p. 95.)

The Worshipful Master's reply to the announcement is: 'Admit him' or 'them,' as the case may be.

The use of additional words subserves no useful end or purpose; redundant forms of expression have crept into the working of Lodges, no one knows whence, or how, or why. Masters of Lodges and Directors of Ceremonies should always be especially careful to nip in the bud the first introduction of all superfluous and meaningless phrases and forms of expression, even as, with the Gavel, the Entered Apprentice is taught 'to knock off all superfluous knobs and excrescences.'

In connection with the Gavel we may mention that it is desirable that the Wardens should be always ready to answer the ▬◖ of the Worshipful Master. When laid again upon the pedestal the Gavel should be replaced silently, so that no other sound is heard than the actual ks.

Much unnecessary energy is too often displayed in the use of the Gavel. One sometimes hears a succession of sounding blows that would not discredit Thor himself, emitting sounds that may be heard far beyond the Lodge room. This is objectionable, for more than one obvious reason. A moderately sharp *tap*, and not a heavy blow, is all that is required upon any occasion.

A very useful precaution for securing the top of the pedestal from injury is to provide (for each pedestal) a flat piece of wood— presumably oak, like the pedestal—say 5 or 6 inches square and $\frac{3}{4}$ inch thick, the underside covered with cloth. This will receive the indentations inevitably consequent upon the repeated taps, or, worse, the blows of the Gavel.

JOINING MEMBERS

If there is a proposal duly made on the summons to admit a joining member, it is well to take the ballot as soon as possible after the confirmation of the Minutes. The proposer and seconder should be called on to state their case in full, vouching for the proposed member and explaining the reasons which lead them to suppose he will be an acquisition to the Lodge. It is assumed that the proposal will have been already approved by the Standing Committee (see pp. 83 and 439).

Assuming the result of the ballot to be favourable, and the Brother in attendance, he should be escorted to the W. M. by the Director of Ceremonies and formally introduced. The W. M. should make a suitable speech to the joining member, bidding him welcome in his own name and on behalf of the Lodge.

At the subsequent post-prandial proceedings a special toast should be given in his honour (see p. 351).

A Past Master of an English Lodge joining another English Lodge becomes a Past Master *in* the Lodge he joins, and takes rank and precedence immediately after the Immediate Past Master of the year in which he joins, and before the Worshipful Master of the year in which he joins.

As a Past Master he immediately becomes eligible for office as Worshipful Master; but it is to be assumed that in ordinary course he would, *cæteris paribus*, rank for office immediately after the last initiate or joining member, according to date.

CANDIDATE

If there is a Candidate duly proposed on the Summons, a Ballot should be taken.

A proposal must be made and seconded on the printed summons, and this proposal should have been already the subject of investigation by the Standing Committee (see p. 83). But that is not all. When that item of the Agenda is reached, the proposer and seconder should make the proposal in open Lodge and *viva voce*, so that the tongue of good report may be heard in favour of the candidate.

The Ballot is a most important proceeding, and should be effected in an impressive manner. When the Worshipful Master directs it to be taken, the Junior Deacon distributes the balls, commencing with the Immediate Past Master, and finishing at the Worshipful Master; and the Senior

Deacon collects them in the Ballot Box in the same order.

Several candidates may be balloted for at the same time; any adverse vote involving a separate ballot for each.

The Ballot is intended to be absolutely secret, so as to give absolute freedom from fear of consequences. A black ball is quite as legal as a white one, and any brother who votes according to his conscience has a right to be protected.

Abstention from voting is permissible, and does not count against the candidate.

The result of the Ballot should be forthwith notified by the Inner Guard to the Tyler, in order that the Candidate may be prepared without delay.

INITIATION

The Ceremony of Initiation may then be taken (see p. 200).

PRAYERS

During the prayers in the various ceremonies, when the attitude of reverence is adopted, the th. is not visible. At the close the h. is 'dropped,' not 'drawn.'

*　　*　　*　　*

Etiquette within the Lodge

OBN.

It should be remembered the Sn. during the E. A. Obn. should be the P. S. of an E. A.

QUESTIONS BEFORE PASSING

If the Ceremony of Passing is to be done, the necessary Questions should be put, and the Candidate entrusted (see p. 210).

OPENING, SECOND DEGREE

All E. As. having been directed to retire, the Lodge may be opened in the Second Degree.

The preliminary points are to be observed as before.

When the Brethren, by direction of the J. W., prove themselves Cn., they should look to the East, and should take their time from the I. P. M. The object is to get the Brethren to make every movement in silence and in unison. This can be done only by taking the time from one man.

Perhaps the best example of discipline in this respect is to be found in military Lodges. The perfection of accuracy and precision of movement and of time are, of course, to be expected from these drilled and trained men;

these qualities, however, are not difficult in practice in private Lodges: the habit is easily acquired, but, unfortunately, so many of the Brethren do not strive after combined and simultaneous action. Every Brother should visit a military Lodge if one such happen to be held 'within the length of his cable-tow,' and he will see how charming and instructive such a visit will be; 'profit and pleasure will be the result,' to a certainty.

They should, thus, in silence and in unison dis. E. A., take Sp., place r. h. before placing l. h. When, however, the W. M. declares 'the Lodge duly open on the S.,' the order is reversed: the l. h. is d. at the word 'open,' and then at the word 'S.' the third portion of the threefold Sn. is given with the r. h. in two distinct motions.

W. M. ━◀ S. W. ━◀ J. W. ━◀.
I. G. ks., and T. replies.

N.B.—If a Candidate is outside, the gavels give gentle ks., and the I.G. does not communicate the ks. to T. He stands in his place and gives ks. on his cuff. This is so done whether in 'opening' or 'resuming.'

J. D. adjusts T. B.
I. P. M. adjusts S. and C.
All sit when W. M. sits—not before.

Etiquette within the Lodge

PASSING

The Ceremony of Passing may now be taken (see p. 212).

OBN.

It should be remembered that the Sn. during the F. C. Obn. is the P. S. of a F. C.

QUESTIONS BEFORE RAISING

If the Ceremony of Raising is to be done, the necessary Questions should be put and the Candidate entrusted (see p. 221).

OPENING, THIRD DEGREE

All F. Cs. having been directed to retire, the Lodge may be opened in the Third Degree.

The preliminary points are to be observed as before.

When the Brethren, by direction of the J. W., prove themselves M. Ms. by Sns., they should, in silence, and in unison, take Sp.; convert F. C. into S. of H.; S. of S.; P. S. from extreme left, and 'recover.' The hand should lie quite flat on the same plane as the floor; not with drooping fingers.

There is no evolution in the whole range of ceremonial observance in the Lodge, in which so many and so wide divergences from the correct forms are to be seen, as in the making of these three Ss., more especially in the first. This Sn. cannot, of course, be described; we can only suggest that in all the movements the body should be quite erect, and the motions should be made with freedom of action, and should be carefully developed, but at the same time with no exaggeration of gesture. The proper movements and positions, once acquired, are perfectly easy, and are never forgotten.

The last answer in the opening in the Third Degree, made by the Senior Warden—'That being a point from which a Master Mason cannot err'—is a very curious one: it is explained at length in the sixth section of the first Lecture, and is referred to in Esotery.

When the W. M. reaches the word 'open,' all draw sharply; when C. is pronounced, all drop in unison, without 'recovery.'

This is the only occasion on which there is no 'recovery.'

W. M. ━╃ S. W. ━╃ J. W. ━╃.
. I. G. ks., and T. replies.

N.B.—If a Candidate is outside, the gavels give gentle ks., and the I.G. does not communicate the ks. to T. He stands in his place and gives ks. on his cuff. This is so done whether in 'opening' or 'resuming.'

Etiquette within the Lodge

J. D. adjusts T. B.

I. P. M. adjusts S. and C.

G. or R. S. all simultaneously.

All sit when W. M. sits—not before.

*   *   *   *

(In some Country Lodges the Worshipful Master alone first gives the G. or R. S., next the Worshipful Master and Senior Warden, and thirdly the Worshipful Master, the Wardens, and the whole of the Brethren. The words accompany the s. . . . in each case—that is, they are spoken first by the Worshipful Master alone, then by the Worshipful Master and the Senior Warden together, and thirdly by all together.)

This is mentioned as the survival of a curious custom; not as an example to be followed.

*   *   *   *

RAISING

The Ceremony of Raising may now be taken (see p. 330).

The Sheet must be fully spread, and never folded either at the commencement or subsequently.

The Master's Light must never be extinguished while the Lodge is open; neither may it by any means be shaded or obscured;

nor may any Lantern or other device, with or without a Star, be permitted.

An official communication on this important point will be found in the Appendix (pp. 420-422).

In this connection reference may be made to an ingenious 'deviation' which has crept into some Lodges in which the electric switch plays a disconcerting part at the Master's solemn allusion to the Morning Star.

The slightest reflection will show the modernity of this undignified innovation.

The proper point at which to restore Ls. and remove the sheet is after the retirement of the Candidate 'to restore,' etc.

OBN.

It should be remembered that the Sn. during the M. M. Obn. is the P.S. of a M. M.

*   *   *   *

ORDER OF BUSINESS

As a general rule, it will be found convenient to commence by opening the Lodge in all the Degrees in which there is work to be done, and the Worshipful Master to 'resume' up and down as occasion requires. This enables the programme to be varied and carried out in any order without confusion. (See p. 337.)

Etiquette within the Lodge

A good rule is observed in many—perhaps the majority of—Lodges, in the order in which the ceremonies are performed. If Initiations, Passings, and Raisings have to be performed at any one meeting, the Raisings are taken first, the Passings next, and the Initiations last. Good reasons can be assigned for this regulation: *inter alia*, the number of Brethren present is, as a rule, greater towards the end of the meeting than at the beginning, and consequently the Lodge is at its best in point of appearance; therefore it is calculated to make a better impression upon the mind of the Candidates.

*   *   *   *

When from any cause either of the Principal Officers leaves his chair for any appreciable period of time, another Brother should take his place. In such cases a good custom prevails in probably the majority of Lodges—namely, the Officer who is leaving his chair takes the right hand of the Brother who is to take his place, and as it were inducts him into the chair which he himself has vacated. If and when the proper Officer returns, his *locum tenens* offers his right hand, and assists the officer back into his chair in the same manner. This is true politeness, and therefore true etiquette. It has in it a grace and dignity worthy of our Ancient and Illustrious Order.

The reason why the Principal Officers should always enter and leave their several chairs in the manner thus described is the same as that which prescribes that the Candidates in each Degree should be led 'up the North, past the Worshipful Master in the East, down the South, and be conducted to the Senior Warden in the West'—namely, that we follow 'the due course of the Sun, which rises in the East, gains its meridian lustre in the South, and sets in the West.' (*Vide* Lecture in the First Degree.)

* * * *

'SQUARING' THE LODGE

This should only be done ceremonially and when prescribed in the Ritual.

In the ordinary peregrinations of the members or officers in the execution of their non-ceremonial duties the attempt to 'square' the Lodge is distinctly a superfluous knob or excrescence which should be knocked off by the gavel.

* * * *

CALLING OFF AND ON

If the programme of business be a long one, it is desirable to make a break at about 'half time.' A definite short period for refreshment is better than the constant disturbance and interruption caused by Brethren retiring and returning in twos and threes.

* * * *

At the conclusion of all ceremonial work the Lodge should be resumed in the Third Degree (if not then working in that degree), and then closed in the Third Degree.

CLOSING THIRD DEGREE

In the closings the L. is proved close tyled.

The com. of the S. Ss. demands considerable care.

The Ws. leave their places by the left side, and stand to order, r.f. in h. of l.

The J. W. takes Sp., gives P. G. leading from 2 to 3, elevates hs., and under them whs. P. W.; recovers, takes Sp., gives S. of H.; S. of S.; P. S.; 5 Ps. of F.; and whs. W. of M. M.; recovers, salutes, and returns to his place the right side.

The S. W. takes up position facing W. M., and asks the W. M. to receive the S. Ss.

The W. M. descends from Ped. by the S. E. side, and take up position immediately in front of it, r.f. in h. of l.

The S. W. then repeats what J. W. has

already done; with the exception that the Ws. are audible.

They both return to places. They should, on resuming their several positions, re-enter their respective places on the side opposite to that by which they left them.

The W. M. confirms S. Ss., and eventually directs the S. W. to close the L.

The W. M. ▬▰ with L. H., still standing to order with P. S. of M. M.

The S. W. closes the L.; all dis. Sn. and recover in unison; gives ▬▰.

The J. W. repeats ▬▰.

The I. G. ks.; T. replies.

The J. D. attends to T. B. The I. P. M. attends to S. and Cs.

All sit if, and when, W. M. sits, not before.

CLOSING SECOND DEGREE

Usually without pause, the L. is proved close tyled.

The discovery of the S. S. in the C. of the Bdg. is announced, and after prayer by the W. M. the S. W. is directed to close the L.; the W. M. ▬▰ with L. H. still standing to order as a F. C.

The S. W. closes L. and gives ▬▰.

The J. W. gives ▬▰.

The I. G. gives ks.; T. replies.

All sit when W. M. sits, not before.

Etiquette within the Lodge

MOTIONS PURSUANT TO NOTICE

The Lodge being now in the First Degree, if there is any motion of which notice has been given, it may now be discussed.

The discussion must follow strictly the ordered lines of regulated debate (p. 330).

The Worshipful Master is the supreme ruler, and when he has decided points of order or other matters of graver importance, he must on no account permit any appeal to the Lodge from his decision.

The only possible appeal from the decision of the Master is to Provincial Grand Lodge or to Grand Lodge, as the case may be.

FIRST RISING

After the conclusion of all ceremonial work and masonic business (if any), and while the Lodge is still open in the First Degree, the Worshipful Master gives one ▬ᗐ, which is followed by the Wardens; he then rises and says: 'Brethren! I rise for the first time to ask if any Brother has aught to propose for the good of Freemasonry in general, or of this (naming it) Lodge in particular.'

On this occasion or 'first rising' initiates and joining members are proposed, and Notices of Motion (other than financial) are given.

It is generally understood that notice of any motion of *more than minor importance* should be given at a regular meeting of the Lodge, and that the motion itself should be set forth in the Summons convoking the meeting at which it is to be brought forward. It is obvious that Brethren who were not present when the notice was given have a clear right to be duly notified by circular of the terms and scope of the motion, and of the meeting at which it is to be discussed.

*   *   *   *

When speaking to the Worshipful Master on occasions other than those prescribed in the Ceremonies, the correct method on commencing to speak is to salute and dis. the Sn. of the degree in which the Lodge is then working; and on finishing to do similarly. It looks awkward, besides being inconvenient, to keep the Sn. up during a speech.

Initial letters, representing the names of the Officers, as, for example, W. M., S. W., J. W., and so on to I. G., are only used in order to save space in printing. No abbreviations of any kind should be used in the Lodge at any time, upon any occasion. The Worshipful Master should never be addressed as 'W. M.,' either during the Ceremonies or at any other period during the meeting. One sometimes hears the Master addressed as 'Worshipful.' This is altogether inexcusable, being totally devoid of the respect due to the high position which the Master holds.

Past Masters may sometimes be heard to address the Worshipful Master as 'Worshipful Sir,' thus implying (we presume) the perfect equality of themselves with the Master. This is a mistaken idea altogether. The Worshipful Master, during the period of his tenure of that Office, is paramount over all, over every member of the Lodge, be he Past Master or Entered Apprentice; there is no exception to this rule.

Unfortunately, habits of this kind are contagious, and we hear occasionally a Junior Warden (not being a Past Master) reply, 'I am, Worshipful Sir'; and others below the rank even of Junior Warden are apt to follow the bad example. All such deviations from established rule and order, and from the etiquette of the Lodge, should be strictly guarded against and repressed, whoever may be the offender in this respect, and whatever may be his status in the Lodge.

In the case of one Past Master addressing another, 'Worshipful Brother' would be a better term. 'Sir' belongs to the outer world; it has no flavour of Freemasonry about it; it is better to leave it behind when we enter the Lodge. In the not improbable case of one Past Master acting as Master *pro tempore*, and another Past Master acting as an officer, in any capacity, if from any cause the officer should have to address the Acting Master, he should address him as 'Worshipful Master.' Although not the reigning W. M., he is, for the time being, the Master of the Lodge, and thereby invested with plenary powers, and fully entitled to the honours due to the actual Worshipful Master.

* * * *

SECOND RISING

After an interval of time the ━▌ are given as before, and the question is repeated, substituting the words 'for the second time.' On the 'second rising' financial matters are disposed of, and notice of motion relating to finance are given.

* * * *

THIRD RISING

Again, after an interval, the ━▌ and the question are repeated 'for the third time.'

It is specially to be noted that the Master asks these questions only when the Lodge is opened in the First Degree, and for a very sufficient reason. In the discussion of any motion, or of any subject that may come up during the meeting of the Lodge, an Entered Apprentice, who is a subscribing member, has as clear a right to vote upon the matter under discussion as any other member of the Lodge. For this reason the questions mentioned in the preceding paragraph are generally reserved until after the ceremonial business of the Lodge has been disposed of.

Another advantage is gained by delaying discussions, and the proposition of Candidates, or of joining members, until the latter portion of the sitting—namely, that Brethren, whose 'public or private avocations' have precluded the possibility of an early attendance at the Lodge, will probably have arrived, and they may then be enabled to make any proposition, or to take a part in any deliberation or discussion having for its object 'the good of Freemasonry in general, or of their own Lodge in particular.'

On the 'third rising,' 'hearty good wishes' are given to the W. M.

Some correspondence appeared in 1890 in the *Freemason* upon the question of the right of visitors to tender to the Lodge in which they are guests 'hearty good wishes' from the Lodges of which they are severally members. Most of the letters were of an inquiring character; the respective writers wanted to know if they had or had not been rightly informed as to Grand Lodge having expressed an opinion 'unfavourable to the continuance of the custom.' Grand Lodge has expressed no opinion favourable or otherwise upon the subject.

The opinion of the late Grand Registrar of the Order was taken upon the question, and he gave it to the effect 'that no Brother has the right to convey the good wishes, hearty or otherwise, of his own Lodge to any other Lodge without the permission of his own Worshipful Master.' Nevertheless, it is an ancient custom, kindly, genial, fraternal, harmless in itself if used in moderation, and genuinely Masonic; it existed before we were born, it will endure long after we are buried.

In the meantime we may safely go on in the old way, giving and receiving 'hearty good wishes,' as the custom has been 'from a time of which the memory of man runneth not to the contrary.'

Closing the Lodge

The Lodge is proved close tyled. The S. W. is interrogated as to his constant place in the Lodge, and after solemn prayer by the W. M., the S. W. is directed to close the L.; the W. M. ◀▬▌ with L. H. still standing to order as E. A.

The S. W. closes the L. and gives ▬▬▌.

The J. W. announces the next meeting, and gives ▬▬▌. J. D. adjusts T. B.

The I. G. gives ks., and the T. replies.

The Lodge must be 'closed.' There is no power to 'adjourn' it.

The I. P. M. calls on the Brethren to lock up the Ss. in a safe repository, uniting in the act F. F. F.

Sometimes the Brethren join in a pious ejaculation: 'May God preserve the Craft,' but it is unorthodox and quite redundant, seeing that the W. M. in the final prayer has already besought the G. A. O. T. U. to preserve the Order by cementing and adorning it with every moral and social virtue.

The Lodge being closed, the customary closing Masonic Ode (see p. 251) may be sung.

PROCESSION

At the conclusion of the Ode the Director of Ceremonies calls on the Brethren to remain standing while the W. M., Wardens, Grand Officers, Members of London Rank, and distinguished Visitors leave the Lodge.

The procession is formed in the following

manner; the Organist, meanwhile, furnishing suitable instrumental accompaniment:

The D. C. signals the J. D. to proceed. The J. D. 'squares' the L. and picks up the S. D. They proceed in company to the left of the J. W.'s Pedestal. He descends and follows them to the left of the S. W.'s Pedestal. The S. W. descends, and the quartet advance to the left of the W. M.'s Pedestal. The W. M. descends and follows the Wardens. The P. Ms. fall in behind, and the Grand Officers, Members of London Rank, and Visitors of high degree join in their order of precedence (juniors first *inter se*), and so all march out; ordinary Visitors and the Brethren of the Lodge following at the end.

CHAPTER XVIII

DRESS, JEWELS, AND PUNCTUALITY

IN discussing 'Freemasonry and its Etiquette,' the question of dress naturally suggests itself for consideration. We may briefly state the conclusions at which the consensus of opinion and of practice, in the great majority of cases, would appear to have arrived.

In Lodges where the members dine together after the business of the Lodge is concluded, evening dress is the rule. This is, indeed, so general that it may almost be said to be invariable and universal.

In other Lodges, where a supper or some moderate refreshment is provided, evening dress is not universal. Still, in some even of these the Brethren make it a rule to wear full evening dress both at their own meetings and when visiting other Lodges. The difficulty in the way of this graceful custom is that the interval between the cessation of the professional or business avocations of many of the members and the hour for the meeting of the Lodge will not allow time sufficient for an entire change of dress.

Freemasonry and its Etiquette

In cities and large towns, where in the Lodges the Initiations are more or less frequent, there are often two, and occasionally three, Ceremonies to be performed on the same evening, and necessarily the hour for meeting must be comparatively early. This will probably account for the fact that some members have acquired the doubtful habit of attending the Lodge in the habiliments of ordinary every-day life. In this respect each Lodge is, as a rule, governed by its own custom and usage; but the members should strive, where it is necessary, rather to attain to a higher standard of propriety in the matter of dress than to degenerate to a lower level.

In certain Lodges the summons states 'Evening Dress.' This, at least, may be expected of every member, whatever be his circumstances in life, and every effort should be made by those in authority in the Lodge to promote uniformity in this respect, as far as may be done without wounding the susceptibilities of any individual member who from any cause may deviate from the general rule.

If morning dress be allowed, it should be black, or very dark in colour; black boots, not brown; and for all outside occasions of ceremony silk hats are *de rigueur*.

Dress, Jewels, and Punctuality

In cases of Lodges of Emergency, Lodges of Instruction, and, indeed, on all Masonic occasions where morning dress is worn, the Apron should be worn outside the coat.

While we are discussing that branch of our subject which relates to 'dress,' a few words may be said about the Jewels which may or may not be worn in the Lodge. Few of our members are ignorant of the rule which strictly forbids the wearing in a Craft Lodge of a Jewel belonging to any Degree which is not recognized by, and is not under the authority of, the Grand Lodge. To this rule there is positively no exception. It is therefore a breach not only of etiquette but of the constitutions, to enter the Lodge wearing the Jewel of the Mark, or some other by-degree, such as that of the Knights-Templar.

It is true that H.R.H. the Grand Master is a member of these Degrees, and has Past Rank in both; and such membership is constitutionally regular (see Act of Union); but although he is at the head of one of them, Grand Lodge does not recognize them, nor exercise jurisdiction over them in any way; therefore the Jewels of those Degrees are not allowed to be worn in a Craft Lodge.

The case of Royal Arch Jewels is entirely

different from these. The degree of the Master Mason includes the Supreme Order of the Holy Royal Arch (Art. 1, Book of Constitutions). H.R.H. the Duke of Connaught is First Grand Principal of the Order, and the Grand Secretary in the Craft is always Grand Scribe E. in the Grand Chapter of Royal Arch Masons, consequently all the Jewels of the Royal Arch Order may be worn in a Craft Lodge.

The Jewels issued to Stewards of the Institutions are by courtesy worn for twelve months—*i.e.*, until the next festival.

The Jewels issued at the Centenary Festivals of the Girls' and Boys' Institutions have been declared Life Jewels, and may be worn permanently.

The Jewels which may with perfect propriety be worn in a Craft Lodge (and in a Royal Arch Chapter also) are those of the Master or Past Master; Permanent Charity Jewels and Clasps; Present Stewards of either or all of the Institutions; Founders'; Centenary; Quatuor Coronati; and the Jewel commemorating the Jubilee of Her late Majesty, the late Patroness of our Order; also the Jewels of the Royal Arch Order, whether of ordinary Royal Arch Masons, or of Present or Past First Principals, or Present or Past Grand, or Provincial, or District

Grand Principals, and some others which need not be specified, with this special reservation, that they must belong to either the Craft or the Royal Arch Order, and no other. Miniature Jewels, each being a facsimile in design of the full-size Jewels, are now very frequently worn by Brethren who have become entitled to wear a considerable number of these honourable badges of distinction.

Many of these Jewels have been presented to the wearers, and are the memorials of the gratitude of their several Lodges for eminent and often long-continued services, and which the recipients may well feel pleasure and pride in wearing. They are something more than mere personal adornments; they subserve an excellent purpose by inciting younger Brethren to increased zeal and energy in the work of the Lodge. 'The hope of reward sweetens labour'; and when work is sweetened by hope and lightened by zeal, it becomes a labour of love; and 'profit' to the Lodge and 'pleasure' to the worker 'will be the result.'

Application by a Lodge for permission for its members to wear a Centenary Jewel must be by petition to the Grand Master, in which petition the necessary particulars as to the origin of the Lodge are to be given, as well as proof of its uninterrupted existence for one hundred years.

When permission has been granted to a Lodge for its members to wear a Centenary Jewel, the privilege of wearing the Jewel is restricted to actual *bona fide* subscribing members, being Master Masons; and for so long only as they pay the stipulated subscription to the Lodge and are returned to the Grand Lodge.

The design for a conventional Centenary Jewel has now been approved by the Grand Master, but about forty ancient Lodges have their own designs, which are, of course, very interesting by reason of their antiquity.

A Brother having served the office of Steward to any two of the Institutions has the privilege of wearing the Charity Jewel, provided he, at each time of so serving, personally subscribed ten guineas at the least.

A Brother entitled to wear the Charity Jewel, and who may have served the office of Steward to any of the Institutions a second time, may wear a clasp attached to the ribbon, and an additional clasp for each occasion of having served the office of Steward if he personally subscribed a like amount.

A Vice-President may wear a rosette attached to the ribbon immediately above the Jewel.

Dress, Jewels, and Punctuality

A vice-Patron may wear the Jewel suspended from a ribbon around his neck.

With regard to the wearing of Grand or London Rank or Provincial Grand clothing, much difference of opinion and of practice exists. Many—probably the majority of—Brethren have undress aprons and collars, which they always wear at the ordinary meetings of their own Lodge. Some even of these wear full dress if visiting a Lodge other than their own, even if it be a regular meeting of the Lodge which they are visiting. Upon Festivals or other occasions out of the ordinary way they would, as a matter of course, wear full-dress clothing, with all proper insignia appertaining thereto, either in their own or in any other Lodge. Instances are not wanting of Brethren considering it to be their duty to wear the full-dress clothing upon every occasion during the year of their tenure of Grand or Provincial Grand Office. No reason can be urged against their doing so. There is no hard-and-fast rule upon the subject. Customs vary in different districts, and individual taste seems to be the chief guide in this matter.

At all the regular meetings of Grand Lodge, and of Provincial, and of District Grand Lodges, full-dress clothing is invariably worn. On all occasions when full-dress clothing is worn, the traditional white tie and gloves should be worn—a comparatively recent fashion of wearing black ties for full dress, to the contrary, notwithstanding. The black tie is not 'in accordance with the ancient usage and established custom of the Order' in this respect.

At meetings of Provincial or of District Lodges, upon special occasions other than the regular meetings, Provincial or District Grand Masters often allow undress clothing to be worn.

In Short, we should show—in so far as outward observance can show—our estimation of and our respect for Freemasonry by always being fitly attired in the Lodge. The advice of Polonius to his son Laertes is of very wide application; it suits the case in question:

> 'Costly thy habit as thy purse can buy,
> But not expressed in fancy; rich, not gaudy;
> For the apparel oft proclaims the man.'

As regards Masonic Mourning dress, see p. 268.

As regards Masonic Mourning dress, see p. 268.

*   *   *   *

Very little needs to be said upon the subject of punctuality in attendance on the part of both Officers and Brethren, but it can

Dress, Jewels, and Punctuality

hardly be passed over without notice In these days of railway locomotion and of high pressure generally in business matters, sharp time is as a rule obliged to be observed by all sorts and conditions of men in the affairs of the outer world. The same rule should, by every possible means, be applied to the meetings of the Lodge. The Master should open the Lodge upon every occasion punctually at the hour stated in the summons. He should be supported in this by his Officers. He and they should always be clothed and in their seats *before the time*, and as the hour strikes the Master's gavel should sound. Certainly the general attendance would be far more punctual and not less numerous.

The time stated upon the summons should be understood to mean that time, and not half an hour or an hour later. In the address to the Wardens after their investiture and their induction into their respective chairs the following sentence occurs: 'You ought to be examples of good order and *regularity*.' Regularity in this sense cannot be separated from punctuality, and the precept applies with equal force to all the Officers of the Lodge. Their acceptance of their several Offices should be taken virtually as a pledge that, with the honour, they also acknowledge their responsibility for a faithful and *punctual* performance of their several duties to the best of their skill and ability.

Unpunctuality, to which is due the frequent paucity in numbers when the Lodge is opened, and even during a Ceremony which may be performed at the earlier portion of the meeting, is not only a bad compliment and a great discouragement to the Worshipful Master: it also produces a bad impression in the mind of new members, and especially those upon whom the Ceremony is being performed.

Further, the interruptions and reports caused by the arrival of late-comers are a great hindrance to the smooth progress of the ceremonies, and a source of delay, and 'late dinner.'

One used to hear *years ago* of members who were seldom in the Lodge 'when the Brethren were at labour,' and seldom absent 'when they were at refreshment,' thereby gaining for themselves the title of 'knife-and-fork Freemasons.' This, however, belongs to an age now happily passed away, and with it the reputation for an inordinate love of feasting, which to some extent our Order once had, as many now living can well remember.

CHAPTER XIX

THE CEREMONIES

IN considering the Etiquette of the Ceremonies in detail, it may be necessary to touch upon questions which would appear to belong rather to Ritual than to Etiquette. The truth is, it is extremely difficult to define the limits and boundaries of each; they so intermix and overlap here and there that it is next to impossible to say where the domain of the one ends and that of the other begins. On the one hand, one is bound to point out errors and defects in practice and procedure; and on the other, to point out the correct way; thus words, and forms of words, must be included, as well as gesture, position, and demeanour.

It is true Etiquette to do the right thing in the right way, at the right time, and in the right place, as it is equally Etiquette to say the right thing in the right way, at the right time and place.

This doctrine, as applied to our Ritual and Ceremonies, forbids us even to wish to add or to alter words or actions, to render the meaning, in our opinion, 'more clear,' or the diction 'more harmonious,' 'more dignified,' or 'more worthy' of 'our ancient and honourable Fraternity.'

The temptation to introduce our own individuality is the source of all deviation, and is the origin of all the trouble which has arisen with regard to the Ritual; and accounts for the very regrettable lack of uniformity which unfortunately prevails.

Once admit the right of one person to make one alteration, and how can the right of any person to make any alteration be denied?

The true principle is to conform completely and unflinchingly to the actual ceremonies of the Ritual as settled by the Lodge of Reconciliation, and approved by Grand Lodge in 1816.

This principle has been steadily kept in view in the preceding chapters; it will be the guiding principle in those which are to follow.

* * * *

The 'superstructure' of eventual excellence in working, 'perfect in its parts, and honourable to the builder,' can only be raised upon a sound foundation of knowledge; both theoretical and practical; and details, apparently small and trivial, but nevertheless subserving some useful end, should not be overlooked. These details, small or great, are more readily committed to memory, and are better carried out in practice, if one *knows the reason why*, as regards time, place, and manner of performance. *Experto crede.*

*   *   *   *

Opinions differ as to the number of Candidates upon whom either of the Ceremonies should be performed at one time—that is, supposing there be more than one Candidate, shall they be taken together, or one at a time?

There is no law upon the subject, for or against. Rule 192 in the Book of Constitutions states that 'not more than two persons shall be initiated on the same day'—nothing more. It is therefore perfectly in accordance with the Constitutions to Initiate, Pass, or Raise more than one Candidate at one time.

Two are easily managed, but it is not desirable to go beyond two. In the case of three, four, or five Candidates presenting themselves, it is better to take them two and one, or two and two, up to and including the Obligation, and (in the Initiation) the restoration; and when the other detachment has reached the same stage, to take all together to the end.

Of course, cases frequently do occur in which two or even three Candidates taken at one time are initiated, passed, and raised, as efficiently and with as much impressiveness as could have been the case if they had been taken seriatim; but this method is not to be commended except under pressing circumstances, and is then only permissible when all the Officers concerned are adepts in their several duties.

The advocates of the custom of performing each Ceremony separately, upon each Candidate—*e.g.*, up to and including the Obligation, and (in the Initiation) the restoration to L., and the explanation of the emblematical Ls.—maintain that the Ceremony is more impressive with one only, than with two together; and that with more than one some confusion is certain to occur. There is solid foundation for these objections. So much depends upon the manner in which the Worshipful Master, the Wardens, and more especially the Deacons, are able to perform their several duties; the impressiveness depends in a great measure upon the Master; the orderliness and the avoidance of confusion and muddle depend upon the other officers.

The 'Golden Rule' will apply here as elsewhere. The governing factor should be due consideration for the rights and interests of the Candidate. He is about to pass through one of the most solemn ordeals of his life— one which will leave its impress upon him for the remainder of his career. It can only happen to him once. Is it worth while to risk the possibility of marring a beautiful spiritual exercise for some mundane consideration such as lack of time or spoiling dinner?

It is a crime to ruin a Candidate's first impressions.

*   *   *   *

A preliminary word of caution may be given here. No Officer should 'help' another. Much confusion is created by interference, however well meant.

The Officers should know their work and each should do his own. If a mistake should occur, give the W. Master time to put it right quietly. Confusion is made worse confounded if everyone tries his hand at correction. Of course, no Visitor, however competent or however highly placed, would dream of saying or doing anything to direct the course of the ceremony. Attendance at the Lodge of Instruction will minimize all risk of error.

*   *   *   *

(A.) Initiation

The preparation of the Candidate for the Ceremony of Initiation is discussed in a later chapter (Chapter XXIII), to which the reader is referred (p. 302), for a full explanation of the origin and the intention of every detail of that preparation. The theory and practice of the various and appropriate Ks. are fully detailed and explained on pp. 305-307.

We will suppose the Candidate to have been properly prepared, the Ks. to have been given, the Report made to the Worshipful Master, and the Candidate ordered to be admitted. The Organist should immediately commence to play impressive and suitable music —*e.g.*, 'Lead, kindly Light'—and should continue until the Candidate reaches the K. S. On his way to the door, the Senior Deacon places K. S.; after which the Inner Guard opens the door, and both the Deacons receive the Candidate at the door; but the Junior Deacon has him in his especial charge, and leads him to K. S. Here an important question is asked, as to the Candidate's eligibility. The Junior Deacon should be from the commencement always on the alert to suggest the proper answers to this and other questions asked by the

The Ceremonies (Initiation)

Worshipful Master from time to time. The two Deacons cross their wands over the Candidate during the Prayer, during which all stand with Sn. of R. At the words 'S. M. I. B.,' whether said by the Immediate Past Master alone or sung by all the Brethren together, the Sn. of R. is 'dropped,' not 'drawn.' When the Prayer is concluded, amid solemn silence that most important question is asked which, with its affirmative answer, constitutes 'the first and most important of the Antient Landmarks of the Order.' The Candidate's answer should come, unprompted, freely and voluntarily from his own heart; but in case of need the Junior Deacon will assist the Candidate. The response having been given and the Worshipful Master having expressed his satisfaction therewith, the attention of the Brethren is called to the fact that the Candidate is about to pass in view before them. When the Worshipful Master has finished speaking, the Senior Deacon replaces K. S., takes the P. to the Worshipful Master, and resumes his seat, unless there is more than one Candidate; in that case the Senior Deacon, as a matter of course, takes charge of one of them; but the Junior Deacon leads throughout the Ceremony.

The Junior Deacon takes the Candidate's

right hand in his own left and they walk side by side ('squaring' the L.) up the N., across the E., down the S.; the Candidate is halted on the Junior Warden's right and interrogated. He is then conducted to the Senior Warden's right; the questions are asked and answered as before and the Candidate again receives permission to 'Enter free,' etc. He is then presented to the Worshipful Master by the Senior Warden, 'a Candidate properly prepared to be made a Mason.'

During the questions which follow the presentation, the Junior Deacon should be ready to suggest the proper reply to each. It is better to prompt the replies than to leave them to the Candidate, whose form of words in reply may perhaps be not well chosen.

'The method of adv. to the P. in due form' is unfortunately often not well understood by the Junior Deacon himself. In the first place the Candidate should be taken 'diagonally' to the suitable spot. The t. ir. Ss. must not be wrongly dictated. They consist of right lines and angles, and morally teach upright lives and well *squared* actions. The position of the feet should therefore be carefully watched. (The Junior Deacon must remember that it is useless to attempt to use his Wand to point out the method of adv.) This position must be carefully distinguished in the minds of the Junior Deacon and Candidate from a later position, as to which the Candidate is informed, 'That is the first R. S. in Freemasonry,' and in which the feet are placed quite differently, as directed by the W. M. The t. ir. Ss. in advancing from West to East, are, and should always be, separate and distinct from the first 'R. S.' The confusion of these Ss., the one form with the other, is inexcusably frequent; it cannot be too strongly reprobated.

The Senior Deacon arrives at Ped. at the same moment as the Candidate.

The instruction given to the Candidate by the Worshipful Master as to his posture during the Ob. contains these words, '. . . your . . . formed in a S.' If he has been properly adv. to the P. by the Junior Deacon, his . . . will be already in that position.

There will therefore be no need for any pulling or pushing, in order to get the position indicated. The Junior Deacon should see that the Candidate's . . . is *well forward*, do the best he can as to the angle, study the balance of the body in an easy position, and accept that position as a sufficient fulfilment of the requirement of the case. Great discomfort—at times amounting to physical pain—must frequently be the result of the Deacon's ill-directed energy.

Deacons cross Wds. during Ob., and all stand with P. S. of E. A.

When the words 'hereby and hereon' are spoken, the Worshipful Master should place his left hand lightly—for a moment—upon the hand of the Candidate, and then upon the V. S. L. The word 'hele' used in the Ob. is an Old English word which signifies 'to hide, or to cover or conceal'. It is derived from the ancient Saxon word 'hælan,' from which we derive, *inter alia* the word 'hell.' The word 'hele' is still used colloquially in Celtic districts (*e.g.,* Cornwall) and is there pronounced 'heel.' In Masonry it is pronounced 'hail.'

On conclusion of Ob. the P. S. is dis. and the Worshipful Master removes Cs.

Where musical services are in use, the sealing of the Ob. on V. S. L. should be marked by an appropriate instrumental *Kyrie eleison*; this must on no account be sung.

The Rn. to L. requires very great care on the part of the Junior Deacon; he has to be ready to suggest the proper word in reply to the Master's question, and at the same time to have all prepared for the denouement *at the proper moment.* It is well also for all the Brethren to look to the

East, so that the salute may be given by all *as by one man.* A volley, and not a dropping fire, should welcome the Candidate on his Rn. to L. The proper motions are P. L. R. ▬▌. The Worshipful Master alone uses the gavel, not the Wardens. The Brethren use their hands, not their Badges. The effect of the whole may be, and often is, marred by want of proper attention to the details here mentioned.

The Junior Deacon restrains the Candidate from movement, and the Worshipful Master then points out to the attention of the Candidate the three great though emblematical Ls., and welcomes the Candidate as a newly obligated Brother among Masons.

After directing the attention of the Candidate to the three L. . . .r Ls. and to other matters, the Worshipful Master communicates the Ss. without leaving his place. He should be careful at the proper moment to take the Sp. and place the f. in the form of the first R. S.

When the Candidate is conducted, still normally 'squaring,' to the Junior Warden, and presented, the examination* should

* The Junior Deacon, after himself saluting the Wardens, does not again give signs or salutes with the Candidate; he merely directs the Candidate to give them.

proceed as far as the W. only, and should not include the derivation and the interpretation, etc. These, however, should always be given to the Senior Warden in full. It should be clearly understood that the import of the W. is *not* S. but *in* S.

The examinations concluded, the Senior Warden presents the Candidate and receives the Worshipful Master's command to invest the new-made Brother with the ancient and honourable distinguishing badge of a Mason —a Lambskin, entirely white: the badge of Innocence and bond of Friendship; a Symbol of a new and spiritual Service; an indication that he is now a Worker and Builder in the service of God and Man; a badge which, if he never disgraces it, will never disgrace him. At this point the Brethren strike their Badges, not their hands.

In adjusting the E. A. badge, the S. W. should see that the 'flap' is up.

After a few observations by the Worshipful Master the Candidate is placed in the N. E. to receive that touching if embarrassing Charge by the Worshipful Master which has thrilled the hearts of thousands on thousands, and to which may be traced the impulse of that Universal Masonic Charity which knows no bounds save those of prudence.

The presentation of the Working Tools,

The Ceremonies (Initiation)

and the exhibition of the Warrant, follow in due sequence.

Mention is made in Chapter XVI, p. 146, of the custom of actually presenting a copy of the Book of Constitutions, and one of the By-laws, to every Entered Apprentice. Good reasons are there given for this practice, and to these the reader will do well to refer.

The newly initiated Brother is told that on his return a Charge will be delivered. He is then conducted along the N. side (no 'squaring') to the L. of the S. W., where the Deacon instructs* his charge to 'Salute the Worshipful Master as a Mason'; and he should, if necessary, correct any informality or slovenliness in the performance of the salute. The hand should be raised at once to the appointed position; and the sign should be completed without bowing or bending of the body before or after. This position, and the manner of assuming it, should be uniformly practised by every member when entering or leaving the Lodge, or when commanded to stand to order. A Perfunctory or solvenly manner of giving the salute or of standing to order is a breach of Masonic etiquette.

The Junior Deacon accompanies the Candidate to the door and resumes his seat.

* See footnote on p. 205.

After a brief interval the Candidate returns. The Junior Deacon receives him, conducts him to the left of the Senior Warden and directs* him to 'Salute the Worshipful Master as a Mason.' The Charge is given to the Candidate at this stage and while he is in this position.

It is by no means a rare occurrence to hear the Senior or the Junior Warden or some Past Master deliver the Charge in this Degree. This is a relief to the Master, and an advantage to the Wardens, as being good practice in anticipation of their higher duties in the future. (See p. 328.)

The Junior Deacon remains in attendance on the Candidate while the charge is given, and at the conclusion of it he conducts the Candidate to a seat and resumes his own.

* * * *

Brethren generally evince a warmer interest in, and will make more strenuous efforts to be present at, the ceremony of Initiation than at either of the other two. It is naturally to be expected that this would be the case, because it is the formal reception of a new member into our Order, and most of us feel an excusable curiosity to see what manner of man the Candidate is, and how he

* See footnote on p. 205.

will conduct himself under the entirely new circumstances in which he will find himself placed.

Most of us have heard newly-initiated Brethren express themselves to the effect that they understood and appreciated the Ceremony of Initiation in far greater measure after having witnessed and heard it performed with some other Candidate than they did at their own Initiation. Naturally this would be the case; the whole surrounding circumstances, the action, the moral teaching, even the phraseology of the Ceremony, being so far removed from anything within the range of their experience in the outer world, so different from any 'opinion preconceived' of that which actually takes place in the Lodge.

A very curious psychological study would be produced by a transcript of the various impressions made upon the minds of the majority of the newly-elected Members of our Order by the First Ceremony. It may be assumed generally that those impressions —favourable or the reverse—would be just in accordance with the degree of carefulness, accuracy, and impressiveness (or with the absence of those qualities) with which the Ceremony had in each case been performed. Instances of very varied results, consequent upon the Ceremony having been well or ill conducted, are within the experience of perhaps every member of mature years among us.

'A tree is known by its fruits,' and increasingly numerous as our Fraternity is, we may conclude that, as a general rule, the seed sown in our Lodges is good seed, well planted, well nourished, or it would not—as it has done, and is doing—'take root downward, and bear fruit upward, a hundred-fold,' as the number of new Lodges year by year added to the registry of the Grand Lodge abundantly testifies. Nevertheless in very many Lodges complaint is made of the falling away of good men and Brethren from our midst, and of the coldness and apathy of many who retain their membership, but whose visits to the Lodge are few and far between. This is perhaps inevitable. It is not given to everyone to appreciate at its proper value our excellent Institution, or to derive 'profit and pleasure' from its moral teaching.

(AB.) Entrusting the Entered
Apprentice

The Junior Deacon with his left hand takes the right hand of the Candidate, and leads him towards the left of the Senior Warden.

The Ceremonies (Entrusting)

The Junior Deacon 'backs,' bringing the Candidate to the proper position, facing the Worshipful Master. There is no 'advance' or 'salute' at this moment. The Worshipful Master examines the Candidate by asking the prescribed questions. If the Candidate should falter it is the duty of the Junior Deacon to correct and prompt him.

At the conclusion of the prescribed questions the Worshipful Master announces that he will put others if any Brother wishes him to do so.

What would happen if any Brother did so 'wish' we will not inquire. At this point some Brethren make a point of ejaculating, 'Very well answered, Worshipful Master!' This is not orthodox, and should be discouraged in all cases; even in those cases where the commendation is earned.

The Junior Deacon (instructing the Candidate, *sotto voce*, about L. F.) then conducts the Candidate, direct (there is no 'squaring' on this occasion), to the N. side of the Worshipful Master's Pedestal, where, after preliminary assurances are given, the P. G. and P. W. are communicated to him.

The Candidate is then taken straight back the way he came (there is no 'squaring' on this occasion) towards the left of the Senior Warden, the Junior Deacon 'backing' as before; and the Candidate is directed* to 'Salute the Worshipful Master as a Mason.' The Junior Deacon conducts him to the door and resumes his seat.

(B.) Passing

It is stated in Chapter XXIII (p. 296, *q.v.*) that when a Candidate for the Second Degree is conducted by the T. to the outside of the door of the Lodge, the Ks. of the First Degree should be given; and the reasons are there fully explained why those Ks., and no others, should be given.

We will, as in the previous Degree, suppose the Candidate to have been properly prepared, the Ks. of E. A. to have been given, the Report made to the Worshipful Master, and the Candidate ordered to be admitted.

The Organist commences his introductory music (which he continues until the Candidate reaches the K. S.). On his way to the door the Junior Deacon places the K. S.; after which the Inner Guard opens the door and both the Deacons receive the Candidate at the door; but this time the Senior Deacon has him in his especial charge, and leads him to the K. S., where he directs the Candidate to 'Advance as a Mason.' Senior Deacons

* See footnote on p. 205.

should note the employment of this phrase when the Candidate is 'advancing' from one Degree to another. The two Deacons cross their wands over the Candidate during the Prayer, during which all stand with the Sn. of R. At the words 'S. M. I. B.,' whether said by the Immediate Past Master alone or sung by all the Brethren together, the Sn. of R. is 'dropped,' not 'drawn.' When the Prayer is concluded the Junior Deacon replaces the K. S. and resumes his seat; unless there is more than one Candidate; in that case the Junior Deacon, as a matter of course, takes charge of one of them; but the Senior Deacon leads throughout the Ceremony.

As soon as the way is clear, and without any preliminary remarks from the Worshipful Master, the Senior Deacon takes the Candidate's right hand in his own left, and they walk side by side, 'squaring' the L.

During the first perambulation the Candidate has to prove to the Brethren that he has been duly initiated; and for this purpose he is halted at the W. M.'s Pedestal, and directed* by the Senior Deacon to 'Salute the Worshipful Master as a Mason.' This the Candidate should do without turning his head or body towards the W. M. He is then halted at the R. of the Junior Warden and

* See footnote on p. 205.

directed to 'Advance to the Junior Warden as such'; he is subjected to an examination, in which he is called upon to show the Sn. and communicate the T. and W. This having been accomplished, the Senior Deacon directs the Candidate to 'Salute* the Senior Warden as a Mason'; he then passes the Senior Warden's pedestal; and having thus made one circuit, the Senior Deacon pauses; and the Brethren are bidden to observe that 'Bro. —— is about to pass in view before them, to show that he is the Candidate properly prepared,' etc. In the second round he has to 'Salute the Worshipful Master as a Mason,' 'Salute the Junior Warden as a Mason,' 'Advance to the Senior Warden as such, showing the Sn., and communicating the P. G. and P. W.,' leading from the First to the Second Degree.

When the two rounds have been completed nothing more in the way of examination has to be done, and the Candidate is presented to the Worshipful Master by the Senior Warden as a Candidate properly prepared to be passed to the Second Degree.

* The Senior Deacon should in all cases bring the Candidate to a complete standstill before issuing directions; and the Candidate should salute without turning the head or body. The Senior Deacon does not illustrate the Candidate's salutes or signs. He merely superintends them.

The Ceremonies (Passing)

The Candidate should be then placed on the North side of the Lodge, about six feet to the West of the Master's pedestal, and facing full South, and the method of advancing to the East in due form should then be verbally explained and physically described by the Senior Deacon; the Candidate's imitation in 'due form' will bring him to the proper place; at which the Junior Deacon should arrive at the same moment on L. of the Candidate.

Some of the remarks made upon the posture during the Ob. in the First Degree apply with equal force to the one in the Second, and the reader would do well to refer to pp. 202 and 203. If the Candidate has been properly instructed, the . . . will already be formed in a S. without any necessity for further movement. A mistake is often made in placing the L. A. in the proper position; the . . . should rest in the angle of the S. with the . . . elevated, with the t.i.t.f.o.a.S., and pointing over the L. S.

The Deacons cross Wds. during Ob., and all stand with the P. S. of F. C.

When the words 'hereby and hereon' are spoken, the Worshipful Master should place his left hand lightly—for a moment—upon the hand of the Candidate, and then upon the V. S. L.

At the conclusion of the Ob. the P. S. is 'drawn,' and the Junior Deacon removes the S. On sealing the Ob. on V. S. L., the Organist plays the *Kyrie eleison*; after which the Worshipful Master says, 'Rise, newly-obligated Fellow-Craft Freemason.'

The Junior Deacon then resumes his seat.

The Senior Deacon places the Candidate at R. of the Worshipful Master for communication of the S. T. and W.

The Worshipful Master should be careful, when he rises, to take the Sp., placing the f. in the form of the Second R. S.

In imparting the Ss., the Worshipful Master should see that the Candidate makes each portion of the three forms accurately, fairly, and squarely; especially in the H. S., in which, not only is the L. A. placed at 'an angle of ninety Degrees,' but the . . . is also, and is clearly pointed over the L. S.; and not, as a visitor to various Lodges in some Northern Provinces too often sees, stretched out across, with the . . . of the hand visible. An opinion upon this point has been obtained from high authority, and the custom here condemned has been pronounced to be entirely wrong.

As to the historical basis of the H. S., a great difference of opinion exists as to the locality in which these words were uttered, as well as in the rendering of the words themselves.

An unprejudiced examination of the facts, which undoubtedly connect the miracle with Joshua, and both with a certain locality (see Josh. x 11-13), must lead to the conclusion that our H. S. is derived from the events recorded in those verses.

The words and signs used in the various portions of the Ritual are 'according to our traditions,' and therefore, not professing that they are the very words of the Bible, the use of them is not open to serious objection.

After the Worshipful Master has finished, the Candidate is conducted to the Junior Warden, and presented by the Senior Deacon for examination. The Senior Deacon, in presenting the Candidate, of course salutes the Junior Warden, but when the Candidate's turn to salute arrives, the Senior Deacon does not duplicate the Sns.; he merely instructs the Candidate what to do. The Junior Warden's examination should proceed, as in the first Degree, as far as the W. only; and should not include the derivation and the interpretation, etc. These, however, should always be given to the S. W. in full.

The examinations concluded, the Senior Warden receives the Worshipful Master's command to invest the Brother with the distinguishing badge of a Fellow-Craft Freemason—a badge which bears two rosettes, and now has the flap down. After a few observations by the Worshipful Master, the Candidate is placed in the S. E. to mark the progress he has made in the Science.

* * * *

The 'Presentation of the Working Tools of the Second Degree' gives occasion to point out one of the greatest anomalies in the Ceremonies of the three Degrees. In the Ritual the explanation of the Square, Level, and Plumb-rule is given with extreme brevity in the Ceremony of Passing to the Second Degree, whereas in the explanation of the Tracing Board of the First Degree they—the Working Tools of the Second Degree—are explained at unusual length.

Very little consideration is needed to show how inconsistent this is. The explanation of the First Tracing Board must of necessity be given when the Lodge is opened in the First, or Entered Apprentice, Degree, and in it the Ritual gives the long Explanation of the Working Tools of the Second, or Fellow-Craft's, Degree; and then in the

The Ceremonies (Passing)

Ceremony of Passing, during which alone the Working Tools of the Second Degree can lawfully be explained, they are slurred over with a brevity not to be found in the Explanation of the Working Tools of the First or of the Third Degree.

This *bouleversement* ought to have been reversed; the lengthy explanation of the uses of these Tools in Operative Masonry, and of their moral signification, should have been expunged from the First Tracing Board, and should have been included in the Ceremony of Passing, to which they legitimately belong.

The implements in question, being the 'Movable Jewels' of the Lodge, and being severally the distinctive badges of the Master and the two Wardens, must of necessity be mentioned in the Tracing Board of the First Degree; but not necessarily described and moralized upon. They should be mentioned only in the quality of Movable Jewels, and as designating the three Principal Officers of the Lodge; it is unconstitutional to explain them in the First Degree.

The description of their uses and the excellent moral lessons which they teach (the latter being far too good to be lost) should have been transferred bodily from the Tracing Board to their proper place in the Second Ceremony. Without this longer exposition of the Working Tools, the Ceremony of Passing is poor and meagre as compared with the Initiation and the Raising; whereas with the full explanation it will compare not unfavourably with the First and the Third Ceremonies.

*   *   *   *

After the presentation of the Working Tools, the Candidate receives permission to retire.

Accordingly the Senior Deacon takes him (no squaring) to the L. of the Senior Warden, and instructs* him to 'Salute the Worshipful Master as a Fellow-Craft, first as an Entered Apprentice.'

The Senior Deacon then accompanies the Candidate to the door, and resumes his seat.

On the return of the Candidate after a short interval, the Senior Deacon (only) meets him, conducts him to the L. of the Senior Warden, and instructs* him to 'Salute the Worshipful Master as a Fellow-Craft, first as an Entered Apprentice.'

The Worshipful Master then proceeds to the head of the Tracing Board.

The Senior Deacon leads the Candidate to the foot of the Tracing Board. The Junior Deacon arrives (L.) at the same moment,

* See footnote on p. 214.

and hands his wand to the Worshipful Master, who gives the Explanation of the Second Tracing Board.

Towards the conclusion of the Explanation, and when the W. M. pronounces the letter 'G,' the I. P. M., S. W., and J. W. successively give ━▌; and *after* the W. M. has said 'denoting God' (not before), the Sn. of R. is placed, and in due course dis.

At the conclusion the Senior Deacon conducts the Candidate to a seat, and then resumes his own.

Sometimes the Worshipful Master delegates the duty of giving this Lecture to some other Brother, thus lightening his own labours and at the same time varying what is apt to become the monotony of the proceedings.

(BC.) ENTRUSTING THE FELLOW-CRAFT

The Senior Deacon, in this ceremony, does exactly as the Junior Deacon does in the ceremony (AB.) Entrusting the E. A. (*q.v.*); except that at the conclusion, on arriving at the left of the Senior Warden, the Candidate is directed to 'Salute the Worshipful Master as a F. C., first as an E. A.' The Deacons ext. Ls. and lay S.

(C.) RAISING

When a Candidate for the Third Degree is conducted by the T. to the outside of the door of the Lodge, the Ks. of the Second Degree are given. The reason for this is given on p. 305.

We will, as in the previous Degrees, suppose the Candidate to have been properly prepared, the Ks. of F. C. to have been given the Report made to the Worshipful Master, and the Candidate ordered to be admitted.

The Organist commences solemn and specially selected music, and continues it until the Candidate reaches the K. S.

On his way to the door the Junior Deacon places the K. S.; after which the Inner Guard opens the door; and both the Deacons receive the Candidate at the door, but, as in the Second Degree, the Senior Deacon has him in his especial charge, and leads him to the K. S., where he directs* the Candidate to 'Advance as a Fellow-Craft, first as an Entered Apprentice.' (Senior Deacons should note the employment of this phrase when the Candidate is 'advancing' from one Degree to another.) The two Deacons cross their wands over the Candidate during the Prayer, during which all

* See footnote on p. 214.

stand with the Sn. of R. At the words
'S. M. I. B.,' whether said by the Immediate
Past Master alone, or sung by all the
Brethren together, the Sn. of R. is 'dropped,'
not 'drawn.' When the Prayer is concluded
the Junior Deacon removes and subsequently replaces the K. S. and follows the
Senior Deacon closely all the time. In the
case of more than one candidate the Junior
Deacon, as a matter of course, takes charge
of one of them; but the Senior Deacon
leads throughout the Ceremony.

As soon as the way is clear, and without
any preliminary remarks from the Worshipful Master, the Senior Deacon takes the
Candidate's right hand in his own left, and
they walk side by side, squaring the L.,
closely followed by the Junior Deacon. They
have to make three perambulations.

During the first circuit, the Candidate is
directed by the Senior Deacon to 'Salute
the Worshipful Master as a Mason,' and to
'Advance to the Junior Warden as such,
showing the Sn. and communicating the T.
and W.' Thus he has to prove to the
Brethren, through an examination conducted by the Junior Warden, that he has
been regularly initiated into Freemasonry.

During the second round the Candidate
is directed to 'Salute the Worshipful

Master as a Fellow-Craft'; to 'Salute the Junior Warden as a Fellow-Craft'; to 'Advance to the Senior Warden as such, showing the Sn., and communicating the T. and W. of that Degree.' Thus he has to prove to the Senior Warden that he has been duly passed to the Second, or Fellow-Craft's, Degree.

The Deacons and the Candidate then halt on the North side of the Senior Warden's pedestal, and the Brethren are requested to observe that the Candidate 'is about to pass in view before them, to show that he is the Candidate properly prepared,' etc.

During the third round the Candidate is directed* to 'Salute the Worshipful Master as a Fellow-Craft'; to 'Salute the Junior Warden as a Fellow-Craft'; to 'Advance to the Senior Warden as such, showing the Sn., and communicating the P. G. and P. W. he received from the Worshipful Master previously to leaving the Lodge.' Thus he has to prove to the Senior Warden that he is in possession of the P. G. and P. W. leading from the Second to the Third Degree.

Now, inasmuch as it is the invariable rule in each Degree that the Candidate shall undergo *one* examination—no more, and no

* See footnote on p. 214.

less—during *each* of these preliminary perambulations, it is clear that the correct rule is that there shall be one perambulation for the First Degree, and no more; two for the Second Degree, no more and no less; and three for the Third Degree, no more and no less.

The Senior Warden then presents the Candidate to the Worshipful Master, 'a Candidate properly prepared to be raised to the Third Degree'; and then, by command of the Worshipful Master, directs both the Deacons to instruct the Candidate to 'Advance to the E. by the proper Sps.'

The Senior Deacon (Junior Deacon still following) takes the Candidate to the N., where the Junior Deacon takes temporary charge of the Candidate.

The Senior Deacon by example instructs the Candidate; the Sps. should be well squared with the body erect; concluding with four distinct Sps. and the completion of the last one. The Junior Deacon arrives at the same time on the L. of the Candidate.

The Deacons cross Wds. during the Ob., and all stand to order with the P. S. of M. M. When the words 'hereby and hereon' are spoken, the Worshipful Master should place his left hand lightly—for a moment—upon the hand of the Candidate, and then on the V. S. L. At the conclusion of the Ob. the P. S. is 'drawn' and 'recovered.'

On sealing the Ob. on the V. S. L., the Organ plays the *Kyrie eleison*; after which the Worshipful Master says, 'Rise, newly-obligated Master Mason,' and the Deacons and the Candidate step back a little.

When the Worshipful Master breaks off in the narrative, and says, 'Brother Wardens,' the Wardens should leave their places, bringing the L. and the P. R., and silently take the places of the Deacons; who open out to R. and L., and then resume their seats. The S. W. stands on the left of the Can., the J. W. on his right; and the J. W. directs him to 'c. h. f.'

The Wardens should be especially careful not to perform their respective functions too soon; a good deal has to be said before the proper moment for action arrives, and the appropriate action should come after the corresponding word is spoken, not before. Each Warden should wait for the cue—*e.g.*, 'temple, 'sink,' &c.; and the instant the Worshipful Master utters the word, the Warden should perform his duty.

At the moment of the final action, the Senior Warden may in a whisper caution the Candidate to be perfectly passive. If, as sometimes happens, the Candidate be allowed to move, he cannot be placed where preparation has been made for him. The Junior Warden c. h. f.

At this point the Organist should play some suitably solemn movement or hymn, such as 'Days and moments, quickly flying,' but on no account must any singing take place.

After the ineffectual efforts of the Wardens, the Worshipful Master descends from his Pedestal, and with their assistance . . . . him on the f. ps. o. f.

The Wardens then resume their seats, and the Worshipful Master, facing N., is left in charge of the Candidate, who faces S.

The Candidate should be placed well back on the North side of the Lodge, having the Emblems of M. and the representation of the . . . on his right; so that in the address which follows, the Worshipful Master may direct his attention to the one and the other without a change of position.

After the solemn address the Worshipful Master reverses the respective positions, and the Candidate then faces N.

In making this movement, the W. M. keeps himself between the Candidate and the Ped.

When the Worshipful Master communicates the Ss. of this Degree, the Candidate is instructed to advance to him as a Fellow-

Craft, first as an Entered Apprentice; and then to take another S. P.

After the Worshipful Master has communicated the Ss. he gives the Candidate permission to 'retire in order, etc.,' and the Worshipful Master resumes his seat.

The *newly-made Master Mason* is conducted by the Senior Deacon (no 'squaring') to the L. of the Senior Warden, and instructed* to salute the Worshipful Master in the three Degrees; (P. S. only of Third Degree on leaving), and he is then conducted by the Senior Deacon to the door of the Lodge.

The Senior Deacon puts his wand by his chair; and both Deacons take up the furniture, restore the Ls., and resume their seats.

* * * *

When the newly-raised Brother is brought back to the Lodge, after a short interval, he is met at the door by the Senior Deacon only, who places him at the L. of the S. W., and directs* him to 'Salute the Worshipful Master in the three Degrees. (Full signs.)' The Senior Deacon then hands him to the Senior Warden, by whom he is invested with the distinguishing badge of a Master Mason.

* See footnote on p. 214.

The Ceremonies (Raising)

After a short address by the Worshipful Master concerning the badge, the Senior Deacon places the Candidate before the Worshipful Master, who gives the remaining portion of the Traditional History, which should always be narrated; the Working Tools with which H. Ab. was S. should be mentioned; and attention should be directed to the Emblems of M. After this, the remaining two of the Ss. are communicated, and the Working Tools presented. After which the Senior Deacon conducts the Master Mason to a seat and resumes his own.

* * * *

The Ritual includes among the Emblems of M. the C. These were unknown in the East before and after the date assumed in the Ceremony. The use of the winding-sheet was universal.

As to 'the Ornaments of a Master Masons' Lodge,' there is no foundation in the Bible for the descriptions given of the 'Porch, Dormer, and Square Pavement'; they never had an existence except in the imagination of the old compilers of the Ritual. See Appendix, p. 415, wherein also the question of the 're-interment' is mentioned.

The proper title of H. Ab. would be 'our Grand Master,' he having been one of the three *Grand* Masters (the others being Solomon, King of Israel, and Hiram, King of Tyre) who presided over the Craft during the building of the Temple.

*   *   *   *

In Lodges here and there scattered about the country the latter portion of the Traditional History is seldom or never narrated; in fact, in very many Lodges the Degree is too often given with maimed rites. This should not be. The Candidate is entitled to know all that we in the Ceremonies have to teach, and if he be of an inquiring mind, and if the narrative, etc., be not completed, he will be led to consider that the Ceremony, which began with great solemnity, and with a most interesting historical narrative, had come to an abrupt and a very lame and impotent conclusion. An imperfect or ill-conducted performance of the Ceremonies is an injustice to the Candidate and to Freemasonry itself.

As it is true etiquette to do the right thing in the right way, at the right time, and in the right place, then the details of position and of action here given are not out of place in the Etiquette of Freemasonry which is intended to be carried through upon the lines laid down in the Introduction. These details, perfectly intelligible and easy of accomplishment though they are, still require considerable care; and it is not too much to expect of the Principal Officers of a Lodge that they should exercise the care necessary to prevent a hitch or a fiasco in the performance of the Ceremonies.

(D.) INSTALLATION OF A MASTER

This ceremony was specially considered and agreed to by the Board of Installed Masters and sanctioned and approved by the Grand Master in 1827. (See pp. 117-118.)

It is one of the prized privileges of the Worshipful Master to instal his successor, and it is becoming quite the rule for the retiring Worshipful Master to exercise this function. To avoid any confusion, however, in the following description of the ceremony he will be styled Installing Master.

While the Lodge is still in the First Degree the Installing Master should appoint Past Masters to the Wardens' chairs.

There should be no declaration that 'all offices are vacant.' In the first place it is not in accordance with Recognized Ritual, and in the second place no one is empowered to make any such declaration. An officer retains his position until the new Worshipful Master appoints and invests a successor.

The Lodge is then opened in the Second Degree, and a Past Master (either the Immediate Past Master or the Director of Ceremonies) presents the Master Elect for the benefit of Installation. On receiving the Installing Master's reply the Past Master resumes his seat, leaving the Master Elect standing alone.

N.B.—No Warden can be installed as Master of a Lodge (except by Dispensation from the Grand Master) unless he has served the Office as an Invested Warden for a full year—that is to say, from one regular Installation Meeting until the next regular Installation Meeting.

No Installing Master may proceed unless satisfied of such service or Dispensation.

After addressing the Brethren generally and the Master Elect in particular, the Installing Master directs the attention of the Master Elect to the Secretary, who reads the Summary of the Ancient Charges, to all of which the Master Elect signifies his unqualified assent by the Sn. of F. taking the Sp. on the first occasion. The Sn. should be given with the same care as all other Sns. There should be no bowing by the Master Elect.

The Master Elect then turns again to the Installing Master, and gives his promise to support them, and then, on instructions,

The Ceremonies (Installation)

advances to take the Ob. as regards his duties as Master of the Lodge.

All the Brethren stand to order with the P. S. of F. C.

At the conclusion of the Ob. the P. S. of F. C. is dis. in unison.

The Lodge is then opened in the Third Degree, the Master Elect standing in his place. All under the rank of Installed Master are invited to retire. Officers should leave their collars on their chairs.

The Master Elect remains standing in his place.

*   *   *   *

☞ (*Here follows the Esotery of Installed Masters. Any Installed Master may have this on application and on establishing his right to possess it.*)

On their re-admission the Master Masons are ranged in the N. Preceded by the Installing Master, they pass round and salute the Worshipful Master as M. Ms. (See p. 336.)

The Installing Master in the E. then proclaims the Worshipful Master for the first time, and leads the M. Ms. in greeting the Worshipful Master.

The Installing Master then presents to the Worshipful Master the Working Tools of a M. M. These *must* be presented *in extenso*; and the Lodge is then closed in the Third Degree. (See p. 337.)

It is, unfortunately, too common to see the Lodge 'resumed' on the plea of 'want of time.' If the Worshipful Master is capable of doing his work he will be well advised to take this opportunity of demonstrating his fitness to rule and direct his Lodge.

The F. Cs. are then admitted, and the same process repeated.

The Working Tools of the F. C. should be presented to the Worshipful Master *in extenso*; and the Lodge closed in the Second Degree.

The E. As. are then admitted, procession and greeting as before, the Working Tools of an E. A. presented, and the Brethren directed to resume their seats.

The Installing Master then delivers the Warrant, presents the Book of Constitutions and the By-laws of the Lodge, each with appropriate advice; and then calls on the Worshipful Master to appoint and invest his officers.

This is done in order of precedence, as set out on p. 91.

All the officers are 'appointed' except the Treasurer and Tyler, who are 'elected.'

If the officer to be invested is already an Installed Master he is conducted to the S. side of the Pedestal; if not, to the N. side.

The Installing Master should, with his left hand, hold the right hand of the officer he is conducting.

When the Installing Master accompanies the newly-invested officer to his place, he should under no circumstances forget to conduct the Past Master, so displaced, to a seat amongst the Past Masters.

On Installation Nights it is customary in some Lodges to salute each officer as he takes his place with a single clap in volley. This is not 'orthodox'; and although it is a kindly and unobjectionable custom, and quite 'Masonic', it were better avoided.

All officers within the Lodge having been invested, the Worshipful Master summons the Tyler or Outer Guard with the proper ━❨.

The Tyler, having saluted on entrance from the L. of the S. W., advances alone to

the Worshipful Master to be invested, and
this having been done, he retires and salutes
alone.

In the event, however, of the Tyler being,
as is often the case, a very old officer and not
quite so active as formerly, the Installing
Master will lose nothing of his dignity if he
fraternally conducts the Tyler also to the
Worshipful Master for investiture.

In either case, if the before-mentioned
unorthodox salute in 'volley' has been given
to the other officers, it should on no account
be omitted on the withdrawal of the Tyler,
who is a Brother; and 'he who is placed on
the lowest spoke of Fortune's wheel is equally
entitled to our regard.'

*　　*　　*　　*

All the officers present having been invested, the Installing Master proceeds to
deliver the three Addresses: the first, to the
Worshipful Master, he delivers from the
left of the Senior Warden; the second, to
the Wardens, from the left of the Worshipful Master. The Wardens should remain
seated during this address. Some make a
point that the Wardens should stand; but
there is not even any logic in it, as they do
not suggest that all the Brethren should
stand during the third and last address,

The Ceremonies (Consecration)

which is delivered by the Installing Master from the left of the Worshipful Master.

*   *   *   *

At the conclusion of these addresses, it is customary for a Past Master to move that a vote of thanks be accorded to the Installing Master and recorded on the Minutes, expressing the appreciation of the assembled Brethren of the admirable manner in which the Installation Ceremony has been performed. Of course if the Installing Master is also the Immediate Past Master, this occasion is taken to pin on his breast, with appropriate words, the P. M. Jewel, which has been, no doubt, already voted to him.

(E.) Calling Off and Calling On

These useful ceremonies will be found in the Ritual *in extenso*, and there is no occasion for any detailed comment thereon, except that there is no legal necessity for the Junior Warden to remain in his seat during the recess as one has sometimes seen.

(F.) Consecration of a Lodge
order of ceremony*

1. The Brethren assemble in the Lodge Room.

2. The Consecrating Officer having entered
   in procession with the Grand Officers,
   takes the Chair and appoints his
   Officers.
3. The Lodge is opened in the Three
   Degrees.

4.   *Opening Ode*
   Hail Eternal, by Whose aid
   All created things were made,
   Heaven and earth Thy vast design;
   Hear us, Architect Divine.

   May our work begun in Thee
   Ever blest with order be;
   And may we when labours cease
   Part in harmony and peace.

   By Thy glorious Majesty,
   By the trust we place in Thee,
   By the badge and mystic sign,
   Hear us, Architect Divine.
                              So mote it be.

5. The Consecrating Officer addressing the
   Brethren on the Motive of the meeting.
   C. O.—'Brethren, we are assembled on
   the present occasion for the purpose
   of Constituting and Consecrating a

* This chronological order is official; but to be
consistent, item 3 should come after item 4.

The Ceremonies (Consecration)

New Lodge, and I am commanded by
the M. W. G. M. to act as Deputy *pro
tem.*, and perform the requisite Ceremony. I therefore call on our worthy
Brother, the Chaplain, to give the

Opening Prayer

Chaplain.—'O Lord, our Heavenly
Father, Architect and Ruler of the
Universe, Who dost from Thy Throne
behold all the dwellers upon earth!
Direct us in all our doings with Thy
most gracious favour, and further us
With Thy continued help, that in all our
works begun, continued, and ended in
Thee, we may glorify Thy holy Name.'

6. Chant (*Omnes*): 'So mote it be.'
7. The Director of Ceremonies addresses
the Consecrating Officer.

'R. W. M., a number of Brethren, duly
instructed in the mysteries of the
Craft, who are now assembled, have
requested me to inform you that the
M. W. G. M. has been pleased to grant
them a Charter or Warrant of Constitution, bearing date the   day of
, 19 , authorizing them to
form and open a Lodge of F. and A.
Masons at. . . . ., in the county

of............, and are desirous that their Lodge should be consecrated, and their Officers installed and invested, according to the ancient usages and established customs of the Order, for which purpose they are now met, and await your pleasure.'

8. The Consecrating Officer replies, and gives directions.

C. O.—'I will thank those Brethren who signed the petition to stand in the body of the Lodge, whilst the D. of C. reads the petition, and also the Warrant or Charter from the M. W. G. M.'

9. The Brethren of the New Lodge are then arranged in order on each side of the Lodge Board.

10. The Director of Ceremonies reads the Petition and Warrant.

11. The Consecrating Officer inquires of the Brethren if they approve of the Officers named in the Warrant.

C. O.—'After due deliberation, the M. W. G. M., by virtue of the authority vested in him by the United G. L. of England, has granted to the Brethren of this new Lodge a Charter, establishing them in all the rights and privileges of our Order, and I now inquire of the petitioners, if they approve of the Officers named in the Warrant to preside over them.'

12. The Brethren signify their approval in Masonic form.

C. O.—'Then we will proceed to constitute these Brethren into a regular Lodge, and to consecrate it according to ancient usage. I therefore call on our worthy Brother, the Chaplain, to deliver an Oration on the Nature and Principles of the Institution.

13. *An Oration*

On the Nature and Principles of the Institution, by the Chaplain.

14. *Anthem*

'Behold how good and joyful a thing it is, brethren, to dwell together in unity!

'It is like the precious ointment upon the head, that ran down unto the beard, even unto Aaron's beard, and went down to the skirts of his clothing.

'It is like the dew of Hermon which fell upon the hill of Zion.

'For there the Lord promised His blessing, and life for evermore.'

So mote it be.

15. *Dedication Prayer (First Portion)*

C. O.—'Almighty Architect of the Universe, Searcher and Ruler of all worlds, deign from Thy Celestial Abode, from realms of light and glory, to bless us in all the purposes of our present assembly. We humbly invoke Thee to give us Wisdom in all our doings; Strength of Mind under all our difficulties; and the Beauty of Love and Harmony in all our communications. Permit us, O Thou Author of Light and Life, great Source of Love and Happiness, to erect this Lodge, and now solemnly to consecrate it to the Honour and Glory of Thy most Holy Name.'

16. Chant (*Omnes*): 'So mote it be.'

17. *Sanctus:* 'Holy, Holy, Holy, Lord God of Hosts; Heaven and earth are full of Thy glory. Glory be to Thee, O God.'

18. The Brethren turn towards the East, and the Consecrating Officer pronounces

The Invocation

C. O.—'O Lord God of Israel, there is no other God like unto Thee, in Heaven above, or in the Earth beneath, Who keepeth covenants and showeth mercy unto Thy servants who walk before Thee with all their hearts.

'Let all the people of the Earth know that the Lord He is God, and that there is none else.

'Let all the people of the Earth know Thy name, and fear Thee.

'Let all the people of the Earth know that I have built this House, and consecrated it to Thy service.

'But wilt Thou, O God, indeed dwell upon the Earth? Behold, the Heavens, and Heaven of Heavens, cannot contain Thee; how much less this House that I have built?

'Yet, have respect unto my prayer, and to my supplication, and hearken unto my cry.

'May Thine eyes be opened towards this House by day and by night; and when Thy servants shall pray towards this House, hearken unto their supplications; hear them in heaven Thy dwelling-place: and when Thou hearest, forgive.'

19. Chant (*Omnes*): 'So mote it be.'
20. The Chaplain reads 2 Chron. ii 1-16.
21. The Consecrating Officer directs Lodge Board to be uncovered.

The Lodge Board is uncovered by the D. of C., who arranged the petitioning Brethren as before on each side of the Board, with a sufficient space between to allow the procession of C. O. and Ws. to pass. The Cornucopia filled with corn, and the vases with wine and oil, are handed by the D. of C. to the C. O. and Ws., and are carried by them round the Lodge, and the elements poured on the floor during their progress. Soft and gentle music.

The Consecration (during which the Elements of Consecration are carried round the Lodge).

22. Before the first circuit the Brethren sing:
'When once of old, in Israel,
Our early Brethren wrought with toil,
Jehovah's blessings on them fell
In showers of Corn, and Wine, and Oil.'

23. The Consecrating Officer scatters Corn—the symbol of Plenty, saying:
'I scatter corn on this L. as a symbol of plenty and abundance. And may the blessing of morality and virtue increase under its auspices, producing fruit an hundredfold.'

24. *Musical Response:* 'Glory be to God on High.'

The Ceremonies (Consecration)

25. The Chaplain reads Ps. lxxii 16.
26. Before the second circuit the Brethren sing:

> 'When there a shrine to Him alone
>   They built, with worship sin to foil,
> On threshold and on Corner Stone
>   They poured out Corn, and Wine, and
>   Oil.'

27. The Consecrating Officer pours Wine—the symbol of Joy and Cheerfulness, saying:

> 'I pour wine on this Lodge as a symbol of joy and cheerfulness.'

28. *Musical Response:* 'Glory be to God on High.'
29. The Chaplain reads Neh. x 39.
30. Before the third circuit the Brethren sing:

> 'And we have come, fraternal bands,
>   With joy and pride, and prosperous
>   spoil,
> To honour Him by votive hands,
>   With streams of Corn, and Wine, and
>   Oil.'

31. The Consecrating Officer pours Oil—the symbol of Peace and Unanimity, saying:

> 'I sprinkle this Lodge with oil as a symbol of peace and unanimity.'

32. *Musical Response:* 'Glory be to God on High.'

33. The Chaplain reads Exod. xxx 25, 26.

34. Before the fourth circuit the Brethren sing:

'Now o'er our work this salt we shower,
Emblem of Thy conservant power;
And may Thy presence, Lord, we pray,
Keep this our temple from decay.'

35. The Consecrating Officer sprinkles Salt —the symbol of Fidelity and Friendship, saying:

'I scatter salt on this Lodge, the emblem of hospitality and friendship; and may prosperity and happiness attend this Lodge until time shall be no more.'

36. *Musical Response:* 'Glory be to God on High.'

37. The Chaplain reads Lev. ii 13.

38. *The Consecrating Officer dedicates the Lodge saying:*

'To God and His Service we dedicate this Lodge! and in memory of the three original G. Ms., under whose auspices many of our Masonic mysteries had their origin.'

39. *Anthem.*

'O how amiable are Thy dwellings, Thou Lord of Hosts! My soul hath a desire and longing to enter the courts of the Lord; my heart and my flesh rejoice in the living God. Blessed are they that dwell in Thy house: they shall be always praising Thee. Hallelujah!'

40. The Chaplain takes the Censer round the Lodge three times, saying:

'And Aaron shall burn thereon sweet incense every morning; when he dresseth the lamps, he shall burn incense upon it, and when Aaron lighteth the lamps at even, he shall burn incense upon it, a perpetual incense before the Lord throughout your generations.'

41. *Dedication Prayer (Second Portion)*

C. O.—'Grant, O Lord, that those who are now about to be invested with the government of this Lodge may be endued with wisdom to instruct their Brethren in all their duties: may brotherly Love, Relief, and Truth ever prevail amongst its members; and may this bond of union increase and strengthen the several Lodges throughout the world. Bless all our Brethren wherever dispersed over the face of the earth and water, and grant a speedy relief to all who are oppressed or distressed. We especially and affectionately commend to Thy especial care and attention all the members of the Fraternity; may they increase in knowledge of Thee, and love of each other. And, finally, may we finish all our work here below with Thy approbation; and then leave this earthly abode for Thy Heavenly Temple above, there to enjoy Light, Bliss, and Joy evermore.'

42. Chant (*Omnes*): 'So mote it be.'
The D. of C. then arranges the petitioning Brethren as before, on each side of the Lodge Board, when—

43. *The Consecrating Officer constitutes the Lodge, thus:*

'I now constitute this Lodge, denominated the.........Lodge, numbered ...... in the Register of the G. L. of England, through the blessing of Divine Providence, to the purposes of Freemasonry, and, in the name of the M. W. G. M., I constitute and form you, my good Brethren, into a Lodge of F. and A. Masons; henceforth I empower you to Initiate, Pass, or Raise Candidates for Freemasonry, and to perform all the Rites and Ceremonies conformably with the ancient Charges, and the Constitutions of the Order. And may the G. A. O. T. U. prosper, direct, and counsel you in all your proceedings.'

44. Chant (*Omnes*): 'So mote it be.'

45.   *Hymn*

'Glory to God on high!
Let heaven and earth reply,
    Praise ye His name.

Masons His love adore,
Arched in their mystic lore,
And cry out evermore,
    Glory to God!'

46.   *Patriarchal Benediction*

'The Lord bless and preserve thee;
The Lord make His face to shine upon
        thee,
    And be gracious unto thee;
The Lord lift up His countenance upon
        thee,
    And grant thee peace.'

47. Chant (*Omnes*): 'So mote it be.'

————————

(*End of Consecration Ceremony*.)

*   *   *   *

48. The Lodge is resumed in the Second Degree.

C. O. to D. of C.—Have you examined the M. nominated in the Warrant, and found him well skilled in the noble science, and duly instructed in our mysteries?

D. of C. to C. O.—I have.

C. O. to D. of C.—Then let him be presented in due form.

D. of C. to C. O.—R. W. M., I present to you Bro. A. B., to be installed Master of this Lodge, whom I believe to be of good morals and great skill, true and trusty, and a lover of the whole fraternity, and who, I feel assured, will discharge his duty with zeal and fidelity.

49. Installation of Worshipful Master.

* * * *

50. Election of Treasurer.
51. Election of Tyler.
52. Appointment and investiture of Officers.
53. Election of Committee to frame By-laws.
54. The W. M. rises for the first time.
   Votes of thanks to Consecrating Officers —Offers of Hon. Membership—Gift of Souvenirs, etc.
   Propositions for Initiation and Joining Members.

55. The W. M. rises for the second time.
56. The W. M. rises for the third time.
57. The Lodge is closed.

58. *Closing Ode*

'Now the evening shadows closing
    Warn from toil to peaceful rest,
Mystic arts and rites reposing
    Sacred in each faithful breast.
God of light! whose love unceasing
    Doth to all Thy works extend,
Crown our order with Thy blessing,
    Build, sustain us to the end.
Humbly now we bow before Thee,
    Grateful for Thine aid Divine.
Everlasting power and glory,
    Mighty Architect, be Thine.'

So mote it be.

59. Procession out of the Lodge as directed
by the Director of Ceremonies.

(G.) LAYING A FOUNDATION STONE, OR CHIEF CORNER STONE

As a rule some high dignitary of the Craft lays the stone. In this copy of the Ceremony the title of Provincial Grand Master will be used.

A Craft Lodge is opened in a convenient room, and there the procession is formed;

the Provincial Grand Director of Ceremonies, assisted by the local D. C., arranging the Brethren in the proper order.

The Provincial Grand Master having arrived at his station on a platform, a flourish of trumpets is given, or a hymn or an ode is sung, or music is played, as may have been arranged.

The Provincial Grand Master delivers an address, either composed to suit the occasion, or in general terms, as follows:

PROVINCIAL GRAND MASTER'S ADDRESS

Men and Brethren, here assembled to behold this Ceremony! Be it known unto you, that we be true and lawful Freemasons, the successors of those ancient Brethren of our Craft, who from time immemorial have been engaged throughout the civilized world in 'the erection of stately and superb edifices,' to the glory of God, and for the service of mankind! From those ancient Brethren have been handed down from generation to generation certain secrets 'by which Freemasons are known to each other, and distinguished from the rest of the world.' These secrets are lawful and honourable, and 'are in no way incompatible with our civil, moral, or religious duties'; and as we have received them from our predecessors in the Order, so we hand them down pure and unimpaired to those who are to succeed us.

Our Order has always been distinguished for loyalty to the Throne, for obedience to the laws and institutions of the country in which we reside, for good citizenship, for goodwill to all mankind, and especially for 'that most excellent gift—Charity!' By the exercise of these qualities we have in all ages enjoyed such distinction, that princes and nobles of high degree have been Members of our Order, 'have patronized our mysteries, and joined in our assemblies.' Under such powerful protection, and by the fidelity and zeal of its Members, Freemasonry has endured through the ages, and has been enabled 'to survive the wreck of mighty empires, and to resist the destroying hand of time.'

We have met here to-day, in the presence of this great assembly, to lay the [Chief Corner] Stone of this building, which is about to be erected to the honour and glory of the Most High, and in humble dependence upon His blessing.

As Freemasons, our first and paramount duty in all our undertakings is, to invoke the blessing from T. G. A. O. T. U. upon that which we are about to do; I therefore call upon you to give attention to the Provincial Grand Chaplain, and to unite in prayer to Him from Whom alone cometh every good and every perfect gift.

(*The stone will now be raised.*)

(*Prayer by the Provincial Grand Chaplain.*)

Chant (*Omnes*).—So mote it be.

P. G. M.—I now declare it to be my will and pleasure that the Chief Corner Stone of this building be laid. Bro. Provincial Grand Secretary, you will read the inscription on the plate. (*Which is done.*)

(*The stone will be lowered about nine inches: during the process of lowering the Choir will sing the first verse of 'Prosper the Art.'*)

SOLO

When the Temple's first stone was slowly
descending,
A stillness like death the scene reigned
around;
There thousands of gazers in silence were
bending,
Till rested the ponderous mass on the
ground.

CHORUS

Then shouts filled the air and the joy was
like madness,
The Founder alone, standing meekly
apart;

The Ceremonies (Laying Stone)

Until from his lips burst—flowing with
 gladness,
 The wish that for ever might prosper the
  Art.

P. G. M. — Bro. Provincial Grand
Treasurer, you will deposit the vessel containing the coins and other articles in the
cavity.

*(The Bottle containing the Parchment, with
an account of the undertaking, and the names
of the principal personages taking part in the
Ceremony, various current coins of the Realm,
and copies of local papers, will be placed in
the cavity. The cavity should now be filled
with powdered charcoal. The plate will then
be cemented in its place over all.)*

*(The Stone is again lowered nine inches,
during which the Choir will sing the second
verse of 'Prosper the Art.')*

SOLO

When the Temple had reared its magnificent
 crest,
 And the wealth of the world had em-
  bellished its walls,
The nations drew near from the East and
 the West,
 Their homage to pay in its beautiful
  halls.

CHORUS

Then they paused at the entrance, with
feelings delighted,
Bestowing fond looks ere they turned to
depart;
And as homeward they journeyed with
voices united,
They joined in full chorus, with 'Prosper
the Art.'

*(The Provincial Grand Master descends
from the platform, the trowel is presented to
him, with some appropriate remarks, and the
Provincial Grand Master spreads the cement.)*

*(Solemn music may be played, or the
'Gloria' may be sung, while the Stone is
lowered into its place.)*

P. G. M.—Bro. Junior Warden, what is
the Emblem of your Office?

J. W.—The Plumb-rule, Right Worshipful Provincial Grand Master.

P. G. M.—How do you apply the Plumb-rule?

J. W.—To try and adjust uprights, while
fixing them on their proper bases.

P. G. M.—Bro. Junior Warden, you will
apply the Plumb-rule to the sides of the
Stone. *(This is done.)*

J. W.—Right Worshipful Provincial Grand

The Ceremonies (Laying Stone)

Master, I find the Stone to be perfect and trustworthy.

P. G. M.—Bro. Senior Warden, what is the Emblem of your Office?

S. W.—The Level, Right Worshipful Provincial Grand Master.

P. G. M.—How do you apply the Level?

S. W.—To lay levels and prove horizontals.

P. G. M.—Bro. Senior Warden, you will prove the Stone. (*Done.*)

S. W.—Right Worshipful Provincial Grand Master, I find the Stone to be level and well founded.

P. G. M.—Worshipful Master, what is the Emblem of your Office?

W. M.—The Square, Right Worshipful Provincial Grand Master.

P. G. M.—How do you apply the Square?

W. M.—To try and adjust rectangular corners of buildings, and assist in bringing rude matter into due form.

P. G. M.—You will apply the Square. (*This is done.*)

W. M.—Right Worshipful Provincial Grand Master, I have applied the Square, and I find the Stone to be well wrought and true.

(*The Provincial Grand Master himself applies the Plumb-rule, the Level, and the Square.*)

P. G. M.—I find the Stone to be plumb, level, and square, and that the Craftsmen have laboured skilfully.

(*The mallet is presented to the Prov. G. M. with some appropriate remarks.*)

(*The Prov. G. M. gives three knocks on the Stone with the mallet.*)

P. G. M.—May T. G. A. O. T. U. look down with favour upon this undertaking, and may He crown the edifice of which we have laid the foundation with abundant success.

(*Flourish of Trumpets, or Music, or the Choir and the Assembly may sing the following Chant:*)

CHAPLAIN.—'Except the Lord build the house: their labour is but lost that build it.

'Except the Lord keep the city: the watchman waketh but in vain.

'It is in vain that ye rise up early, and late take rest: for so He giveth His beloved sleep.

'If the foundations be destroyed: what can the righteous do?

'Her foundations are upon the holy hills: the Lord loveth the gates of Zion more than all the dwellings of Jacob.

'That our sons may grow up as the young plants: and that our daughters may be as the polished corners of the temple.

The Ceremonies (Laying Stone)

'Happy is the people that is in such a case: yea, happy is that people whose God is the Lord.'

(*The Provincial Grand Superintendent of Works, or the Architect, presents the plans.*)

P. G. S. of W.—Right Worshipful Provincial Grand Master, it is my duty to present these Plans of the intended building, which have been duly approved.

(*The Provincial Grand Master inspects the Plans and returns them to the Architect.*)

P. G. M.—I place in your hands the Plans of the intended building, having full confidence in your skill as a Craftsman; and I desire that you will proceed without loss of time to the completion of the work, in conformity with the plans and designs now entrusted to you.

BEARER OF THE CORN.—Right Worshipful Provincial Grand Master, I present to you Corn, the sacred emblem of Plenty.

(*The P. G. M. strews Corn upon the Stone.*)

CHAPLAIN.—'There shall be a handful of corn in the earth upon the top of the mountains: the fruit thereof shall shake like Lebanon: and they of the city shall flourish like grass of the earth.' (*Psalm* lxxii 16.)

BEARER OF THE WINE.—Right Worshipful Provincial Grand Master, I present to you Wine, the sacred emblem of Truth.

(*The P. G. M. pours Wine on the Stone.*)

CHAPLAIN.—'And for a drink-offering thou shalt offer the third part of a hin of wine, for a sweet savour unto the Lord.' (*Numbers* xxviii 14.)

BEARER OF THE OIL.—Right Worshipful Provincial Grand Master, I present to you Oil, the sacred emblem of Charity.

(*The P. G. M. pours Oil upon the Stone.*)

CHAPLAIN.—'And thou shalt make it an oil of holy ointment, an ointment compound after the art of the apothecary: it shall be a holy anointing oil.

'And thou shalt anoint the tabernacle of the congregation therewith, and the ark of the testimony.' (*Exodus* xxx 25, 26.)

P. G. M. (*or Chaplain*).—May the All-bounteous Creator of the Universe shower down His choicest blessing upon this (*names the building*), and grant a full supply of the Corn of nourishment, the Wine of refreshment, and the Oil of Joy.

Chant (*Omnes*).—So mote it be.

(*The Provincial Grand Master reascends the platform. Some money for the workmen is placed on the Stone by the Provincial Grand Treasurer. If the building be for a charitable institution, a voluntary subscription is made in aid of its funds during the singing of the Anthem or Te Deum.*)

The Ceremonies (Laying Stone)

After which the Chaplain pronounces the

Benediction

CHAPLAIN.—May the Glorious Majesty of the Lord our God be upon us; prosper Thou the work of our hands upon us, yea, the work of our hands establish Thou it.

Chant (*Omnes*).—So mote it be.

(*The following Masonic Version of the National Anthem may be sung:*)

God save our gracious Queen,
Long live our noble Queen,
   God save the Queen.
Grant her victorious,
Happy and glorious,
Long to reign over us,
   God save the Queen.

Hail! mystic light Divine,
Long may thy radiance shine
   O'er sea and land.
Wisdom in thee we find,
Beauty and strength combined;
May we be ever joined
   In heart and hand.

Sing, then, ye Sons of Light,
In joyous strains unite,
   God save the Queen.

The Ceremonies

Long may Queen Elizabeth reign
Lord of the azure main.
Freemasons! swell the strain,
God save the Queen.

*   *   *   *

(*End of the Ceremony.*)
(*Procession, formed as before, returns to the place from which it started, and the Lodge is closed.*)

(H.) FUNERAL CEREMONY

(*To follow the usual funeral service of the religious denomination to which the deceased Brother belonged.*)

The Worshipful Master reads as follows:

Brethren.—The melancholy event which has caused us to assemble on the present occasion cannot have failed to impress itself on the mind of everyone present. The loss of a friend and Brother—especially of one whose loss we now deplore—conveys a powerful appeal to our hearts, reminding us as it does of the uncertainty of life, and of the vanity of earthly hopes and designs.

Amid the pleasures, the cares, and the various avocations of life we are too apt to forget that upon *us* also the common lot of all mankind must one day fall, and that Death's dread summons may surprise us even in the meridian of our lives, and in the full spring-tide of enjoyment and success.

The ceremonial observances which we practise during the obsequies of a departed Brother, are intended to remind us of our own 'inevitable destiny,' and to warn us that we also should be likewise ready, for we know not the day nor the hour when in the case of each of us 'the dust shall return to the earth as it was, and the spirit shall return unto God who gave it.'

Then, Brethren, let us lay these things seriously to heart; let us strive in all things to act up to our Masonic profession, to live in accordance with the high moral precepts inculcated in our Ceremonies, and to practically illustrate in our lives and our actions the ancient tenets and established customs of the Order. Thus, in humble dependence upon the mercy of the Most High, we may hope, when this transitory life, with all its cares and sorrows, shall have passed away, to rejoin this our departed friend and Brother in the Grand Lodge above, where the world's Great Architect lives and reigns for ever.

Chant (*Omnes*).—So mote it be.

(*The following supplications are then offered by the Master:*)

MASTER.—May we be true and faithful, and may we live in fraternal affection one towards another, and die in peace with all mankind.

RESPONSE (*to be sung*).—So mote it be.

MASTER.—May we practise that which is wise and good, and always act in accordance with our Masonic profession.

RESPONSE (*to be sung*).—So mote it be.

MASTER.—May the Great Architect of the Universe bless us, and direct us in all that we undertake and do in His Holy Name.

RESPONSE (*to be sung*).—So mote it be.

(*The Secretary then advances and throws his roll into the grave, while the Master repeats, in an audible voice.*)

MASTER.—Glory be to God on high! on earth peace! goodwill towards men!

RESPONSE (*to be sung*).—So mote it be, now, henceforth, and for evermore!

There is a calm for those who weep,
    A rest for weary pilgrims found;
They softly lie and sweetly sleep,
    Low in the ground! low in the ground!

The storm that wracks the winter sky
    No more disturbs their deep repose
Than summer evening's latest sigh,
    That shuts the rose! that shuts the rose!

The Ceremonies (Funerals)

Ah, mourner! long of storms the sport,
   Condemn'd in wretchedness to roam,
Hope thou shalt reach a sheltering port,
   A quiet home! a quiet home!

The sun is like a spark of fire,
   A transient meteor in the sky;
The soul, immortal as its sire,
   Shall never die! shall never die!

(The Master then concludes the ceremony at the grave in the following words:)

MASTER.—From time immemorial it has been the custom among the Fraternity of Free and Accepted Masons, at the request of a Brother on his death-bed, to accompany his corpse to the place of interment; and there to deposit his remains with the usual formalities of the Order. In conformity with this usage, and at the special request of our deceased Brother, whose loss we deeply deplore, we are here assembled as Freemasons, to consign his body to the earth, and, openly before the world, to offer up in his memory the last tribute of our fraternal affection, thereby demonstrating the sincerity of our esteem for our deceased Brother, and our inviolable attachment to the principles of the Order.

Freemasonry and its Etiquette

* [With all proper respect to the established customs of the country in which we live, with due deference to all in authority in Church and State, and with unlimited goodwill to all mankind, we here appear as Freemasons, clothed with the insignia of the Order, and publicly express our submission to order and good government, and our wish to promote the general interests of mankind. Invested with 'the badge of innocence, and the bond of friendship,' we humbly bow to the Universal Parent; we implore His blessing on our zealous endeavours to promote peace and goodwill; and we earnestly pray for His grace, to enable us to persevere in the *practice* of piety and virtue.]

The Great Creator having been pleased, in His infinite wisdom, to remove our worthy Brother from the cares and troubles of this transitory life, and thereby to weaken the ties by which we are united to the world, may *we* who survive him, anticipating *our* own approaching end, be more strongly cemented in the bonds of union and friendship, and, during the short space which is allotted to us in our present existence, may we wisely and usefully employ our time in

* The paragraph between the brackets [   ] may be omitted.

the interchange of kind and fraternal acts, and may we strive earnestly to promote the welfare and happiness of our fellow-men.

Unto the grave we have consigned the body of our deceased friend and Brother, there to remain until the general resurrection, in the fullest confidence that both body and soul will then arise to partake of the joys which have been prepared for the righteous from the beginning of the world. And may Almighty God of His infinite goodness, at the last grand tribunal, extend His mercy towards him, and all of *us*, and crown our hope with everlasting bliss, in the realms of a boundless eternity! This we beg, for the honour of His Name, to Whom be glory, now and for ever.

Chant (*Omnes*).—So mote it be.

It is decreed in heaven above,
That we, from those whom best we love,
    Must sever.
But hard the word would be to tell,
If to our friends we said farewell,
    For ever.

And thus the meaning we explain—
We hope, and be our hope not vain,
That, though we part, we meet again.
A brief farewell; then meet again
    For ever.

(Then the Brethren, led by the Worshipful Master, pass round the grave, and each Brother casts a sprig of acacia on the coffin.)

(End of Funeral Ceremony.)

Masonic Mourning

In the event of the death of any high dignitary in the Craft, an order is sent by the Grand Secretary to each Lodge that mourning shall be worn by every Brother for a certain period of time. In the case of a similar loss in a Province or District, the Provincial or District Grand Secretary would send a like order to every Lodge in his Province or District.

The regulation form of mourning dictated on these occasions is as follows: For Officers present and past of Grand Lodge, or of Provincial or District Grand Lodges, and for Officers of private Lodges, a black crape Rosette near the point of the collar above the jewel; and for all Master Masons, Officers included, a similar crape Rosette to cover the three blue Rosettes, one just above the point of the flap of the Apron, and one on each of the lower corners.

For Fellow-Crafts and Entered Apprentices, two black crape Rosettes, to cover the blue Rosettes on each corner of the bottom of the Apron.

Black or white ties, and white, or, *preferably*, grey gloves, with black stitchings, should be worn. In either case uniformity is much to be desired; on this point an expression of the wish of the Worshipful Master may be added to each circular.

If it be thought necessary or desirable that the Lodge-room should be put into mourning, the following plan or any portion thereof may be adopted:

Each of the three pedestals may have a black cloth cover to fit the top, with a fall round the front and the two sides eight inches deep, with a black bullion fringe of five inches round the lower edge.

The Master's and the two Wardens' chairs may have a cap of black cloth fitted to the shape of the top of the back of each chair, about twelve inches deep, fringed on the lower edge the same as the covers on the pedestals. The three candlesticks and the columns should each have a trimming of crape; so also should the Deacon's wands.

If the Banner of the Lodge be displayed, it should have a large black crape Rosette on or near the top of the staff, and one of the same size (or nearly) on each of the four corners. If there be cords and tassels, they may be trimmed with crape.

If the occasion justify any further demonstration of mourning, advantage may be taken of any salient portion of the room and the furniture, such as the tops of windows and doors, and the Secretary's table, the organ or harmonium, upon which crape or cloth may be placed. Much may depend upon the occasion of the mourning, whether it be for a high dignitary in the Craft (as previously mentioned), or for one of the then Principal Officers, or a Past Master of the Lodge.

In the case of the death of an ordinary member, it is unusual for the Lodge room to be put into mourning; the Brethren wear their crape Rosettes at the next meeting; and a letter of condolence to the family of the deceased, signed by the Master and the Wardens, is generally considered to be proper and sufficient. This mark of respect should not by any means be omitted.

(I) THE CEREMONY OF OPENING A PROVINCIAL OR DISTRICT GRAND LODGE

The Craft Lodge having been opened in the three Degrees, the Provincial or District Grand Master and the Provincial Grand

The Ceremonies (Prov. G. L.)

Officers, present and past, make their formal entry (see p. 70).

(We will use the initials of a Provincial Grand Master with the prefix of R. W. for Right Worshipful. A District Grand Master is also Right Worshipful. If a Deputy Provincial or Deputy District Grand Master should preside, he would be addressed as Very Worshipful, etc.)

R. W. P. G. M. (━▌ *followed by Provincial Grand Wardens*).—Brethren, assist me to open this Provincial Grand Lodge.

(All rise.)

R. W. P. G. M.—Bro. Provincial Grand Pursuivant, where is your situation in Provincial Grand Lodge?

P. G. P.—Within the Inner Porch of Provincial Grand Lodge Right Worshipful Provincial Grand Master.

R. W. P. G. M.—What is your duty?

P. G. P.—To give a proper report of all approaching Brethren, and to see that they are properly clothed and ranged under their respective banners.

R. W. P. G. M.—Do you find them so placed?

P. G. P.—To the best of my knowledge, Right Worshipful Provincial Grand Master.

R. W. P. G. M.—Where is the situation of the Provincial Junior Grand Warden?

P. G. P.—In the South, Right Worshipful Provincial Grand Master.

R. W. P. G. M.—Bro. Provincial Junior Grand Warden, whom do you represent?

P. J. G. W.—...., the Prince of the People on Mount Tabor.

R. W. P. G. M.—Bro. Provincial Junior Grand Warden, where is the situation of the Provincial Senior Grand Warden?

P. J. G. W.—In the West, Right Worshipful Provincial Grand Master.

R. W. P. G. M.—Bro. Provincial Senior Grand Warden, whom do you represent?

P. S. G. W.—...., the Assistant High Priest on Mount Sinai.

R. W. P. G. M.—Bro. Provincial Senior Grand Warden, where is the situation of the Deptuy Provincial Grand Master?

P. S. G. W.—At the right of the Right Worshipful Provincial Grand Master.

R. W. P. G. M.—Bro. Deputy Provincial Grand Master, whom do you represent?

D. P. G. M.—H. A. B., the Prince of Architects.

R. W. P. G. M.—What is your duty?

D. P. G. M.—To lay lines, draw designs, and assist the Right Worshipful Provincial Grand Master in the execution of the work.

R. W. P. G. M.—Very Worshipful Deputy

Provincial Grand Master, where is the situation of the Provincial Grand Master?

D. P. G. M.—In the East.

R. W. P. G. M.—Whom does he represent?

D. P. G. M.—The Royal Solomon, on his throne.

R. W. P. G. M.—Then, Brethren, after the Worshipful Bro. Chaplain has invoked the blessing of T. G. A. O. T. U., I shall, in the name of the Royal Solomon, declare this Provincial Grand Lodge open. (*All adopt the sign of R.*)

[*The Prayer by the Chaplain.*]

(*At the conclusion of the Prayer the Sn. of R. is 'dropped,' not 'drawn.'*)

R. W. P. G. M.—Brethren, in the name of the Royal Solomon, I declare this Provincial Grand Lodge opened in due* form. (⬛ *followed by the Provincial Grand Wardens; the Provincial Grand Pursuivant gives ks., and the Tyler replies.*)

*   *   *   *

P. G. D. of C.—Brethren, I call upon you to salute the Right Worshipful Provincial Grand Master with seven, taking the time from me. To order, Brethren!

(*All present, including Provincial Grand Officers, give the Gr. or R. Sn. seven times.*)

* See No. 79, 'Book of Constitutions.'

Freemasonry and its Etiquette

P. G. D. of C.—Brethren, I call upon you to salute the Very Worshipful Deputy Provincial Grand Master with five, taking the time from me. To order, Brethren!

(*All present give the Gr. or R. Sn. five times. Then the Provincial Grand Officers sit down.*)

P. G. D. of C.—Brethren, I call upon you to salute the Provincial Grand Officers past and present, with three, taking the time from me. To order, Brethren!

(*This is done by those who have remained standing.*)

P. G. D. of C.—Brethren, be seated.

CEREMONY OF CLOSING PROVINCIAL OR DISTRICT GRAND LODGE

R. W. P. G. M. (▬▌ *followed by Provincial Grand Wardens*).—Brethren, assist me to close this Provincial Grand Lodge.

(*All rise*)

R. W. P. G. M.—Bro. Provincial Grand Pursuivant, prove the Provincial Grand Lodge close tyled. (*This is done.*)

P. G. P. (with Sn.).—Right Worshipful Provincial Grand Master, the Provincial Grand Lodge is close tyled.

(*The Ceremony proceeds exactly as in the opening.*)

(*At the proper moment all adopt the Sn. of R.*)

The Ceremonies (Prov. G. L.)

[*Prayer and Praise by the Chaplain.*]

(*At the conclusion of Prayer and Praise the Sn. of R. is 'dropped,' not 'drawn.'*)

R. W. P. G. M.—Brethren, in the name of the Royal Solomon, I declare this Provincial Grand Lodge closed in due* form. (*Gives the* ▬Ḻ, *followed by the Prov. Grand Wardens.*) (*The Provincial Grand Master, followed by his Officers present and past, leaves the Lodge, the Brethren all standing, and the Organist performing his duty.*)

(*End of Ceremony of Closing Provincial or District Grand Lodge.*)

*   *   *   *

(*The Worshipful Master, and the Officers, resume their several places, and the Craft Lodge is closed in three Degrees.*)

(J) CEREMONIES OF OPENING AND CLOSING GRAND LODGE

The Ceremonies of Opening† and Closing Grand Lodge are precisely the same as detailed on pp. 270-274, except that—

1. The Pro-Grand Master is styled *Most Worshipful*.
2. The words 'Provincial' are omitted.
3. Grand Lodge is not 'proved close tyled.'

* See No. 79, 'Book of Constitutions.'
† See No. 51, 'Book of Constitutions.'

CHAPTER XX

THE CHAPLAIN AND HIS DUTIES

THE Constitutions provide that the Master 'may' also appoint a Chaplain; and in any Lodge which has among its members a duly qualified Brother, it is desirable that a Chaplain should be appointed; and, as a matter of course, all the devotional portions of the opening and the closing in each Degree and in each of the three Ceremonies would then be performed by him. The impressiveness and the solemnity of the whole proceedings may be enhanced by having a Chaplain to perform those important duties.

The following optional address may be delivered to the Chaplain on his investiture:

(W. M.) 'W. Bro......., I appoint you Chaplain of the Lodge, and now invest you with the Jewel of your Office, the Open Book. This represents the Volume of the Sacred Law, which is always open upon the Master's Pedestal when the Brethren are at labour in the Lodge. The V. of the S. L. is the greatest of the three great, though emblematical, lights in Freemasonry. The Sacred

The Chaplain and his Duties

Writings are given as the rule and guide of our Faith. The Sacred Volume will guide us to all Truth, direct our steps in the paths of Happiness, and point out to us the whole Duty of man. Without it the Lodge is not "just"; and without an openly avowed belief in its Divine Author, no Candidate can be lawfully initiated into our Order. Your place in the Lodge is near the Worshipful Master, and as, both in the opening and the closing of the Lodge in each Degree, as well as in each of the three Ceremonies, the blessing of the Almighty is invoked on our proceedings, it will be your duty, as far as may be possible, to attend all the meetings of the Lodge, in order that you may exercise your sacred office in the devotional portions of our Ceremonies.'

*   *   *   *

If the Chaplain recites the Prayers, he must follow the Worshipful Master in this manner:

OPENINGS

First Degree

W. M.—The Lodge being duly formed before I declare it open. . . .

CHAPLAIN.—. . . . let us invoke, etc. . . . . harmony.

I. P. M.—So mote it be.

Second Degree

W. M.—Before we open the Lodge in the Second Degree. . . .

CHAPLAIN.—. . . . let us supplicate, etc. . . . science.

I. P. M.—So mote it be.

Third Degree

W. M.—We will assist you to repair that loss. . . .

CHAPLAIN.—. . . . and may Heaven aid our united endeavours!

I. P. M.—So mote it be.

CLOSING

First Degree

W. M.—Brethren, before we close the Lodge. . . .

CHAPLAIN.—. . . . let us, with all reverence, etc. . . . . . virtue.

I. P. M.—So mote it be.

CHAPTER XXI

THE DIRECTOR OF CEREMONIES AND HIS DUTIES

THE Director of Ceremonies is not a 'regular' Officer of a Lodge, and no place is assigned to him in the Recognized Ritual of the Regular Ceremonies of Initiation, Passing, Raising, and Installation.

Nevertheless, a capable Director of Ceremonies is of great advantage to any Lodge which appoints him. His duties are multifarious and onerous, and his influence for good can be made to extend to every department of Lodge working.

It is very desirable that he should be a Past Master, not only by reason of the experience he has gained in serving the various offices, but because a continuity of service in that capacity is important.

He should, of course, be well versed in the Ritual and in the requirements of the various degrees, so as to guard against all imperfection in the ceremonies.

It is he who organizes the processions in and out of the Lodge, receives the visitors and assigns to them their correct precedence in the Lodge, and at table; settles all questions of etiquette among the Brethren; and contributes to the dissipation of difficulties when they arise.

He will probably be consulted by the Worshipful Master on points of procedure; and on the order of business; and if any Officer should be prevented, by the pressing emergencies of his avocation, from fulfilling his duties, he will most probably be asked to advise as to a substitute.

In the Ceremony of Consecration important duties are assigned to him, and in public ceremonial he is, of course, an indispensable factor.

One important duty attached to the Office of Director of Ceremonies is 'to marshal all processions and demonstrations of the Brethren.' We may remark in connection with this subject that a rule exists which gives to the Rulers of the Order the power to put a check upon too frequent public demonstrations of the Brethren. Rule No. 178 of the Book of Constitutions expressly states that no Brother shall appear in Masonic clothing in public without a dispensation from the Grand Master or the Provincial or District Grand Master.

As a matter of course, the petition for a

Dispensation would set forth fully and clearly the object of the demonstration. The petition would necessarily be sent to the Grand Secretary, or in the Provinces or Districts to the Provincial or District Grand Secretary, as indeed etiquette demands that all written communications to the high dignitaries mentioned should invariably be so sent.

One general rule would appear to apply to the marshalling of all processions of our Order, some details being occasionally superadded to suit the varying purposes of the demonstration. The Tyler, with a drawn sword, heads the procession; next follow Entered Apprentices two and two; then Fellow-Crafts, followed by the Master Masons, juniors leading; next the Assistant Officers of the Lodge, the lowest first; then Past Masters, juniors first; next the Immediate Past Master; the Banner of the Lodge; the Worshipful Master, supported on the right by the Senior Warden, and on the left by the Junior Warden, each of the Wardens carrying his Column. After these come Provincial or District Grand Officers, the lower in rank going first, Grand Officers bringing up the rear; among the Provincial, or District, or Grand Officers, being probably the one appointed to perform the Ceremony, if any. He would be in the last rank, supported on each side by Brethren of distinction and of high rank in the Craft.

It is necessary that all (except those mentioned as being supported right and left) should form *two deep*, as will be seen in the next sentence. On arriving at the appointed place, the Tyler halts, and the whole of the Brethren, down to, but not including, the rear rank, separate and form two lines. Those in the rear rank walk forward between the lines, and each two of the Brethren as they are reached fall in behind, and so on until the whole order of the procession is inverted, and those—the juniors—who were first, become the last.

*   *   *   *

If the occasion be the laying of a foundation, or Chief Corner Stone, the requisite number of distinguished Brethren are appointed to bear the Square, the Level, and the Plumb-rule, the Heavy Mall, and the Trowel, the Corn, the Wine, and the Oil. Others carry the bottle containing the coins, etc., the brass plate with the inscription, and whatever else it may be thought necessary to carry in the procession. The Architect carries the plans of the building.

If the edifice to be erected be a Church or

Church Schools, the open Bible with the Square and Compasses is carried frequently by the Tyler. A board of the necessary size, covered probably with crimson velvet or cloth, with a cushion upon it, would be provided. Two broad straps or ribbons passed over the Tyler's shoulders would enable him to carry the whole with perfect ease, and he would have his right hand free to carry the sword.

On one occasion the open Bible was carried upon a board made for the purpose, having four handles extending horizontally, two in front and two at the back. The bearers were four little boys, *each boy a Lewis.* Nothing in the whole procession attracted so much interest as those four little bearers of the Bible, all apparently under ten years of age. The Deputy Provincial Grand Master who laid the Chief Corner Stone, afterwards sent an enduring memento of the occasion to each of the boys. It would be interesting to know if they—or any of them—eventually became Freemasons.

Once the members of a Lodge in the far West of England erected a Masonic Hall. The Chief Corner Stone was laid by the Deputy Provincial Grand Master, assisted by a number of Provincial Grand Officers. One of these of high rank regulated the whole proceedings. On that occasion the Tracing Board of the First Degree, on a light frame with four handles—an enlarged edition of that mentioned in the preceding paragraph—ornamented white and gold, was carried by four Past Masters of the Lodge. This Tracing Board was supposed to represent the Lodge in a symbolic sense.

It would probably have been more correct to have had the three Tracing Boards. At the Consecration of a Lodge in a large public building—not the Lodge-room—the three Tracing Boards, piled (horizontally) one upon another, were placed upon a stand in the centre of the hall, presumably representing the Lodge. A Very Worshipful Brother, high in Office in Grand Lodge, was the Presiding Officer; the Wardens were also Very Worshipful Members of Grand Lodge, and the then Grand Director of Ceremonies assisted, so no doubt can be entertained of the strictly correct manner in which everything was carried out.

Customs, however, vary in different Provinces, and a practice which is held to be strictly correct in one Province would be utterly condemned in another. In all cases of Public Ceremonial, if any doubt or difficulty should arise, application should be made to the Grand or Provincial, or District

The Director of Ceremonies and his Duties

Grand Secretary, according to locality, for counsel and guidance.

When the chief Functionary is the Provincial, or District Grand Master, or his Deputy, or any of his past or present Officers specially appointed to officiate in his stead, the Provincial, or District Grand Secretary, would, as a rule, take the control of the proceedings, assisted, of course, by the Officers of the Lodge, or Lodges, chiefly interested in the Ceremony to be performed. In the case of the Grand Master himself, or the Pro-Grand Master, or the Deputy Grand Master, or other high Officer of Grand Lodge officiating, the Grand Secretary would dictate the course of the proceedings, and would give his instructions to the Brethren who, under him, would have the charge of the preparations.

The Ceremony of laying a Foundation, or Chief Corner, Stone will be found on pp. 251 to 264.

*   *   *   *

One other occasion for a 'public procession of Freemasons clothed with the Badges of the Order' is a Masonic funeral. Widely divergent opinions will be found to exist in different Provinces, and even in different portions of the same Province, as to the desirability, or otherwise, of continuing the

285

practice of this undoubtedly ancient custom in the Craft. In some Provinces it may be considered obsolete, or is possibly almost, or altogether unknown.

In one Province, where the custom of burying with Masonic Ceremonial was rather frequently practised, a feeling adverse to the custom was known to exist on the part of some two or three Provincial Grand Officers (not the highest in authority), and an attempt was made to pass a resolution in Provincial Grand Lodge interdicting the practice in that Province; the motion, however, was negatived by a substantial majority, chiefly representative of Lodges favourable to its continuance.

Very much may be said upon both sides of the question. Of its lawfulness there is no doubt whatever; it is upon its expediency that the doubt may arise. As supplementary to the comprehensive and beautiful Burial Service of the Church of England, the tacking on of our Masonic Service at the end appears to many to be a supererogatory proceeding; to some an anti-climax. Many, on the other hand, especially older members of the Craft, regard it with an extreme reverence, and believe in its impressiveness and solemnity, and in its possibly lasting good effect upon the hearers.

The Director of Ceremonies and his Duties

Three cases may here be cited. A Nonconformist Brother, a zealous Freemason, and an old Past Master, had—on his deathbed (a necessary condition)—expressed the desire to be buried with Masonic Ceremonial. A programme of the full Ceremony was furnished, a few days previously to the funeral, to the minister who was to officiate on the occasion. He, the minister, being bound by no rule or Ritual, so composed and arranged his portion of the service as to lead up to and to fit in with the Masonic Ceremony. The result was that all went admirably and harmoniously as two component parts of one perfect whole. There was no incongruity, no superfluity.

The second case was that of the oldest Past Master in the district in which he had spent a long and active life; he had been highly distinguished in Freemasonry for many years, and had borne high office in Provincial Grand Lodge. He had a long, lingering illness, the fatal result of which he never doubted. He repeated his wish again and again, that his obsequies should be performed with Masonic Rites.

The interment took place in a country churchyard, near to the birthplace of the deceased. The Vicar (who had been made fully aware that some Masonic Ceremonial would be performed), immediately upon the conclusion of the Burial Service of the Church, took his departure, without a word, and remained in the vestry until those concerned went in to pay the fees, after the conclusion of the Masonic Ceremony. Very many present, including a number of non-Freemasons, considered that the Vicar had showed a bigoted and intolerant spirit. It is possible, however, that he acted in accordance with his conscientious convictions; he probably felt that a service, not sanctioned by the Church, should not be performed upon ground consecrated by the Church. Such a view may be narrow; but if it be conscientiously held, it is entitled to respect.

The third instance was the interment of the remains of a Provincial Grand Master—a man of mark in his county, a territorial magnate, and a zealous Freemason. A very large gathering of the Brethren of the deceased's own and of the neighbouring Province assembled, including the majority of the then present and past Provincial Grand Officers. A choir—Freemasons, with some female voices—had been provided. Two at least of the sons of the deceased, who were Freemasons, were 'clothed with the Badges of the Order.' The aged widow sat by the grave-side. The Burial Services of the Church and that of our Order were admirably rendered—there appeared no want of harmony between them; the effect of the whole was solemn and impressive in a high degree. The clergy remained throughout, up to the end. The eldest son became Grand Master of his Province, and a Warden in Grand Lodge.

The foregoing have been given here in order to show that the advocates for the retention of the custom in question are not without precedents, supplying good arguments in favour of their views: that the practice—if it be at all an anachronism—is not obsolete; that men of high degree, as well as those of a lower grade, continue to express the wish that the Brethren with whom they have been associated in life should join with their immediate connections in 'paying this last sad tribute of respect to departed merit.'

The fact, also (previously mentioned), should not be lost sight of, that no such Ceremony, nor, indeed, any demonstration of Freemasons (in clothing), can take place without the permission of the Grand Master, or of those to whom he may delegate the authority to grant dispensations for such public occasions. The power of veto therefore always rests with the authorities, and we may presume that in every case good cause must be shown for the application or it would not be granted.

(See Masonic Mourning, p. 268.)

CHAPTER XXII

THE ORGANIST AND HIS DUTIES

THE adoption of instrumental music is on the increase; hence the office of Organist has become much less of a sinecure than it used to be. It is not a regular office; the Organist being one of those whom the Worshipful Master 'may' appoint. His duties are set forth in the following optional address, which may be delivered to him when he is invested with the jewel of his Office, as follows:

'Bro....., I appoint you Organist of the Lodge, and I now invest you with the Jewel of your Office. The Lyre is the emblem of Music; one of the seven liberal Arts and Sciences, the study of which is inculcated in the Fellow-Crafts' Degree. The records of Ancient History, both sacred and secular, testify that from the earliest times Music has borne a more or less important part in the celebration of religious rites and ceremonies; that Pagans and Monotheists, the Ancient Hebrews, and the more comparatively modern Christians, have in all Ages made full and free use of music, as an aid to devotion, and in the expression of praise and thanksgiving in the services of their several systems of religion. In like manner Freemasonry, from the earliest period of its history, has availed itself of the aid of music in the performance of its rites and ceremonies; and we must all feel how much of impressiveness and solemnity is derived from the judicious introduction of instrumental music into those ceremonies. Music has been defined as "the concord of sweet sounds." In this aspect it typifies the concord and harmony which have always been among the foremost characteristics of our Order. Your Jewel, therefore, the emblem of Concord, should stimulate us to promote and to maintain concord, goodwill, and affection, not only among the members of our own Lodge, but with all Brethren of the Craft.'

* * * *

A few words must, however, be added upon the subject of the musical services in the three degrees.

Any Brother who visits other Lodges is able to mark the contrast between a Ceremony performed with accompanying instrumental music, and one without that accompaniment, and in which the voice of

The Organist and his Duties

the Worshipful Master alone is heard from the beginning to the end, with only the slight break here and there of the little which the Wardens have to say. The impression made upon the mind of the Candidate by the musical addition to the Ceremony is far deeper, and consequently is calculated to be far more enduring than that formed by a Ceremony unrelieved by the effect of the Divine Art of Music.

Great care must be taken to exercise this art within the boundaries of the Constitutions.

At one time there was a tendency to introduce the singing of hymns and anthems during the ceremonies, the perambulations, and at certain noticeable points.

This was dangerous. Masonry is universal, and finds adherents among the followers of many creeds, demanding from them only the common acknowledgment of a supreme Governor of the Universe.

Hymns and anthems, therefore, which would seem innocuous to some might contain words and references which, if vocalized, would offend others; and thus friction might arise.

It was in these circumstances that on April 20, 1875, the Board of General Purposes passed a resolution that: 'Hymns form no part of the Masonic Ritual; and the singing of hymns in a Lodge is an innovation to which the Board of General Purposes strongly objects.'

On June 17, 1902, there was a Resolution of the Board of General Purposes reaffirming above; and on September 3, 1902, a similar Resolution was reported by the Board of General Purposes to Grand Lodge, and adopted.

There is no objection to singing the Masonic Opening Ode before the Lodge is opened; and none to singing the Masonic Closing Ode after the Lodge is closed.

There is no objection to chanting 'So mote it be' at the conclusion of the Prayers because that is part of the Ritual.

What is objected to is the interpolation of words not found in the Ritual. Thus, while there is no objection to the Organist playing a kyrie eleison at the conclusion of the Obn., there is objection to the Brethren singing the words, although free from dogma.

The plain rule to be deduced is therefore that no words other than those used in the Ritual may be sung in any part of the ceremonies.

There are many points in the ceremony when the introduction of suitable instrumental music is very useful; but it should always be unobtrusive, furnishing a gentle accompaniment to a solemn occasion; in fact, when it becomes noticeable it is a nuisance.

*   *   *   *

Besides the musical portions of the ceremonies within the Lodge, it often becomes the pleasurable duty of the Organist to arrange and supervise the musical entertainment during and following the Banquet.

On important occasions, such as Installation, professional artistes are usually engaged by the W. M.; but on ordinary occasions it is possible to construct an enjoyable programme by the aid of the talent of the members. (See p. 355.)

This scheme of pleasure is not restricted to musical performance. Many greatly varying items may be included—*e.g.*, Anecdotes, Glees, Part Songs, Recitations, Sleight-of-hand, Records of Travel, Masonic Facts, and even Masonic Fictions.

It is respectfully submitted that so-called 'comic songs' should be rigidly avoided, and that no 'smoking-room stories' of questionable colour should be permitted.

CHAPTER XXIII

THE TYLER AND HIS DUTIES

IT will be convenient at this stage of our work to consider in some detail the multifarious duties of that very useful Officer the Tyler, some of whose duties will be found to have a distinct bearing upon our subject.

We will first, however, discuss briefly the Tyler himself, and consider what manner of man he should be. Experience gained in a number of different Lodges enables one to divide them into at least three classes.

The first of these would consist of old Past Masters. These are now comparatively few in number, and are gradually becoming more and more rarely to be found. These may be subdivided into two classes, one class consisting of those who continue to subscribe to the Lodge, and are unwilling to be out of Office, and who perform the duties of Tyler with perfect efficiency without fee or reward. The other subdivision will include those 'who perhaps from circumstances of unavoidable calamity,' etc., are glad to retain their connection with

The Tyler and his Duties

Freemasonry by serving the Office of Tyler, the fees of membership being remitted, and the small emoluments of the Office being of value to them in their low estate.

The second main division would comprise members of certain Lodges in which it is the custom to have no permanent Tyler, paid or otherwise, that Office being year by year filled by a junior member, and constituting the first step upon the Official ladder, and without which no one can attain to any higher Office.

This custom has certain advantages. It goes to the very root of the matter, and if the aspirant should go on step by step through all the gradations of Office, until he attains to the chair of Worshipful Master, his experience will be unquestionable, and he will have the satisfaction of feeling that, having begun at the very beginning, he has literally worked his way upward to the Chair. Against this custom may be set the disadvantages of the want of age and of experience in the work of the Lodge. Zeal and ability, care and attention, will, however, soon enable even the youngest in experience to perform his duty with a fair degree of efficiency and success.

The third, and by far the most numerous division, will comprise those who are paid for their services (excluding the second sub-division of the Past Masters mentioned in the first division). Some of these are Initiated with this express intention. They are called 'serving brethren,' and in many Lodges they act as waiters at Banquets, etc. Where Lodges are held in Hotels, it is not unfrequently thought desirable to initiate one of the waiters (preferably the head of his department), but in this case he does not always undertake the duties of Tyler.

Other paid Tylers are older Freemasons (who have not passed the Chair) who have fallen upon evil days, and who are glad to serve the Lodge in a humble capacity, and to receive the small emoluments of the Office, and who rank as ordinary members of the Lodge, but without paying any subscriptions. These are as a rule faithful and efficient Officers, zealous and energetic in the performance of their duties.

Some mention should be made of those who have formerly been members of Military Lodges—generally pensioners—and, foremost among these, retired non-commissioned officers are especially to be commended. If they possess medals and a goodly number of clasps, and have testimonials of good conduct, as most of them have, so much the better. Old soldiers, if they have encouraged habits of sobriety, may be depended upon to keep sober under all circumstances. They have in addition learned the lesson of perfect obedience. They have been accustomed to rigid discipline, and have become strict disciplinarians themselves, and when— in the event of any public procession of the Order—they march at the head of their Lodge, they handle the sword and set and maintain the pace as few civilians are able to do.

*   *   *   *

The duties defined in the address to the Tyler at his Investiture, and partially repeated by the Junior Warden in the opening of the Lodge in the First Degree, are these: 'To see that the Candidates are properly prepared; to give the proper reports on the door of the Lodge, when candidates, members, or visitors require admission; to keep off all intruders and cowans to masonry, and suffer none to pass but such as are duly qualified.'

In addition to the before-named duties of a Tyler, others of equal importance and indispensably necessary to the working of the Lodge, and to the convenience of the Officers and Brethren, come within the scope of his supervision. The furniture and implements, the collars and jewels, and, in short, all the belongings of the Lodge, are under his care, and he is responsible for their being kept always in good condition. He has to prepare the Lodge for all its meetings, and to see that everything that can be required in each Degree shall be in its proper place ready for use.

The Tyler's multifarious duties have much to do with 'Freemasonry and its Etiquette,' which may be freely rendered, as 'the right way in which to do the right thing, at the right time, and in the right place.' This, applied to the work of the Lodge through the several Degrees, will show that the Tyler, in the preparation of the Lodge, and in providing that everything that can possibly be wanted shall be in its proper place, has a very close connection with the subject of this treatise.

Foremost among all the duties previously detailed, must be mentioned the duty of the preparation of the Candidates in each of the Degrees, and of a thorough comprehension of the theory and practice of the Ks. or proper reports on the door of the Lodge. The word 'theory' may well be applied to both these subjects, for one can seldom go wrong in the practice of either of them if one knows the reason why a certain form is practised at one time and not at another. These subjects will be discussed in the following pages.

*　　*　　*　　*

PREPARATION OF CANDIDATES

Attention may here be called to the desirability of the Director of Ceremonies (or some Past Master) leaving the Lodge and superintending the preparation of the Candidates in each Degree, or, at least, inspecting them before they claim admission. The Tyler is liable to have his attention distracted by members or visitors coming or going, by having to answer the Ks. upon the door when the Lodge is being opened in the higher Degrees; and in many ways his thoughts may be diverted from the work in hand; and a mistake may be made in the preparation of the Candidate, however efficient generally the Tyler may be.

Another equally cogent reason may be given for the Tyler having the assistance of some Past Master. In the preparation of a Candidate for the Ceremony of Initiation, there are certain processes which may well cause some surprise in the mind of a stranger. In such a case—perhaps it would be well to say in all cases—it is desirable that a Past Master should assure the Candidate that nothing is being done without a meaning; that there is a good historical or traditional reason for every detail; and that in due time the whole will be explained, and will be made perfectly clear to him.

Probably some few of the Officers and Brethren who witness or assist at this preparation of a Candidate for Initiation are themselves partially, or even totally, unaware of these reasons. In order that such of those as may read these pages may be instructed upon this subject, and that when in office they may be enabled to give the assurance contained in the previous paragraph with perfect truthfulness, a full explanation, of the origin of and the reasons for the several processes of the preparation, is here given.

Preparation in the First Degree

The following explanation consists chiefly of excerpts from the second section of the First Lecture.

The Candidate is divested of m....l and h. w. d., his r. a. l. b. and k. m. b., his r. h. s. s. and a c. t. placed about his n.

He is divested of all m....l, firstly, that he may bring nothing offensive or defensive into the Lodge to disturb its harmony; secondly, having been received into Freemasonry in a state of p....y, he should always thereafter be mindful of his duty to relieve indigent Brethren, as far as may be consistent with his own circumstances in life, and with the needs, and more especially with the merits, of the applicant; and thirdly, because at the erection of King Solomon's Temple 'there was not heard the sound of metallic tool.' Following the pious example of King Solomon at the building of the Temple, we do not permit the Candidate to enter the Lodge with any metallic substance about him, except such as may necessarily belong to the articles of clothing which he may have upon him.

In 1872 the then Grand Secretary, Bro. Hervey, wrote a letter, *with the personal approval of the Grand Master*, stating 'that in the present day the rule was to be taken to represent metals of value, money, or weapons.'

The Candidate is h. w., firstly, that in the event of his refusal to go through any of the Ceremonies which are usual in the Initiation of a Freemason, he may be led out of the Lodge without discovering its form; secondly, as he is admitted into Freemasonry in a s. of d., it should remind him to keep all the world so with respect to our Masonic mysteries, unless they come legally by them, as he is then about to do; and, thirdly, that his heart may conceive before his eyes are permitted to discover.

The r. a. of the Candidate is m. b., to show that he is able and ready to labour; his l. b. is made b., so that nothing may be interposed between it and the p. of the P. extended thereto by the Inner Guard at the door of the Lodge; and further, in order to distinguish beyond a doubt the sex of the Candidate. The l. k. is m. b., in accordance with the immemorial custom of the Order, which prescribes that the Obn. of an Entered Apprentice shall always be taken upon the l. k. b. and b.

The r. h. is s. s., in allusion to a certain passage of Scripture, where the Lord spake thus to Moses from the Burning Bush: 'Put off thy shoes from thy feet, for the place whereon thou standest is holy ground.'

The Candidate has a c. t., with a r. n. about his n., to render any attempt at retreat equally fatal.

This completes the preparation in the First Degree, and, being thus properly prepared, he is conducted to the door of the L., where, after having sought in his mind, asked of his friends, and knocked, the door of Freemasonry is opened to him, and after strict examination he is admitted.

The Tyler and his Duties

Then, after solemn prayer, being neither naked nor clothed, barefoot nor shod, but in an humble, halting, moving posture, the Candidate is led round the Lodge, figuratively to represent his seeming state of poverty and distress.

PREPARATION IN THE SECOND DEGREE

The Candidate's preparation in the Second Degree is in a manner somewhat similar to the former, save that in this degree he is not h. w. His l. a. b. and r. k. are m. b. and his l. h. s. s. He is admitted by the Ks. of an E. A. on the S.

PREPARATION IN THE THIRD DEGREE

The Candidates b. as b. bs. and b. ks. are m. b. and b. hs. s.s. He is admitted by the Ks. of a F. C. on b. ps. of the Cs. presented to b. bs.

*   *   *   *

REPORTS

The next subject in connection with the duties of the Tyler which demands our attention is the series of Ks. or reports on the door of the Lodge. Either from carelessness or from an innate maladroitness, the Ks. are too often jumbled, or so imperfectly sounded as to necessitate correction, which to a great extent interferes with the smooth and correct working of the Lodge. The Ks. severally of the three Degrees are simple in the extreme, and when the theory of their arrangement is once understood, a mistake need never be made in giving them.

When a Candidate for Initiation is conducted to the door, the Ks. of the Can. must be given by the Tyler, in allusion to an ancient and venerable exhortation: seek and ye shall find; ask, and ye shall have; knock, and it shall be opened unto you.'

(See remarks on p. 161.)

When a Candidate for Passing is brought to the door (the Lodge being at that time open in the Second Degree), the Ks. of the First Degree should be given, in order that the Brethren within the Lodge may be warned that one who is not a Fellow-Craft is seeking admission.

The same reason exactly applies to the Third Degree. When the Candidate for Raising is brought to the door the Ks. of the Second Degree should be given, and the Brethren within the Lodge are thereby informed that the Candidate (necessarily a Fellow-Craft) seeks admission.

The Tyler and his Duties

In brief; for a Candidate in the First Degree the Ks. of the Can.; for a Candidate in the Second Degree, the Ks. of an Entered Apprentice; and for a Candidate in the Third Degree, the Ks. of a Fellow-Craft.

When the Lodge is open in the First Degree, for a member or a well-known Visitor seeking admission, the Ks. of the E.A. Degree are given by the Tyler. In the Second Degree, for a member or a visitor who is known to have taken that Degree, the Ks. of the F.C. Degree are given. In the Third Degree for a member or visitor those of the M.M. are given. In each and in all of these cases the Ks. so given are respectively the Ks. of the Degree in which the Lodge is opened at that particular time.

In the case of late comers, the Tyler should be particularly careful not to disturb the Lodge by making his announcement on the door of the Lodge at an inconvenient moment. If, for example, a ceremony is in progress, it must not be interrupted except at recognized points; and, however important the late arrival may be, the Tyler must remember that the interests of the Candidate are even more important.

*   *   *   *

Admission of Visitors

Pleased as we are to receive Visitors, their admission into our Lodges should be the subject of careful attention.

The W. M. promises that no Visitor shall be received into his Lodge without due examination and producing proper vouchers of his having been initiated in a Regular Lodge.

Most of our Visitors are naturally our own friends who are members of English Lodges, and about them there is no need to say anything. The fact that they are introduced by members of the Lodge is ample warranty, and quite sufficient authority to the Tyler to announce them. But occasionally come Visitors from other Constitutions, and then arises the necessity for caution. In the event of a stranger professing to be a Freemason seeking admission, the Tyler should immediately summon the Junior Warden to his aid, so that the responsibility of either granting or refusing admission to the Lodge may not rest upon himself alone. Etiquette, even ordinary politeness, requires that a probably well-qualified Brother shall not be turned back simply upon the *ipse dixit* of the Tyler, but that one of the Principal Officers of the Lodge—that is, the Junior Warden—shall be the arbiter in such a case.

The Tyler and his Duties

It is not sufficient that the Brother himself should express his belief in the G. A. O. T. U. He must have been initiated on the V. S. L. in a Lodge acknowledging the same supremacy. There is no compromise possible, and no exception may be made. All strangers must be proved with Masonic rigidity, and the Tyler must suffer none to pass but such as are duly qualified.

*　　*　　*　　*

A custom appears to prevail in the United States of admitting strangers who profess to be Freemasons, but who have no friend or acquaintance to vouch for them, who have with them no certificate, and who apparently are subjected to little or no examination, but who nevertheless are received into the Lodge upon taking that which they call the Tyler's obligation. This is, in plain English, the meaning of the words in italics in the following extract from Bro. Dr. Mackey's Masonic Law. The words mentioned are capable of being thus paraphrased: '. . . they may still be admitted by the production of their certificate, or by an examination as to their knowledge of Freemasonry; or, dispensing with both these safeguards, they may be admitted by the Tyler's obligation.' A very loose and reprehensible custom, which we devoutly hope may never be imported into this country. The extract runs thus:

'But many brethren who are desirous of visiting are strangers and sojourners, without either friends or acquaintance amongst the members to become their vouchers, in which case they may still be admitted *by certificate, examination, or the aid of the sacred volume*—commonly called the Tyler's obligation, which in the United States runs in the following form: "I, A. B., do hereby and hereon solemnly and sincerely swear that I have been regularly initiated, passed, and raised to the sublime degree of a Master Mason in a just and legally constituted Lodge; that I do not stand suspended or expelled, and know of no reason why I should not hold Masonic communication with my Brethren." ' The doctor concludes with the dictum: 'And this is all that Freemasonry needs to provide'! We in England think this is not *all* by a very long way.

CHAPTER XXIV

MISCELLANEOUS MATTERS

LODGES usually have two classes of Members. those who pay a full rate of subscription, which is fixed to cover Banquets, etc.; and those who pay a lower rate, which does not include, or which does only partially include, refreshments, as may be fixed by the By-laws.

The former are usually termed Full Members or Dining Members (happy phrase!). The latter are usually styled Country Members or Non-Dining Members.

No such distinction is recognized so far as Grand Lodge is concerned.

The same Quarterage is payable to Grand Lodge, and they are all equally Members of the Lodge, and have the same right of voting.

In some Lodges Country Membership is considered a disqualification for Office, and common sense and convenience generally would seem to support that view; but apart from any By-law bearing on the subject, there does not seem to be any constitutional disability which would preclude a Non-Dining Member from accepting Office if able to discharge its duties satisfactorily.

* * * *

In some Lodges, where the rate of subscription is insufficient to cover all the outgoings, especially where some of those outgoings are of a personal nature (such as a Past Master's Jewel), there may be found a more or less surreptitious form of income under the denomination of Fees of Honour.

This impost is usually levied in a graduated scale upon all the Officers of the year. Commencing at, say, 10s. from the Inner Guard, 20s. from the Junior Deacon, 30s. from the Senior Deacon, 40s. from the Junior Warden, 50s. from the Senior Warden, 60s. from the Worshipful Master, it amounts to the respectable sum of £10 10s.

This is the amount which many Lodges vote to the Master's List if he goes up, as he ought during his year of Office, as a Steward for one of the Great Masonic Charities.

* * * *

The subject of Honorary Membership is hedged with difficulties. The status of an Honorary Member must be strictly confined to the Lodge which so elects him, and can in no way give him any position in the Craft outside the door of that Lodge.

He cannot therefore hold any Office in the Lodge, or vote on any subject which might even remotely affect the Craft at large.

In short, his status and privileges as an Honorary Member entitle him to attend the meetings, and partake of its refreshments, without the necessity of being introduced by a subscribing member. Honorary Members have no other right or privilege whatever.

Until recently there was an additional pitfall. Constitution No. 127 says: 'No Brother who has ceased to be a subscribing member of a Lodge shall be permitted to visit any one Lodge more than once until he again become a subscribing member of some Lodge,' and this Law was invoked against an Honorary Member who had been unfortunate enough to bring himself within its provisions (by a Secretary who must have desired to exemplify that 'the letter killeth, but the Spirit giveth Life'). Accordingly, March 4, 1914, Grand Lodge added: 'But this Rule shall not apply to the visits of a Brother to any Lodge of which he has been elected a non-subscribing or Honorary Member.'

This is the first recognition by the Book of Constitutions of an Honorary Member.

An Honorary Member must not be included in the Returns to Grand Lodge. Even his refreshment is a matter of doubt in the minds of the meticulous. It is suggested that the above phraseology merely entitles the Honorary Member to dispense with an introduction to the table; but that he must pay for his own meal!

It is apprehended, however, that if the Lodge Subscription covers, as is usual, the subsequent refreshment, the Honorary Membership of that Lodge would do so likewise.

A Brother is even ineligible for Honorary Membership while he is an ordinary member of the Lodge in which it is proposed to 'honour' him.

It will be seen therefore that current and generally accepted ideas as to Honorary Membership, and the dignity thereby conferred, are not applicable in Freemasonry.

An Honorary Membership of a Lodge would appear to be a negligible quantity (such as when conferred on Consecrating Officers, who are never likely to see the inside of that Lodge again), and not by any means to be classed as a reward (*e.g.*) for meritorious service to a Lodge rendered by one who has perhaps been a member of it for many years, and who, with increasing age and diminishing resources, might have gladly accepted such honorary membership as a token of appreciation.

Grand Lodge recognizes, as Members of Lodges, only those whose dues to Grand Lodge are duly paid, and whose subscriptions to the Lodge are not further in arrear than the By-laws of the Lodge, and ultimately the Constitutions (B. of C., 148), permit. The dues to Grand Lodge must be paid in respect of Secretaries (and others) whose services are considered equivalent to their subscription (B. of C., 104).

A Lodge has no power to elect a Life Member, and Grand Lodge does not permit the commutation of future dues by a single payment or otherwise.

It would seem, therefore, that an Honorary Member is not a Member of the Lodge at all. He possesses:—

(a) The ordinary unrestricted right common to all Masons of visiting the Lodge, without invitation, so long as he is a Subscribing Member of some other Lodge (Const. 167).

(b) The recently conferred right of visiting unrestrictedly the Lodge (in which he has the title of

Honorary Member), even though he is not a Subscribing Member of some other Lodge (Const. 127, as amended).

(c) The right to sit at the table of the Lodge without invitation (the question of payment for his refreshment being determined by the custom of the Lodge).

(d) The right to employ his Honorary Membership as a cloak to conceal the fact that he is really a Visitor, though signing the Attendance Book as a Member.

* * * *

It sometimes happens that a Warden of a Lodge is unable or unwilling to accept election as Master, and therefore he stands aside.

This is unfortunate, as when he ceases to be a Warden he ceases to have the right to attend Grand Lodge.

* * * *

If, however, he has completed his full year of service as Invested Warden (see p. 92), he will always be eligible, *cæteris paribus*, in any Lodge, as its Worshipful Master, without any further qualifying period of service as Warden.

Miscellaneous Matters

It occasionally happens that from circumstances quite beyond control the investiture of a Warden does not take place on the regular date of Installation, and the full qualifying period cannot be legally satisfied. In such a case—but only on good cause shown—a remedy may be provided by Dispensation (Const. 109).

It has also been known that a Warden served part of a year as Junior Warden and part of a year as Senior Warden, and under the special circumstances of his case the broken periods (amounting to sixteen months) were allowed to be equivalent to the regulation year from Installation to Installation.

*　　*　　*　　*

When a Brother, usually the Senior Warden, has been elected to fill the Worshipful Master's Chair for the ensuing year, he receives the title of Master-Elect. It is quite wrong to style him 'Worshipful-Master-Elect,' as he does not become entitled to the prefix 'Worshipful' until he has been 'placed in the Chair of K.S. according to ancient Custom.'

It often happens, however, that a Brother who is already a Past Master in another Lodge is elected to the Master's Chair.

That Brother, being already entitled to the prefix 'Worshipful,' is, in fact, a Worshipful Master-Elect (not a Worshipful-Master Elect); but in view of the confusion likely to arise in the minds of junior Members, it is most advisable to adhere in all cases to the term 'Master-Elect.'

* * * *

As regards the necessity of confirming the [Minutes of] the Election of Master before the Installation Ceremony can proceed (p. 156), the employment of the word 'Minutes' in Law 105 is perhaps a little misleading in this connection. It is the election itself which must be confirmed, and until the election is so confirmed the Master is not 'deemed to be elected.' The interval is evidently intended as an opportunity for reflection on so important a subject. Minutes as such can only be confirmed or rejected on the score of their accuracy or inaccuracy of record. Strictly speaking, therefore, if the Minutes of a Lodge accurately record *inter alia* the fact of the election of a Master, the Minutes ought to be confirmed even though the election itself be not confirmed.

The motion for the non-confirmation of the election might properly be based on the substantial ground of a change of opinion; or on the more formal ground that the Master-Elect was not eligible, and that consequently his election was invalid; or on the technical ground that the election itself was improperly conducted, and was, therefore, void.

Neither of these reasons would form a proper basis for refusing to confirm the Minutes.

The principle, therefore, cannot be too clearly urged upon the attention of Masters and Secretaries that the mere formal confirmation of the Minutes does not *ipso facto* include, however much it may imply, the confirmation of those matters mentioned in the Minutes which may in themselves require confirmation.

Those matters 'arise out of the Minutes,' and should be so dealt with.

* * * *

A reigning Worshipful Master is not only paramount in his own Lodge, but he is entitled to precedence over all Past Masters during his year of Office.

* * * *

The status of a Past Master of a Lodge is not achieved solely through having been elected and installed as Worshipful Master of that Lodge.

A Worshipful Master must have filled that office in that Lodge for one year (see Const., No. 9) (and that year is usually, though not invariably, counted from the regular date of Installation 'until the next regular period of election within this Lodge and [not or] until a successor shall have been duly elected and installed in his stead') before he becomes entitled to rank as a Past Master of that particular Lodge; so that if for any cause a Worshipful Master is displaced before the completion of his period or 'year of Office,' he thereby, and to that extent, fails to become entitled to the position and status of a Past Master of that Lodge. It is conceivable that he might be already, or might subsequently become, otherwise qualified for that position.

Having regard to the obligation taken by a Master-Elect, the voluntary resignation of his Office by a Worshipful Master is not contemplated by the Constitutions; indeed, it would be quite unmasonic, and in a strict sense illegal.

Constitution 119 provides that 'if the Master shall die, be removed, or be rendered incapable of discharging the duties of his office . . .' (see p. 94).

Now, it is not at all clear by whom the Master could 'be removed.' Certainly his own Lodge has no power to remove him. And if the conduct of the Master were such as to justify his impeachment before Grand Lodge, his rights and privileges as Master and Past Master would be determined by, or deducible from, the judgment of that august Tribunal.

If the Master were 'rendered incapable'— *e.g.*, by accident or illness of body or mind, no doubt his year of office would run its normal course, the Lodge being ruled in his absence in accordance with the provisions of Constitution 119.

Therefore the mere absence, from whatever cause, of an Installed Master during the greater part of his year of office is not necessarily or *ipso facto* a disqualification for his Past-Mastership of that particular Lodge.

Occasionally, however, a vacancy occurs by the death of the Worshipful Master, and consequently a broken period has to be filled. In such a case it is advisable to elect a Past Master of the Lodge to fill the vacancy, as the broken period would not qualify a new occupant of the Chair for a Past Mastership, and to complete the full year would necessitate breaking in upon another regular year, and so on.

On the other hand, an Installed Master of an English Lodge becomes thereby entitled to certain privileges as such. For example, he becomes entitled to attend any Board of Installed Masters under English, Irish, or Scotch Constitutions, and to count as one of necessary quorum. If invited to do so, but not unless, he may preside, and may instal a Master under the English Constitution; and he may do the like under Irish or Scotch Constitutions in the remote contingency that no Master or Past Master of that Lodge's own Constitution is present.

Of course, a Past Master of any Lodge retains the privileges of Grand Lodge to which he has become entitled so long as he continues a subscribing member of any Lodge (see p. 60).

When a Past Master of a Lodge visits another Lodge, he is not legally entitled to sit with the Past Masters of that Lodge on the left of the Worshipful Master. To do so would be to displace some Past Master of that Lodge, and would therefore be a breach of etiquette.

When a Past Master joins another Lodge (see p. 164), he is entitled to sit with the Past Masters of that Lodge according to the rule of precedence there mentioned.

A Brother who becomes a Past Master of one Lodge while remaining an ordinary member of another or others, becomes, under the same rule, entitled to rank and precedence in all Lodges of which he is a member, without altering his number on the Lodge List.

*　　*　　*　　*

On vacating the Master's Chair, the Immediate Past Master finds himself on a pedestal entirely his own. His title is recognized in the Constitutions, and in the Ritual; his place in the Lodge is settled by established custom; and on certain occasions, notably in the absence of the Master, he has the first right to the Master's Chair; but his rank and precedence are nowhere defined. He is not mentioned in the Table of Precedence of Regular Officers. His status is, apparently, the growth of immemorial usage.

In the Lodge he sits on the immediate left of the Master.

Most Lodges assign to him during the year of his Immediate Past Mastership a precedence ranking immediately after the Worshipful Master and before the Wardens, though how far this can be theoretically justified is open to doubt, as the Government of the Lodge is vested in the Master and his two Wardens, *tria juncta in uno* (see 'Landmarks,' p. 65).

Nevertheless, he is a very useful sort of

person, and no one grudges him the consolations which accompany and, let us hope, soften his journey from his high estate of Worshipful Master through the paths of his Immediate Past Mastership, to the abysmal depths of his position as Junior Past Master, from which only the lucky incident of a Past Master joining can save him.

* * * *

Should a member be three years in arrear he thereupon ceases to be a member of the Lodge, and can only become a member again by regular proposition and ballot. Secretaries and others whose services to the Lodge are deemed equivalent to the payment of their subscriptions should see that due provision concerning them is made in the By-laws of the Lodge, otherwise trouble may arise.

* * * *

The length of the Cable Tow is the distance within which attendance at the Lodge is deemed obligatory upon a Master Mason. In the old charges it varies from five to fifty miles. Nowadays it seems to be made of elastic. The collars worn by the Officers are said to be survivals of the Cable Tow.

* * * *

324

Miscellaneous Matters

In these days of feminine association with some masonic and semi-masonic functions, such as Ladies' Festivals, Lodge Dances, etc., and the consequent admission of non-Masons of both sexes to Banquets, etc., it may not be amiss to recall what the Antient Charges enjoin with respect to 'Behaviour in presence of strangers not masons:—

'You shall be cautious in your words and carriage that the most penetrating stranger shall not be able to discover or find out what is not proper to be intimated.'

And with respect to 'Behaviour at home and in your neighbourhood':—

'You are to act as becomes a moral and wise man; particularly not to let your family, friends, and neighbours, know the concerns of the Lodge, etc.'

*   *   *   *

Dispensations are permission granted (on due cause shown) by the M.W.G.M. for a temporary or occasional infraction of the General Law.

Dispensations are frequently required in the administration of a Lodge—*e.g.*, to hold a Lodge on an irregular date or at an unusual place; to wear Masonic clothing in Public—*i.e.*, outside the Lodge; to be Worshipful Master of more than one Lodge at the same time; to continue as Worshipful Master of a Lodge for more than two years; to initiate more than five Candidates on the same occasion; to initiate any person under the age of twenty-one. All these and other occasional circumstances require a Dispensation and, needless to add, a fee—10s. 6d. for London, 5s. for a Province.

Apart from the benefit thus created for the Fund of General Purposes, these Dispensations are of value as manifestations of loyalty to the Constitutions and as indications of good Masonic discipline.

* * * *

One of the proudest moments of a Freemason's early career is that when he receives his Certificate from Grand Lodge. It is of course signed by him at the Secretary's table in open Lodge, and the Worshipful Master should then present it to the newly-fledged Master Mason with appropriate words, which will ring in his ears and be remembered by him in years to come, even as the Senior Warden's address when investing him with the badge can never be effaced from his memory.

* * * *

'The Charges of a Freemason extracted from the Antient Records of Lodges beyond Sea, and of those in England, Scotland, and

Ireland, for the Use of Lodges, to be read at the making of new Brethren, or when the Master shall order it,' will be found *in extenso* in the Book of Constitutions.

These Ancient Charges are, unfortunately, greatly neglected in the majority of Lodges, and it is suggested that the Worshipful Master of every Lodge should find or create opportunity for their being read at least once during his year of Office.

When there is 'no work to do,' the time could not be better occupied than in reminding ourselves of what our Ancient Brethren considered the Code of Good and True Men.

The announcement of such intention on the Summons convening the meeting would add importance to the occasion.

William Preston, in his 'Illustrations of Masonry' (twelfth edition), writes:—

'A rehearfal of the Ancient Charges properly fucceeds the opening and precedes the clofing of the Lodge. This was the conftant practice of our ancient brethren, and ought never to be neglected in our regular affemblies. A recapitulation of our duty cannot be difagreeable to thofe who are acquainted with it; and to thofe to whom it is not known, fhould any fuch be, it muft be highly proper to recommend it.'

*   *   *   *

Strictly speaking, the Charge after Initiation ought to be delivered by the Master himself, and, of course, from the Master's Chair.

If a Past Master delivers it, he should temporarily occupy the Master's Chair for that purpose.

If the Master is unwilling to vacate his position, although delegating some of his duties, the next best thing is for the Past Master to deliver the Charge from the left of the Worshipful Master; and if a Warden or a brother of lesser degree be invited to deliver it, it should be recited from the left of the Worshipful Master. The Warden should not deliver it from his Pedestal, and the position of the Candidate at the left of the Senior Warden's Pedestal should not be varied.

* * * *

Any procedure by which the secrecy of the Ballot is or may be infringed is entirely irregular. Consequently a proposal—usually made on the score of 'saving time'—that the 'Ballot shall vest in the Worshipful Master' is quite out of order.

Any public announcement by a Brother of how he intends to vote, or how he has voted, is an infringement of the secrecy of the ballot, and may entail the annulment of the proceedings.

If the Master, on inspecting the Ballot Box, has reason to believe that by some accident or carelessness the result of the ballot is not what was intended, he may, in his absolute discretion, order a Second Ballot to be taken then and there, warning the Brethren of the fatal consequences of a second mistake.

* * * *

A few words may not be out of place as to the Ethics of Balloting. Although the use of the black ball is provided for in the Constitutions, and although the power of employing it is one which it is essential to possess, and to keep in reserve, it is a power which should only be employed in extreme cases. There are other means of effecting the same object more masonically.

If there are serious reasons for objecting to the admission of a new Member, representation may be made, confidentially if need be (but, better, quite openly), to the Standing Committee, or, if that does not exist, to the Worshipful Master or Secretary. In this way opportunity may be given to the Proposer to withdraw the name without the infliction of any indignity upon the Candidate.

Hundreds of reasons may be considered sufficient reasons for refusal of admission, without implying any reflection on the Candidate. Even personal dislike or political differences—though not very noble—can be understood and accepted as amply sufficient, as it is inadvisable to introduce into a Lodge any element likely to cause resignations or destroy the Love and Harmony which should characterize all Freemasons.

The Golden Rule is the unfailing Guide, and happy the Lodge whose Minutes record the passing of its Resolutions 'unanimously'!

*　　*　　*　　*

There are various Rules and Regulations as to voting in Lodge, according to the subject-matter of discussion.

Rule 105, Book of Constitutions, provides on the occasion of the ballot for the election of a Master for a bare majority of those present who vote—that is to say, if there are any present who do not vote, their abstention from voting does not count against the Candidate for the Chair.

The same principle applies in the case of the ballot for a Candidate for Initiation (see p. 165), the ballot for a Joining Member

(p. 164), the ballot for the Treasurer (p. 93), and the show of hands for the Tyler (p. 93).

All the general questions which come before the Lodge are determined by show of hands and a bare majority (see p. 338). But for the removal of a Lodge a majority is required of two-thirds of those present who vote at a special meeting convened for the purpose (Const. 141*b*).

In the case of a formal complaint by the Master against any of the Officers, Const. 120 provides that the matter shall be dealt with at a Regular Meeting, with seven days' notice in writing to the Brother complained of (see p. 94).

Nothing is said about the matter appearing in the Agenda of the Summons convening the meeting.

In this case a majority of the Brethren present is required, and it is apprehended that if there were any present who did not vote, their abstention from voting would be counted against the complaint.

In the case of a proposal to exclude a Member, Const. 181 provides that the power of exclusion can only be exercised by a majority of not less than two-thirds of the Members present at a meeting appointed for the consideration of the complaint of which the said Member shall have had due notice.

Nothing is said about giving notice to the other Members in the Summons convening the meeting, but it is assumed that such notice would be given.

In these circumstances, if there were any Brethren present who did not vote, their abstention from voting would count against the motion for exclusion.

Assuming, therefore, an attendance of, say, thirty-five, twenty-four would have to vote for the motion to entitle the Master to declare it carried.

The Second or Casting Vote of the Master in the Chair (p. 99) should (if necessitated) be judiciously exercised, and, generally speaking, should be used to negative the proposal, and to preserve the *status quo ante*.

It is a counsel of perfection to suggest that motions should as far as possible be carried unanimously.

In every case, however, a ready acquiescence in all votes and resolutions duly passed by a majority of the Brethren is expected from all good Masons.

*   *   *   *

A Resignation of Membership is effectual and irrevocable as soon as it is communicated to the Lodge; it may be withdrawn by the writer at any time before being so communicated. If a Brother intimates his resignation, and if it is desired to ask him to reconsider his intention, care should be taken not to read his letter to the Lodge until after his final decision has been ascertained.

On the other hand, the resignation, when so communicated to the Lodge, is effective from the date on which it is written, and not from the date on which it is communicated to the Lodge. It does not require 'acceptance'; being complete without it.

On the Minutes it may be 'recorded' with regret.

Resignation takes effect, as above stated, whether dues are in arrear or not; but if any Member resigns without having complied with the By-laws of his Lodge, or with the general regulations of the Craft, he is not eligible to join another Lodge unless and until that Lodge has been made acquainted with his former neglect.

Any Lodge failing to make proper inquiry is liable to pay the arrears due to the other Lodge.

When a Member resigns, he may require a certificate stating the circumstances under which he left, and this must be produced to any Lodge he proposes to join.

In the case of a joining Member who has not resigned, a similar inquiry as to dues must be made, and a certificate procured from the other Lodge or Lodges that he is 'in good standing.'

This certificate is commonly called a Certificate of Clearance.

* * * *

Occasionally it happens that a man wishes to become a Mason in circumstances which necessitate haste, and constitute what is known Masonically as an emergency.

If in the opinion of the Master the emergency be real, he may direct the Secretary to include the necessary particulars of the proposed Candidate in the Summons; and if the ballot be in his favour, he may be Initiated.

This procedure is known as the FIAT of the Worshipful Master. But in no case can a Candidate be initiated unless full particulars appear on the Summons, and at least seven days' notice given.

* * * *

Although a brother has, so long as he continues to be a subscribing member of a Lodge, an inalienable right to visit (if duly vouched) any Regular and Recognized Masonic Lodge without any invitation, and to remain during the whole time of the transaction of its masonic business (see 'Landmarks,' p. 65), there are occasions when it would be good taste to retire voluntarily.

He has, for example, a complete right to hear the reading of the Minutes; and if the conduct of a member were under consideration with a view to his exclusion from the Lodge, the Visitor would have an undoubted right to remain and to hear the discussion, as the decision of such a matter would affect the interests of the whole Craft. He is entitled also to remain during the performance of any ceremony which his masonic rank may entitle him to witness.

On the other hand, discussions as to a Lodge's finances (in which even Grand Lodge has no *locus standi*) are matters in which the presence of a visitor might be irksome, both to himself and the Lodge, and his temporary retirement would be a testimony to his Masonic good feeling.

This right to visit is, however, subject to the power of the Master to refuse admission to any visitor whose presence may disturb the harmony of the Lodge; or to any visitor of known bad character (Const. 126).

*   *   *   *

An Inventory of the Furniture and other possessions of the Lodge should form an integral part of the annual Audit of the Accounts of the Lodge; and this opportunity should be taken to consider the question of repairs and renewals, thus keeping the Furniture and appointments of the Lodge in a state of efficiency.

Many — perhaps most — Lodges content themselves at their Audit with a Statement of Receipts and Expenditure for the year; but it is submitted that a Balance Sheet is a desirable form in which to exhibit the result of the year's working and the present financial position.

* * * *

When the Board of Installed Masters is closed, the Master Masons, on re-entering the Lodge, do not salute until directed to do so by the Installing Master; but all Master Masons, Visitors as well as Members, should pass round and salute. If there are too many for comfort, perhaps Visitors might be seated after saluting as M.M.s.

On this subject Brother Henry Sadler, in his 'Notes on the Ceremony of Installation,' says: 'I will merely direct attention to another innovation, which, although of less moment, is, in my opinion, almost as objectionable. I allude to the practice now in vogue of visitors below the chair resuming their seats on their return to the Lodge after the Installation, and not performing the usual perambulations, etc. Certainly no such privilege was allowed in my early days, and I must confess that I fail to see any reason why visitors in particular should be exempt from the customary act of homage and respect paid to the new Presiding Officer. I can only account for the omission by the knowledge that at recent large gatherings of the fraternity, such as Consecration Meetings, the Director of Ceremonies has permitted the visitors to resume their seats—(I presume more as a matter of convenience than for any other reason)—and hence the idea has got abroad that it is the right thing to do at all Installations. I know many old Masons who feel rather strongly on this point, and the sooner we revert to the ancient custom the better it will be for those who, like myself, occasionally perform the ceremony of Installation, and do not believe in innovations, however trivial they may appear, and are sometimes under the necessity of insisting upon visitors taking their places in the ranks instead of acting the part of mere spectators of the proceedings.'

* * * *

Although, for the convenience of working the Programme of Business in the Lodges, it is permissible, after opening in the three Degrees, to 'resume' up and down (see p. 172), the Lodge should, at the conclusion of ceremonial work, always be resumed in the third Degree, and formally closed in each degree. Any other procedure is not only technically incorrect, but implies inability on the part of the Master and his Officers. The excuse of 'want of time' is too thin.

*   *   *   *

The Deacons' Jewel is now, and has been since the Union, officially 'a dove bearing an olive branch'; but 'in the olden time before then' the 'Athol' or 'Antient' Lodges used to employ a figure of Mercury. In some of the older Lodges this emblem is still retained upon the Deacons' collars, presumably through a disinclination to discard such interesting evidences of antiquity.

*   *   *   *

In certain circumstances, and on good cause shown, a Lodge may (with the approval of the M.W. Grand Master) change its name (Const. 98), but not its number.

No provision is made in the Constitutions as to the voting necessary to achieve this result; but official requirements, in certain instances, have been—

Miscellaneous Matters

(*a*) Notice of Motion, in open Lodge, at a Regular Meeting.

(*b*) Printed Notice, on Summons of such Regular Meeting.

(*c*) Bare majority of those present and voting.

(*d*) Printed Notice of Confirmation on Summons of next Regular Meeting.

(*e*) Bare majority at such meeting.

(*f*) Extracts of Minutes transmitted to Grand Secretary.

(*g*) Endorsement of Warrant, with subsequent publication in the Transactions of Grand Lodge.

* * * *

When the accuracy of the Minutes has been confirmed, either in their original form or as amended, the Minute Book should be taken, by the Senior Deacon, to the Worshipful Master in order that it may be signed by him as a correct record.

In adjusting the Minute Book for signature, the Senior Deacon should take care not to place it on the V.S.L.

In some Lodges the minutes are signed by the Wardens also.

* * * *

No excuse, except sickness or the pressing emergencies of public or private avocations, is available as a justification for failure to attend the duties of the Lodge (see p. 88).

Of course, if an Officer is unavoidably prevented from attending in his place, timely notice to the Worshipful Master, enabling the provision of a substitute, is the least which may be expected; and no doubt this intimation should be accompanied or followed by suitable explanation and apology for absence.

Ordinary members might very well accept it as incumbent on them also (though not perhaps so obligatory) to render similar courtesy to the Worshipful Master in the event of inability to obey the summons.

Such thoughtful manifestations of respect to the Chair are greatly appreciated and reciprocally bring their own reward.

*   *   *   *

Brethren should not be too ready to believe the mere verbal assertion that Grand Lodge wills this, or disapproves of that, as such observations are often made in good faith, but with very imperfect knowledge. The truth or otherwise of such statements is to be discovered without much difficulty through the proper official channels, and in cases of grave doubt or difficulty no Brother need hesitate to make inquiry; he may be sure of a courteous reply, always presuming that the case is of importance. Perhaps we may say that the Secretary of a Lodge would in most cases be the best channel of communication for obtaining information as to all matters affecting the interests of a particular Lodge.

*　　　*　　　*　　　*

We may here mention briefly the mode of addressing any written communication to those in authority over us. No one would be so presumptuous as to address H.R.H. the Grand Master, except in the form of a petition, which would be forwarded to the Grand Secretary. The heading of such a petition will be found in Article 94 of the Book of Constitutions. The Pro. Grand Master is entitled to the prefix Most Worshipful, in virtue of his Office as the immediate representative of the Grand Master. The Deputy-Grand Master, and all Provincial and District Grand Masters, are entitled Right Worshipful. Deputy-Provincial Grand Masters, and the higher Officers of Grand Lodge, including the Grand Secretary and the Grand Registrar, are Very Worshipful. The Master of a Lodge, as every Freemason knows, is entitled Worshipful. Whether it be in oral or written addresses, the several titles should always be strictly observed. We venture, however, again to caution Brethren that all written communications to the higher authorities should always pass through the hands of the Grand, or Provincial, or District Grand Secretary; and, even then, that Brethren should not address those high Officers without good and sufficient reason.

* * * *

The following are the nineteen Lodges now entitled to recommend Grand Stewards:

1. Grand Master's .. .. (c.), †1759
2. Antiquity .. .. Time Imm.
4. Royal Somerset House and
Inverness .. (c.), Time Imm.
5. St. George's and Corner Stone, †1756
6. Friendship 1721
8. British .. .. .. (c.), 1722
14. Tuscan .. .. .. (c.), 1722
21. Emulation .. .. (c.), 1723
23. Globe .. .. .. (c.), 1723
26. Castle Lodge of Harmony (c.), 1725
28. Old King's Arms .. (c.), 1725
29. St. Alban's .. .. (c.), 1728
46. Old Union .. .. (c.), 1735
58. Felicity .. .. .. (c.), 1737

c. = Centenary warrant.
†'Athol' or 'Ancient' Lodge.

Miscellaneous Matters

60.	Peace and Harmony	..	1738
91.	Regularity	.. ..	(c.), 1755
99.	Shakespeare	.. ..	(c.), 1757
197.	Jerusalem	.. ..	(c.), 1771
259.	Prince of Wales ..	..	(c.), 1787

These Lodges are colloquially termed 'Red Apron Lodges,' from the red edging worn on the aprons by their members.

CHAPTER XXV

'THE FESTIVE BOARD'

THE etiquette of the table, or in old Masonic parlance 'the festive board'—Brethren are besought not to call it 'the Fourth Degree'— differs in no material degree from the order and rules observed when a number of men meet and dine or sup together upon any occasion.

It is not generally remembered that theoretically all 'refreshment' is under the immediate supervision of the Junior Warden 'as the ostensible Steward of the Lodge.'

The Worshipful Master will already have announced in Lodge whether the brethren are to dine 'in full Masonic clothing' or only 'officers in collars.'

The duty rests upon the Director of Ceremonies to see that the places at the table for visitors and for members are assigned in accordance with their rank in the Craft; allowing, of course, a certain degree of freedom of choice; that is to say, if a distinguished visitor be assigned a place at, or near the top of the table, and if he prefers a lower seat beside the Brother who introduces him, or with whom he may be more or less intimate, his wish would, of course, be complied with. On the other hand, it would be bad taste for a Brother who bears no rank of any importance to aspire, on the plea of sitting next to a friend, to occupy one of 'the chief seats at feasts, lest haply a more honourable man than he come in,' etc.

Visitors should be ranged in the order of their rank and precedence on the right of the Worshipful Master. The only exception is the Initiate, who, on the night of his Initiation, takes precedence of visitors, Grand Officers included, and sits on the immediate right of the Worshipful Master.

Past Masters of and in the Lodge should be ranged, in the order of their Masonic rank and of their seniority in the Lodge, on the left of the Worshipful Master; the Immediate Past Master being, of course, on his immediate left (pp. 164, 322-323).

There is as a rule more freedom from form and ceremony at the table after the ordinary meetings of the Lodge; still, order and regularity should not be neglected; rules should be observed as far is as compatible with freedom from unnecessary restraint, but they should not by any means be ignored. At Festivals (annual or other) a certain degree of state and ceremony should be observed, and the ordinary rules regulating the proceedings on such occasions should be even more strictly enforced; and precedence should be given to rank and station in the Craft.

*   *   *   *

When Grace is said (that is, when it is not sung), if the Chaplain be present he should say it.

We have a good old Masonic form of 'Grace before meat,' and of 'Grace after meat,' which should not be allowed to fall into disuse. They run thus: 'May T. G. A. O. T. U. bless that which His bounty has provided for us. So mote it be'; and 'May T. G. A. O. T. U. give us grateful hearts, and supply the needs of others. So mote it be.'

*   *   *   *

During the meal the Worshipful Master 'takes wine with the Brethren.' This operation is sometimes performed in sections; and sometimes the ingenuity of the Immediate Past Master or of the Director of Ceremonies is responsible for a great variety of excuses for the 'taking of wine.'

It is usually: 'Brethren, the Worshipful Master will take wine with the Brethren on his left'; then with those 'on the right.'

'The Festive Board'

On these occasions the Worshipful Master should always stand. He is in the capacity of a host welcoming his friends to his table, and courtesy demands that he should rise. It is perhaps for this reason that he makes these occasions collective rather than individual.

The Brethren, on their part, have an inveterate habit of 'challenging' each other in the course of the meal; but even in this free and easy habit etiquette prevails.

No one may challenge the Worshipful Master at all. No one may challenge a Grand Officer or superior officer or senior member. He should wait until the superior or senior challenges him.

Of course in the case of a little forgetfulness or too great absorption of—mind—on the part of the 'high and mighty,' there is nothing to prevent a succession of 'nods, becks, and wreathed smiles' to indicate that the junior is anxious and willing to be challenged.

In this connection it may be remarked that Officers of the Lodge should be spoken to and spoken of by the name of their Office —*e.g.*, 'Worshipful Brother Immediate Past Master,' 'Brother Senior Warden,' 'Worshipful Brother Treasurer,' 'Brother Inner Guard.'

*　　*　　*　　*

During refreshment the Stewards should be quietly and unostentatiously active in looking after the comfort and satisfaction of all the Brethren, but especially of the Visitors, that they may be encouraged to wish to come again.

*   *   *   *

The custom of proposing certain regular toasts, and occasionally of drinking to the health of any particular Brother or Brethren who may be present, if not universal, is still general as of old. Numbers of men advocate the entire abandonment of the practice; and suggest that, as at military mess dinners, one toast only—'The Queen'—should be given.

It may well be doubted if the abolition, or even the partial abandonment of the custom, or the serious curtailment of the lists of toasts which we have been accustomed to find upon the programmes of our Festivals, would be acceptable to any but a very small minority of the Members of the Craft. The custom of giving toasts and of drinking healths at social gatherings, dinners, etc., in our own houses, is happily a thing of the past; but with Masons the case is different. We profess to be, and we are, very properly tenacious of 'The ancient Landmarks of the Order.' The custom of toasts at our festive meetings is so old as to have become a social landmark—it should not be lightly abandoned, or tampered with to any serious extent.

Some of the peculiar Masonic toasts are said to have been 'revived' in 1719 by Dr. Desaguliers, who was then Grand Master.

The forms will necessarily vary to some extent in different Provinces or Districts, or even in neighbouring Lodges; but in their main features and in their order of sequence there is no great variation.

Even in the same Lodge some difference is generally made between the number of toasts given at an ordinary meeting and those included in the list intended for an Installation dinner, or an Anniversary, or any other special occasion.

At the ordinary meetings of the Lodge, it is not expected that the full complement of toasts shall be given, although, even then, a certain routine should be observed, such as: 'The King and the Craft'; 'The high dignitaries and the Rulers of the Order, supreme and subordinate'; 'The Worshipful Master,' and some others at discretion, and in accordance with the probable duration of the sitting.

The list of toasts, however, should not be cut down to poor dimensions upon extraordinary occasions, such as Festivals, Installations, and so on, when large numbers—members and visitors—are expected to be present.

Where so great a variation of practice is certain to exist in different Lodges and different Provinces, one feels some degree of hesitation in even suggesting, and much more in dictating for general adoption, any programme of toasts.

The following is culled from programmes recently used at Installation and Anniversary banquets:

1. The Queen and the Craft.

2. The Most Worshipful Grand Master, His Royal Highness the Duke of Connaught and Strathearn, K.G., K.T., K.P., etc., etc., etc.

[See note on p. 357 as to smoking.]

3. The Most Worshipful Pro Grand Master, the Lord Ampthill, G.C.S.I., G.C.I.E., the Right Worshipful Deputy Grand Master, the Right Honourable Thomas Frederick Halsey, and the rest of the Grand Officers, Present and Past.

4. Brother (name, and titles, if any), Right Worshipful Provincial (or District) Grand Master of (insert the Province or District).

5. Brother (name and rank), Very Wor-

shipful Deputy Provincial (or District) Grand Master, and the Provincial (or District) Grand Officers present and past.

6. The Worshipful Brethren of London Rank (instead of 4 and 5; see p. 380).

7. The Worshipful Master.

7a. The Initiate.

8. The Visiting Brethren.

8a. The Joining Member.

9. The Immediate Past Master, the Installing Master, and the other Past Masters of and in the Lodge.

10. The......Chapter, No.....

11. The Masonic Charities.

12. The Treasurer and Secretary.

13. The Senior and the Junior Warden, and the other Officers of the Lodge.

14. Prosperity to the Lodge (name), Number......

15. All Poor and Distressed Masons (wherever dispersed over the face of Earth and Water, etc., etc.). (See Charge after third section of first Lecture.)

*   *   *   *

It is, perhaps, unnecessary to remind the responsible reader, that no Masonic toast should be proposed, honoured, or acknowledged unless the Banqueting Room be 'close tyled.'

When about to propose the Toasts, the Worshipful Master, or the Brother whom he has deputed, or whose duty it is to propose the Toast, after satisfying himself that the Lodge is 'close tyled,' usually inquires (seated) of the Wardens: 'Brother Senior and Junior Wardens, how do you report the glasses under your respective Columns?' and, having been assured by them that they are 'all charged in the West, Worshipful [Master],' and 'all charged in the South, Worshipful [Master],' he calls upon them to rise, saying, 'Principal Officers upstanding!' so that, in effect, the Toast is proposed by the three Principal Officers, 'the Worshipful Master, and the Senior and Junior Wardens.'

These formulæ are not employed for the Toast of 'The Officers,' or for the 'Tyler's Toast.'

It is a custom in certain Lodges for all the members of the Lodge to stand while the Toast of the Visitors is being proposed.

*   *   *   *

It is no uncommon thing to find on programmes of Festivals and other occasions 'The Queen' as the first toast, without any reference to 'The Craft'; this is wrong.

In the united toast, we express at once

our loyalty to the Throne, and our reverence for 'our ancient and honourable Fraternity.' 'The Queen and the Craft' is the
original and very ancient form among Freemasons; whereas 'The Queen' alone is the
form used at ordinary meetings in the outer
world. We should retain the combined
form by all means; and we should do so
whether the reigning Monarch is or is not a
Freemason.

Similarly, full Masonic Honours should be
given to the combined toast. A circular
issued in 1911 to Masters of Lodges on this
subject concludes with the expression of the
Pro Grand Master's hope 'that the ancient
form of toast "The King and the Craft"
will be generally retained.'

* * * *

Visitors may be present whose rank socially
or Masonically may entitle them to special
mention and a separate toast. No hard-
and-fast line can be or should be attempted
to be drawn upon the subject. All that has
been aimed at above has been to give a
good, useful, practical programme, fairly
comprehensive, and not wearisome.

With regard to 'the honours' after the
Toasts in Provincial Lodges, the following
have been obtained from a very efficient

Provincial Grand Director of Ceremonies, and are those which generally obtain in the Provinces—

The Queen and the Craft	3 times	9
The W.M. Grand Master	3 ,,	9
The W.M. Pro. G. Master	3 ,,	9
The R.W. Dep. G. Master	3 ,,	7
The Grand Wardens	3 ,,	5
The Rest of Grand Officers	3 ,,	3
The R.W. Dist. or Prov. G. Master ..	3 ,,	7
The R.W. Dep. Prov. G. Master (in chair)	3 ,,	5
The W. Dep. Prov. G. Master (not in chair)	3 times	3
The Prov. G. Wardens	3 ,,	3
The Rest of Prov. G. Officers	3 ,,	3

N.B.—When any of the foregoing are grouped, the Honours given are those to which the highest Officer of the Group is entitled.

The W.M.	3 ,,	5
The P.M.s	3 ,,	5

N.B.—Occasionally the W.M. and P.M.'s toast is honoured with twenty and one—or Running Fire.

Visitors and Brethren generally ..	3 ,,	3

They appear to have been well arranged, and are fairly proportioned to the individual rank of the several subjects of the various toasts. There is no authoritative rule and no universal custom. The Worshipful Master and the Director of Ceremonies must always arrange the programme either in accordance with precedent in their Lodge or at their own discretion.

The 'Fire,' after the Toasts in London Lodges, is usually restricted to the P. L. R.

This is often imperfectly given, owing to want of observant attention on the part of those who copy it from those who know; or, still worse, to the misfortune of copying it from those who do not know the absolutely correct method; which is—

P. L. R. P. L. R. P. L. R. one. two. three. (Sn. of E. A.) 1 2 3 (Sn. of E. A.) 1 2 3 (Sn. of E. A.) 1 2 3.

The 'Fire' after the Tyler's Toast is sometimes given with what is called 'silent fire.' This is utterly wrong in principle. It is not a funeral. It is a toast to poor and distressed Freemasons, who may yet, and we all hope they may, find a relief from all their sufferings. So they are entitled to the same joyous 'open fire' as the rest of us.

*　　*　　*　　*

On Anniversaries or Installation banquets as a rule each toast is followed by a song or glee, or some musical performance. These are within the province of the Organist, and whatever may be arranged is set forth— each piece in its proper place—in the Programme. If the songs, glees, etc., be well

355

selected, with some care as to their appropriateness to the toasts which they respectively follow, and if they be fairly well rendered, the entertainment as a whole will be successful and enjoyable, at least, let us hope, to the majority—to those who desire to be happy themselves, and, if it be in their power, to communicate happiness to their Brethren.

In some Lodges a custom exists for the Worshipful Master to propose the first toasts. He then calls upon some Past Master or Senior Warden or the Junior Warden to propose the next. After these have been duly honoured, various Brethren selected by the Worshipful Master (assisted perhaps by the Director of Ceremonies) are requested to propose certain of the remaining toasts; these being allotted to the several speakers according to their special fitness for the duty; derived, it may be, from an intimate knowledge of the subject of the toast with which each speaker is entrusted; or for other good and sufficient reasons.

It is important, however, to be noted that the Brother whom the Worshipful Master deputes to be the proposer of any Toast is entrusted for the time being with the Worshipful Master's gavel. This symbol indicates that the Toast is being proposed by and with the authority of the Worshipful Master, and it is intended to be as great a compliment as if proposed by the Worshipful Master himself.

*   *   *   *

Immediately after the toast of the Grand Master permission is given to the Brethren to smoke; then, and not till then, cigars and other means and appliances for the enjoyment of the nicotian weed are brought into requisition.

No apology can be needed for the mention of tobacco in connection with the symposia of our Order, the habit is so generally, indeed universally, practised at our meetings. Still less need we hesitate to allude to the subject in these days, when, from the lordly club or social gathering in which princes occasionally disport themselves, down through all grades—to the working men's political or social club—'smoking concerts' are, as our American cousins would aptly say, in *full blast.*

*   *   *   *

Some mention must be made of the speeches of the Brethren in proposing the various toasts; and of the replies (returning thanks) of those whose healths—either singly or in connection with others—have formed the subjects of the personal toasts.

A considerable amount of ridicule is cast upon the quality of post-prandial oratory.

The kind, the manner, and the quality of the speeches one hears at the table at Masonic meetings differ, perhaps, quite as much as the speakers themselves differ the one from the other, and as the toasts vary in importance, and in general or individual interest. It is, therefore, clearly impossible to lay down rules for general adoption.

One hesitates to go so far even as to hint at, or to make the slightest suggestion upon, a subject so varying in all its surrounding circumstances as a list of toasts must necessarily be, comprising, as it does, subjects of the highest dignity and of world-wide interest down to subjects of local interest, and so on. Who shall prescribe—with any hope of even partial success—rules or suggestions for their several introduction in speech?

A Demosthenes is not born every day. Nevertheless, among the members of our Order we may occasionally meet men capable of investing common subjects with the charm of their own fancy, affording an intellectual feast to their hearers. From such men we do not expect brief utterances—we should be disappointed with a short address—we expect something above the average in quantity as well as in quality, and generally we are not disappointed.

Except from men of superior attainments, and of unusual facility and happiness of expression, long speeches upon well-worn topics, such as the routine toasts given at our meetings, are a weariness of the flesh; they should be studiously avoided. There are, however, certain toasts, such as the health of the Worshipful Master, particularly if by the performance of the duties of the lower Offices, and during his Mastership, he have shown exceptional zeal and ability; in such a case a moderately lengthy address is not only permissible, but is eminently desirable.

Again, the toast wishing 'Success to the Masonic Charities' is one that demands much more than a brief introduction. It is very desirable that at least 'once in every year' the members of the Lodge should learn, from some well-informed Brother, the excellent, the beneficent work, which year after year our various Charities are engaged in performing. Some well-selected, and not too minutely-detailed statistics, may well be given upon such occasions. The facts and figures thus produced tend to foster the virtue of Charity in the best possible way—namely, by convincing the Brethren that the various Institutions are conducted with care and efficiency, that the large revenues are carefully administered, and that the results bear in all cases a full proportion to the means employed.

In many Provinces, every Lodge elects yearly a member, whose duty it is to attend to all matters connected with the Charities, both Metropolitan and Provincial, so far as the interests of his own Lodge are concerned. In the Provinces alluded to, there are Charities, educational and otherwise, the benefits of which are restricted to the Provinces in which they exist; and the Brother mentioned is the representative of his Lodge upon the Central Committee of the Province, which conducts the affairs of the Institution. In the case also of an application to the Board of Benevolence in London, the same Brother goes to the meeting of the Board, to support the application, and to answer the searching questions which are always, and very properly, asked before the application is decided upon.

In many Lodges the same Brother is re-elected year after year, with the good result that he becomes as a rule thoroughly well versed in the working of the Charities, and so is able to render eminent service to the Lodge. Who, then, can be a more 'fit and proper person' to propose the toast of 'The Masonic Charities,' or perhaps, better still, to respond to the toast? In the latter case some Brother, selected for his fitness for the duty, might dilate at reasonable length upon 'the distinguishing character-istic of a Freemason's heart—namely, Charity,' in the abstract; and the Charity Representative would follow with such moderate detail of the results of the benefi-cence of the Craft as will interest and not weary his hearers.

This subject has been here somewhat fully discussed, because Charity being, as it were, the watchword of our Order, the younger Brethren should learn that it is no unmeaning cry, no 'sounding brass or tinkling cymbal,' but a substantial reality among us; that we do minister to the relief of 'our poor and distressed Brethren, and their widows, and their helpless orphan chil-dren'; that all is done without degrading the recipients, and without wounding their self-respect; that, judged by results, our Charities are the best managed and the most successful organizations in existence; that, with scarcely an exception, the scholars who have passed through the Boys' and the Girls' Schools respectively have done credit to the Institutions, and in some instances have achieved eminent success in their after-life; and that the closing years of life are rendered comfortable and happy for many an aged Brother, and many an otherwise unprovided for and hopeless widow. Having the knowledge of these good works of our Order imparted by 'one who knows,' 'the best feelings of the heart may be awakened to acts of Beneficence and Charity,' to the lasting advantage of our Charitable Institutions, and to the realization on the part of the givers of the fact that in very deed 'it is more blessed to give than to receive.'

There may be other occasions, such as the presence of a visitor of distinction, or the presentation of an address, or a testimonial (a jewel, or something of the kind), as an acknowledgment of eminent services rendered to the Lodge, when something more than a hasty and perhaps ill-considered address is required of the speaker. A very nice discrimination is necessary in treating these subjects; the speaker is required to avoid, on the one hand, excessive laudation, manifestly beyond the merits of the recipient, and, on the other hand, the equally manifest falling short in the expression of appreciation of those merits, and in giving utterances to the sentiments of those of whom he is the mouthpiece.

A difficult task, generally, is that of replying to the toast of one's own health, or of expressing one's grateful feelings as the recipient of the testimonial mentioned, whatever form it may take. There is always the initial difficulty of having one's self as the topic upon which to dilate.

We should never cease to be natural in our utterances; 'the tongue, being an index of the mind, should utter nothing but what the heart truly dictates,' and if our utterances bear the stamp of truthfulness, if they have the ring of the true metal, be they the utterances of a novice or the well-rounded periods of a practised speaker, they will not fail of their full effect upon the hearers.

A good old custom, in general use some years ago, is now perhaps less observed than it formerly was; but on every occasion when there is an Initiation, immediately after the newly initiated Brother's health has been duly proposed, the Loving Cup should be circulated, and the Entered Apprentice's Song should be sung as a matter of course; indeed, the Brethren should as soon think of omitting the Charge as of foregoing the

E. A.'s Song, with its chorus and the cordial hand-grasps all round during the singing of the last verse. All the older Brethren, and certainly the majority of the younger generation, would consider the ceremony incomplete without the good old song.

(Full notes on the Entered Apprentice's Song will be found in the Appendix, p. 423.)

THE SECRETARY'S TOAST

One interesting toast which is of remote origin and rarely heard, is one proposed occasionally by the Secretary.

To enable it to be proposed properly the Brethren must arrange themselves all seated, if not in a circle, in a conveniently continuous chain, which may for this purpose be deemed to be an irregular circle, as it is requisite that each Brother should be in immediate whispering contact with a left-hand neighbour.

The Secretary commences by whispering to his left-hand neighbour the words, 'The Secretary's toast'; and each Brother in turn whispers the same words to his left-hand neighbour, until in due course the Secretary is reached. He then starts the whisper similarly, 'What is it?' and that question is passed round the table. In exactly the same whispered way the following phrases are circulated.

'There's no harm in it!'

'The Mother of Masons.'

'Who is she?'

'No. . . .' (the No. of the Lodge).

Then, in an audible voice, this message is sent round:

'Glass lip high.'

Then the order is similarly circulated:

'Drink.' [And, as each Brother passes on the command, he drinks.]

Then the Secretary, in a loud tone, says:

'Drink all, and all drink.' [And simultaneously all the Brethren drink, and (theoretically) drink all—*i.e.*, to the last drop.]

The 'fire' is correspondingly unique. The Secretary commences with a single knock, and that single knock is passed round the table one after the other until it has made three complete circuits.

Then, led by the Secretary, all the Brethren 'fire' three times rapidly, and raising the firing glass high in the air, finish with one tremendous volley.

CHAPTER XXVI

THE ROYAL MASONIC INSTITUTIONS

1. The Royal Masonic Benevolent Institution

THIS Institution was founded as the result of efforts initiated by Dr. Crucefix about 1834-35 to found a home for aged Freemasons. An annuity fund was formed in 1842 (during the Grand Mastership of the Duke of Sussex), and Grand Lodge voted the sum of £400 a year towards the granting of Annuities to Aged and Distressed Freemasons. As the Institution steadily progressed, it enlarged its sphere of usefulness by establishing, in 1849, a Fund for the Widows of Freemasons. The two funds were later amalgamated, and in recent years help has also been given to the aged and needy Spinster Daughters and Sisters of Freemasons. In 1849 also an amalgamation of this Institution was effected with the Asylum for Aged Freemasons at Croydon—where there was a home for thirty-two residents.

The Royal Masonic Institutions

The majority of the Annuitants to-day live in their own homes, but about one hundred of them can live in the self-contained flats which are being built at Harewood Court, Hove. Here they live rent free and are allowed heating and light in addition to their annuities. Medical attendance and nursing are also provided free.

In 1867, the earlier system of classifying the Annuitants according to age was abolished. The maximum payment to a married Brother is now £156 per annum, and to other classes of Annuitants, £104 per annum.

Apart from the Annuitants who are now living, about 550 widows and 200 Brethren have received over £1,000 each from the funds. Nineteen Brethren and sixty-one Widows have been paid over £1,500 each.

There are now about 2,300 Annuitants on the Funds of the Institution, who are paid in the aggregate no less a sum than £183,000 per annum.

2. The Royal Masonic Institution for Girls

(Incorporated by Royal Charter.)

This Institution was founded in 1788 by the Chevalier Ruspini, P.G.Sd.B., a 'Modern.'

Since the foundation nearly nine thousand Girls have been trained or assisted in their education.

One Hundred and Seventy Five Girls were admitted to the benefits of the Institution *without ballot* during the year 1953.

Four hundred special Naval, Military and Air Force Nominations have been reserved for the benefit of the Daughters of Brethren killed or incapacitated during the War.

The *Senior School* (400 Girls) is situated at Rickmansworth, Hertfordshire. The *Junior School* (120 Girls) is situated at Weybridge, Surrey.

Girls are admitted to the Junior School at the age of eight, and proceed to the Senior School at about the age of ten. They remain normally until the age of sixteen, but many are retained until seventeen and even later should circumstances justify that course.

The Royal Masonic Institutions

At present 1,038 girls are receiving the benefits, 520 of whom are in the schools, the remaining 518 being in receipt of Out-Education Grants varying according to age and circumstances from £50 to £75 per annum. In cases of exceptional necessity these grants may be increased up to £150 per annum. Where a Boarding School is necessary an amount up to £200 per annum may be paid and in cases of exceptional necessity may be increased by a further £100.

The school has been very successful in the results attained in the General Certificate of Education Examinations. During the year 1953 14 girls passed at advanced level and 50 at ordinary level.

During the same year 169 girls received grants for further education after their school career was over, 53 of whom studied at University or other Training Colleges.

The income from investments last year was £39,368.

The annual expenses of the Institution approximate to £238,000 per annum, and are likely to increase in future.

3. The Royal Masonic Institution for Boys

(Incorporated by Royal Charter.)

The Royal Masonic Institution for Boys was founded in 1798, mainly by Brother Burwood, an 'Athol' or 'Ancient' Mason, since which time 9,826 sons of Freemasons have been elected to receive benefits of education, clothing and maintenance.

The object of the Institution is to receive under its protection, to maintain, clothe and educate the sons of Freemasons under the English Constitution of every religious denomination who from circumstances arising from the death, illness or misfortune of either or both parents are reduced to and continue to be in a position requiring the benefits of the Institution.

This object is achieved within the Schools of the Institution at Bushey, Hertfordshire, and also by assistance to boys educated at schools near their homes or in boarding schools. For boys out-educated adequate grants are made for school fees (if any) and maintenance, while for ex-pupils substantial scholarships are available for post school education at Universities, Medical Schools, etc. Extensive provision is also made for ex-pupils to assist them during their early years of employment by paying apprenticeship premiums and supplementing wages until they are able to be self supporting.

1,029 boys are now actually receiving benefits, 691 being at Bushey, 265 being out-educated and 73 being ex-pupils aided from the funds of the Institution.

Boys are admitted by election to the Institution's benefits at five, and are educated at schools near the residences of their parents or guardians until eight years of age, when, according to seniority of age, they may be drafted in the Bushey Schools.

In the Great War 1914-1919, 750 old boys served their King and country; 106 laid down their lives, and many others were wounded. Many distinctions were gained including a C.M.G., O.B.E., D.S.O., forty-nine Military Crosses and Medals, etc.

In the World War 1939-1945, about 1,398 Old Boys were serving in the Services and Merchant Navy. Of this number 533 held Commissioned Rank. 128 laid down their lives or were 'missing.' The many distinctions gained included O.B.E., M.B.E., D.S.O., M.C., D.F.C., D.C.M., D.S.M., D.F.M., A.F.M., B.E.M., etc.

There are four elections in each year, and 144 boys were admitted to benefits in the year 1953. Since 1910, 5,758 candidates have been admitted without a ballot, thus relieving their friends from much anxiety and expense. In addition, 666 duly qualified boys, whose fathers were killed or became incapacitated on or through active service in time of war, have been similarly admitted without a ballot to the benefits of the Institution.

A Royal Charter of Incoporation was granted to the Institution by Letters Patent dated June 15, 1926, and the Institution now enjoys the Royal Patronage of her Majesty the Queen.

CHAPTER XXVII

THE MASONIC LECTURES

THE Masonic Lectures are an elaborate explanation and commentary, not only of the ceremonies of the three Degrees and of the Tracing Boards appertaining to them, but of many important subjects connected with the higher phases of Masonry and Masonic thought. As at present constituted, they are divided as to seven sections in the First Lecture, five sections in the Second Lecture, and three sections in the Third Lecture, making fifteen sections in all. They are catechetical in form, and at some Masonic festivals all the fifteen sections are worked on the same evening!

The system of Lodge Lectures is, as compared with Masonry itself, of modern growth.

Some of the questions would seem to be intended merely to test the *bona fides* of the person examined, as both question and answer are distinctly arbitrary.

Freemasonry and its Etiquette

It may be accepted as historical fact that previous to 1717 the fraternity was without any such system.

Prior to that time the Charges and Covenants explanatory of the duties of Masons to each other seem to have been read 'at the making of a Freemason,' but these charges contained no instruction as to the symbolism of the Order. (See p. 326.)

The earliest authorized Lectures were apparently arranged by Drs. Anderson and Desaguliers, but they were imperfect and unsatisfactory, and in 1732 Bro. Martin Clare, M.A. (afterwards Deputy Grand Master), was commissioned by Grand Lodge to prepare a system of Lectures 'which should be adapted to the existing state of the Order without infringing on the Ancient Landmarks.'

Oliver says that Clare's version of the Lectures was so judiciously drawn up that its practice was enjoined on all the Lodges.

But Clare's Lectures did not long occupy their authoritative position in the Order. About 1766 Thomas Dunckerley—'that truly Masonic luminary'—was authorized by Grand Lodge of 'Moderns' to prepare a new course of Lectures.

Dunckerley's Lectures were a considerable amplification of those of Clare, but a considerable modification also, as in them he dissevered the Master's Word from the Third Degree, and postponed it into the Royal Arch Ceremony.

Even Dunckerley's had to give way to the Lectures of William Hutchinson, of the North of England; and while Hutchinson was labouring in the North, another light, of almost equal splendour, appeared in the South, and a system of Lectures was prepared by William Preston, which soon superseded all those that had previously been in use. It is supposed that Hutchinson and Preston united in this undertaking, and that the Prestonian Lectures which were afterwards universally adopted were the result of the combined labours of the two.

In 1787 William Preston organized the Grand Chapter of Harodim in order to thoroughly teach the Lectures he had prepared. Some of the most distinguished Masons of the day became members of the Order.

The Prestonian Lectures continued to be used authoritatively until the Union in 1813, when it was determined to 'revise' the system of Lectures. This duty was entrusted to the Rev. Dr. Hemming. Many alterations of the Prestonian system were made by Dr. Hemming, principally, it is said, in consequence of their Christian references.

It appears from a letter from Bro. Philip Broadfoot (who was one of the members of the Lodge of Reconciliation and founder of the Stability Lodge of Instruction), that Bro. Hemming, after arranging the First Lecture, could not be induced to go on with the Second and Third, and that Bro. Philip Broadfoot was obliged to arrange them himself!

As may well be imagined, this was the subject of debate and controversy, as in 1819 complaint was made 'against Philip Broadfoot and others for working unauthorized Lectures.' Into this we need not enter very deeply. The Board of General Purposes recommended that the Lecture complained of should not be further promulgated, but Grand Lodge thought it unnecessary to adopt the recommendation, and, indeed, the M. W. Grand Master, the Duke of Sussex, stated that it was his opinion that so long as the Master of any Lodge observed exactly the Landmarks of the Craft he was at liberty to give the Lectures in the language best suited to the character of the Lodge over which he presided. This will explain why the Lectures practised by the Stability Lodge of Instruction have since claimed to be considered as legally 'orthodox' as those of the Emulation Lodge of Improvement; but the same considerations apply, though not in the same degree, to the Lectures as to the Ritual, as to the desirability of adhering to a precise and uniform method of working.

In 1819 the Perseverance Lodge of Instruction unanimously passed a resolution 'that the Lectures as heretofore worked in this Lodge be continued.' This was seconded by Bro. J. H. Wilson, subsequently a founder of the Emulation Lodge of Improvement.

In 1821 a similar resolution was carried unanimously.

In 1823 the Emulation Lodge of Improvement was founded by 'several Brethren who considered that the Masonic Lectures were not worked in Lodges upon a sufficiently regulated system, and that if those whose attainments as working Masons placed them as a prominent authority were to meet together and to work efficiently, they might be the means of effecting much improvement.' The work of this Lodge of Improvement was at first confined to the Lectures, but afterwards the Ceremonies were introduced. The Grand Stewards Lodge was, until that time, the only recognized authority for a recognized system of Lectures. The

Lectures then worked at the Grand Stewards Lodge were probably the 'Prestonian' Lectures formerly worked in the Lodge of Antiquity No. 2, William Preston's favourite Lodge. Accordingly, some members of the Grand Stewards Lodge conceived it to be their duty to watch the proceedings; and some Grand Officers, with Bro. Harper, the Grand Secretary, attended, and were greatly pleased with all they saw.

'For how long a period the Lectures as now worked at Emulation were previously in vogue it is impossible to state definitely, but we have every reason for believing that they are almost identical with the Lectures worked in the Perseverance Lodge of Instruction, which were described as "Ancient" in 1821, and they certainly bear a striking resemblance to Lectures known to have been in use about 1798.'

Bro. Thomas Fenn in 1893 stated that Bro. Stephen Barton Wilson admitted having made a few additions to the Lectures. No alteration has been made since, and in their present form they are regularly practised by the Emulation Lodge of Improvement.

William Preston died in 1818, and was buried in St. Paul's Cathedral. He bequeathed, among other Masonic gifts, £500 Consols to the Board of Benevolence, and

The Masonic Lectures

£300 Consols as an endowment for the annual delivery of the Prestonian Lecture. This was delivered somewhat intermittently until 1862, since which date it appears to have been forgotten.

CHAPTER XXVIII

LONDON RANK

LONDON RANK was instituted in December, 1907, as a consequence of a widespread feeling that Past Masters of London Lodges should have an opportunity, until then denied them, of attaining a dignity analogous to, and equivalent to, that of Provincial or District Grand Rank.

The honour is the direct gift of the M. W. Grand Master, and exists only during his pleasure, but the recipient is nominated by the Master of the Lodge to which he belongs, and this nomination is usually the result of consultation between the Master, Past Masters, and Wardens, in response to an invitation to that effect from the M. W. Grand Master.

The honour is therefore very highly esteemed as being the result of an expression of confidence by the Lodge itself.

London Rank entitles the holder to precedence in any London Lodge, next to

London Rank

Grand Officers; beyond the London area, or, in other words, outside the 'Province' of London, that precedence ceases.

The holder is of course entitled during the Grand Master's pleasure to wear the London Rank clothing, consisting of a distinctive Jewel Collar and apron, at all Masonic Meetings, whether in London or elsewhere; with a modification, however, with respect to meetings of Grand Lodge.

On the occasions of his visits to Grand Lodge every holder of London Grand Rank (like his brother holding Provincial or District Grand Rank) attends Grand Lodge in virtue only of his Past Mastership.

The honour is now conferred on about 263 Past Masters every year, representing about one-third of the London Lodges.

There are at present about 1,500 Worshipful Brethren of London Rank, of whom about 450 are members of a voluntary association called London Rank Association.

Proposals have been submitted to Grand Lodge and rejected to divide London into ten Metropolitan Districts and establish ten Metropolitan Grand Lodges. Under that Scheme no further appointments would have been made to London Rank, but the holder of London Rank would have retained his right to wear his London Rank Jewel and

Clothing, and he would have had the same rank and precedence as a Past Metropolitan Grand Senior Deacon; but he would have had this rank and predecence only in the Metropolitan Grand Lodge containing the Lodge originally nominating him for London Rank.

CHAPTER XXIX

MARK MASTERS, AND ROYAL ARK MARINERS

THE Degree of Mark Master is recognized by the Grand Lodge of Scotland and Ireland. It is regrettable, however, that the Degree of Mark Master was not recognized by the United Grand Lodge of England in 1813 as coming within the definition of 'pure and ancient Masonry.'

As part of Speculative Masonry it existed before 1813; indeed, there are authentic records dating September, 1769. It is a complement of the Fellow-Crafts degree of a particularly interesting character. It is, however, conferred only on Master Masons.

In former times it was the custom, in all Fellow-Craft Lodges, for each Fellow-Craft to choose a mark by which his work might be known to his Overseer, the mark selected being one not previously chosen by a Brother of the same Lodge. This mark he presented at the Senior Warden's wicket to receive his wages as a Mark Man.

In due course, when he became a Master

Mason, he had the degree of Mark Master conferred upon him.

It is at this stage that the Legend of the Mark Master who prepared a curious stone commences. He has the mortification of having rejected in the first instance, and subsequently has the ecstatic joy of seeing it placed in one of the most important positions in the Building.

In 1855 a Committee appointed by Grand Lodge reported that, whilst not positively essential, it was a graceful appendage to the degree of a Fellow-Craft.

In March, 1856, it was resolved by Grand Lodge 'that the degree of Mark Mason or Mark Master is not at variance with the Ancient Landmarks of the Order, and that the degree be an addition to, and form part of, Craft Masonry'; but at the subsequent meeting in June this was not confirmed.

Three months afterwards the Grand Lodge of Mark Master Masons was formed, and has proved very successful, controlling 654 Lodges, and has recorded 66,616 advancements of Candidates.

*   *   *   *

The degree of a Royal Ark Mariner is conferred only on Mark Master Masons. It has been worked from 'time immemorial' (!). The earliest records are of a date *circa* 1790.

In 1870 the Royal Ark Mariners came under the jurisdiction of the Grand Lodge of Mark Master Masons, and since then these Arks have been 'moored' to Mark Master Masons' Lodges.

The ritual goes back to the time of Noah, and refers to the despatch of the dove which returns with the olive branch. It is distinctly a side degree, and bears no apparent relation to Craft Masonry or its Etiquette.

It is not recognized by the United Grand Lodge of England, but is recognized by the Supreme Grand Chapter of Scotland.

It is only mentioned here on account of its relationship with the Mark Masters.

CHAPTER XXX

THE SUPREME ORDER OF THE HOLY ROYAL ARCH

THE Supreme Order of the Holy Royal Arch is not a degree; it is the completion of the Master Mason's degree, which is interrupted in such an untimely fashion; and without it no Master Mason can consider himself 'fully fledged.'

In early times it was, no doubt, incorporated in the Third Degree; and the true word which constitutes the Royal Arch was found by Dr. Oliver in a Master Mason's Tracing Board, *circa* 1725. The earliest mention of it as a separated ceremony is about 1740, just two years after the separation of the 'Ancients' and the 'Moderns.' Its creation is attributed to the 'Ancients.'

As late as 1758 the 'Moderns' had no Royal Arch, and in the Lecture of the Third Degree the true Master Mason's word was revealed to the Master Mason by the 'Moderns' in the latter ceremonies of the Third Degree, thus precluding the necessity for the Royal Arch.

The Supreme Order of the Holy Royal Arch

About 1766 Dunckerley was commissioned by the 'Modern' Grand Lodge to revise the Lectures, and he did so by, *inter alia*, dissevering the true word from the Third Degree, and transplanting it into the Royal Arch ceremony, and to that extent assimilating the Ancient and Modern systems. This radical move owed its success to Dunckerley's popularity and the influence of the Grand Master. It was no doubt a great factor in preparing the ground for the reunion in 1813, when the Royal Arch was declared a part of 'pure and ancient Masonry'; and so it has ever since remained.

The Royal Arch is not recognized by the Grand Lodge of Scotland.

In 1817 the two Grand Chapters of the Royal Arch were amalgamated.

In 1834 the ceremony of exaltation was considerably altered by the Rev. G. A. Browne, at the request of M. W. G. M. the Duke of Sussex; but the general outline of the system was preserved.

In 1853 a Chapter of Promulgation was authorized for the purpose of disseminating the revised Ritual with a view 'to establish a uniformity of Practice and Working throughout the Order.'

The Supreme Grand Chapter governs the Order, and its Ruler is denominated the

Most Excellent First Grand Principal. The most important Grand Officers of Grand Lodge are entitled *ex officio* to similar offices in Grand Chapter (if they are R. A. Masons), so that the government is in practically the same hands.

In former times the ceremony was restricted to those who had passed the Chair. In 1843 the Regulations required only twelve months' service as a Master Mason; while since 1893 any Master Mason who has exercised himself in that capacity for four weeks and upwards is eligible for 'exaltation' in the Order; and there can be no impropriety in urging a brother to complete his Third Degree.

From a practical point of view, it is also very desirable, if otherwise convenient, that a young Mason should join the Royal Arch as soon as possible. While in the first place it gives him a greater comprehension of his 'blue' Masonry and assists him to take an intelligent interest in that, the practical advantage is that of saving time, by enabling him to take office in the Royal Arch as soon as his progress in the Craft warrants it.

No Mason can occupy a Principal's Chair in the Royal Arch until he is an Installed Master in the Craft, but conversely, if he can mount in rotation in the Royal Arch at the same time as he is nearing the Chair in the Craft, there need not be such a long interval as there would be if he were not a member of the two organizations concurrently.

At the present time there are 250 London Chapters and 612 Provincial Chapters.

*   *   *   *

On May 7, 1902, a Resolution 'that it is expedient that all Royal Arch Masons be permitted to be present at the Opening of Private Chapters' was proposed in Grand Chapter and carried 'almost unanimously.'

Prior efforts to achieve the same object in 1880, 1893, and 1896, had been defeated by large majorities.

CHAPTER XXXI

LODGES OF RESEARCH

It is natural that so vast a subject as Free-masonry should induce a spirit of inquiry in those whose thoughts are not circumscribed by the physical aspects of their Lodges.

Our Masonry is to us what we make it. If we confine it to social enjoyment and mundane ambitions, it will yield these things abundantly, and give us the sweets and bitters associated with such matters. If, on the other hand, we enlarge the outlook, then the possibilities are infinitely greater, and we reap a correspondingly greater result.

Simple investigations into the origin of the Fraternity from the historical point of view are interesting if illusory. Speculation as to the more recondite spiritual meaning of our mysteries, and their association with the same mysteries of preceding ages, is an absorbing study; for we must surely realize that our researches are prompted by the same desires as prompted the researches of the ancient seekers after TRUTH.

Lodges of Research

The labours of our investigators have been limited by the paucity of record, and yet their industry has produced so much that a lifetime would be insufficient to read it all.

And if we could read it and retain it, what more should we know of the Infinite and Eternal than our ancestors knew? Who can say?

But it is a most satisfactory feature that the desire to know more is perennial, and this very proper inquisitiveness has gathered together some of our Brethren, who have encouraged themselves and others to form Lodges of Research, charged with the pleasurable duty of acquiring and disseminating useful knowledge in all branches of Masonry.

Prominent among these is the Quatuor Coronati Lodge, No. 2076, which was established in 1884, to provide a centre and bond of union for Masonic students, and to imbue them with a love for Masonic research. Its membership is limited to forty, but it has an unlimited Correspondence Circle extending to all parts of the world. It meets as a Regular Lodge at Freemasons' Hall six times in the year. At every meeting an original paper is read, which is followed by discussion. Once a year an excursion is arranged.

The fee for the Correspondence Circle is

1os. 6d., and that entitles the subscriber to the Transactions 'Ars Quatuor Coronatorum,' published three times per annum.

The Lodge of Research, Leicester, was founded in 1892.

The Humber Lodge of Installed Masters was consecrated 1894.

There are many other Lodges, Clubs, and Associations having objects similar to these, among which may be mentioned, Manchester Association for Masonic Research, Leeds Installed Masters' Association, Masonic Veterans' Association.

It is to be hoped that every Brother who reads these pages will become a member of at least one of them.

CHAPTER XXXII

OPERATIVE MASONRY

WE have seen in Chapter I (p. 11) that Speculative Masonry is derived from the various systems of Operative Freemasonry which have existed since the earliest periods; and that it is, more immediately, based upon the secret organizations of the Operative Masons of the Middle Ages; but it is insufficiently known and realized by present-day members of our Speculative Lodges that the Craft to which they profess their devotion was, originally, wholly operative; and that the members of it were real Free Masons, engaged in actual construction of buildings; dependent, for their subsistence, upon the excellence of their work; that the Lodge was the place in which the work was carried on; and that the ceremony of Initiation was an actual ordeal through which the candidate had to pass before he could be permitted to learn the practical secrets of the Craft by which he expected to earn his daily bread.

Freemasonry and its Etiquette

It was only as a concession, and as a compliment to sympathizers of the types mentioned in Chapter I, that the Craft from time to time admitted or 'accepted' a sprinkling of non-working or Speculative Masons, who were not actually Free Masons, but were known as 'Accepted' Masons.

Thus the membership of the Operative Lodges, while almost entirely composed of Operative Masons, consisted, in many instances, of Free Masons on the one hand, and of 'Accepted' Masons on the other.

This was the state of affairs down to 1717 when the Grand Lodge of that date was formed, and Anthony Sayer, himself an Operative, was elected Grand Master.

In this connection attention may be called to the Entered Apprentice's Song, as printed in 1722 (see p. 423), in which the toast is to a Free OR Accepted Mason.

Under the Speculative Grand Lodge the non-working element gradually increased, and indeed soon predominated, to the utter exclusion of the working element, until nowadays the very existence of an Operative is lost sight of in a Speculative Lodge.

We are often reminded in the Ritual that we are not all Operative Masons; but, for the above reason, the phrase is meaningless to most. It is unquestionably a survival of the times when Operatives and Speculatives sat side by side in the same Lodge.

It must not, however, be supposed that Operative Masonry died in giving birth to Speculative Masonry.

The Operative parent system, now enfeebled by various causes, especially by Trade Unionism, continued its existence, notwithstanding the birth, separate life, and extraordinary growth of the Speculative offspring.

Bro. R. B. Grant writes: 'The existing Operative Lodges in England, which are under the Worshipful Society of Free Masons, Operative, have never come under the control of the Grand Lodge of England; and they continue to work their old Ritual, as revised in 1663 and 1686, and as it was before the Speculative Grand Lodge was formed in 1717.'

To Masonic Speculative students the present-day existence of these Operative Lodges must be a matter of intellectual interest, since the ancestry is common to both.

It will be readily conceded that a right understanding of the practical trade of Masonry, the methods employed in delineating the building in a draft or plan for the instruction and guidance of the workmen, and the working tools and implements used by them in executing the work, cannot but be helpful to a clearer appreciation of the meaning—often the hidden meaning—of the corresponding speculative aspect of Masonry, " . . . for many parts are quite incomprehensible even to learned Free Masons, without the technical part which only the Guilds of the Free Masons can supply." Hence, any research which will bring us into closer contact with the actual Operative Lodges of ancient times is likely to give us clearer insight, and to widen our range of Masonic vision and comprehension. On the other hand, it must be admitted that the endeavour to distinguish and appreciate the connection of our whole system and the relative dependency of its several parts will lead us into a very wide field of research—one in which, regrettably, there is more opportunity for developing imagination than for discovering incontrovertible facts.

There are many worthy Speculative Masons who, feeling mentally unsatisfied with the meagre and imperfect explanations provided for their acceptance from speculative sources, and feeling that there must be a rich harvest of additional knowledge to be reaped in the field indicated, are devoting their attention to the Operative aspects of

Operative Masonry

Masonry; and are attending Operative Lodges; as a result of which Speculative Masonry is, to them, illuminated from the Operative point of view.

These Operative Lodges work their own Operative Ritual, and purport to carry on the work as practised in the ancient Operative Lodges from which they claim to trace their descent both immediate and remote— that is to say, their remote origin is claimed to date from the beginning of building, while their more immediate History, although we read in our Masonic Year Book that St. Alban formed the first Lodge in Britain, A.D. 287, may be said to date from Athelstan, A.D. 926, and the granting of the Charter at York in that year.

Dr. Charles Hope Merz, President of the Masonic Library of Sandusky, Ohio, writes: 'By the Athelstan Charter, granted A.D. 926, the Operative Society had the inherent right to form a kind of private law court in order to preserve its rights. The Masters and Passed Masters held an Assembly regularly, and at this meeting a Charge was read to them. Edward died A.D. 924, and was succeeded by his son Athelstan, who appointed his brother Edwin patron of the Masons. This prince procured a charter from Athelstan, empowering them to meet annually in

communication at York, where the first
Grand Lodge of England was formed in 926,
at which Edwin presided as Grand Master.
Here many old writings were produced (in
Greek, Latin, and other languages), from
which the Constitutions of the English
Lodges were originally derived. From this
era we date the establishment of Freemasonry in England. There is to-day in the
city of York a Grand Lodge of Masons, who
trace their existence from this period
(Masonic Minstrel, 1818).

'Athelstan (926) gave the Operatives power
to correct within themselves faults . . .
done within the Craft. This, with the
system of fines, is in operation to-day.'

Between A.D. 926 and A.D. 1717 the
records are very meagre and tantalizingly
insufficient.

The following dates and facts are interesting and indicative, although not in all cases
free from doubt:

1349. Ordinance of Labourers (23 Ed. III)
respecting Operative Masons (ce-
mentarii).

1350. Statute of Labourers (25 Ed. III) respecting Operative Masons, "Mas-
ter Mason of Free Stone," and
"other Masons."

1356. Regulations by the Mayor, Aldermen, and Sheriffs of the City of London concerning Operative Masons.

1358.* Edward III revised the Constitions.

1360. Statute of Labourers (34 Ed. III) "Masons . . . Congregations, Chapters, Ordinances, and Oaths . . . wholly annulled."

13—. Probable date of Halliwell MS.

1376. Two Operative Societies in London (Herbert's Livery Companies). "The Worshipful Society of Freemasons in the City of London," and "The Free Masons Company of London."

1377. Will Humbervyle, styled "Magister Operis," and a "Free Master Mason," was employed as a teacher at Oxford.

1380-1400. Approximate date assigned to document from which the Regius MS. appears to have been copied.

1390-1410. Approximate date assigned to document from which the (Matthew) Cooke MS. appears to have been copied.

1425.* Masons yearly General Chapters prohibited (3 Henry VI). This

* See *Masonic Year-Book*.

Act was virtually repealed in 1562 by (5 Eliz., Cap. 4), and was formally repealed in 1825 bv (6 Geo. IV).

1445. Statute of (28 Henry VI) refers to Frank Mason. This would appear to be the earliest expression in the Statutes which could bear the rendering of Free Mason.

1450.* Henry VI (said to have been) initiated (at the age of twenty-nine).

1481. The City of London made further regulations *re* Operative Masons.

1495. Statute of (11 Henry VII). The words Free Mason appear for the first time in the actual Statutes (see A.D. 1445). Repealed 1497.

1515. 7 Henry VIII. "On the humble petycyon of the Free Masons, rough Masons . . . wythin the Cytie of London."

1550-1575. Probable date of Lansdowne MS.

1562. 5 Eliz., Cap. 4, giving Masons and others the right to take Apprentices.

1583. "Grand Lodge" version of the Operative Constitutions.

1598. Schaw Statutes (No. 1) written in the

*See *Masonic Year-Book.*

Minute Book of the Lodge of Edinburgh.

1600. John Boswell, Laird of Auchenleck, a non-Operative Mason, attended Lodge of Edinburgh and attested the Minutes with his mark like his 'Operative Brethren.'

1607.* Inigo Jones constituted several Lodges.

1637.* Earl of St. Albans "regulated" the Lodges.

1646.* Elias Ashmore (Windsor Herald) initiated October 16 at Warrington.

1655. The Free Masons Company discontinued the use of the word 'Free,' and elected members who had not served seven years at the Trade.

1663. Robert Padgett rewrote the Operative Ritual.

1675. Foundation Stone of St. Paul's Cathedral laid June 21 by Operative Free Masons.

1677. King Charles II granted to the Operative Masons Company another Charter.

1685.* Sir Christopher Wren was Grand Master of Operative Free Masons.

1686. Robert Padgett further revised part of Operative Ritual.

* See *Masonic Year-Book*.

1690.* King William III was initiated.

1691. Sir Christopher Wren (said to have been) 'adopted' a Free Mason.

1708. Last stone laid on dome of St. Paul's, October 25.

1710. Dr. Anderson appointed Chaplain to St. Paul's Operative Lodge.

1715. Dr. Anderson's connection with Operative Masonry severed.

1717. Constitution of Speculative Masonry by the formation of the Grand Lodge of England. (See p. 20.)

It must be remembered that many of the statements made in this chapter emanate from Operative writers, and from Operative sources only, and upon them the responsibility for their accuracy rests, and must, of course, rest, until the production of independent corroborative testimony permits, or, indeed, compels, their unreserved acceptance by Masons generally.

It is stated that Robert Padgett, who was 'the Clearke' of the Operative Society, rewrote their Ritual in 1663; and it is also stated that at Wakefield in 1663 the General Assembly sanctioned the ancient prayer which is still in use by the Operatives.

This Revised Operative Ritual is appar-

* See *Masonic Year-Book.*

ently the Ritual which was taken in hand before 1717 by the Rev. Dr. James Anderson.

Dr. Merz writes: 'In order to show the close relation existing between them, it is only necessary to place the two rituals side by side, and all the remarkable points of similarity will at once become apparent; and the "digestions" of Dr. Anderson may be readily detected.'

Dr. Anderson is said to have been appointed Chaplain to St. Paul's Operative Lodge in London in January, 1710; but it appears that he never became a Master Mason in the seventh degree. It is even alleged that he was expelled from the Operatives in September, 1715, and that he then conceived a system of Speculative Masonry for 'gentlemen who did not work at the trade.'

Dr. Anderson was, of course, an important factor in the organisation of the Grand Lodge of England in 1717, and he was its first Grand Secretary. This Grand Lodge was composed of both Operatives and Speculatives, and the first Grand Master, Anthony Sayer, was an Operative; and, of his Wardens, one was an Operative, the other a Speculative.

The establishment of this Grand Lodge was, therefore, no 'revival' of Freemasonry as some write of it. It was rather a 're-visal' of it.

It was apparently intended to be an alliance between the Free and the Accepted; more or less on the same lines as before, but with their status equal; but events falsified prognostications, and the remarkable growth of the Speculative side of its membership completely overshadowed and eventually crowded out the Operatives.

In September, 1721, Dr. Anderson was commissioned by the Grand Lodge of England, under John, Duke of Montagu, to write a Digest collated from the existing Gothic (*i.e.*, manuscript) documents. In 1722 this Digest was approved, and ordered to be printed under the style of the 'Ancient Constitutions of Freemasonry.' On January 17, 1723, 'G. Warden, Anderson, produced the New Book of Constitutions now in print which was again approved.'

A second edition was published in 1738, in which Dr. Anderson made important alterations, which were unauthorized by Grand Lodge, and gave offence.

One of the most striking of these important alterations is that two degrees—the Apprentice Part and the Fellow-Crafts' or Masters' Part—are officially recognized in the constitutions of 1723, and three—En-

tered Apprentice, Fellow-Craft, *and* Master
—by the Constitutions of 1738.

Dr. Anderson's characteristics would have
delighted some of the Ritual Reformers of
the present day, as he appears to have
altered the Operative Ritual radically and
ruthlessly, and often 'without rhyme or
reason.'

For instance, in Operative Masonry the
three Masters sit in the West, to see the sun
rise in the East. The Senior Warden sits
in the East 'to mark the setting sun.' The
Junior Warden sits in the North to 'mark
the Sun at its [high] meridian.' The thoughtful Speculative Mason will perceive many
reasons why this arrangement is more suitable.

Operatives open the Lodge in the seventh
degree, and work downwards.

The Degrees are:

VII. Three Ruling Masters.
VI. Certified Master.
V. Intendent and Super-Intendent.
IV. Super-Fellow Erector.
III. Super-Fellow.
II. Fellow.
I. Apprentice.

Operatives explain that, as Dr. Anderson
did not know the seventh degree work, he

opened in the first degree, and worked upwards.

For this reason also, they assert, he was unable to give the Secrets of a Master Mason, and invented the legend of the loss of them; and this is the explanation also why, although the Operatives have three Masters, the Speculatives have only one.

There are numerous other examples which could be quoted; but enough has been said to show that Dr. Anderson found the Operative Ritual very 'indigestible' fare, and this will explain the errors, anachronisms, and confusions, which occur in what may be termed the technical part of our present-day Speculative Ritual.

Let us, however, be thankful that those parts of Operative Masonry to which he had access have enabled him to transmit so much of it pure and unpolluted.

CHAPTER XXXIII

THE SUPREME COUNCIL OF THE ANCIENT AND ACCEPTED SCOTTISH RITE (33°)

'On May 1, 1786, the Grand Constitution of the Thirty-third Degree, called the Supreme Council of Sovereign Grand Inspectors-General, was finally ratified by His Majesty the King of Prussia, who, as Grand Commander of the Order of Prince of the Royal Secret, possessed the sovereign Masonic power over all the Craft.'

'In the new Constitution this power was conferred on a Supreme Council of nine brethren, in each nation, who possess all the Masonic prerogatives in their own District that His Majesty individually possessed, and are Sovereigns of Masonry.'

'Every Supreme Council is composed of nine Inspectors-General, five of whom should profess the Christian religion' (Dalcho, 1802).

The English Supreme Council was established in 1845.

The following is a list of the thirty-three degrees:

Freemasonry and its Etiquette

SYMBOLIC LODGES

1. Entered Apprentice.
2. Fellow Craft.
3. Master Mason (inc. Royal Arch*).

LODGES OF PERFECTION

4. Secret Master.
5. Perfect Master.
6. Intimate Secretary.
7. Provost and Judge.
8. Intendant of the Buildings.
9. Elect of Nine.
10. Elect of Fifteen.
11. Sublime Elect.
12. Grand Master Architect.
13. Royal Arch of Enoch.
14. Scotch Knight of Perfection.

COUNCIL OF PRINCES OF JERUSALEM

15. Knight of the Sword and of the East.
16. Prince of Jerusalem.

CHAPTER OF PRINCES OF R.C.

17. Knight of the East and West.
18. Knight of the Pelican and Eagle and Prince of the Order of Rose Croix of H. R. D. M.

* See definition of Pure Antient Masonry, Art I, Book of Constitutions.

Supreme Council of Scottish Rite

COUNCIL OF KADOSH

19. Grand Pontiff.
20. Grand Master of Symbolic Lodges.
21. Noachite, or Prussian Knight.
22. Knight of the Royal Axe, or Prince of Libanus.
23. Chief of the Tabernacle.
24. Prince of the Tabernacle.
25. Knight of the Brazen Serpent.
26. Prince of Mercy.
27. Knight Commander of the Temple.
28. Knight of the Sun, or Prince Adept.
29. Grand Scottish Knight of St. Andrew.
30. Knight Kadosh.

CONSISTORY OF PRINCES OF R.S.

31. Inspector Inquisitor Commander.
32. Prince of the Royal Secret.

SUPREME COUNCIL

33. Sovereign Grand Inspectors-General.

APPENDIX (A)

LITTLE needs to be remarked upon the Tracing Board of the First Degree. It is far from being all that can be desired, but it is not open to the strong objections which exist against the other two.

The Explanation of the Second Tracing Board, as given in the Ritual, is almost from the beginning to the end a series of statements having little or no foundation in fact; and in several of its details it is diametrically opposed to the descriptions in the Bible of the things alluded to. There is no Scriptural warrant for the assertion that 'the Entered Apprentices received a weekly allowance of corn, wine, and oil; the Fellow-Crafts were paid their wages in specie.' This, however, may be ranked among the *traditions*, and it is of small importance.

In the Ritual it is stated that 'after our Ancient Brethren had entered the Porch they arrived at the foot of the winding staircase, which led to the middle chamber.' This idea is partially embodied in the Tracing Board itself. There are depicted two columns under an arch, at the very entrance of the Temple, with a picturesque view of the open country, but *no Porch* at all. Almost from between the two columns springs a huge winding staircase, leading to a large and lofty vestibule, at the end of which is a doorway, with not a door, but a pair of curtains. The staircase clearly winds up to the *left side* of the building. The only description of the 'Chambers' is in 1 Kings vi 5, 6, and 8. Verse 8 runs thus: 'The *door* for the middle chamber was in the *right side* of the house.' It is clear, therefore, that the staircase, so far from facing the very entrance of the Temple, was not seen at all until the door at 'the right side of the house' was opened; consequently, all that is said about the Porch and the Pillars applies to the main entrance to the Temple, and not in any sense to the middle chamber.

It is clearly stated in the Volume of the Sacred Law that the three chambers were 'built against the wall'; and they measured, respectively, five, six, and seven cubits—that is, about nine feet, ten feet nine inches, and twelve feet six inches in breadth (length not stated); therefore the Porch and the

Pillars, etc., as applied to the middle chamber, are an absurdity. The two Pillars are asserted to have been 'formed hollow, the better to serve as archives to Masonry.' Now, supposing such Records to have been then in existence, and to have been deposited in the two Pillars, how could they have been made accessible?—how arranged for reference? The thing is too absurd for argument. The Pillars were formed hollow then, as they would be now, because solid Pillars would have involved a vast waste of metal, and, from their enormous weight, such difficulty in moving and rearing, as would have taxed the skill of the Craftsmen to the uttermost. It is said 'those Pillars were further adorned with two spherical balls, on which were delineated maps of the Celestial and Terrestrial Globes.' In I Kings vii 41, mention is made of 'the two *bowls* of the *chapiters*, that were on the top of the two pillars.' In verse 20 of the same chapter are these words, 'and the chapiters upon the two pillars had pomegranates also above, over against the *belly* which was by the network.' In these two extracts it would appear that '*bowl*' and '*belly*' both mean the swell of the capitals of the Pillars. These capitals were fixed at the tops of the shafts *in the usual way*; and the old compilers have here supposed that the *bowls* mentioned were identical with *spherical balls*, and those balls they have placed on the top of a square *above the chapiters*. The idea of these balls being covered with the delineations of the celestial and terrestrial Globes is sublime in its audacity. The first terrestrial Globe on record is that made by Anaximander of Miletus, 580 B.C.—that is, considerably over *four hundred years* after the date of the building of King Solomon's Temple; the celestial Globe would probably be of even later date. The height of those Pillars was seventeen cubits and a half each, and the chapiter five cubits, equal in the whole to forty-one feet (one account, 2 Chronicles iii 15, makes them, the Pillar thirty-five cubits, and the chapiter five cubits). Students of geography and astronomy must have had some difficulty in consulting globes placed at an elevation of from forty to fifty feet above the ground. The assertion about these globes is as wildly improbable as that the Pillars were 'formed hollow the better to serve as archives to Masonry.'

The meaning of the P. W. S. . . . is literally 'an ear of corn,' in some sentences in the Bible and a 'flowing stream' in others, and therefore correctly depicted in the Tracing Board. The *word* does not *mean* 'P. . . . y,' but its double signification may, when united, be said to denote 'P . . . . y.' Eminent Hebrew scholars have been consulted as to the interpretation of the word, and there exists no difference of opinion between them, except that one rather favours the 'stream of water,' inasmuch as the word was used as a *T . . . . beside a stream.* Nevertheless, a multitude of texts have been quoted in which the word is used in such connections that no other meaning *in those places* can be assigned to it than 'an Ear of Corn'; but no case can be cited in which the word alone can by any means be rendered 'P . . . . y.'

The remaining portion of the 'Explanation' needs little comment. The winding staircase may or may not have comprised flights of three, five, and seven steps. There is no mention of this in the Bible. The Tracing Board shows fifteen continuous steps, without a break, or any indication of these three flights. It is stated in the last clause of the Explanation of the Tracing Board that 'when our ancient Brethren were *in the M. C.* their attention was peculiarly drawn to certain Hebrew characters.' This is, of course, a pure invention. It is of little moment, but it does not agree with the Tracing Board, in which 'certain Hebrew characters' are shown *above the doorway* at the end of the vestibule and *outside* the M. C., while in the centre, at the top of the Tracing Board, is a letter 'G' in a radiated triangle. The Tracing Board shows a strongly marked Mosaic Pavement, whereas in 1 Kings v. 30 it is clearly *stated*, 'and the floor of the house he overlaid with gold, within and without,' meaning, probably, the Temple proper, the Holy of Holies, and the Porch. *Not one word* indicating a Mosaic Pavement can be found in either of the two accounts of the building of the Temple.

The Porch and the Mosaic Pavement were evidently in high favour with the old compilers of the Ritual. They have both of these in their explanation of the Sanctum Sanctorum.

They have given their fancy very free play, and have paid but scant attention to the clear descriptions of the Temple in the Kings and the Chronicles.

Freemasonry and its Etiquette

The following remarks embody all that needs to be said upon the Tracing Board of the Third Degree.

Perhaps the grossest absurdity of all in this connection is the statement 'he was not buried in the Sanctum Sanctorum, because nothing common or unclean,' etc. Evidently the old compiler considered it the height of *respectability* to be buried in the church, according to the bad old fashion existing in England some years ago, and he thought that H. A. B. would certainly be buried within the Temple, and he gives a reason (*in words borrowed from the New Testament*) why he was not buried in the Holy of Holies itself, being evidently ignorant of the fact that intra-mural interment was expressly forbidden by the Jewish Law. The Coffin is made a prominent object in this Degree. It is cited as one of the emblems of mortality, it is the most conspicuous (indeed, almost the only conspicuous thing on the older Tracing Boards. An actual Coffin, sometimes in miniature, sometime of full size, used to be (and in many places still is) brought into the Lodge, and actually used in the Third Degree. Many instances can be brought to prove that Coffins were not in use (then at least) in Judea. The Winding Sheet alone was used, and the body was carried on a Bier. In 2 Kings xiii 21 it is related that a man was hastily cast into the 'sepulchre of Elisha, and when he touched the *bones* of Elisha, he revived and stood on his feet.' Now it is clear from this that neither the man nor Elisha could have been in a Coffin, and Elisha was one to whom all honour in burial would have been paid. In the Christian era clear proofs are found of the use solely of the Winding Sheet. Then, again, the B. of our Master was found very indecently i. ..d, and although it was afterwards re-......d, it is as little likely that a coffin was used as that it was ever contemplated that he should be buried in the Holy of Holies, and was only prevented 'because nothing common or unclean was allowed to enter there.'

Equally absurd is the statement that 'the same fifteen trusty Fellow-Crafts were ordered to attend the funeral clothed in white aprons and *gloves*.'

As to the Ornaments of a Master Mason's Lodge. 'The Porch, Dormer, and Square Pavement,' there is not in the Bible any foundation for supposing that they ever formed part of King Solomon's Temple. There is no room for doubt upon the subject; nothing can be more clear than the description given in the Bible of the whole internal arrangement of the Temple; and the references given in the following remarks will show how entirely the Scripture accounts differ from the description in the Third Ceremony.

There could have been no 'Porch' to the entrance to the Sanctum Sanctorum. The only Porch was outside, at the entrance to the Temple, on either side of which the Two Great Pillars stood. The 'Dormer' is a pure invention. No such thing is mentioned (see 1 Kings vi and 2 Chron. iii). None was needed. The High Priest alone, and he only once a year, entered the Holy of Holies; and the Shekinah was there, the visible manifestation of the Divine Presence in the Pillar of Cloud and of Fire. In 1 Kings (vi 30) it is distinctly stated, 'the floor of the house he overlaid with gold, within and without'—that is, in every part—and certainly the Holy of Holies would not be less richly floored than the rest; consequently, 'the square pavement' is an error. As a matter of course, the High Priest must walk on the floor of the Holy of Holies, be it what it might, as he must go in at the door; but it would be absurd to say that the door was for the High Priest to enter by. The floor was just a necessary part of the structure, as were the walls and the ceiling, the whole being not simply or even primarily for the use of the High Priest, seeing that he entered it but once a year. The Holy of Holies was the receptacle for the Ark of the Covenant, and the Mercy Seat, with the Cherubim, etc. (see Exod. xxxvii). Then it is stated in the Ritual that the office of the High Priest was to burn incense once a year; that is true, but he had many other things to do on the Great Day of Atonement (see Levit. xvi). He had to offer a young bullock and two kids; then the Ceremony of the Scape-goat had to be gone through, and much in the way of 'Atonement.' The whole chapter is full of the various acts of 'Atonement,' but it has not one word to justify the assertion that the office of the High Priest on that day was 'to pray fervently that the Almighty . . . peace and tranquillity upon the Israelitish nation during the ensuing year.' He did nothing of the kind as a perusal of Leviticus xvi will clearly show. It may be mentioned that the words 'peace and tranquillity' are used twice in the Third Ceremony; such a conjunction occurs nowhere in the Bible.

APPENDIX (B)

'The Master's Light'

'Freemasons' Hall,
'*December* 7, 1839.

'Dear Sir and Brother,

'In reply to your questions as to the propriety of extinguishing the Master's Light, and, if extinguished, of introducing a Lanthorn with a Star, etc., I feel no difficulty of stating that such extinguishment is not only improper, but positively in violation of a most maturely considered and unequivocal direction of the Grand Lodge, and that the introduction of a Lanthorn, etc., is equally against the order.

'In the Lodge of Reconciliation, the extinguishment had been proposed, and occasioned much dissatisfaction; in order, therefore, to settle that, and some other points, or, more properly speaking, to carry out the intention and direction of the Act of Union, that there should be a conformity of working etc., a Special Grand Lodge was convened on May 20, 1816, to witness the ceremonies proposed by the Lodge of Reconciliation. These concluded, the several points were discussed—amongst others, the Lights in the Third Degree: and decisions were come to upon them. But to afford opportunity for the most mature consideration, and to leave the subject without a possibility of objection, another Special Grand Lodge was holden on June 5 following, to approve and confirm what had been done on May 20.

'At these Meetings, the M. W. G. Master presided, and the attendance of Members was larger than at any other I recollect (excepting the day of Union).

'The decision was, that the Master's Light was never to be extinguished while the Lodge was open, nor was it by any means to be shaded or obscured, and that no Lanthorn or other device was to be permitted as a substitute.

'One of the reasons is, that one of the Lights represents the Master, who is always present while the Lodge is open, if not actually in his own person, yet by a Brother who represents him (and without the Master or his representative the Lodge cannot be open), so his Light cannot be extinguished until the Lodge is closed; the two other lights figuratively represent luminaries, which, at periods, are visible—at other times, not so.

Freemasonry and its Etiquette

'As to the penalty with which the Grand Lodge might think fit to visit a Lodge acting in contravention of its positive order, I venture no opinion; you are as capable as myself to decide upon that point.

    'I remain,

        'Dear Sir and Brother,

            'Yours fraternally,

(Signed)   'WILLIAM H. WHITE, G.S.'

APPENDIX (C)

THE ENTERED APPRENTICE'S SONG

THIS ancient and very famous Masonic ditty was originally called 'The Freemason's Health.'

It is said to have been composed by Bro. Matthew Birkhead, who died on December 30, 1722, but it is quite possible that it was only 'arranged' by him, as it is said to have been in general use among Operative Masons about 1650, and that ancient Freemasons' jugs exist which have the song thereon, and which were made in the days of Matthew Birkhead the elder; not his son above referred to.

The earliest impression of it is taken from Read's 'Weekly Journal, or British Songster' (December 1, 1722), where it is printed in the following form:

423

Freemasonry and its Etiquette

I

Come, let us prepare; We Brothers that are.
　Met together on merry Occasion;
Let's drink, laugh and sing; Our Wine has a
　　Spring.
　　'Tis a health to an accepted Mason.

II

The world is in pain Our secret to gain,
　But still let them wonder and gaze on;
Till they're shown the Light, They'll ne'er
　　know the Right
　　Word or Sign of an accepted Mason.

III

'Tis this and 'tis that, They cannot tell what,
　Why so many great Men of the Nation,
Should Aprons put on, To make themselves
　　one
　　With a Free or an accepted Mason.

IV

Great Kings, Dukes, and Lords Have laid
　　by their swords,
　This our Mist'ry to put a good grace on;
And ne'er been ashamed To hear them-
　　selves named
　　With a Free or an accepted Mason.

Appendix (C)

V

Antiquity's pride We have on our side,
It makes each man just in his station;
There's nought but what's good To be under-
stood
By a Free or an accepted Mason.

VI

Then joyn hand in hand, T'each other firm
stand;
Let's be merry and put a bright face on:
What mortal can boast So noble a toast
As a Free or an accepted Mason.

☞ Note the use of the word 'or.'

* * * *

In early days an accepted Mason was a sort of 'honorary' Free Mason. The phrase 'A Free or an Accepted Mason' embraces, therefore, either an (Operative) Free Mason or a (Speculative) Accepted Mason.

* * * *

The words and music are given in the First Edition of the 'Book of Constitutions' issued in 1723.

Subsequently, about 1730, the following stanza was composed by Bro. Springett, Perm. Deputy Grand Master of Munster—

We're true and sincere, We're just to the
    Fair;
They'll trust us on any occasion;
No mortal can more The Ladies adore
    Than a Free and an Accepted Mason.

The song appeared in the 1738 Edition of
the 'Book of Constitutions' with this stanza
added.

Various trifling and seemingly unnecessary
alterations have been made from time to
time by our irrepressible modernizers and
reformers until the following seems to be the
generally accepted present-day version of it.

(N.B.—Organists are respectfully reminded, that for the comfort of elderly voices
—and therefore the general good of the
occasion—it is advisable to play it in F.)

THE ENTERED APPRENTICE'S SONG

Come, let us prepare; We Brothers that are
    Assembled on merry occasion;
To drink, laugh and sing; Be he beggar* or
    King,
    Here's a health to an Accepted Mason.

* In the first section of the first Lecture we
read: 'Brother to a King, fellow to a Prince or
to a beggar, if a Mason and found worthy.'

Appendix (C)

The world is in pain Our secret to gain,
    And still let them wonder and gaze on;
They ne'er can divine the word or the
    sign
    Of a Free and an Accepted Mason.

'Tis this and 'tis that, They cannot tell
    what,
    Why so many great men of the Nation,
Should aprons put on, And make themselves
    one
    With a Free and an Accepted Mason.

Great Kings, Dukes, and Lords Have laid
    by their swords,
    Our Myst'ries to put a good grace on;
And ne'er been ashamed To hear them-
    selves named
    As a Free and an Accepted Mason.

Antiquity's pride We have on our side,
    To keep us upright in our station;
There's nought but what's good To be
    understood
    By a Free and an Accepted Mason.

(All rise and join hands.)

427

Then join hand in hand, By each brother
firm stand;
Let's be merry and put a bright face on:
What mortal can boast So noble a toast
As a Free and an Accepted Mason?

(*Repeat.*)
What mortal can boast So noble a toast
As a Free and an Accepted Mason?

APPENDIX (D)

Proposition Form

....Lodge, No..........

Form to be signed personally by the Candidate, as well as by his Proposer and Seconder, and then read by the Master or Secretary in open Lodge before the Ballot takes place.

1. *Name (in full) of Candidate*..................................

2. *Full Postal Private Address*..................................

3. *Business Address*..

4. *Age*..................... *Occupation*...........................

5. *Has a proposal for Initiation been made before to any*

    Lodge ? ....

    Signature of Candidate................................

    Date........................., 19.........

We, the undersigned Members of the........................
Lodge, No.........., do hereby declare that we, from personal knowledge, believe that the Candidate who has signed above is a fit and proper person to be initiated as a Member of this Lodge.

Name of Proposer........................... *Rank*............

Name of Seconder........................... *Rank*............

Date........................, 19.........

I have had due inquiries made (Constitution 183), and the Candidate has been approved by the Standing Committee of the Lodge.

        Signature...

            W.M., Lodge No..........

Date..............................., 19.........

It is suggested that the proposed Candidate should be 'sounded' as to the answer he will be likely to give to that important question concerning 'the first and most important of the Antient Landmarks' (see p. 64), and that he should be made aware of the contents of the Declaration which he will be asked to sign (Const. 162); also that he should be given an opportunity of making himself acquainted with the By-laws of the Lodge of which he is to become a member, as his acceptance thereof at his Initiation is deemed to be a declaration of his submission to them. It is only fair, therefore, that he should see them beforehand.

APPENDIX (E)

INFORMATION FOR THE GUIDANCE OF ANY LODGE OF INSTRUCTION WHICH MAY BE DESIROUS OF OBTAINING THE OFFICIAL RECOGNITION OF THE COMMITTEE OF THE EMULATION LODGE OF IMPROVEMENT

1. The Lodge of Instruction must hold its meetings 'under the sanction of a Regular Warranted Lodge' (Const. 132).

2. Its By-laws must, *inter alia*, provide—

(*a*) That the Lodge of Instruction shall be governed by a Committee which 'shall be answerable for the proceedings, and responsible that the mode of working adopted has received the sanction of the Grand Lodge' (Const. 132).

(*b*) That of this Committee the Honorary Preceptor, and at least one other member, shall be approved in writing annually by the Committee of the Emulation Lodge of Improvement.

(c) That the mode of working shall be in complete conformity with:

(1) The Ancient Ceremonies of Initiation, Passing and Raising as approved, sanctioned and confirmed by the United Grand Lodge on June 5, 1816; and

(2) The Ceremony of Installation as agreed by the Board of Installed Masters, and sanctioned and approved by the Grand Master in 1827; and

(3) The Lectures corresponding with the said Ceremonies and the ancient usages and established customs of the Order;

that is to say, in complete conformity with the recognized system of the Emulation Lodge of Improvement.

(d) That no discussion on the Ritual or Working shall be permitted while the Lodge of Instruction is open for business.

(e) That neither smoking nor refreshment shall be permitted in the Lodge of Instruction during Masonic business.

(f) That the Lodge of Instruction shall furnish annually to the Committee of the Emulation Lodge of Improvement a report on the condition of the Lodge of Instruction and a summary of the past year's work.

(g) That any alteration of the By-laws affecting these requirements shall be forthwith communicated to the Committee of the Emulation Lodge of Improvement.

3. It is suggested that the Programme of Work should correspond as far as practicable with the work to be done at the Emulation Lodge of Improvement on the following Friday evening.

"What one fool could do,
another fool could do, too."

Thales of Miletus (625–547 B.C.)

Thales was one of seven sages of antiquity. He is credited as being the inventor of options.

MANAGING DERIVATIVES RISK

Establishing Internal Systems and Controls

DIMITRIS N. CHORAFAS

IRWIN
Professional Publishing®
Chicago • London • Singapore

Library of Congress Cataloging-in-Publication Data

Chorafas, Dimitris N.
     Managing derivatives risk / Dimitris N. Chorafas.
       p.   cm.
     Includes index.
     ISBN 1-55738-778-8
     1. Derivative securities.   2. Risk management.   I. Title.
   HG4352.N35 1996
     658.15′5—dc20   95–22503

Printed in the United States of America

BB

1 2 3 4 5 6 7 8 9 0

JB

"What one fool could do,
another fool could do, too."

Thales of Miletus (625–547 B.C.)

Thales was one of seven sages of antiquity. He is credited as being the inventor of options.

Table of Contents

Preface

Benjamin Franklin, when asked what form of government had emerged from the American Constitutional Convention of 1787, replied: "A republic, if you can keep it." Paraphrasing Franklin's dictum, when asked what form of financial instruments emerged from the competitive markets of the 1990s we can reply: "Derivatives, if we can keep them"—and the way to keep them is through rigorous risk management.

Few processes are simpler in principle, more demanding in their study, more difficult to put into practice, and so far-reaching in implication as derivatives risk. In the course of the research that led to this book, banks with experience in off-balance-sheet financing commented that risk is

❑   Hard to master.

❑   Impossible to make uniform.

Therefore, said these financial institutions, it is important to share experiences on how to approach derivatives risk management, to elaborate on the methods chosen, and to examine the models used as well as the results obtained.

This book is built on this premise. Based on the experience of premier financial institutions in three continents, it addresses itself to the challenges that derivatives risk management presents and to the established methods of facing them.

Reflecting the results of an extensive research project on derivatives risk management, this book is written for practitioners in the financial industry: bankers, traders, treasurers, investors, financial analysts, and consultants. It can also be used as a textbook and reference book for graduate courses in economics, banking, and finance.

The text is composed of 17 chapters divided into three parts. Part One examines the components of a risk-management policy and presents a number of practical examples—some from successful risk-control operations, others from cases that leave something to be desired.

Chapter 1 offers the reader an appreciation of the most recent evolution of financial instruments and of solutions that have been applied for risk-management purposes. Since the theme underpinning derivatives trades is the notional principal amount, Chapter 2 is dedicated to this subject—the metrics that can be used and the effort some banks have made in converting notional principal to loans equivalent amounts.

The valuation of any financial product is, in itself, a crucial issue. The methods of calculating a fair value change with time, as Chapter 3 suggests. The major transition is from marking-to-market to marking-to-model. Metrics of exposure are cash flow and liquidity; their importance and their impact are discussed in Chapter 4.

While credit risk and market risk are the foremost issues in the bankers' thinking, an equally lethal exposure may result because of legal risk. Chapter 5 addresses this subject. Chapter 6 presents the issues associated with the next layer of risks, in connection to payments, clearing, and settlement.

Financial institutions, whether banks or nonbanks, as well as the treasury departments of industrial corporations, do not enter into derivative deals just for the fun of it. Theoretically at least, they deal in off-balance-sheet vehicles in order to hedge—but hedging should be an integral part of the organization's strategic plan. This is the theme of Part Two.

The six chapters in this part of the book examine the risks associated with both the traditional derivatives instruments and the exotics. These are new and complex off-balance-sheet products that come to the fore practically every day. They contain many unknowns, and the skill necessary to manage them has not yet been built up.

A few of the banks met in the course of the research let it be known there is no evidence they are taking inordinate risks with their off-balance-sheet trades. But the majority responded to this argument by saying that the absence of evidence is not evidence of absence.

If we ignore contradictory facts and observations, we might claim to have a robust reason there is no risk. This, however, is not good management. The sound approach is to take all evidence into account—starting with the targets set by the strategic plan.

This is precisely what Chapter 7 does, following the viewpoints expressed by first-tier financial institutions. It also examines risk as a function of market opportunity. Chapter 8 goes into further detail, restructuring the responses into a pattern that comprehensively outlines how banks, nonbanks, and treasury operations attempt to control their derivatives risks.

One of the questions that came up in these meetings is whether it is better to finance through debt or equity. This is the issue Chapter 9 addresses, while Chapter 10 is dedicated to synthetics and exotic derivatives: long futures, embedded options, straddles, strangles, binary options, and so on.

Hedging is the topic of Chapter 11, and with it the exploitation of market inefficiencies. While there is plenty of argument about whether the market is efficient or inefficient, off-balance-sheet trades are often done in inefficient markets—as the reader will see in this chapter. There are also practices that result in superleverage. Chapter 12 starts with a brief history of financial bubbles and panics; it ends with securities lending.

Whether on-balance-sheet or off-balance-sheet, no new financial instrument can be successful in the marketplace, as well as handled at an affordable cost, if it is not supported through high technology. This is the message conveyed to the reader in Part Three. The concept underpinning the next five chapters is "Don't underestimate technology's contribution to the control of risk."

The term *technology* is used in the broadest possible sense. It not only refers to telecommunications, computers, databases, networked workstations, and software, but also to advanced organizational solutions. Methods, systems, and procedures constitute the lion's part of Chapter 13, the theme of which is how to effectively use technology to control risk and keep ahead of competition.

The focal point of Chapter 14 is the models and metrics necessary for derivatives risk management. Therefore, emphasis is placed on the contribution of rocket scientists in the banking industry: the physicists, engineers, and mathematicians who came into finance from atomic research and aerospace. The new metrics of exposure and risk—delta, gamma, theta, kappa, and rho—are explained in Chapter 15.

By themselves, models and metrics will not make a difference. A new culture is necessary in finance, and its fundamentals make up the better part of Chapter 16, always with derivatives risk management as the central theme. Finally, computers and databases are discussed in Chapter 17 under a title that sets the tone of the whole presentation: "Strategic Decisions in Technology for Greater Professional Clout."

If Chapter 17 concerns itself with technology's nuts and bolts, this is not the case with the other four chapters of Part Three. Their emphasis is on a complete and coherent derivatives risk-management system—which they outline from alpha to omega. The text is based on personal experience with risk-control projects.

To a substantial extent, the presentation of a risk-management methodology in Part Three is applicable to banks, nonbanks, and treasury operations alike. The solution being outlined is based on

❑ The concept of risk capital as distinct from, but complementary to, other equity.

❑ A factual and documented conversion of notional principal amounts in loan risk equivalent as the common denominator.

Some financial institutions say the notional principal amount is useless as a derivatives risk-management tool. But others, including central banks, are using it most effectively—pointing out that with instruments such as binary options, the whole notional principal effectively corresponds to the risk the bank is assuming.

A growing number of financial institutions consider cash flow the best metric for estimating derivatives risk. At least one central bank, the German Bundesbank, designed regulations in 1993 that focus on cash flow for risk-control reasons. There are, however, a number of banks that have chosen to put cash-flow estimates on the back burner.

The sense of these references is that there is no uniformity of views and practices on how derivatives risk management should be approached. Therefore, what I did in this research was to identify the best methods and models currently in practice and unify them into a system that is both complete and consistent.

The book is written in a comprehensible manner so that readers without experience in derivatives can follow it. Risk management is the responsibility not only of staff and line, but also of board members and chief executive officers. "He who is chosen the people's king can choose little for himself thereafter," the Magi advised Alexander after he conquered Persia and became its monarch. Quite similarly, Chief Executive Officers are *not* free in increasing the company's compound risk.

* * *

I wish to express my appreciation for the reception and assistance I received from the 293 senior managers, financial experts, and systems designers in the United States, England, Germany, Austria, Sweden, Switzerland, Denmark, and Japan who participated in this research.

One hundred financial institutions, computer manufacturers, communications companies, and university laboratories participated in this research effort. A complete list can be found in the Acknowledgements.

Let me close by expressing my thanks to everyone who contributed to this book: to my colleagues for their insight; to the company executives and technologists for their collaboration; to Dr. Heinrich Steinmann for the imaginative project on derivatives he entrusted me with; to Mark Butler, who has been instrumental in seeing this book into print; and to Eva-Maria Binder for the drawings, typing, and index.

Dr. Dimitris N. Chorafas
Valmer and Vitznau

Acknowledgments

The following organizations, their senior executives, and their system specialists participated in the 1992 and 1993 research projects that led to the contents of this book.

UNITED STATES

Bankers Trust

Dr. Carmine Vona, Executive Vice President for Worldwide Technology
Shalom Brinsy, Senior Vice President, Distributed Networks
Dan W. Muecke, Vice President, Technology Strategic Planning
Bob Graham, Vice President, Database Manager
  One Bankers Trust Plaza, New York, NY 10006

Citibank

Colin Crook, Chairman, Corporate Technology Committee
David Schultzer, Senior Vice President, Information Technology
Jim Caldarella, Manager, Business Architecture for Global Finance
Nicholas P. Richards, Database Administrator
William Brindley, Technology Officer
Michael R. Veale, Network Connectivity
Harriet Schabes, Corporate Standards
Leigh Reeve, Technology for Global Finance
  399 Park Avenue, New York, NY 10043

Morgan Stanley

Gary T. Goehrke, Managing Director, Information Services
Guy Chiarello, Vice President, Databases
Robert F. De Young, Principal, Information Technology
  1933 Broadway, New York, NY 10019
Eileen S. Wallace, Vice President, Treasury Department

Jacqueline T. Brody, Treasury Department
  1251 Avenue of the Americas, New York, NY 10020

Goldman Sachs

Vincent L. Amatulli, Information Technology, Treasury Department
  85 Broad Street, New York, NY 10004

J.J. Kenny Services

Thomas E. Zielinski, Chief Information Officer

Ira Kirschner, Database Administrator, Director of System Programming and Data Center
  65 Broadway, New York, NY 10006

Merrill Lynch

Kevin Sawyer, Director of Distributed Computing Services and Executive in Charge of Mainframe to Client-Server Conversion Process

Raymond M. Disco, Treasury/Bank Relations Manager
  World Financial Center, South Tower, New York, NY 10080-6107

Teachers Insurance and Annuity Association/ College Retirement Equities Fund (TIAA/CREF)

Charles S. Dvorkin, Vice President and Chief Technology Officer

Harry D. Perrin, Assistant Vice President, Information Technology
  730 Third Avenue, New York, NY 10017-3206

Financial Accounting Standards Board

Halsey G. Bullen, Project Manager

Jeannot Blanchet, Project Manager

Teri L. List, Practice Fellow
  401 Merritt 7, Norwalk, CN 06856

Massachusetts Institute of Technology

Dr. Stuart E. Madnick, Information Technology and Management Science

Dr. Michael Siegel, Information Technology, Sloan School of Management

Patricia M. McGinnis, Executive Director, International Financial Services

Peter J. Kempthorne, Project on Non-Traditional Methods in Financial Analysis

Dr. Alexander M. Samarov, Project on Non-Traditional Methods in Financial Analysis

Robert R. Halperin, Executive Director, Center for Coordination Science

Prof. Amar Gupta, Sloan School of Management

Prof. Jean-Luc Vila, Finance Dept., Sloan School of Management

Prof. Bin Zhou, Management Science, Sloan School of Management
  292 Main Street, Cambridge, MA 02139

Eric B. Sundin, Industrial Liaison Officer

David L. Verrill, Senior Liaison Officer, Industrial Liaison Program
  Sloan School of Management
  50 Memorial Drive, Cambridge, MA 02139

Henry H. Houh, Desk Area Network and ViewStation Project, Electrical Engineering and Computer Science

Dr. Henry A. Lieberman, Media Laboratory

Valerie A. Eames, Media Laboratory

Dr. Kenneth B. Haase, Media Arts and Sciences

Dr. David Zeltzer, Virtual Reality Project
  Ames St., Cambridge, MA 02139

Santa Fe Institute

Dr. Edward A. Knapp, President

Dr. L. Mike Simmons, Jr., Vice President

Dr. Bruce Abell, Vice President, Finance

Dr. Murray Gell-Mann, Theory of Complexity

Dr. Stuart Kauffman, Models in Biology

Dr. Chris Langton, Artificial Life

Dr. John Miller, Adaptive Computation in Economics

Dr. Blake Le Baron, Non-Traditional Methods in Economics

Bruce Sawhill, Virtual Reality
  1660 Old Pecos Trail, Santa Fe, NM 87501

School of Engineering, University of California, Los Angeles

Dr. Judea Pearl, Cognitive Systems Laboratory

Dr. Walter Karplus, Computer Science Department

Dr. Michael G. Dyer, Artificial Intelligence Laboratory
  Westwood Village, Los Angeles, CA 90024

School of Business Administration, University of Southern California

Dr. Bert M. Steece, Dean of Faculty, School of Business Administration
Dr. Alan Rowe, Professor of Management
  Los Angeles, CA 90089-1421

Prediction Company

Dr. J. Doyne Farmer, Director of Development
Dr. Norman H. Packard, Director of Research
Jim McGill, Managing Director
  234 Griffin Street, Santa Fe, NM 87501

Simgraphics Engineering

Steve Tice, President
David J. Verso, Chief Operating Officer
  1137 Huntington Drive, South Pasadena, CA 91030-4563

NYNEX Science and Technology

Thomas M. Super, Vice President, Research and Development
Steven Cross, NYNEX Shuttle Project
Valerie R. Tingle, System Analyst
Melinda Crews, Public Liaison, NYNEX Labs
  500 Westchester Avenue, White Plains, NY 10604
John C. Falco, Sales Manager, NYNEX Systems Marketing
David J. Annino, Account Executive, NYNEX Systems Marketing
  100 Church Street, New York, NY 10007

Microsoft

Mike McGeehan, Database Specialist
Andrew Elliott, Marketing Manager
  825 8th Avenue, New York, NY

Reuters America

Robert Russel, Senior Vice President
William A. S. Kennedy, Vice President
Buford Smith, President, Reuters Information Technology
Richard A. Willis, Manager, International Systems Design
M. A. Sayers, Technical Manager, Central Systems Development
Alexander Faust, Manager, Financial Products, USA (Instantlink and Blend)
  40 E. 52nd Street, New York, NY 10022

Oracle Corporation

Scott Matthews, National Account Manager
Robert T. Funk, Senior Systems Specialist
Joseph M. Di Bartolomeo, Systems Specialist
Dick Dawson, Systems Specialist
   885 Third Avenue, New York, NY 10022

Digital Equipment Corporation

Mike Fishbein, Product Manager, Massively Parallel Systems
   (MAS-PAR Supercomputer)
Marco Emrich, Technology Manager, NAS
Robert Passmore, Technical Manager, Storage Systems
Mark S. Dresdner, DEC Marketing Operations
   146 Main Street, Maynard, MA 01754
   (Meeting held at UBS New York)

UNISYS Corporation

Harvey J. Chiat, Director, Impact Programs
Manuel Lavin, Director, Databases
David A. Goiffon, Software Engineer
   P.O. Box 64942, MS 4463, Saint Paul, MN 55164-0942
   (Meeting held at UBS in New York)

Hewlett-Packard

Brad Wilson, Product Manager, Commercial Systems
Vish Krishnan, Manager, R+D Laboratory
Samir Mathur, Open ODB Manager
Michael Gupta, Transarc, Tuxedo, Encina Transaction Processing
Dave Williams, Industry Account Manager
   1911 Pruneridge Avenue, Cupertino, CA 95014

IBM Corporation

Terry Liffick, Software Strategies, Client-Server Architecture
Paula Cappello, Information Warehouse Framework
Ed Cobbs, Transaction Processing Systems
Dr. Paul Wilms, Connectivity and Interoperability
Helen Arzu, IBM Santa Teresa Representative
Dana L. Stetson, Advisory Marketing, IBM New York
   Santa Teresa Laboratory, 555 Bailey Avenue, San Jose, CA 95141

UBS Securities

A. Ramy Goldstein, Managing Director, Equity Derivative Products
299 Park Avenue, New York, NY 10171-0026

Union Bank of Switzerland

Dr. H. Baumann, Director of Logistics, North American Operations
Dr. Christian Gabathuler, Director, Information Technology
H. Shrikantan, Vice President Information Technology Department
Roy M. Darhin, Assistant Vice President
299 Park Avenue, New York, NY 10171-0026

Evans and Sutherland

Les Horwood, Director, New Business Development
Mike Walterman, Systems Engineer, Virtual Reality Applications
Lisa B. Huber, Software Engineer, Three-Dimensional Programming
600 Komas Drive, P.O.Box 58700, Salt Lake City, UT 84158

nCube

Michael Meirer, President and Chief Executive Officer
Craig D. Ramsey, Senior Vice President, Worldwide Sales
Ronald J. Buck, Vice President, Marketing
Matthew Hall, Director of Software Development
919 East Hillside Blvd, Foster City, Ca 94404

Taligent

Dr. Jack Grimes, Manager, Technology Evaluation
Catherine Jaeger, Manager, Market Development
10201 N. De Anza Blvd, Cupertino, CA 95014-2233

Visual Numerics

Don Kainer, Vice President and General Manager
Joe Weaver, Vice President OEM/VAR Sales
Jim Phillips, Director Product Development
Dr. Shawn Javid, Senior Product Manager
Dan Clark, Manager, WAVE Family Products
Thomas L. Welch, Marketing Product Manager
Margaret Journey, Director Administration
John Bee, Technical Sales Engineer
Adam Asnes, VDA Sales Executive
William Potts, Sales Manager
6230 Lookout Road, Boulder, CO 80301

University of Michigan

Prof. John H. Holland, Electrical Engineering and Computer Science
Dr. Rick L. Riolo, Systems Researcher, Department of Psychology
Ann Arbor, MI 48109-2103

UNITED KINGDOM

Barclays Bank

Peter Golden, Chief Information Officer, Barclays Capital Markets,
Treasury, BZW
Brandon Davies, Director of Financial Engineering
David J. Parsons, Director, Advanced Technology
Christine E. Irwin, Group Information Systems Technology
Murray House, 1 Royal Mint Court, London EC3N 4HH

Bank of England

Mark Laycock, Banking Supervision Division
Threadneedle Street, London EC2R 8AH

Association for Payment Clearing Services (APACS)

J. Michael Williamson, Deputy Chief Executive
14 Finsbury Square, London EC2A 1BR

Abbey National Bank

Mac Millington, Director of Information Technology
Chalkdell Drive, Shenley Wood, Milton Keynes MK6 6LA
Anthony W. Elliott, Director of Risk and Credit
Abbey House, Baker Street, London NW1 6XL

Natwest Securities

Sam B. Gibb, Director of Information Technology,
Don F. Simpson, Director, Global Technology
Richard E. Gibbs, Director, Equity Derivatives
135 Bishopsgate, London EC2M 3XT

Oracle Corporation

Geoffrey W. Squire, Executive Vice President and Chief Executive
Richard Barker, Senior Vice President and Director, British Research
Laboratories

Giles Godart-Brown, Senior Support Manager
Paul A. Gould, Account Executive
   Oracle Park, Bittams Lane, Guildford Rd, Chertsey, Surrey KT16 9RG

Virtual Presence

Stuart Cupit, Graphics Engineer
   25 Corsham Street, London N1 6DR

Valbecc Object Technology

Martin Fowler, Ptech Expert
   115 Wilmslow Road, Handforth, Wilmslow, Cheshire SK9 3ER

Credit Swiss Financial Products

Ross Salinger, Managing Director
   One Cabot Square, London E14 4QJ

Credit Swiss First Boston

Geoff J.R. Doubleday, Executive Director
   One Cabot Square, London E14 4QJ

E.D. & F. Man International

Brian Fudge, Funds Division
   Sugar Quay, Lower Thames Street, London EC3R 6DU

SCANDINAVIA

Vaerdipapircentralen (VP)

Jens Bache, General Manager
Aase Blume, Assistant to the General Manager
   61 Helgeshoj Allé, Postbox 20, 2630 Taastrup, Denmark

Swedish Bankers' Association

Bo Gunnarsson, Manager, Bank Automation Department
Gösta Fischer, Manager, Bank-Owned Financial Companies Department
Göran Ahlberg, Manager, Credit Market Affairs Department
   P.O. Box 7603, 10394 Stockholm, Sweden

Skandinaviska Enskilda Banken

Lars Isacsson, Treasurer
Urban Janeld, Executive Vice President, Finance and IT
Mats Andersson, Director of Computers and Communications
Gösta Olavi, Manager, SEB Data/Koncern Data
  2 Sergels Torg, 10640 Stockholm, Sweden

Securum Ab

Anders Nyren, Director of Finance and Accounting
John Lundgren, Manager of IT
  38 Regeringsg, 5 tr., 10398 Stockholm, Sweden

Sveatornet Ab of the Swedish Savings Banks

Gunar M. Carlsson, General Manager
  (Meeting at Swedish Bankers' Association)

Mandamus Ab of the Swedish Agricultural Banks

Marie Martinsson, Credit Department
  (Meeting at Swedish Bankers' Association)

Handelsbanken

Janeric Sundin, Manager, Securities Department
Jan Aronson, Assistant Manager, Securities Department
  (Meeting at Swedish Bankers' Association)

Gota Banken

Johannsson, Credit Department
  (Meeting at Swedish Bankers' Association)

Irdem Ab

Gian Medri, Former Director of Research at Nordbanken
  19 Flintlasvagen, 19154 Sollentuna, Sweden

AUSTRIA

Creditanstalt Bankverein

Dr. Wolfgang G. Lichtl, Director of Foreign Exchange and Money
  Markets
Dr. Johann Strobl, Manager, Financial Analysis for Treasury Operations
  3, Julius Tandler-Platz, 1090 Vienna

Bank Austria

Dr. Peter Fischer, Director of Treasury
Peter Gabriel, Deputy General Manager, Trading
Konrad Schcate, Manager, Financial Engineering
   2, Am Hof, 1010 Vienna

Association of Austrian Banks and Bankers

Dr. Fritz Diwok, Secretary General
   11, Boersengasse, 1013 Vienna

Aktiengesellschaft Fuer Bauwesen

Dr. Josef Fritz, General Manager
   2, Lothringenstrasse, 1041 Vienna

Management Data of Creditanstalt

Guenther Reindl, Vice President, International Banking Software
Franz Necas, Project Manager, RICOS
Nikolas Goetz, Product Manager, RICOS
   21-25 Althanstrasse, 1090 Vienna

GERMANY

Deutsche Bundesbank

Eckhard Oechler, Director of Bank Supervision and Legal Matters
   14, Wilhelm Epstein Strasse, D-6000 Frankfurt 50

Deutsche Bank

Peter Gerard, Executive Vice President, Organization and Information
   Technology
Hermann Seiler, Senior Vice President, Investment Banking and Foreign
   Exchange Systems
Dr. Kuhn, Investment Banking and Foreign Exchange Systems
Dr. Stefan Kolb, Organization and Technological Development
   12, Koelner Strasse, D-6236 Eschborn

Dresdner Bank

Karsten Wohlenberg, Project Leader Risk Management, Simulation and
   Analytics Task Force Financial Division
Hans-Peter Leisten, Mathematician
Susanne Loesken, Organization and IT Department
   43, Mainzer Landstrasse, D-6000 Frankfurt

Commerzbank

Helmut Hoppe, Director, Organization and Information Technology
Hermann Lenz, Director, Controllership, Internal Accounting, and
   Management Accounting
Harald Lux, Manager, Organization and Information Technology
Waldemar Nickel, Manager, Systems Planning
   155, Mainzer Landstrasse, D-60261 Frankfurt

Deutscher Sparkassen Und Giroverband

Manfred Krueger, Division Manager, Card Strategy
4 Simrockstrasse, D-5300 Bonn 1
   (Telephone interview from Frankfurt)

ABN-AMRO (Holland)

Schilder, Organization and Information Technology
   (Telephone interview from Frankfurt)

Media Systems

Bertram Anderer, Director
   6, Goethestrasse, D-7500 Karlsruhe

Fraunhofer Institute for Computer Graphics

Dr. Martin Goebel
Wolfgang Felber
   7, Wilhelminerstrasse, D-6100 Darmstadt

GMD First—Research Institute for Computer Architecture, Software Technology, and Graphics

Dr. Wolfgang K. Giloi, General Manager
Dr. Peter Behr, Administrative Director
Dr. Ulrich Bruening, Chief Designer
Dr. Joerg Nolte, Designer of Parallel Operating Systems Software
Dr. Matthias Kessler, Parallel Languages and Parallel Compilers
Dr. Friedrich W. Schroer, New Programming Paradigms
Dr. Thomas Lux, Fluid Dynamics, Weather Prediction and Pollution
   Control Project
   5, Rudower Chaussee, D-1199 Berlin

Siemens Nixdorf

Wolfgang Weiss, Director of Banking Industry Office

Bert Kirschbaum, Manager, Dresdner Bank Project
Mark Miller, Manager, Neural Networks Project for UBS and German
 banks
Andrea Vonerden, Business Management Department
 27, Lyoner Strasse, D-6000 Frankfurt 71

UBS Germany

H.-H. v. Scheliha, Director, Organization and Information Technology
Georg Sudhaus, Manager IT for Trading Systems
Marco Bracco, Trader
Jaap Van Harten, Trader
 52, Bleichstrasse, D-6000 Frankfurt 1

SWITZERLAND

Bank for International Settlements

Claude Sivy, Director, Controllership and Operational Security
Frederik C. Musch, Secretary General, Basel Committee on Banking
 Supervision
 2 Centralbankplatz, Basel

Swiss Bank Corporation

Dr. Marcel Rohner, Director, IFD Controlling
 Swiss Bank Center, 8010 Zurich

BZ Bank Zurich

Martin Ebner, President
Peter Sgöstrand, Finance
Roger Jenny, Analyst
 50 Sihlstrasse, 8021 Zurich

BZ Trust Aktiengesellschaft

Dr. Stefan Holzer, Financial Analyst
 24 Eglirain, 8832 Wilen

Ciba-Geigy Ag

Stefan Janovjak, Divisional Information Manager
Natalie Papezik, Information Architect
 Ciba-Geigy, R-1045, 5.19, 4002 Basle

Olsen and Associates

Dr. Richard Olsen, President
   233, Seefeldstrasse, Zurich

Eurodis

Albert Mueller, Director
Beat Erzer, Marketing Manager
B. Pedrazzini, Systems Engineer
Reto Albertini, Sales Engineer
   Bahnhofstrasse 58/60, CH-8105 Regensdorf

Ecole Polytechniqaue Federal De Lausanne

Prof. Dr. Jean-Daniel Nicoud, Director, Microinformatics Laboratory
Prof. Dr. Boi Faltings, Artificial Intelligence
Prof. Dr. Martin J. Hasler, Circuits and Systems
Dr. Ing. Ropman Boulic, Computer Graphics
   1015 Lausanne

JAPAN

Bank of Japan

Harry Toyama, Counsel and Chief Manager, Credit and Market
   Management Department
Akira Ieda, Credit and Market Management Department
   2-1-1, Kongoku-Cho, Nihonbashi, Chuo-ku, Tokyo 103

Dai-Ichi Kangyo Bank

Shunsuke Nakasuji, General Manager and Director, Information
   Technology Division
Seiichi Hasegawa, Manager International Systems Group
Takahiro Sekizawa, International Systems Group
Yukio Hisatomi, Manager, Systems Planning Group
Shigeaki Togawa, Systems Planning Group
   13-3, Shibuya, 2-Chome, Shibuya-ku, Tokyo 150

Fuji Bank

Hideo Tanaka, General Manager, Systems Planning Division
Toshihiko Uzaki, Manager, Systems Planning Division
Takakazu Imai, Systems Planning Division
   Otemachi Financial Center, 1-5-4 Otemachi, Chiyoda-ku, Tokyo

Mitsubishi Bank

Akira Watanabe, General Manager, Derivative Products
Akira Towatari, Manager, Strategic Planning and Administration,
    Derivative Products
Takehito Nemoto, Chief Manager, Systems Development Division
Nobuyuki Yamada, Systems Development Division
Haruhiko Suzuki, Systems Development Division
   7-1, Marunouchi, 2-chome, Chiyoda-ku, Tokyo 100

Nomura Research Institute

Tomio Arai, Director, Systems Science Department
Tomoyuki Ohta, Director, Financial Engineering Group
Tomohiko Hiruta, Manager, I-STAR Systems Services
   9-1, Nihonbashi, 1-Chome, Chuo-ku, Tokyo 103

Mitsubishi Trust and Banking

Nobuyuki Tanaka, General Manager, Systems Planning Division
Terufumi Kage, Consultant, Systems Planning Division
   9-8 Kohnan, 2-Chome, Minato-ku, Tokyo 108

Sakura Bank

Nobuo Ihara, Senior Vice President and General Manager, Systems
    Development Office VIII
Hisao Katayama, Senior Vice President and General Manager, Systems
    Development Office VII
Toshihiko Eda, Senior Systems Engineer, Systems Development Division
   4-2, Kami-Osahi, 4-Chome, Shinagawa-ku, Tokyo 141

Sanyo Securities

Yuji Ozawa, Director, Systems Planning Department
K. Toyama, Systems Planning Department
   1-8-1, Nihonbashi, Kayabacho, Chuo-ku, Tokyo 103

Center For Financial Industry Information Systems (FISC)

Shighehisa Hattori, Executive Director
Kiyoshi Kumata, Manager, Research Division II
   16th Floor, Ark Mori Building, 12-32, 1-Chome
   Akasaka, Minato-ku, Tokyo 107

Laboratory For International Fuzzy Engineering Research (LIFE)

Dr. Toshiro Terano, Executive Director

Dr. Anca L. Ralescu, Assistant Director

Shunichi Tani, Fuzzy Control Project Leader

Siber Hegner Building, 89-1 Yamashita-Cho, Naka-ku,
Yokohama-shi 231

Real World Computing Partnership (RWC)

Dr. Junichi Shumada, General Manager of RWC

Hajime Irisawa, Executive Director

Tsukuba Mitsui Building, 1-6-1 Takezono,
Tsukuba-shi, Ibarahi 305

Tokyo University

Dr. Michitaka Hirose, Dept. of Mechano-Informatics, Faculty of
Engineering

Dr. Kensuke Yokoyama, Virtual Reality Project

3-1, 7-Chome, Hongo Bunkyo-ku, Tokyo 113

Tokyo International University

Dr. Yoshiro Kuratani

9-1-7-528, Akasaka, Minato-ku, Tokyo 107

Japan Electronic Directory Research Institute

Dr. Toshio Yokoi, General Manager

Mita-Kokusai Building - Annex, 4-28 Mita, 1-Chome,
Minato-ku, Tokyo 108

Mitsubishi Research Institute (MRI)

Masayuki Fujita, Manager, Strategic Information Systems Dept.

Hideyuki Morita, Senior Research Associate, Information Science Dept.

Akio Sato, Research Associate, Information Science Dept.

ARCO Tower, 8-1 Shimomeguro, 1-Chome, Meguro-ku,
Tokyo 153

NTT Software

Dr. Fukuya Ishino, Senior Vice President

223-1 Yamashita-Cho, Naka-ku, Yokohama 231

Ryoshin Systems (Systems Developer Fully Owned by Mitsubishi Trust)

Takewo Yuwi, Vice President, Technical Research and Development
9-8 Kohman, 2-Chome, Minato-ku, Tokyo 108

Sanyo Software Services

Fumio Sato, General Manager, Sales Department 2
Kanayama Building, 1-2-12 Shinkawa, Chuo-ku,
Tokyo 104

Fujitsu Research Institute

Dr. Masuteru Sekiguchi, Member of the Board and Director of R&D
Takao Saito, Director of the Parallel Computing Research Center
Dr. Hiroyasu Itoh, R&D Department
Katsuto Kondo, R&D Department
Satoshi Hamaya, Information Systems and Economics
9-3 Nakase, 1-Chome, Mihama-ku, Chiba-City 261

NEC

Kotaro Namba, Senior Researcher, NEC Planning Research
Dr. Toshiyuki Nakata, Manager, Computer System Research Laboratory
Asao Kaneko, Computer System Research Laboratory
3-13-12 Mita, Minato-ku, Tokyo 108

Toshiba

Dr. Makoto Ihara, Manager Workstation Product Planning and
   Technical Support Dept.
Emi Nakamura, Analyst, Financial Applications Dept.
Joshikiyo Nakamura, Financial Sales Manager
Minami Arai, Deputy Manager, Workstation Systems Division
1-1, Shibaura, 1-Chome, Minato-ku, Tokyo 105

Microsoft

James Lalonde, Multinational Account Manager, Large Accounts Sales
   Dept.
Sasazuka NA Bldg, 50-1 Sasazuka, 1-Chome,
Shibuya-ku, Tokyo 151

Apple Technology

Dr. Tsutomu Kobayashi, President

25 Mori Bldg, 1-4-30 Roppongi, Minato-ku, Tokyo 106

Digital Equipment Japan

Roshio Ishii, Account Manager, Financial Sales Unit 1
   2-1 Kamiogi, 1-Chome, Suginamiku, Tokyo 167

UBS Japan

Dr. Peter Brutsche, Executive Vice President and Chief Manager

Gary P. Eidam, First Vice President, Regional Head of Technology

Charles Underwood, Vice President, Head of Technical Architecture
   and Strategy

Masaki Utsunomiya, Manager, IT Production Facilities
   Yurakucho Building 2F, 1-10-1 Yurakucho,
   Chiyoda-ku, Tokyo 100

Abbreviations

Abbreviations Used with Financial Algorithms

AI	accrued interest receivable (also written AIR)
bp	basis points
C	cash flow
C_s	stochastic cash flow
c	covariance
CC	cost of carry
CE	capital expenditures
CTD	cheaper to deliver
CR	credit risk
CPR	current project revenue
D	duration
D_t	depreciation value per year
E_i	return on stock i
E_m	overall market return
FC_s	stochastic funding cost
FP	future price
fV	face value
FV	future value
k	an estimated drift parameter
L_r	ratio of liquid to illiquid instruments
MP	market price
MR	market risk
MM	marking-to-model
NPV	net present value
NFV	net future value
NAV	net asset value
NC	normal cash flow
NP	notional principal amount
OE	operating expenses

P_i	price of stock i
$P_{i,t}$	price of stock i in period t
PF	pay frequency
PP	periodic (fixed) payments
PME	potential market exposure
PMR	potential market risk
PC	projected cost
PR	projected risk
PV	projected value
RR	rate of return of a portfolio
rr_i	rate of return of asset i
R	receipts, revenues
R_f	receive frequency
RC	real cash flow
RF	risk factor
RP	risk premium
RR	rate of return
RE	risk equivalence
RE_c	equivalence to credit risk
RE_m	equivalence to market risk
RF	risk factor
R(w,t)	1-year rate process at time t
SP	strike price
SPP	spot price
T	remaining term to maturity
TP	transaction price of a bond
t	a given time period
ζ	tax rate
TD	tax shield from depreciation
TI	taxes on income
W(w,t)	standard Wiener process at time t
w	a stochastic sample scenario
x_t	interest payment of a bond in period t
Y	annual yield of a bond
YY	convenience yield

ABBREVIATIONS USED WITH FINANCIAL INSTRUMENTS

ADR	American Depository Receipt
ARM	Adjustable-Rate Mortgage
CAT	Certificate of Accrual on Treasuries
CMO	Collateralized Mortgage Obligation
DPA	Deferred Payment American Option
FRA	Forward Rate Agreement
IAR	Index Amortizing Swap
IPS	Index Principal Swap
IRS	Interest Rate Swap
MBF	Mortgage-Backed Financing
MBS	Mortgage-Backed Securities
OAS	Option Adjusted Spread
OEM	Original Exposure Method
OTC	Over-the-Counter
RORC	Return on Risk Capital
STRIP	Separate Trading of Registered Interest and Principal Securities

PART ONE

COMPONENTS OF A RISK-MANAGEMENT POLICY

1

Financial Instruments and Risk-Management Systems

1. Introduction

A *financial instrument* is cash; evidence of ownership in equity or debt; a bilateral or multilateral contract that meets obligations and rights. Financial instruments are subject to many risks, among which *credit* and *market risks* are the better known and more generally feared:

- ❑ *Credit risk* is the possibility that a loss may occur from the failure of the counterparty to perform according to the terms of a contract.

- ❑ *Market risk* concerns the chance that future changes in market prices may make a financial instrument less valuable or more onerous.

Credit and market risks denote the presence of an exposure to accounting losses. The same is true of legal risk, country risk, currency risk, interest rate risk, placing risk, settlement risk, inventory risk, fraud risk, and many others.

Many of these risks have existed through the ages and separately or together are present with all financial instruments, for instance, loans. Inventory risk regards the investment vehicles in the portfolio. Fraud risk addresses the issue of unauthorized issuance of payment orders and is a widespread source of worry for commercial banks as well as for central banks.

3

There is no absolute protection against the resourcefulness of criminal minds, even if cooperation between banks and state-of-the-art security systems permits the implementation of procedures that can substantially reduce the risk of fraud. This, however, is more difficult to do with new financial instruments, such as derivatives, for the simple reason that banks and bankers have not yet mastered them.

In order to control the risks associated with both the old and new financial instruments, bankers must *rethink their mission*. They must appreciate that new markets, new products, demands of new clients, and high technology have accentuated the need for nontraditional research, rigorous financial analysis, and first-class risk-control systems. There is also the need for lifelong learning because without steady training, experience becomes obsolete, making it much more difficult to control risk.

2.   Classical and Exotic Derivative Instruments

A *derivative* financial instrument is a security or contract whose value is determined (or derived) from the value of a specified underlying asset, liability, or index: the *underlier*. Many derivatives are bilateral agreements, but others are traded in exchanges. The ratio of the former to the latter typically varies between 33 percent and 50 percent.

Off-balance-sheet (OBS) financial products are used to hedge as well as to take positions that (it is hoped) enhance returns. Given that different types of derivatives dominate the financial markets, there is a crying need for a method to measure exposure as well as a comprehensive risk-management system—which very few banks presently possess.

Off-balance-sheet is a better term than *derivatives* because "derivatives" misleadingly lumps together different classes of instruments, some of which are not derivative at all. For example, in most cases, swaps are simply exchanges of cash flows, and commitments to extend credit do not derive their prices from an underlying instrument.

Derivative instruments can be classified into traditional and nontraditional. Some vehicles are considered *traditional* because they have matured over the years. As a result, they are better known by bankers, traders, and investors—or, at least, this is the leading hypothesis.

Derivatives are relatively recent financial instruments, many among them being nontraditional.

In America, the Financial Accounting Standards Board (FASB)—which depends on the Securities and Exchanges Commission (SEC)—has defined the following off-balance-sheet operations as typical:[1]

---

[1] See also D. N. Chorafas and H. Steinmann, *Off-Balance Sheet Financing* (Chicago: Probus, 1994).

- ❑ Commitments to extend credit.
- ❑ Standby letters of credit.
- ❑ Financial guarantees written (sold).
- ❑ Options written.
- ❑ Interest rate caps and floors.
- ❑ Interest rate swap agreements.
- ❑ Forward contracts.
- ❑ Futures contracts.
- ❑ Resource obligations on receivables sold.
- ❑ Obligations under foreign currency exchange contracts.
- ❑ Interest rate foreign currency swaps.
- ❑ Obligations to repurchase securities sold.
- ❑ Outstanding commitments to purchase or sell at predetermined prices.
- ❑ Obligations arising from financial instruments sold short.

Derivative trades are called *off-balance-sheet* because in the early 1980s the Federal Reserve permitted banks to write these contracts off-balance-sheet. At the time, these trades were the exception and carried little weight in terms of a firm's financial results. Today, however, trading in derivatives roughly represents two-thirds of the credit line assigned to counterparties. Such deals generally include the following:[2]

- ❑ Futures and options on futures.
- ❑ Forward interest rate agreements (FRA).
- ❑ Equity and currency options.
- ❑ Interest rate swaps (IRS).
- ❑ Currency, commodity, and equity swaps.
- ❑ Interest rate caps and floors.
- ❑ Stripped Treasuries, or STRIPs.[3]
- ❑ Mortgage-backed financing (MBF).

---

[2] This is only a birds-eye view. Exotics are covered in detail in Chapter 10.

[3] STRIP is an acronym for Separate Trading of Registered Interest and Principal Securities.

❏   Floating rate for fixed-rate payments, on a notional principal amount.[4]

❏   Other, custom-made financial vehicles, many of which are exotic.

These ordinary options, futures, and swaps typically have a long life cycle. By contrast custom-made, complex instruments such as *exotic* options have a time horizon that depends on client needs. The more custom-made and unusual the instrument is, the shorter its market appeal and life cycle will tend to be.

Therefore, averages regarding a derivative instrument's time horizon are meaningless. Every OBS vehicle has to be considered on its own merits. The same is true of

❏   Risk characteristics.

❏   Market liquidity.

❏   Reward for risk.

The number and variation of the so-called exotic derivatives is wide and is growing quickly. Typically, the term *exotic* stands for new and complex instruments, which in today's market include derivatives known in the trade as the following:

❏   All-or-nothing.

❏   Barrier.

❏   Binary.

❏   Butterfly.

❏   Complex chooser.

❏   Compound (nested).

❏   Down and out (or in).

❏   Discount swaps.

❏   Embedded options (Embedos).

❏   Inverse floaters.

❏   Knock-in and knock-out.

❏   Lookback.

❏   One touch.

❏   Outperformance.

---

4 For the definition of the notional principal, see Chapter 2.

❑ Path dependent.

❑ Quanto.

❑ Step-lock.

❑ Up and in (or out).

There is always a new invention, accompanied by a rather significant amount of unknown risk. For this reason, the excuse that derivatives trades are engaged in hedging does not really hold water.

While pure hedging operations do take place, by far the number one reason for engaging in an off-balance-sheet trade is lust and greed—or easy profit. But most often profits with derivatives resemble profits in a lottery. No one really knows in advance how the market will behave or, therefore, how the chips will fall.

3.   The Personalization of Financial Products—Opportunities and Risks

If a company is in the business of making a product that has become indistinguishable from those of its rivals, this means that its goods have turned into a commodity. Thereafter, they will sell chiefly on price. This happened indeed not only to consumer goods but also to technology; for instance, makers of inexpensive clones knocked down names such as the IBM PC.

The makers of many goods and services now live in terror of the same thing happening to them, and this is true all the way to banking. All over the world, look-alike competitors are elbowing aside financial institutions that have been famous for so long they became reckless enough to forget about market whims and drives.

Because of changing market tastes and the increasing sophistication of counterparties, one way of looking at the customer base is the personalization and customization of financial products. This strategy aims to reverse the commodity-oriented trend. If the appeal of the brand name is declining, the bank is well-advised to redefine itself and resurrect its fortunes.

What is happening to brands has a significance that goes well beyond the makers of commodities such as soft drinks, cigarettes, and soap powders. It is an axiom of capitalism that the winner in the market is the one who makes a better mousetrap at the lowest cost.

The fact that puts wind in the sails of the derivatives market is that, in terms of traditional banking, it has become so much harder to make a product that is genuinely different from or better than a competitor's. And it is even harder to stay ahead without investments in research and development (R&D) and high technology implementation.

**Figure 1–1.   Derivative Financial Instruments Are
Addressed to the Clients and Corresponding
Banks at the Peak of the Pyramid**

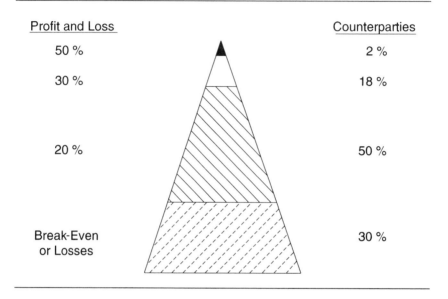

Profit and Loss		Counterparties
50 %		2 %
30 %		18 %
20 %		50 %
Break-Even or Losses		30 %

This is enough of a reason why steady innovations in new financial instruments are welcome—but not at the cost of bringing down the
financial system through an inordinate systemic risk. The trouble is that
many banks enter derivatives without having the needed expertise in
this trade and without really being able to control the amount of risk
they are taking.

A fact that should never be lost sight of is that while bread-and-
butter derivatives are now being offered through retail banking and insurance companies to medium- and low-net-worth individuals,
personalized products—including exotics—are developed for big companies, institutional investors, and high-net-worth individuals.

This sounds reasonable enough. As every banker should know,
nearly 50 percent of the company's profits come from 2 percent of the
clients, while the next 18 percent of the clients account for another 30
percent of the profits. Figure 1–1 presents this correlation between a selected group of clients and the potential profits they generate. But
higher profits also mean higher risks.

As exotics become the instrument of choice of many trades, the
risks taken by corporate treasurers and many bankers are making headlines. Few people really appreciate that *custom-made* and *exotic* derivatives bring with them a host of new requirements, including the ability
to perform rigorous analytics before commitment and the wisdom to

control exposure before it becomes deadly to the investor and to the financial system.

J. Copenhaved, director of derivatives at Sumitomo Bank Capital Markets, says, "I am certain that people do not understand the risks of some of the transactions they are putting on. Not only the endusers but, I suspect, some of the supposedly sophisticated dealers."[5]

Complex derivatives and synthetics present both opportunities and problems. Through them, it is possible to build personalized instruments that, bankers suggest, can meet any financial need. This attracts both institutional investors and corporate treasurers, who often have little understanding of what the new vehicles involve and the amount of exposure that is assumed.

"It has not yet reached epidemic proportions, but it is a growing problem," says Robert Studer, president of the Union Bank of Switzerland.[6] The reference is to the tendency for banks' corporate customers to run their treasury for profits rather than for cash management and pure risk control.

A senior banker stated in a recent meeting in Monte Carlo that one of the priorities in financial institutions is *how to package* products to guarantee risk and return. Many customers call and say, "I give you $1 million, or $5 million, and I am willing to forego the interest for higher return. What do you have to offer?"

A valid answer to this query requires not only new product design and associated experimentation—including risk control—but also pooling. To optimize, it may be necessary to group up to 10 parties to make a $50 million investment fund. Pooling has its own risk and return characteristics.

Whether individually or in pools, options, futures, forwards, swaps, and exotic derivatives instruments are today widely traded by an increasing universe of companies, banks, other financial institutions, and industrial corporations. They are disseminated quickly in the markets and so are the risks that go with them.

4.   An Industry in Rapid Evolution

There has been a very rapid development of financial derivatives since they were first launched on Chicago's Mercantile Exchange (CME) in June 1972. It is no accident that their advent coincided with the breakup of the Bretton Woods system of fixed exchange rates and the new business opportunities that came along.

---

5 *Institutional Investor*, September 1992.
6 *The Economist*, London, June 4, 1994.

An integral part of these opportunities is that derivatives contracts reflect not *real* but *virtual* assets, as we will see in the next section. Their value mirrors the changing price of an underlying asset—shares, currencies, or other commodities—making it theoretically possible to hedge risk or diversify.

This is considered the reason most corporate treasurers and fund managers now use derivatives routinely to guard against exchange-rate and other movements in prices that could reduce the value of earnings. Their strategy is to revamp their portfolios more quickly and at lesser cost than by buying and selling securities directly.

There is an evident logic in this argument, but it is unwise to forget there is a price for the many unknowns included in the deal. There is also plenty of room for arbitrage as astute investors, investment funds, banks, and securities firms spot a profit in momentary inconsistencies between

❑ Cash.

❑ Underliers.

❑ Derivatives prices.

Back in the 1980s, when the whole off-balance-sheet business got its momentum, derivatives were an extension of an underlying financial instrument and its "cash" market. The value of an equity index futures contract when it expires is based on the underlying shares in the index. But values do not move mechanically in line with a given cash market. In many cases, the derivatives markets themselves actually determine prices in the underlying instruments. Prediction is very important in exploiting business opportunity and controlling risk, but it becomes ever more complex because of the plethora of new financial instruments.

Let's take a bird's-eye view of what the derivatives market really involves. While thousands of different derivatives exist, and new ones spring up every day, they can be classified into four main categories:

1. *Options* give the holder the right to sell (a put option) or buy (a call option) something in the future at a price determined at the outset.

An institutional investor wanting to protect the gains he or she has made in an equity portfolio might buy put options. These would guarantee a minimum level at which he or she could sell the shares in the future—without at the same time limiting the potential gains.

2. *Futures and Forwards* require the holder to buy or sell an underlying asset or other commodity, such as a currency, at some time in the future. Unlike an option, the holder cannot simply let the contract lapse. Forward contracts are bilateral agree-

ments that practically have no active secondary market. By contrast, futures are traded in exchanges and have a market[7]— except, of course, in the case of panic.

3. *Swaps* involve two parties who agree that for a certain period they will exchange regular payments according to a contract.

What the counterparties are essentially exchanging, or swapping, is forward obligations. In an interest rate swap, for instance, one party exchanges fixed-rate interest payments for the other party's floating-rate interest payments.

4. *Exotics*, discussed earlier, are of many different types. Binary or digital options, for example, provide discontinuous payoffs.

Under a binary option, the buyer will pay or receive one of two different flows *if* a particular level is reached, the most common being *all-or-nothing* and *one touch*. As the name implies, the first provides an "all" or "nothing" payout depending on the value of the option at expiration. If the option is in-the-money at maturity, *then* the purchaser will receive a value equal to the notional principal of the contract.

But if the option ends out-of-the-money, the purchaser will receive nothing, and the writer will have no further obligation to the buyer. This sharply contrasts to the conventional option, which pays the buyer the difference between the current market and the strike price times the notional amount of the contract.

Binary options are the nearest thing to a financial lottery. Their huge risk comes from the fact that they involve the whole notional principal amount. This differentiates them not only from other options but from swaps as well—where the notional principal concept originated.

In an interest rate swap, for instance, one institution pays the other a fixed rate of interest based on some notional principal amount, while the other pays a variable rate of interest, which changes as market interest rates change. Interest rate swaps enable companies to turn floating-rate liabilities into fixed-rate, and vice versa or execute a number of other bilateral transactions where the notional principal is only a reference level never to be paid out or received.

The problem with all four classes of transactions, and most particularly those that are the most risky, is that the fragmented structure of regulation is badly organized to deal with the fast-growing derivatives markets—and there are also many disagreements among regulators how to handle systemic risk.

---

7 See also D. N. Chorafas, *Advanced Financial Analysis* (London: Euromoney, 1995).

In early 1993, the Basel Committee, Bank for International Settlements (BIS), issued three papers connected to derivatives financial products. The Market Risk Amendments and Interest Risk Amendments were proposals made to improve upon the capital requirements specified by the 1988 accord. A netting process was also proposed.

All these documents have been studied and discussed by the central banks, commercial banks, and other institutions. But as of November 1994, when I last checked with BIS, only the netting paper had gone through. The others are still on the high seas. It is not easy to obtain international regulatory agreements.

In the absence of clearly set regulations for cross-border trades, the markets become dominated by some of the big dealers who manage to completely escape government control. As we will see in section 7, there are reasons why this happens—and, as it happens, it compounds the systemic risk.

5.   Real Versus Virtual Assets

Physical commodities are *real assets*, whether we talk of wheat, soybeans, pork bellies, copper, gold, diamonds, or the family home. These assets have intrinsic value and can be used as an exchange for other goods and services taken at their prevailing market price. Real assets tend to be limited in supply and, short of trading, generate no income stream. Further, they differ significantly from *financial assets*, in the sense that the latter are nominal, not physical.

Contrary to the real or physical asset, a financial asset is virtual. It is also expandable and easier to manipulate—as it resides on a piece of paper or, more recently, in a database. But a financial asset generates an *income stream* based on the value of the underlying physical asset. This reference concerns all financial assets, not just derivatives. All financial assets, for instance loans, are derivatives of a physical asset. What we currently call "derivatives"—that is, off-balance-sheet instruments—are in essence derivatives of derivative products.

All financial vehicles are virtual assets and have in common the fact that their value is set in nominal terms. Hence, the value of financial products—and, therefore, of financial investments—can be more severely influenced by market forces than that of commodities.

Along the same lines, the value of off-balance-sheet instruments is more severely influenced than the value of balance sheet instruments, hence the reason for *higher order* risk metrics such as delta, gamma, theta, kappa, and rho, which will be discussed in Chapter 15.[8]

---

[8] The term *high order risk metrics* reflects the mathematical concept of higher order differentiation, rather than magnitude of risk.

Furthermore, given certain economic conditions, the value of commodities and that of nominal assets can vary in an opposite sense. An example is inflation. The value of real assets can be enhanced in inflationary conditions. But currency depreciates under inflation, and the bond market unravels.

It is not surprising that real assets such as housing and commodities, which have intrinsic value, perform best in periods of high inflation. Nominal assets such as stocks and bonds, whose value is based on today's assessment of a future income stream, are typically not good performers under inflationary conditions.

Few people appreciate the fact that off-balance-sheet financial instruments are essentially the derivatives of derivatives and are therefore highly sensitive to price changes of the basic price function with regard to the underlying physical asset—as the bond bloodbath of February/March 1994 documents.

❑ If $F(x)$ is the price function of the physical asset, then

❑ $\dfrac{dF(x)}{dx}$ is the price function of the balance sheet financial product, and

❑ $\dfrac{d^2F(x)}{dx^2}$ is the price function of the off-balance-sheet instrument.

These algorithms should not be confused with the increasingly popular metrics delta, gamma, and so on, which will be discussed in Chapter 15. When we reach that point in our discussion, we will try to reconcile the two issues of price function and its metrics.

One of the particularities of the financial markets is that while, strictly speaking, real assets do not possess an income stream, most institutional investment in commodities can be structured to generate a yield. Typically, a tangible asset will underlie the revenues:

❑ The securitized instrument will be linked to a collateralized commodity product.

❑ The real asset will perform more like the nominal assets in terms of risk and reward.

The challenge is to present these relationships in a way that can be kept dynamic but also easily comprehensible by management. A three-dimensional frame, such as the one shown in Figure 1–2, allows easy visualization of risk and return. Presentation of ad hoc queries must be done interactively in three-dimensional color graphics.

As the reader will appreciate, Figure 1–2 is very simple. There are two reasons why this figure and many similar figures, have been included in the text. First, it is always wise to try to present fairly complex

Figure 1–2. **The Reporting Structure Must Present Management with Risk Figures That Are Both Comprehensive and Comprehensible— Preferably in 3-D**

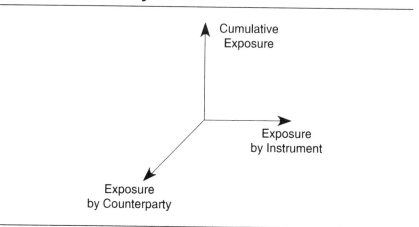

issues in simple form. Second, I am convinced this is the best way to acquaint the reader with a three-dimensional view of data—an approach that should characterize all senior management reports.

This can be stated in conclusion: The issues treated in this and the preceding sections cover a great deal of the risk associated with derivative financial instruments as well as the profits that can be expected from them. The risks are by no means negligible, which a growing number of references helps to document.

6.   Stopping the Flow of Red Ink

There have been many spectacular losses with derivatives by industrial corporations. One of the better known is Procter and Gamble, whose treasury lost $102 million in 1993 by taking ill-judged bets on future movements in interest rates. Other American companies that lost a lot of money are Gibson Greetings and Piper Jaffray.

In Italy, in September 1994, Olivetti reported a loss of $223.4 million, of which only $3.4 million was from the company's main business line of computers and office equipment. The origin of 98.5 percent of the losses was officially stated to be bonds—or, more precisely, derivatives based on bonds.

In the United States, Dell Computers is said to have lost $32 million from derivatives in 1994. Over the preceding three years it had made profits, but this represented only 72 percent of the money it lost in one year. This has not discouraged other players. Intel invests big in derivatives,[9] and the same is true of Enron, the Houston oil and gas company. Neither of these companies seems to have lost a great deal of money in OBS trades so far.

Banks have also been taking major exposures. A report released in May 1994 by the Government Accounting Office (GAO) states that one of the U.S. money center banks with an exposure of $1.8 trillion in notional principal has in its books OBS products worth $27.2 billion at risk. While this is expressed in notional principal amounts, as we will see in Chapter 2, the $27.2 billion roughly corresponds to $1 billion when converted to loans equivalent. This bank is rumored to have lost $400 million in 1994, or 40 percent of its loans equivalent derivatives exposure.

Four hundred million dollars is a lot of red ink, though optimists might say that, after all, it is only a fraction of the $2 billion the treasury of Orange County, California, lost in late 1994. Subsequently, on December 7 it had to file for bankruptcy. We will talk of this event and its aftermath in Chapter 13, but it is wise to keep in mind that losses with derivatives are getting out of control.

Though off-balance-sheet trades are booming in all G-10 countries, Japanese companies seem to be among the biggest gamblers and losers with derivative vehicles. They do so with billions of dollars.

Kashima Oil lost a breathtaking $1.5 billion on foreign exchange speculation and probably finds little consolation in the fact that other companies in America and Europe are also licking their wounds from forex "hedging." Showa Shell lost over $1 billion in 1993 as a result of massive foreign exchange deals done through derivatives—which amounted to a speculation. Both companies have stated that at least part of these deals were unauthorized. "Victory," an old proverb says, "has many fathers, but defeat has none."

The Japanese Postal Savings Bureau (Kampo) and an Indonesian bank have also been reported to have lost several billion dollars in currency exchange during 1992 and 1993. Metallgesellschaft, the German conglomerate, speculated in oil futures and lost a cool DM 5 billion ($3.3 billion), which grew to DM 8 billion counting other losses.[10]

In 1994, Japan Airlines (JAL) declared a huge loss on foreign exchange hedging, reputedly as much as 45 billion Yen ($450 million). Declarations of currency losses are now mandatory in Japan.

Nippon Mortgage specialized in lending money to property developers. It collapsed with liabilities of more than Yen 518 billion ($5.2 billion). This was Japan's third largest corporate failure since World War II.

---

[9] *Business Week*, October 31, 1994.

[10] See also D. N. Chorafas, *Derivatives Financial Instruments* (London and Dublin: Lafferty, 1994).

Compared to billions of dollars of red ink, millions of dollars in losses seems like peanuts. Yet such losses are indicative of the riskiness of derivatives trades. In the autumn of 1992, Sumitomo Finance International, the London-based arm of the Sumitomo Bank, suffered losses of about $3 million on its interest rate options book, after an employee apparently concealed his true trading position from senior management.

As every banker should know, excesses don't change the bitter facts. Unchecked, the losses mushroom. In the Sumitomo Finance case, they were linked to the partial breakdown of the Exchange Rate Mechanism (ERM), which overturned the assumptions about volatility and market correlation on which options prices are based and made the market extremely difficult to trade, let alone to speculate in.

A long list of American, European, and Japanese companies and financial institutions join those mentioned here, evidently including hedge funds. While Steinhart's hedge fund may be the better known example of the February/March 1994 debacle—with $1 billion in red ink, or 25 percent of its capital—there are scores of others who lost big money with off-balance-sheet gambles.

The heart of the matter is that people and companies neither really master the complexities nor have a valid risk-management system. Yet doing so is possible, as Part Three will explain in detail.

7.   Is Management in Control of Derivatives Trades?

In an October 1992 speech to IOSCO, Dr. Henry Kaufman said, "In many cases, senior management does not have a good handle on what risks are being taken. The fact is that sizeable losses have been incurred in such areas as mortgage derivatives, even by well-run institutions." In a November 1992 speech to the U.S. Securities Association, M. Carpenter said "Bad risk management could sink a firm in 24 hours." Bad risk finally cost Carpenter his job as CEO of Kidder Peabody. In October 1994, General Electric sold Kidder Peabody to Paine Webber, losing $1.5 billion in this process.

The lack of transparency from the growth of derivatives trades has rendered the nature and distribution of risks connected to financial instruments and their transactions much more invisible that they used to be. Some visibility can be regained through worst-case scenarios and experimentation, but many banks confuse the worst-case scenario with the nightmare scenario connected to panics.

In general, these two scenarios are not the same, but they tend to merge because in addition to the big banks, there is a rapidly growing number of small outfits anxious to enter the derivatives game at any price—without having the appropriate know-how and high technology.

Big and small banks and other companies are the crowd Dr. Felix Rohatyn probably had in mind when he stated that "26-year-olds with computers are creating financial hydrogen bombs."[11] This is a good paradigm to keep in mind when we talk about the control of risk.

The fact is that nobody really knows the web of interconnections established in the financial markets through derivatives. Even an understanding of OBS trading and its longer-term effect is relatively inadequate—and this is true not only of commercial banks but also of central banks in the United States, Europe, and Japan.

That is one of the main reasons it was said in section 4 that many off-balance-sheet deals escape supervision. At best, the control exercised by the regulators is weak, not for lack of want, but for another fundamental reason.

The big players in the derivatives markets are typically financial institutions and other companies versatile in advanced technology and the methods it puts at their disposal. These companies have years of experience with

❑   Rocket scientists.

❑   Distributed deductive databases.

❑   High-performance computers.

❑   Intelligent networks.

❑   A very flexible market approach.

By contrast, the regulators and their governments excel in none of these criteria of modern business and are therefore left in the dust. This makes risk control by supervisory authorities singularly ineffective.

There is a counterpart to this in the rapid development of new products in manufacturing. Nowadays, competitors rated to survive the steady market tests are no longer locked into assembly lines that take months to retool. They are also able to draw on a global web of technically competent manufacturers.

Rapid time-to-market has become a basic criterion of business success. That's good, but let's not underestimate its challenges. In rolling over thin ice, protection is in speed, as secret recipes and formulas—be they for banking, colas, or medicines—are not only harder to come by, they are also hard to protect.

As we have seen in section 3, branded products increasingly make up a shrinking proportion of sales. There is also some evidence that it is the better off and better educated who are the most likely to go for innovation. Both wealth and education make consumers and businesspeople buy more rationally—as well as take more risks.

---

11 *International Investor*, July 1992.

❑ On the one hand, the use of derivatives is by now deeply imbedded in the financial markets, and it cannot be legislated away.

❑ Only in new and less sophisticated financial markets can the government forbid "this" or "that" type of derivative trades, as happened in 1993 in China.

Nor should off-balance-sheet trades be put altogether on the back burner, even if this were feasible. What is wrong is not derivatives per se, but the fear many people have about invoking the risks they entail. They are equally fearful about doing something constructive in controlling them.

This fear among derivatives lovers of being pointed out as a black sheep can be expressed no better than in the words of a reviewer of an earlier book of mine on derivatives exposure. Everyone is free to express his opinions, but the concepts written by this reviewer reveal the phobia:

> I do not share and cannot agree with the author's viewpoint that derivatives are complex, mysterious, explosive, dangerous. I have spent a good part of the last two years reviewing every official study and report on derivatives that has been written and, based upon (their) findings, I strongly believe that the author's thesis is unsupported. How can one claim to discuss seriously the benefits and risks of derivatives without reference to the established facts: the official studies or reports on derivatives?

In other words, is it enough to commission an "official" study by any think tank that says there is no risk connected to derivatives in order to waive away all exposure? This, in spite of all the evidence that exists to the contrary, as documented by meetings with confident executives and organizations who know what they are doing.

Barings, the British investment bank, was one of the most prestigious of London blue-blood financial institutions. Founded in 1762, it was once described as the sixth great power of Europe, after Britain, France, Austria, Russia, and Prussia. But on the weekend of February 25–26, 1995, Barings desperately searched for a rescue takeover to avert bankruptcy.

The disaster was caused by a loss of $1.5 billion by a dealer in its Singapore office trading Nikkei Index derivatives on the Osaka financial market. It was said in the City that the deals that cumulated to 20,000 off-balance-sheet contracts were unauthorized by management—but this made matters even worse by showing that management was not in control.

Such cases do not just happen with Barings. They characterize large chunks of the financial industry where banks and company treasuries get involved with derivative financial vehicles they don't master—

and do so without sophisticated real-time systems for risk management, which operate for any product, at any time, anywhere in the world.

8. A Sound Procedure for Risk Management

A sound procedure for risk management must be both rigorous and generic. It must be established in full appreciation of the fact that exposure is an integral part of all financial instruments. Risk identification should be done "without the scare of calling a spade a spade" as Confucius advised 25 centuries ago.

A basic characteristic of a valid solution is its consistency. A sound procedure for derivatives risk management does not deal with the random trivia of the day but with the fundamental problems, problems involving each individual issue of exposure and all the many phases of global risk. A sound solution is concerned not with things as they are, but with things as *they might be*. It does not just record or photograph, but forecasts, creates, and *projects*.

This is the sense of modeling, experimentation, extrapolation, deduction, and induction, which will be discussed in Part Three. Not only must we identify the risks incurred with each instrument, counterparty, and transaction, but we also estimate compound exposure due to ongoing trades and events.

We should always be aiming to define in the most accurate manner the risk that our organization is taking in its day-to-day operations as well as in the longer-term commitments that management makes. To properly evaluate risk, responsible managers must require information about

- ❏ Income and expense performance.
- ❏ Credit lines to counterparties.
- ❏ Statistics on trading volumes.
- ❏ Key indicators such as market volatility liquidity, and other sensitivities.
- ❏ Resulting balance sheet and off-balance-sheet risks.

Such information must be presented in a way that allows exposure to be managed, making it possible to run the bank's business in a properly controlled manner. And while the information in the above list is necessary, as Part Two will demonstrate, it is not enough.

The problem is that traditional financial reporting tools rarely, if ever, provide the type or level of detail needed to make critical decisions in a timely manner about product pricing, risk control, and costing—or the real-time management of resources, their allocation, and optimization. What is necessary is

**Figure 1-3. Tolerances and Control Limits According to the
              Heisenberg Principle**

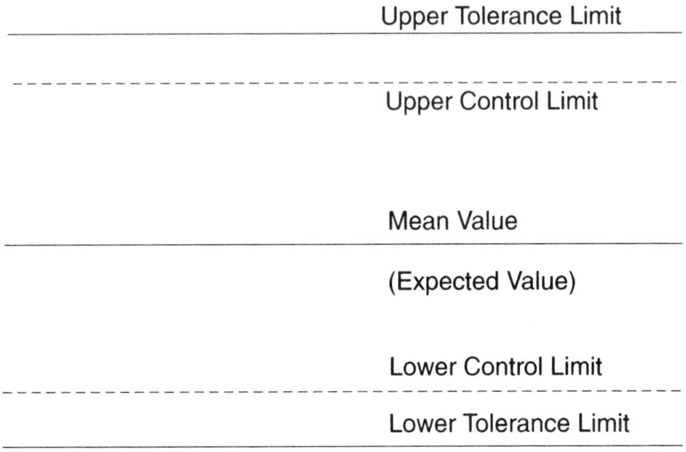

Upper Tolerance Limit

- -

Upper Control Limit

Mean Value

(Expected Value)

Lower Control Limit
- -
Lower Tolerance Limit

❏   Quick access to very current information on all transactions, from
    atomic elements to compound events.

❏   Powerful algorithms permitting the manipulation of such infor-
    mation in a polyvalent and meaningful sense.

The result must be a consistent view of performance across legal
entities, product lines, customer groups, individual counterparties, market sectors, specific markets, or any other well-defined business criterion. With such consistency, risk-management decisions can be made
based on a clear perspective about where and when to invest financial
resources and capitalize on new opportunities.

For every transaction the bank makes, risk management involves a
thorough evaluation of strategic and tactical moves made both on a
steady and on an exceptional basis.

This concept is no different from that of good management at
large, but it is focused on all issues involving trades, their profitability,
and associated exposure. The underlying principle, shown in Figure 1-3,
was defined in the early 1930s by Dr. Werner Heisenberg, the nuclear
physicist, who stated that nothing moves along a straight line—and we
can predict nothing with zero tolerance. We have tolerances and control
limits.

The basic characteristics of whatever we do, of every transaction
we make, move within control limits, which can be preestablished in a
mathematical sense. As long as these limits are within acceptable toler-

Figure 1–4.   A Frame of Reference Within Which Can Be Expressed Exposure in Any Instrument, Toward Any Counterparty, in Any Market

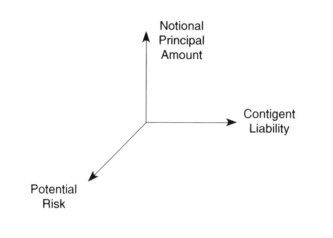

ances, the process is under control. The tolerances are the responsibility of the board. What the rocket scientists must do is assure that tick-by-tick the OBS processes stay within control limits.

All physical processes and all financial transactions have key characteristics that essentially constitute determinants of value. In oil exploration, for instance, the three most influential determinants of exploration venture value are target size, discovery probability, and finding cost.

Correspondingly, with derivative financial instruments, I see the three most influential determinants as notional principal amount, potential risk, and contingent liability (see Figure 1–4).

We have briefly spoken of notional principal and will do so in detail in Chapter 2. The notion of *contingent liability* is practically the alter ego of off-balance-sheet financing.

Contingent claims are assets where a new variable can occur and fluctuate—hence affecting the payment stream of a contractual agreement. This impact on liabilities and assets is engineered by the agreement that has been signed. Examples of contingent claims are

❑   Options contracts.

❑   Floating-rate loans

❑   Loans with caps and floors.

❑   Different types of warrants.

In other words, for any practical purpose, off-balance-sheet essentially means contingent liabilities, no matter what the derivatives traders might say. Such a concept may seem confusing at first glance.

❑   Although a bank loan is counted as an *asset* on a bank's balance sheet, a promise to make a loan is a *liability* because it constitutes an obligation.

❑   But while these contingent liabilities do not represent actual money lent by the banks, they do represent *potential risk.*

These three key factors in the measurement of exposure constitute a three-dimensional coordinate system, a frame of reference that can be helpful in expressing the exposure taken with off-balance-sheet deals transaction by transaction, toward any counterparty, with any financial instrument, in any country, and in a compound sense.

Potential risk may concern the ability of a counterparty to repay. Hence, there is credit risk. It may be market risk, legal risk, currency risk, or any other—including compound risk. In fact, Figure 1–4 can be extended from three-dimensional to n-dimensional by using fractals, as I have explained in a previous book.[12]

9.   Accounting for Past-Due and Sour Derivatives

Classical bankers may say that an n-dimensional solution space for risk management is a motion totally unfamiliar to them, if not indeed one that is fuzzy. This fuzziness essentially replaces what used to be clear-cut assets and liability cases:

1.   The use of derivative financial instruments radically changes the concepts dominating our balance sheet and income statement, even to the point of calling a liability an asset.

That means no more vanilla ice cream banking. The practices we inherited from the 1980s defined debt as being better than equity. Tax laws pushed further in this direction. They even created disincentives for banks to hold bonds.

A cushion for major declines in bonds is the fact that banks and individual investors seem to be satisfying their need for income by buying Treasury notes and bonds with the idea of holding them. However, rather than promoting this strategy, legislation has built in contrarian forces.

American financial institutions no longer buy and hold bonds because accounting rules have made it less and less interesting for banks

---

[12]*Chaos Theory in the Financial Markets* (Chicago: Probus, 1994).

to invest in them. When bonds go down, they could impair a bank's book value because new accounting rules require that the bank marks the bonds to market. FASB Statement 105 is a case in point.[13]

As loan demand grows, banks are selling bonds in order to lend the money out to commercial, industrial, real estate, and consumer borrowers or to provide a credit line to counterparties for derivatives trades.

2. As this trend gains momentum, off-balance-sheet and other debt-swapping practices will not go away just by hoping they will; but by remaining uncontrolled and unregulated, they may lead to disastrous results.

Cash-flow problems and lack of confidence can be converted into a crisis. Since the financial markets of the developed world are networked, major defaults in one country—or in one money center bank—can reach global proportions, hence the need for having as collateral real assets that are not somebody else's liability.

In full understanding of these facts, regulatory authorities are now trying to work out a pattern that permits financial institutions to better appreciate risks from derivatives per se as well as in connection to other instruments such as loans. Figure 1–5 presents an integrative approach:

❑   *Past-due derivatives* have a market risk similar to that of *bad loans* traded at huge discounts.

❑   *Sour derivatives* are contracts in trouble because of credit risk.

❑   *Past due* and *sour derivatives* are both off-balance-sheet exposures.

❑   *Sour derivatives* and *bad loans* are related because of counterparty troubles.

Sour derivatives are the counterpart of bad loans. Past-due derivatives are not yet sour, but they have to be very carefully watched. Past-due derivatives fall in this bin mainly because of market risk, while sour derivatives have a high quotient of credit risk.

Serious readers will appreciate that the risks involved in this frame of reference are *metastasizing* through crossovers rather than simple mutations. Let's keep this in mind every time we speak of the management of risk.

Regulation and eventually legislation will take care of past-due and sour derivatives. In the United States, the Office of the Controller of the Currency (OCC) now requires banks to disclose the dollar value of

---

[13] This is not a critique of FASB or of 105. FASB has done a first-class job so far, but there are always consequences that were not seen ahead of time.

Figure 1–5. A Coordinate System for Controlling and Reporting Transactions That Have Become Highly Risky

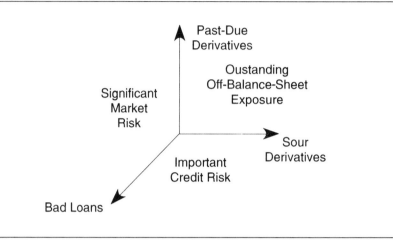

all their derivative contracts *gone sour*. They must also account for the compound effect of *bad loans*.

The OCC also sees to it that banks must assure their exposure is *aggregated* for sound risk-management reasons. Because a very large part of what enters a derivatives trade is a *book entry*, it might be that everyone *wins*, and it might be that everyone *loses*. But eventually, the *bubble bursts*. To keep the financial system in control, we must be able to see the trouble coming.

In conclusion, due to the complexity of the modern financial environment and the compound effect of derivative instruments, positioning a portfolio or the whole bank is a strategic consideration full of perils: Positions are taken and exposures assumed on the basis of leading hypotheses, but the market can turn around, invalidating even the best-laid plans. The dramatic drop in the value of bonds and options on bonds in February/March 1994, among so many other examples, confirms this statement.

As it will be remembered, in early 1994 following the hike of short-term interest rates by the Federal Reserve, a couple of hedge funds lost $600 million each, and one lost $1 billion. All of them found themselves exposed on the wrong side of the balance sheet when the market sell-off occurred. Therefore, positioning studies should carefully evaluate many alternative market hypotheses—something that can be nicely done through real-time simulation and high-performance computers.

2

Understanding the Notional Principal Amount and Its Metrics

1. Introduction

As we have seen in Chapter 1, the term *notional principal* is widely used with derivatives. It has been borrowed from the swaps market where it signifies the quantity of money never actually to be paid or received. By contrast, the actual cash flows resulting from the trade will be paid or received; for instance, by applying the corresponding difference in fixed or floating interest to the appropriate calendar periods. Today, the same notional principal concept is used in connection to caps and floors, forward rate agreements, future or forward contracts for Treasury bonds, guilds, and bunds, as well as exotics such as binary options.

Not every derivatives trade is expressed in terms of notional amounts. The concept of notional principal is not so useful with vehicles derivatives such as stock index futures and commodity options, where the bases for calculations are, correspondingly, number of shares or bushels of wheat or soybeans—which cannot be meaningfully aggregated. But in many cases, aggregation is possible, especially if we convert to a common denominator. Loans equivalent constitutes a good frame of reference because practically any banker understands the notion of loans.

Some bankers suggest that, in general, the notional principal amount is a fairly fuzzy but useful concept. Others would prefer not to use it to measure exposure. The Financial Accounting Standards Board defines the notional principal as a hypothetical amount on which, for example, swap payments are based.[1] In this sense, the contract or notional amount does not represent in its totality potential credit risk. Yet, in an exotic derivatives context, it may do just that—as Chapter 1 demonstrated.

With the more classical derivatives, such as interest rate swap agreements, notional principal amounts are often used to express the volume of the transactions taking place. They do not represent the much smaller amounts potentially subject to credit risk and market risk. This notion, however, changes as new instruments come into play.

2. The Changing Aspects of Notional Principal

The chapter introduction made the point that, for some banks, while the notional principal or contractual amount of interest rate and foreign exchange contracts does not represent the market risk associated with those contracts, it gives an indication of it—by identifying the volume of the transactions. This, in turn, can be used for risk control purposes.

What about credit risk? For any given financial institution, the credit exposure for interest rate and foreign exchange contracts is represented by the amounts of recognized gains in the market valuation of those contracts. These fluctuate as a function of

❑   Maturity.

❑   Interest rates.

❑   Foreign exchange rates.

A similar statement can be made about other financial products. The problem is that following up on exposure is a multidimensional business that becomes more complex as counterparty, currency, country, settlement, and legal issues enter the picture, in addition to the market exposure concerning the instruments themselves.

That is the reason for the reference made in the chapter introduction about the facility for aggregation a common denominator can provide. *If* we are able to structure a common ground, *then* we can have an operations-wide view of our derivatives exposure, apart from being able to study better our OBS strategy.

If such an approach were available, and we will see in this chapter that it can be made to work, then we would be able to aggregate market risk and credit risk, as well as perform profit and loss analysis ahead of a commitment. Figure 2–1 explains the component parts of such a solu-

---

[1] Financial Accounting Series No. 109-A, November 18, FASB, Norwalk, CT, 1991.

Figure 2–1. Developing an Operational View of the Derivatives Strategy

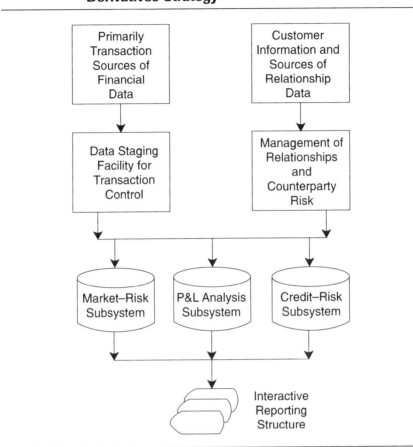

tion. The approach that Figure 2–1 presents is very flexible and can be extended to cover other risks. Databases and direct inputs can, for instance, be used for legal risk, settlement risk, currency risk, and so on.

The counterargument to this approach is that the notional value of a bank's derivatives portfolio usually confers imprecise information about the market-risk exposure, to which these activities give rise. Such imprecision arises from a number of factors:

❑ Some derivatives embody market risk limited to differences between financial market indices or prices, not to gross market price movements.

❑ A derivatives portfolio is itself to a large extent matched or hedged, with exposure intended to hedge on-balance-sheet market risks.

❑ Notional totals include written contracts such as deeply out-of-the-money options that are unlikely to be exercised and, therefore, have little risk.

At the same time, in credit-equivalent terms, the share of exposures incurred toward other banks is often smaller than when measured in the corresponding notional figures. A smaller credit equivalent share probably reflects a greater preponderance of contracts with an original maturity of less than one year or, alternatively, the presence of out-of-the-money contracts.

There is also a risk variation by type of instrument. For instance, because of greater volatility, exposures arising from foreign exchange contracts tend to be much larger than exposures resulting from interest rate derivatives.

To a large extent, these arguments are valid. Exposure can, however, have compound effects, as a substantial portion of a bank's risks in derivative contracts is incurred vis-à-vis corresponding banks. On the basis of notional amounts, more than 85 percent of foreign-exchange-rate-related exposures of German, Italian, and Luxembourg banks arose from interbank transactions. In other countries, the interbank proportion averages around 60 percent; but in the case of interest-rate-related derivatives, it reaches or exceeds 70 percent.

All this talks volumes of a systemic risk in the banking industry. At the same time, the fact that the product mix varies by country makes it even more urgent to establish the *common denominator* we have been discussing since the beginning of this chapter. My thesis is that establishing a common denominator is doable by using the notional principal amount.

Derivatives can be converted into notional principal amounts equivalent to on-balance-sheet positions and slotted into the maturity ladder alongside other assets and liabilities. This can be done even if there is no exact definition of notional amount for all trades, as the following points suggest:

❑ As we saw in the introduction, according to FASB and the American approach in general, notional principal is *a hypothetical* amount on which payments are based.

❑ British authorities look to the notional principal amount as the *face*, or principal, value upon which the performance of a derivative contract rests.

Continental European banks largely agree with the British definition. Where both parties are in accord is that, in general, notional values are not paid or received. But with the emergence of binary options and some other instruments, even this notion may become obsolete.

3. Examining Contrarian Approaches to Risk Tolerance

The best way to approach a contrarian argument is to look at it head-on. In a March 4, 1993, article in the *Financial Times*, David Walker, deputy chairman of Lloyds Bank and former chairman of the British Securities and Investment Board, suggested that derivatives do not add risks to the system. Rather, they provide the ability to identify, price, and transfer existing risks.

This is, of course, the optimist's argument, which Chapter 1 demonstrated is practically unattainable. In a way, David Walker must be aware of this fact, since in the same article he apptly suggests that a balanced approach to regulation is needed, neither tolerating inadequate standards or risk, nor cramping the energy and innovation of these markets.

This argument is very sound, and it implicitly admits that there are risks embedded in derivatives. The classical conflict between regulators and bankers rests on the difference in viewpoints. The regulators look at the systemic risk that excesses can bring to the financial industry and at the dangers that follow. Bankers and traders want a free hand in entering into further deals, looking more at the profits than at the losses they may entail.

Legislation, regulation, and business opportunity are essentially balancing acts and, in the last analysis, David Walker's approach is not as contrarian as it might seem. The only problem is that it does not offer a different or better metric than notional principal.

Other bankers have made the point that both national and international standards for the control of risk must be anchored on firm ground. There are not too many alternatives available, and as every financial expert should know, one of the first questions a manager must ask him- or herself is "What are my alternatives?"

As far as I can see, in terms of anchoring ground for off-balance-sheet risk, there are three possibilities. Each has its strengths and its shortcomings. None is perfect, but together, as Figure 2–2 illustrates, they provide a good three-dimensional frame of reference:

- ❑ Notional principal amount.
- ❑ Fair value estimates.
- ❑ Cash flow predictions.

Figure 2–2 shows how a three-dimensional reporting scheme can be constructed for risk-management reasons. As we will see in regard to fair value estimates in Chapter 3, we are talking about *marking-to-model* more than marking-to-market because for many over-the-counter deals there is no active secondary market. This, too, is a limitation.

**Figure 2–2.   A Coordinate System That Presents a Good
Solution Space for Risk Management**

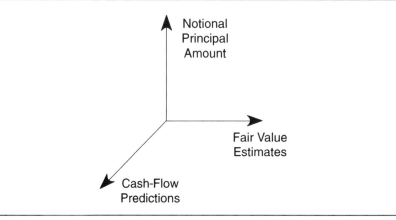

Quite similarly, while projected cash flow is a good metric for risk control, the best we can do is an estimate that itself is exposed to credit risk. The cash flow method, too, has its proponents and its contrarians—each with good arguments why it should or should not be used. No metric may be perfect in itself. Perfection is not part of real life. However, three of them taken together provide a solution space in which we can work with a good degree of confidence.

The concept of notional principal amount and subsequently that of the fair value of the deal and of cash flow—which will be discussed in Chapter 3—are important because once properly established they are useful for accounting, risk management, and reporting purposes.

The way the regulations under development at the Bank of International Settlements will probably move, in the future there will be no particular reason to differentiate between off-balance-sheet items and the regular on-balance-sheet items in the reporting framework. This further emphasizes the need for common ground.

By contrast, for monitoring and statistical purposes, BIS advises it will be useful to separately identify the positions taken in the main derivative products. A pro forma reporting form can make that distinction provided transnational agreements can be reached.

More questionable is the BIS recommendation that positions are netted and that the resulting net position for each time band should be weighted by an estimate of its duration—with weights adjusted to reflect the relative volatility of interest rates across the term's structure. This way, the net balance of individual weighted positions might form a basis for evaluating interest rate risk.

Many banks do not agree with this thesis, some because the BIS definition does not yet provide a theoretical background for vertical and horizontal netting; it only gives a few examples. One of the major Japanese banks, however, considers this approach to lack a solid foundation, calling it "junior high school stuff." The wheels of financial transactions rarely grind at one speed long enough to permit easy netting. Chances are that at any given moment it is either becoming easier to trade in a given instrument, or it is becoming more difficult.

One universal lesson of the banking experience taught through hard lessons over the centuries, is that no financial, monetary, or control system is fullproof—and it surely is not foolproof. Market gyrations are a difficult and relentless master. "What one fool could do, another fool could do too," said Thales of Miletus—one of the seven sages of antiquity and the man who invented options 2,600 years ago.

4.   A Demodulator for Estimating Risk Based on Notional Principal

Looking at the subject in a rather superficial way, there is really no all-inclusive algorithm for calculating risk out of the notional principal values of off-balance-sheet operations. Every financial instrument has its own ratio that permits it to convert notional principal to loan-type exposure. But, as we will see in this section, banks have invented ratios that can be instrumental in converting the total notional principal amount outstanding and reaching a comprehensive and manageable risk form.

Starting with the fundamentals, whether we talk of the swaps market, caps and floors, forward rate agreement, futures or forward contracts for Treasury bonds, gilts, and bunds, we either explicitly or implicitly make reference to a notional principal. FASB Statement 105 required that these amounts be disclosed in the financial statements as an indication of the size of contracts. The term *contract* means a legally enforceable agreement, which would include most deals but would exclude an informal arrangement that had no legal standing.

FASB has not provided a minimum threshold below which disclosure is not required, other than the general minimum threshold of *materiality* that applies to all FASB requirements. Therefore, there are no threshold levels recognized in the size of an obligation.

If the notional principal is the hypothetical or face value, what may be the risk associated with a transaction? In a forward rate agreement that includes a fixed rate and a variable rate, *in the short term* either party is exposed to a fluctuation of 100 to 200 basis points, but

1.   Many interest rate swaps are long-term and getting longer.

This dramatically changes the volatility of the transaction to 500 basis points or beyond. "I believe some intermediaries are writing 30 year options," says P. Kent of the Bank of England.[2] "Quite how confident anyone can be that the premium received for such options is an adequate reward for the risks taken is a subject which falls into my personal knowledge gap."

If historical volatility is taken over a 30-year period, we no longer talk of 100 or 500 basis points, but of 1,000 and 1,500 basis points. In fact, the 1,500 basis points will come within only 15 years, not 30 years of historical volatility. In other terms, while for short-range interest rate swaps a demodulator of the notional principal amount by 50 can provide a conservative risk estimate, with long-range IRS, the whole notional principal is on the block. Therefore, the demodulator is equal to one. We will see more examples to this effect in Part Three.

It is, of course, proper to emphasize that the notional amount for measurement of exposure is not so useful with other instruments. This fact was mentioned in the chapter introduction. But we also said that in a significant number of off-balance-sheet deals, notional principal metrics can be applied.

2.   The amount of money involved in a derivatives trade is often huge.

Therefore, even a high demodulator of the notional principal involved in the deal represents a very great exposure. This is not always appreciated by bankers, traders, and investors, yet it constitutes a sword of Damocles hanging over their heads. Let's not forget the effect of some exotic derivatives where

Risk = Notional Principal Amount

The point has already been made in Chapter 1 that this is the case with binary options, which provide discontinuous payoffs. All-or-nothing digital options provide the buyer a payout of all or nothing, depending on the option's value at expiration. If the option is in-the-money, the buyer will receive a sum equal to the notional principal amount or, alternatively, a different amount specified by the contract and unrelated to the intrinsic value of the option.

One-touch options are similar to the all-or-nothing, but they are exercised once the strike price is reached. Hence, the holder does not need to wait until maturity to collect the profits. Both one-touch and

---

2 *International Financial Review*, November 1992.

all-or-nothing have a very high premium—but also an extremely high risk. This will be discussed further in Chapter 10.

5.   Converting the Notional Amount to Loans Equivalent

Management of one of the major European central banks mentioned during our meeting that of its over 5,000 employees only 5 persons— one per thousand—really know how to manage derivatives risk. This statistic is typical in the banking industry, and it can be even worse among commercial banks.

Another reserve bank emphasized that it is questionable whether five or six of the largest commercial banks have mastered the off-balance-sheet game and are in control of their risks. The others are simply rolling along, taking an inordinate exposure because they do not quite appreciate the OBS risks in their trading book and portfolio.

But if very few bankers really know how to evaluate derivatives risk and how to protect their institutions from its consequences, the majority are well aware of loans risks. It can therefore be rewarding to convert notional principal amounts from off-balance-sheet trades to loans equivalent.

This can be of significant interest for another reason. Developing and applying the proper demodulator can help to downsize the trillions of dollars in exposure that is currently prevalent in the financial industry. Each of the 30 largest money center banks and brokers has an exposure that varies from $2.7 trillion to $700 billion in notional principal amounts.[3]

In mid-1992, Arthur Andersen released a survey on derivatives trades that included roughly two-thirds of the major market participants. This study was commissioned by ISDA and indicated that the *notional amounts* of derivatives among the surveyed firms reached $3.1 trillion at the end of 1991.[4] But in terms of gross *marked-to-market exposure*, the amount stood at $77 billion.

Assuming for a moment that this marked-to-market figure is reasonable in terms of reflecting the risk for the entire span of the trade, it could be taken as the nearer possible estimate to *loans equivalent*.

This is the sense of the *demodulator*, divisor, or demultiplier, which was discussed in the preceding section. Its function is to convert one amount of the notional principal into another amount: the *loans equiva-*

---

3 For details see D. N. Chorafas, *Risk and Reward With Derivative Financial Instruments* (London and Dublin: Lafferty Publications, 1994).

4 On the BIS basis of counting a bilateral agreement only once as exposure, with which I do not agree since I consider the traded amount to reflect on both parties—once for each.

lent. In the Arthur Andersen study, we observe that the ratio between notional principal amount and marked-to-market exposure stands at 1:40. The 1:40 demodulator addresses the cumulative exposure in off-balance-sheet risk and helps give management a snapshot of the current derivatives risk. Every derivative financial instrument has its own conversion ratio, which can vary from 1:1 to nearly 1:100, but it takes very detailed calculations to analytically establish the exposure.

In section 4, we have seen examples of interest rate risk, where the variation can be 200 basis points in cases with short maturities. This will represent an exposure of 2 percent on the notional principal; hence a demodulator of 50 can be acceptable. But we also said that with long maturities the change in interest rate might reach 1,000 basis points. Then, a demodulator of 10 should be used—always in connection to interest rate risk.

A general demodulator of notional principal exposure and specific demultipliers by instrument complement one another—they are not a contradiction. Analytical studies on general trend but also specific metrics such as duration are necessary for rigorous derivatives risk management. In nervous markets, it is important to get real-time information on current commitments and exposure figures.

While an instrument-by-instrument demodulator of notional principal will give more precise results, let's not forget that the resulting exposure also needs to be sorted out by counterparty, by market, and by other criteria. Better, then, to be accurate than to make errors in precision.

Can the ratio of 1:40, which we have seen with the Arthur Andersen example, be seen as an average demultiplier in terms of conversion to loans equivalent? The answer is that it may be. The reasons for this reply are based on responses of some of the bankers I met during my research. Conservative bankers prefer to use a 1:30 ratio. They reduce it to 1:20 when the market gets very nervous or they are expecting unfavorable developments.

By contrast, high-risk-taking banks tend to use a ratio of 1:50 or even 1:60. This means assuming a very high exposure in terms of OBS, with all that that means in risk terms if the market turns against the bank or the investor.

Personally, I see the 1:30 to 1:20 range as reasonable, and in my projects I use a demultiplier of 30 to 20 depending on normal or tightened inspection. As my finding reveals, the majority of banks keep an eye on notional principal amounts whether or not they admit it publicly. A significant number of them apply the demultiplier principle by notional principal on a specific instrument, on the sum of notional principals, or both.

One of the best examples in this connection has been given by Bankers Trust, which takes the sum of all instruments, generally calcu-

Figure 2–3. At Bankers Trust, the Demodulation and Normalization of OBS Trades Permits Real-Time Risk Control

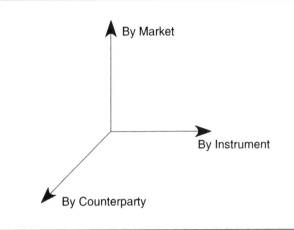

lated to the equivalent of a risk-free four-year Treasury bond. Some of the swaps transactions are seen in a frame of two-year bonds equivalence. Above this are set exposure limits and charges for risk services.

Such a strategy permits the steady measurement of risk by market, by instrument, and by counterparty, as shown in Figure 2–3. This should be a real-time operation steadily enriched with agents that track exposure and inform interactively according to criteria set by the board.

"Even with large positions, you can take less risk through the development and use of advanced analytical tools," says Dr. Carmine Vona, executive vice president of Bankers Trust. "Once the basic reference frame is in place, we can enrich the model. For instance, we can calculate exposure on the basis of adverse news."

6.   Using Military Standards to Gauge Derivatives Exposure

Let's start by creating an integrated approach to the concepts and procedures section 5 has presented as well as the rationale for adopting them. Well-managed banks appreciate the need for norms and standards in exposure measurements. "We found that derivations risk is a system with a unified pattern," said Colin Crook, chairman of Citibank's Corporate Technology Committee.

Other senior bankers made similar statements. They emphasized in the course of our meetings that whether in the trading book or in the banking book, off-balance-sheet risk is very similar to dealing with a once big client, not with independent trades dispersed in an end-user population.

My research helped to document that, in terms of off-balance-sheet exposure, typically, a money center bank today has a notional principal in the range of $1 trillion to nearly $3 trillion.

In section 5, we spoke of the interest in bringing such figures to the equivalent level of loans exposure. Banks, it was said, apply a reduction factor of 1/10, 1/20, 1/30, 1/40, 1/60—or something in between these ratios.

I have also emphasized that the 1/10 ratio characterizes the more conservative institutions, and the 1/60 those which are the most risk prone. Hence, it is wiser not to use it.

One of the banks I met with in the course of the London meeting challenged the idea of addressing the total exposure in notional principal, emphasizing that the notional amount should be controlled separately *by financial instrument.* No summation of notional amounts is done because "It would be a meaningless number like all the fruits in the world." That's an opinion like any other—and it has its merits.

The problem for this bank, and for a large number of other financial institutions, is that it is so submerged in the backwards culture of its mainframes and their high priests that it cannot possibly handle the huge detail an instrument-by-instrument conversion of notional principal requires. I don't advance the use of the summation of exposure because it is pretty or precise. I suggest it because generally, given the prevailing low technology, it is a reasonable compromise.

I have also made the statement that, based on my experience, in terms of cumulative exposure in notional principal amounts, I consider the 1/30 demodulator to be right under normal conditions. But a bank must calculate it within its stream of OBS deals, not in the abstract.

It was also suggested that in tough times it is wise to switch to 1/25 and 1/20, by stages, accounting for systemic risk. This transition from reduced inspection to normal inspection and tightened inspection has a mathematical basis developed in the World War II years at Columbia University for the Manhattan Project. The necessary methodology and tables can be found in MIL-STD-104.[5] As a matter of principle, all derivatives transactions should be considered to be high risk in nature and put under this methodology:

❑ Some are high risk because the OBS instruments are not so well known.

❑ Others are high risk because the loss exposure can be unlimited.

---

5 United States Printing Office, Washington, D.C.

Figure 2–4. A Qualitative and Quantitative Frame of Reference for Risk Control in Off-Balance-Sheet Transactions

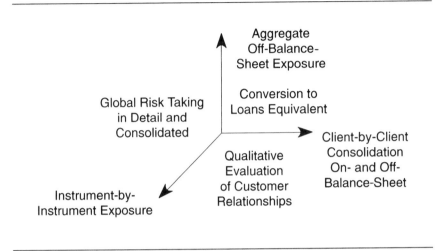

□   And still others are high risk due to the long maturity horizon they cover.

The use of already established military standards in quality control and in reliability engineering is very helpful because these risks are not so easy to hedge—in contrast to what is so often said in public on this subject. Military standards can help those banks that look favorably toward the calculation of a *loan risk equivalence. If* the conversion of notional principal is done in a sound manner as it has been explained, *then,* the Cooke Committee standard of BIS can be applied in terms of capital requirements.

Then it also becomes feasible to integrate balance sheet and off-balance-sheet exposure. By the same token, this approach makes it possible to pay attention to other crucial factors that enter the risk equation.

Figure 2–4 sets in a three-dimensional frame three of the factors mentioned in the preceding paragraph: client-by-client consolidation for on-balance-sheet and off-balance-sheet deals, and the calculation of instrument-by-instrument exposure.

Client-by-client consolidation should start with transactional detail, evidently based on the instruments on which risk is taken. Instrument-by-instrument exposure should also be detailed, reaching down to desk level and eventually to the trader, as well as to the client with whom the deal is made.

Finally, I would like to emphasize that even if the associated derivatives risks are computed in a risk-equivalent form, and steadily tracked, off-balance-sheet trades are appropriate only for institutions of high credit quality. According to the prevailing unwritten norms:

❏ The higher the quality of the institution, such as those with a AAA rating, the longer-term the deals may be—up to 7, and in some cases 10, years being a reasonable limit.

❏ Upper-medium quality institutions, for instance those with a AA rating, are generally regarded as suitable for medium-term derivative transactions, from 1 to 5 years.

❏ Banks and other companies with lower investment ratings are considered suitable only for short-term maturities—for instance, up to 3, 6, or 9 months.

Even short-term maturities for lower-middle-grade institutions can be questionable in terms of counterparty risk. A similar statement is valid about extremely long-term maturities for AAA banks; for example, up to 20 or 30 years.

Let's recall what P. Kent of the Bank of England said about correspondent banks that are writing 30-year options. Can they be confident that premiums received for such options are an adequate reward for the risks taken? Do they have the financial staying power to withstand adversity in such a long time frame?

7.   Arguments Favorable to Risk Conversion

Some of the arguments advanced against the use of notional principal amount as a tool of gauging exposure rest on the fact that several types of derivatives are *inherently illiquid*. They may be a modern instrument in their conception, but they are a *slow asset* which—in times of crisis—must wait for its maturity, with all this means in counterparty risk.

Besides this, in spite of what is so often said—that derivatives exchange market risk with credit risk—banks also have to face market risks; for example, interest rate risk in derivative products. Therefore, regarding market risks, it is wise to convert all debt derivatives and off-balance-sheet instruments that react to changes in interest rates into positions in the relevant underlying security. These include forward rate agreements (FRAs), futures and options on debt instruments, interest rate and cross-currency swaps, and forward foreign exchange positions.

Futures and forward contracts in the same currency, including forward rate agreements, would in principle be treated as a combination of a *long* and a *short* position in a notional sense. The maturity of a futures or an FRA would be the period until delivery or exercise of the contract. It is also important to know the life of the underlying security, where applicable.

Forward foreign exchange positions would be slotted within their appropriate currency ladders, according to the maturity of each contract. For instance, a four-month forward contract to sell U.S. dollars for British pounds would be slotted as a short position in the three- to six-month band of the dollar ladder, and a long position in the three- to six-month band of the pound ladder.

Swaps can be treated as two notional positions in securities with relevant maturities. An interest rate swap under which a firm is receiving floating-rate interest and paying fixed rate can be seen as a long position in a floating rate instrument of maturity equivalent to the period until the next interest fixing and a short position in a fixed-rate instrument of maturity equivalent to the residual life of the swap.

The separate legs of cross-currency swaps can be accounted for in the relevant maturity ladders for the currencies concerned. Knowledge-enriched software can be helpful in real-time updates of these positions and in answering interactive reporting requirements.

Rules currently under study by BIS tend to incorporate in the measurement of OBS risk those debt derivatives and other off-balance-sheet instruments that react to changes in interest rates and thus affect the institution's exposure to market risk. These include

❑ Futures and options on debt instruments, interest rate and cross-country swaps, and forward foreign exchange positions.

❑ Other option-like products, such as caps, floors, and options on futures or swaps.

The treatment of *options* poses problems in calculating exposure because of the asymmetrical risk and the nonlinear relationship with the underlying securities. According to BIS, the most practical method of measuring the risk in options is to report options on a delta-weighted basis, or a simplified proxy of delta, subsequently slotting them into the maturity ladders.

As we will see in Chapter 15, *delta* is the first derivative of the price function F(x). It gives the expected change of an option's price as a proportion of a small change in the price of the underlying instrument. An option whose price changes by $10 for every $20 change in the price of the underlier has a delta of 0.5. The delta rises toward 1 for options that are deep in-the-money and approaches 0 for deep out-of-the-money options.

Delta hedging is a method that option traders use to hedge risk exposure of options through purchase or sale of the underlying asset in proportion to the delta. Delta-neutral positions are established through delta hedging when the underlying instruments are left unaffected by small changes in the price of underlying securities. We will return to these concepts in Part Three.

In slotting deltas into time bands, a two-legged approach can be used. Some people see no need for time bands at all if the method is maturity-specific. Most specialists, however, emphasize the need for time bands in order to calculate the horizontal disallowances.

In the 1993 Market Risk Amendment and the 1993 Interest Risk Amendement, proposed by BIS, currently considered by central banks and commercial banks, it is suggested that a further measure of risk should be added to take account of the fact that deltas do not capture all the risk of loss in trading options. But there seems to be no agreement on this issue. The counterargument is that the use of deltas can account for interest rate risk. Under whichever light it is seen, this constitutes a good example of how mathematically oriented the control of off-balance-sheet risk has become.

Any way one wants to look at the subject, the principle is that all derivatives would be converted into positions in the relevant underlying instrument and become subject to norms for applying specific and general market risk under a building-block approach. Converting positions recorded in a maturity ladder into a measure of exposure to future market movements requires assumptions about likely directions in market response. It also requires correlations between the perceived trend and the time horizon over which a bank is likely to be exposed to changes, for instance in rates, before it can take action to protect its position. Appropriate assumptions must be used to determine open position weights that indicate the riskiness of holding a single long or short position and rules governing the offsetting of long and short positions within and across time bands.

The Bank for International Settlements advises that positions in each time band of the maturity ladder can be weighted by a factor designed to reflect the price sensitivity of those positions to changes in interest rates. But as we have already seen in an earlier section, vertical and horizontal netting are not generally accepted as valid schemes by the banking industry.

8. Going Beyond Risk Equivalence

Notional principal amounts-to-loans risk equivalence is a process of calculation and adjustment that observes and exploits the characteristics of the exposure. But while the conversion ratios we studied in sections 5 and 6 are just a common denominator and have been advanced to address the financial industry as a whole, every institution will be well advised to reevaluate its portfolio in a detailed manner in terms of specific

❏ Rating of the counterparty.

❏ Type of derivative instrument.

❑ Maturity of trade and time dimension.

❑ Initial rate or other crucial factors.

❑ Frequency of payments.

❑ In-the-money, at-the-money, and out-of-the-money market valuation.

❑ Possible all-or-nothing components in complex derivatives.

❑ Prevailing market liquidity and volatility.

❑ Initial and marked-to-model value.[6]

❑ Other factors it considers critical.

A $50 million, three-year unsecured loan by a bank represents a $50 million risk extended to the counterparty. A $3 billion interest rate swap may "only" represent $60 to $75 million in risk because only the interest flows are exchanged.

Section 6 has presented the reasons why this $60 to $75 million exposure can be said to represent loans equivalent risk. This conversion is not very precise, but in the longer run it tends to be accurate enough for management control reasons. The bank needs a compass to assess the direction it is taking.

The demultiplier algorithm advanced in this chapter is essentially a model designed to assist management in its decision in connection to derivatives risks. Such loans equivalent estimates can be improved in terms of precision by improving some of the parameters we just saw. However, it should be appreciated that the more detailed the model is, the more sophisticated its structure must be, and the higher the level of required skill and technological resources will be.

As with loans, risk-equivalent exposure calculation concerns the end user of the instrument as much as the market response. Some banks tend to look at loan equivalent risk as just credit equivalent risk. This is, however, an incomplete approach.

Starting with the premise that in the majority of derivatives trades the notional principal amount per se is not involved, risk equivalence aims to produce a *quantitative result* so that actual and potential risks are appropriately estimated. But a sound solution will permit real-time response and reporting, rather than provide figures to be given long after the facts, which makes them meaningless.

But no model solves all of the risk-related problems single-handedly. Well above modeling are corporate policies and procedures aimed

---

[6] Discussed in Chapter 3.

to assure that the bank does not sleep on its laurels but has a constant watch over exposures.

Though these policies and procedures will vary from one bank to another, the following principles are fairly general; I consider them a viable approach. They are advanced for this purpose.

1. Take initiative in a derivatives risk management sense and do so on an international basis.

The flexibility and mobility of derivatives trading means that the possibilities for great differences from one instrument to another, and one country to another, are present if playing fields are not level. But a common level requires a basic, shared understanding of OBS problems.

2. All key practitioners from traders to risk managers should be involved in the elaboration of the method and the model.

Given the complexity of modern financial derivatives markets, no single division or department can be said to have sufficient understanding of all the aspects of the problem. For the same reason, regulators require the players' input rather than working in an ivory tower.

3. Since derivatives contracts provide a good means of covering against specific forms of market risk, the focus is often on credit risk.

But market risk, legal risk, settlement risk, and other risks cannot be forgotten. While credit risk should be examined very carefully, under no circumstances can the other risks be overlooked.

4. There is a huge need for improvement in real-time reporting within the bank and in disclosure standards to the supervisory authority (or authorities).

Such improvements are necessary to promote management's appreciation of the amount of derivatives risk. They should be set in the right direction to provide incentives and to help understanding, among market players, of the complex risks they are undertaking—particularly in writing options and in exotics.

Most important is the establishment of valid procedures for fair value calculations, credit assessment, and audit arrangements to be done separately from the trading desk. The lack of clear-cut organizational lines is, in many cases, part of mainstream risk.

5. In cases where there are doubts, national regulators should question and even curtail the operations of local players.

Since most of the off-balance-sheet activity is concentrated in the financial centers of the G7 countries, it is easy to identify the national regulators primarily concerned with setting of national and international standards.

National and international standards should be compatible and homogeneous. Short of this, it is difficult to manage the derivatives risk of a money center bank and impossible to avert systemic risk in the world's financial markets.

Let me add this important afterthought. While this book was going to press, a seminar on "The Management of Market Risk in Banks" organized by the New York University Salomon Center, Leonard N. Stern School of Business came to my attention. Its focal point is a better understanding of the financial business through properly recognizing market risk.

Designed for senior executives of financial institutions, treasury managers, financial controllers, and financial planners, this program focuses on strategic options for a modern bank. Its special characteristic is that it underlines two of the themes which have constituted the pillars of this chapter:

1. The wisdom of using the notional principal amount of calculate loan equivalent risk, and

2. The need to proceed with risk aggregation by product, market, and counterparty as a means to bring exposure under control.

3

Estimating Fair Value by Marking-to-Market or Marking-to-Model

1. Introduction

A bank has trading positions and an investment portfolio. Both need to be valued on a steady basis in order to know in a fairly accurate manner what the assets, liabilities, and exposure are. The problem lies in choosing the best way to do this valuation as well as how often.

Bankers and other investors often say that the market is the better judge of the fair value of assets and liabilities. This is true *if* there is a market for the securities in the trading book and in the portfolio, which, however, does not necessarily need to be the case. Futures and many options have an active market. But forwards, swaps, and other bilateral agreements do not benefit from a secondary market.

Some traders are quick to suggest that the over-the-counter market is so huge that there is no worry in valuing OTC-traded products. While it is true that the OTC market has gained impressive dimensions, no one can guarantee that all of the instruments in a bank's portfolio are active. The way to bet is that they are not.

Therefore, alternative ways have to be found for estimating *fair value*. Not only bankers, but regulators are coming around to the idea that there are two avenues for fair value estimates:

❑ Marking-to-market.

❑ Marking-to-model.

For bank supervision purposes, however, the models to be used for valuation must not only be sound but proven to be sound. Little is made of the fact, however, that they should be accepted by the central banks of the G-10 countries as well as by BIS and the International Monetary Fund (IMS).

This has slowly started to take place in the United States, where the Financial Accounting Standards Board recommends the use of the Black-Scholes option pricing model for marking-to-model. There are also other algorithms. The problem is not just one of selecting the best but also, if not primarily so, of normalizing the marking-to-model practices and providing a lender of last resort on a global financial basis.

Markets and models for pricing financial instruments are not designed for panics, yet bubbles and market disruptions are distinct possibilities. Cognizant executives and troubleshooters must be around in a major upheaval to handle the crisis. Otherwise, marking-to-market and marking-to-model would have been fruitless exercises.

2.   Why Is It Important to Estimate Fair Value?

In Statement 107 and other places where FASB uses the term *fair value,* the price desired is *not* to be computed on the basis of a possible collapse in the market or other worst-case scenario. The desired price is the amount at which the instrument could be exchanged *in a current transaction* between a willing buyer and a willing seller, in cases other than in a forced or liquidation sale. If the market has collapsed at the time the valuation must be made, Statement 107 requires an entity to produce its best estimate of fair value, unless that is impracticable.

This valuation, of course, can be subjective. Faced with thin markets, some American financial institutions have estimated the contents of their portfolio and trade book at values based on similar instruments that are trading, while others have concluded that valuation is impracticable.

Regulators are not unaware of the subjective elements and sometimes bias that may enter a process of valuing assets and liabilities. Therefore, how banks should value their assets is a long-running debate involving policy decisions and basic principles in accounting.

Traditionally, companies value their assets and liabilities at their historic costs and ignore fluctuations in their value. That makes accounting *simple but inaccurate* in terms of what the figures represent. Reformers want companies to value assets and liabilities according to their current value in the marketplace.

In the United States, the Financial Accounting Standards Board has taken the lead through a ruling requiring companies to account for investments in debt and equities at market value. This is not unrelated to the fact that FASB depends on the Securities and Exchange Commission.

SEC is a promoter of *market-value accounting*. But the Federal Reserve tends to think that market-value accounting would put banks' profits and solvency at the mercy of markets.

This will discourage the banks from investing in long-term securities. We have already seen an example with bonds. Both the SEC and the Fed arguments have value.

Banks mainly buy securities issued by federal and local governments and their agencies. There is little risk that these issuers will default, but SEC fears that while the credit risk may be low the market risk may be high—as for instance with interest rate futures.

There is also the issue of the product mix in a bank's inventory. No two financial institutions have the same composition in their portfolios. One international bank active in derivatives mentioned the following items as constituting the bulk of its off-balance-sheet assets. The roughly $500 billion in notional principal amount was comprised of the following:

❏ 59 percent in interest rate swaps.

❏ 28 percent in interest rate caps and floors.

❏ 7 percent in currency swaps.

❏ 6 percent in other instruments, including forward rate agreements.

Slightly less than 20 percent of the outstanding were written with affiliated companies. The valuation of the swap book at the end of the preceding year was a rumored unrealized loss of $320 million.

This was part of the market risk, but in the financial industry at large, the difference between credit risk and market risk is not always seen in the proper perspective. Although, contrary to 19th century practice, in the 20th century American municipalities do not default, the value of their bonds drops when interest rates rise.

Until quite recently, under the going accounting rules, banks did not need to recognize this in their balance sheets. Yet, the SEC is right in insisting on recognition because the banks' exposure to risk may be growing. The SEC fears that, encouraged by rules that demand a great deal of bank capital for loans and little for government obligations, banks are replacing credit risk with market risk.

This evidently runs contrary to what many people say, which is that the net effect with derivatives is to replace market risk with credit risk. Because of historic-cost accounting practices, banks can take profits on successful investments and ignore losses on bad ones.

Yet, due to the exponential growth of off-balance-sheet instruments, big changes in interest rates, in foreign exchange rates, and other sensitivities could reveal huge swings in the value of banks' capital. Fair value estimates may not provide an outright answer to this challenge, but they make it possible to know with some degree of accuracy the assets and liabilities of the bank.

3.   Marking-to-Market for Better Risk Management

Banks are reasonably looking at a meaningful intersection between sizeable accounts and accounts that they expect to be around for some time. These are *target accounts* that they wish to actively trade with and that they need to value dynamically in order to be able to estimate exposure figures, lines of credit, and profits and losses.

It is precisely for these reasons that banks like to mark-to-market some assets and liabilities that are related to past deals with counterparties and their securities holdings, which would reduce swings of the type section 2 has discussed. But deciding which liabilities are related is no easy task, and valuing them to market can be even harder.

From a worst-case scenario viewpoint, it all adds up to the capital that will be available when there is an urgent need for it—and, if possible, in the case of a panic or a run on the financial system such as occurred in 1932.

Banks lend a line of credit assuming that they will carry the loan or derivatives transaction at its full value until the borrower repays. But the loan's illiquidity binds the bank to the counterparty, and this too has to be recognized.

If the counterparty runs into trouble, it is a foregone conclusion that it will expect help from the bank. However, in the case of loans, fair value estimates, which apply market valuation accounting, would make such assumptions irrational. The same is also true of many derivatives trades.

If banks begin to value loans in the same manner they value securities, they will trade loans just as readily, as already happens with mortgage-backed financing. The Federal Reserve has been pointing out that today there is no market for most bank loans. But such a market can nicely develop as already happens with mortgage-backed securities and with corporates. Banks have also been packaging credit card loans into securities for years, and doing so rather successfully.

Once the links between borrower and banker are served, banks can buy and sell loans to commercial and industrial companies, mutual funds, pension funds, insurance companies, and other investors.

As technology improves, more information about a golden horde of borrowers will become more widely available. Securities markets will use this data to price and trade their loans. This will make the classical argument of core deposits nearly irrelevant.

One of the issues in evaluating the possible effect of funds withdrawals is that while depositors can cash in their demand deposits at any time, traditionally they tend not to do so all at once. Banks reckon that their core deposits can fund five- to seven-year assets without risk. They want to value those liabilities accordingly.

SEC opposes such a move because core deposit means little in a crisis. When a bank is in trouble, depositors rush to pull out their money. This accounts for the interest in advancing a scheme that would subject all financial assets and liabilities, not just debt and equity securities, to market value accounting. FASB took a first step in 1992 by requiring companies with more than $150 million in assets to disclose the fair value of most financial assets and liabilities. For securities, the fair value is the market price or something close to it. For loans, it is the banks' best guess, but it has to be reasonable.

At first, these disclosures nestle in the safe obscurity of notes to company accounts, but eventually the FASB may require financial institutions to mark-to-market the bulk of their balance sheets. That would revolutionize banking.

Marking-to-market or original value, *whichever is lower*, is a good rule for risk management. A similar policy should be followed with marking-to-model, the latter substituting for the marking-to-market chores when they are impractical.

Marking-to-market can be tough not only because of the lack of a secondary market for some OTC deals, as already mentioned, but also for other reasons. A good deal of the future of the derivatives business rests in cross-border transactions, passive investing such as indexation, and customized product offerings.

Customized product offerings and globalized business can only be done effectively by using models and computers. Figure 3–1 suggests this by presenting how databased information elements can be used to give an ad hoc view of the business and to feed information in real time into the bank's risk-management system.

This effort must be consistent and well orchestrated. Because of the difficulty in defining overexposure, solutions must be both flexible and dynamic. Board members, the president of the bank, and the president's immediate assistants must have online access to a risk/asset ratio updated in real time, whenever they wish to do so.[1] They must have available to them the tools for evaluating exposure from interest rate agreements, forward foreign exchange deals, money market instruments, and commodity trading, among other transactions.

The chief executive officer of a multinational bank must be able to access fully updated risk and return, as well as assets and liabilities information and do so worldwide. Short of this, the bank's employees

---

1 Chapter 16 presents systems and procedures required for such a solution.

Figure 3–1. A P&L and Risk-Analysis System for Custom-Made Derivatives

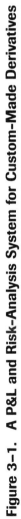

View of the Business

Return on Assets

Ad Hoc Performance Analysis

Fair Value of Assets and Liabilities

Risk-Management System

Any Location

Any Product

Any Customer

should not be pushed to take more interest rate risk, more yield risk, more currency risk—even if the current profitability is lackluster. Banks that jump into the market imprudently are turning belly-up.

4. Analogical Reasoning and the Art of Marking-to-Model

The average banker is sort of shy when he hears about marking-to-model the trading book and the portfolio. Yet the process is fairly simple. Every model rests on the premise of *analogical reasoning*, along with some simplification of the real situation as perceived by its developer.[2]

The development and testing of models made for financial analysis reasons, and for pricing, is dependent on the accuracy of our assumptions, the parameters we choose, and the computer programs we design. The accuracy associated with marking-to-model can be higher or lower depending on the quality of the work embedded in them. Not only do we have to be attentive and meticulous, we must also be suspicious of every detail throughout the whole analytical exercise. It is not possible to emphasize strongly enough the importance of end-to-end testing for the model as well as for its critical components.

The models we develop are essentially simulators. *Simulation* is an artifact based on analogical reasoning. When analogous systems are found to exist, experimentation and observation done with one of them can be used in predicting the behavior of the other.

Simulations are only as good as the assumptions on which they are based, and so is the model that we construct through algorithms and heuristics. The roles of modeling and testing must be considered as inseparable, with particular attention paid to the quality of the product that will be used in a decision-making sense.

As the preceding paragraphs have explained, fundamentally the modeling mechanism the banker uses is nothing more than an analogical reasoning process. The block diagram in Figure 3–2 shows its main components, which lead from problem definition to a justification process. The model we develop for fair value reasons may regard a single transaction, an instrument, or a whole portfolio. Its goal may be to help regulate an investment policy, valuate the trading book, offset risk versus return, or any issue critical to risk management.

The model of the system will invariably consist of algorithms relating to the product and the market and/or to risk and return of each instrument. The model may be simple or complex. In many cases, while

---

2 See also D. N. Chorafas, *Simulation, Optimization and Expert Systems* (Chicago: Probus, 1992).

Figure 3–2. Structural Decomposition of an Analogical Reasoning Process

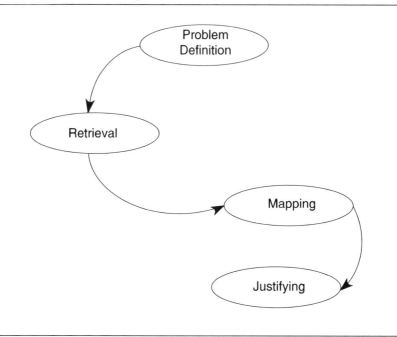

simplicity is at a premium, simple equations are not sufficient, and other relationships must be considered as better alternatives for modeling.

Additional issues with pricing models, beyond the price of the instrument and the market's behavior, may include transaction costs associated with the execution of orders, the restructuring of existing commitments, or other constraints and restrictions. For instance, the need to allocate a minimum or maximum proportion of the assets to a certain type of investment, or account for credit line limitations in connection to counterparty risk.

In modeling, this is done through control parameters. These are the elements generally within the user's discretion to change—such as the allocation of funds to particular investment forms or the rating of counterparties.

Notice that allocation and optimization can be greatly assisted through models—from the now commonplace linear programming to genetic algorithms.[3] The same is true of scoring credit risk. Recently,

---

[3] See also D. N. Chorafas, *Rocket Scientists in Banking* (London and Dublin: Lafferty, 1995).

British banks have used genetic algorithms to modernize their credit rating for loans.

Pricing models do not have to address optimization, but they have to be sensitive to optimization needs—or they may be part of a larger aggregate we will have to optimize. Among the issues to be borne in mind for an optimization is which allocations should be changed within a given portfolio in order to maintain the best risk and return ratio within certain guidelines of maximum risk or minimum return.

Still other objectives to be considered may include the liquidity of assets, a subject we address in Chapter 4. This information on previous performance of investments is important as it helps in pricing instruments and in optimizing the portfolio in the future.

To be of value to their users, models must be flexible, even if they involve a certain level of complexity. This brings into perspective the concept of *parametric modeling*. Both in the scientific community and among financial institutions, there is a move toward parametric design. This is also known as *variable-driven* modeling, and it interests companies of all sizes that are investing in technology for competitive reasons.

5. Highlighting the Role of Parametric Modeling

Parametric approaches are important both in drawing up the original design specifications and in reengineering the product development process to leverage technology and achieve meaningful results. A parameter-driven design is important with concurrent banking, concurrent engineering, and for training reasons.[4] It permits product and process designs to remain flexible, without requiring that the entire model be constrained from the start. Through parameters, the designers can input important elements as well as develop patterns to speed modeling, without having to restructure the model every time. This is done through the dual approach of explicit modeling and parametric changes. With *explicit modeling*, the designer works with and alters the model through parameters that can be interactively manipulated.

Flexible, knowledge-enriched software sees to it that the model is associated with all of its previous stages all of the time. It is manipulated and changed not in terms of its current form, but in terms of how it was built from the outset. This is an important feature in connection with the pricing of financial products and the valuation of trading books and portfolios.

Fundamentally, whether we price the instruments in our trading book and in our portfolio through marking-to-market or marking-to-model is often decided by circumstances. These may be due to the exist-

---

4 As those discussed in Chapter 17.

ence of a market and/or to constraints posed by regulation and bank supervision. However, it is important to understand that the two marking processes have much in common. A realistic model effectively reflects the market's behavior.

In terms of developing and/or implementing parametric pricing models, a good deal can be learned from engineering because of the experience that exists in the field of science. The primary choice for product and process designers today is a parametric-type hybrid model. Hybrid approaches offer the capability to import legacy data[5] and market data into the model. The key to such a solution is a nondisruptive migration path. Handling legacy data is important because almost every organization has it from its work with earlier systems, especially with formerly popular financial instruments.

Legacy data might include previous, simpler versions of a product, procedures, customer files, or recurring references that have been carried over from one generation of product to the next. Examples include the following:

❑   *Leverage.* This is in essence an investment form in itself, with the relevant parameters such as gearing level, factors of cost, higher return, higher risk, correlation of risk categories, and so on.

❑   *Risk limits.* For institutions and others that follow stringent guidelines, the modeling process to be adopted should require certain caps on high-risk and floors on low-risk investments, or other tolerances.[6]

❑   *Product guarantees.* For instance, the ability to guarantee a certain return followed by the optimized risk/return mix for the remainder of the portfolio.

With variational design of a financial instrument, the driving dimensions of the model can be based on a fairly complex set of equations, which is the job of the rocket scientist, not the end user. Variational approaches allow users to manipulate the design of an instrument without being concerned about the order in which constraints are placed or solved.

In conclusion, parametric modeling can be used for many purposes: for reasons of prognostication, optimization, or capturing a transaction history of operations. The chosen variables constitute the design intent. We record the design process by mapping the relationships among information elements and providing the user with a valid experimentation tool.

---

[5] From classical data-processing applications.
[6] See also the discussion on the Heisenberg principle in Chapter 2.

6. Why an Object-Oriented Solution Is the Better Alternative

The advent of object-oriented solutions in information technology has brought with it a wave of change. One of its crucial advantages is the simplification achieved through semantics, and the ability to give meaning to our queries when communicating with the sprawling distributed databases we have constructed and use daily.

Let's begin with a few definitions to provide a common background. The word *object* is used to describe an entity that encapsulates an information element as well as operations on it. In other words, objects can be *passive*, such as abstract data types, or *active*, including data but also rules for operations.[7]

We are particularly interested in active objects because these are capable of initiating independent actions. Knowledge artifacts such as *agents* are objects residing at network nodes and activated by a message-passing mechanism.

All this may seem out of place in a book on finance, yet it is highly relevant in connection to marking-to-model. Object-oriented models can differ from one another in terms of their internal behavior, but as a class they are more sophisticated and more capable than other models— whether these are relational or rest on hierarchical solutions. Object-oriented solutions provide an ephemeral hierarchical representation, which enhances semantics but disappears when the operation is completed. This sustains systems flexibility and makes feasible the use of *metaknowledge*—that is, knowledge about knowledge.

Object-oriented features serve well the parametric modeling approach we examined in section 5. Objects are better fit to express the way the market behaves using rules and attributes. They also allow financial analysts to communicate with their system using familiar terms.

Feature-based modeling performs functions once done manually in most banks because legacy approaches through mainframes, Cobol, and naive protocols cannot handle modeling. Besides this, interactive solutions based on advanced technology are well-suited to today's team-oriented environment, where a product and process design, or design segments, is often passed from one person or company to another and the ability to quickly make changes to the model is crucial, even without having complete knowledge of how someone else will react to it.

There are parallels between engineering and finance that are worth exploiting in a creative sense. Engineering is primarily concerned with the materials sciences and their assets. Finance is primarily concerned

---

[7] See also D. N. Chorafas and H. Steinmann, *Object-Oriented Databases* (Englewood Cliffs, NJ: Prentice-Hall, 1993).

Figure 3–3.   Physical and Logical Channels in Nature and in Business

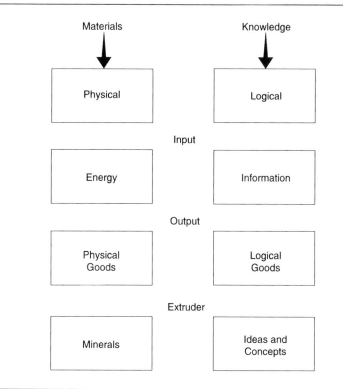

with logical or virtual assets and the knowledge these require. Information is a resource common to both. A similar statement can be made about knowledge. Figure 3–3 shows a conceptual comparison between physical and logical channels that are dominant both in nature and in business. In order to function properly, both processes need input, output, and an extruder function.

Input and output have values that must be estimated and optimized. The whole concept of fair value calculations rests in these simple terms and can be served through an object-oriented parametric model along the lines that Citibank has followed in restructuring its information technology for retail banking.[8]

What can be learned from simulation experience in the sciences that is helpful in marking-to-model? While its adoption by leading-edge

---

[8] See D. N. Chorafas, *Intelligent Multimedia Databases* (Englewood Cliffs, NJ: Prentice-Hall, 1994).

banks is recent, parametric modeling burst upon the engineering scene in the late 1980s. It provided significant productivity gains by virtue of its ability to capture the design process, and assured effective interrelationships between the various parts of the design.

When product designs and market scenarios are altered, object-oriented parametric approaches permit the entire set of algorithms to be automatically updated to reflect those changes. Also, while the idea of working in terms of features has existed in a number of three-dimensional modeling systems prior to the introduction of parametric modeling, it is the most recent software that makes this feasible in a seamless sense.

In conclusion, by employing sets of rules that define how changes to products and prices will be handled, the user is establishing an editing framework. There are also situations where the user is conceptualizing something and doesn't want to be locked in to constraints right away. Hence the user needs an intelligent constraint management and the ability to leave some of the parameters unspecified.

As the user keeps working, the rocket scientist and the financial analyst can add or delete constraints and include parameters later on or have the model updated. Parametric solutions leave aspects of the model unconstrained and unbounded, as elements simply exist in space in whatever form the designer of the model, and the user, have temporarily decided upon.

7.   Shortcomings of Methods of Estimating Fair Value

No model is fail-safe. The same is true of the marking-to-market estimates we do, as well as of traditional approaches to the calculation of net present value. These typically rest on the choice of a single risk-adjusted factor, such as discounted rate of return, to compute the probability distribution of a payoff function.

Many of the methods financial analysts classically used do not properly capture the value of a designer's or a trader's ability to modify a financial product as uncertainty is resolved or, alternatively, as it increases, or as an investor comes forward or holds back changes for whatever reason. For instance, as uncertainty unfolds and risk grows or shrinks, so does the risk-adjusted discount rate. Essentially, this means that no single discount rate may be appropriate for all cases or the same case at all times.

The ability to adapt a financial operation or trade to futures contingencies can be effectively faced through object approaches and parametric modeling, as we saw in sections 5 and 6. But we must be careful not to introduce asymmetries in future project values resulting in an overall increase or decrease in value as contrasted to the static type of net present value analysis.

None of the methods that have been used in pricing financial instruments is free of constraints and approximations. All present similar challenges, *net asset value* being an example. Net asset value is equal to the market value of the total assets belonging to a portfolio, including all cash, cash equivalents, securities, and other investments, minus the total liabilities. Each asset and liability in the portfolio must be determined on the basis of generally accepted accounting principles consistently applied under the accrual method. Net asset value includes, but is not limited to, any unrealized profit or loss on open positions and realized profits and losses on closed positions.

All commodity positions shall be valued at their fair value, by marking-to-market—which means the settlement price, as determined by the exchange on which the transaction is effected or the most recent quotation as supplied by the clearing broker or banks through which the transaction is effected.

In the past, if such a settlement price or quotation was not available on the date the net asset value was determined, commodity positions were valued at their fair value as determined in "good faith." This is of course very subjective. A more objective alternative is marking-to-model.

Another shortcoming of the net asset value method lies in the fact that, by and large, the data it uses are old—hence obsolete. This hardly answers the requirements of a fast-moving market, as the method provides estimates of relatively low accuracy.

No approach can do everything. As the FASB research that led to Statement 107 helped document, current practices followed by organizations that estimate fair value for internal management purposes vary along with specific methods, assumptions, and models.

In the course of the research that led to this book, several banks commented that fair value as it has been practiced in the past implies a *steady state*. This, they said, is an illusion because a steady state does not exist in the financial markets.

Not everyone is on the same wavelength. Some banks stated that the management role of fair value is unquestionable. For instance, the fair value of liabilities provides information about the company's success in minimizing financing costs on a continuing basis. This is typically done by timing borrowing decisions to take advantage of favorable market conditions.

FASB Statement 107 points in a more dynamic direction by building extensions on the more classical practice and disclosure requirements—for example, FASB Statement 12, Accounting for Certain Marketable Securities, and FASB Statement 15, Accounting by Debtors and Creditors for Troubled Debt Restructurings. The latter provides guidance on determining the fair value of assets without active markets, for instance when transferred in settlement of troubled debt.

FASB also advises adding certain descriptive information pertinent to the value of financial instruments that would help investors and creditors make their decisions, such as the carrying amount of a financial instrument, its expected maturity, and the effective interest rate.

It is the opinion of a growing number of financial experts that the benefits to investors and creditors of having some timely information about fair value outweigh the disadvantage that this information is less than fully comparable. Let's not forget that information about financial instruments based on historical prices is also not comparable—whether from one market to the other or from a given company to another.

8. Exploiting the Potential Fair Value Offers

The shortcomings of the fair value method, which we have seen in section 7, bring to mind the limitation some banks attribute to the use of the notional principal amount in connection to the control of risk. No solution is perfect, and for this reason Chapter 2 emphasized the wisdom of taking a frame of reference with three crucial variables rather than betting strictly on one of them.

Are there examples where even an approximate estimate of fair value can be put to profitable use? To answer this question effectively, it is important to understand that no company necessarily needs to settle a debt financed at a rate below prevailing market rates to realize a gain. The gain could be realized over the period of repayment of that debt. But information about the fair values of assets and liabilities permits an assessment of an institution's success in managing its finances.

This reference has many aspects that concern not only banks but also treasury departments of corporations. Treasuries are not being supervised by the reserve banks or other regulatory agencies. Yet they increasingly engage in financial operations, many of them having become nonbank banks.

There is the beginning of regulation in reporting by treasuries, but not yet in terms of a generic approach to fair value. In the United States, corporate treasurers as well as nonfinancial entities in general are directed to the following normalization guidelines regarding disclosures about financial instruments:

- ❑ For cash and short-term investments, the carrying amount approximates fair value because of the short maturity.

- ❑ For long-term investments, fair value is to be estimated based on quoted market prices for those or similar investments.

- ❑ The fair value of foreign currency contracts used for hedging purposes is to be estimated by obtaining quotes from brokers.

❏ For investments for which there are no quoted market prices, a reasonable estimate of fair value should not be made.

The fair value of long-term debt can be based on the quoted market prices for the same issues or on current rates offered to the company for debt of the same remaining maturities. Existing regulation is missing the point that current value estimates can be significantly improved through *real-time simulation*, utilizing experience developed by and for the military.

Figure 3–4 highlights this approach, which I have explained in detail in my book on rocket scientists and their job. This solution involves a family of models for market data filters, simulation, multimedia, three-dimensional color graphics presentation, and real-time response—whether or not the end user is immersed in a virtual reality setting:

❏ *Data streams* from the environment arrive in parallel to an input box and are processed through one or more market filters.

❏ *Reformatting* is done at two levels of reference: one for historical data to be reported in real time, the other for predictive purposes—also online.

❏ The *end user(s)* can be passive, receiving information, or *active*, interacting with this information and formulating ad hoc queries.[9]

Let's assume that a company entered into interest rate swap agreements to reduce the impact of changes in interest rates on its floating-rate long-term debt. These interest rate swap agreements mature at the time the related notes mature; still, the company is exposed to credit loss in the event of nonperformance by the other parties to the interest rate swap agreements.

Besides this, if in terms of foreign exchange contracts a company enters as a hedge against foreign accounts payable, market value gains and losses must be recognized. Theoretically, the resulting credit or debit offsets foreign exchange gains or losses on those payables; but, depending on the strategy that was followed, this may not necessary.

What real-time simulation does is provide senior management with a flexible, ad hoc evaluation of positions; the end user chooses this fair value information stream at the moment he or she needs it, not the way data processors decided five years ago that it should be done. Regulators can also benefit from this flexibility.

Interestingly enough, a similar approach can be used in the evaluation of new proposals, such as the 1993 Market Risk Amendment by

---

[9] For the definition of hard data and soft data, see Chapter 17.

Figure 3–4. A Real-Time Simulation Solution to Help in the Presentation of Fair Value

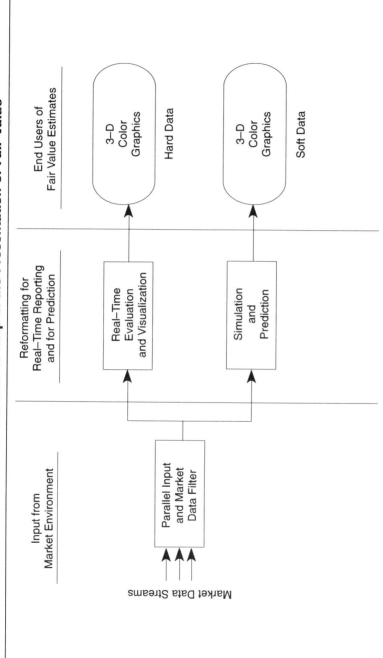

BIS or other regulatory issues. Prior to finalizing its Statements, FASB brings out a draft for comments. Respondents to the 1990 Exposure Drafts commented that some valuation techniques require sophisticated assumptions as well as advanced valuation models; for instance, the expected prepayments on a portfolio of loans assuming various future levels of interest rates. Manual evaluation, however, is very limited. It carries the risk that it could force even the smaller companies to incur significant costs.

Because of this, regulators tend toward simplified assumptions, which, however, do not give a reliable estimate of fair value. Nor do they always provide appropriate disclosure. Through real-time simulation, the reporting entity could estimate market value by separately calculating changes in market value due to changes in overall general interest rates and changes in market value due to cash flows affected by market premiums for credit risk.

In conclusion, reliable fair value information about financial instruments comes at the cost of developing, implementing, and maintaining a measurement and reporting system able to generate disclosures. Financial and industrial organizations should have real-time systems in place to monitor and manage the market risk and credit risk of their portfolios—and simulation is a good way to do this.

9. Fair Value Estimates Must Be Commensurate to the Amount of Exposure

The thesis supported in section 8 is that, if properly done, fair value estimates can serve management in a significant way. But the procedures we adopt must be reasonable, follow normalization principles, present both current data and predictive estimates, and permit the end user to experiment through simulation—in real time. These principles should be universal in business and industry, because today it is increasingly difficult to distinguish banks from nonbank banks and from the treasury departments of major corporations.

The attention to be paid to fair value estimates and the accuracy required from them—whether by marking-to-market or marking-to-model—should also be a function of the amount of exposure a financial institution or industrial organization has taken. Today, each of the 30 largest international banks has more than $700 billion in derivatives in notional principal. Of these, 24 have more than $1 trillion, and the three most exposed money center banks have more than $2 trillion in derivatives exposure.[10]

---

[10] See also D. N. Chorafas, *Derivative Financial Instruments* (London and Dublin: Lafferty, 1995).

Such exposures are so huge that the budget should be made available as a matter of course, by each financial institution, to develop real-time simulation systems of the type described in section 8. One major advantage that marking-to-model has over marking-to-market is that the models are built once, but they can be used for current estimates and for predictions.

Predictive capabilities are particularly crucial when exposure mounts fast. In a more or less official manner, it was said during the research meetings that three of the largest United States institutions involved in interest-rate-related derivatives have seen in the last three years an increase of 35 percent per year in the value of these instruments in their banking books.

There are also misconceptions. Some banks suggested that though the trades increased, off-balance-sheet risks shrank in 1994. The argument behind this statement is that the pace at which their derivative portfolios are growing is not necessarily adding to their real exposures—a statement that is very difficult to support.

According to the banks' own measurement of derivatives risks, the reason for such a curious statement is that the exposed amount is not directly related to the scale of the contracts, but to the extent to which each contract is showing a gain in fair value. If a counterparty stopped paying the fixed-rate leg of an interest swap agreement, the scale of the loss would depend on how profitable the swap has become to the bank. If the payments of an interest-related swap were at 7.0 percent, compared with a market interest rate of 5.5 percent, the bank would face a cost from the lost income stream.

That lost income, discounted back to present value, is the replacement cost of the contract. But is this argument sound? What if there is no replacement market because of market disruption, which is not necessarily a panic?

A more reasonable assumption seems to be that fair value estimates and risk calculation should be made on the basis of closing the contract altogether. This would require calculating a fair value that can be affected by the nonexistence of a market, for any reason.

Similar issues are raised in regard to off-balance-sheet trading volume in the foreign exchange market. Three of the largest United States banks are dominating this field, each adding several hundred billion dollars per year in exchange-related derivatives in terms of notional value.

While the credit risks associated with these trades are particularly important with the larger banks, they concern all financial institutions whose exposure rose significantly during 1993 and 1994, whether they admit it or not. Taking the six largest money center banks as a group, the volume of their OBS trades grew by about a third over the last 12 months—and this seems to be consistent across most of the different exchange and interest rate products: swaps, options, futures, and forwards.

By contrast, there were sharp differences between the banks in terms of the instruments in which each has been most active. The careful reader will appreciate the fact that such differences are not a modeling constraint. If anything, they provide an opportunity for better modeling solutions—which constitute a competitive advantage.

The development of simulators must be highly modular, not monolithic. Different modules will need to be built for different financial products, and parametric approaches must take care of the variations that are bound to occur within the same vehicle. Object orientation will allow flexible solutions that permit the bank to benefit from the use of semantics—while real-time simulation will effectively answer the requirements for derivatives risk management.

4

Capitalizing on Cash Flow and Liquidity

1. Introduction

Different types of portfolios can generate identical or nearly identical cash flows. This is the case with a forward contract and a leveraged position in the spot asset, with a bond denominated in one currency and a bond denominated in another currency, and with a cross-currency forward contract and a leveraged coupon bond position.

Cash-flow matching may be sustained even if the portfolios tend to differ for a number of reasons or are subject to different valuation rules. Cash flow is crucial to any investment, and its valuation is feasible even if differences exist across markets, such as supply and demand imbalances. The calculation of cash flow as a measure of the risk taken with off-balance-sheet instruments makes sense for many reasons. The most important is that fundamentally a financial product is a claim on a stream of future cash flows.

The term *cash flow*, however, is far from being homogeneously interpreted in business and industry.[1] For instance, in typical industrial accounting practice, cash flow is the total of net earnings and depreciation, minus dividends.

Depreciation costs are part of the cash flow and are subtracted from net income. This is a big reason for the depressed profits of many

---

1 See also D. N. Chorafas, *Financial Models and Simulation* (London: Macmillan, 1995).

companies, but it also means that much of the cash that would otherwise move to the bottom line and be taxed is hidden from view.

If a company depreciates $200 million, shows net earnings of another $300 million, and pays no dividend, it has actually generated a cash flow of half a billion, with all the leverage this provides.

Companies that plan to capitalize on this fact must take notice that not all the cash flow will become available for acquisitions and operating expenses. Rather, it is the *free cash flow* that is calculated as cash flow less capital expenditures.

Another metric of exposure we will treat in this chapter is *liquidity*, which is the market's ability to buy or sell commodities, securities, and derivative products (options, futures, forwards, swaps, and so on) at a competitive price—at any time and, more recently, in any place at any time.

2.   Advisable Practices in Connection to Cash Flow

Some companies follow a simple and others a complex procedure for calculating cash flow. The simplest way to think of cash flow is dollars received minus dollars paid out. This is just as true of the whole firm as of any of its departments or projects and the financial instruments it trades.

$$\text{Cash Flow} = \text{Money Received} - \text{Money Paid Out}$$
$$= \text{Inflow} - \text{Outflow}$$

Figure 4–1 suggests that a sound management policy should concentrate on cash flow not only from one market source, but from all markets that are currently active in a global banking sense, hence the outlined three-dimensional framework for interactive reporting. We will follow up on this subject when in section 7 we speak of *liquidity*.

Both cash flow and liquidity should be steadily evaluated in a detailed and global sense. The global approach is necessary for an integrative view, and can be subsequently sorted by

- ❏   Client relationship,
- ❏   Country of operations,
- ❏   Currency of exposure,
- ❏   Short-term, medium-term, long-term, or other criteria.

When we evaluate on a project-by-project basis or instrument by instrument, we should consider only the cash flows from the project (or instrument). But we should include all incidental effects and opportunity costs and always use after-tax cash flows. Some banks, however, consider sunk costs irrelevant.

Figure 4–1.   A Sound Management Policy Focuses ᴜᴎ Cash Flow and Liquidity in All Three Markets

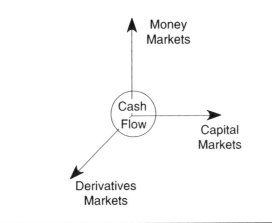

After the policy questions have been settled, the evaluation procedure starts, and matters might become a little more complex. In a manufacturing environment, for instance, the cash flow includes depreciation—and the money pool it creates will be used for capital expenditure, working capital, and other purposes.

Procedures vary by company, but good practice suggests that once a machine is retired it should be treated in an accounting sense the very year it is retired. It is highly advisable to be very careful with general accounting data. For example, don't treat depreciation as a cash flow unless it creates tax shields, and watch out for overhead because it has adverse effects on profits, and it consumes cash flow.

One of the important features of depreciation is that it creates tax shields that themselves are a cash flow. With taxes and depreciation, the cash flow equation becomes

$$C = R - OE - CE - TI + TD$$
$$T = \zeta (R - D - OE)$$
$$TD = \zeta D$$

and
$$C = (1 - \zeta)(R - OE) + TD - CE$$

where

$$C = \text{cash flow}$$
$$R = \text{receipts, revenues}$$
$$D_t = \text{depreciation value per year}$$
$$OE = \text{operating expenses}$$
$$CE = \text{capital expenditures}$$

$$\text{TI} = \text{taxes on income}$$
$$\zeta = \text{tax rate}$$
$$\text{TD} = \text{tax shield from depreciation}$$

There are different ways of looking at depreciation. The *depreciation value* is equal to initial cost minus salvage value. *Salvage value* is the liquidation value of capital equipment. When we estimate depreciable life, we essentially focus on the number of years over which it is exercised. With straight-line depreciation it is

$$D_t = \frac{1}{t} \text{ (Depreciable Value)}$$

where

$$D_t = \text{depreciation value per year}$$
$$t = \text{the number of years the law permits for depreciation}$$

With accelerated depreciation:

$$D_t = \text{(Depreciation Algorithm) (Depreciable Value)}$$

Some other rules are important to keep in perspective. Interest payments are not a cash outflow. They are already accounted for in the investment cost and are part of the financing equation and associated decisions.

The payoff from a project or financial instrument varies over time because cost and revenue varies; the same is true of the cash flow. For example, there can be more competition as time elapses, which changes the risk and rewards equation. However, with every project or instrument, inflation should be treated consistently. Otherwise, cash-flow comparisons are unsound and could even be misleading.

An important metric is the *present value of expected cash flows*. Those are both inflows and outflows resulting from transactions that can be expected to happen in the ordinary course of business.

Discount rates could be historical, that is, the rate stated on the date the transaction was originally consummated; a current rate as of the date the financial statements are being prepared; or some other rate such as the average expected rate over the life of the asset or obligation—or possibly some kind of average cost of capital.

Whichever rate is used is likely to cause criticism. In the case of an asset or obligation with a long life, the rate being chosen could significantly affect the cash flows. This is most important inasmuch as investors greatly value the ability of a company to generate net cash inflows. They look at its *assets* as a source of prospective cash inflows and its *liabilities* as obligations that probably will require cash outflows.

Positive or negative cash flow must be thoroughly investigated, with the resulting financial plans and statements comprehensible to investors and creditors. Reports should always convey a reasonable understanding of business and economic activities reflected in financial accounting—as well as trends and deviations from plans.

3. Looking at Cash Flow from a Financial Statement Viewpoint

There are other important issues to consider in connection to the cash flows. First, what is the basis of financial plans and the focus of financial statements? Should such statements emphasize balance sheet and off-balance-sheet evaluation of assets and liabilities, or should the matching of income and expense be emphasized in determining income and reflecting changes in assets and liabilities?

The *balance sheet* view would use changes in the value of assets and liabilities during a given period to determine net income. The increases in net assets would be obtained from the changes in value of the bank's resources and obligations. This valuation would necessarily require the adoption of some form of fair value measurement for resources and obligations.[2]

The *income-expense* view forms the basis for financial statements determining net income by matching revenues and expenditures. An alternative, often referred to as the nonarticulated method, is in essence a combination of the balance sheet and the income and expense approach, involving decisions about how to treat differences that might arise under this presentation.

The second key reference revolves around the definition of capital. The *financial capital* approach says that capital is measured by the resources that are contributed by shareholders either directly or indirectly. Present, generally accepted accounting practices embrace this definition of financial capital.

In the manufacturing industry, for instance, changes in value of inventory and productive assets are included in earnings. But in times of high-level inflation, some commentators have criticized the existing definition of capital. They say that there is a need for a definition that will recognize the effects of inflation, and that the financial capital concept will eventually impair the company's ability to build and replace productive capacity in the future.

This reference is important in a banking framework because both the trading book and the portfolio (particularly the latter) can be seen as

---

2 See also Chapter 3.

an inventory of financial assets. In fact, several banks look at it in that way. This inventory of logical or virtual assets is subject to rules similar to those affecting an inventory of physical assets.[3]

The alternative definition of capital is the *physical capital* concept. In industry, this approach includes holding gains on inventory and productive capacity in shareholder equity, so that when inventory or productive asset replacement is required at inflated prices the company will have funds to use for the purchase. A physical capital definition can be thought of as capital maintenance or a replacement cost approach.

The third key reference to bring to the reader's attention regards the need for *multidimensional analysis*.[4] It became relevant in the 1980s with the globalization of business, though a good deal of the approach has to do with conglomerates that feature many product lines.

Taking the financial industry as an example, we typically compare our bank to other banks, the capital market, and the money market, and we evaluate the results accounting for the prevailing macroeconomic factors at home and abroad. But what about the lines of business we are in? How do we value their contribution to our bottom line?

A monolithic approach to evaluation of a company as a going concern falls short of capitalizing on *our* strengths, and it limits the ability to strangle *our* weaknesses. Nor does it permit us to exploit the business opportunities the market may provide. A modern bank of some size has at least two dimensions: retail and wholesale.

While some banks have one focal point—wholesale or, alternatively, retail—many divide their lines of business along a greater number of product clusters—or channels—such as the following:

❑   Retail banking.

❑   Business loans (mid-size portfolio).

❑   Corporate loans.

❑   Traditional securities.

❑   Derivative instruments.

❑   Foreign exchange and international.

❑   Leasing, factoring, and other.

No bank is strong along each and every one of these lines; and even if it were, its revenues from business would not necessarily be evenly distributed. The same reference is valid with reference to manufacturing companies and any other branch of industry.

---

[3] See also the discussion on parametric modeling in Chapter 3.
[4] See also section 7 on liquidity and diversification.

**Figure 4–2. A Frame of Reference Permitting Better
Appreciation of a Bank's Financial Strengths
in a Given Business Environment**

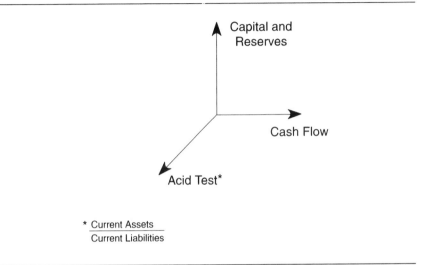

* Current Assets
  Current Liabilities

Figure 4–2 presents a frame of reference I have been successfully using for many years in evaluating the financial staying power of a company. It can be employed both by banks and with manufacturing or merchandizing firms—but the results are much more accurate when the model is applied by *product line.*[5]

To evaluate manufacturing, merchandizing, and financial companies, Yamaichi Securities has developed a multidimensional classification scheme that helps to clarify strengths, weaknesses, and income sources, arranging them in a taxonomical sense. The same principle can be applied in banking. An example of a multidimensional analysis matrix is shown in Table 4–1.

This classification according to business strengths by channel of operations considers six financial institutions—A, B, C, D, E, F—and weights their market performance along the line of reference we have just discussed. By so doing, it emphasizes the markets each business line appeals to, bringing attention to their relative strengths.

Each one of these channels can generate a cash flow that contrasts markedly to that of another channel. The same is true regarding the stream of profits. Often banks keep subsidizing inefficient product lines because in the compound results they don't see how inefficient they are.

---

5 The acid test is the ratio of current assets to current liabilities. In Section 9, it
  will be discussed in connection to derivatives.

Table 4–1.   Multidimensional Analysis of Financial Companies

	BANK					
	A	**B**	**C**	**D**	**E**	**F**
Retail	45%	5%	20%	–	10%	10%
Business loans	20%	–	40%	25%	10%	15%
Corporate	5%	10%	5%	25%	20%	–
Securities	15%	30%	10%	12%	20%	30%
Derivatives	10%	30%	13%	18%	20%	25%
International	5%	25%	4%	10%	20%	15%
Leasing	–	–	8%	10%	–	5%

When we are looking at the cash flow from the viewpoint of a consolidated financial statement, we see one pattern emerging. This is not necessarily the same pattern the channel-by-channel analysis gives. Greater focus is a major advantage of a multidimensional analysis, which permits us to distinguish between product lines hungry for capital and those that are cash cows; channels that are profitable and those that are dry holes.

4.   Results Provided Through Multidimensional Analysis

Using a multidimensional approach along the lines discussed in the previous section, a bank's business can be reflected in any one of a range of well-established categories. Such classification permits a more accurate assignment of cash flow, one that reflects the financial line of business.

Let's, however, also consider that the term *multidimensional* has another meaning as well—which can be important in analytical work. The analytical factors that enter the Yamaichi Securities model focus on

❑   *Macroeconomics*, such as inflation, rates of interest, employment, foreign exchange, and political factors.

❑   *Microeconomics*, including market rate of return resulting from the overall price movements as well as corporate fundamentals and technical indices.

The inclusion of this range of variables in financial modeling results in a much more thorough assessment of stock value than is possible through simpler models. In the Yamaichi implementation, the multidimensional analysis uses both algorithms and heuristics, focusing on the following:

❏ *Entities* such as corporations, other units active in business and industry, and economic reference points.

❏ *Market themes* from macroeconomics to microeconomics, including market returns, corporate fundamentals, and technical factors.

❏ *Methods* from time series analysis to cross-section evaluation, Monte Carlo, and expert systems.

Balance sheets and income statements are thoroughly investigated within this perspective, including critical ratios. Yamaichi made the point that the same ratio, in strictly numerical terms, can have different meanings in different industries—or at different times.

This is another way of emphasizing the importance of multidimensional analysis, as it provides the detail an analytical effort requires. Averages can be of no real help in judging the health of *our* company—or of other companies whose statements we analyze. Vertically integrated industries and conglomerates spanning many markets and products should be studied according to the multidimensional perspective. Variations in performance can be significant from one industry sector to another; therefore, they have to be analyzed appropriately.

The service-oriented operations of a conglomerate, for instance, tend to be less cyclical than its manufacturing business. The service industry now accounts for over 75 percent of employment—up from 65 percent a few years ago; hence, it is labor-intensive. But manufacturing features greater productivity improvements. These are differences that have to be reflected in the analytical models.

Manufacturers have implemented just-in-time inventory management techniques, which permit them to make production adjustments more rapidly than in the past. They also use robotics extensively. Excessive and unintended production capacity is less likely to occur in a highly automated environment.

Hence, a service industry-and-manufacturing conglomerate may have a split personality in terms of performance. From this fact comes the wisdom of approaching business performance in a multidimensional way after having properly identified the lines of business a company is in and giving them the proper weights. Cash flow will vary from one industrial sector of operations to another. Hence, we need to separately analyze each operations domain, using knowledge engineering.[6]

In a similar way, using a combination of high-frequency time series and cross-sectional analysis, a recently constructed knowledge artifact

---

6 See also D. N. Chorafas, *New Information Technologies—A Practitioner's Guide* (New York: Van Nostrand Reinhold, 1992).

provides its users with an ongoing interactive picture of changing events in terms of a financial company's strengths and weaknesses. Another module focuses on the company's impact on the marketplace.

The artifact was constructed on the premise that a highly competitive environment must be steadily watched. The expert system mimics what financial analysts have classically done in their research. This solution incorporates both quantitative and qualitative measures, mounts a 24-hour watch, and is able to justify its opinions.

A more sophisticated model, built by another financial institution, uses a pattern-recognition process to capitalize on a visual analysis of events at any given time. It also reflects on trends from past to present. These include

❑ The predominant trends in the bank itself, by operating division.

❑ Changes in its relationship with other financial institutions.

❑ Changes in its relationship with clients: manufacturers, merchandising firms, and consumers.

As these examples help document, both heuristics and algorithms should be used to assure that management can always investigate even minute changes in cash flow created within the broader perspective of market trends and influencing financial performance. Such an approach should be analytic and multidimensional. Subsequently, an integrative feature will bring together diverse inputs to provide a consolidated viewpoint for decision purposes.

5.   Attributes of a Qualitative Evaluation of Cash Flow

Bankers, and most particularly derivatives traders, can learn a great deal about the use of cash flow for qualitative and quantitative evaluation by studying policies and practices in other industries. Particularly important is a group of tools often referred to as *current value accounting*.

The attributes of this approach are primarily related to the balance sheet. The parameters selected should be applicable to both assets and liabilities as well as embedded into the parametric model. In terms of analysis, we can distinguish between two types of cost and two types of value:

1.   Historical costs, which are easily verified.

Their use has been criticized because they often ignore subsequent price changes. Yet, with few exceptions, we cannot account for real changes in the value of, say, depreciable assets until a transaction occurs.

2.   Current cost.

Accounting defines current cost as the "amount of cash or its equivalent that would have to be paid if the same assets were acquired currently." This is the sense of the fair value we discussed in Chapter 3.

One of the principal objectives for using current cost measurements is to provide management an opportunity to keep control over income by varying the replacement cost assumptions. In manufacturing, current cost of production is often modified to reflect technological improvements that could result in significant savings. In banking, we mark-to-model.

3. Current exit value.

This is a way of saying orderly liquidation. The current exit value of assets basically uses some hypothetical transactions and is subject to many of the same criticisms as current value.

Management's intent is important in considering current exit value. What is management's intended course of action in regard to a particular resource? To determine the current exit value of an asset, market quotes must be available in sufficient numbers to be reliable.

4. Expected exit value.

This alternative looks at exit value in the due course of business. The major difference between 3 and 4 is that the latter is based on a going concern rather than liquidating value. Expected exit value reflects cash flows from expected transactions in the future. It treats those cash flows net of any costs in making the exit value estimate.

As we saw in section 4, a multidimensional analysis along a chosen frame of reference can help capture causal relationships, including those with high levels of uncertainty—which can be handled through fuzzy engineering. It can also deal with variables exogenous to the bank.

The proper estimate of environmental factors can be instrumental in measuring an organization's ability to effectively use its cash flow, by gauging the level of resources available and the level necessary. Analytics along a multidimensional approach contribute to greater efficiency in the allocation of resources. Cash flows, balance sheets, budgets, and P+L statements are planning instruments.

Their effective use requires they be combined into an integrated framework, which takes account of the continual changes in the market environment. This can be effectively done by modeling. The essence of good cash planning is to recognize and discard assumptions that no longer hold true.

This can be done by using relevant knowledge in its rich detail. Effective execution requires a combination of qualitative reasoning and algorithmic procedures to show cash-flow fluctuations and their meaning, as well as accounting gain or loss on the acquisition or sale of assets along each of the multiple dimensions we have taken care to consider.

The management accounting gain or loss must be determined by product within a given line of business. In industry, the tax accounting gain or loss is determined by comparing the pretax asset recovery value to the tax basis less the total of all tax depreciation deductions taken to date.

The challenge is to present the differences and similarities in reporting in a multidimensional manner. Through expert systems, computers can help to automatically determine which type of gain or loss and which rate to apply. The decision of when to use the capital gain rate, for instance, must be made in a documented manner in the context of each product line's dimension. The same reference is true regarding the valuation of derivative instruments. Valuation is where all our forecast information comes together to show how worthwhile it is to undertake a given business opportunity. Financial theory tells that it is cash and timing that count—and high technology is at our service to provide real-time tools if we truly master its use.

6.   Comparison of Cash Flow, Duration, and Effective Duration

The examples we have seen in sections 4 and 5 come from industry. They have been included to enlarge the domain of reference and provide some practical cases concerning both the problems connected to cash-flow estimates and the solutions that have been found.

To complement this discussion and provide an opening to derivatives trades, in this section we will follow in detail a financial example on the estimation of cash flow from a bonds portfolio. The key word is *duration*.[7] Duration is a measure of the sensitivity of a bond's price to changes in yield. A low-duration bond will show a lesser change in price for a given change in yield than will a high-duration bond.

The way to look at duration is as a function of *discounted cash flow* of the coupon stream: the amount by which the bond's price is changing for a unit change (one basis point) in interest rates. In general

❏ High-duration bonds are characterized by long maturities and low coupons.

❏ Low-duration bonds have short maturities and high coupons.

❏ Floating-rate bonds usually have very small interest rate sensitivity and hence low duration.

---

[7] The algorithm for Macaulay's duration is given in Chapter 14, section 10.

The algorithm for cash-flow durations is known as the Macaulay duration measure.[8] It expresses the price sensitivity of a security to yield changes. The principle is that a portfolio has a duration equal to the weighted average of the duration of its securities.

Modified price duration is the percent change in bond price for a given change in yield. Dollar duration is approximately equal to the change in bond price for 100 basis points change in yield. It can be given by the algorithm

$$(\text{Modified price duration}) \ (\text{Bond price})$$

Taking Macaulay duration as the weighted average time to return a dollar of price,

$$\text{Modified duration} = \frac{\text{Macaulay duration}}{(1 + \text{yield}/1,200}$$

To compute this measure, we multiply the present value of the cash flow C(t) by the time t at which it is received. Then, we sum up from t = 1 . . . T and divide by the price.

$$\frac{\displaystyle\sum_{t=1}^{T} t \, \frac{C(t)}{(1 + \text{yield}/1,200) \, t}}{\text{price}}$$

The division by 1,200 must be applied if bonds pay interest on a monthly basis.

This algorithm is used to measure the price sensitivity of an option-free instrument for which cash flows are independent of interest rates, such as Treasuries and straight corporate bonds. Only if cash flows are independent of interest rates do we have the relationship

$$\text{Modified duration} = \frac{(-1)}{\text{price}} \cdot \frac{\partial \, \text{price}}{\partial \, \text{yield}}$$

$$= \text{Effective duration}$$

For instance, for a straight bond with price above par, say at 105 percent, and modified duration of 2.5 years, if yield goes up by 1 percent, the price would fall roughly by:

---

8 This will be discussed further in Part Three, when we consider how to build a comprehensive model for derivatives risk management.

$$\frac{105.0 \times 2.5}{100} = 2.62 \text{ points}$$

This algorithm should be used in full recognition of its properties. For instance, it is only valid for option-free securities with deterministic cash flows. It should not be used in connection with contingent claims, and it becomes extremely inaccurate for instruments such as collateralized mortgage obligations (CMOs), adjustable-rate mortgages (ARMs), and so on.

Notice that the equation for modified duration also gives *effective duration*—which is an important metric. It represents the rate of percent change in actual price with respect to changes in yield.

To calculate it, we generate two different sets of cash flows and the corresponding prices for two scenarios: up 50 basis points (bp) and down 50 bp. Then, we divide the price differences by the base case price.

$$\frac{\text{price (down 50 bp)} - \text{price (up 50 bp)}}{\text{(base case) price}}$$

One of the interesting applications of this algorithm is to measure the price sensitivity of any fixed-income security with or without embedded options. For instance, for a fixed-income security with a price of 93 percent and an effective duration of 2.7, if interest rates go up 1 percent, the price would drop roughly by

$$\frac{93.0 \times 2.7}{100} = 2.51 \text{ points}$$

Among the properties of this approach to be kept in perspective is that it can handle interest-rate-contingent claims as well as straight bonds. But the result is much longer than modified duration for deep discount MBF and CMO companion bonds—and much shorter than modified duration for high premium MBF and ARM.

7.   Paying Attention to the Fundamentals of Liquidity

Liquidity is the quality or state of being liquid, particularly in respect to securities and other assets. Liquidity emphasizes the ability to be instantly converted into cash. This is no different from the banking definition of liquidity.

Every market and every financial instrument has liquidity characteristics of its own. While futures markets are liquid, very large orders might have to be broken down into smaller units to prevent an adverse price change, which often happens when transactions overwhelm the available store of value. In general, and with only very few exceptions, it is wise to stay liquid. Liquidity is ammunition, permitting quick mobilization of money, whether for defensive reasons or to take advantage of business opportunities.

In their seminal book *Money and Banking*[9] Dr. W. H. Steiner and Dr. Eli Shapiro say that the character, amount, and distribution of its assets conditions a bank's capacity to meet its liabilities and extend credit, thereby answering the community's financing needs.

"A critical problem for bank managements as well as the monetary control authorities is the need for resolving the conflict between liquidity, solvency, and yield," say Steiner and Shapiro. "A bank is *liquid* when it is able to exchange its assets for cash rapidly enough to meet the demands made upon it for cash payments."

"We have a flat, flexible, decentralized organization, with unity of direction," says Manuel Martin of Banco Popular. "The focus is on profitability, enforcing strict *liquidity* and *solvency* criteria, and concentrating on areas of business that we know about—sticking to the knitting."[10]

A bank is solvent when the realizable value of its assets is at least sufficient to cover all of its liabilities. The solvency of the bank depends upon the size of the capital accounts as well as the stability of the value of its assets. This is a central issue in terms of capital requirements. *If* banks held only currency, which over short time periods is a fixed-price asset, *then* there would be little or no need for capital accounts to serve as a guarantee fund.

The currency itself would be used and the assets sold at the fixed price at which they were acquired. But over the medium to longer term, no currency or other financial assets are fixed in price. "They fluctuate," as Dr. J. P. Morgan wisely advised a young man who asked about prices and investments in the stock market.

Given this fluctuation, if the need arises to *liquidate*, there must be a settlement by agreement or legal process of the amount of indebtness. Maintaining a good liquidity permits avoiding this possibility. It makes it easier to clear up the affairs of the business, settling the accounts by matching assets and debts. An orderly procedure is not possible, however, when the bank faces problems of liquidity.

Another crucial issue connected to the same concept is *market liquidity* and its associated risks. Financial institutions tend to define market liquidity with reference to the extent to which prices move as a result of their own transactions. Normally, market liquidity is usually said not to have diminished, and this is true in most markets. But in-

---

9 New York: Henry Holt, 1953.
10 "Profit from Change," ICL Report on the 1994 European Banking Conference in Budapest (London, 1994).

creased transaction size and more aggressive short-term trading see to it that market makers are sometimes swamped by one-way market moves.

Since market moves are not predictable with certainty, it is wise to use tools that permit an experimental approach. We have seen in Chapter 3 the benefits that can be obtained through real-time simulation. But how many banks are ready in a cultural sense, as well as in terms of skill and in technology, to apply this solution?

8.   Aspects of Liquidity

Several of the financial institutions that took part in this research commented that it is very difficult to define *liquidity* and *diversification* in a sufficiently crisp manner, to be used for establishing a common base of reference.[11] Criteria for liquidity typically include turnover and number of market makers.

Diversification can be established by the portfolio methodology we are adopting, based on some simple or more complex rule, reflecting stratification by established threshold. A model is necessary to estimate concentration or spread of holdings.

Market characteristics are crucial in fine-tuning such distribution. The same is true of the policies the board is adopting. For instance, what really makes the bank kick in terms of liquidity? What are the thresholds?

Other critical queries relate to the market(s) the financial institution addresses itself to and the part of the pie it wishes to have in each of them by instrument class. Figure 4–3 gives an example from the global market by asset class. Confronted with such statistics, senior management must ask itself the following two questions:

❑   Which is our primary target: fixed-income securities, equities, or other vehicles?

❑   What is the cash flow in each class? The prevailing liquidity?

No financial institution can afford to go lightly over these subjects. Two sets of answers are necessary. The one regards the global pie chart and that of the main markets to which the institution addresses itself. The other is specific to the company's own trading book and portfolio.

Generally, banks have a different approach than securities firms in regard to cash liquidity and funding risk, but differences in opinion also exist between similar institutions of different credit standing. Cash liquidity risk appears to be more of a concern in these situations:

❑   The greater a firm's involvement in the derivatives businesses.

---

[11] See also sections 3 and 4 on multidimensional analysis.

Figure 4–3. $28 Trillion in the Global Market by Asset Class

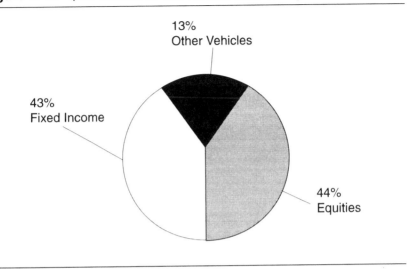

- ❏ The higher its reliance on short-term funding.
- ❏ The lower its credit rating in the financial market.
- ❏ The more restricted its access to central bank discount or borrowing facilities.

Therefore, in spite of the shrinkage of the deposit market and the increase in their derivatives activities, many banks with access to central bank funding seem less concerned about liquidity risk than do banks without a direct link to the central bank. Among the latter, uncertainty with respect to day-to-day cash flow causes continual concern.

By contrast, securities firms find less challenging the management of the cash requirements arising from a large derivatives portfolio. This has much to do with the traditionally short-term character of their funding. Cash liquidity requirements can arise suddenly and in large amounts when changes in market conditions or in perceptions of credit rating

- ❏ Necessitate significant margin payments or
- ❏ Adjustment of hedges and positions.

The issue connected to bank liquidity, particularly for universal banks is, as Bundesbank suggested during our meeting, far more complex than it may seem at first sight. "Everybody uses the word 'liquidity' but very few people really know what it means," said Eckhard Oechler, and he identified four different measures of liquidity that need to be taken simultaneously into account, as shown in Figure 4–4:

Figure 4–4. Four Dimensions of Liquidity a Bank Should Take into Account

1. *Money market liquidity*, practically equal to the liquidity in central bank money.

2. *Money market liquidity* in an intercommercial bank sense based on the bank's own money.

3. *Capital market liquidity*, or the ability to buy and sell securities.

4. *Swaps market liquidity*, the liquidity necessary to buy or sell off-balance-sheet contracts.

Swaps market liquidity is novel. As the Deutsche Bundesbank aptly explained, not only will the notion of *swaps liquidity* not be found in textbooks, but it is also alien to many bankers. Yet these are the people who every day have to deal with swaps liquidity in the different trades they are executing: players in markets that are growing exponentially and therefore require increasing amounts of swaps liquidity, and buying, selling, or holding options, forwards, swaps, and other derivative products in bilateral deals that may be illiquid.

The crucial question in swaps market liquidity is whether the bank in need can really find a new partner to pull it out of a dry hole. This is very difficult to assess a priori or as a matter of principle. Therefore, the rule at Bundesbank is that to assure swaps market liquidity, there should be a definition of what constitutes the ability to replace the contracts a bank has in this market.

9.   Cash Liquidity, Funding Risk, and Derivatives Acid Test

Despite the differences between commercial banks and brokers, a common problem of all financial institutions is that large derivatives portfolios can at times give rise to unexpected, sizable, and costly cash liquidity needs. Such needs come both from the inventory in off-balance-sheet instruments and from ongoing derivatives transactions. Some institutions forecast cash needs by adding together (1) the cash requirements whose origin can be found in the passage of time, holding prices, and volatilities constant; and (2) the cash requirements arising from potential price and volatility changes at each point in time, mostly computed by using historical data.

In this manner, estimated cash requirements are compared to funding availability and used to draw up new funding plans. Other financial institutions run regular liquidation analyses to determine whether the firm can survive a run resulting, for example, from a sudden downgrading or a market panic. There are plenty of reasons why market risk is connected to liquidity risk. The risk of cash liquidity can be further exacerbated by any default, that is, by credit risk.

As the case of the forced liquidation of part of the Orange County fund portfolio documents, there can be liquidity problems with over-the-counter options. It is often difficult to find a counterparty to close out or sell the option position. The following algorithm can help a bank or an investor in evaluating the liquidity of a derivatives portfolio.

$$L_r = \frac{\text{Exchange–Traded Instruments}}{\text{OTC and Bilateral Agreements}}$$

$$= \text{Derivatives Acid Test}$$

where L_r indicates the ratio of those instruments that tend to be more liquid to those that can be manifestedly illiquid. Both the numerator and the divisor have credit risk and market risk. However, market risk dominates in the numerator, while credit risk is more pronounced in the divisor.

There are no established tables of L_r ratios to help quantify and judge the numerical result given by this algorithm, but a case can be made in using known facts from the *acid test*—that is the ratio of current assets to current liabilities—since this, too, deals with liquidity.

Let's first define *acid test* in classical terms:

$$\text{Acid test} = \frac{CA}{CL} = \frac{\text{Current Assets}}{\text{Current Liabilities}}$$

It is generally accepted that a liquid enterprise has a $\dfrac{CA}{CL} \geq 2$.

If $\dfrac{CA}{CL} = 1$, the company is in trouble. And if $\dfrac{CA}{CL} < 1$, it is illiquid, and it should deposit its balance sheet.

In a similar manner, it could be stated that in terms of its off-balance-sheet business, given that exchange traded financial instruments tend to be significantly more liquid than OTC and bilateral agreements,

❑ $L_r \geq 2$ shows a liquid financial institution which, other things being equal, has fewer liquidity problems.

❑ $1 < L_r < 2$ is an indicator that the bank is heading for trouble.

❑ $L_r = 1$ is a limiting case indicating that the bank has entered a turbulence region.

❑ $L_r < 1$ can be used as proof that the OBS portfolio tends to be rather illiquid.

Notice that what has been outlined above can be nicely expressed in a fuzzy engineering diagram, as shown in Figure 4–5.[12] The statements that have been made to characterize the *derivatives acid test* are not crisp, but the resulting pattern can be most helpful in positioning *our* bank against the market forces.

The importance I attach to the use of the L_r metric comes from the fact that the liquidity of the OBS portfolio is rarely if ever given the importance it deserves. At the same time, practically all other metrics we have seen have been designed to respond to normal conditions—not panics—while the derivatives acid test can be improved upon for use in exceptional situations.

L_r is a metric that can be sensitive to turbulence and panics. It helps to indicate how much of the OBS portfolio of a bank or an investor can be liquidated under prevailing market conditions, even if at a loss, and capital recovered to sustain the business that faces cash-flow challenge.

This can be stated in conclusion. Financial markets need normalization and uniformity of metrics and measurements in order to be able to judge if liquidity is sufficient. Derivatives not traded in exchanges are by definition illiquid—but in terms of size of commitment, they also constitute the bigger deals and therefore the bigger risks.

---

[12] It is of course possible to develop a fuzzy diagram with a much finer grid for L_r.

Figure 4–5.   A Fuzzy Engineering Diagram to Position *Our* Bank Against Market Forces in the Derivatives Acid Test

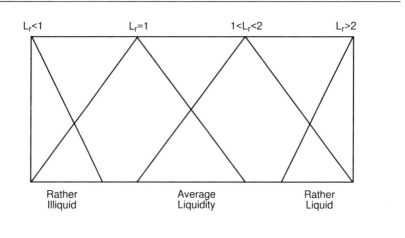

$L_r<1$ $L_r=1$ $1<L_r<2$ $L_r>2$

Rather Illiquid   Average Liquidity   Rather Liquid

5

Aspects of Legal Risk and Possible Aftermaths

1. Introduction

New financial instruments, such as futures, forwards, options, swaps, and exotic derivatives, pay little regard to national borders. The competitive development of cross-border mechanisms tends to overcome many of the barriers that existing regulation has erected—but further growth in trading requires improvements in settlements systems as well as improved and more homogeneous legal frameworks.

Uncertainties and legal risks complicate both trading and the management of derivative financial products in the trading book and the portfolio. Legal ambiguities associated with new vehicles can be substantial, and, though they lessen over the product cycle, they do impede the control of risk. To overcome this situation, many banks assume that adherence to well-established market conventions provides adequate legal protection. Yet, even in respect to business involving established financial products, many players learn the hard way that *legal surprises* may occur.

Legal risk is the risk of loss due to legal, legislative, or regulatory rules, which vary from one country to the other, while derivatives require a global market setting. One type of legal risk may be, for example, the inability to enforce an in-the-money contract in connection with bankruptcy or insolvency.

Another type of legal risk is in connection with exposure in regard to counterparties and clients. International banks would like to calculate client-to-client exposure; this, however, is both complex and imprecise because of legal issues.

The laws differ from one country to another, and in many cases they are less practical than one would imagine. The laws are also heterogeneous in the way they address cross-country trades. Both individual investors and companies active in off-balance-sheet markets typically operate in a global sense. But there are no laws able to cope with global needs in terms of financial responsibility and exposure.

That is why legal risks and uncertainties complicate both trading and asset management. It is therefore not surprising that they are now receiving considerable attention. The time has come to address the legal ambiguities associated with financed transactions, whether they use new or old instruments.

2.   Legal Issues with Cross-Border Financial Trades

Significant legal uncertainties can arise in cross-border trades involving financial products that have not been well established or routinely traded in the counterparty's country. Legal uncertainties can also arise when domestically traded derivatives contracts are based on underlying instruments that are funded and settled abroad.

While bilateral netting agreements are used for some transactions, they can be difficult to enforce. Their legal status may not be clear in domestic law, or, in the case of cross-border transactions, differences across country bankruptcy laws can bring up problems with settlements.

Experience with international financial trades teaches that the prevailing uncertainties about the laws in individual countries and how they would apply to international activities pose a risk to financial markets and complicate risk-management policies.

This is true even if most derivative instruments are documented with master agreements that contain the basic terms of the parties' relationship. The economic terms of each trade are usually set forth on separate confirmations supplementing the master.

Masters are prepared by the International Swap Dealers Association (ISDA). The terms of a master agreement will, among other things, permit a party to terminate that agreement and all related trades upon the counterparty's bankruptcy or insolvency. But rules defining bankruptcy are not universal: they vary among countries.

The ISDA master may provide for close-out netting, whereby the nondefaulting party calculates the market value of each trade at termination based on a methodology stipulated in the contract. Then, it aggregates all resulting values to reach a single, *net termination value* payable to or by the nondefaulting party.

Also, the master agreement permits a nondefaulting party to apply collateral it holds toward any termination payment owed to it by the defaulting party. ISDA, however, is not a sovereign government, and the law of the land prevails. Hence, this procedure does not alleviate the legal risk.

Therefore, each counterparty should carefully consider the effects of applicable bankruptcy laws on the enforceability of its master agreements. In many countries, bankruptcy laws raise concerns over the ability of a nondefaulting party to enforce early termination rights, close-out netting provisions, and related contractual rights.

In the United States, the Bankruptcy Code previously prohibited a nondefaulting party from exercising contractual rights against the bankrupt defaulting party without the bankruptcy trustee's consent. Hence, prior to receiving consent, a nondefaulting party would have been exposed to swings in its portfolio's market value and, despite bankruptcy protections, in the value of its collateral.

One of the aspects of legal risk for which there are no evident solutions unless universally valid rules are established is that, in the case of bankruptcy and insolvency, legislation can permit a trustee or receiver to handpick or outright reject an insolvent dealer's out-of-the-money contracts or to accept or continue only its in-the-money contracts.

It is evident that selective choices can cause serious losses because solvent counterparties would have to continue making full payment on their losing trades while receiving only a claim in bankruptcy for their gains. Such legal issues can best be understood if we appreciate the way in which—in general—the law itself is structured.

Figure 5–1 brings into perspective the fact that the establishment of a fault is only the first condition. The prejudice then has to be proved, and subsequently the cause-effect relationship needs to be verified. The norms for this verification vary from one country to another. Estimates of the consequences and subsequent corrective actions also vary.

While bankruptcy concerns have diminished for American banks due to recent amendments to the Bankruptcy Code, and to similar laws governing the insolvency of financial institutions, this is not the case in other countries. Even when there are rules that permit the exercise of termination rights and rights to apply collateral, their scope is somewhat limited if they can be invoked to apply only to expressly enumerated types of products.

This does not mean that with U.S. banks everything is clear. Amendments to U.S. law—for example, rights of parties to equity derivatives that are enumerated—do not fully protect all trades. Most importantly, significant enforceability concerns remain with respect to

Figure 5–1.   The Legal Procedure Is Typically Modular—Cross-Country Differences Can Exist at Every Step

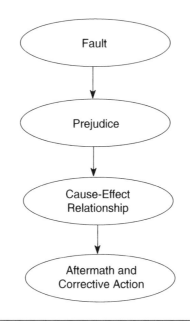

foreign counterparties whose bankruptcies would not be subject to U.S. laws.

For these reasons, it is advisable that before entering into a master agreement, a financial institution or any other party carefully study the legal nature of the proposed transaction(s), most particularly, the bankruptcy rules applicable to the country where the counterparty originates and operates.

3.   Polyvalent Nature and Uncertainty of Legal Aspects

Lawyers are often caught between a rock and a hard place: between duty to clients and duty to the state as an officer of the court. In the case of Lincoln Savings and Loan, for example, the lawyers seem to have rather quickly detected that the institution lacked the loan documentation that regulators would demand. Dozens of loans, many in excess of $1 million, had been granted without any risk analysis or proof of the borrower's credit. The savings and loans often had not obtained even routine appraisals or cash-flow projections of properties.

As reported by *Business Week*, auditors found that a Lincoln employee had backdated documents that had the directors' names on board minutes. Outside lawyers who audited such documents urged Lincoln's in-house lawyers to notify regulators and to remedy such practices.[1]

Valuable lessons can be learned by the legal and financial aftermath that hit Prudential Securities. The company says that during the reign of George Ball as its CEO, management made many unwise commitments, mainly connected to new and untested products. Customers to whom these products were sold brought the company to court. Untangling the legal maze behind this action took nearly eight years. The estimated cost to Prudential Securities stands at $1.4 billion.

This is the risk the company assumed for very meager rewards, and the eight-year-long delay happened with customers who are primarily based in the United States. Cross-country legal tangles can be much longer.

The message Lincoln S&L and Prudential Securities convey is that both top management and the lawyers must be very careful about the legal side of the transactions the bank enters into. They must also carefully watch their own morale. There is a counterpart to this in the military business.

"Enlisted men may be entitled to morale problems, but officers are not," general George Marshall once said. The same is true of executives and lawyers. "When a general complains about the morale of his troops," added Marshall, "the time has come to look for his own morale."

The fact that derivative deals today represent trillions of dollars in capital spread across political and country borders makes the legal issues, including the accompanying risk, all the more complex. Banking and trading laws were written long before there were off-balance-sheet vehicles, and there is a great deal of work needed to seal the gaps left where derivative transactions do not fit into an old-fashioned legal structure. The problem starts with defining the following:

- ❑ What each derivative instrument is.

- ❑ Who is allowed to trade with that instrument.

- ❑ How to enforce standard agreements designed to reduce transaction risks.

This is written in full appreciation of the fact that these are major issues in banking today. Interest rate swaps are a case in point. Their risk is judged illegal under the gambling laws of countries as diverse as

---

[1] May 4, 1992.

Japan, France, Canada, and Brazil—and, until recently, under the commodities regulations of the United States. In some countries, swaps risk has been classified as usury, which is illegal. But changes in the legal environment have also come in important areas.

In 1993, U.S. commodity regulators declared that swaps were exempt from futures regulations. But in France, in September 1992, national financial authorities issued a circular that defined who is allowed to use swaps, and under what conditions they can trade. Sometimes the law is vague or has contradictions. In France, local governments cannot speculate in derivatives. But they can use them to hedge—as though it is possible to draw the line.

Changes or redefinitions of the law have occurred under conditions still in flux. Uneasiness about the risks that derivatives pose to the banking system as a whole prompted the U.S. Congress to reserve final word on derivatives regulation. Some legislators view the swaps exemption from commodity law as simply an interim step on the way to more structured swaps regulation.[2]

Counterparty risk is another major topic of uncertainty. Governments, particularly municipalities, can be attracted to derivatives deals, but their qualification for a swaps marriage is far from clear. That much was said in England, in 1991, when the House of Lords ruled that the London Borough of Hammersmith and Fulham, an active sterling interest rate swaps trader, did not have the power to enter into derivative contracts.

That decision voided five years worth of contracts and forced both the local authority and the financial institutions involved in the trades to take losses. The decision also voided similar deals between more than 130 U.K. councils and 75 of the world's largest banks, stirring up legal appeals that are still in the courts—and will probably stay there for some time.

4.   Is There Immunity from Legal Risk?

All companies experience legal risks, particularly in a time of change. This happens not only with financial instruments and their trades, but with classical banking operators; with mergers, acquisitions, or divestitures; and in cases of reorganization that may involve legal issues. Contests over corporate control often go hand-in-hand with major litigation. Board members and officers of companies undergoing a change in control are still the most likely targets of a claim.[3]

---

[2] See also D. N. Chorafas, *Derivative Financial Instruments* (London: Lafferty, 1995).

[3] See also section 5 on CEO responsibilities.

One major area in litigation is shareholder claims. An important issue is complaints of inaccurate or inadequate disclosures in quarterly and other reports. Inaccuracies may exist as well in filings with the Securities and Exchange Commission, transactions in which management did not exercise due diligence—whether in loans or derivatives—and statements issued by directors and officers in connection to exceptional cases, routine corporate transactions, or simply daily business.

The chair and the managing director of a financial institution might be held liable because they had circulated inaccurate profit and loss information to the press. Or they may be judged responsible for the losses suffered by minority shareholders.

The lack of appropriate diligence may not just be a matter of poor management, but may also involve personal misdeeds such as conflicts of interest, misappropriation of trade secrets, or insider trading. Plenty of cases can serve as warning to officers and directors of the consequences that may follow if these legal obligations are breached. Shareholder activism is a spreading phenomenon for two reasons:

1. Many legislative changes favor the shareholder.

2. Shareholder muscle is due to pension fund and other institutional investors.

Taken together, these two reasons erode, and will continue to erode, management defenses. At the same time, corporate boards can ill afford to brace for litigation from angry shareholders, employees, creditors, and the regulatory authorities.

To effectively face the challenges presented by this situation, board members, the officers of the company, and other professional managers should be educated on the nature of their responsibilities in connection to legal risk. It is essential that the company advise its directors and officers on the specific legal and regulatory standards they must observe.

A well-researched program should be designed to assure compliance with all statutory, common law, and bank supervision requirements. The issues to be thoroughly addressed go beyond conflicts of interest and must include the following:

❑ Derivatives trades.

❑ Share dealing.

❑ Accounting and solvency.

❑ Unlawful payments.

❑ Political contributions.

❑ Authority for execution of documents.

❑ Tax issues with new financial products.

According to *The Wall Street Journal*, in Germany the Frankfurt prosecutor's office was recently engaged in an investigation of about 400 bankers and brokers for alleged tax evasion related to questionable securities dealings and another 20 individuals for alleged breach of trust.

This is one of the recent incidents suggesting that both regulation and the law are likely to increase pressure on officers and directors who may be jointly liable for a breach by any one of them. To avoid liability, a member of the board will be obliged to prove that he or she was not personally at fault. The directors' and officers' liability is a worldwide problem. The risks associated with serving as a corporate director will continue to grow.[4]

Yet, in day-to-day practice many officers and directors assume risks without a clear awareness of their legal duties. This means that they are prone to step outside the legal framework, and at the same time they lack the necessary insurance.

This statement is valid both in regard to financial transactions taking place within the same country and in a cross-border sense. In fact, as the preceding sections documented, cross-border cases are much more complex and therefore require a higher level of awareness in terms of legal risk.

5.   CEOs Can Never Be Too Careful

Chief executive officers whose personal accountability is connected with high-risk instruments would be wise to check out the biography of Louis XI of France. The monarch spent a lifetime dealing with problems of authority and reform analogous to those that the financial industry is currently undergoing.

Louis XI (1423–1483) was born in the twilight years of the Middle Ages. The kingdom he inherited was weakened by incessant warfare, disunity, and economic decline. But many of the challenges he faced have a curious similarity to cross-border derivatives trades. Poor leadership at the top had allowed the great noblemen to grow powerful, hence arrogant, like some derivatives traders today. These local chieftains were jealously guarding their personal interests and privileges, conspiring to usurp those of the Crown.

Barings offers an excellent example on how things can get out of hand in the far fringes of modern corporations, as was the case in me-

---

[4] See also D. N. Chorafas, *Membership of the Board of Directors* (London: Macmillan, 1988).

dieval kingdoms. The fatal flaw that in a couple of weeks destroyed 235 years of banking tradition was created by an English derivatives trader operating out of the bank's Singapore office—who played with Nikkei Stock Exchange instruments in the Osaka exchange—and fed by deficient internal control that proved incapable of giving warning signals.

Both in the medieval kingdoms and in modern corporations, it has consistently been easier to import new technology than to import new attitudes. Just as important is the fact that there are clear limits to the king's, the chairman's, or the president's zest for risk-management systems.

Can one really sustain that there are parallels to the way medieval nation-states and present-day financial institutions are being managed? During my research in Germany, I was told of one of the largest and most successful German banks, whose board, in the late 1980s, wanted to enter the derivatives trades.

❑ Having found no German banker willing and able to fill the OBS bill, it hired an American and gave him "carte blanche."

❑ The American derivatives expert was indeed enterprising. He did so many deals, and such large ones, that he scared the hell out of the board members.

The board of the German bank finally fired the American banker and put German derivatives connoisseurs to work untangling the portfolio the other had left behind. But this proved to be an impossible task. So the board rehired the American banker, charging him with creating order out of the mess he had left behind.

Here comes the Louis XI precedent. After his coronation in 1461, the king moved quickly to reform the kingdom. New men, mostly talented commoners, were brought to the government. Many tax privileges of the great lords were disallowed—and so was the king who, at the hands of his arrogant noblemen learned a great lesson.

Meeting a wall of resistance from the feudal structure of his state, Louis XI abandoned his frontal attack on the old order in favor of one based on subtlety. While the great dukes were impulsive, he was patient. Thoughtfully, he struck at their weaknesses, separating his enemies from one another through cunning and bribery, then overcoming them one by one, spinning a web of stratagems far more intricate than anything known among his contemporaries.

Louis XI was never much loved by his people, whom he taxed heavily, but over the course of a long reign the great dukes were brought to heel, the economy of the kingdom was restored, and the English invasion came to an end.

The great lesson of this reign is that those who create change find themselves alone, exposed, and imperiled by those who have an investment in the status quo. But a thoughtful and patient approach can carry the day, provided it is consistent in the longer term, and it uses skill rather than brute force.

Boards can learn a lesson from this reference, which is particularly applicable to legal risk and its management. They should learn, for instance, to appreciate the fine distinction between events and nonevents. A little-known and therefore unappreciated, yet important, fact is that amounts that are notional[5] have no legal standing. But once a transaction is accepted for netting by the clearinghouse, it becomes legally binding to each counterparty.

Using analogical reasoning in connection to the experience of Louis XI, it seems necessary to elaborate a web of stratagems far more intricate than those needed with classical financial products. Such stratagems should aim to overcome the legal contradictions that develop because of the gap between the nature of new financial product and legislation.

Finally, like the French monarch, the CEO must also be careful in handling his great dukes who are based abroad and have reason to resent central authority, even though without central authority it is not possible to exercise derivatives risk management in a global sense.

6.   Paying Attention to Issues of Personal Responsibility

One of the lessons to be learned in terms of legal consequences is that legislation in connection to derivatives increasingly focuses on the responsibilities of the board. This is true not just in one country, but internationally.

In October 1993, the Office of the Comptroller of the Currency issued 26 pages of guidelines concerning how national banks should manage the risks of their derivatives business. These guidelines specifically mention more than a dozen times how responsibilities fall on the bank's board.

While this warning might seem to be no more than a reprise of past efforts by regulators to make directors understand they are on the firing line for the deeds of their banks, its consequences could be significant. Comprehending derivatives trades has become a basic responsibility for a director.

As a way of enhancing derivatives legislation, several members of the U.S. Congress pushed for a federal derivatives commission composed of SEC, CFTC, the Fed, OCC, the Treasury's Working Group on Financial Markets, and FDIC. This Commission could establish the following requirements for off-balance-sheet instruments:

---

5 See Chapter 2.

❑ Capital.

❑ Accounting.

❑ Disclosure.

❑ Suitability.

For its part, the General Accounting Office (GAO) proposed not only legislation, but the *independent auditing* of the *risk management* policies and practices of all players. The bet is that once the new U.S. legislation is in place, the other G-10 countries will follow.

Because there are so many uncertainties and possibilities for pitfalls, prudent executives tend to avoid off-balance-sheet trades. An example is Dr. John F. Welch chairman of General Electric. In an article in *Fortune* magazine, Welch said that derivatives were something that as a company they had "chosen to miss."[6]

But, as the experience of Louis XI suggests, the CEO may be in for surprises because his dukes do things their own way—and could not care less about what the monarch thinks or says.

Welch and other wise executives see off-balance-sheet instruments as producing trading surprises they don't really care for. Their experience in financial businesses has made them aware of the excesses these businesses can spur. Welch was also quoted as saying, "Things tend to grow to the sky, get a momentum. 'Let's make it a little higher, a little higher.' I think we have learned a lot about that." But M. Carpenter, then the CEO of Kidder Peabody, and his people thought otherwise. On Sunday October 16, 1994, as a result of mounting losses with derivative financial products, the decision was made to break up Kidder Peabody, the troubled investment banking subsidiary of General Electric. Its most attractive businesses were to be transferred to Wall Street rival Paine Webber. This announcement ended GE's eight-year ownership of Kidder Peabody, which in the late 1980s had been rocked by an insider trading scandal and loss-making junk bond holdings and in 1994 had been hit by tumbling bond markets and an alleged bond trading fraud that resulted in fictitious profits of $350 million.

Companies typically call managers on the carpet when their results are below expectations. Yet, whether out of negligence or for medieval "quality of management" reasons, most never ask apparent "superstars," such as Kidder Peabody trader Joseph Jett, to explain results that far exceed expectations. This lends credibility to the saying that most frauds are not detected by control systems, but are picked up by people who ask knowledgeable and cutting questions. It also confirms the fact that one person's excesses are other people's misfortunes.

---

6 March 7, 1994.

This is the main message one gets from the fact that General Electric agreed to sell Kidder Peabody after the loss of $85 million in the third quarter of 1994. Chopping off deadwood became unavoidable even if GE's deep pockets temporarily saved the old-line firm from going under in the face of mortgage-backed securities losses and the Joseph Jett trading scandal.

General Electric said it would take a charge of around $500 million as a result of the sale, taking the total cost of its ill-fated involvement with Kidder to more than $1.5 billion. This is one of the better recent examples of the attention that needs to be paid to issues of personal responsibility at all organizational levels.

In principle, the strategy of an industrial corporation keeping out of derivatives is sound. But did it protect General Electric from mishap? A few months after John Welch's "chosen to miss" statement, adversity struck its Kidder Peabody financial subsidiary, leaving a gaping hole precisely because of derivatives trades.

7. The Laws, the Lawyers, and the Legislators

A growing number of legislators, as well as lawyers, see the need for a legal infrastructure that is more precise concerning OBS trades, more clearly enforceable, and more technology-specific, since technology is an integral part of all trades. The issues usually being raised include familiar topics such as the following:

- ❑ Liability.

- ❑ Malpractice.

- ❑ Default.

- ❑ Financial crimes.

In these and other areas, difficulties arise not only in terms of new legislation, but also in applying the existing laws, which often were not written with all of the idiosyncrasies of off-balance-sheet finance in mind. Examples include the definitions of *authorization* and *misuse*.

From regulators to public attorneys, law enforcement agencies typically seek more arrests and more prosecutions. These might become less relevant, however, if solutions were on hand that help control the risks both to the bank and to its clients and regulate the meaning of negligence and financial responsibility.

Social scientists have identified many needs that transcend financial technology and the law. Examples include the need to restructure our concept of financial responsibility, to provide better education about the nature and exposure of new financial instruments, and to encourage greater interaction and disclosure in order to reinforce and promote ethical behavior.

Such a diversity of perspectives is typical when new products and new technology emerge, whether in finance or in engineering. At any one time, certain interest groups may seek economic or industrial leverage, and each party may view its goals as predominant, ignoring those of the others. Solutions to these problems must be rigorous. It is dangerous to believe that one issue has a higher priority than another. Each solution must contribute positively to the company's survival and be geared to work in synergy with other solutions.

Within a coordinated effort, each perspective must be respected. But the laws, the technology, and the social norms must also evolve further to reflect the current realities of the social and financial environment in which we live. How many laws should there be to regulate the new instruments? Should these laws be detailed or spell out general principles?

Four and a half centuries ago, Tommaso Campanella wrote in *Città Solaris* that the laws should be very few and very simply expressed.[7] Today, precisely the opposite occurs, and we see the results.

In the United States, the Financial Institutions Reform, Recovery, and Enforcement Act of 1989 has 467 pages, and this is just the conference report. The actual law is three times as long. Any bank or other organization that needs to use it must not only know this book inside out but also follow all the subsequent changes in accounting standards, legislation, oversight practices, regulation, and so on.

This requires a swarm of lawyers and regulators ceaselessly trying to get information on the developing situation. They need the latest version of a voluminous reference in order to bring both guidelines and details to the attention of managers, traders, investment advisors, and other experts.

Financial products, incidentally, are not alone in being shaken up by technology, in a legal sense. Members of the National Writers Union now claim that electronic publishers are violating their copyrights, and they have filed a lawsuit against a handful of major media companies in a federal court in New York City. Defendants include the *New York Times*, Time Warner, Mead Data Central[8] and Bell & Howell's University Microfilms International unit.

Since the U.S. Copyright Act was written before electronic databases were commonplace, there are no provisions covering electronic transmission. A Writers Union spokesman said the rights of hundreds, if

---

7 *La Città del Sole e Poesie*, first published in the mid-16th century. Recent edition by Feltrinelli, Milano, 1962.
8 Which operates the Nexis database.

not thousands, of writers are being infringed as their work is placed on electronic databases and CD-ROMs without their consent or payment.

8.   Taking Account of the Law and Legal Decisions

French legal practice makes a very fine distinction between the letter of the law itself and the interpretation of the law by judges that establish a precedence but that may change over time. The latter is called *jurisprudence*.

A similar process exists in all countries. The examples we will see in this section come from legal decisions concerning management responsibility. The examples are from U.S. and British companies, but can occur anywhere.

A 1992 court decision in the United States brought nearer the day when directors have a legal duty to shareholders and partners. The case of *Brane v. Roth* was not handled in New York and involved no Wall Street investment bank, just a small grain cooperative in Indiana, yet it could set a nationwide or even international precedent. America has thousands of agricultural co-ops that buy and sell produce on behalf of their shareholders. The latter are usually local farmers who entrust their annual harvests to co-ops in the hope of getting the best price.

When the manager of the Indiana co-op finished selling his farmers' crops in 1980, a year in which the price of grain collapsed, the co-op had a gross loss of $424,000. The manager might have avoided the loss by using grain futures on the Chicago Board of Trade to hedge against falling prices, as the co-op's accountants had advised him to do. But he had only hedged a tiny amount—$30,000 out of a value of $7.3 million.

Losses mounted as the price of grain tumbled, and the shareholders sued the co-op's manager as well as four directors. After long proceedings, the Indiana courts agreed to the case of negligence, citing the failure to hedge as the reason. Regarding the directors, the judge said they had a duty to understand hedging techniques and they should have watched over the manager more carefully.[9]

This case seems to be the first ruling of its kind. Though it has no legal force outside Indiana, it may prove an irresistible precedent elsewhere: Ignorance of derivatives is no excuse for not using them, but both investors and financial institutions must also be able to manage financial risk.

The other reason that makes the Indiana court decision a milestone is that it emphasized the board members' responsibility and accountability. Two years down the line, faced with a totally different case, a British court ruled in the same way.

---

[9] In June 1992 the co-op's directors lost their final appeal.

More than 3,000 investors in the Lloyd's of London insurance market were awarded compensation by the high court that could amount to £504 million (about $790 million), based on an October 4, 1994, judgment.

Although Lloyd's "Names"[10] have unlimited liability, the ruling found that underwriters for the Gooda Walker syndicate negligently exposed them to high-risk markets that suffered huge losses from the *Exxon Valdez* oil spill, Hurricane Hugo, the Piper Alpha disaster, and other gaping holes in insurance.

This was the first case of its kind concerning insurers' negligence related to Lloyd's of London, which used to be like the Rock of Gibraltar. Other similar suits wait in the wings.

The central issue before the high court in the Gooda Walker case was whether the underwriters had been negligent in leaving the syndicates so heavily exposed to a series of catastrophes. The Names argued that the Gooda Walker underwriters were negligent in leaving the syndicates so exposed; the underwriters failed to manage their businesses adequately by not properly monitoring their total exposure to risk; and they failed to arrange sufficient reinsurance or exercise sufficient care in dealings with the *excess of loss* spiral.

Notice that all of these arguments are most relevant in a derivatives setting. The careful lawyer will see that though the example concerns insurance, it applies equally well to off-balance-sheet trading.

The Gooda Walker agents responded by arguing that the sequence of catastrophes was unprecedented and unforeseeable, that underwriting excess of loss cover (LMX) was an *intrinsically* high-risk business, and that Lloyd's regulations did not oblige underwriters to calculate their total exposure or probable maximum losses.

The careful reader will notice that many derivatives are also intrinsically high-risk. If there is negligence with insurance, there could be even more with off-balance-sheet instruments, which involve a great many more unknowns.

In the Gooda Walker–Lloyd's case, Justice Phillips ruled that underwriters had failed to exercise the skill and care expected of competent professionals:

> The growth of the LMX market in the 1980s and, in particular, the growth of the spiral business raised special problems in relation to the assessment of risk, exposure, and rating that called for special consideration.

---

10 Individuals who supply Lloyd's with insurance capital.

The verdict continued with the concept that the exposure for which the underwriters were held at fault "was culpable because it was unintended, unplanned and unjustified by any proper analysis of risk." The principal negligence was in failing to buy sufficient reinsurance protection—something derivatives players are supposed to do for hedging reasons rather than adding to the risk.

9. Can the Gooda Walker–Lloyd's Ruling Create a Precedent?

Having tried and failed to play peacemaker in 1993, Lloyd's now prefers to leave Names to fight individual underwriters, while it tries to attract new capital from corporate investors. But many observers think the company's underwriters do not have the resources to meet the huge compensation bills and that it is time Lloyd's had another go at settling disputes that will otherwise drag on. The issues in the Gooda Walker case fell into two main areas:

❑ The nature of competent underwriting practice in the Lloyd's market and more generally in high-risk insurance.

❑ The approach that responsible underwriters should have taken with regard to excess loss cover on existing and new contracts—avoiding the "spiral."

Justice Phillips ruled that there are basic principles of insurance underwriting that should be adhered to. These are particularly important in connection to off-balance-sheet deals because they have direct counterparts in derivatives trades.

1. An underwriting account should be balanced in the sense that all the risk being taken should not be exposed to the same loss.

The judge rejected the agents' argument that Names should accept that, having agreed to unlimited liability, their underwriters could deliberately expose them to such a risk. Notice that this argument also exists with OBS, where about 33 percent of all contracts are forwards in interest rate risk.

"On the contrary," the judge said, "the Name will reasonably expect the underwriter to exercise due skill and care to prevent him suffering losses." If an underwriter intended to expose Names to periodic losses, he must make sure that they were aware of this and the scale of the potential losses.

Justice Philips did not enter into derivatives practices and trades, but in Chapter 12 the reader will find a first-class example with the securities lending superleveraging—which risks leaving financial institutions and investors in an unprecedented wasteland.

2. According to the Phillips judgment, accounts should be properly planned and documented so that an underwriter knows what he is doing.

This includes monitoring the total liabilities and probable maximum losses to which accounts are exposed. This is also a key issue in derivatives trades—including the need for real-time response.

"In my judgment, it was a fundamental principle of excess of loss underwriting that the underwriter should formulate and follow a plan as to the amount of exposure that his syndicate would run," the Judge stated. Banks had better take notice. It may be their turn next time around.

3. The ever present issue of risk management and reinsurance policy is worthy of great attention.

The judge ruled that an underwriter must know the exposure he intends to run and ensure that it is not exceeded. This should be done by having a thoroughly researched, detailed reinsurance policy. The judge rejected the agents' argument that LMX business was widely known to be high-risk:

> It is quite plain from the evidence before me that this was not the perception of LMX business shared by many of the defendants at the time. I have no doubt that there are many plaintiffs who would understandably have felt outraged had they heard the plea being advanced on behalf of their members' agents that Names had no cause for complaint because the type of business they had chosen to write was well-known to be dynamite.

Showing considerable knowledge of this matter, Justice Phillips also described the spiral: the complex arrangement under which catastrophic excess of loss risks were insured and reinsured, "rather like a multiple game of pass the parcel." This, too, has surprising similarities with derivatives.

Whether Names or investors, those left holding the liability are those who first exhaust their resources. "The last ducat always wins the war," Louis XIV once said, and his dictum is fully applicable in insurance as well as in off-balance-sheet finance. In the case of the Names, the exhaustion was caused by layers of LMX reinsurance. The effect on individual syndicates was to magnify the impact of a particular loss many times.

But isn't this a basic characteristic of aggressive financial instruments and of players who enter into huge bilateral agreements, thus exposing themselves and the markets at large to a domino effect?

10. Legal Issues, Country Risk, and Off-Balance-Sheet Instruments

In the Gooda Walker–Lloyd's case, Justice Phillips quoted the views on the spiral of Richard Quothwaite, the underwriter who gave expert evidence for the agents. Quothwaite explains his reluctance to write spiral business because of the exposure involved.

But at the same time, the judge dismissed the agents' argument that the Gooda Walker underwriters should be judged according to the standards of competence of other participants in the spiral. This sets a good precedence on the need for understanding what risk and exposure means.

"Suppose a profession collectively adopts extremely lax standards in some aspect of its work. The court does not regard itself as bound by those standards." Justice Phillips also ruled that the performance of one underwriter was "far short of reasonable competence." He could not believe the underwriter's claim that he monitored his aggregate exposures and that his approach to buying reinsurance was rather clear.

The London judgment ruled that the underwriter's failure to properly assess cover for such a loss was negligent. The verdict for another underwriter was that as he had not calculated probable maximum losses, they formed no part of his reinsurance policy, a policy which proved unsound.

But Justice Phillip did not award a waterfall of damages to the plaintiffs either. He rejected the Names' claim that they should be compensated for all the losses they had suffered through their involvement with the Gooda Walker syndicate. Instead, the damages he awarded were based on the losses sustained from the negligent conduct. Let's take good notice of this ruling. There are significant similarities between LMX and derivatives.

Trading in off-balance-sheet financial instruments raises other issues as well. There is always a new wrinkle that makes the current legislation incomplete, or even contradictory. It is no accident that some financial executives characterize derivatives as "the unknowables, owned by the unknowing."

One of the unknowables is the cross-border tangles that continue to develop. The streamlining of legal issues is urgently needed, but it cannot be one-sided. Legislation and regulation should both involve all G-10 countries and chop off the off-shores.

Otherwise, there is a significant risk that the over-the-counter derivatives activity could be driven largely offshore, if the regulation or legislation is finely tuned in developed countries but totally substandard in developing countries.

Since there is no international body with legal standing to do that job, the best solution is to work by way of an inverse delegation, as shown in Figure 5–2. International legislation and regulation for both

Figure 5–2. **An International Derivatives Legislation Should Work by Way of an Inverse Delegation from the Periphery to the Center: That Is How IMF, the World Bank, BIS, G-7, and G-10 Work**

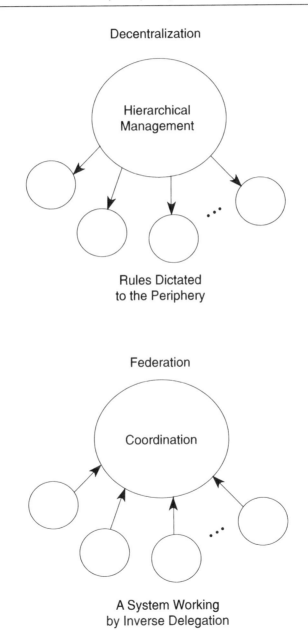

balance sheet and off-balance-sheet instruments must be properly coordinated—it cannot be dictated from above.

Focal points of cross-border streamlining of legal issues have to be the redefinition of *negligent conduct*, which Justice Phillips spoke of, and also of *financial responsibility*. Whether or not it is appreciated, both constitute part of *country risk* as well as of credit risk at large.

But it will not be easy to redefine financial responsibility in a cross-border sense. The appropriate analysis will include a detailed political, social, and economic study, covering all crucial aspects of the targeted country. Among the factors that should be examined are the following:

❑ The criminal law.

❑ The political stability.

❑ The participants in the financial structure.

Characteristics of the socioeconomic environment include socialization and socioeconomic tensions, future economic perspectives, trade balances, and the government deficit, as well as the country's infrastructure and its diversity. This is all relevant to legislation, as it is influenced by, but also defines, the pressures being exerted on the economic and social fabric.

Another characteristic of country risk centers on previous events involving governmental abrogation and interference, as well as compensation history. A careful study of the laws as well as of legal actions and court decisions can be revealing. This type of analysis should preferably be done in different time frames. A study of the laws and of past court decisions is part of the investment necessary for entering a new market.

Quite similarly, the cross-border and multicurrency exchange and settlement systems should be examined in detail. A prudent course is that in all circumstances the risk should be limited to the net balances, and payments already made should never be brought into question because of a default by one of the participants. But the attitude of some jurisdictions is still hesitant on these matters. Only some of the players seem to have a clear understanding of the risks they are incurring.

6

Payments, Clearing, and Settlement Risk

1. Introduction

The payments system is the alter ego of the credit system. Its clearing depends on the receipt of a payment, be it for physical goods or a financial transaction. The recipient, too, must have complete confidence that the asset will be transferred to his or her ownership—at par and in an acceptable form.

In most exchange-cleared transactions, the two parties involved have little detail concerning the creditworthiness of their opposite number. They rely on financial institutions acting as intermediaries to provide the checks they cannot assure for themselves. This is why a banker's draft is as good as cash, and the check system gives assurances that payment will be made.

The difficulty for regulators is that as financial institutions are still mostly the means by which payments are made, the payments system itself is vulnerable to failures of those institutions. That is why in some countries, for instance Denmark, the reserve bank and the Ministry of Finance have set up a jointly owned escrow service.[1] Even the failure of small banks dealing only with retail payments can spread nervousness

---

1 On the Danish Vaerdipapircentralen, see D. N. Chorafas and H. Steinmann, *Off-Balance Sheet Financial Instruments* (Chicago: Probus, 1994).

through the financial system. If problems touch the wholesale institutions involved in electronic funds transfer (EFT), the results could bring a panic.

A *settlement risk* between two counterparties is the risk that one of them to whom the other has made a delivery of assets (or money) will default before the amounts due have been received. It is also the risk that technical difficulties will interrupt delivery or settlement even if the counterparties are able to perform.

In the latter case, payment is likely to be delayed but remains recoverable, while default of one of the parties puts the other one under stress. In this sense, settlement risk is a composite of factors exposing a no-fault party to credit risk, cash liquidity risk, country risk, and electronic funds transfer risk.

2.   National and Cross-Border Payments

Though different in many respects, national and cross-border payments have a number of characteristics in common. One of the most important is the fact that, in a wholesale electronic payment system, the transaction volume is huge and composed mostly of financial transactions, such as the buying and selling of funds and securities among banks or sales of foreign exchange. As the dollar is still the world's reserve currency, dollar-denominated transactions involve not only thousands of financial institutions in the United States, but institutions around the world. The main financial markets are no more than a computer link away. Because of globalization, the credit interdependencies have become frightening. The credit exposures are even more so, despite the fact that some may be short-lived.

Transactions may be short-lived because access is by computer and payment is provisional, subject to final settlement each working day. But this argument overlooks the fact that the large majority of banks are still working batch for clearing—hence the exposure is practically 24 hours or longer.

This is what J. M. Williamson, deputy chief executive of the Association for Payment Clearing Services (APACS), calls the *Follow-the-Sun Overdraft*. As we will see in section 5, with *intraday* payments, the amount of exposure of the settlement system is staggering.

Let's face it. In spite of huge budgets for technology, the solutions banks provide for themselves and the financial system are substandard. Because it does not fit with networked financial markets that work 24 hours per day, batch should have been outlawed—but batch is still king.

Fully real-time execution is a necessity, since financial transactions increasingly dwarf the cash balances in the system that are meant to act as liquidity cushions against disruptions. These cushions include interbank demand deposits—the reserve balances of banks held by the Federal Reserve, the Bank of England, and so on—and demand balances held at banks by their customers using CHIPS, CHAPS, or other clearers.

The possibility of a frightening intraday or overnight exposure alarms many regulators. Without the real-time operation of the whole-sale dollar electronic payments, and of the banks themselves, the whole financial system is at risk—and with it the world economy. This is an area in which it is in the public interest to assure the strictest standards of supervision, not just in finance but also in technology. Even a computer glitch at one of the handful of big financial organizations could cause chaos.

Because current EFT networks as well as the banks' own computers and communications systems are a patchwork of machines and software, the whole is only as strong as its weakest link. Each participating institution and the system as a whole need to restructure their technology. *If* one or the other of the subsystems goes down more often than is consistent with the maintenance of financial responsibility, *then,* the financial system as a whole will suffer serious disruption.

This is not a far-fetched hypothesis if we account for the fact that over the past two years disruptions have occurred at individual banks. Such disruptions help to identify the technological weaknesses of payments, clearing, and settlement and can have both national and international financial consequences.

Just as complex are the legal issues characterizing cross-border payments. In March 1989, the Group of Thirty, a think tank based in Washington, D.C., issued a report that contained a number of recommendations for improving national clearance and settlement systems.[2] However, this study did not address the problems of settling cross-border trades, even though the volume of such trades is most important and increasing.

Problems with cross-border trading caused Euroclear to undertake its own study, with a report published in 1993.[3] This addressed a number of problems in connection with settling cross-border trades, and it contains recommendations regarding initiatives that may assist both in countering some inherent problems and in developing an international securities market.

Based in Brussels and largely owned by the Morgan Bank, Euroclear is one of two clearers of transborder bond transactions. The other

---

2 Clearance and Settlement Systems in the World's Securities Markets (Washington, D.C.: Group of Thirty, 1989).

3 *Crossborder Clearance, Settlement, and Custody: Beyond the G30 Recommendations* (Brussels: Euroclear, 1993).

is Luxembourg-based Cedel. Both Cedel and Euroclear have a keen interest in cross-border payments and settlements.

3. The Need for Fast Response to Cross-Border Money Flows

Central banks have dealt with sources of risks in the clearance and settlement of securities trades. Several studies have concluded that the largest financial risk occurs during the settlement process, where *delivery versus payment* (DVP) of securities takes place between the buyer and the seller. There is risk of chain reactions in the settlement of securities trades if a major market participant becomes insolvent. This risk can only be countered if the settlement system assures the strongest possible ties between delivery and payment.

Many professional associations of international depository banks, stock exchanges, central securities warehouses, and the authorities supervising the financial sector have addressed these issues. Invariably, the discussion centers on requirements that effective clearance and settlement systems must live up to at national as well as international levels.

Properly designed netting arrangements can reduce risks associated with cross-border financial activity. As we saw in Chapter 5, to reach such an outcome a number of issues need to be addressed, with the top priority being the resolution of *legal* uncertainties involving the enforceability of netting arrangements both within countries and across countries.

As Chapter 5 explained, part and parcel of the legal infrastructure is the development of methods to assure that the financial system has the capacity to achieve settlement in the event of the default of one or more participants in the context of cross-border multilateral and multicurrency clearing.

When there is pertinent legislation, some of the problems are eased. When not, clauses must be included in any bilateral cross-border contract to close the legal loopholes.

Settlement risk is also present when payments are conditional or revocable until final settlement. Such risk occurs when a bank enters into a net credit position with another bank, providing its customers available funds based on anticipated settlement. Therefore, settlement systems have to be very carefully defined in terms of financial responsibility. The overriding concept of a cross-border solution is finality of payments.

Through their continuous gross settlement, real-time settlement mechanisms, such as the Swiss Interbank Clearing system (SIC), tend to make each individual payment immediately final, eliminating settlement risk. CHIPS in New York and CHAPS in London work on the same basis—a basis that characterizes automatic clearinghouses (ACH)—but a real-time global system for the world's markets, commensurate with 24-hour banking, is still lacking.

The need for rapid and secure cross-border clearing of assets and liabilities cannot be emphasized too strongly. About a quarter of the turnover of Britain's top 100 quoted companies is generated by subsidiaries on the Continent, compared with 12 percent in the mid-1980s. Business has become transnational whether or not investors like it, or even realize it.

What could be the effect on risk management of this undeniable evolution? Is the problem getting better or worse? Modern portfolio theory teaches that diversification reduces risk by spreading exposure among several markets, the investor hopes to reduce his or her risk for a given level of return. This assumes that the different markets are imperfectly correlated; they are not moving in step.

But from the investor's viewpoint, managing a process of international diversification is not that eaᶜy, though it is the trend. In the past decade, Britain's pension funds have increased their holdings of foreign securities from 7 percent to 20 percent of their portfolios. In the United States, the proportion has risen from 1 percent to 10 percent; in Japan from 1 percent to 18 percent. All this is happening without a rigorous analysis of foreign markets and investment vehicles, as is done with domestic investments, and without benefit of high technology, which could be instrumental in closing some of the knowledge gap.

In connection to national and international payments and settlements, this chapter has pointed out that although a rigorous cross-border legal and analytical infrastructure is necessary, it is not enough. The technological infrastructure must also be significantly upgraded—not by adding more deadwood in the form of mainframes, but by converting systems and intelligent networks to real time.

Figure 6–1 describes a solution space that should characterize future investments in technology. The bank of the 1990s is *the network*—and the same statement is valid about payment and settlement systems. The technology of the years to come must be more efficient and more responsive than it has ever been before.

4.   The Increasing Correlation of Cross-Border Markets

Derivative financial instruments play a major role in the increased correlation of cross-border markets and therefore on the strains of the international payment and settlement system. Because of the risks involved with derivatives, the solutions we develop cannot have the luxury of being mediocre.

Figure 6–1. A Solution Space Able to Sustain the Tighter Coupling between Markets in a Cross-Border Sense

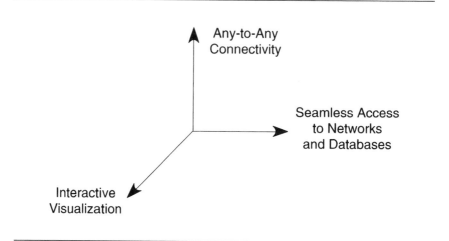

Cross-border trades, investments, and payments are the main cause of a tighter coupling between markets. Cross-border money flows grow as investors tend to choose the foreign shares and markets, supposedly to reduce equity risk. But they rarely account for settlement risk, even if it is always present.

While settlement risk increases, the promise of modern portfolio theory, that there will be risk reduction due to diversification, remains elusive. Many investors buy the companies they have heard of, which often means the international ones that sell to them at home. By contrast, wise investors seeking to reduce risks would buy into companies with fewer links to their home country, and well-informed investors would factor into their equation payment-settlement currency and country risk.

Such factoring will tend to reduce the lure of some "emerging" markets. It will also bring into perspective the costs and the exposure associated with some of the deals. Another positive result is that it will focus attention on existing substandard technological supports, adversely influencing payments and settlements.

We can better appreciate the sense of this last paragraph if we look at electronic payments and settlements during the last 30 years. The key question is, How fast should this settlements procedure take place?

Since the time of Fedwire I in America, which means the mid-1960s, it has been thought that overnight clearance is good enough. Many systems in other countries were designed along the same logic—

which at the time, with the available technology and the relatively small size of money transfers, was not wrong.

Today, however, such a slow-moving procedure is an aberration. Thirty years after Fedwire 1, overnight clearance proves totally inadequate, even though very few clearance houses are ready to act in real time, as for example, Denmark's Vaerdipapircentralen (VP).[4] VP was established in 1983. Ten years later, it benefitted from much-needed changes in rules and regulations, altering its technology. In the past, a full day has been the smallest registration unit used in the VP system to create a legal right. But on September 10, 1993, this was replaced with on-time notification—and the next goal is real time.

The general manager of VP said during our meeting that growing internationalization and increasing trading speed necessitated this change. They made it necessary to create faster settlement of securities, to assure safe payment through escrow, and to rapidly handle the increasing volume of clearing and settling of all trades.

In fact, a couple of years after Vaerdipapircentralen became operational, its management saw system redesign as a necessity. Over the elapsed decade, major changes in the market have called for significant innovations in clearing and technical developments—which go hand in hand.

The rapidly growing volume of activity gradually reduced system flexibility and made the introduction of new functions a painful and resource-demanding process. Upgrades are steadily necessary for improved handling of stocks, bonds, and derivative financial products, for immediate settlement and same-day trades. In the case of Vaerdipapircentralen, it became imperative to correct failed transactions without counterparty risk as well as to proceed with other innovations ahead of competition. "There is competition not only among banks but also among cross-border clearers," said VP's general manager.

The legal basis for more than one settlement between the same two counterparties within a 24-hour period and for delivery versus payment at individually selected times (trades for immediate settlement) was created at VP, following the amendment of section 8 of the Danish Securities Center Act. This Act went into effect on September 10, 1993.

The legal amendment means that the effect of a registration in VP is no longer limited to a full day as the minimum unit, but instead occurs at the time the appropriate notification is received. Hence, a technological change was necessary so that the clearers could execute trades and notifications without delays.

---

4 See also D. N. Chorafas and H. Steinmann, *Off-Balance Sheet Financial Instruments* (Chicago: Probus, 1994).

This is only an example of the evolution taking place in the payments, clearance, and settlements systems. Though in this example the impulse for change came from the letter of the law, as cross-border settlements grow and the competition among clearers intensifies, all countries will be moving toward more efficient legislation and regulation. Therefore, the time to act is *now*.

5.   The Critical Case of Intraday Payments

The proliferation of derivative instruments has contributed to the very significant growth of intraday credit exposures, not just settlement flows themselves. This problem is now recognized by financial institutions as representing a potential threat to market stability.

There are several types of risks arising from off-balance-sheet and on-balance-sheet obligations and settlement positions. For this reason, in many countries bank regulators are placing renewed emphasis on risk reduction in the payment system.

Both the financial institutions and the regulators must factor into the costs of the system the payment risk involved in each transaction being processed. They should be increasingly concerned with economic risks in their home countries and systemic risks in the global environment. Concerns about risk are not new to regulators, as risk assessment has been part of banking activity for hundreds of years. But the huge volumes today represented by the over-the-counter market and the exchanges radically alter the more cozy past approaches.

Bankers get paid to mitigate risk, but as the financial instruments multiply and get more complex the result is more, not less, potential exposure to risk for banks, with settlement risk an integral part of this picture.

Studies and statistics by international organizations such as the International Monetary Fund, the Bank for International Settlements, and OECD have documented the growth over the past 20 years—and most importantly during the last decade—in the number of financial instruments and markets. In some areas, such as foreign exchange markets and various derivatives markets, such growth has been explosive.

This deepening and broadening of financial markets is the sign of a vigorous economy, which, however, requires a rigorous settlements solution. Payment risk surfaced as a significant issue during the late 1970s and early 1980s, with market forces and computer technology in the background.

The market demanded, and in a way technology provided, the means for overnight settlement of increasingly large amounts. Economic historians will most likely attribute this vast market demand for cross-border money flows to the Smithsonian Agreement of the early 1970s and the high interest rates for dollars of the early 1980s. Both provided the motive to dramatically increase the velocity of money. However, the evolution the market has gone through since then saw to it that payments are not being funded by deposits, but by other payments, greatly increasing the settlements risk.

The potential for a domino effect in defaults if this payment flow is interrupted has become a major source of concern. In May 1985, the Federal Reserve Bank introduced the Payments System Risk Program. It's objective is a reduction in intraday overdrafts—that is, daylight overdrafts.

Capital markets transactions typically involve the borrower returning funds each morning and repurchasing them each afternoon, creating a daylight overdraft at his or her bank in the interim. Many large banks feature significant intraday overdrafts. To discourage the rapid growth of these overdrafts, a *cap* (overdraft limit) was implemented as a function of risk-based capital and a self-evaluation process.

The self-evaluation process typically takes into account assets, liabilities, creditworthiness, operational controls, and credit controls. But many bankers say it is more subjective than objective. Analytical models are required to bring this type of risk under control.

Enriched with knowledge-engineering software, a real-time system can be instrumental in supporting intraday cash accounting, enabling bankers to determine availability of cash for same-day processes. Knowledge artifacts should be an integral part of the procedure for validation and acceptability of individual transactions.

This applies not only to intraday payments, but also to DVP. Critical to the success of any delivery versus payment facility is the guarantee that stocks, bonds, and derivatives vehicles move in connection to the agreed-upon payment.

The acceptance of a transaction must be validated by the clearer or settlement service against the availability of cash in the counterparty's cash account. Once accepted, such cash must be earmarked as awaiting settlement. Settlement will occur when the asset is available for delivery, and the clearer has approved the acceptance. But stocks, bonds, and other instruments should not be available for delivery if they are used as cover for collateral or for securities lending.[5]

This strict assurance of availability is the principle my professors at the University of California taught me 42 years ago. Today, however, with lending activities ranging widely, the standards have become shaky, which in itself represents a significant risk.

In conclusion, settlement must involve the equity, liability, or derivative instrument being transferred from the deliverer to the taker in

---

5 See also the risks posed by the securities lending bubble, in Chapter 12.

return for a cash account transfer. Any outstanding transfers from the clients should be recorded and handled in real time.

6.   Using Risk Pricing to Swamp Intraday Exposure

The redepositing of international intermediated funds between a larger number of banks as well as a pronounced increase in interbank flows associated with trading and portfolio investments lead to the buildup of paper balances that characterize the international position of many banks. This surge evidently increases *systemic risk*.

As the wave of financial activity mounts, the payment system runs on the basis of intraday overdrafts that are tacitly granted by banks or by the central banks. These overdrafts are accepted in the course of the exchange of payment instruments, but are not definitely settled until irrevocable payment is made in central bank money.

The fact that the reserve banks grant the overdrafts sees to it that commercial, investment, and other banks frequently have a poor perception of the risks involved in the payment system or underestimate them. In their way, bankers tend to have blind faith in the counterparties to their transactions, particularly the AAA-rated companies. Therefore, they are tempted to do without preventive measures because the costs seem out of proportion with the remote possibility of a default.

This is an evident misapprehension of the follow-the-sun overdraft, which justifies central bank intervention in payment systems through the setting of appropriate international norms. It is the central bank's job to guarantee and maintain the stability of the financial fabric.

In spite of the fact that the intraday overdraft is the rule of the game, the payment system as a whole cannot afford large unmonitored daylight overdrafts in accounts at central banks or private settlement centers. Over the years, this led to multilateral netting, but in an awkward way, using designs based on the 19th-century check clearing houses and relying on the unwinding of payments as the ultimate remedy for settlement failures.

However, as time went by, it became evident that more sophisticated solutions were necessary. Presently, large-value payment concepts are a core part of the monetary institutions in every country as well as in the international financial landscape, as the 1993 BIS proposal on netting suggests.

Practically every banker who took part in this research agrees that payment systems must be stronger than their individual member banks if they are to provide a stable foundation for the financial community. As experience demonstrates, in times of financial stress large-value payment systems must be able to accommodate potentially huge transfers of money in a cross-border sense and do so without interruption, inspiring market confidence that settlements will work as planned.

At the same time, one of the lessons of the past two decades is that the costs of creating and running large payment systems must be weighted against the potential costs of systemic instability in troubled times, not just against operational alternatives in times relatively free of bubbles and panics.

The proper design of a global risk-management solution for payments and settlements must account for the fact that demand for the availability of intraday funds to payees has resulted in the growth of intraday credit exposure to the banking system. The intraday risks incur to the banks as providers of payment services. Hence, they should also be proportionate to the capacity of an individual bank to bear them, and they should be measurable by transaction, corresponding bank, currency, and country—as well as cross-border.

Since settlement failures can happen, it is necessary to have a reliable solution able to protect against a chain of defaults. At the core of this statement is interbank credit exposure in large value payments.

Exposure arises from the practice of giving unconditional value to payee customers before the interbank settlement has taken place. Real-time control and steady experimentation are the only sure way to keep intraday risks in check. Simulations done by leading-edge banks help document that intraday exposures can be massive. Sometimes they exceed the capital of the banks concerned.

The daylight overdraft cap on a bank's account at the Federal Reserve is a function of that bank's creditworthiness relative to its peers. Such caps can help reduce the risk per dollar transferred, even if absolute risk in the system is higher today than at any other time. From this consideration comes the concept that intraday credits must be priced in a way similar to insurance premiums. Pricing of intraday credits is a free market's response to risk, while avoiding overregulation.

The Federal Reserve's costing of intraday credits will most likely lead to their pricing in the private banking sector as well. This will provide incentives to reduce usage of that credit, correspondingly reducing intraday risk.

In conclusion, the proper pricing of intraday and follow-the-sun overdrafts will reduce the provision of subsidized daylight credit to the banking sector through the payment mechanism. The fees should help stimulate market-based responses to managing daylight payment flows and settlement risks, thereby leading to increased safety and soundness for the payment system.

7.   Clearinghouses and the Concept of Margins

Stocks, futures, and some options are traded in exchanges. Bonds and swaps are largely handled through bilateral agreements between two banks or brokers. Forwards and other options are traded over-the-counter. No matter how the buying and selling of financial instruments is done, a clearing mechanism is required.

Typically, a commodity futures exchange is affiliated with a clearinghouse. Member firms are expected to clear all purchases and sales that they transact. The clearinghouse will require the member firm to deposit original margin for the trades it clears. Membership requirements for the clearinghouse are stringent in regard to integrity and financial staying power. The amount of money the member firm must have on deposit with the clearinghouse changes, as changes occur in the market of futures and other contracts.

A clearinghouse uses the settlement price established by the exchange as the basis for determining if more money is due from the member firm. If the price of a futures contract moves in an adverse direction, causing a decrease in equity, the member firm would be required to deposit additional margin.

Both original margin and additional margin must be deposited with the clearinghouse before the opening of trading on the next business day. If a market is especially volatile, the clearinghouse has the right to call for variation margin during the trading session, and such a request must be answered within one hour.

The concept of margins is a rather classical way for reducing systemic risk, since it serves as a buffer to leveraged positions in regard to market movement. Margin requirements start at the investor level, since the broker requires margins from clients for exchange-traded contracts.

Margins are good-faith deposits to be made with a commodity broker in order to initiate or maintain an open position in a futures contract. When futures contracts are traded, both buyer and seller are required to post margins with the broker handling their trades as security for the performance of their buying and selling operations and to offset losses on their trades due to daily fluctuations in the markets.

Brokerage firms carrying accounts for traders may impose margins whether or not they are otherwise required and may increase the amount of necessary margin as a matter of policy in order to afford themselves further protection.

Minimum margins are usually set by the exchanges, but they can be adjusted from time to time by the regulatory authorities, according to the prevailing market conditions. There may also be temporary emergency margin levels on any futures contract.

The use of margins provides a safeguard; however, no system is foolproof. Leverage exercised by means of futures contracts can lead to significant profits in trading, but leverage can also prove to be a double-edged sword. A margin is a relatively modest cash outlay posted for each futures contract traded. Hence, even a small adverse move in the price of an underlying commodity can wipe out a trader's initial margin deposit.

Once a margin call is issued by a broker, an investor must post additional margin immediately or face the prospect of having his or her futures position liquidated at a loss. This happens from time to time, particularly with overleveraged accounts as well as in cases where the investor(s) tries to corner the market and, as is usually the case, loses the gamble.

Margins with respect to transactions on certain foreign exchanges generally are established by member firms rather than by the exchanges themselves. An independent clearinghouse, such as the International Commodity Clearing House (ICCH), requires margins and deposits from its members, and such members generally ask their clients to put up amounts at least equal to the ICCH charges.

8. Commodities and Futures Exchanges

COMEX, which stands for Commodity Exchange, Inc., was founded on July 5, 1933. It was the result of a merger of four exchanges: National Metal Exchange, Rubber Exchange of New York, National Raw Silk Exchange, and New York Hide Exchange.

Today, COMEX is the world's most active metals market for gold, silver, aluminum futures, and copper futures as well as for options trading. The exchange operates as a not-for-profit organization, with its 772 seats held by individuals on behalf of firms who meet financial requirements designed to assure the integrity of the marketplace.

In a generic sense, a futures exchange is a market where contracts for the future delivery of various commodities are bought and sold. Since these contracts are normalized, each represents a specific amount and grade of a commodity, designated for delivery at a specified date.

Such date may be months or years in the future. The only negotiable aspect of a contract is its price, which is settled through competitive auction by supply and demand. This price is determined on the floor of the exchange, allowing investors to hedge against the financial risk associated with fluctuations in commodity prices.

COMEX trading is conducted in New York City's World Trade Center, on a trading floor the exchange shares with other New York futures exchanges: the New York Mercantile Exchange (NYMEX); the Coffee, Sugar and Cocoa Exchange; the New York Cotton Exchange (NYCE); and the New York Futures Exchange, under the auspices of a company called Commodities Exchange Center, Inc. (CEC).

The COMEX Clearing Association (CCA) is an organization of COMEX members, incorporated independently from the Exchange. Both collectively and individually, the association's members look after the clearance of every trade executed on the COMEX floor. Acting indirectly as the counterparty to every trade, CCA itself becomes the ultimate buyer to every seller and seller to every buyer. This intermediary role assures the integrity of the exchange as well as a liquid marketplace.

A clearinghouse performs important functions, including netting and the assurance that all accounts of clearing members are balanced at the end of each trading day. The exchange settles all gains and losses resulting from trading and acts as the opposite party to every completed transaction.

In this function, the clearinghouse is guarantor to every trade up to a point. It serves the original buyer and seller, relieving them from direct obligation to each other except for the fulfillment of the contract.

Clearinghouses usually say that, due to their intermediation of futures, market participants need not be concerned with the creditworthiness of the opposite parties to their trades. As we have seen in section 7, each clearing member is required to deposit funds with the clearinghouse on a daily basis in proportion to the number of contracts cleared. These deposits, along with the guarantee funds and surplus reserves of the clearinghouse, are available against default by any clearing member.

Recalling, however, that the clearinghouse is a party to every trade, the careful reader will appreciate that what has just been said is only half true. Deposited funds do not necessarily cover all trades, particularly in days of high activity.

Because of the intermediation of the exchange the failure of one of the parties to fulfill its obligations may not result in credit risk to the other party or parties, but it may involve market risk. For instance, an unfulfilled deal might have featured favorable terms to the party suffering the loss.

Along with 10 other American futures exchanges, COMEX is regulated by the Commodity Futures Trading Commission (CFTC). CFTC is an independent government agency established in 1975 to administer the provisions of the Commodity Exchange Act, which subjects all commodity futures and options trading to federal oversight. It also restricts trading to futures exchanges designated and licensed by the Commission.

While supervision by the government is necessary, the best and toughest supervisor should be the management of the exchange itself. This is true all the way from avoiding criminal activities, controlling the behavior of the member firms and the quality of the services offered by the exchange, and keeping in check all issues relating to costs; for instance, costs for computers and networks.

Following this principle of cost control, since 1994 futures exchanges in France and Germany have been linked to reduce costs for financial institutions trading between the two countries. Such a link gives members direct electronic access to futures contracts in Deutsche

Terminbörse (DTB) and the Marché à Terme International de France (Matif). DTB and Matif represent 17 percent of the global trading in futures and options.

9.   Electronic Trading Technology at Exchanges and Member Firms

Advancements in computers, communications, and software see to it that exchanges electronically accept buy and sell orders, handle trading of most assets automatically, and provide their members with computer-to-computer support for transaction confirmation and market data updates.

To realize the impact of trading automation, it is necessary to understand the workings of an automated securities and commodities exchange. The infrastructure is not just a matter of machines but also, if not primarily, of cultural and economic links that give a member firm an advantage over its competitors.

Section 8 made reference to the Deutsche Terminbörse, which will be used here as an example of the extent to which systems and software support are necessary. To start its operations, DTB bought the Swiss-made Sofex software and adapted it to the German market. But its members had to choose software packages and provide for a front-desk/back-office integration.

The implementation of new systems and procedures connected to operations has not been free of problems. The majority of German banks connected to DTB chose Devon Software. Some went for Rolfe and Nolan back-office routines with Barra front-desk software. However, these two commodity software offerings are not integrated, which led some banks to switch to Optas front-desk programming support offered by the Swedish Front Capital systems firm.

One advantage of front-desk/back-office software integration is that it makes feasible a trade that is matched with a corresponding bank by computer and sends the information to all participants in the deal. Other advantages include direct hookup to accounting routines and updating of the risk database.

But there are also disadvantages. For instance, the different software modules often run on different machines, which makes it difficult to provide for transparency of the prevailing heterogeneity. This has effects all the way from poorly integrated databases to the deplorable situation of two or three keyboards parked on the trader's desk.

Another disadvantage with some of the packages offered in the market is that the supported screens are not ergonomic. One of the traders in Frankfurt working online with DTB said "I could lose my eyesight in a few years because of the twisted formats used for order entry and for reporting on market prices."

Valid software support will see to it that the human interfaces are friendly to and appreciated by the end users. It will also provide the end users with an array of analytical routines and instruments for handling options, futures, forwards, and swaps. However, even if the details are sound, the system may not stand the market's test if the quality of its grand design is questionable. Both at the Deutsche Terminbörse and in all other commodities and futures exchanges, the performance of the adopted solution has been a direct function of technical characteristics.

To improve upon the technological supports offered on a commodity basis, self-respecting financial institutions set up a conceptual design team to study the strategic, functional, and technical components of operation. The solution underpinning the DTB concept has been divided into three parts:

❑ The conceptual part provides a high-level overview of the adopted solution.

❑ The design part covers the trading, clearing, and settlement aspects.

❑ The technical part provides the detailed information on hardware and software.

The objective of a conceptual study such as this is to determine the strategic direction of the project with regard to products traded and trading structures. The objective of the design study is to identify all installation components for trading, and so on, to estimate their installation effort, and to propose a detailed implementation plan. The technical study aims to determine the hardware and software specifications for front desk and back office.

A sound systems approach makes it necessary to address the functional and technical specifications of all internal and external interfaces, fitting such interfaces within the chosen architecture. This presupposes a sound organizational structure for front-office, back-office and information technology support, and a definition of procedures for domestic and global clearing.

The implementation model should be properly determined, identifying all legal reporting requirements and proposing a solution that incorporates the key elements not only of training needs, but of the marketing plan and personnel requirements. All of these elements play a role in the elaboration of the appropriate systems and procedures for trading and clearing products—particularly in a real-time environment.

Above all, any valid work plan should include *risk control* procedures as well as software to support the management of exposure for any deal, at any time, anywhere in the world. Both traders and the company's management must be provided with flexible means to monitor and analyze market information, preevaluate the exposure taken by individual deal, and obtain a live picture of changes in the bank's risk pattern.

10. ECHO: A Case Study of Failure

Daily settlement payments in the global foreign exchange markets average $1.3 trillion to $1.5 trillion and peak much higher. This results in a huge number of confirmation and settlement messages. Most are handled via SWIFT, but the sheer volume of transactions means that processing, administration, and reconciliation costs are relatively high.

Settlement risk is evidently present, particularly as forex operations are not handled through exchanges. For each bank, there is the possibility that one of its counterparties may be unable to honor the deals it has made. For instance, a corresponding bank could fail to make a payment in one currency while taking receipt of the second currency involved in the foreign exchange deal.

The potential loss if a bank defaults is the entire amount of all the deals due for settlement by that bank on the day of default. There is also a *replacement risk*—the cost of dealing in the market to replace forward contracts that the defaulting bank will no longer honor. The potential loss for a financial institution facing replacement risk is the difference in rates between the original deal with the defaulter and those achieved upon replacement of all of the counterparty's forward contracts.

To confront these risks and assure a niche for itself in the financial market, an initiative by several banks brought forward the London-based Exchange Clearing House Organization (ECHO).[6] Theoretically, ECHO has not been projected to substitute for the banks in forex dealing. The plan was that its members would continue to trade with other banks as they were presently. Where their counterparty was another ECHO member, a copy of the dealing confirmation would be routed to the central clearinghouse.

This will enable each bank to settle with the clearinghouse for the net amount due or owed in each currency, in respect to its deals with all other ECHO members. The exchange will keep track of each member's position and initiate the actual payments.

Settlement netting has been expected to reduce the number of payments required from one per bank per transaction to one per bank per currency per day. In other terms, ECHO projected a process of *contract netting*.

---

[6] Not to be confused with the European Commission Host Organization, also known as ECHO.

❏ In the event of a member failing, ECHO will view the overall position with the member, rather than each bank looking at each of its individual transactions with that member.

❏ This however is accounting information, not affirming action, and it has been one of the shortcomings of the whole scheme.

Another, and more important, shortcoming lies in the fact that forex dealing is a very lucrative business for banks, which see to it that they are not willing to do away with the benefits they derive because of interfacing by an exchange. Hence, the very cool reception accorded to ECHO, which found it difficult to take off.

"ECHO netting might be nice for small banks with *low* standing, but not for big banks," said one of the largest German financial institutions. British clearers criticized ECHO's plan to start by handling 45 different currencies and banks from nine countries.

Each one of these countries has different jurisdictions. "It's a legal nightmare," said one of the London clearers, forecasting that ECHO would go down like the 13th database of the European exchanges[7] because of unsolved legal and other problems. Far from being pessimistic, this prognostication proved to be a realistic assessment. Apart from the major banks' hostility, many unresolved problems stood in its way.

In the case of a bank failure, ECHO wanted to play a protective role, replacing the defaulted net forward positions by dealing in the market directly with the replacement counterparties. It was projected that the net cost or profit of doing this would initially be claimed from or paid to the liquidator, shared among the other members on the basis of their individual exposures with the defaulting member. But the arrangement left much to be desired from legal and operational standpoints.

ECHO also planned to take other functions upon itself by assessing the credit standing of each member, based on the judgment of the major agencies such as Moody's and Standard & Poor's, as well as the capital adequacy requirements of the Bank for International Settlements. This assessment was expected to serve in determining the dealing limits through ECHO for each member as well as their contribution to the liquidity of ECHO itself.

The way banks looked at ECHO, its deeds were a long way from substantiating the claim made in mid-1992 that the proposed netting service had been designed primarily to limit the risk of a global banking crisis through significant reduction of trading and settlement risk. Nor was there solid evidence that member banks would benefit from lower transaction costs.

---

[7] See D. N. Chorafas and H. Steinmann, *Do IT or Die* (London: Lafferty 1992).

The original theme had been that instead of processing each contract separately they would be able to net off their forex trades and make just one payment for each of up to 24 currencies to the clearinghouse. This, however, substantially increased intraday risk.

Finally, the whole effort capsized after a number of successive delays and some hurdles. Originally there had been 40 members in ECHO, including European and U.S. institutions. But tensions seem to have developed between them, and the Americans pulled out. Eventually, a two-tier approach was created, involving a first tier of 16 founding members (of which only 3 signed) and a second tier of members with no voting rights. Neither tier still expects ECHO to take off.

PART TWO

CONTROL OF EXPOSURE AS PART OF THE STRATEGIC PLAN

7

Strategic Plans by Financial Institutions, Risk, and Market Opportunity

1. Introduction

Strategy is a master plan, not just a list of individual actions, and it involves competition. In fact, competition is, or at least should be, a basic ingredient in any strategy—as it establishes the best way for positioning your bank against the forces of the market.

Strategy has been applied to war and to propaganda, but fundamentally it is a much broader concept, with implications in politics, finance, industry, and commerce. Strategy is not an object in itself, and there are prerequisites to strategic planning as well as to the execution of a chosen strategy.

Strategy can also be defined as the determination of basic long-term goals and objectives, followed by the adoption of one or more courses of action, and the allocation of resources necessary for carrying out these plans. Strategy involves decisions about expanding the volume of activities, operating internationally, offering new financial products, or becoming diversified.

New courses of action must be devised and resources allocated and reallocated in order to reach established goals. Strategic plans are not made in the abstract, but represent a consistent effort to serve well-defined aims, such as

❏ Maintaining or expanding the bank's activities.
❏ Responding to shifting market demands.
❏ Capitalizing on the new technology.
❏ Counteracting the actions of competitors.

The adoption of a strategy may bring with it the need for new skills and different technologies—or may even alter the business horizons of the financial institution. Such changes can be prerequisites to the proper execution of a strategy, but the first crucial questions management should ask itself are

❏ What is *our* strategy?
❏ What is the strategy of our *competition*?
❏ Can we overtake them with our strategy?

These questions have to be answered in a factual and documented manner prior to even thinking about possible moves. While strategy is the exercise of skill, forethought, and artifice, it is also the means by which we clarify our plans and goals. In establishing and carrying out our plans, particular attention must be paid to products and markets.

The fact that strategy is a master plan against an opponent means that strategic moves are not just a list of individual actions. They involve competition, a basic ingredient of any strategy. It is on these premises that the present chapter has been built.

2.   What Is the Real Reason for Forecasting?

The introduction has pointed out that any valid strategy has prerequisites. The first is *planning*, and therefore *forecasting*. Forecasting not only focuses on future events, it focuses on the effects of current decisions. In fact, the latter is the number-one goal of forecasting.

In the business world, forecasting involves three major activities:

❏ Looking into the evolution of general business conditions, including evaluating how the economy of the nation, and the world, is progressing.

❏ Estimating banking industry trends, both nationally and internationally, and, more particularly, in the area in which your bank is active.

❏ Evaluating your bank's strengths and weaknesses and its positioning in terms of products and services within the current and future markets.

The number-one purpose of forecasting is not to predict the future precisely, but to determine the effects that current decisions will have on the scope, direction, profitability, and success of the bank. A forecast should not be rigid or inflexible.

Well-done forecasts aim to identify the probable course of coming events, always keeping in mind that *prognosis* is not concerned with future decisions. As I will never tire of repeating, prognosis is concerned with the future impact of present decisions.

This is why we are interested in learning about the *future course* of events—from *opportunities* to *risks*. On this probable future course will rest the milestones in management decision, including timing, commitments, costs, exposures, and expected results.

These are the basic characteristics of forecasts made for strategic planning. As such, they pave the way for the commitment of resources that ensure the best returns while preserving capital. If done effectively, the forecast represents the best estimate that can be made about a situation at the time of its preparation. Even though forecasts can never be as accurate as a wristwatch, they should reflect learned assumptions about specific cases.

In other words, forecasts have to be specific. They should be tailored to fit the needs of the financial institution for which they are being made, leading to valid planning assumptions.

Planning requires forecasting, yet planning is always done in the light of incomplete information. A plan must be flexible and readjustable in a changing world, its function being to minimize the unknown.[1] Planning problems arise every day. "The plan is nothing," President Dwight Eisenhower once said, "planning is everything."

Forecasting and planning are essential because strategy is based on the hypotheses bank management makes concerning the strengths and weaknesses of the competitors, their probable actions, and the possible effect of these actions. The introduction to this chapter made the point that strategy is essentially the exercise of skill, forethought, and artifice in carrying out plans. But the basis on which the plans are established must be fairly solid, hence the need for forecasts.

If we look at the functions of management as a pyramid, as shown in Figure 7–1, we will see that forecasting stands at the top and operates in an unstructured information environment. But the questions asked and answered can be concrete.

Crucial questions that management should ask itself—and expect clear answers to—are: What are our products? What are our *future* products? What is their current and future market appeal? Their profit margins? Their costs? Their risks? In essence we are asking

---

1 See also D. N. Chorafas, *Handbook of Management for Scientific and Technical Personnel* (New York: McGraw-Hill/TAB Books, 1990).

Figure 7–1. The Six Basic Functions of Management Range from an Unstructured to a Structured Information Environment

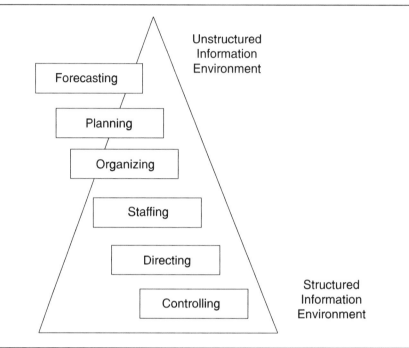

- ❏ How do our products appeal to the market compared to those of our competitors?

- ❏ How much risk are we taking when we sell them? When we hold them?

- ❏ How much risk do our correspondents, clients, and competitors take with their products and with our products?

When we talk about products, we are also talking about markets. What is the primary market we appeal to? What are the other markets? The *future* markets? How do we stand in our primary market against our competitors? How fast is this market growing? How fast does it shift? What are its special risks? How well do we manage them?

3.   Strategic Plans and Structural Prerequisites

Strategic planning details the policy followed in making moves during the interaction of two or more entities, whose action is based on some sort of expectation about moves by the other, over which neither party has control. Having a *master plan* is critical in that it sets strategy apart from other plans or moves.

Many strategies are based on intentions, but implicit intentions are not good enough, both because they are unclear and because they shift. They cannot bring management the focused and disciplined approach that is required. To focus on subjects, we need a master plan that is able to distinguish correctly between what is essential and what is only wishful or superficial. Time and competition see to it that clear distinctions bring the highest returns by permitting us to concentrate our efforts and to gain market thrust.

I worked for 16 years as a personal consultant to the chairman of a large banking group who was very concerned about the ability of the presidents of his banks to focus on a subject. He considered focusing more important than the decisions that were ultimately reached, his basic idea being that lack of focus will eventually destroy the enterprise.

The same is true of lack of structure. *Structure* can be defined as the organizational design through which the enterprise is administered. Whether made formally or informally, this design has two functions:

1. To clarify the lines of authority and responsibility between the different officers and their offices.

2. To establish the information and knowledge flow through these lines of communication and accountability.

The third of the management functions identified in Figure 7–1 is *organizations*. This addresses the structural prerequisites that have been outlined in points 1 and 2. An additional point is that structure should be flexible, but it should not change too fast or it will destabilize the organization.

Organizations, however, are made up of people. Therefore, the fourth of the management functions that Figure 7–1 outlines is *staffing*, the selection, training, and promotion of the organization's human capital—which is any bank's tier-one asset.

The structural lines as well as the accountability and the information flow defined in an organizational and staffing sense are essential to assure the effective coordination, appraisal, and planning necessary to carry out basic goals and policies. They also are necessary to knit together the total resources of the institution, including

❑ Financial capital.

❑ Products and services.

❑ Marketing plans.

❑ Human capital.

❑ Technological infrastructure.

These five resources constitute the major components of a strategy. Current and future plans will use them to reach objectives. But as already stated, structured dimensions as well as structural concepts change over time—and, by so doing, they affect the other two functions of management: *directing* and *controlling*.

As Figure 7–2 demonstrates, in terms of structure, direction, and control, the modern approach is to focus on federated organizations rather than inflexible hierarchical organizations to manage the resources of a financial institution in products, markets, moneys, information, and know how. This concept of federation is not alien to the reader: It was discussed in Chapter 5.

Charles Handy aptly comments that organizations used to be perceived as gigantic pieces of engineering, with largely interchangeable human parts.[2] We viewed these structures as systems of inputs and outputs with local and central controls. However, the troubles that monolithically organized large organizations have developed raise questions about whether these companies can work anymore. In many cases, the arteries of knowledge and information are clotted, and the outfit resembles a recording studio run by deaf people.

It is not therefore surprising that today organizational monoliths are dying, just as the dinosaurs did. Even decentralized organizations have been nothing more than a transitional phase.

Banks that wish to remain flexible in their global operations practice a federated structure, which implies inverse delegation from the periphery to the center. It is characterized by independent business units with their own cultures, knowledge, products, markets, and networks held together with a common interest—and a strategic plan.

4. Capitalizing on the Many Aspects of Strategic Planning

Planning is fundamentally choosing. The selection and setting of criteria necessary to guide decisions is very important in establishing plans. Like strategies, plans must fit the objective(s) of the financial institution making them. Forecasts should not fit objectives; they should be made with objectivity. The following are examples of the multiple dimensions of planning:

❑ The establishment of planning premises.

❑ The planning periods being chosen.

❑ The coordination of short-range plans with the long-range plan.

---

[2] *The Age of Unreason* (London: Arrow Books, 1980).

Figure 7-2. The Change in Structure from a Monolithic Hierarchical Organization to a Federated Concept Is the Most Significant Event in Corporate Governance

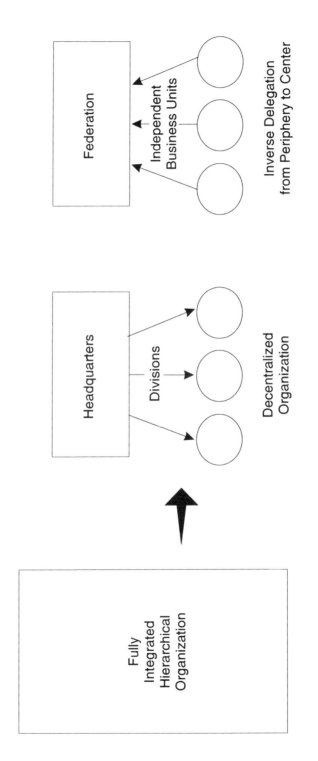

❑   The search for alternative courses of action.

❑   The formulation of necessary derivative plans.

The tools of planning are programs, budgets, and schedules; policies, procedures, and priorities; information services, qualifications, and quantification of results. Budgets are plans expressed in financial terms. The same is true of profit plans. Planning involves the following steps:

❑   Setting objectives.

❑   Elaborating possibilities.

❑   Collecting facts.

❑   Ascertaining causes and effects.

❑   Choosing among alternatives.

❑   Detailing course(s) of action.

❑   Assuring that the chosen course of action fits the overall strategy.

Any financial institution that has established a planning procedure has gone through these phases. Every successful enterprise has found out that structure follows strategy and that some complex structures are the result of the linking of several basic strategies.

A company's decision to expand into new markets called for the building of a multidepartmental structure and a central office. The development of new lines of products brought the need for research and development in banking.

Leading-edge financial institutions have found out that since structure follows strategy, there should be no delay in developing the new organization needed to meet the business demands of the new strategy, and that the new strategy, which calls for a change in structure, should come first, before the structural change, since it conditions the latter.

This precedence is assured through the strategic plan. The process of strategic planning integrates decisions and actions. This is a continuous activity and must be tuned in a way to help the bank adapt to changing conditions. A strategic plan allows the organization to take a proactive role, to influence the environment before it feels its impact.

As a process, strategic planning is often divided into logical steps, from the determination of the objectives to feedback and evaluation. Prognosis sees to it that potential problems may be avoided by appropriately tuning management decisions.

Knowing where the bank is headed is a good incentive to employees and management for better performance. A well-organized master plan also serve as a communications tool. Successful strategic planning systems include five key features in terms of their development and organization:

❑ Objectives are established by the board of directors and senior management.

❑ The overall master plan is divided into component plans for each operating unit and geographic area.

❑ Strategic planning procedures follow a regular cycle, phased in with the operational planning and control process.

❑ Periodic reviews are made both regularly and by exception, to ensure *plan versus actual* performance and to correct deviations.

❑ Highlights are steadily provided in an interactive form to assure that the strategic plan remains valid and dynamic.

Many banks accept the idea that strategic planning is important, but few follow a valid procedure. The trick is in the implementation of the principles outlined in this and the preceding two sections.

Key questions must be posed and answered to help identify goals and the way in which they will be reached. Starting with the fundamentals, What is a bank? What is a deposit? What is a loan? What is a derivative financial product? What business is *our* bank in?

The answers to these questions are quite different today than they were a decade or two ago, and they will continue to change. But the layers in Figure 7–3 alter themselves rather slowly—even if the characteristics of each layer change rapidly in order to adapt to developing market conditions in the function of risks and rewards.

Today, as in so many other times throughout its long history, the banking industry is in a critical phase of its development. To survive and prosper, financial institutions need a comprehensive and well-defined long-range plan, based on a forecast of events to come—but also on choices made by management. A critical responsibility of a good manager is to answer in a factual and documented manner the following question: What are *my* alternatives?

5.   Banking Plans, Globalization, and the Changing Financial Industry

The future belongs to those who can create the structures needed for today's and tomorrow's more complex and more uncertain financial environment. By all accounts, the beginning of the 21st century will see banking and financial services as a key battleground, while the scope and structure of commercial banking will radically change in form.

Traditionally, competition among banks was primarily confined to one's own country, as many examples from Europe help demonstrate. But this is no longer the case. While the three big Swiss banks moved into Frankfurt in an open bid for domestic German business, the Deutsche Bank moved aggressively into the domestic banking business in Italy. Crédit Lyonnais did the same. These are just a few examples.

Year after year, the financial results presented by money center banks tend to show a further shift in the balance of their businesses toward global operations. This is due to their determination to break out of an overcrowded and very competitive home market and to be a pacesetter for the world's financial markets.

But the transformation from commercial banking to global banking carries risks, even if it succeeds. The range of businesses on which financial institutions are building an international strategy is narrower than in their home country, where they mix retail banking with wholesale banking and some investment banking.

Like Ferdinand Magellan's voyage, which shrunk the world instead of expanding it, the globalization of banking shrinks the spatial nature of the world's financial markets. To face challenges, some money center banks establish a two-tier strategy:

❑   At home, retail and wholesale commercial banking, and investment banking.

❑   Abroad, wholesale only commercial banking, and investment banking.

With only a few exceptions such as Citibank and Crédit Lyonnais, which invest in retail banking internationally, commercial banks want to rival global investment banks, particularly in derivative financial instruments. By doing so, they risk their earnings becoming more dependent on the activity of global financial markets, and hence subject to a more volatile environment.

The shift also dearly affects the banks' culture. A solid, hierarchical approach is being loosened by the deal-making aspects of their international arms. Big banks have decided to run such risks in exchange for the prize of developing an earnings stream to supplement their home profits. According to Benjamin Graham's adage, "Most new issues are sold under *favorable* market conditions—which means favorable for the seller."

Favorable market conditions, however, do not develop out of the blue. Therefore, global banks will be well advised to ask themselves a number of critical questions, as suggested in Figure 7–4, and to answer them in a factual and documented manner.

The careful reader will appreciate that there are parallels between Figure 7–3 and Figure 7–4. Both address key planning questions but at a different level of detail. Both bring into perspective the integrative nature of a master plan.

Though it may be argued that many banks have been reasonably successful without strategic planning, let's not forget that even though

**Figure 7–3. Functional Layers Change Slowly, but the
Characteristics of Each Layer Change Rapidly
as a Function of Risk and Return**

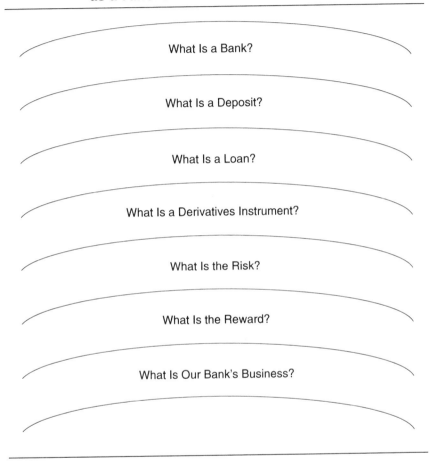

What Is a Bank?

What Is a Deposit?

What Is a Loan?

What Is a Derivatives Instrument?

What Is the Risk?

What Is the Reward?

What Is Our Bank's Business?

no formal master plan may exist, this function has been usually performed at the general management level. But, as Drucker aptly suggests,

> There is nothing more treacherous—or, alas, more common—than
> the attempt to make a precise decision on the basis of coarse and
> incomplete information.[3]

Particularly within a global market perspective, planning means
preparation in full appreciation of the fact that markets change. Man-

---

3 From a lecture by Dr. Peter Drucker.

Figure 7–4. Decision Layers in a Banking Strategy Connected to International Expansion

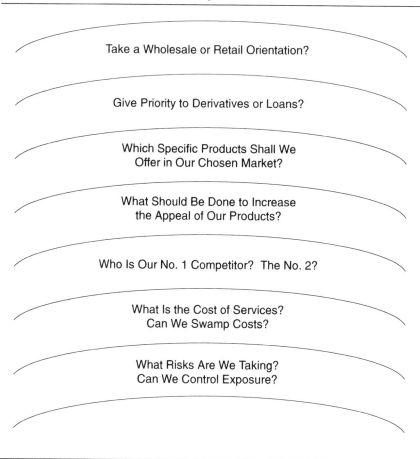

Take a Wholesale or Retail Orientation?

Give Priority to Derivatives or Loans?

Which Specific Products Shall We
Offer in Our Chosen Market?

What Should Be Done to Increase
the Appeal of Our Products?

Who Is Our No. 1 Competitor? The No. 2?

What Is the Cost of Services?
Can We Swamp Costs?

What Risks Are We Taking?
Can We Control Exposure?

agement needs a prescience, meaning foreknowledge of events. The management of financial institutions is no exception to this principle. Webster's defines a prescience as the human faculty or quality of being able to anticipate the occurrence or nature of future events—in other words, foresight. At no other time is foresight more badly needed than in times of turbulence such as those in which we live—and with products as risky as derivatives.

Banking is not the only industry at the crossroads. In the Middle Ages, alchemists labored to make gold. With the crisis in the formerly formidable chemical industry, the challenge for modern chemists is to find money. Banks have the money. The puzzle is how to invest it in such a way that the risk is controllable.

6.   Can We Develop and Sustain a Winning Strategy?

A winning strategy must have a vision and a message. Business opportunity, risk management, and cost control are inseparable elements of such a strategy. The same is true of high technology employed in an instrumental way to permit real-time appreciation and control of global exposure.

Technology should be competitively used not only to develop products faster and gain new clients, but also to swamp clerical costs and assure that services being offered are *rich in content* and *lean in manual* intervention. Professionals should be used for creative jobs:

- ❑   Advising clients.

- ❑   Financial analysis.

- ❑   Marketing and sales.

- ❑   Auditing.

- ❑   Risk management.

Income-producing, imaginative work should be performed by high-grade professionals. Routine work should be done by the computers—and delivered online to the clients. Hence, there is a need for rapid deployment of new systems and of knowledge-enriched software.

Left alone, both the business opportunities and the profit picture will deteriorate. One of the best-known banks suggested in our meeting that, according to its statistics, during the last 10 years the operational income of German banks increased by 184 percent, but the allowance for losses grew by 670 percent—nearly four times faster.

Partly, but only partly, this has been the result of an international expansion. Many money center banks have a pressing motive for expanding abroad. Their home market has become very competitive in retail banking, and profit margins are too low to compensate for persistent bad debt problems. But is it not true that costs in international operations can be higher, cutting deep into the bottom line? Information technology at home is not necessarily information technology abroad. Without a real-time risk control system, exposure can get out of hand.

Every bank needs to watch its bottom line. Return on equity falls because of high bad debt and dubious OBS deals and is unlikely in the medium term to recover to levels that prevailed in the 1970s and 1980s. Nor is it wise to forget that internationally money center banks face fierce competition from securities firms, which currently dominate the brokerage and corporate finance business and from other large banks that are also trying to build a global network.

A winning strategy will not automatically fit into place as a result of expanding abroad. Globalization is taxing both managerial and financial resources, and care should be taken that it does not weaken the bank's credit standing. A triple-A rating is increasingly important in international business, particularly in selling financial derivatives and in dealing with complex instruments.

In both cases, survival requires sound and detailed management controls and proper forecasts about clients, markets, and products—which many banks are not properly tooled to do, partly for cultural reasons and partly because of substandard technology.

Entrusted by the board with developing a winning strategy, top management must carefully balance the risks and opportunities of multinational expansion. Many banks depend on in-house experts in law, accounting, insurance, finance, and other areas to help them assess the business opportunity, its costs and rewards, and the risks posed by globalization and/or an active role in derivatives trades.

Other financial institutions bring in outside experts such as accounting firms, investment bankers, insurance brokers, and other consultants. In terms of risk management, such advisors might provide financing or hedging mechanisms to offset some of the risks, but only a culture of rigorous risk management can guarantee that a winning strategy is in place.

7. Elaborating a Banking Strategy That Emphasizes the Client

Any bank aiming to survive in times of turbulence must spend significant time and effort in studying and trying to anticipate trends in the financial markets. This includes market drives affecting not only products and services but short-term price movements, as well as those responsible for the long-term evolution of the financial system itself.

Out of the concepts developed from these studies evolve dynamic business strategies. But they remain dynamic only when the critical examination of strategic factors becomes a steady process. Master plans must be kept in a continuous state of evolution and change affecting five classes of resources:

❑   Products.

❑   Markets.

❑   Human resources.

❑   Financial staying power.

❑   Technological infrastructure.

Since products, markets, human resources, and financial master plans have priority, they determine the direction of technological strategies. This being said, it is no less true that a great deal of thought and research must be invested in the development of a technological infrastructure tailored to support the financial institution and its business, as well as its clients.

There is no doubt that technology, particularly high technology, is a vital component of any financial institution's future success. But the number-one priority is the master plan of the business and how it can affect the client base generally enough to reflect the basic functions of the financial system and specifically enough to answer the needs of the market and, more specifically, of the top 20 percent of clients.[4]

Components of the client-oriented section of the master plan are financing, advising, trading, positioning, processing transactions, and managing risk. All have to be examined fully. As Bankers Trust aptly suggests, today these functions should be looked upon in a very different manner than was the case with classical banking. Rather than deposits, loans, and securities, the main theme now is *the management of wealth*. Financial intermediation remains a core function since it facilitates the movement of funds from suppliers to user. But it involves more than the identification of users and suppliers, requiring the provision of new services and products to satisfy both.

The able management of wealth increasingly calls for a great deal of advising clients how to make better decisions for themselves. This leads to the following questions: Who are our clients? What should we do to satisfy their requirements? What kind of hand-holding should we provide?

A thorough study by one of the leading financial institutions attempted to answer the first and second queries concerning *client profile* and *customer requirements*. It focused on asset allocation and portfolio management and led to the 1 percent rule. Out of a total of 2,000,000 customers, the top segment had highly sophisticated requirements; one percent of customers, or 20,000, advanced a torrent of demands; and the next 5 percent of customers, or 100,000, had to be satisfied with significant effort.

The requirements posed by the next 14 percent of the bank's clients also gave the rise to exception routines in products and services, while the remaining 80 percent of customers were satisfactorily handled through established procedures.

The top 20 percent of customers was composed of institutional investors (at the upper level of the pyramid), multinational corporations, some of the corresponding banks, high-technology industries, and high-net-worth individuals. All classes posed significant customer handling and real-time reporting challenges.

---

4 See also Chapter 1. Pareto's Law is applicable to the customer population and the profits the bank derives.

Particularly felt by alert managers has been the tough level of required new functionality. This was found necessary in practically all cases, from institutional investors to high-net-worth individuals, which is not unreasonable since there is a growing practice among high-net-worth people to create a company as a legal entity that handles their assets.

At the peak of the client pyramid, derivatives trading and the management of wealth are nearly inseparable. In all of its many evolving forms, trading encompasses the buying and selling of claims on wealth. The bank must position itself in a way that provides liquidity to its clients and to the market: moving market prices while making these prices more visible and reliable and permitting the establishment, as well as the maintenance, of a fair value setting.

Transactions processing is not only the effective execution of client transactions, but also the transferring, storing, safeguarding, verifying, and reporting of claims on wealth. This is becoming an increasingly demanding task because of the complexity involved in financial transactions, such as off-balance-sheet deals.

But none of these operations, nor the concept of overall performance, will be complete or profitable for long without *risk management*. This is seen by the most important clients as the process of providing *them* with risk identification and risk protection.

It is a process of moving them closer to their desired *risk profiles*. The mission is not just hedging but also, if not primarily, helping clients to shed unwanted risks or acquire new risks that suit their strategy, thereby appropriately structuring their portfolios. This involves not just trading and record keeping, but analytically unbundling, transforming, and repackaging risks.

Such operations should be performed in a way that is tailored to the particular needs of the client in the short, medium, and longer term. The effective application of such a strategy requires a clear vision of the financial products and markets of the future, as stated throughout this chapter.

8. Information Technology and the Redefinition of Financial Intermediation

People and people, *our* clients and *our* personnel, are the two top assets of *our* bank. We have also seen that strategic plans on products and markets as well as financial staying power constitute the vital components of a master plan. But we should not forget high technology, particularly as it is the catalyst in the redefinition of financial intermediation.

To better appreciate the last statement, it pays to take another look at the fundamentals. If companies and private individuals are the depositors, who are the ultimate borrowers? For a money center bank, they are the governments and multinational business firms. For other banks, they are the household for personal loans, mortgages, and so on.

Because private individuals have more money in the banks than companies do, the ultimate lender is the households. This is the case even if books on economics and finance state that the reserve bank is the lender of last resort. Without intermediation, the *direct finance* algorithm is that the ultimate lenders buy securities issued by the ultimate borrowers. However, this direct type of finance does not exist when individuals do not have access to the markets. Furthermore, individuals suffer from insufficient information, such as the risk of *default*.

Indirect finance requires the existence of intermediaries. They get deposits from the ultimate lenders as well as buying primary securities. Then they issue their own securities, which in turn are bought by ultimate lenders—for instance, the funds. Checking accounts in a bank are used by the bank to make business loans. The checking account, or demand deposit account, is essentially a security issued by the bank. By contrast, the loan is a security issued by the business firm or, more precisely, a primary security.

Commercial banks, savings and loan associations, credit unions, pension funds, and insurance companies act as financial intermediaries. They channel funds from depositors to the market, through a process of indirect finance.

There is nothing new in this description of the process of intermediation, but there is something new in its opposite: *disintermediation*. Disintermediation hit the financial sector because of nonbanks and the fact that big borrowers now go directly to the market and issue warrants as well as commercial paper.

Also new is the fact that the rather leisurely pace of financial intermediation has, as of recently, enormously quickened. From loans to derivatives trades, business is now done on-line, and successful business is supported through the following:

❑ Knowledge artifacts, or agents.

❑ Distributed deductive databases.

❑ Intelligent any-to-any networks.

❑ High-performance computers.

Part and parcel of the new vision of banking—and the new process of intermediation—is technology because technology is also the primary driving force for change. Computing speed and capacity, interactive databasing, interactive three-dimensional color visualization, and real-time communications are the new tools of intermediation.

Through satellites, fiber optics, coaxial cable, and other media, broadband networks—increasingly called *information superhighways*—link depositors, intermediaries, lenders, loan takers, derivatives traders, investors, and financial markets. This trend will continue, resulting in a truly global interactive market. In this greatly evolving global financial market, the key currency will be *wealth accounts*. Companies and investors will hold their assets and liabilities in broad-based and readily accessible interactive databases.

Investors and traders will still hold and exchange today's financial instruments such as stocks, bonds, and derivatives as well as physical wealth such as buildings, farms, and vehicles. But computers will continuously track these items in the individual's wealth account, constantly *mark them to market* or *mark them to model*, and try to make them liquid.

9.   What's Behind the Concept of Wealth Cards?

Section 8 ended with a reference to *wealth accounts*. These have little to do with the demand deposit accounts of old, though they also constitute a security issued by the bank. The difference is not just in the three to five orders of magnitude in their worth as compared to current accounts, but is primarily in their great *reach* and *flexibility*.

Like all finance, wealth accounts are a *virtual asset* but they are polyvalent, including all forms of assets—from cash to stocks, bonds, derivative vehicles, and real estate. Wealth accounts are *transnational*, permitting their holder access to wealth in any financial product, in any place, at any time.

Some of the tier-one banks, which invest a great deal in forward planning and research, talk of a first incarnation of the wealth account—the so-called individual *wealth card*. It would allow its owner to pay for, for example, a new car by instantly drawing on part of the wealth inherent in, say, a vacation house in some other country or anywhere in the world. These wealth cards will not be physical, but virtual, essentially a subset of the individual wealth account. They will be accessible on-line in real time by their owner as well as by the authorized banker, who would use them for transactions.

In this new definition of financial intermediation, virtual assets and liabilities will be traded globally at any time, in any currency, anywhere in the world. Global exchanges will essentially be electronic bulletin boards and will constitute the principal medium through which buyers and sellers will post their needs and execute transactions.

Banks that have done their homework in prognosis and in strategic planning have developed a fairly concrete picture of how the new intermediation environment will shape up. In terms of value, the majority of these transactions will be different from those we know today.

Starting with forward and exotic derivative financial instruments, the trend will be *customization* for each market segment, down to the individual investor. Through the use of high technology, many of the existing and all of the new financial products will be tailored to a client's needs at a reasonable price.

This trend will increasingly include highly personalized services from financial companies selling to market niches made up not just of one institutional investor, but of a single household or a single individual investor.

It is not for nothing that Wall Street firms are engaging more and more experts in mathematical modeling of financial phenomena to explore a range of new portfolio opportunities. Rocket scientists are using asset pricing algorithms, option pricing heuristics, and market efficiency theories.

One of the goals is customized products and services. A second objective is innovation to gain a market advantage. A third is the early identification of transient market opportunities where profits can be made.

This is the shape of the new financial companies that will flourish by the end of this decade and well into the 21st century. Any strategic plan that does not allow for such evolution is a sitting duck to the competition, particularly those competitors able to read tomorrow's newspaper today.

10. A Strategy for Dealing in Derivative Financial Instruments

As with any other trade, the key to successful dealing and investing in options, forwards, futures, swaps, and exotic derivatives is the ability to develop an appropriate strategy for any market at any time. As we have seen throughout this chapter, crucial to a successful financial enterprise is the clear definition of goals to be reached as well as the study of ways to reach them.

Taking options as an example, no investor is likely to ever employ all the possible strategies, for the simple reason that no one is likely to need all of them to attain her or his goals. Prior to establishing *an individual* strategy, however, an investor should be keen to examine the options. The investor should then elaborate through simulation several scenarios, so that his or her choices are factual and documented.

At one time or another, the knowledge the investor has acquired about investing provides a significant advantage over those who lack this knowledge. This advantage is precisely what creates "lucky" traders and investors. Luck is what happens when preparation meets opportunity.

Taking derivative financial products as an example, properly used and in moderation, they can help in terms of protection against declining prices or rising prices—according to the strategy adopted. They can also be employed to achieve short-, medium- or long-term objectives, again depending on the strategy.

The introduction to this chapter stated that a strategy is a master plan against an opponent. It is intended to position a company (or an investor) against the market. Strategic evaluations must, therefore, serve a triple purpose, and derivatives are no exception to this rule:

1. Demonstrate the options that exist as well as their nature.

2. Achieve a higher level of familiarity with the way the market works.

3. Provide a reference guide to the implementation of the chosen alternative.

This triple purpose is present in all strategic evaluations, from military to market-oriented evaluations, and can be instrumental in assuring that as opportunities become available for using derivative financial instruments they can be exploited at a rapid pace, within a specific course of action.

A sound policy is not to try to master every OBS vehicle, but to focus on those that seem most pertinent to the business problem at hand and that correspond most closely to the objectives. This is as true with classical banking as it is with derivatives.

Let's apply these principles to a market setting. In deciding which option to buy and sell, the first basic factor is that of creating a common denominator of all options strategies after having outlined the possible alternatives. To decide which option to buy, hold, or sell we must decide on the type of option we are after. Then we must make up our mind whether we want an option with a short or long period of time remaining until expiration or an option that is currently out-of-the-money, at-the-money, or in-the-money.

A choice among alternative instruments and associated scenarios is vital because option premiums reflect both the time remaining until expiration and the option strike price relative to the quoted futures price. This sees to it that different options have different risk-reward characteristics.

Other things being equal, the longer the time until the option expires, the higher the premium will be. This is similar to having to pay more money for a one-year insurance policy than for the same insurance policy valid for six months. It is, therefore, a fairly common strategy.

More complex is choosing the option strike price. In this case, there is no easy rule of thumb. The investor's decision may be influenced by considerations such as the following:

- ❏ Are one's own price expectations bearish or bullish?

- ❏ What is likely to happen to the price of the underlying futures contract?

- ❏ How much risk is one willing to take in order to realize a potentially larger reward?

Being bullish or bearish is a fuzzy concept rather than a black-or-white proposition. In the past, investors and traders had to be either outright bullish or bearish to enter the futures market, expecting to make a profit on a speculative position. This has changed in the sense that new financial instruments permit tonalities of grey. One can be slightly bullish, slightly bearish, or even neutral and still trade profitably. Options on futures offer investors and traders profit opportunities that did not formerly exist.

The same statement can be made about the characteristics of the new financial instruments. This raises further questions. If, for instance, the objective is price protection, should one pay a smaller premium for less protection or a larger premium for more protection? There are plenty of such queries because options provide a wide range of alternatives—each fitting within a specific strategic move.

8

Control of Risk by Banks, Nonbanks, and Treasury Operations

1. Introduction

Chapter 7 defined banking strategy, the processes it involves and its components. Not only the banking sector, but the financial industry at large has come to a strategic crossroad. Winners and losers will be separated by their ability to add value to the services provided to their customers and to control the risks taken in transactions as well as those inherent in portfolios.

The distinction between the banking sector and the financial industry at large is significant. The latter does not only include *banks*, though this term is broad and often ill-defined. Many institutions tend to go under this general term—commercial banks, investment banks, industrial banks, and so on—but many others do not qualify and are currently being called nonbanks.

Governments have typically adopted bank incorporation acts, which permitted a group of investors capable of meeting a standard set of legal requirements to open a bank. In the United States, for instance, in the 1838 to 1850 time frame this procedure of organizing a bank came to be known as *free banking* and resulted in the establishment of thousands of institutions.

Free banking has not meant freedom from all constraints. Bank statutes have imposed fairly rigid specifications, from the granting of a charter to making sure the organizers are competent and trustworthy.

For national banks, this scrutiny is in the hands of the following federal agencies:

❏ The Office of the Controller of the Currency (OCC) of the Treasury Department.

❏ The Federal Reserve Board, which exercises bank supervision.

❏ The Federal Deposit Insurance Corporation (FDIC).

Nonbanks—which may be savings and loans, insurance companies, brokers, credit associations, department store chains, mutual funds, acceptance corporations, and so on—do not have these constraints. Though ultimate authority in all cases of banks and nonbanks rests with the stockholders, charting and supervision makes a difference, particularly in the mode and range of operations, the responsibilities assumed by the institution, and the legally defined control of risk.

Therefore, whether a company is a bank or a nonbank, a basic choice to be made at the level of the strategic plan is whether it will take some types of risks—and how it is going to manage its exposure.

Different types of risk are often suggested by traders and loan officers whose intent is to show high profits. The alternative is to follow a prudent policy aimed at protecting depositors and shareholders as well as abiding by the prevailing regulations regarding the bank's charter. But this also means slower growth and lower profits.

2. The Concept of Risk and Its Management

The raw material of banking is money, and this money must come from somewhere. The ability to attract credit depends on the quality of management, its policies, and its risk-control procedures. The same is true of the ability to manage investments.

Financial institutions that run their affairs well will always have deposits and credits, while those that don't will perish. Yet, it is surprising how often in the banking industry, as well as in industrial organizations, "improvement" in management means that mediocrity replaces ineptitude.

The foregoing proposal is not written in a sense that sound management is synonymous with risk aversion. Profits depend on taking, risks and risk is no alien concept in banking. However, today more than ever, bankers should appreciate that the positions taken by the financial institution must be controlled. One troubling development is the increasing magnitude of losses and the number of defaults. Another source of worry is that in the middle of many risk calculations there are often one or two mythical assumptions.

Some risks are kept under control, while other risks are uncontrolled or even uncontrollable. Uncontrollable risk is a testament to the shallowness of the management function. By contrast, effective management constantly monitors the total performance of the financial institution; establishes warning signals for all activities, avoiding moves it cannot master; and shows decisive action as soon as danger signals are detected—before it is too late.

Technology can help achieve this goal. Real-time response, simulators, and knowledge artifacts permit us to detect and control risks that in large measure are inherent in the way we do business. The block diagram in Figure 8–1 shows the necessary flow of information; later on, we will talk about the needed models.

Figure 8–1 makes a distinction between *risk policies* and *risk data streams*. Risk policies include, but are not limited to, criteria for credit risk and market risk, overall limits on risk and exposure, necessary risk structures, and the targeted distributions of risk.

Risk data streams involve detailed data on transactions, the corresponding risk and exposure, information on how policy has been implemented, and information on deviations from policy.

Most of this information will come from day-to-day operations, from loans to dealing rooms.

The reason for channeling information on risk and exposure is to create a response. This response must take place in real space, utilizing the capabilities technology offers to compress long distances into a single reference point:

❏ Bringing markets on different continents into one solution space.

❏ Mapping markets, products, and transactions into intelligent models.

❏ Providing us with an exceptionally good decision tool as well as monitoring capability.

While it is true that if we have the know-how we can use technology to enrich our operations and help ourselves with first-class tools, this will be of little use unless we have a clear concept of the following:

❏ Risk proper.

❏ What precisely we wish to control.

Let us therefore briefly look at definitions. Risk is the chance of injury, damage, or loss; it is a hazard. In insurance and in banking, risk is expressed quantitatively as the degree of probability of loss. Such probability is not a question of pure mathematics. It is a business proposition and therefore a function of the type of loss that is covered.

The type of loss can be in such areas as life, fire, or accident insurance, or, alternatively, fluctuation in exchange rates, interest rates, legal issues, settlement problems, or counterparty failure.

Figure 8–1. Position for Risk Control Requires Steady Information Flows as Well as Uninterrupted Management Attention

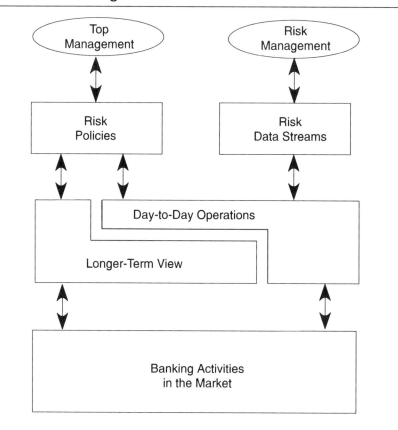

❑ The risk that is involved in a transaction.

Such risk may be due to the type of person and/or company, hence credit risk. Or it may have its origin in a commercial or financial operation, centered on market risk.

Mathematically, risk is the measure of variance around an expected value. Algorithmic formulae aim at pinpointing the target (expected value) and calculating the probability of reaching the goal (or coming close). The whole science of statistics is based on this concept, including vagueness and uncertainty.[1] A heuristic approach is more applicable

---

[1] See also D. N. Chorafas, *Advanced Financial Analysis* (London: Euromoney, 1994).

with foreign exchange rates and interest rates. An algorithmic approach is preferable when we deal with the loan's principal and interest.

Algorithms and heuristics will underpin the models, to which a brief reference was made in connection to Figure 8–1. Part Three will discuss management purposes at length, while this and the other chapters in Part Two will focus on the types of risk we wish to control.

3.   Risk Management as a Philosophy of Banking

Developing the mathematical models for the control of risk and providing the necessary information flows is the easier part. The more difficult is cultural change, which has to do with the philosophy of banking that a financial institution has adopted. That is where the concept of *managing risk* originates.

Risk management is a complex issue because quite often the banker, the trader, and the investor are part of the target they wish to hit. In highly dynamic markets, risk cannot be controlled independently of the players. This is indeed a peculiar characteristic of derivative vehicles, which is only recently being recognized for what it is.

According to the Hungarian financier George Soros, it is generally believed that the stock market anticipates recessions. But it would be just as correct to say that it can help precipitate them. The anticipatory concept lead Soros to the assertions that

❑   Markets are always biased in one direction or another.

❑   Markets can influence the events they anticipate.[2]

Soros calls this *reflexivity*. An example has been the descision by the British chancellor Kenneth Clarke and Eddie George, governor of the Bank of England, to increase base rates from 5.25 to 5.75 percent in September 1994, with the attitude of financial markets playing an important role in that decision.

Kenneth Clarke noted that the markets were expecting interest rates to be raised sooner rather than later. He was concerned that if the expectation was not realized, markets could become more *volatile*, and the eventual increase in rates might need to be larger.

Eddie George, who had proposed the interest rate increase in the first place, said there were arguments for delaying it but worried that such a delay would have its dangers in the financial market. Accounting for what the market likes or does not like is in itself a philosophy of management. What any philosophy teaches is *living with*—finding a path in the midst of an unknown environment.

---

2 George Soros, *The Alchemy of Finance* (London: John Wiley, 1993).

Philosophy and risk management have issues in common, starting with the fact that neither progresses in a linear fashion or along a horizontal dimension. Their evolution is toward the depths, and their advance consists in questioning that which previously has not been questionable.

Whether connected to risk management or the exploitation of business opportunity, both analytical results and new policies influence the market's expectations. In turn, the market's expectations alter the course of events because of the impact they have on people with the power to fulfill those expectations. Therefore, the alert investor needs to do more than consider the relevant fundamentals in a market. He or she must weigh the opinions of other influential investors and how people in the real world are likely to react due to their perception of those opinions.

But it is also important to react without preconceptions. George Soros once commented, "I make as many mistakes as the next guy. Where I excel is at recognizing my mistakes." A good risk-management system can make a significant contribution in helping to recognize the mistake(s) and altering the wrong course of action.

Sam Walton called this faculty "being able to turn on a dime,"[3] and he considered it to be the foremost factor in the success of Wal-Mart. Turn on a dime is, of course, a matter of personal philosophy—and most specifically of the philosophy one adopts in risk management.

Only the most successful people are willing and able to recognize their mistakes when it comes to business opportunity and risk. Quite similarly, very few financial institutions have in place the models, simulators, knowledge artifacts, computers, databases, and networks able to identify and calculate the risk inherent in banking operations. To do so, we must do the following:

❑ Establish in detail all important risk factors.

❑ Determine linkages and establish metrics in their regard.

❑ Take measurements and reach conclusions in real space.

❑ Elaborate dynamic correction capabilities and take decisive action.

Figure 8–2 presents in a nutshell the tools that can promote a risk-management philosophy. It identifies the risk factors we are after, the distributed databases that should be interactively accessible, and the models that must operate in real time.

Whether a company is a bank or a nonbank, the people responsible for its management must be able to elaborate risk parameters and

---

3 Sam Walton, *Made in America—My Story* (New York: Bantam, 1992).

Figure 8–2. A Sound Risk-Management Philosophy Should Underpin the System's Architecture

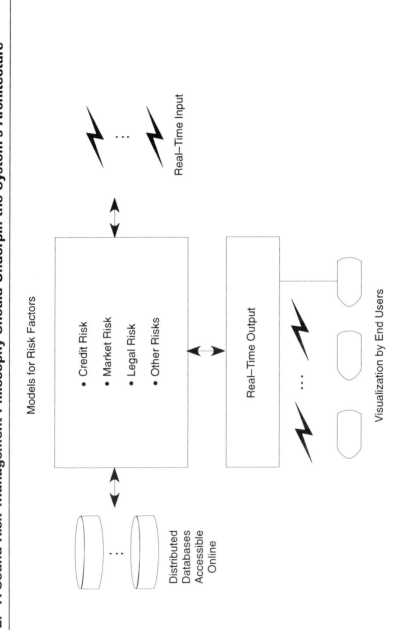

control the execution of orders. Napoleon once stated that even the most thought-out order is useless if the commander fails to see it through.

In conclusion, for a contribution to risk management to be enduring, it must be based on sound policies, on the proper infrastructure, and on a personal philosophy about risk. With these prerequisites, a good solution can be built only when expert bankers and first-class technologists closely collaborate to establish the means for a sound pursuit of business opportunity commensurate with manageable risk.

4.   Risks Associated with Investments and Credits

The careful readers of financial history have been able to appreciate that bankers, traders, investors, and the institutions themselves have remarkably short memories. This is true both of banks and of nonbanks, as well as of the majority of individuals.

Nowhere is this reference more valid than in matters of allocating *credits*, which medium and large banks today roughly distribute between trading and investing in derivative financial instruments, and loans given to companies and counterparties. The prevailing ratio is roughly 2/3 for derivatives and 1/3 for loans.

Etymologically, the word *credit* derives from the Latin *credo*—"I believe."[4] It is correct, however, to add that all money is a matter of belief—and there is much hype in many if not most of the calculation about what we get in return for our investments.

Credit provides the markets with liquidity. But at the same time there has never been a crash without an explosion of credit lines, extended on the assumption that the good times would continue indefinitely.

A similar set of beliefs propels investment decisions. In the background of many investments by banks, nonbanks, other companies, and private individuals is the hope that they will appreciate. Yet, the unalterable fact of life is that prices never rise to the levels expected. Nor do they progress in a straight line.

Both booming investments and a significant credit creation lead to unserviceable assets and liabilities, which in turn brings a crash. This is the object lesson to be learned and to guide us in the years to come, whether credits and investments are made by banks or by nonbanks.

Says Robert Beckman in his book *Crashes*:

> Credit is nothing more than single-entry bookkeeping. If banks fail, businesses go bankrupt and the value of assets disintegrates, those

---

[4] It is a combination of the Sanskrit *cred*, meaning "trust" and the latin *do*, "I place."

credits—which represent money—disappear, and there are insufficient funds available to pay for the inflated prices or to cope with the requirements of production and commerce.

This is where the key to the banking crisis of the 1930s lies. The likelihood of a recurrence of such a crisis can be directly traced to the heart of the system that governments have perpetuated in their own interests.[5]

While president of the Federal Reserve, Dr. Marriner Eccles, a commercial banker by origin and a reserve banker later on in his career, made a statement which fits perfectly with the foregoing concept:

There is no limit to the amount of money that can be created by the banking system, but there are limits to our productive facilities and our labor supply which can be only slowly increased and which at present are being used near capacity.[6]

These are the words of a worried central banker, and his time, the 1930s, has much in common with our own. Now, as then, there has been a peculiar interpretation of the four Cs of credit: character, capacity, capital, and collateral.

❏   *Character* is a measure of the moral risk and constitutes the most important factor in the debtor's ability to repay credit.

❏   *Capacity* measures the business risk, as investments and credit are based on leverage rather than real assets.

❏   *Capital* is the property risk measure. Banks have capital reserves to protect themselves against losses.

❏   *Collateral* means guarantees whose value can be determined easily and that can be converted into cash at no major loss of value.

In an overleveraged society such as ours, whether gearing comes from banks or from nonbanks, collateral must be something other than someone else's debts. Yet, as we will see in Chapter 12 when we talk of securities lending, it is precisely this "other debt" that today constitutes the basis of collateral.

As a matter of fact, in spite of the enormous economic activity that characterizes the last 20 years of this century, character, capacity, capital, collateral—and therefore credit—are generally not very well understood. Deposit credit can be defined as an obligation on the part of a bank to pay a certain sum of money on demand. This obligation is iden-

---

5 Robert Beckman, *Crashes* (London: Grafton, 1988).
6 William Greider, *Secrets of the Temple: How the Federal Reserve Runs the Country* (New York: Touchstone/Simon and Schuster, 1987).

tified only by an entry in the books of the bank, without any currency or other transferable documents being involved.

While deposit credit was originally established as the result of a specific specie, the extension of such credit on the basis of collateral such as property, shares, bonds, insurance policies, and so on, or simply on the presumed good faith of the borrower, has been practiced for centuries. Loans credit, whether for investment or commercial reasons, is likewise a matter of evaluation and of collateral. Credit for trading in derivatives stands on more shaky ground than loans credit, if for no other reason than because the money is more leveraged.

Bankers usually talk of loans advanced for OBS business as "investment credit." Investment credit is used to acquire assets whether fixed, as plants and equipment, or financial assets of different sorts. Investment credit is typically longer-term, while commercial credit is short-term.

Commercial credit is used for current operations, to finance production, to purchase materials, or for payroll. Repayment of debt is made with the proceeds of sales, but commercial credit is self-liquidating only to the degree that current operations are successful. This is often overlooked in the calculation of risk.

5.   How Can the Financial System Face the Challenge of Added Leverage?

The negatives presented above are not meant to discourage investment and credit, but to bring into focus what is involved on the risk side— whether the operations are undertaken by banks or nonbanks. A great deal behind current exposure lies in the fact that externally secured and nonsecured bank credit has become the dominant instrument of finance.

The possible effects are not that difficult to detect, but who whats to see them? The value of money and the reliability of bank credit rest heavily on the prudence and discretion of bankers and nonbankers who have entered the banking business. Borrowers do not draw their line of credit in cash, but simply transfer this credit to others by means of electronic funds transfer. Hence, very little actual money is needed by a bank to support the credit it extends. The rest is bookkeeping.

Dr. Marriner Eccles was right to suggest that bank credit can be multiplied endlessly as checks drawn on created bank credit can be deposited in other banks. Add to this the fact that EFT helps to create new deposits and more credit. The problem few people appreciate is that this means added leverage.

Added leverage is created by the financial system that turns itself into ready money by the magic of bank credit. Nowhere is this more apparent than in the high exposure with derivative financial instruments—which now features a cumulative $50 trillion amount, as we have seen in Part One.

The use of bank credit as ready money has become part and parcel of the modern financial structure. Therefore, most people are rather astonished to learn that the actual amount of currency available, both in circulation and held by banks as reserves, would redeem only a small fraction of deposits in banks and other financial institutions.

When I make this statement in my seminars, adding that the amount of cash available at the Federal Reserve is no more than 10 percent of the money changing hands every 24 hours in New York,[7] many people respond that

1. The Federal Reserve can create all the money it wants.

2. It is unthinkable that, as lenders of last resort, the Fed and the government will not salvage the financial institutions.

Both statements are only half true. The Federal Reserve can create money, but the huge sums of $2.5 trillion dollars that change hands overnight in New York would result in an awful inflation that would spread like brushfire around the financial markets of the world.

This process of colossal money creation will in itself destabilize the markets because of the lack of confidence that will follow. As for a massive salvaging operation that would cover every bank and nonbank, there is no way it can be done—nor is there a precedent.

Small size salvaging is another matter. In the early 1980s the Federal Reserve pulled Continental Illinois Bank by nationalizing it, but it let Penn State and other smaller- to medium-size banks go down the drain.

Thanks to FDIC, the depositors got up to $100,000 per depositor per bank, but above that the capital was lost. This brings home the message that, from a depositor's standpoint, the entire affair is a matter of confidence. If depositors believe their money is sitting safely in the bank, they will leave it there. If they lose confidence in their bank or in the banking system as a whole, they will rush to pull out their money.

In this case, both the bank(s) on which there is a run and the whole banking system become unsafe. The same is evidently true of nonbanks, even if they do not have the right to take deposits, nonbanks will not be the first to be affected by the withdrawal of money by private individuals, but will suffer from the shakedown in confidence. Eventually, nonbanks will be obliged to return money to the banks that

---

7 Typically, $200 to $280 billion, while overnight clearing can reach $2.5 to $3.0 trillion.

gave them a line of credit and who now feel obliged to call back their funds.

All this excessive risk can be avoided if there is a strong sense of risk control—a *philosophy of risk management*, as section 4 suggested. This is vital in defining the style of management, whether of a bank or non-bank. Books discuss two traditional approaches: Tight control and free rein.

However, these are extremes not usually encountered in common practice. Any and every financial institution has policies and procedures that establish both the mechanics and the dynamics of control action. Together, they should be seen as constituting the prevailing philosophy of risk management.

6.   Running the Treasury for Profits and Its Risks

There used to be a time when a corporate treasurer's job was simply to make sure there was enough money to pay the bills. But by making their treasury a profit counter, companies brought hedging into the treasury department, and with it exposure to financial risk.

Today a typical treasury department tries to control the impact on the firm's profits due to movements in interest rates, currency exchange rates, raw materials, and stock market moves. To serve this function, the finance industry has come up with an ever expanding array of products whose core is derivatives.

The use of derivative financial instruments by company treasurers, however, is far from risk-free. In Chapter 1, we saw examples of huge losses that have occurred during the last couple of years. Increasingly, there is news of companies—multinational and national, large and medium-sized, in manufacturing, merchandising, and finance—that have lost large sums of money from both simple and complex off-balance-sheet products. Some manufacturing and merchandising firms now accuse banks of being more inclined to sell products that earn them fat fees than products that best suit the firm's interests. But they fail to define the firm's "interests."

Some years ago, I worked as a consultant to the president of a bank that had no strategic plan. When I asked him what his institution's strategic objective was, he said, "You tell me my strategic goals." Many companies do this today with derivatives—then when things go wrong they accuse the hedgers of not protecting their interests.

Even if the treasury is run for profit, which is not necessarily the best idea, risk management should be the cornerstone of its activities. This requires both a strategic plan, under which the treasury works, and a philosophy of risk management. At the board level, risk control should be seen as an integral part of management control in appreciation of the fact that the act of controlling ensures progress toward objec-

Figure 8–3. A Family of Curves That Help Define Audit Costs Versus Risks

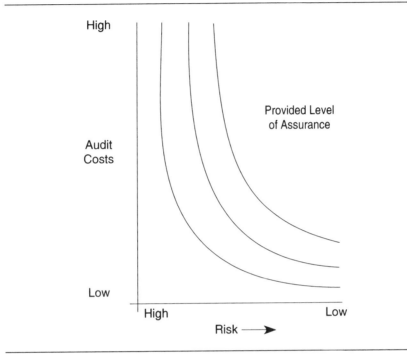

tives. Because the assurance of conformity to plans is part of the board's responsibility, it must have the ability to ascertain the extent of deviations.

Because the board is responsible for corrective action, it must also have the means to adjust plans. Controls can be of an auditing nature: financial, operational, and managerial. Whatever their goal, they require

- ❏ The existence of performance standards.

- ❏ Aims expressed in a quantifiable way.

- ❏ Measurable results to compare against standards.

- ❏ A steady, accurate, reliable feedback mechanism.

There is a family of curves defining audit costs versus risks, which is applicable to treasury and other operations. As shown in Figure 8–3, the level of assurance we are after suggests that when risks are low, the costs of extensive audits are high. But when risks are high, the cost of most careful audits is low and justifiable.

The treasurer himself, and general management at large, has every interest in following exception-reporting procedures, in keeping communications channels open, in using a control language that is fully understood, and in evaluation procedures being timed in such a way that all persons in the bank understand the impending danger.

First at the board level and then in the treasury, risk-control policies must be clearly phrased and leave no ambiguity as to management's intentions. Policy is a guide for thinking, a mental framework on which the planning process will be built.

The policies established by top management help eliminate many trivial day-to-day decisions, but to be effective they must be dynamic and constantly reevaluated. This is far more true regarding derivatives risk management.

Like strategies, risk policies cannot be set once and then forgotten. Besides this, policies are general, not specific, statements. In order to channel their decisions and actions in accordance with risk-management policies, subordinates must interpret these policies. Properly established procedures help to aid in this interpretation.

In conclusion, whether the treasury is run for profit or it concentrates on its more traditional cash-management function, there is no substitute for *derivatives risk management*. This requires clear policies and a high-technology system—as well as the redefinition of financial responsibility and accountability.

7. The Cultural Evolution Among Company Treasurers

Company treasurers used to be a conservative lot. As we saw in section 6, traditionally their mission has been to assure the liquidity and cash to run the company's businesses and pay bills on time. Lately, however, some treasury operations are taking inordinate risks with derivatives.

Losses in a domain that few treasurers master hit the bottom line hard—as can be seen in quarterly, semester, and annual financial statements. Big companies are reporting hefty losses because of blunders made by their treasuries, as we have seen in several examples.

It is indeed ironic that so much money is being lost by treasurers, whose traditional job is to reduce the risks a firm encounters rather than increase them. While to protect against currency exchange loss, the treasurer may enter a few forward contracts, hedging exposure to forex movements, interest rates, or raw-material prices should never become a sort of gambling.[8]

For managers who once had $7.5 billion in real money to invest and tried to leverage it to nearly $22 billion, the people running the Orange County Fund are now trying hard to appear as financial inno-

---

[8] "Isn't hedging the same as gambling?" asked one of the readers. Theoretically, the two terms are the absolute antithesis of one another. But because of lust and greed, in some cases they become synonymous.

cents. In testimony before a special state senate panel, county executives said they were unaware of the risks that led to the county's bankruptcy filing and losses of nearly $2 billion.

"I had never owned a share of stock," testified former Treasurer Robert Citron, who said he relied on investment houses such as Merrill Lynch.[9] Citron's deputy, Matthew Raabe, said he didn't grasp "the somewhat bizarre aspects" of the high-risk investments that sank the fund. Unfortunately, this is not the exception, but a case found quite frequently in business and industry.

As the pace of reported losses by treasury departments quickens, it lends credibility to current estimates that over the next several years the competition for money will become more and more sophisticated and risky.

An increasing number of companies will seek out the best returns. The price of money will be set on an international basis and various derivative products will take the foreground for profits and for hedging.

The massive entry by treasury departments into derivatives trades and the effects this has, not only on daily transactions but also on the values held in their portfolios, fairly significantly changes the definition of nonbank.

As Chapter 7 pointed out, it used to be that nonbanks were institutions working in finance but not qualifying for a banking charter; for instance, insurance companies, brokers, savings and loans, and credit unions. To these were added the credit operations of department store chains and other organizations, acceptance corporations, mutual funds, and—why not?—pension funds.

Now it has become evident that, given their active dealing in the financial markets, the treasury departments of industrial companies—manufacturing as well as merchandising—are also nonbanks. In fact, a growing number of companies are hiring bankers to head their treasuries.

As the whole concept of what is and is not possible in the financial business changes, the price of money will be set within a given risk spectrum and with an associated risk premium.[10] Many results will follow. For instance, the calculation of interest rates versus inflation will be less and less useful in determining interest-rate trends—which may be set by the derivatives market.

A new equilibrium will eventually be reached, defying current financial principles. During the transition, however, we can expect some spectacular failures aggravated by the new and curious fact that the treasury departments at so many companies register big losses.

---

[9] *Business Week*, January 30, 1995.

[10] We will talk extensively of this subject in Part Three and show how to use it for risk control.

The most favorable hypothesis concerning the causes of this significant change is that treasuries do not lack ethics or have an extraordinary amount of lust, but rather they simply fail to understand the strategies that need to be used with derivatives, their mechanics, and the dangers of some of the novel financial instruments.

On many occasions, the line between a classic hedge and a risky bet can become blurred. It therefore comes as no surprise that treasurers are not necessarily aware of the risks they are taking and the exposure they have assumed.

People knowledgeable in the field suggest there is another more fundamental reason for what is happening. Increasingly, boards of directors encourage risk taking by looking at the treasury department as a profit center. Setting profit targets for treasury departments can create many hazards *if* it rewards the treasurer for making money but not for reducing the risks associated with the company's core business.

A treasury that is losing money is pulled into even riskier bets, in a bid to meet the profit target. This is particularly so if the board does not place strict controls on how the company's treasury operates. In a rational sense, every board member must be closely involved in the following:

❑   Deciding when the treasurer should hedge risks or take them.

❑   Giving clear objectives about how much risk the treasurer is allowed to take on.

❑   Assuring that those executing deals are not involved in settling or valuing them.

It should also be appreciated that the "gambling treasurers" trend has much wider implications. One of them is that investors should think twice before buying shares in an industrial company if they know that most of its profits came from speculation rather than manufacturing.

8.   Can External Advisors Help?

Because the whole business of financing has radically changed, regulators will be well advised to extend their authority over the treasuries of industrial and merchandising companies; for instance, making all firms disclose in their accounts the outstanding value of their trading positions and the highest and lowest levels these reached during the year. It is a sound policy to ask that companies disclose the following:

❑   What they expect of their treasury.

❑   How much freedom it has been given to take risks.

❑   The controls imposed upon it.

❑   The amount of profit and loss it makes.

This will not stop treasurers from losing money in derivative products, but it will significantly increase accountability and reduce the propensity to gamble. It will also make treasury departments more sensitive to the need to get advice on *derivatives risk management*, until they are able to fly on their own.

There is no free lunch. For many users of derivatives, the real problem is very basic: lack of goals and lack of know-how about how to *choose* and *manage* OBS instruments. For these reasons, many companies now look for outside help to educate them in derivative products and risk management.

The banks themselves are tapping this rich source of business. Bankers Trust is among the leaders in the risk-management consulting field.[11] There are also other companies that specialize in giving advice on risk control, such as Tokai Bank Europe, an affiliate of a Japanese bank, and Emcor Risk Management Consulting in the United States.

Bankers Trust claims to have been successfully handling some companies' risk management for about three years. It currently advises over 20 firms on risk control. Its clients are both bigger and smaller companies, and they turn over all or a portion of their risk management duties.

Tokai's risk-advisory business got into gear in 1993. Its boss says his team is doing as much business as it can handle all the way to Thailand, where it contracted with the Industrial Finance Corporation (IFC), a government organization that lends to domestic companies. The project aims to help the treasurer of the firm analyze risks better, provide the client with the technology for managing risk, and educate the IFC staff about risk-management products and their usage.

However, some treasurers are not sure, and for good reason, whether banks that are also selling derivatives products can be impartial advisors. Therefore, independent risk consultants are springing up to give them more impartial advice. Emcor Risk Management Consulting, for example, currently advises some 30 companies on risk control, while certified public accountants are also becoming active in this field.

How well suited are these advisors for derivatives risk management? It depends on their experience and their research facilities. Rocket scientists contributed models and knowledge artifacts to help manage exposure. Their presence serves two major purposes:

❑   Opening up new business opportunities.

❑   Helping control risks.

Because of their background and training, rocket scientists provide the know-how necessary to establish the financial equivalent of the mi-

---

11 *The Economist*, October 1, 1994.

croscope in the derivatives business, particularly in connection to complex products. They determine the exact nature of the investments to be made and define how to control the risks embedded in the different deals.

However, every board and every treasurer should know and appreciate that mathematical experimentation, analytical finance, and good advice are not the end of the risk-control business, but the beginning. Carrying out a risk-management strategy is the board's responsibility, and it must be a continuous concern. It can also be an expensive process, as simulators and real-time computers and networks are needed to track positions.

Both mainframes and PCs are unable to handle anything but the simplest transactions. Approaches able to analyze an investment portfolio and handle more complex transactions involve sophisticated software, knowledge-enriched artifacts, and high-performance computers, as well as rocket scientists and staff well versed in risk-management instruments.

Many problems can be solved through skill and funding, but only a few companies have the skills, and only a few hundred firms do enough risk-management business to justify the cost, hence the conclusion reached by some treasurers that it may be cheaper to pass risk-management to someone else.

Responsibility, of course, can never be delegated. The board and senior executives of the client companies have to make the final decisions, even if they rely on the risk management advisors to decide which derivatives products to buy, which execution capabilities to acquire, and which systems can best keep track of open positions.

In conclusion, advisory services on risk management seem to have a good future, both with medium-sized and large client firms. Having a knowledge consultant enables the bigger company to have a benchmark against which it can compare what it can do for itself, assisting the treasurer in his or her risk-management functions—provided these functions are properly defined.

9.   New Perspectives for Risk Management

The message that sections 6, 7, and 8 have conveyed is that there is a major cultural change in the way industrial companies conduct their treasury operations, converting themselves into nonbanks. The problems are many, but by far the most important is lack of skill in derivative financial instruments. Contrarians might say that not everything that is happening is all that new.

Multinational industrial companies have been entering into currency contracts for nearly two decades. At the same time, futures and options trading on exchanges has been hot for more than 10 years. But it has not happened at the pace or involved the vast amounts of money today on the block.

The dazzling growth in off-balance-sheet dealing takes place in OTC derivatives—the tailor-made contracts which really took off in the mid-1980s, and the pace accelerated in the 1990s. Because many over-the-counter deals are custom-made, they are making the business complex and difficult for treasurers, bankers, and regulators to get their arms around.

The derivatives portfolio of a given OTC dealer may still include many plain vanilla swaps, in which the bank and an end user—say the treasurer of a manufacturing firm—will have exchanged floating rate for fixed rate, dealing entirely in one currency. But these plays and players are recently outweighted by the more exotic contracts that get beyond *binary risk* and into a *combination* of risks.

For instance, interest rates and currencies. Or call and put contracts, which theoretically counterbalance one another but in reality compound risk. We will talk more about them in Chapter 10.

Take an oil company that faces the risk of oil prices dropping and interest rates rising. To hedge, it might buy an oil price floor and an interest rate cap. But it might also enter into a contract that would pay out only if oil prices are low and interest rates are high at the same time. This is a distinctly *nonlinear* combination.

Just as complex is the case of a British bank whose loans so far have been made almost entirely to British companies and a California bank whose loans are almost totally on the West Coast. The two institutions decide to diversify by swapping exposures. The British bank takes over some of the California risk and vice versa. Such a deal might even make sense, but it is hardly controllable in a sound management sense.

For instance, presently there is no dependable index of credit losses in Britain that is valid for California, and vice versa. This puts both banks at a disadvantage in valuing their exposure. Those kinds of indices are in their infancy—and this is a good indicator of how convoluted the derivatives business has become.

The difficulty in understanding all the particularities and future results of a deal is compounded by an organization and technology that does not live up to the task. In terms of risk management, not only industrial companies but also banks typically run separate and incompatible books:

- ❑   A spread book.

- ❑   A volatility book.

- ❑   A basis book.

- ❑   A yield-curve book.

❑   A currency book.

❑   A country book.

The spread book trades swap spreads using Treasuries to hedge medium- to long-dated swaps and a combination of futures and Treasuries for the short term. This is complex enough, but it is not integrated with the volatility book, which tracks deals in caps, floors, captions, floortions, swaptions, and spread options.

Lack of integration also characterizes the basis-book deals with spreads between different floating-rate indices, such as prime and commercial paper versus LIBOR. Other books are structured to arbitrage changes due to movements in interest rates, while the bank's rocket scientists run their own show in calculating delta, gamma, theta, kappa, and rho.

10. The Special Case of the Offshores

Still other problems arise from investments that have been made in dubious companies and obscure holdings—and sometimes in not-so-well-known markets or illiquid markets. A case in point is the growing horde of offshores.

The word *offshore* raises images of exotic places, but offshore investment can be as close to home as Dublin or Luxembourg. Starting with the fundamentals, with offshore and onshore, there are major differences between unit trust and investment trust funds.

The distinction regards open-ended funds, such as unit trusts, and closed-ended funds, the investment trusts. Funds tend to be launched this way because it is quicker and cheaper than setting up a new investment trust in one of the major financial markets. Regulation is lighter, and the tax treatment is more favorable. Also, managers have greater freedom to invest in the newest, riskiest emerging markets than they would with a New York-, London-, Paris-, or Frankfurt-based fund.

Offshore closed-ended funds tend to plunge into emerging markets. A number of recent offshores are single-country investment funds, which are riskier than broader-based regional or international ones. Most are aimed at institutional investors. Though there is sometimes the possibility of spectacular gains, the investor also runs much bigger risks by putting money in untried markets.

There are also other problems to consider. Putting aside Cayman Island and its likes, even markets such as Dublin and Luxembourg are much smaller and less liquid than New York, London, or Tokyo. Therefore, it can be difficult to get the size of order you want, and the bid-offer spreads may be wide.

Also, most of the offshore markets do not have market makers. Deals go through on a matched-bargain basis. If turnover in a particular fund's shares is low, the investor could have to wait for a counterparty to surface.

Investors may have to buy shares without knowing the real current asset value. This can be particularly worrisome in the more volatile emerging markets, which may fall 20 percent from one month to the next. For these reasons, closed funds have a limited life, and the majority of investors are expected to stay in from launch to windup—as every treasurer, banker, or other investor should appreciate.

9

Derivatives Financing Versus Debt or Equity Financing

1. Introduction

When we deal in derivative financial products, and most particularly in equity derivatives, we had better be sure what is in store for us in terms of risk and return. Chapter 8 pointed out that the fact that corporate treasurers engage in off-balance-sheet operations in an increasingly intense way changes the valuation procedures regarding equity in industrial companies. There are also other factors to keep in mind.

Several years ago, Dr. Franco Modigliani of the Massachusetts Institute of Technology and Dr. Merton Miller of the University of Chicago developed what is now known as the Modigliani-Miller theory. Leading economists today believe that this theory made two distinct breakthroughs.

1. It proved that under certain conditions the value of a firm is the same whether it finances itself with debt or equity.[1]

---

1 A conclusion that tends to favor debt over equity, as we will see in section 2.

This suggests that the corporate treasurer who worries about how to raise the firm's capital might actually be wasting his time. If the Modigliani-Miller theory is correct, he can choose debt or equity as he pleases.

2. It advanced a new economic methodology: the law of *one price*, which says that two similar assets must cost the same amount.

The law of one price has since become the backbone of several models in finance, but it is not generally accepted. By contrast, the law of equal value (see No. 1 above) seems to have more or less established itself and also been justified by tax issues, as taxation tends to favor debt over equity.

For tax reasons, there is no simple trade-off between debt and equity financing. Debt financing is cheaper than equity financing because investors take on less risk when purchasing debt, which results in their accepting a relatively lower return. But debt financing also has a greater volatility due to interest rates and is therefore more generally seen as a burden.

When a company swaps some of its equity for debt, it may reduce its cost of capital and increase its value. Part and parcel of the equation, however, is the fact that the firm becomes too heavily indebted. Equity holders and debt holders will start demanding higher returns to compensate for the risk.

This reaction means that the firm's cost of capital will rise. Hence, between the extremes of issuing all debt and all equity, there must be some cost optimization by establishing the appropriate debt-to-equity ratio. We will be looking into this matter, starting with the Modigliani-Miller hypothesis.

2.   Prevailing Forms of Financing

When a company needs cash, it issues equity, primarily addressing itself to its current stockholders. Alternatively, it issues debt in the form of corporate bonds or makes bank loans. Each one of these methods has variations. Common stock pays a variable dividend, nonvoting stock pays a higher dividend, and preferred stock pays a fixed dividend.

Bonds pay a fixed rate of interest, but there are bonds with variable interest rates, and there are zero-interest bonds. There are also distinctions between bullet (straight) bonds, redeemable bonds, and many others—some 25 main types.

Warrants give rights to buy stocks at a given price. Convertible bonds can be converted into stock. Bank debt usually pays a fixed interest, but there are also loans with variable interest rates, for which companies buy caps and floors, a derivative financial instrument.

❑   The loan the bank gives may be secured or unsecured.

❑   Senior debt is serviced first.

❑   Preferred stocks are senior to common stocks.

When a firm issues new equity, the price of its stock falls because managers, who are also shareholders, have better information than the other shareholders and are likely to sell when stock is overvalued. This looks like insider trading, and in a way it is; it is not quite legal, but it is not quite illegal when it is not done in a massive sense.

There are other reasons why the price of a share falls. For instance, it falls after there is a decrease in dividends or when an expected dividend increase does not materialize. In general, dividends are smoother than earnings. Directors do not like to increase dividends if they have to decrease them next time around. In a way,

❑   A company's equity is like an option. Acting on behalf of equity holders, management may undertake very risky projects.

A similar principle is true for investors. Gold mine shares, for example, can be seen as a call on gold.

❑   Under normal conditions, debt is less risky than equity. But because management cares mainly about shareholders, there may be debt overhang problems.

In principle, debt imposes discipline on managers. It also eliminates uncommitted cash flows. Not all managers, however, like to be disciplined, and they can always find a way to break ranks.

❑   This is also true with equities. That's why modeling equities and debt is a taxing job.

❑   For the same reason, it is often quite difficult both to prove and to disprove the different theories regarding equity and debt.

Usually, reasons given to substantiate a new theory are qualitative rather than quantitative, though because of the influence of macroeconomics and of the analytics associated with derivatives trades, quantification has entered into finance in a big way .

In their original paper, as well as in subsequent cases, Modigliani and Miller tilted towards debt over equity. Other economists have done the same, citing the fact that

❑   A company that issues debt can deduct interest from profits before paying taxes, but

❑   It cannot deduct from profits dividend payments or the capital appreciation of shares.

Other economists have the opposite opinion, arguing that the tax advantages of debt are balanced by the risk that a heavily indebted firm might be unable to pay its creditors.[2] Optimal debt-equity ratios usually weigh tax savings against bankruptcy risk and its costs.

However, for most well-managed companies the threat of bankruptcy is insignificant. The risk could hardly offset a potential corporate tax saving of 34 cents a dollar after the tax reforms of 1986. Other countries have an even higher tax burden on equity dividends, in some cases in excess of 50 percent.

In spite of the Modigliani-Miller theory, however, because of the culture surrounding debt many economists think that replacing debt with equity is a healthy policy—and so do investment managers and market analysts. For the individual company, lowering interest costs can increase profits and give companies a financial cushion to fend off hard times and/or face increasing global competition.

But is the market according higher price-earnings ratios to companies issuing equity? The answer is situational. In the 1980s, the more leverage a company had, the better the market liked it. By contrast, in the 1990s it *looks* as though investors see the issuance of equity as positive.

In spite of theories and countertheories, there are no fast and dirty answers to this equity versus debt problem. Every case must be answered within the perspectives of each time and market sentiment—as well as the conditions prevailing in a given company. Theories are good, but practice—and therefore actual decisions—might be a different matter.

3.   Company Stocks and Financing Through Equity

Textbooks say that corporate *common stocks* represent ownership. In reality, what shares represent is *residual* claims on assets, after the parties with priority claims have been satisfied. This is substantially different than what an "ownership" argument seems to suggest.

What the ownership of common stocks does not provide is in a way offered by *preferred stocks*. The latter constitute a sort of priority claim, and they are considered by many experts to be nearer to the concept of debt than that of equity. Preferred stocks and convertible bonds are two different sides of the same coin, though legally they do not represent the same issue. They are both hybrids of stocks and bonds, where preferred stocks

---

[2] "I would like to have a one-arm economics advisor," President Truman is rumored to have said, "so that when he advises me he does not add: 'On the other hand . . .'."

❏ Pay a fixed dividend.

❏ Take priority over common stocks.

Some preferred stocks are convertible to common stock. In this sense, preferred stocks are similar to convertible bonds, as the foregoing paragraphs have suggested.

The reason investors buy preferred stocks is that they offer protection against dividend cuts. Much of their attraction comes from the fact that the cash-strapped issuer is required to cut the dividend on its common stock before it cuts the preferred payout. This provides not only a cushion, but also a warning signal. For these reasons,

❏ The ability to calculate the fair value of an equity is not as forward as it might seem.

❏ Marking-to-market is one thing. But what is the *real* value?

As defined by some financial analysts, the *cost of equity* is the return on equity required to get the market value of a company's equity shares to equal its book value. This can be expressed as a spread for the majority of companies whose shares often trade at a discount to their net book value.

But what is the book value? The answer might look simple, since the books are there for every knowledgeable person to see, and companies, at least in most developed countries, publish their balance sheets. But in reality, it is not that simple.

First comes the question of what is written in the books. Aside from the fact that some companies keep double books, each quite different from the other, even one set of books in one company does not really compare with those of another firm:

❏ The laws vary quite significantly between different countries in terms of disclosure.

❏ Even within the same country, management is keen to exploit the loopholes and flexibilities in the law to its advantage.

A good example in terms of the first reference is the listing of German shares an the New York Stock Exchange (NYSE). Time and again, Germany's biggest companies have hit a brick wall in their drive to list their stocks directly on Wall Street because their accounting system, with its hidden crash reserves, runs directly against the American way of disclosure for small investors—and SEC regulations.

This impasse symbolizes a roadblock to the globalization of financial markets but also tells a story about the way in which different markets value their stocks and bonds. No two countries have the same legislation regarding securities.

According to SEC regulations, companies must provide information allowing investors to align their accounts with the rules governing U.S. balance sheets. German companies have refused to do this because they would have to disclose their hidden reserves of cash. They argue that

❑ These secret pools of money allow them to take longer views of their markets and investments.

❑ Hidden reserves make it possible to iron out yearly fluctuations that necessarily occur in any firm. U.S. regulators and exchange managers reply that the practice of hidden reserves facilitates insider trading and can deceive stockholders. Therefore, they don't accept the argument.

The hefty number of 200 German blue-chip stocks are involved in this issue of applying for listing in the United States and are being refused. Many of them now trade as American Depository Receipts (ADR), which permit investors to participate in dividend payments and capital gains of foreign stocks deposited with U.S. banks but do not require issuers to conform to U.S. accounting standards.

ADR has been a loophole in American securities legislation, which was discovered and exploited in the 1920s by Dr. J. P. Morgan. ADRs are now institutionalized and continue to be a loophole in SEC regulations because they are not really registered shares in exchanges in the United States.

The German ADRs generally trade via the so-called pink sheets, daily price listings of over-the-counter issues. The market is not as liquid as the main exchanges, and it usually attracts notice among the narrow, albeit growing, circle of American investors putting their money outside the United States. That's a sort of "in-house offshore" of the kind we saw in Chapter 8.

4. Can Value Investing Determine the Fair Value of Stock?

Sections 2 and 3 posed the question What's the fair value of a company's stock? The corollaries to this question are How can we tell when a stock is overvalued and when it is a bargain? Such questions cannot be answered simply; they require a fairly complex response.

The theory runs that *if* we can see smarter pricing criteria than the markets, *then* we will win. But that's theory. The credibility of so-called *value investors* was bruised in the soaring bull market of the 1980s and again in the early 1990s, as followers of the smart stock-picking styles trailed market averages badly.

❏ As the great bull market of the 1980s became increasingly speculative, investment strategies that measured the relative cheapness
of stocks fell out of favor.

❏ What often mattered most was whether a company could be spun
off into separate businesses, streamlined, or otherwise radically
transformed.

According to conventional logic, in a bear market value investors
should have staged a comeback. When the stock market takes a broad
hit, the only shares likely to outperform would be those already selling
cheaply.

But reality does not always follow that logic. At the end of 1989,
the cheap stocks proved to be banks, insurance companies, and brokerage firms. These companies were hurt badly by severe collapses in the
real estate and junk bond markets; their prices reflected that fact.

There were also bubbles. One of them hit the Australian Stock Exchange with several collapses, the more notorious being that of Alan
Bond, the Australian highflier who spent the 1970s and 1980s building a
brewing, media, and real estate empire on debt. Said one disgruntled
London broker, "A bunch of us were trying to calculate whether it
would be cheaper to use [Bond Corp. debt] certificates or wallpaper to
cover the walls."[3]

While in some cases value investing might help save the money
that goes down market drains, it offers no sure course. Developed by
two Columbia University business professors, Benjamin Graham and
David Dodd, value investing is a method for analyzing the intrinsic
worth of companies in the wake of the 1929 crash and rests on three
basic criteria.

1. *Price/earnings (P/E)* ratio measures the annual earning power of
   a company relative to its stock price.

The higher the multiple, the higher the prices people are paying
for a company's growth prospects. The ratio is arrived at by dividing
the current stock price either by last year's earnings per share or by an
estimate of the following year's earnings per share. Value investors usually target firms trading at least 20 percent below the average S&P 500
multiple.

2. *Dividend yield* measures the relative size of the annual dividend or payout the investors receive versus the current stock
   price.

---

3 *Business Week*, August 13, 1990.

Dividend yield, which is found in the financial pages of newspapers along with the P/E multiple, is expressed as a percent of the current stock price. Theoretically, the higher the dividend payment relative to stock price, the better. Practically, dividends are manipulated, with some companies selling assets to pay higher dividends—a practice discouraged both by SEC and by the Fed (for banks).

3. *Price-to-book* ratio measures the value of the company's assets versus the current stock price.

This multiple is determined by dividing the current stock price by a company's total value per share: assets minus debts. This can be calculated from financial statements found in annual reports and gives an indication of a company's value if it is liquidated. But, as already stated, the values written in the books are sometimes questionable.

If they act according to the theory, value investors must go through a two-tier selection process. First, they must establish the criteria they like best and by which they think the market will eventually come to judge stocks and therefore upgrade the prices.

Once this is done, value investors have a list of suitable candidates. Thereafter, they must use their judgment and pick the firms whose business they believe has the best prospects. This, too, is theory. However scientific the definition of *value* might be, investing remains an inspirational business—and a risky one at that. Nor is any one of the three metrics listed above applicable with derivatives. Instead, the metrics delta, gamma, theta, kappa, rho[4] are applicable, but since they involve the value of the underlying, it is a good policy to keep these value ratios in mind—for whatever they are worth.

In conclusion, the question posed in the title of this section is answered in a rather negative way. Value investing cannot tell what the fair value of stocks is, and in some cases it might give misleading answers. A much more thorough financial analysis is necessary. If it is unavailable, the investor makes her bets and takes her chances. Miracle answers to not exist, but the proper homework can provide considerable insight.

5.   Profit and Loss with Equity Derivatives

In the financial markets of America, Europe, and Japan, trading of derivative securities, such as stock options and futures, is growing fast. Although the European markets started later with off-balance-sheet in-

---

[4] Which will be discussed in Chapter 15.

struments, today their business is growing about three times faster than U.S. trading.

There are several reasons for this trend, other than speculation. Futures and options contracts are cheap to trade and don't involve any copyrights. Stocks do not travel as easily. Already, daily trading of NYSE-listed stocks through the London Stock Exchange amounts to at least 20 million shares, more than 10 percent of NYSE volume.

Eventually, a *stateless* electronic market trading several hundred world-class securities is likely to develop. Much like the Eurodollar, it could become a prime capital-raising mechanism for corporations besides serving the global market of stocks and bonds.

It is not difficult to understand how *equity derivatives* derive their value and their risk. Say, for instance, we do not buy Exxon stock, but instead buy a call on Exxon. That's an option entitling us to buy Exxon stock within a specified time at a specified price. From this point on, the value of our call—which is a derivative vehicle—is going to be determined by what happens to the price of Exxon stock, which in trading is known as the *underlying*. For instance, what will be the effect of the $5 billion judgment for damages in the *Exxon Valdez* disaster?

❑ The cost of the call, or the premium, will be relatively small and this gives us great leverage if the stock does well.

❑ But if the stock falls, the call could be worthless, and the investor will lose what he or she paid for the option.

Options, such as the Exxon call, are one of the basic kinds of derivatives. Another is forwards, such as forward rate agreements. An example of a forward contract is the swap.

As the Exxon example helps document, equity options have their challenges. Interest rate exposure is another interesting case, and the two can be related. Most experts agree that the most difficult risk hedge in the European Exchange Rate Mechanism (ERM) crises, particularly the one of September 1992, has been the interest exposure on equity options.

Equity derivatives are influenced by interest rate levels. The latter are fundamental to the pricing of equity options because option models assume funding at a risk-free rate. However,

❑ Changes in interest rates affect the value of the option, a sensitivity known as *rho*.[5]

❑ In the case of a call, an interest rate hike increases the price of the option to cover higher funding costs.

---

5 See Chapter 15.

A rate reduction has the opposite effect on calls. But the reverse holds true for puts: Interest rate increases reduce the value of the option and vice versa. These are variables that must be factored into any model aiming at a more or less accurate valuation.

Other factors are also important. The shorter the option, the less effect interest rate changes have on the option's price. This is the general principle, but the effects can be magnified if it is particularly hard to get hold of very short interest rates.

As a matter of fact, in the case of the ERM crisis, the most difficult risk to hedge in some markets was short-term rates. This posed significant problems of coordination within the bank, along the concurrent engineering lines: If trading takes place in a way that the interest rate and equity derivatives desks are not closely linked, big problems lie ahead in achieving a reasonably good equilibration between the price-determined factors.

Linkage between desks with different interests, and therefore integration of trades, is a culture in itself. Not only does it require first-class specialists, it also requires advanced technology and sophisticated knowledge-enriched software—all the way to the ability to capture and exploit high-frequency financial data.[6]

Another type of equity derivative that is used for hedging but also involves risks is stock index futures. A stock index futures contract is an agreement in which its writer (seller) agrees to deliver to the buyer an amount of cash equal to a specific dollar amount times the difference between the value of a specified stock index at the close of the last trading day of the contract and the price at which the agreement is made.

No physical delivery of the underlying stocks in the index is made. The successful use of stock index futures contracts, and options on indices, depends upon the investment adviser's ability to predict the direction of the market and is subject to various risks. The correlation is imperfect between

❑ Movements in the price of the stock index future.

❑ The price of the securities being hedged.

The risk from imperfect correlation increases as the composition of a portfolio diverges from the composition of the relevant index. There is no assurance that liquid secondary markets will exist for any particular futures contract or option at any particular time.

---

6 See also D. N. Chorafas, *Rocket Scientists in Banking* (London and Dublin: Lafferty Publications, 1995).

6.   Using Commercial Paper and Disintermediation

Traded by securities affiliates of commercial banks, bank holding companies, and other institutions, equity derivatives provide a significant source of income—and of exposure. As we have already discussed, new sources of income are necessary as banks have lost much of their role of intermediation between deposits and loans. Big-name companies no longer pay fees to an intermediary to sell all their commercial paper. They market large chunks of it themselves.

IBM has taken this one step further, setting up the IBM Money Market Account, which is marketing commercial paper to its shareholders but is open to anyone with $2,500 to invest. British Petroleum set up its own in-house investment bank that

❑   Issues commercial paper.

❑   Performs interest rate and currency swaps.

❑   Performs mergers and acquisitions.

Du Pont has a mergers and acquisitions unit that averages about 20 deals a year, ranging from $5 million to $500 million. Until it sold its derivatives unit in October 1995, Eastman Kodak conducted foreign exchange trading and hedging, up to $25 billion yearly.

General Motors Acceptance Corporation, the financing arm of the automaker, was one of first to handle its own commercial paper. Today it has a total portfolio of $26 billion. Philip Morris bought Jacobs Suchard, a Swiss coffee and candy producer, for $4.1 billion, using its own staff. It only engaged investment bankers for market analysis and fairness opinion.

Much of the money that flows with a bank's intermediation comes from direct placement with institutional investors. But since 1990, SEC elaborated new rules that tend to make direct placements more difficult. Under them, money-market funds could not hold more than 5 percent of their assets in paper rated below top investment grade as opposed to the 10 percent they used to hold with no cap.

The curbs put on commercial paper—such as short-term, highly liquid, corporate IOUs—have companies howling that they will be forced to pay a lot more for loans. Those affected include such household names as Philip Morris, Marriott, and Union Carbide, which loaded their balance sheets with debt in the 1980s. Concerned over several defaults by commercial paper issuers, SEC aimed to protect investors in money-market funds from future debacles. That is a reasonable concern because today funds hold one-third of the outstanding commercial paper.

Historically, failures by commercial paper issuers have been rare. But the 1990 defaults by Integrated Resources and Philadelphia-based Mortgage & Realty Trust sent a shiver through the financial community, even though the funds maintained their record of never passing losses along to customers. SEC of course fears that investors won't always be this fortunate.

Critics of the new measures bring up the daunting example of the savings and loan bailout bill, which required thrifts to divest themselves of junk bonds. In doing so, the measure helped to sink the junk bond market:

❑ While it saved the thrifts from a much greater exposure,

❑ It closed off a reliable method of financing for fledgling companies.

Part of the fear of regulators is that with an R&D arm in full swing, the financial industry may bring to the market more risk instruments, such as *high-high* bonds and LYONs[7] or other inventions.

The message the reader should retain from this discussion is TINA: *There Is No Alternative* to a rigorous analysis of *risk* and *reward*. Not everything that shines is gold. Bankers, traders, and investors who go for the crust of the cake will be left with a bitter taste after they have made a commitment.

7. How Investors Get Trapped with High-High Bonds and LYONs

Optical illusions happen in finance as they do in any business. High yields don't really need to be high if the price of the instrument is huge, too. Low yields might be higher—and sometimes asking whether high is low and low is high is like arguing about whether a zebra is black with whites stripes or white with black stripes.

The title "high-high bonds" was coined in Japan where they originated, by all accounts, at the beginning of 1994. In the months until the end of 1994, Nikko Securities alone is said to have underwritten around 500 billion Yen of them ($5.2 billion).

High-high bonds got their name because they have a high coupon, giving the impression that their yield is high. But they are sold at a high price, which makes the real yield lower than average. The World Bank and Sweden were among the borrowers that took advantage of this cheap source of money—because investors don't take the time and care to analyze what they buy prior to commitment.

Some of Nikko's rivals claim that mutual funds run by its investment management affiliate were forced to swallow these high-high bonds. Others suggest that the indifference of small investors to risk

---

7 Both are explained in section 7.

explains why such bonds can be sold. Indeed it seems that smaller Japanese investors, including regional banks and municipal pension funds are not too fussy about what they buy. They simply don't look at the bonds' overall return—or for that matter the risk involved.

Yen-denominated bonds also look relatively attractive to Japan's small investors because returns on alternative investments are even lower. In mid-1994, for instance, banks offered an annual compound rate of 2.9 percent on four-year deposits. That is well below the yield on the World Bank's yen-denominated paper—even if it is "high-high."

The other example mentioned in section 6 is the *Liquid Yield Option Note* (LYON). It is a convertible zero bond which, however, assumes peculiar risks over and above those the zero bond itself features.

The concept behind zero convertible bonds is that investors buy them at a large discount from face value. They give zero interest payments until the bonds mature, typically in 15 to 20 years, when they are redeemed at face value, but they are convertible into stock at any time. If the stock shoots up, the LYON suddenly becomes a lot more valuable. That's a gamble.

For brokerage houses, these instruments can mean handsome fees. Issuing corporations are interested in them because they raise money from the public at below-market rates and also defer the interest payments for years. But the product is not universally appreciated, precisely because of its embedded risk.

Critics of LYONs say buyers can be disappointed, while from the issuer's point of view, it is almost a no-lose proposition. This seems to be one of the rare cases where finance becomes a zero-sum game. To make money with LYONs, the stock has to keep going up at a rapid rate. Only then do investors profit. But there is always the risk that the company issuing them will file for protection under Chapter 11 and that creditors will be left holding the bag.

Treasurers who have rocket scientists and a couple of smart lawyers to work with them have found new ways of financing that are neither via equity nor via debt, but fall somewhere in between. Investments may be blown "this way" or "that way" depending on a never ceasing series of discoveries.

8.   The Great Variety in the Securitization of Mortgages

Like many of the traditional financial instruments, mortgages are the raw material that Wall Street restructures into the securities that investors have been buying for years. Mortgage-backed financing (MBF) relies on a pool of individual mortgages that serve as its collateral. The MBF market is huge, with issuers raising $418 billion in 1993 alone. But as these securities get more complex, staggering losses mean much smaller issuance of mortgage derivatives.

In the early 1990s, a large number of the successful trades in MBF were done on the basis of the lowest interest rates in 10 years. The sudden increase in short-term interest rates in 1994 brought a sharp price drop, which led to greatly reduced trading in the MBF market—it also led to a vicious cycle.

Big investors sold Treasuries to meet margin calls, further boosting overall interest rates. The biggest hits were at two of Wall Street's most innovative creations:

❑ Interest-only (IO) strips.

❑ Principal-only (PO) strips.

To make them, rocket scientists strip apart the two elements that underlie mortgages, packaging interest and principal payments into separate securities. Both offer some of the highest fixed-income returns available—but they evidently have significant risks.

To understand why the IO and PO markets imploded, we must appreciate what individual homeowners do when interest rates move. This is fairly predictable for small changes that affect behavior, but the computer models are usually not geared to face sharp market moves, nor have they been built for the whole variety of MBF vehicles available.

Mortgage derivatives are fairly complex instruments and can be of many kinds. There are PACs, TACs, Z-tranches, and a whole alphabet soup of variations on the IO/PO theme. They are all part of the so-called Collateral Mortgage Obligations (CMO), which range from the rather predictable to the highly risky.

❑ Plain vanilla CMOs are the basic product, consisting of income from a pool of mortgages.

❑ Planned-amortization class CMOs are a version less vulnerable to risk of mortgage prepayment.

❑ With interest-only strips, investors receive only the interest portion of mortgage payments.

❑ With principal-only strips, investors receive only the principal portion of mortgage payments.

❑ Z-tranche CMOs are highly risky because payments are made only after other investors get paid.

Rapidly rising rates halt mortgage refinancing. For a holder of a PO, that means waiting longer than expected to get the principal repaid. Since the PO's initial price was based on a shorter payout period, it plunges in value. By contrast, IOs benefit from rising rates, because as repayments slow, interest streams lengthen, and the holder gets interest for a longer period.

If you are thinking of following the practice of offsetting, take notice that the two risks don't necessarily balance out. Even professionals went wrong in thinking they could hedge IOs with POs. It seems logical that a price drop in the PO could be offset by a price rise in the IO. But hedges work only if there is liquidity in the market.

As investors fled the MBF, prices on POs tanked; IOs moved up slightly but hardly enough to offset the fall in the POs. Market-neutral positions that hedged IOs with POs turned upside down—and this is a good example of what happens with many schemes that are supposed to hedge.

Derivatives risk management is not that easy. On the mathematics side, the rocket scientists have to revisit their analysis of MBF securities and their derivative products. The tools used to project returns will have to

❑   Deal with a broader array of potential outcomes.

❑   Take liquidity well into account.

But there is also a managerial and marketing side that needs reengineering. It regards the crying need to pay attention to bondholders who, after all, put their money on the line.

Bondholders used to be an afterthought in a corporation's investor relations; they were also of secondary importance to brokers and investment banks. The main focus has always been the shareholders. Yet bondholders are most crucial, particularly for

❑   Debt-burdened companies.

❑   Securitized products.

To stay alive, companies that carry an inordinate debt level often have to persuade creditors to swap high-interest junk bonds for cash, stock, or less valuable paper. That means these companies must step up efforts to please bond investors, soliciting their goodwill. The same is true of MBF issuers.

Keep in mind, however, that not all public relations campaigns and the financial deals underpinning them work. Even the threat of imminent demise does not always carry the day. Bondholders are doing their own computing about who to trust.

In September 1990, as it was sinking deeper into trouble because of failed loans, the Bank of New England tried to engineer a $700 million swap with bondholders. Yet creditors backed away, thinking the move was too late. They were right. Regulators seized the bank three months later, on January 6, 1991.

9.   Virtual Financial Products Are All over the Market

The big exchanges in Chicago learned they could make an easier living by selling virtual wheat and virtual hogs in the commodities pits. Dealers and investors could buy a hog future and turn a nice profit before the real hog ever showed up. Virtuality is the freedom that the market gives with futures and options.

After having taken farming and changed it into high finance, the Chicago exchanges turned their attention to financial products themselves. They introduced futures and options so that investors could buy and sell virtual stocks and virtual bonds—altering the traditional meaning of debt and equity.

These vehicles became a big hit among professional and fund managers, who used derivatives to hedge their positions whenever they were afraid they owned too many real stocks or underliers. Wall Street caught up with this business and started to develop new lines of virtual financial products, which were popularized under a variety of curious names:

❑   ELKS, or equity-linked securities.

❑   YEELDS, yield-enhanced equity-lined securities.

❑   CHIPS, common-linked, higher-income participation securities.

❑   REMICs, real estate mortgage-investment conduits.

Designers of derivatives like to say their products are used mostly by people who are trying to reduce risk to themselves and the market. Bankers and traders downplay the fact that off-balance-sheet financing provides exciting betting opportunities for billion-dollar speculators. Potential payoffs are very high, and so are the risks.

Some people are in the derivatives trade without even knowing it. As we have seen in section 8, if you have a home mortgage, you are most likely involved in securitization, whether you like it or not. There is a good chance your mortgage will not be kept in one piece by the banks that lent the money. Instead, it will be part of a pool of mortgage-backed securities, which in turn can become raw material for other derivatives—the REMICs.

While being restructured into a new entity, it is quite possible that your mortgage has been chopped apart. We spoke in section 8 about the principal-only (PO), and interest-only (IO) securities.

Bond funds use IO derivatives to add yield to their portfolios and make aggressive bets on the direction of interest rates. But as we have already seen in examples of the February/March 1994 bond bloodbath, this strategy can turn belly-up.

Let's add another case. A portfolio reportedly worth about $500 million has been badly bruised after playing a forward rate agreement (FRA) game. The fund that owned this portfolio speculated on the price difference between two sets of mortgage-backed securities. When interest rates rose quickly, the speculative scheme fell apart.

Leaving aside what individual players may be suffering, the case of systemic risk is always in the background. Two trillion dollars in mortgages is now bound up in mortgage-backed securities, up from zero in 1970. Just like MBF trades on the strength of the underlying mortgages, other derivatives are floating over the real world of stocks, bonds, wheat, and hogs.

This situation has a great resemblance to the 1920s, with its investment pools and trusts. A series of shell companies was piled on top of a real company, most often a dividend-paying utility. Each shell company offered a dividend that was dependent on its receiving the dividend from below. Yet, its price reached such lofty heights that the value of the original company, the underlier, was lost from sight.

Eventually, the investment trusts of the 1920s came crashing down. One of the most celebrated operators, Samuel Insull, erected a structure of 65 companies that operated utilities in 32 states. By 1932, the Insull empire had completely collapsed in a $750 million loss for investors—more than $10 billion in today's currency.

10. The Popularization of Financial Software

Whether they place more emphasis on financing through debt or equity, banks need to rise to the market's demands rather than just stand by and watch their primary income sources continue to shrink as today's customers become tomorrow's competitors. If they fail to take control while there is still time to develop and implement strategic alternatives, their customers or their competitors and shrinking profit margins will make the decision for them.

As the examples we have seen in this chapter help document, methodology and technology are the most important components of risk management, and R&D is the key ingredient in developing new value-added services for customers. Indeed, the real issues for this industry from any point of view—strategic directions, new services, revenues creation, cost control, and risk management—is the choice of a course of action that responds to the market's drives and its effective implementation. This increasingly means sophisticated and personalized investment proposals, since the bank's most important customers are willing and able to shop around both for better service and lower costs.

A sound investment proposal must be based on a financial analysis that is customized and focuses on all issues that could affect the level of risk and return. Increasingly, product design factors include specific experiments on

- ❏ Credit risk.
- ❏ Market risk.

For international proposals, they involve the visibility the investment will have in the host country; outline the prevailing laws in terms of ownership, majority, and minority shareholder rights; and provide documented information on the protection of proprietary trade secrets, patents, and other issues.

In the past decade, a significant amount of attention was paid to project financing. Today, it tends to be generalized to a growing number of financial products. The very competitive markets and the most wealthy clients are no longer satisfied with the vanilla ice cream banking that is taught in many business schools.

Vanilla ice cream banking is presently done through commodity software, and the foremost providers of programming products position themselves in that market. "Managing finances is a pre-eminent application that the electronic world will advance. Microsoft wants to be there," said Bill Gates, Microsoft's chairman, when he made public his intention to purchase Quicken for $11.5 billion.

Had it gone through, this deal would have been the largest acquisition in the history of the software industry, demonstrating the ability of Microsoft to bolster its market leadership through acquisitions when it lacks products. Intuit's Quicken is used by about 6 million PC owners, or 75 percent of all active personal finance software users. Microsoft's competing Money program has captured only a tiny share of the market since its introduction in 1992.

The acquisition was projected to roughly double Microsoft's sales of software specifically designed for personal computer users. It would also have given Microsoft an immediate entry into the emerging market for home banking which, after 16 years of going nowhere (since Viewdata in 1979), seems to have taken off.

Through partnerships with Visa International and Checkfree, Intuit has established direct on-line links with financial institutions and a system to allow individuals to pay the bills electronically.

In addition to its home-banking arrangements, Intuit offers on-line updates of mutual funds' performance and other financial data to the users of its software. Intuit had itself recently acquired the National Payment Clearing House, an electronic bill-paying service, which had been processing payments for users of Microsoft Money.

Let's take notice that anything offered as commodity software becomes commonplace, even if it used to be sophisticated. Every one of our competitors can have it and every end user as well. Therefore, we have to move forward with more advanced developments able to leave our competitors behind. Eventually, they will catch up—but hopefully by then we will be way ahead once again.

10

Synthetics and Exotic Derivatives

1. Introduction

In an attempt to reduce risk in trading, banks, investors, and speculators tend to employ sophisticated strategies that might decrease exposure in the highly leveraged off-balance-sheet market. Or at least they *hope* that through synthetics and exotic derivatives they will be able to bring their risk under control.

One of the more widely used strategies involves the use of spreads, known as straddles, which we will study in this chapter. As market transactions, spreads enable the trader to profit not from the rise or fall of a single commodity futures contract but from a widening or narrowing in the price differential, involving varying charge between two futures contract months.

Are "financial exotics" appropriate? To a large measure, the answer depends on what is meant by *exotics*. For analogical reasoning purposes, the concept of *noise* can be used to explain that everything is relative.

In physics and in engineering, noise is defined as any unwanted input. Even chamber music can be noise when one wants to sleep. A more fundamental definition, however, is that noise distorts other signals that are the focal point of our measurement. In that sense, financial derivatives are not noise; they are part of the signal. They are the result of the steady pressure for innovation in the financial markets. But complexity introduces noise in risk calculation, possibly distorting other signals.

Proponents of synthetics and exotics are quick to suggest that this effect will disappear as these vehicles become more popular. This might be so, but the fact remains that a major risk lies in the lack of redefinition of financial responsibility.

In this chapter, we will examine a number of derivatives trades known as "exotics." Let's not lose sight of the fact that a financial instrument considered exotic today because it is not that well-known can become commonplace tomorrow. It happened with what are now considered the more traditional types of derivatives.

2.   Synthetic Positions: An Example with Currencies

The stated objective of OBS transactions is to reduce risk and enhance returns. But the statements being made are often contradictory, and the risk-free solutions, which they promise to provide, are, for evident reasons, rather elusive.

Synthetic positions usually consist of a combination of derivatives products, such as the examples we will see in this chapter. The term *synthetic long position* refers to the use of an option and a future with the same effect as one long option position. Whether we talk of calls or puts, the algorithm is

Synthetic long option position =
futures position + long options position

A good example of synthetics can be taken from foreign currency trading. Currency futures in $; £, DM, yen, or other moneys can be used to create synthetic foreign currency futures contracts.

Buying one currency future and simultaneously selling another helps to generate the equivalent of a currency futures contract. This derivatives vehicle is either denominated in a money other than the basic currency of reference or provides a cross-currency futures spread.[1]

If, for instance, a German trader expects the British pound to appreciate relative to the dollar, he can buy pound futures and sell dollar futures. A future exchange rate between the pound and the dollar will be expressed by the algorithm

$$\text{FV (\$/£)} = \frac{\text{FV (DM/£)}}{\text{FV (DM/\$)}}$$

---

[1] See also the example on straddles with exchange rates in section 5.

where

FV = the future value of the money, expressed as the ratio of two currencies

This synthetic position will be profitable *if* both the £ and the $ appreciate with respect to the DM, but the pound appreciates more; or, alternatively, both the £ and the $ depreciate in respect to the DM, but the $ depreciates more.

Most particularly, this trade will make sense if the prognosis is that the £ appreciates relative to the DM, while the $ loses ground in the DM/$ exchange rate. Notice that in the first two cases, one leg of the foreign exchange spread loses money, but the other leg gains more money than these losses, leaving a net profit.

By contrast, in the third case, which can be the more profitable, both legs make money. This is the optimal result to be obtained from a synthetic position.

Bankers, traders, and investors active in the market of off-balance-sheet financial vehicles who are long or short in underlying instruments are increasingly interested in combining such positions with long/short puts or calls on the same underlying. This job is done through synthetics and exotics:

❏ Synthetics are usually custom-made products.

❏ Exotics, too, are customized instruments such as embedded options.

This is precisely the reason why from synthetics to spreads, straddles, and strangles, which we will study later on in this chapter, the instruments are difficult to evaluate in terms of market and credit risk.

Some investment banks do not advise over-the-counter trading of exotic options, preferring the liquidity and transparency of exchange-traded financial instruments. Indeed, there is a large number of possibilities that analysts and traders can exploit through a combination of exchange-traded derivatives.

At the same time, there are occasions where the flexibility of OTC options outweighs other disadvantages. For instance, "knocked-in" or "knocked-out" options can result in considerable cost savings compared to exchange-traded deals—*if* traders and investors know how to establish the pricing and control the risk.

3. Synthetic Long/Short Option

Sophisticated option strategies employ a number of positions involving calls, puts, different strike prices and expiration dates. Some are long, owning, or short of the underlier. Many combinations are possible through the use of synthetics because there is equivalence between certain options positions, as shown in Table 10–1.

Table 10–1. Synthetics Through Options and Underliers

If you are exposed in options	Then you are having a synthetic
Long put at price P and long on underlier	Long call at price P
Long call at price P and long on underlier	Long call at price P
Short put at price P and long on underlier	Long call at price P
Short call at price P and long on underlier	Long call at price P
Long call at price P and short put at price P	Long instrument
Short call at price P and long put at price P	Short instrument

A long underlier, short call position has the same effect as a short put position. This is shown in Figure 10–1, which presents an example from equity derivatives.

This analogy has evident implications on the interdependence of put and call options of the same strike price and same expiration date. However, as the market turns, these don't need to balance each other out the same way.

Forget about offsetting. What is good to remember is that at any given time, and for a period that is reasonably limited, short call, short put, and underlier positions can be combined into an overall P+L framework. The levels and slopes of the lines entering the pattern in Figure 10–1 can be derived by constructing a table.

❑   Calculates P+L for a range of underlying prices.

❑   Subsequently helps to plot individual graphs per instrument, as well as a composite graph.

For instance, buying the equity and selling a call on that equity produces a situation equivalent to a put whose price must be related to the price of the call. But we must also take into account different times at which cash flows occur. If the deal is not balanced, there will be an arbitrage opportunity.

Similarly, synthetic futures are created by combining two options. A trader aiming to customize a financial product in response to client

Figure 10–1. Synthetic Graph of a Long Underlier, Short Call Position, Equal to a Short Put Position

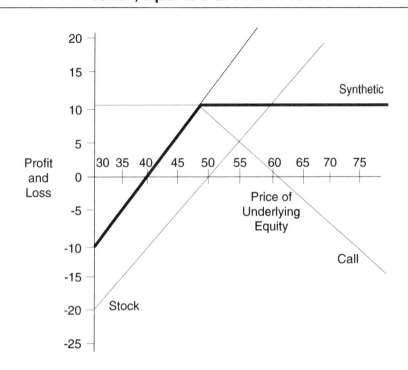

requirements can generate a *synthetic long futures* by combining long call options and short put options of the same strike price. Conversely, synthetic short futures are made by combining long puts with short calls, also with the same strike price.

Synthetic futures sales use a combination of put and call options. By simultaneously buying a put option and selling the corresponding call option, a trader can construct a position analogous to a short sale in the futures market.

For instance, a synthetic stock index future can be used to create a synthetic index fund. The investor may purchase futures as a substitute for cash, investing the proceeds in a short-term credit product. If the position is held until expiration of the futures contract, when cash and future prices converge, risk and return are about identical. But if the position is liquidated prior to expiration, the synthetic index deal faces greater risks than a comparable cash index instrument.

The synthetic has the advantage of lower overall cost, lower custodial cost, no cash outlay, and no tracking error. It has the disadvantage of market risk, which in this case is composed of price risk, rolling risk, and variation margin. Among the advantages of a long stocks position (cash) are dividends and the fact that the operation is simpler. The disadvantages include higher initial costs, custodial costs, and possible tracking error.

In a synthetic futures transaction in gold, for example, the holder of a synthetic short future will profit from a drop in the price of gold and will incur losses if gold prices increase. A long position in gold call options combined with a short sale of gold futures creates price protection that is analogous to that gained through purchasing put options.

The position holder will tend to profit from a decline in gold prices and will face a loss if the price of gold rises. The synthetic put seeks to capitalize on disparities between premiums. An analogous statement can be made of synthetic calls.

Other synthetics can be generated by combining options and futures positions. For instance, a synthetic long call option is made by a long put option and a long futures option. A synthetic long put option is created by combining a long call option and a short futures option.

As these examples help demonstrate, synthetic futures are proxies for short or long futures positions. Two reasons synthetics may be more attractive than outright futures positions are that they can be less costly, and they have lower margin requirements.

A more potent reason, however, is that synthetics provide the traders with the opportunity to develop new financial instruments that appeal to investors, even if they do not quite understand their consequences if the market turns against them.

As it cannot be repeated too often, the more sophisticated the financial product, the more knowledge is necessary not only to design it and sell it, but to hold it.

4.   Hedging with Spreads and Synthetics

There is a wide range of synthetic options offered in the financial markets. Among the simpler are those that actively combine puts and calls, doing so in various ways. As a rule, credit risk and market risk are much greater with synthetic options than with simple option positions. As we have already seen, with market transactions spreads

- ❑   The trader does not profit from the rise or fall of a single commodity futures contract.

- ❑   The trader gains from the widening or narrowing in the price differential between two options or futures contract months.

Spread trading can be done both by writing and by purchasing puts and calls contracts. After taking account of costs and premiums, the change in the differential between the two contracts corresponds to the trader's profit or loss.

In spread trading, one futures contract is sold. After taking account of the costs, the change in the differential between the two contract months corresponds to the trader's profit or loss.

The problem with synthetics starts with the design of the option itself. The first basic step is to look at the financial market and its evolution, subsequently focusing on the sector of the market where the option addresses itself. As always the *actual* versus *projected* price fluctuation is at the origin of the profit or loss to the bank and to the investor. But this price fluctuation is much more difficult to forecast in the case of synthetic derivatives because the price-driven positions multiply.

A relatively simple case of synthetics may involve long calls, long puts, short calls, and short puts in some ingenious combination. Figure 10–2 offers an overview of what a synthetic position may involve. Traders tend to think that combinations similar to this example are relatively simple and sure profit makers. But this is far from being the case. As the market turns, one position does not compensate the other. To avoid inordinate risks, traders have to bring their undivided attention to all four quarter spaces—and their combination.

This example explains why, in general, synthetics are created by putting together long and short options as well as long or short underlying financial instruments. Therefore, for risk-calculation purposes, it is wise to unbundle a synthetic package to its atomic level. This permits

❑ The individual examination of long and short positions.

❑ The attribution of risk by element, followed by the integration of risk factors.

Simple synthetics deals may not be difficult, but they get increasingly complex as the number of combinations and permutations increases in handling them. This requires both first-class knowledge and advanced technology in models and computers.

While the basic idea underpinning a synthetic option may be reasonable, the execution might leave much to be desired. For example, say that in 1991 a manufacturer of gold jewelry made a large purchase of physical gold when the metal was selling at $400 per ounce. The drop in gold's value forced the manufacturer to discount the retail price of his jewelry. Hence, he immediately established a short position in gold futures, hoping to hedge his risk.

Following up on this scenario, the first news that came in from the market was positive to his view. The gold price collapse of 1992 saw to it that his hedge protected him from almost $72 an ounce in losses. Therefore, he continued his hedge. As a contract approached final delivery, he rolled into a later contract.

Figure 10–2. Even a Relatively Simple Synthetic Option of Four Quarter Spaces Can Be Complex Enough

	Calls(s)	Puts(s)
Long	Premium Strike Price	Premium Strike Price
Short	Premium Strike Price	Premium Strike Price

The jewelry manufacturer's calculation showed that his exposure was equivalent to owning 500 ounces of gold. Hence, he maintained a five-contract short position in gold futures.

But at the end of 1992, his broker advised him to buy gold, as there was a low in gold prices. If gold rose in price, the extra profits from jewelry markups would be offset by losses from the short futures position. If, however, the manufacturer removed the futures position and gold prices fell again, he would have nothing left to offset his mark-down losses.

In theory, if he had a gold call position rather than owning physical gold, he would have control over losses. In practice, he could not dispose of his physical gold unless he elected to go out of business.

As a solution, he followed the advice of his broker. With the broker's help, the gold jewelry manufacturer synthesized his position, given that physical gold correlates well with the near-term gold futures contract.

The principle is that if one is long on the underlying instrument and wishes to have the equivalent of long calls in options at exercise price P, he need only purchase puts of exercise price P. The long position in the underlier, and the long put position synthesizes a long call position.

This approach saw to it that the gold jewelry manufacturer's downside losses stopped at the level of the put option he bought. His profits, however, would be open-ended if gold prices rallied. His net position would be synthesized a long call with price at the put options specified price.

On the other hand, if gold prices rose, the manufacturer would lose the premium he paid for each option. This is an acceptable cost for the gold price protection he received, but let's not forget that the betting is done by a professional who uses gold as raw material in his work—and the betting is reasonable, not speculative.

For instance, if the gold jewelry manufacturer bought 100 contracts of 100 ounces each for the 500 ounces of metal he owned, he was not hedging but speculating. The first five contracts would be fitting in the scenario we have seen. The others will be positions open to fluctuations in the gold market—for better or for worse.

The same principle applies in the banking industry. *Backspreads* are established when an institution buys more contracts than it writes—whether these are puts or calls. While all contracts may have the same maturity, for delta-neutral reasons the bank may have to buy a different number of puts and calls, as higher and lower strike prices have different premiums.

5. Straddles

A *straddle* consists of the purchase or sale of both a put and a call, on the same underlying futures contract, with the same expiration date and exercise price. In this sense, it consists of a put and call with everything else the same. Taking exchange rates as an example, the put and the call in a straddle are struck at the same exchange rate and have the same expiration date. As we will see, by buying both the call and the put in a long straddle, the trader or investor bets that exchange rates will become volatile. The assumption is that this volatility will push either the put or the call in-the-money by more than the total cost of the two options.

By contrast, the writer of a straddle—who is faced with a short call and a short put—expects (or more likely hopes) that the premium he receives from the sale of the two options will cover the amount either option is in the money and will leave a profit. In essence, the writer is *selling volatility*, while the purchaser buys volatility.

A different view of the same type of trade is that bankers and investors spread to reduce risk, since changes in the price differential between their long and short positions, the so-called *legs*, are usually more gradual than the price changes on either leg and because due to the reduced risk associated with spreads, exchanges tend to have lower initial margin requirements for this form of dealing.

Another trader might purchase a long straddle if he believes the underlying futures contract is going to make a sizeable move, but he is not sure in which direction. By purchasing both a put and a call, he hopes to make money in either direction if he properly places his bets.

A trader might write a short straddle if he has the opposite outlook on the market, that is, if he is hoping for little or no movement in the price of the underlying futures contract. As we have seen in the foregoing example on interest rates, a short straddle is written by a bank or investor who believes that the market will remain relatively quiet for some time. If there is little volatility, the short put or call positions will not move significantly, resulting in no or only a little payout to the buyer.

By contrast, long straddles are established when the investor anticipates significant volatility and associated price movements in the financial market. Therefore, both short and long straddles should be designed, in response to the investor's sentiment as to which way the market will move.

There are risks associated with straddles. The P+L of a short straddle of, say, selling at-the-money calls and puts on the same U.S. long bond can change dramatically on a –5 to +5 percent change in the futures. Figure 10–3 shows that the underlying exposure of the short call and put options is equal to half the portfolio value.

This graph helps to explain why there has been so much painful experience related to writing options and why it is so important to have a good risk-management system able to keep track of exposure with derivatives on a real-time basis and through interactive access to market information and databases.

This need is particularly pronounced when, in an attempt to reduce risk in trading, banks, investors, and speculators employ sophisticated strategies. These are thought to decrease market exposure in the highly leveraged futures market. But if the available know-how *and* the supporting technology are not fine-grain, the result will be exactly the opposite.

6.   Strangles: One Step Further in Complexity

As we have seen in this and the preceding chapters, with all trading strategies there are different market views. These lead to scenarios adopted by investors that are usually conditioned by a given risk/reward ratio. Generally, in developing a scenario on how to bet, the following concepts apply:

❑   In the so-called carrying-charge markets, or *contango*,[2] nearby delivery months trade at a discount to more distant contract months.

---

[2] See section 7.

Figure 10–3. Change in Portfolio Value as a Result of a Change in Futures Price, in Connection to a Short Straddle

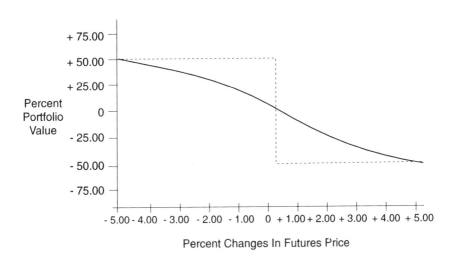

Percent Changes In Futures Price

❑ The legs of a spread will tend to move in the same direction in response to price changes, but not always by the same amount.

The opportunity for profits or losses on spreads finds itself in the variable rate of movement. Price changes in the distant contract months tend to exceed spot price changes because of the effect of the carrying charge, due to the prevailing interest rate:

❑ A rally would cause the distant contract months to gain on the nearby months, therefore widening the commodity's spreads.

❑ A decline in price would prompt the distant months to fall faster than the nearby months, causing a narrowing of the spread.

Under market conditions such as severe shortage, demand for the commodity can push up prices in the nearby months to a premium over the distant contracts. When this occurs, the market has inverted and is said to be in *backwardation*.

For these reasons, the experienced spread trader must be aware of the possibility that inverted markets will occur. Such markets can materially affect potential profits and losses. Spreads do not behave in textbook fashion. We will discuss this further in sections 7 and 8, when we look into greater detail into contango and backwardation.

A *strangle*, is a strategy that leads one step further in complexity. A strangle consists of the purchase or the sale of both a put and a call, on the same underlying futures contract, with the same expiration date but different exercise prices.

❑   The call is above the market.

❑   The put is below the market.

Hence, the two exercise prices bracket the market. In principle, traders and investors consider strangles to be more aggressive than straddles; but in terms of design, the two have considerable similarities:

❑   Short strangles are taken when projected market volatility is very low.

❑   Long strangles are made by buying puts and calls with the same expiration date but different strike levels.

A trader would purchase a long strangle if he believes the underlying futures contract is going to make a sizeable move, but he is not sure in which direction. Breakeven is determined by adding the premium paid to the call and subtracting it from the put exercise price.

The buyer's risk is limited to the total premiums paid. Therefore, he would be hurt by time delay in a nonvolatile, reasonably stable market. His hope is that his potential profit is unlimited—this being somebody else's risk.

A trader would sell a short strangle if he believed there was going to be little or no movement in the price of the underlying futures contract. Breakeven is determined by adding the premiums collected to the call and subtracting them from the put exercise prices. In this case the writer's maximum profit is limited to the premium collected. In contrast, his risk is unlimited.

There are other trading strategies more complex than straddles and strangles. For instance, a *butterfly* is a combination of four separate puts and calls.

❑   A *long butterfly* is similar to a short straddle, but tends to have a somewhat more limited risk.

❑   A *long butterfly* is structured by buying the low and high strikes and selling the middle strikes.

When strikes of the different options are further apart, traders talk of a *condor*. The condor has the potential for greater profits but also for more significant losses, depending on the way the market moves.

7.   Capitalizing on Contango and Backwardation

Bankers, traders, and investors have three main strategies in connection with any commodity. They can go *outright long* through futures, forwards, and swaps; they can use *options* alone or in combination with outright positions; and they can implement a bull spread strategy through a backwardation swap.

In most commodities markets, the crucial determinant of the price differential between two contract months is the cost of storing that commodity over the chosen time frame. Hence, markets tend to compensate an investor for *carrying charges*, including

❑   Interest rates.

❑   Storage.

❑   Insurance.

These are known as full *contango* or full carrying markets. Futures contracts in the precious metals markets almost always reflect the interest charge above the others. Because the cost of storing gold, platinum, and silver is very low in relation to the total value of the contract, one can interpret the price differential between spot and futures contract months with precious metals as an interest rate plus a small insurance and storage cost. Carrying costs vary, however, as institutions and sophisticated investors attempt to arbitrage implied interest rates in the gold, platinum, and silver markets.

In principle, the contango structure of the futures market in gold is kept intact by the ability of bullion dealers and financial institutions to bring carrying charges back into line through arbitrage. When carrying charges are greater than prevailing interest rates, dealers will buy the physical commodity and sell futures, therefore earning the charges.

When carrying charges are below prevailing interest rates, dealers will sell their physical gold and buy futures, moving their cash into instruments offering more attractive returns. The net effect of these transactions is to keep carrying charges in the futures market in line with interest rates.

Another profit opportunity that might be significant exists when a distant month trades at a lower price relative to a nearby month. *Backwardation* is also known as inverted market, and might occur in situations where there is exceptional short-term demand for the commodity in the face of tightening supplies.

Backwardation can take place in commodities such as oil or copper in cases where storage and transportation problems may make it difficult to bring substantial quantities to market quickly. This happens due to major events impacting the market.

Taking as an example the oil market in the 1985 to 1994 time frame, we can see the following significant events. In the autumn of 1985, Saudi Arabia implemented netbacks in order to regain market share. The spring of 1986 saw a very strong demand for gasoline in America. Then, in August 1986, OPEC agreed to cut output by four million barrels per day (Mbbl/d).

The summer of 1987 saw the Tankers War. In August 1988, the Piper Alpha disaster occurred, which shut down 13 percent of North Sea production in addition to costing Lloyd's underwriters a fortune. In that same time frame; the autumn of 1988 experienced an OPEC overproduction. But in the 1988–89 winter, OPEC cut output by three Mbbl/d to regain control over prices.

In the Spring of 1989 the *Exxon Valdez* oil spill occurred in Alaska; while a year later in the 1989–90 winter, the East Coast of the United States experienced the coldest December in nearly a century.

Among significant events in the 1990s in the oil industry in the 1990s, the spring of 1990 brought OPEC overproduction, which depressed prices. But the invasion of Kuwait by Iraq on August 2, 1990, sent the barrel to $40, as shown in Figure 10–4. January 1991 saw Operation Desert Storm, and in the second half of 1993 oil prices slid on overproduction and weak demand.

All these events had a significant impact on oil prices. The future is not necessarily known, in spite of all the efforts at prognostication; but now that we have a scenario written with hard data, we can use it to develop a good example of what can be achieved through algorithms and heuristics—in terms of business opportunity and derivatives risk management.

8.   Setting the Stage for a Backwardation Swap

Let's start with the hypothesis that an investor has a view of the market that fits within the landscape defined by the events we have seen in section 7. In connection to oil prices, he has established his view on the term structure of the oil market, and he chooses to exploit this term structure—rather than the spot prices. Strategically, the investor positions himself to benefit from an appreciation of the price of the first nearby contract versus the third nearby contract. Such a backwardation swap rests on a spread scenario he sees as a means to gain long exposure—and it can be viewed as bullish.

Learning from past events, as described in section 7, the investor plans a three-year backwardation swap starting in May 1995 when he buys the first nearby West Texas Intermediate (WTI) contract and sells the third nearby at a fixed differential of –0.17 $/bbl. This means a contango of 0.17 $/bbl.

Figure 10–4. Outright Prices on the First Nearby Contract for West Texas

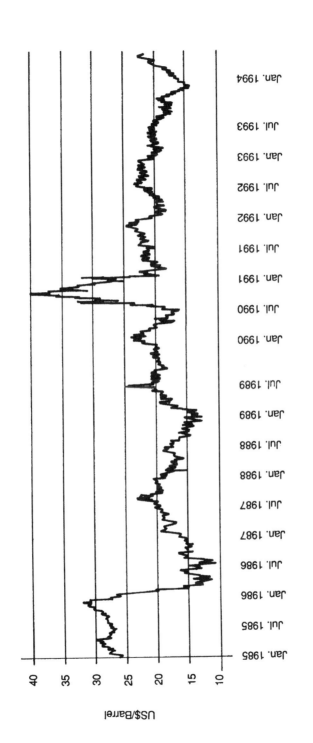

The settlement is quarterly, and the notional quantity is X barrels per quarter. The way this deal works, at the end of every quarter of the period May 1995–April 1998, we must compare the metrics S and F.[3]

❏ If $S - F + 0.17 > 0$, the buyer of the backwardation swap would receive $(S - F + 0.17).X$ at the end of the quarter.

❏ If $S - F + 0.17 < 0$, the buyer of the backwardation swap would have to pay $(F - S - 0.17).X$ at the end of the quarter.

where

S = average of the daily settlement prices of the NYMEX WTI first nearby contract during the quarter.

F = average of the daily settlement prices of the NYMEX WTI third nearby contract during the quarter

X must be selected in view of the size of the initial portfolio and of its yield. The whole trade is based on investors' expectation of the declining price. Looking back to the relationship between spot and futures prices, the algorithm is

$$SPP - FP = YY - RP - CC$$

where

SPP = the spot price
FP = the futures price
YY = convenience yield
RP = risk premium
CC = cost of carry

YY is essentially an insurance premium against the risk of a physical shortage of the product. In the event of a crisis due to supply or demand shock, YY is going to increase sharply.

In cases of war, major accidents, or extremely cold weather, there is no theoretical limit to the level of YY. But $YY = 0$ in the case of an oversupplied market, when buyers are quite relaxed and don't care to hedge.

RP, the risk premium, might be seen as an insurance against the risk of an adverse price change in the future price of the product. It

---

[3] These two symbols are the only ones that do not have a consistent meaning throughout this book.

represents the money an investor will demand in order to take the off-setting side of a hedge. Any scenario will rest on hypotheses:

- ❑ *If* hedgers are producers, hence net sellers, and investors are net buyers, then RP < 0, which is Keynes' Normal Backwardation theory.

- ❑ *If* hedgers are end users, therefore net buyers, and speculators are net sellers, then RP > 0.

In the case of strong prices, producers will have an incentive to hedge; hence, RP < 0. But when prices are weak, end users will have an incentive to hedge the other way around, and therefore RP < 0.

CC has two components. One is a pure financial cost, a direct function of interest rates and prices levels. The other is the cost of holding physical inventories and tends to be the predominant one of the two. CC is the maximum level that the contango can reach

$$FP - SP \leq C$$

Otherwise, a physical arbitrage becomes possible, buying the physical product, storing it, and selling it forward. Nevertheless, when inventories reach high levels, the cost of storing increases very sharply, as happened with the record contango in the spring of 1990.

The way to bet is that a strong market is likely to be associated with an oil shock, leading to high positive values for YY—or producers hedging. Hence, RP < 0. Then, a backwardation scenario is the way to bet

$$SP > FP$$

A weak market is likely to be associated with an oversupplied situation where YY = 0; end users hedging, or RP > 0; and full inventories. Also, high positive value for CC. By contrast, the strong market has normal CC.

A contango scenario is limited by the cost of storing. There is no theoretical limit to the level of backwardation. This is a fact investors often forget.

Regardless of a contango or backwardation market, over time, as a futures contract approaches its last day of trading, the futures price and the cash price will get closer together. This is known as *price convergence*, and it takes place in practically all markets. Therefore, it should be reflected in the algorithm.

Observance of this background information permits the step-by-step development of a model that can be nicely programmed for processing by computer, thereby making it feasible to experiment on different hypotheses on the basis of the investor's market view. This is the algorithmic part.

When seemingly everybody in the investment community is on pins and needles as to any hint of spike in oil prices, this algorithmic part has to be enriched with a fuzzy engineering artifact. The reader's attention has already been brought to the fact that fuzzy engineering can be instrumental in defuzzifying subjective opinion.[4]

9.   Embedded Options

The term *embedded options* (embedos) is used in connection with tailor-made derivatives deals. Among the different types are knock-ins, knock-outs, and look-backs—also known as path-dependent, or barrier, options. Other examples of high risk are

❑   Digital or binary options.

❑   Time-dependent or preference options.

❑   Outperformance options.

❑   Basket options.

❑   Quanto.

❑   Equity call and put spreads.

❑   Deferred payment American options.

Path-dependent options have a payout directly related to the movement of the underlier. A barrier option either comes into being (knocked in) or is eliminated (knocked out) when the market price reaches a predetermined strike level, that is

$$MP = SP$$

where

MP   =   Market Price

SP   =   Strike Price.

The better known barriers are

❑   Up and out.

❑   Down and out.

❑   Up and in.

---

[4] See also D. N. Chorafas, *Chaos Theory in the Financial Markets* (Chicago: Probus, 1994).

❑ Down and in.

From the buyer's viewpoint, the aim of buying a path-dependent option is to lower the premium paid to the writer, who is assuming a lower degree of risk than would otherwise be the case. By contrast, as its name implies, in a look-back option, the buyer will receive from the seller the greater profit regardless of the day of expiration.

The binary option has some interesting characteristics. It will provide continuous protection or payoff—with the purchaser paying or receiving one of two particular flows if a given price level is reached. The more popular binary types are

❑ All or nothing.

❑ One-touch.

The first provides the buyer payout, which is *all* or *nothing*, depending on the option at expiration. If it is in-the-money, the holder will receive a sum of money equal to the notional principal amount of the contract, which can be a big sum. If it finishes out-of-the money, the buyer will get nothing.

The risk implications of this type of contract are significant. While the writer of a digital option, or any other option, cannot be certain at the time the transaction is made that the stipulated money is at stake, he will be well advised to approach the digital option issue from a worst-case viewpoint. The writer's market risk equivalent exposure will be

$$RE_m = NP - Premium \tag{1}$$

where

RE_m = risk equivalence to market exposure

NP = notional principal amount

The buyer also has a risk, which in a credit exposure sense is RE_c. He is particularly open to the counterparty's ability to fulfill the contract in case he overcomes the market risk. It will be

$$RE_c = Premium + NP \tag{2}$$

Notice that some all-or-nothing binary options have a payout different from the notional principal. In this case, in equations (1) and (2), in place of NP should be written the total payout agreed in advance between writer and buyer.

The amount of risk being assumed with this type of exotic derivatives should be clear to bankers, traders, and investors. Provided the fundamental notions are put right, analogical reasoning can help in understanding the change in exposure, even in those cases that are considered to be less well settled.

Bonds, of which we talked extensively in Chapter 9 in connection to mortgage-backed financing, provide an example. Traditionally, they used to be the instrument vehicles of conservative investors, but since the last decade this has changed twice:

❑ First, in the 1980s, came the junk bonds (mascarading as high interest), with which some banks made a fortune and others lost one—or were even forced to liquidate.

❑ Then, in the 1990s, a growing number of bond derivatives became the instrument of choice for some investors and most speculators.

But in February 1994, as the era of relatively steady low interest rates came to an end, there was an earthquake in the bond market—without regard to which currency they were issued in.

Recalling the facts in a nutshell, the wave of selling started in New York and spread like a brush fire in Europe. February to November 1994, the price of bonds dropped anywhere from 7 percent to 20 percent, breaking historical patterns, and no one can be sure that the sellout has ended.

Traditionally, the price of bonds fluctuates up to 10 or 12 percent on either side; that's why they are conservative investment vehicles. A fluctuation of 15 percent is exceptional for AAA bonds, AA bonds, and government bonds. But in 1994 the downturn hit 20 percent of value because of derivatives leverage, and the prognostication was made by many experts that this might not be the end.

As can be appreciated, with derivatives at large, and most specifically synthetics and exotics, it becomes increasingly more important to calculate the level of exposure, subsequently bringing it under control—because the stakes are so much higher. It is the responsibility of top management to see to it that risks are

❑ Isolated at the atomic level.

❑ Computed in an accurate manner.

❑ Integrated into a valid exposure algorithm.

It goes without saying that computation should be interactive, provided through real-time simulation. Since binary options tend to be customized, they have to be supported through mathematical models and knowledge artifacts. It is unwise not to engage in trades unless the appropriate software is on hand. Able trading depends on fast software deliverables.

10. Guaranteed Bonds and Other Risky Derivatives

Superficially, *guaranteed bonds* appear the same as other bonds: They are fixed-income instruments. But contrary to what their name implies, they are really guaranteed by nothing. Also known as *structured bonds*, these are firmly rooted in the highly leveraged derivatives market with all this means in terms of investment risk. As far as bonds are concerned, generally we distinguish between real bonds and guaranteed bonds.

❑ *Real bonds* are issued by governments (gilts) or corporations. They offer a fixed income for a period of years, and what varies is the price at which the investor buys the income stream.

To calculate the yield of the so-called real bonds, we divide the coupon rate of the bond by the price, accounting as well for the time left to maturity.[5] This is compared to interest rates on bank deposit accounts and other investment vehicles competing for money.

❑ *Guaranteed bonds* are usually offered by mutual funds and other organizations investing in derivatives contracts, who promise that the investors' or treasurer's capital will be returned after a number of years.

This assurance is the sense of the guaranty which, as many investors fail to appreciate, is virtual rather than real. There is an unspoken credit risk: The counterparty offering the guaranty may fail.

There is, of course, a certain amount of confusion about the difference between a bond and a fund using derivatives and offering a vehicle that calls itself a bond. This confusion has been heightened by the recent trend for new fund launches to be sold to bond investors.

The so-called guaranteed bonds coming onstream are seeking to tap the liquidity of the huge bond market. *High income* and other misleading qualifications are just names invented by marketing people to persuade investors they are buying something that has the assurance of a real bond, as happened in the 1980s with junk bonds.

Another variety is guaranteed equity bonds, which theoretically combine a capital guaranty with some exposure to the stock market. In the United Kingdom, these products are aimed mainly at building society investors, who are more or less unaware of the risks they are taking.

Guaranteed equity bonds are fairly complex instruments, and even professional advisers find it difficult to assess them. There is no easy way to pick out the best buys; the answer depends on one's own assumptions, but some guidelines can help:

❑ All these bonds have slightly different minimum repayments.

❑ Different percentages of starting capital are linked to different multiples of stock index growth.

❑ Some have a cap limiting the maximum return, or have other constraints.

---

5 See also D. N. Chorafas, *Rocket Scientist in Banking* (London and Dublin: Lafferty Publications, 1995).

What the investor gets depends on his tax rate. Comparisons with other investments have to adjust for the fact that these bonds have many complex features attached to them, even if they are being sold to people who are believed to have no real grasp of how the market works.

Exactly because the name *guaranteed bond* is tricky and in a way inappropriate, serious traders and financial analysts warn individual investors to educate themselves about the nuts and bolts of derivatives as well as about their many nuances. They should do so before entering the structured bond market. But few people listen.

Hard lessons can be learned through failures. In the United States, James Carville, the Democratic political consultant, said:

> The day the 30-year bond rate dropped another 11 percent, I was beginning to understand real power. I used to think if there was reincarnation, I wanted to come back as the president or a .400 baseball hitter. But now I want to come back as the bond market. You can intimidate everybody.

The irony of all this is that structured bonds were originally designed to protect corporate treasurers against adverse movements in financing costs. If a company needed to hedge a loan against a possible rise in interest rates, a bank would be called upon to structure a bond whose income grew when interest rates rose.

This facility rests on the fact that structured bonds use the cash from standard fixed-income securities to gain exposure to highly geared derivatives. However, such a strategy involves laying out more money than going directly into derivatives, and it does not cut the risk, contrary to what dealers say.

Hedging through guaranteed bonds is just a way of talking, since an increasing number of players use them for speculation rather than for risk management. The attraction of structured deals is that they can be tailored to cover almost any view an investor takes of the market as well as the level of risk he wants to assume—in case he knows what he is after.

The point many people do not follow is that the high gearing of structured bonds can quickly turn significant profits into huge losses. As a matter of fact, a number of major losses made by the treasury departments of large corporations in recent years have been publicly announced as being due to "bonds," conveniently forgetting the adjective "guaranteed," which can be interpreted as speculation.

The fact that there is confusion in terminology is in itself a negative because many investors may think they have chosen a conservative scenario—which is not the case. Lack of appreciation of the major differences between bonds and "bonds" also raises fears that many investors are taking risks in this complex derivatives market without fully understanding what they are doing.

11

Hedging through the Exploitation of Market Inefficiencies and the Emerging Markets

1. Introduction

Hedging is a protective procedure designed to minimize losses that may occur because of price fluctuations. Investment instruments available in the commodity markets enable the hedger to shift the risk of price fluctuations with the goal of protecting his or her position. This, however, is true only up to a point, beyond which what is thought to be hedging may involve significant risks.

Uncontrolled risks have many consequences. One of the main stumbling blocks in the Mellon Bank–Dreyfus Fund merger has been the divided management attention because of troubles at Mellon's Boston Company. This is an investment management firm that Mellon bought from American Express for $1.4 billion in May 1993.

In November 1994, Mellon said it would write off $130 million as a result of losses on derivatives holdings by Boston Company's securities lending business (whose risks are detailed in Chapter 13), rather than pass the losses on to clients. Dreyfus sources thought these pressures have prompted deeper cuts in spending for business development, com-

pensation, and technological improvements than either company originally contemplated.[1]

A similar statement is valid about the ability to exploit *market inefficiencies* as well as the procedures and tools involved in this process. Up
to a point, we exploit market inefficiencies for hedging reasons, which
means we are protected from market surprises. Beyond that point, market inefficiencies are exploited for profit. As with hedging, this involves
considerable risk.

People able to capitalize on market inefficiencies can be both investors and speculators. The same is true about investing in the so-called
emerging markets, a euphemism coined to lump together securities markets of the developing world as having great ups and downs—hence,
high volatility. Investors and speculators do so for profits, but quite
often they sustain some hefty losses. The difference between them is
that

❏ Investors risk their own capital with the hope of making profits
from price fluctuations sometime in the future.

❏ Speculators risk the capital of others—usually borrowed or
trusted money. This is what the hedge funds do.

Speculators assume the risks that investors seek to avoid. But both
investors and speculators rarely stick to the investments they make in
the emerging markets—just as they rarely take delivery of the actual
physical commodity in the futures market. They close out their positions
by entering into offsetting purchases or sales of futures contracts.

One of the knowledgeable financial executives participating in this
research suggested that another way of sorting out investors and speculators concerns their propensity to write options. Conservatively managed firms have eliminated the practice of options writing. They also
see to it that counterparty risk is controlled by strict limits on the size of
deals done with companies listing less than AAA credits. But in emerging markets, AAA counterparties are rare birds indeed.

There is no ideal risk hedging, but a sound policy, whether with
derivatives or other instruments, requires frequent monitoring and
equilibration. The rebalancing of risks with options, futures, forwards,
and exotics has to be steady, preferably done in real time, and assisted
with models and computers. Swaps pose somewhat less critical time requirements, but no one is investing only in swaps.

---

[1] *Business Week*, January 16, 1995.

2. Goals and Procedures for Hedging Policies

Theoretically, the primary interest of hedgers is not in making a profit through the purchase and sale of options, futures, and other derivative instruments. Rather, it is to shift the risk of loss due to an adverse price change.

The hedging operation is made, for example, through a forwards or futures purchase or sale, to serve as a temporary substitute for a cash market transaction that will be made at a later date. According to this definition; the hedger

❑ Produces or uses the actual commodity.

❑ Uses the futures market primarily as a means of shifting risk.

The risk is shifted to other people who, for whatever reason, are willing to assume the hedger's exposure. Again theoretically, it is a speculator who assumes the risk that the hedger is trying to avoid. This *transfer of risk* is considered one of the most important benefits that investors and speculators provide to the futures market.

In practice, however, things are a little different because, as we have seen in the chapter introduction, hedging and speculation are divided by a very thin and flexible line. Companies and individuals who trade in derivative contracts are neither hedgers nor speculators all of the time. More often than not, they buy and sell futures and other derivatives for the purpose, not only of hedging, but of making a profit.

Treasurers and traders will take a long position in a given commodity when they anticipate that its price will rise, or take a short position when they anticipate that its price will fall. This may partly be a protective measure, but it is also partly an attempt to reap profits based on market sentiment.

If bankers, investors, and speculators are correct in their judgment, they will make a profit by entering bids and offers for a commodity. By so doing, they add to the liquidity of the market. That's the good news. The bad news is that at the same time they take significant risks.

Prognosis is neither always "right," nor always "wrong." Both right and wrong guesses are the moving gear of the market. By making them, traders, investors, and speculators help sustain a liquid market, which enables instruments to be quickly bought and sold. All hope to profit by correctly anticipating the direction and timing of price changes, and all who play in the market say that they do so for *hedging*.

After Procter & Gamble lost $102 million after taxes in leveraged swaps transactions in 1994, top management stated that its philosophy was to use financial instruments to manage risk and cost but not to speculate. Subsequently, the company announced the formation of a risk-management council, chaired by its vice president and comptroller.

The new policy, said the company's chairman, Edwin L. Artzt, was another "level of scrutiny" extending "well beyond normal corporate operating controls."[2] The risk-management council reports directly to the CEO and board of directors. It consists of senior managers from the various financial and purchasing units and meets monthly to assure that "hedging is hedging."

The objective of true hedging is the reduction of price risk for a defined volume of a specific commodity and for an established time period. Hedges for physical commodities using futures and options markets can be either straightforward or complex, designed with sophisticated objectives in mind. In both cases

❑ While the hedge programs reduce the *price risk* in the physical market,

❑ The hedger becomes subject to *basis risk* and other risks.

Therefore, a successful hedge program must consider all the alternatives available to achieve the proper balance among cost, reduction of price risk, and assumption of basis risk. The *basis* is the difference between

❑ The cash price of the commodity being hedged.

❑ The futures market price providing the hedge.

Some hedging scenarios may have only a small basis risk, while in others it may be substantial. There is no general rule good for all hedges, and therefore all types of risk and reward must be carefully studied.

Because investors and speculators may take either long or short positions in the futures markets or play with exotics, it is possible for them to earn profits or incur losses regardless of the direction of price trends. The same is true of market participants who, while not literally hedging their positions or requirements, use the futures and forward markets in following strategies designed to reduce overall risk—including that of cash positions they are holding.

Prior to the introduction of options to the commodities markets, the prospective hedger could use futures but was limited to choosing the timing and the degree to which he desired to limit his exposure. While he locked in a price, he lost the opportunity for further gain on a long hedged position if the prices moved down.

Hedging with options increases both risk and reward. It can provide protection against large losses while still permitting higher profits, at the cost of the option premium. Combinations of futures and options

---

2 *Business Week*, October 31, 1994.

are also employed, assuring a mix of cost, risk, and opportunity for added profits, as we have seen in Chapter 10 in the discussion of exotic derivatives.

3.   Hedging, Speculation, and Price Differentials

The usual approach to hedging is to trade futures or options in an underlying commodity that is closest to the quantity and quality of the commodity being hedged. But, at times, selective use of other contract vehicles can be advantageous.

In the energy markets, for instance, crude oil futures can be used for hedging heating oil. The selection can be influenced by the expectation of the future pattern of oil prices, both crude and its derivatives, choosing the hedge strategy in which the basis risk is considered most favorable.

Particular conditions existing at the time of initiating a hedge program will be the chief determinants of the hedge instrument and the scenario to be followed. A given strategy may exploit seasonal and inter-commodity price patterns in two ways:

❑   As a guide to selecting the hedge vehicle.

❑   In the evaluation of a hedge program.

However, the historical pattern of the direction of a commodity's price, or the extrapolation of the futures prices from the current spot price, is not a reliable guide to the pattern that spot prices will actually take.

Underlying seasonal variation in prices is the market perception of the general direction of prices in one or more commodities. As we have seen in Chapter 10, futures contracts can be flat as opposed to current spot prices for the same commodity. They may show steadily rising prices from the current spot price—a contango effect—or steadily declining prices from the current spot price—a backwardation. Both hedging and speculation involve risks but of a different type. Also, the motivations behind each form of trading can be different.

By means of hedging, producers, processors, salesmen, and users of commodities—or treasurers handling derivative financial instruments—try to obtain a form of price insurance that takes the guesswork out of projecting future costs or allows them to hold on to property without sustaining losses as a result of volatility.

Though a hedge is generally applied against a corresponding position in a given commodity, it is not necessarily a substitute for a cash market transaction sometime down the line. Like speculative positions, hedges are generally closed out prior to contract expiration, and there are bound to be profits and losses.

In its most genuine form, a hedge involves establishing a position in the futures market that is equal but opposite to a position in the actual commodity. For example, a silver producer long 100,000 ounces of physical metal may hedge by going short in futures contracts, establishing an equal and opposite position.

The concept of taking such equal and opposite positions in the cash and futures markets is that a loss in one market could be offset by a gain in the other market. In this manner, the hedger can fix a futures price for his commodity in today's market by using a protection from derivative instruments.

Theoretically, this process works because cash prices and futures prices tend to move in tandem, converging because of basis risk as each delivery month approaches and reaches expiration. In practice however, because the hedges are fairly complex, it does not turn out this way. One of the best recent examples, where heaven broke loose, are the oil deals in America of Metallgesellschaft (MG), of which we spoke in Chapter 1.

Theoretically, even if the difference between the cash and futures prices of a given commodity widens or narrows as they fluctuate independently, the risk of an adverse change in this relationship is considered less than the risk of going unhedged. This is also taken to be true of exchange rates of major currencies—since money is a commodity.

In a way that contrasts the strategy of the hedger, who seeks to avoid risk, the speculator willingly assumes risk by trying to predict price movements before they occur, thereby profiting from market volatility. In this sense, speculators make decisions to buy or sell based on their evaluations of the following:

❑ The supply/demand outlook.

❑ Psychological factors.

❑ General market trends.

Contrary to the hedger, who seeks merely to assure a certain stabilized economic result, the speculator makes his profits from the uncertainty frequently associated with fluctuations in commodity prices. Speculators tend to capitalize on the highly leveraged nature of futures contracts and other derivatives. Typically, leverage

❑ Depends on the amount of capital needed to establish and manage a trading book, and

❑ Is high in commodities futures trading because initial margins are relatively small in relation to the total value of the contract.

But this simple fact is also something that hedging and speculation have in common. Relatively small margins permit hedgers to turn to speculators—when they get greedy and think they can make a fast buck with no risk.

Therefore, as will be discussed in Part Three, the metrics we use must reflect risk adequately. It is wise to use *risk types* as a basic unit of analysis applicable to all kinds of hedges—whether speculative or not. We will return to this issue.

The concept we will examine from Chapter 13 onward is that of *value-at-risk*, with capital adequacy level being flexible and adjustable, depending on the bank's trading book and investment portfolio. What we will call in-house *risk capital* will give extra protection without having to cope with the argument of whether a given investment or trade was done more for hedging reasons or, inversely, for speculative purposes.

Figure 11–1 gives in a nutshell the sense of value-at-risk simulation, which will be fully explained through practical examples in Part Three. Real-time simulation can be a valuable assistance in derivatives risk management but only as far as there is a strong sense of responsibility among bankers and traders—accompanied by a system of accountability.

4. Dynamic Solutions and Wrapped Hedges

While the calculations leading to a hedge scenario may be sound, and the chosen hedge strategy may initially work, as the market changes the way to bet is that the chosen solution will become less effective. This is why there is a need for a dynamic hedging policy that sees to it that both *simulation* and *optimization* play a significant role:

❑ Through models and real-time input, we rehedge sufficiently, often to minimize risk.

❑ But we don't do so in a way that the execution of small transactions significantly increases dealing and settlement costs.

As I have emphasized on several occasions, costs should in a way be part of the hedging algorithm and of its optimization procedure. Otherwise, simulation is a theoretical exercise. Attention should also be paid to retaining the natural smoothing effect that time can have on market prices.

The balancing act with dynamic hedging is complex, as we wish to control risk while at the same time not miss the effects of an increase in volatility—and to avoid excessive costs and brokerage fees. Optimization can be done through models, and genetic algorithms are a good approach for reaching this goal.

Once the model has been built and is able to handle conflicting aims effectively, computers must be used in real time to monitor expo-

Figure 11–1. Real-Time Simulation Should Target Key Factors That Significantly Help in Derivatives Risk Management

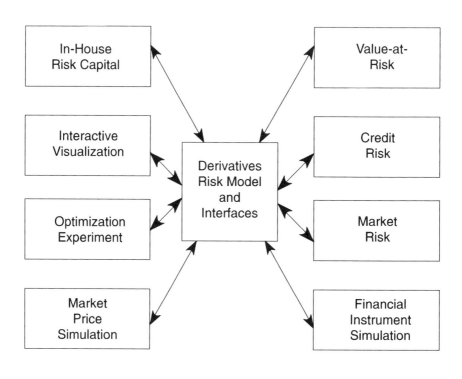

sure very carefully. By performing *what-if* analyses, traders—as well as the bank's management as a whole—will be able to judge if and when potentially risky positions are being accumulated.

The more complex the off-balance-sheet instruments being handled, the more this interactive approach to sensitivity analysis and experimentation is necessary. An example of a strategy where experimentation cannot only provide significant insight but is crucial is the *wrapped hedge*.

The wrapped hedge is a defensive strategy that locks in the gains made, for instance on a stock index, while letting the investor share in some of the upside potential that may be left in the issue. The technique involves buying a put option on, say, shares of General Motors, as a form of insurance when the market price for the stock is XX. The put allows the holder to sell the shares to the writer of the option at XX at any time until it expires. If the price of GM erodes before then, losses to the investor will be offset because the put will gain in value by a similar amount.

The other half of the hedge involves selling (writing) a call to recoup some of the cost of buying the put option. The call lets the buyer purchase GM at a price higher than XX, so the owner of the shares is capping his potential profits at that price, up until expiration.

Theoretically, the wrapped hedge is a good way to carry gains into next year to defer taxes while, also theoretically, eliminating the risk that one might lose the profits in a price correction down the line. Practically, however, this scenario must be rigorously tested in a through models and computers to avoid future surprises.

Some financial analysts think they have the perfect formula because theoretically there are certain nearly perfect hedges such as *put-call parity*. This is a relationship between the value of a European-type call and a European put option. Theory says that at any time before expiration, the difference between the value of a call and a put

❏   Orchestrated at the same strike price and

❏   Having the same expiration date,

is equal to the difference between the present value of the strike price and the present value—for instance, of the principal quantity of foreign exchange, using the foreign currency interest rate. But, once again, that's theory.

When adversity struck the bond markets in February/March 1994, similar put–call parity schemes made for hedging purposes turned sour. Huge losses made in one leg of the transaction were far from being covered by minor gains realized in the opposite leg—yet, that ingenious scheme was supposed to be fullproof as well as foolproof.

Another, more aggressive, options technique known as *covered call writing*, works best in gradually rising markets. The action resembles the second half of the wrapped hedge, in which the investor sells call options on shares he owns in order to gain premium income.

However, unlike the original wrapped hedge, covered call writing does not offer downside protection. For example, if a given stock on which the investor was betting tanks, he or she bears all the losses offset only by the amount of premium income taken in. The strategy also can backfire spectacularly if the stock zooms because it is a takeover target or for other reasons.

The notion of such risks may not be unknown to investors and speculators. The unknowns lie in the effects of leverage. Hence, a wise policy will see to it that experimentation precedes commitments and involves all crucial factors that may vary in function of future market behavior.

5.   Is There Profit in Exploiting Market Inefficiencies?

The first question to be asked is whether or not *market efficiency* exists, as Dr. Harry Markowitz and his Modern Portfolio Theory (MPT)[3] tend to suggest. The Efficient Market Theory is based on the premise that all outstanding information about companies is built into their share prices. By extension, this means that such shares are always fairly valued— which is not true.

One implication of efficient market theory is that there is no sure way of making gains in the stock market unless one is trading on inside information. This is also a false assumption, because even if a market is quick to digest earnings data, it can be grossly inefficient in valuing everything else.

In the long run, a variety of factors affect a company's performance. These may include the products in its laboratories, its sensitivity to market drives, internal cost controls, the quality of its production facilities, inventory surpluses and shortages, the land of the company's origin, the loans outstanding, and the quality of company management.

Not only are financial markets characterized by a more or less *inefficient* operation, but this could not be otherwise. At least four different levels of inefficiency are built into the financial and economic system:

1. Companies, whose equity and debt is traded in the market(s), are inefficient in one or (usually) more of the factors discussed above.

2. Market(s), in which companies are quoted, are inefficient because pockets of corporate weaknesses are not easy to uncover.

3. The sprawling market-to-market transaction process, which overwhelms practically all securities houses, is very inefficient.

4. Increased market complexity, introduced by global 24-hour trading as well as currency risk and country risk, is inefficient because there are few theories on how it should be handled.

Taking currency risk as an example, if the market(s) perceived every currency as equally risky, implied volatilities would be similar.

---

[3] Which, of course, is not that modern anymore. Since the early 1960s, many things have changed.

But as every currency trader knows, this is far from being the case—which is why it is difficult to evaluate and compare the implied volatilities embedded in currency option prices. Option prices convey better information about risk and return than the cash market does. But, this approach only goes so far and, as we have seen, there are layers of inefficiency affecting the price of money or of stocks.

Aside from the psychology of the markets, there are other reasons that all moneys and all stocks cannot be fairly priced. If they were, investment managers would not be necessary; trading would not improve investment performance; and brokers would earn large commissions for providing a useless service.

In the 1950s, prior to MPT, investors did not generally think about mathematical models when they set prices and built portfolios. Most thought about earnings growth prospects when they assessed price-to-earnings ratios. They considered single stocks rather than portfolio aggregates when selecting investment strategies.

The fact that the Efficient Market Theory—which, in fact, has never been more than a hypothesis—is a dubious proposition does not hinder securities experts from taking a methodical approach to the market. Because they perceive market inefficiency, leading securities houses focus on locating pockets of

- ❑ Overpriced stocks.
- ❑ Underpriced stocks.

While some brokers believe these can be identified by common factors such as price/earnings ratios, yield, and market capitalization, the more analytically minded traders and investors also investigate factors such as a company's strengths and weaknesses; forecasted growth rate in earnings and product leadership; and turnaround potential in P/E, documented by steps taken by management.

A sound strategy in unearthing a company's hidden efficiencies as well as its inefficiencies. Both are behind its past surprises in terms of performance. This tells a lot about management quality, which must be evaluated on a steady basis as well as through exceptional events.

On a national stock exchange (one on which country and currency risk are not factors), forward-thinking investment bankers and traders start from the premise that a market system is *inherently inefficient*—and they know that this inefficiency can be exploited to their advantage. This exploitation, however, gets more complex in an international market setting, particularly so with emerging markets where

- ❑ A still greater amount of inefficiency is built into the system.
- ❑ Information is scarce and filtered, therefore unreliable.

❏ Factors unknown to the home market come into play to upset existing models.

❏ Legislation is lax and spotty, with insider trading being the rule.

The New York Stock Exchange is very tough about admitting foreign companies into anything other than American Depository Receipts (ADR), and for good reason. The legislation in their country of origin is different and often lax, which alters the rules of the game and creates an uneven playing field.

By contrast, American investors—and most particularly institutional investors—take big risks in the stock exchanges of emerging countries where they believe the rewards could be higher. By so doing, they fail to properly appreciate the inefficiency and the risks.

A wise strategy is to have financial analysts specializing in foreign markets and foreign companies one by one. This will not increase the efficiency of the markets, but will improve the efficiency of the investment process—which is, after all, the process of exploiting market inefficiencies.

6.   Capitalizing on Market Inefficiency

The best way to capitalize on market inefficiency is by doing analytical studies substantiated through person-to-person interviews and followed up by thorough database mining: experimenting with simulators. Knowledge engineering artifacts and high-performance computers are invaluable, but they only supplement the human touch. They don't substitute for it.

Eventually, but with some delay, the results of a thorough financial analysis, and therefore the information that individuals use in their investment decisions, is incorporated into security prices. Inversely, investors use the information contained in security prices in their decisions to buy, hold, or sell.

Given these two premises, it is naive to think that market prices are arbitrary, but this does not mean that they are efficient. There are many factors impacting market prices, some of them psychological:

❏ Investors partially base their decisions on what they expect other investors to do, whether this is subjective or objective.

❏ Psychology plays a key role and investors do not only or always take into account the assets' expected payoffs.

As a general rule, the less speculative the investor is, the more he will base his decisions on estimates of the assets' expected payoffs and market appreciation (or depreciation) as well as other objective factors—though subjective factors will always be present.

It is generally said, or at least thought, that mutual funds and other institutional investors use their knowledge to predict future security prices. This is believed to enable them to earn abnormal returns. Such a claim evidently contradicts the strong form of market efficiency other people believe to exist, unless mutual fund managers can obtain and retain private information. It follows that if this is not the case, which is plausible, then the market is inefficient.

In fact, empirical studies find that when measuring net returns, on average, mutual funds do not perform any better than a passive investment strategy would. In addition, there is evidence that a "good" mutual fund manager does not necessarily repeat his performance in subsequent years, which suggests that one year's success might be a lucky strike.

In the presence of market inefficiency, investors can expect to prosper only by possessing either better information than other investors or by having superior know-how. The more complex the financial instruments get, the more this superior know-how is supported through models, and most particularly real-time simulation.

Models are the domain of rocket scientists, who have a major role to play in modern investment practices. They help analyze the rationale and possible consequences of investment decisions by

❑ Experimenting on expected payoffs.

❑ Evaluating the expected resale value of assets.

When prices are formed on the basis of simulated information, we must reflect in a rigorous way on what is available and on whatever other information financial analysts can unearth. This goes beyond the better-known types of economic and financial studies.

Technical analysis cannot achieve abnormal returns because current market prices already reflect past prices as well as risk and return information. No investor can achieve great returns by using trading rules based on historical information of a simple time-series nature.[4]

Fundamental analysis does not achieve abnormal returns either, given that prices reflect all publicly available information, past and present. This includes annual reports of corporations, newspapers, investors' newsletters, public databases, and data streams from information providers.

In conclusion, because the market is generally inefficient but also features pockets of greater inefficiency, the competition is on, with rocket scientists performing in-depth studies. But there is also the fact that information acquisition and analysis is not without cost.

---

4 See also D. N. Chorafas, *Chaos Theory in the Financial Markets* (Chicago: Probus, 1994).

Rocket scientists and financial analysts do make profits for the companies they work for, but they are also competing with each other as new analysis tools continue to enter the industry. As this competition becomes more rigorous, financial analysis pushes toward a process of great risk and return, which leaves the old tool users in the dust.

7.   Investment Uncertainties and the Efficiency Frontier

A rigorous financial analysis should take into full account the covariation of crucial factors affecting market prices at all levels of their aggregation. As any rocket scientist should know, the omission of dependencies among variables can lead to seriously distorted results.

Statistical analysis and reasoning by analogy can be employed to account for covariation prior to building simulators and optimizers that will help in decisions about allocation of financial resources. A careful study will distinguish between

❑   Systematic risk.

❑   Unsystematic risk.

Unsystematic risks are those that can be reduced by diversification of investment activities, whereas systematic risks are more or less immune to diversification. In other words, diversification cannot reduce risk factors, at least within a given domain.

What both types of risks have in common is the fact that analytical studies of prices and of market behavior require algorithms and heuristics, most particularly *nontraditional* tools for financial research. Besides this, the exercise of expert judgment for risk reduction requires a consistent real-time monitoring effort, which increasingly focuses on high-speed financial data.[5]

A simple taxonomy of *risk classes* faced by the banker, the analyst, and the investor sets the stage for a more rational look at uncertainty and risk. It has already been discussed that object-oriented approaches can be very helpful because they permit the construction of perishable hierarchies, making the artifacts we develop so much more flexible.

Real estate property is an example of a coarse-grain approach to the balancing of different risk classes, to the extent that investors seek protection against systematic risks to financial assets. Such property has been the preferred real asset. However, there may be a case for commodities fulfilling part of property's role in a portfolio, particularly in a derivatives sense.

---

[5] See D. N. Chorafas, *Rocket Scientists in Banking* (London and Dublin: Lafferty Publications, 1995).

The traditional response of an investor who targets a portfolio strategy has been to diversify between financial assets—for instance, between stocks and bonds—while holding a small amount of cash. Liquid markets, allowing funds to enter and exist fairly easily, have reinforced this tradition. But any strategy should be steadily under test because markets change so rapidly.

Because they lack the concept of risk classes, many investors have almost no concept of the *degree of uncertainty* in their portfolio. As a result, the prevailing pattern is one of overconfidence. This bias is nearly universal and expresses itself specifically in forecasts that are upset by subsequent events.

❏ In their quantitative predictions, experts usually set their predictive ranges far too narrowly.

❏ In qualitative forecasts, this bias is expressed by a strong tendency to rely on only one hypothesis, rather than on many, in carrying out an investigation.

One of the hypotheses that has found favor in the last few years is that *portfolio diversification* takes the wind out of risk. Yet, as already noted, portfolio diversification does not necessarily protect from systematic risk.

Much is built on hope rather than rationality. For instance, apart from the hope for above-average returns, it is postulated that investment in emerging markets may help to raise the risk-adjusted return by diversifying risks—which is another hope, and, as the 1994/1995 Mexico disaster shows, it is as well irrational.

Diversification gains when stock markets move independently of one another or when their movements are very weakly correlated. The study of covariation, however, alters this perspective, because the financial markets of the world are increasingly interlinked.

The misconception of independence is promoted by the fact that studies using monthly data have "demonstrated" investor gains from diversification into emerging market stocks. Such studies aim at computing *efficiency frontiers* for portfolios with different proportions of emerging market and traditional market stocks—a concept that has yet to prove itself in practical terms.

An example on the efficiency frontier is given in Figure 11–2, which is based on historical dollar returns in a combined index for major world markets, and on the index for returns on equities available to international investors in emerging markets.[6]

---

6 For a discussion on fact and hype regarding emerging markets, see section 9.

Figure 11–2. Bounded Efficiency Frontiers by Diversifying into Emerging Markets

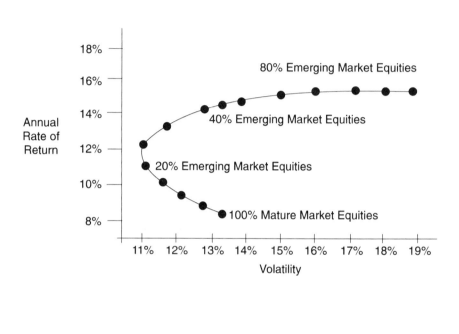

As the reader will appreciate, the efficiency frontier plotted in Figure 11–2 suggests that a mix of 70 percent industrial country and 30 percent emerging markets stocks might have more than doubled the return of a portfolio invested only in traditional markets. In the 1989 to 1993 time frame, a portfolio that was 60 percent invested in the emerging markets and only 40 percent invested in traditional markets would have provided a 17 percent annual return. As plotted, the efficiency frontier tends to suggest that this would have taken place with roughly the same risk faced at traditional markets. But it's always easy to forecast the past.

This mode of presentation is relatively new, and it is open to a contrarian frontier hypothesis. The concept of an efficiency frontier might eventually prove to have merit after it is worked out in a more rigorous manner, but the word *efficiency* should not be confused with the concept of an efficient market. If anything, it denotes exactly the opposite.

The concept of an efficiency frontier is worth exploiting in a factual and documented manner because, properly used, it can provide *insight* on the risks taken with derivatives. We always need to carefully experiment with financial instruments that provide protection against the shifting values of commodities and other assets. Let's keep in mind that use of derivative financial products neither fits the traditional definitions of assets and liabilities, nor is served by the traditional tools used in financial analysis.

Off-balance-sheet instruments are in a world of their own, and the more widespread their use becomes, the more we need to analyze our own hedging scenarios. That is where, properly worked out, the calculation of an efficiency frontier has its merits.

An efficiency frontier should be studied, not in connection to the past, but the future—including the financial instruments we use (or plan to use) to take a position on future price change(s). This may involve currencies, interest rates, and commodities—agricultural and other.

But the model we build must account for the fact that off-balance-sheet vehicles are geared instruments, offering a much greater market exposure for a smaller outlay than the more traditional financial tools. Hence, it must introduce the concept of *risk capital*. Let's remember this when we reach the risk capital discussion in Part Three.

8. An Efficiency Frontier in Diversification Strategies

Section 7 explained the sense of an efficiency frontier and how the concept works. Two examples were given, one from emerging markets, the other from derivatives. A similar argument can evidently be made with other diversification hypotheses targeting risk and return.

Figure 11–3 shows a series of points at which varying portions of managed futures are added to hypothetical traditional portfolios of stocks, bonds, and cash. Each dot on the plot indicates a different mix of assets, as the following paragraphs document.

Portfolio 1 represents 50 percent stocks, 45 percent bonds, and 5 percent cash. Each portfolio (dot) between 2 and 15 represents a change from Portfolio 1, according to the following algorithm:

❑   An incremental addition of 2 percent to managed futures and

❑   A corresponding 1 percent decrease from both stocks and bonds.

The allocation of 5 percent to cash remains unchanged throughout the different scenarios in Figure 11–3. Notice, however, that this example also forecasts the past.

The object of the model is to show how an efficiency frontier diagram can be developed and used for *visualization* of experimental results. The best use would be through an interactive presentation based on *database mining*. The model must be flexible, giving the experimenter

Figure 11–3. Bounded Efficiency Frontier with Managed Futures

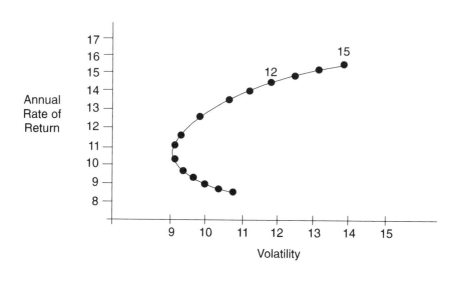

the option to choose which factor(s) should be kept constant and which should be varied.

For instance, a different scenario can be built that focuses on cash—but in different currencies, such as $, £, yen, DM, and Swiss francs in varying proportions.

Such models can be instrumental in the exploitation of market inefficiencies. Let's recall that in Figure 11–3, Portfolio 12 represents 38 percent stocks, 33 percent bonds, 24 percent managed futures, and 5 percent cash. Comparing Portfolio 1 and 12, we see that

❏   Both have approximately the same degree of volatility. But Portfolio 12 seems to exhibit a much higher rate of return.

By contrast, Portfolio 15, which contains the greatest allocation of managed futures, also demonstrates a significantly greater risk. Its volatility stands at 15 percent, versus 12 percent for portfolios 1 and 12.

Any serious financial analysis should be keen to bring into perspective the fact that *product mix* in an investment portfolio can feature a lot of misconceptions—and quite often hype. For instance, the argument for diversifying into emerging markets is subject to four important qualifications.

1. Available statistics are based on the recent past, and there is no reason why events will repeat themselves in the future.

If a lesson can be learned from the past, it is that investors found emerging markets to be a new, higher-risk, higher-return playground. This tended to bid up the prices of a relatively fixed quantity of equities from a broad spectrum of countries, whatever their underlying earnings prospects might have been.

2. Emerging markets are now well publicized, and their existence has been built into their prices.

A different way of making this statement is that future discoveries are likely to come from still smaller country markets and from second-tier stocks, which also involve a much higher amount of risk. This market will involve a lot of uncertainties.

3. The exchanges of emerging markets are tiny, and so is their capitalization. Foreign investors moving in and out would create waves of volatility.

This means that booms and busts are and will increasingly be induced by foreign investors who rush in and out of the emerging market(s) like a herd. It happened in Australia in the 1980s and in Turkey as well as in many other countries in the 1993–94 time frame—and will happen frequently in the future.

4. Picking new bright stars early enough to make a profit will require a large research investment and a strong local presence.

In other words, not only the risks will be increased, but the costs as well. As I have already emphasized, serious international players in the world's stock exchanges must not only have a local presence, but must also employ analysts who are very versatile in the culture characterizing these exchanges—as well as in the foreign companies being quoted, where investments are made.

A similar case can be made about derivatives. Futures trading is challenging, but sophisticated investors should be very analytical in their approach when they choose to participate in options futures, forwards, swaps, and exotics. Returns might be improved through a professionally managed strategy—but under no condition can they be guaranteed. That people try to capitalize on the market forces is not surprising. What is surprising is the fact that they try to do so without an appreciation of the risks involved.

Analytical tools, such as simulators, and interactive visualization solutions like three-dimensional color graphics, radar charts, and the efficiency frontier, provide the possibility for improving performance. But they also require factual documentation—not merely plotting a graph.

Genetic algorithms, for instance, can be instrumental in building up a nonlinear optimizer that uses crossovers and mutations to structure a portfolio of assets. Our models and our data must be objective and accurate, even if it is inescapable that subjective judgment will enter into the interpretation of the results.

Failing to exploit market inefficiencies is one thing, but being inefficient in portfolio management is another. Prudently, the different managed funds advertise that they seek to capitalize on the profit potential of a professionally managed portfolio of futures, forwards and options. There can be no assurance, however, that the Fund will achieve its objective.

This leaves the investor with the need to do her own research in order to protect her property. Capital appreciation as well as higher dividends don't come at zero cost. Risk and reward from the perspective of a public fund and that of a private investor may well be two totally different issues.

9.   Examining Investment Trends in Emerging Markets

As we have seen throughout this chapter, there is a change in strategy regarding investments and portfolio management at large. Yesterday's investments were typically done in one country. Today, they are concentrated in a few countries, an example being the international bond market. Tomorrow, investments will be in many different countries and markets.

Because of credit risk and country risk, in terms of bonds it has been customary that G-10 countries accounted for nearly all net new issues, while the less-developed countries retired more outstanding bonds than they issued new ones. Since 1992, however, this too has changed. There is now a new pattern.

In 1993, Mexico issued international bonds of over $10 billion, Argentina of $7 billion, and Brazil of nearly $6 billion. In a way, international bond issues replaced the capital that in the 1970s had been pumped into these three countries by the money center banks, leading to the debt crisis of Central and South America.

Not to be outdone, also in 1993, South Korea and Hong Kong borrowed more than $4.5 billion each, while Greece, Hungary, and Turkey fell just shy of the $4 billion mark. China, Portugal, Thailand, and Venezuela each borrowed about $2 billion—while other countries retrieved an estimated $1.8 billion in net redemptions. A dozen relatively new entrants to the international bond market are said to account for more than 80 percent of equity portfolio inflows. By contrast, some 130 other

Figure 11–4. An International Strategy in Investments and Portfolio Management

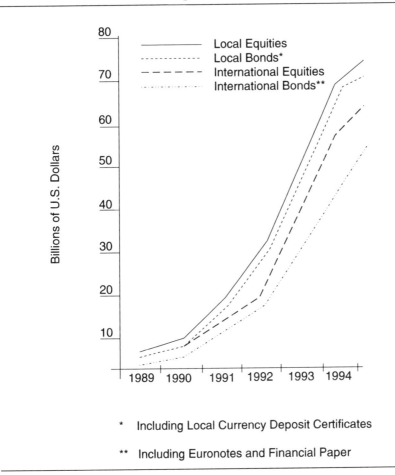

	Local Equities
	Local Bonds*
	International Equities
	International Bonds**

*   Including Local Currency Deposit Certificates

**   Including Euronotes and Financial Paper

countries in the nonindustrial world remain largely on the sidelines or are out of sight altogether.

As Figure 11–4 illustrates, there is an ongoing internationalization of the bond market. This explosive growth really took off in 1990 and started to move exponentially two years later. Hence, it is a very recent phenomenon whose study calls for answers to tough questions:

❑   What should a financial institution assume regarding the future of stock markets, bond markets, and derivatives markets in a multinational sense?

❑   And what about today's national monopoly of the local exchange, which is highly profitable for the domestic banks?

Given the fact that national exchanges are known entities and that they are protected by interest groups, it is small wonder that governments are committed to the perpetuation of the current regime. But can it survive?

Institutional investors, and most particularly the pension funds, are rapidly becoming the dominant sources of funds in Europe and elsewhere in the world as they were in the United States 10 years ago. And to optimize both the deals they do and their portfolios, these institutional investors operate cross-border. Perceived business opportunities are one reason for the change, but not the only one. The local markets do not have the liquidity major institution need, and they are suffocating under the high costs of the current narrow-aperture system.

Global banks, institutions, and other investors should therefore appreciate that local exchanges might survive as the places where prices are officially registered. But the actual trading will be done on-market and off-market by transnational brokerage firms, especially for their institutional customers.

As nonbanks, large brokerage firms are positioning themselves for this case. A more radical hypothesis is that the existing stock exchanges will become irrelevant, especially for large institutional investors, being replaced by

❑   Transnational networks.

❑   Party-to-party deals.

❑   Over-the-counter discount markets.

This is what is happening already, to a large extent, with derivatives. Taking debt as an example, in the past, internationalization was limited to issuers that more or less were members of the Group of Ten; therefore, the new trend is in itself a huge departure from past practices. The events of February/March 1994 with the huge losses in the bond market, slowed down this trend somewhat, but did not appreciably alter the direction.

There are financial analysts who believe that, while a wider internationalization is good, the ongoing explosion of investments and their concentration in a dozen emerging countries raises several risks. An example is the so-called knock-on effect:

❑   *If* problems in one country generate substantial losses,

❑   *Then* investors could respond by withdrawing from other emerging markets.

This would generally depress prices and encourage further withdrawals, leading to a snowball that central banks in the G-10 countries would have great difficulty counteracting since the country (or countries) where the snowball starts is (are) out of their jurisdiction.

One of the shortcomings of current models—and the bankers who develop them—is that they don't take snowballs and bursting bubbles into consideration. For the time being, investors are more interested in discovering new opportunities than in calculating these risks, which is a mistake.

One of the best examples along this line of reference is provided by the Mexican crisis of December 1994–February 1995. Mexico attracted $64 billion of portfolio investments in the 1990–1994 time frame, or roughly 10 percent of the money that went during that period to emerging markets. Hence, a default in Mexico would have had a snowball effect putting the currencies of all of the lesser developed countries under pressure.

But there exist as well other significant differences between countries which are not accounted for by most models, therefore reducing their degree of accuracy. When the debacle came:

❑ Mexico's debt-service ratio stood at about 30 percent of Gross National Product, compared to 16 percent of GNP for the Philippines.

❑ Over 80 percent of Mexico's debt was short-term, compared with about 25 percent in the Philippines.

The current-account deficit of the Philippines is about 4.5 percent of GNP and has narrowed as a proportion of the country's Gross National Product since 1993. When the most recent crisis broke, Mexico's deficit was about 8 to 9 percent of GNP and widening.

Other factors also contributed to Mexico's downfall. The Mexicans had pledged to defend a fixed exchange rate and so depreciation of the currency seemed a threatening issue—which proved to be one with significant impact on market psychology.

Finally, according to some experts, the December 1994–February 1995 Mexican peso crisis may as well have resulted in part from currency speculation using OTC derivatives. Though there is not yet enough information to support this thesis, there have been studies that suggested the same type of trading contributed to the collapse of the Italian lira in September–October 1992.

12

Securities Lending: How to Precipitate a Banking Crisis

1. Introduction

Chaos theory suggests that bubbles and panics in the financial markets have a mathematical shape, one that is familiar to nuclear engineers, aerospace designers, and other scientists. Prices in a bubble climb, pass beyond the point at which they can be sustained, and push through, as confidence noses down and the market sharply falls.

❏ The bubble follows the line of an explosive curve.

❏ The panic shows a vertical drop, after a critical point in time.

This pattern occurs because psychology can change very rapidly between a situation in which there are no sellers and one where there are no buyers. Typically a one-way market goes all the way up or down, as both selling and buying are driven by expectations. This underpins the volatility we observe in the markets.

One of the swords of Damocles hanging over the head of the financial market is the process of lending securities—whether equities or debt—with a repurchase clause. It is generally known as a *repo* agreement and is a derivative financial product.

This chapter focuses on *securities lending,* the Ponzi game, which during the last few years has become the favored pastime of the financial system. It does not take a genius to see that repos are vehicles that run without brakes toward their eventual downfall.

Risk takers would respond to this statement by claiming there is nothing to worry about because "there is no danger from repos." Some would provide as documentation the fact that, when it comes to securities lending, the Swiss National Bank has been doing it with Swiss commercial banks for 50 years. This argument purposely forgets two basic facts:

❏ The reserve bank does securities lending in a measured way to assist, not speculate.

❏ The reserve bank is the lender of last resort, using all assets at its disposition to perform this function.

Other repo gamblers would argue that the practice is fairly old. Before securities lending, repos were done with gold—selling the same real asset four or five times—hence, through leveraging.

The response to this argument is that whether it's done with gold or with securities, this process is highly leveraged and therefore very risky. But in the last analysis, a physical commodity such as gold puts the brakes on because the supply is limited.

By contrast, with securities lending, the leveraging is multilayered. Repos are a high-level gearing, because commercial and financial paper is itself a leveraged vehicle. Therefore, there is a much greater exposure in lending the same security four or five times than in doing something similar with gold.

No better example can be found in connection to the risks than the bomb that exploded in Orange County, California. On December 7, 1994, less than a week after disclosing that its investment fund had lost over $2 billion with reverse-repurchase agreements, Orange County was forced to file for bankruptcy. This is the largest bankruptcy case involving a municipality in the United States. Its cause was gambling in derivatives and most particularly in repos.

2. Bubbles, Bursts, and Panics—A Common Denominator

Bubbles, bursts, and panics don't always have known causes such as the Great Depression of 1929–1933 did. They often spring from unexpected sources, such as the Tulip mania of the 17th century and the South Seas adventure of the 18th century—or securities lending of the late 20th century. The common thread of these events is lack of financial responsibility.

The story of providing adequate regulation and supervision for avoiding bubbles, bursts, and panics is about four people named Everybody, Somebody, Anybody, and Nobody. There was an important job to be done and Everybody was asked to do it.

❑   Everybody was sure Somebody would do it.

❑   Anybody could have done it.

❑   But Nobody really did it.

Somebody got angry about that, because it was Everybody's job. Everybody thought Anybody could do it, but Nobody realized that Everybody wouldn't do it. This is what is happening today with the control of supergeared financial vehicles.

It ends up that Everybody blames Somebody when Nobody does what Anybody could have done. Legislators and central bankers usually blame commercial and investment bankers for being unable to police themselves or not providing the pertinent information in time, while the public usually blames all of the bankers for not having paid due attention to the risks. That's how banking crises are precipitated.

❑   In 1889, the California residential property bubble burst, and land prices had plunged to a quarter of their real value by the time the market stopped falling.

❑   In the 1929–1932 time frame, banks had little reserves, and the first drain in deposits caused some of them to become insolvent. As they were shut down, they precipitated a panic.

❑   In 1974, share prices in Britain fell to little over a quarter of their peak value in 1972—as though to confirm that shares are inherently risky, particularly in panic selling.

Bubbles burst when confidence in an ever greater price of a commodity fizzles and nobody is left pushing the speculative instrument even higher. The careful analyst will, however, detect some basic axioms underpinning the build-up-and-crash cycle.

The first, and most important, axiom is that nothing is immune from becoming a speculative vehicle at one time or another. High-quality bonds used to be investment instruments for conservative investors. Then, in the 1980s, came the wave of so-called "high-interest bonds"—a name coined to hide the fact that they were in reality junk bonds, many of which eventually defaulted.

In the 1990s, a new speculation developed with bonds: the derivatives play. Examples range widely, from mortgage-backed financing to a hoard of other leveraged products, which after skyrocketing in value in 1993 went down like a stone in February 1994 when the time of low and stable dollar interest rates came to an end.

Figure 12–1 dramatizes the fact that in 1994 the formerly conservative bond investments performed much worse than the stock market. While in early 1994 the S&P 500 index went into negative territory, in

Figure 12–1. In a Reversal of the Past, Because of High Leveraging in 1994 Bonds Had Greater Risks Than Stocks

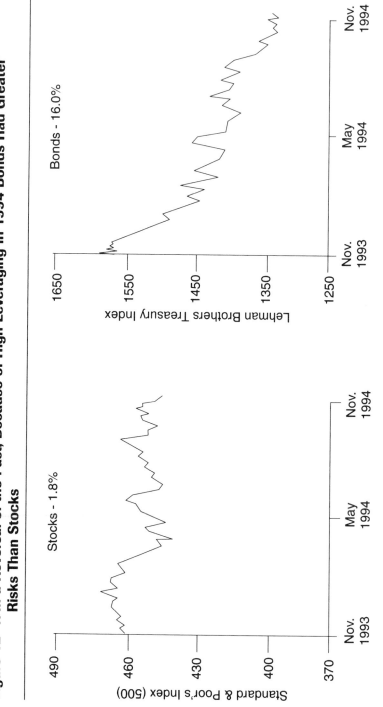

sympathy with the bond market, later on in the year it recovered. By contrast, the bond market continued to fall.

The second axiom addresses the way in which the criteria are chosen for the selection of the financial instrument. It says that a bubble will eventually burst and crash—downgrading the process as well as propelling this vehicle to new heights. There are basically two strategies for leveraging:

- ❏ Catch the eye of bankers, traders, major investors and, most particularly, minor investors in the general public as a fast and fat profit opportunity.

- ❏ Make believe that the price of the instrument has only one way to go: UP! The gimmick is to sell the idea that it can never fall in value.

Yet the price of every commodity is bound to fluctuate. And the faster it rises, the steeper it will fall. Whether it is bonds, stocks, oil, soybeans, copper, or gold, in a market economy no commodity can have a higher price than what people are willing to pay for it, not just in the short term, but also in the longer term.

Many bubbles build up because there is no shortage of sharp operators in the market, with considerable experience in engineering flashy products that burst. Ironically, such products are launched with considerable success, but the more they remain in the system, the more they poison the market. Rigorous financial analysis by central bankers can identify and kill bubble-prone financial products. This is a political decision that should be made before they tear the financial fabric apart.

Interestingly enough, two of the three earliest and most famous bubbles—the Tulip Bubble, the South Sea Bubble, and the Mississippi Bubble, took their names from the financially hollow companies that had managed to lure the public in. The collapse of the South Seas Company and the Mississippi Bubble in the 18th century prompted the English government to pass the *Bubble Acts*.

These acts were aimed at preventing illusionary schemes, and as far as I know have never been repealed. Therefore, they can be effectively used in the case of overgeared derivative financial products—not only for whole company strategies and awesome-looking financial vehicles, but also for daily trading reasons.

3.   "Strategies for Growth" and Tulip–Type Bubbles

With real-time networks and 24-hour banking setting the pace of the financial markets, a trader can create a small bubble in derivative equities through the illegal practice of "goosing" the market. A *goose* consists of forcing up the price by buying outstanding shares for the purpose of creating demand for the stock and/or its derivatives.

The goosing strategy was not invented yesterday. While the concept is as old as humanity, the first written evidence of using it to push the price of a product to new heights dates back to the 17th century with the tulip trade.

Imported in the early 17th century to Holland from Turkey, the tuplip was at the origin of the first major bubble in financial history. The year this pyramiding started seems to be 1620, with a number of factors contributing to it:

❑   Status-conscious Dutch and other Western Europeans were easily lured by an oriental novelty.

❑   The fact that Amsterdam was Europe's major trading center helped push the product.

❑   A search for new, more efficient investment vehicles was already underway.

New techniques were developed in 17th-century Holland for bulb growing and subsequently for tulip picking, harvesting, and marketing. These were the four essential ingredients for advancing prices faster than tulips could be grown, and their rigorous study can be seen as the oldest known example of R&D in investment banking.

New and more rapid methods of transportation became necessary, and once they were on hand, very expensive tulips, which could cost thousands of gilders to develop, were packaged and traded internationally. Most of Europe became a market for the Dutch tulip trade.

Prices were rapidly advancing for the most rare varieties to which the higher technology of the time was addressed. It is said that one inventor even studied ancient Egyptian arts and attempted to market tulip-mummifying machines to give permanent protection to the product. Another Dutch inventor developed a new insurance policy for tulips, which immediately flourished. Some collectors held tulips as investments, and others lodged them as security against loans. Bankers came into the fray, and it is said that some economists challenged the gold standard in favor of a tulip standard.

In a way reminiscent of some exotic derivatives, lust and greed flourished as people—from producers to sellers and investors—made fools of themselves. The market rise suppressed reason, and the desire for fast profits in the tulip trade became the primary purpose of tulip dealing, *Tulpewoerde* in the Dutch language.

The more sophisticated Dutch businessmen used tulip brokers who, through messengers, transmitted all relevant changes in the price of the leading tulip types to their clients. Tulip jobbers were on the alert for new speculative possibilities, making use of all the methods then known to gain from fluctuation in prices, in a way that is not too different from what happens with derivative trades today.

By 1636, regular markets had been established for selling and buying tulips through the exchanges of Amsterdam, Rotterdam, and other cities. These trades had become so profitable that many people thought it was silly to restrict the activities to the winter months. Thereafter, a *futures market* developed for tulips. Traders would issue contracts at any time during the year, with delivery specified in the following winter. Such contracts could be sold and bought several times before the tulips actually arrived.

History books suggest that the futures market was followed by an *options market* with calls and puts on the favored tulip—and with investors as well as speculators betting that tulip prices would keep going up. This scenario became known as *Windhandel*, or trading air.

The financial analysts of the time were quick to array a number of reasons why the price of tulips should continue to go up, downplaying the negative side in the same way as happens today with calls and puts on

- ❑ Commodities.
- ❑ Equity derivatives.
- ❑ Securities lending.
- ❑ Swaps and other trades.

Then as now, the value of a vehicle—in this case the tulip—related only to what the market was willing to pay for it. Prognosis was done by tulip analysts, whose luck eventually ran out because folly, too, has its limits.

The time came when the tulip trade blew its fuses. A few people saw this change in market sentiment before they were hit by bad luck. These were the people who studied the excesses, becoming aware that the tulip bubble could not last indefinitely—regardless of what the tulip analysts and other economists suggested.

Similar cases exist with trading equities. It is said that Joseph P. Kennedy sold his portfolio and stepped out of the stock market right before the Great Depression, after a shoeshine boy gave him a "hot tip" on which stock to buy. After all, who would invest in market assets on the advice given by a shoeshine boy?

With the burst of the tulip bubble and the end of the tulip mania, the Netherlands was plunged into a depression. The credibility of Amsterdam and Rotterdam was obliterated in the international markets—a plight that was to last for several decades. Has the reader heard of major financial centers that today play a similar role with derivatives?

4.   Speculation, False Information, and King George I

In 1497, the Genoese Giovanni Caboto, better known as John Cabot, sailed under the orders of King Henry VII and found a continent to the north of Columbus's explorations. In 1513, Vasco Nuñez de Balboa crossed the Panama isthmus and reached the Pacific Ocean. Another great navigator, Ferdinand Magellan, was, in the 15th century, assured by his mathematician friend Ruy Faleiro that the "South Sea" could be only a couple of thousand miles across.

What motivated many of the 15th- and 16th-century explorers and those who financed their expeditions were stories about lands with untold riches. Such stories are not new; they reappear under new names every hundred years or so.

The reason behind these stories about untold riches within easy grasp are opportunities for the exploitation of naive bankers and investors. This is the setting for the South Sea bubble and the nonexistent assets of the South Sea Company on which it rested. It hit England and continental Europe in the beginning of the 18th century.

In 1711, the South Sea Company, which practically came out of nowhere, received a royal warrant. King George I became its governor, which led to increased credibility—not only in England but in all the rich countries of the world. Investors were out for quick profits. The stage was set in 1717, after the King's speech in Parliament and the South Sea Act.

Big investment plans were made, rosy profit pictures were painted, and all was publicly announced in imaginary details—accompanied by even more audacious proposals. One proposal was to pay off the entire national debt in one act—a massive undertaking—by incorporating England's national debt with the South Sea Company shares.

Speculation carried the day, and the South Sea Company's shares shot up, even though no interest was being paid to investors. In 1720, three years down the line, it was resolved that the proposals made by the South Sea Company were likely to be of great advantage to the whole of England, and therefore the company was authorized to create £1 of new stock for every pound of national debt it took over.

The price of company shares rose by 250 percent, and everyone who had the good fortune to participate in the investment tasted the flavor of easy money—but not for long. As it became apparent that the bubble would not last, the King and his government engaged in desperate measures to save the South Sea Company from bankruptcy. Nevertheless, the South Sea Bubble eventually burst, ruining its investors, and England plunged into a deep financial crisis.

Optimists will say that this is long past and that it has nothing to do with derivatives speculations, since as "everybody knows" off-balance-sheet financial instruments have underliers, which was not the case with the South Sea Bubble. What Everybody, however, does not know is that

1. These underliers are someone else's debt or paper asset, whatever its value might be.

2. Most of the underlying instruments are being lent many times over, in an unprecedented spree of leveraging.[1]

3. Practically all major companies today speculate with derivatives, though some are doing it much more than others.

Intel, the chip manufacturer, Enron, a Houston oil and gas company, and Dell, the PC maker, have made the most daring use of hedging. Their management insists that the risks of not using derivatives vastly outweigh the risks of using them. Olivetti, too, had the same concept and policy, but in the first six months of 1994 it lost from guaranteed bonds and other derivatives trades $220 million versus the $3.4 million it lost from its main business lines.

A *Business Week* report[2] stated that Intel treasurer Arvind Sodhani saw that excess returns could be achieved by doing complex OBS transactions. His opinion was that he was not making bets on currencies or using leverage, though in managing Intel's $5 billion cash he used put options to reap windfalls on the company's stock-buyback program.

This strategy seems to have produced gains of $183 million since Intel began using derivatives in 1990. Some critics, however, suggest that since the company both knows its buyback plans and can time them as it pleases, this is essentially the nearest thing to insider trading exercised in the OBS domain.

In the first half of 1994, Dell Computers lost $32 million after having made $13 million on derivatives in the 1991–1993 time frame. Like the South Sea Bubble, speculative strategies bode fine until they burst. "You can fool some of the people all of the time or all of the people some of the time," said Abraham Lincoln, "but not all of the people all of the time."

On October 20, 1994, the top management of Kodak made a wise move when it sold its portfolio of derivatives, and its treasury operations got out of OBS trades. But who is to guarantee that vanilla ice cream bonds and stocks are a safe bet when speculation has reached such heights—and they are being lent many times over?

---

1 As we will see in sections 5 and 6.
2 October 31, 1994.

5.   The Art of Securities Lending and Borrowing

The massive use of *securities lending and borrowing* is a relatively new business aimed at providing investors and speculators with an opportunity for added returns. But it also constitutes a major risk to the financial system because

❑   It significantly increases the level of leverage in the market as a whole.

❑   It introduces uncertainty about how safe the financial assets deposited at the bank are.

Securities lending is the loaning of securities for a commission. Though this is not a product of the 1990s, as it has been around for decades, it is in the last few years that it has become a major business. Worse yet, practically everyone is yearning to be in the game.

As with many other rather recent financial products, technology has been instrumental in promoting securities lending operations. The reason lies in the significant easing of *delivery problems* encountered in connection with stock market transactions and with bonds dealt over-the-counter.

❑   The possibility of borrowing securities for trading while avoiding delivery delays helps make traders and investors more aggressive.

❑   Theoretically, this operation reduces the settlement risk facing market participants.

❑   Practically, it increases the level of exposure of both players.

Not only commercial banks, but also clearing organizations such as Euroclear, Cedel, the German Securities Deposit Association (Kassenverein) and other clearers, exchanges, and custodians offer market operators securities lending services involving someone elses assets, thereby increasing the leverage in securities trading by a very significant margin.

The complete transaction cycle is shown in Figure 12–2. There is a collateral posted by the borrower for what it is worth. As transactions with borrowers are consumated, the collateral being provided is cash, bonds, commercial and financial paper,[3] or standby letters of credit issued by banks. Depending on the type of collateral being provided, its market value typically lies between 105 percent and 110 percent of the

---

[3] The term *financial paper* is not often used, the reason being that the term *commercial paper* is misused. Strictly speaking, commercial paper results from a commercial transaction; the rest is financial paper.

Figure 12-2. The Complex Transactions Underpinning Securities Lending and Borrowing Operations

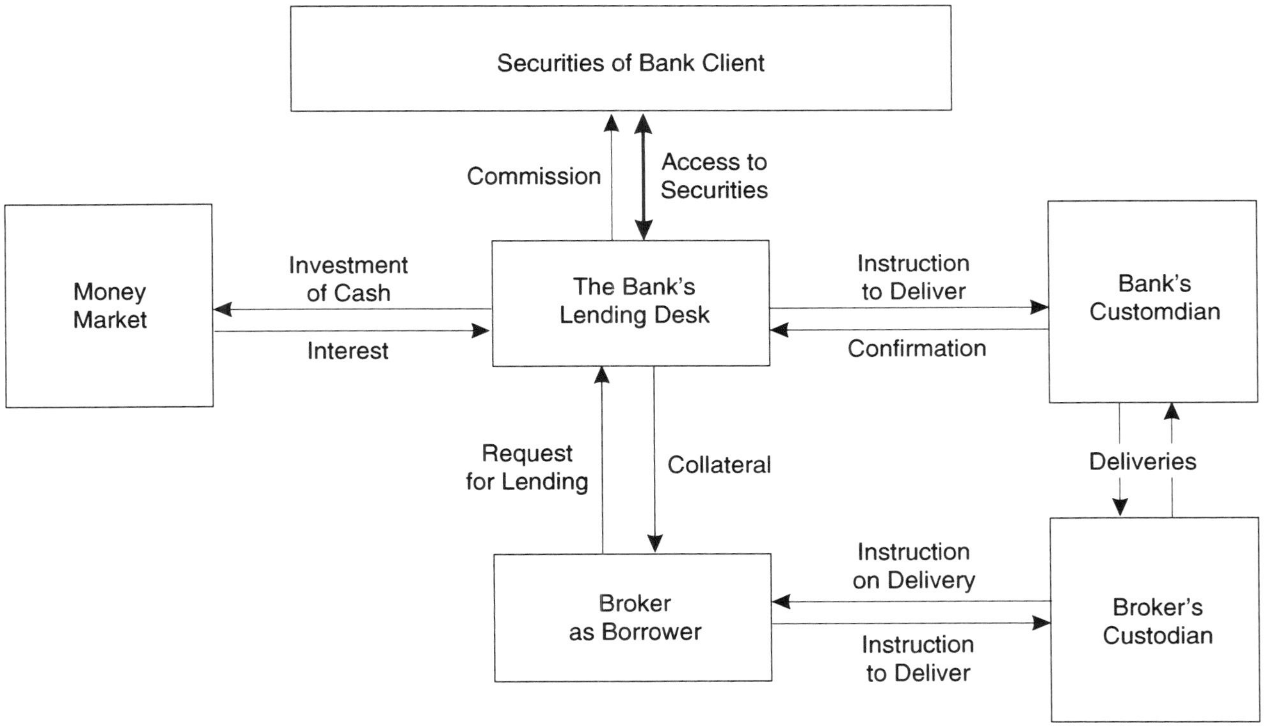

market value of the securities on loan—which is a very thin margin. This compares poorly with the collateral securities given for loans, where banks usually offer between 60 and 70 percent of market value—practically a 50 percent markup.

Repo transactions are typically expressed in terms of the market value of the securities being loaned, the value being inclusive of any accrued interest for fixed-income instruments. In general, however, this calculation does *not* reflect the risks involved in the transaction.[4]

In general, during the lending and borrowing operation, dividends, interest payments, and other entitlements are transferred to the borrower. The lender, however, will be authorized to receive full compensation from the borrower.

When dividends, interest payments, or other benefits are due on securities that have been lent out, these will be credited on the correct value date *as though* the securities were not on loan. This makes the lending operation transparent to the owner of the securities—who typically is the bank's client. But failures do happen, particularly with banks and exchanges that use old mainframe technology—and the legal owner ends by paying the bills of these lending practices.

It is the bank's responsibility to reclaim the amounts due from the borrower, but there can be a loss of value date, as a recent case I personally experienced helps document. Even that error is up to the client to discover—rather than being flushed out by the bank in whose custody the securities were left.

Let's further notice that the exposure with repos varies not only in terms of credit risk and market risk, but also depending upon the quality of the actual securities being borrowed. Therefore, there are distinct percentages to be applied both between and within two classes:

❑ Equity vehicles.
❑ Fixed-income instruments.

One of the critical factors that led to the development of a trend in securities lending as a lucrative financial product is the need for the market maker to acquire positions on all sides:

❑ Bull and bear.
❑ Long and short.

These contrasting positions can be taken on the basis of securities borrowing, even if the market maker is not covered. With the popularity of such operations on the increase, over the past few years securities lending has been employed increasingly to support strategies such as the following:

---

[4] In Part Three, we will see how such risks can be taken into account.

❑   Futures arbitrage.

❑   Options arbitrage.

❑   Warrants arbitrage.

❑   Short sales.

Among commercial banks, securities lending and borrowing was conceived for their long-standing safekeeping account customers. For these customers, the main incentive for taking part in the bank's lending program is the potential for cutting custody costs. Banks kick back to the customer part of the profits they make in securities lendings. But customers rarely appreciate the other side of the coin:

❑   The bank's portfolio becomes highly exposed, as big chunks of it are in essence lent out,

❑   The customers' assets are integrated with those of the bank and can also disappear if the bank fails.

Banks try to reassure their customers that they will not lend out their assets without their accord. A letter by a major financial institution to a customer who complained about securities lending stated; "Please be informed that we will never arrange a lending transaction on your behalf without your written approval."

This letter further stated that the bank was engaging in securities lending on a collateralized basis (cash, bonds, money market papers, standby letter of credits) of 105 percent, which made such transactions "very safe."[5] But in direct contradiction to this statement, it was further written that "the bank is indemnifying every client against a loss." Securities lending, said the letter in question, is a new service that "allows our clients to generate extra income and benefit from an indemnification based on our AAA rating."

What the bank's letter did not say is that done through averages, which are often meaningless, and supported by slow-moving mainframes, this "collateralized basis" is very approximate at best and at worst it can be disastrous. The stated 105 percent does not make transactions "very safe"; it simply compounds the leveraging—and the risks.

The bank's statement that the securities lending service is very new is true. It is also untested, with possibly disastrous effects in the case of a panic, which nobody has yet seriously studied. The practice is part and parcel of *repo* agreements, which are themselves a darling of big players in the derivatives markets. But big players can also be burned, as we will see in section 6.

---

5 Which is ludicrous.

6.   Repurchase Agreements and Gaping Holes

One of the factors playing an important role in market psychology is the expansion of credit, whether through the classical means of the banking system or through junk bonds, derivatives, and other instruments. Basically, what a repo agreement does is significantly expand the credit basis. When credit is easy and trading seems effortless, people and companies borrow in a big way in order to invest in the new fashion, and everyone hopes to make huge profits at the expense of everyone else.

Financial history shows that *credit inflation* is always followed by *credit deflation*. The most famous bubbles—Tulips, South Sea, and Mississippi—as well as bubbles in the real estate market, stock market, and bond market—are practical examples of what can go wrong with a credit inflation attitude.

Another key factor that helps to burst a bubble is *pyramiding*, the Ponzi game, so named after its inventor, who in the 1920s in Boston developed the scam that cheated naive investors of their savings as they rushed to profit from exceptionally high interest rates.[6]

Here is how a classic pyramiding operation works. First comes an advertising barrage to make the "newly available," very high return on investment widely known. Then, the money deposited by the many buying into the company's "success story" funds the higher interest and the return share prices paid to the few cashing in their IOUs, the term often used for financial paper issued by a debtor.

This process, which is a full-fledged con game, can continue until the influx of new investors dries up or until investors' confidence is shaken, and a run on the company begins. This bursts the bubble, and the many are left holding the bag. But usually the "inventor" and a very few smart operators get the money and run.

Securities lending can be a double-edged sword. While many market-making operations would not be possible without this practice, the typical depositor of securities does not understand the risks involved in gearing synthetic long positions—as is the case with several options and futures—in refinancing the market maker's holdings.

True enough, this process is not indiscriminate. Yet there are no real guarantees either. Typically, the lenders taking part in a particular transaction are selected on the basis of an algorithm conceived to assure that every participant in the operation has a share. But what does this mean in terms of risk? In general,

---

[6] The latest Ponzi game is that of the Foundation for New Era Philanthropy, a Philadelphia-based organization specializing in "matching gifts" which in May 1995 crashed with losses estimated at $550 million hitting 300 charities and other nonprofit organizations and donors.

❑   The securities in the lending pool are offered for bids from borrowers around the clock, worldwide, to all the major financial centers.

❑   The target is to present the individual borrower (investor or speculator) with a pool of securities so that he or she does not need to turn to different lenders to find the type and numbers of securities he or she requires.

Not only the lender, but also the borrower takes a risk, as, depending on his grade and liquidity, the lending bank may decide at an inopportune moment to recall the securities on loan. Far from being a conservative policy, this aggravates the risks and can lead to a snowball effect.

What happened in early December 1994 with the Orange County bankruptcy is a case in point. A $7.5 billion fund used repos and other derivatives to leverage its portfolio up to $20.5 billion—betting in the wrong direction in terms of interest rates and other vehicles for which there was little demand in the market. As the value of the highly geared fund dropped to $18.5 billion from $20.5 billion, CS First Boston asked for payments.[7] Orange County had no more funds left to care for its obligations; it defaulted and filed for bankruptcy.

Many bankers, treasurers, and investors playing with derivatives fail to appreciate that while their accounts are highly leveraged, the losses they suffer are real money. The gaping hole of over $2 billion in the Orange County fund will be missing from the original $7.5 billion, which represents a cool 26.6 percent of its capital.[8]

Few people really understand the two-way exposure involved in securities lending. Yet this has been one of the reasons why, in some countries, the regulatory authorities have not welcomed securities lending and borrowing. They see that such transactions point to an ever greater risk because the system can run out of control.

For instance, until May 1990 securities lending in Switzerland was restricted to those securities exempt from withholding tax. The Swiss federal tax authorities were concerned that any withholding tax paid on interest or dividends due might be reclaimed by both the borrower and the lender.

Eventually, it was established that the risk of double tax reclamation could be avoided by adopting the Anglo-Saxon system of manufactured dividends. This prompted Switzerland's tax officials to allow securities lending operations involving both domestic and foreign stocks

---

7   It is said in Wall Street that CSFB also lost big money in the transaction—the rumored amount being between $200 and $400 million.

8   Ironically, in February/March 1994, Steinhart's hedge fund also lost 25 percent of its capital with derivatives, mainly leveraged bonds—$1 billion in red ink out of $4 billion in total capital.

and bonds. As a result, not only securities exempt from withholding tax, such as Eurobonds, can be lent out, but other types of financial paper as well.

Reserve banks are in a better position to put the brakes on transactions than legislators, if for no other reason than due to power games legislators are never in agreement. "If they had a fire at the U.S. Congress and needed a vote to pull the fire alarm, the whole place would be burned down to the ground," said an American banker—and this is true of the financial system as well.

7.   Can You Spare Someone Else's Assets for a Repo?

A bank or investor holding an inventory of assets—for instance, bonds—can fund his or her position in the *repo* market, doing so either on term or overnight. The holder of a bond—such as another bank, another investor, an exchange, or a clearinghouse—may agree to sell it and buy it back. Repurchase will take place on a specified day in the future, for a higher price. This effectively means that the seller is borrowing money, but the consequences go further than that.

The repo operation is a derivatives transaction that connects the underlying cash market and the futures market. The difference between the buyback price and the selling price is, for all practical purposes, the interest.

Given the weight repos have assumed during the last 10 years, and most particularly in the 1990s, it is important to understand the exposure involved in a *repurchase agreement*. A financial institution may enter into such agreements, whereby, as the seller of a security, it agrees to repurchase it at a mutually agreed-upon *time* and *price*:

❑   The repurchase is usually within a day or two of the original purchase, though it may extend over a number of months.

❑   The resale price is in excess of the purchase price, reflecting an agreed-upon rate of return effective for the period of time the purchaser's money is invested in the security.

The problem arises from the fact that what the bank, the clearer, or the exchange is selling and repurchasing[9] is not necessarily its own property but someone else's—someone who thought it was safe to leave his or her financial assets in custody and who even pays a custody fee for safekeeping.

Repo strategies essentially amount to *unsafekeeping*. While supposedly prudent policy sees to it that repurchase agreements will at all

---

[9] Which essentially means *lending* out.

times be fully collateralized in an amount at least equal to the purchase price, including accrued interest earned on the underlying securities, this is not enough. As section 5 has explained, such a practice means two things:

1. A risk that in some cases can be unlimited has to be squeezed into the 5 percent or so of the margin. This is totally inadequate for facing market gyrations, let alone a crash.

Instruments held as collateral should be valued daily. If the value of negotiable vehicles left as guaranty declines, the bank should ask for additional collateral. But the low technology employed by the large majority of banks, exchanges, and clearinghouses does not permit this steady process of revalution. Therefore, a major gap can develop.

2. An even larger and more ominous part of the risk is the practice of lending the same piece of financial paper—bond, stock, or other—many times over.

This supergearing results from the fact that the bank's repository of the securities lends them out; the bank which has assigned these securities for safekeeping to the repository also lends them; the exchange handling these securities lends them; and the clearinghouse through which the transaction transits lends them.

"There is no limit to the expansion of money supply by the banking system," Dr. Marriner Eccles, president of the Federal Reserve in the Roosevelt years, once said. Paraphrasing Dr. Eccles, there is no limit to the expansion of a finite amount of securities by banks, brokers, and exchanges. Figure 12–3 gives a bird's-eye view of what this means.

To face the requirements posed by this supergearing operation, banks, brokers, exchanges, and clearinghouses have instituted a *repo desk*. And as we have already seen, this is not just a passive enterprise, but a very active one, aggressively going after borrowers, with all this means in terms of risk.

Active securities-lending policies have been made possible by advancements in technology. Say that a bank or clearer receives on-line a repurchase agreement from two parties. One party sends dollars; the other sends securities as collateral. The operation is known as delivery versus payment (DVP).[10] The bank or clearer

❑ Gets the request to lend over the network channel.

❑ Records the repo in the database to generate all instructions required to settle this transaction.

---

[10]See section 10.

Figure 12–3. There Is No Limit to the Virtual Expansion of Real Securities by Banks, Brokers, and Exchanges

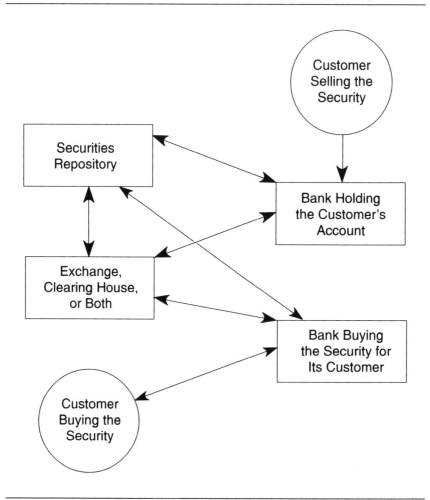

The procedure to be executed typically is "receive cash, pay cash" or "receive securities with repo, pay cash." Quite often, this can be a complex (long) transaction, but the existence of sophisticated software permits relatively easy processing.

I said sophisticated software. As far as technology is concerned, impotent mainframes, naive SQL, and monolithic DB2 or other centralized database management systems would be both highly expensive and incapable of handling the requirements in real time. Yet, as we have seen in the preceding paragraphs, it is necessary to update the market price of securities and to produce interactive reports on

❑ Individual and cumulative exposure.

❑ The different counterparties and their risks.

❑ Single transaction and consolidated statements.

Solutions have to be polyvalent. Repo operations may concern securities versus securities, securities versus cash, and so on. The best approach is to *assure flexibility* by developing advanced software through rapid prototyping. Most banks, brokers, and exchanges, however, still depend on aged and inflexible COBOL programs to handle highly risky deals as well as very large sums involved in complex transactions— which is simply nonsense.

8. A Mortgage-Roll Arbitrage Model for Repos

Mortgage rolls are a variation of repurchase agreements. A writer agrees to sell mortgage-backed financing (MBF) instruments to a buyer and to repurchase an equal amount of substantially the same securities at a specified future date and at a set price.

The writer/borrower receives cash equal to the spot market price on the opening settlement date in return for the securities. On the closing settlement date, the seller pays the buyer the forward price, and the securities are returned. What happens can, in principle, be expressed in these terms:

❑ The difference between the spot and forward prices (drop) provides the seller with incentive to enter the roll transaction.

❑ The buyer/lender receives the interim cash flows from the securities as compensation for lending the cash.

Mortgage rolls benefit sellers and buyers in a similar manner to repos, but they also carry risks. They allow sellers to convert MBFs into cash at a short-term, low-cost rate; to reinvest the funds for the term of the contract at a higher rate; and to earn a spread on the transaction. For their part, the buyers often use rolls to cover their obligations to deliver mortgage securities.

Mortgage rolls differ from repos in that the ownership of the securities is actually transferred, and therefore the buyers are entitled to receive the intermediate cash flows from these securities. Over and above this, roll buyers need only return substantially similar securities but are under no obligation to give back the identical pools on the repurchase date.

The two primary considerations in the mortgage-roll analysis are the *cost of carry* and the *drop*. A mortgage-roll arbitrage model is needed to determine the profitability of possible roll transactions under different prepayment assumptions:

❑ Detailing mortgage security information.

❑ Providing arbitrage graphics of forward drops by prepayment scenario.

Results should be presented in terms of both arbitrage dollar amount and implied cost of carry. A break-even drop for a given market repo rate must be computed for each prepayment assumption, and this requires models, computers, and experimentation.

Because mortgage-roll arbitratge repos are, so to speak, a derivative of a derivative, the exposure has to be followed very carefully. This requires the support of both rocket scientists[11] and high technology.

Also, given that the money center banks and other large institutions operate not just in one location, but as a network, and can do mortgage-roll arbitratge cross-border, any valid solution would have to pay due attention to the ability to control risk in a networkwide sense. Short of this, problems may arise:

1. *Business type*: When does a transaction become a commitment, when it arrives or when it is booked?

2. *Legal type*: How well are local laws observed? How valid are transborder agreements?

3. *Technical type*: Is the bank able to handle in real-time cross-border trades in different currencies in connection to repo transactions?

Let's keep in mind that we are talking about very large deals. Transactions of $100 million or more are nothing exceptional—and references also exist to up to $1 billion, hence to very high risk.

As emphasized in section 7, the problem is both one of superleveraging and of technology. Highly innovative financial instruments simply cannot be handled effectively, if at all, through obsolete technology and worn-out tools. Yet, many banks, brokers, exchanges, and clearers have not yet made the transition to high-technology solutions.

Personal computers (PCs) can process simple transactions, but they cannot consolidate reports. Neither mainframes nor PCs can handle very complex transactions. They cannot assist in the management of new products such as intermediary lending in the securities versus securities business, nor are they the platforms necessary for rigorous risk management.

---

[11] See Chapter 14.

9.   How the Regulators Look at Securities Lending

According to Securities and Exchanges Commission (SEC) regulations, investment funds must specify in writing in their prospectus the rules according to which they may enter into securities lending and borrowing. For instance, a given fund may only lend or borrow securities through one of the following:

- ❏   A standardized system organized by a recognized clearing institution or

- ❏   A first-class financial organization specializing in this type of transaction.

As part of securities-lending procedures, the fund must in principle receive a guarantee, the value of which, at the conclusion of the contract, must be at least equal to the total valuation of the securities lent and the accrued interest, if any.

However, as with any system, there are exceptions. One of the more common is that such a guarantee shall not be required if the securities lending is made through Euroclear or Cedel or through any other organization assuring the lender a reimbursement of the value of the securities lent by way of a guarantee or otherwise. This evidently involves credit risk.

In principle, the guarantee in question must be given in the form of liquid assets and/or of securities issued or guaranteed by a member state of the OECD, by their local authorities, or by a supranational institution. Also, the securities borrowed by the fund may not be disposed of during the time they are held by the fund. But there are exceptions; for instance, in some cases they are covered by other sufficient financial vehicles. This enables the fund to restore the borrowed securities at the close of the transaction.

Exceptions of course open gaping holes in a system that otherwise aims to be fullproof. And there are other weaknesses in current legislation, which is largely national in a financial world that is increasingly multinational.

What is still missing, and it is regrettable, is the existence of transnational agreements that cover companies operating cross-border. As the securities lending and borrowing market continues to grow, new transnational legislation is necessary to support arbitrage transactions; for instance, derivative products on the securities of blue-chips-companies no matter what their country of origin.

A similar statement can be made about commissions. The commissions that a lender can normally expect to earn per securities category and market are the bait that sees to it that this market is growing in size, sophistication, and potential, not only in the United States, Europe, and Japan, but in other markets, such as Hong Kong and Singapore.

In their fundamentals, supply and demand also determine the prevailing individual rates in a particular market. But regulation sees to it that the train stays on its tracks. One of the key factors is the safety margins to be observed.

As we have seen in sections 5, 6, and 7, the margin taken for securities lending operations on the collateral is usually 5–10 percent for more conservative deals. But even 10 percent can be totally inadequate if the market turns against the counterparties.

To compensate for the thin safety margin, collaterals need to be marked daily to the market, and lending banks must be made liable for any loss suffered in securities lending despite the provision of collateral. The case of banking failure should also be covered, but current legislation and regulation is falling far short in regard to this type of credit risk.

There are also other problems that have to be legally sorted out. For instance, in the case of capital market transactions entailing options, it is basically the borrower who decides what to pick. While normally the borrower is able to meet the lender's choice, if there is one, this is not legally guaranteed.

Another case in point is voting rights. When securities are on loan, the voting right is passed on to the borrower, depriving the lender of his entitlement to vote on such shares. Should the lender nonetheless wish to exercise his voting right, he must either exclude the securities in question from being lent out or call them back in good time. This is an operation few investors whose assets are lent out are able to perform.

In conclusion, securities lending opens up an arbitrage opportunity, since the futures contract may be bought at the same time it is acquiring a short position in the corresponding securities on the spot market. However, this operation includes major risks, and very few people or companies are able to properly estimate them.

From the Federal Reserve and other central banks to the SEC, FDIC, and OCC, the regulatory bodies have a lot of homework to do in bringing repo agreements, and their many ramifications, under control. A significant part of this effort must focus on the legal and regulatory aspects of delivery versus payment, recasting them to cover the risks associated with the freedom that technology has given to the contracting parties.

10. Delivery Versus Payment

Fundamentally, delivery versus payment (DVP) is a good application since it does away with paperwork. It is also a necessary transition to wealth management and is aimed at the automation of the trading cycle, as shown in Figure 12–4. That's the good news.

Figure 12–4. Working Toward the Automation of the Trading Cycle

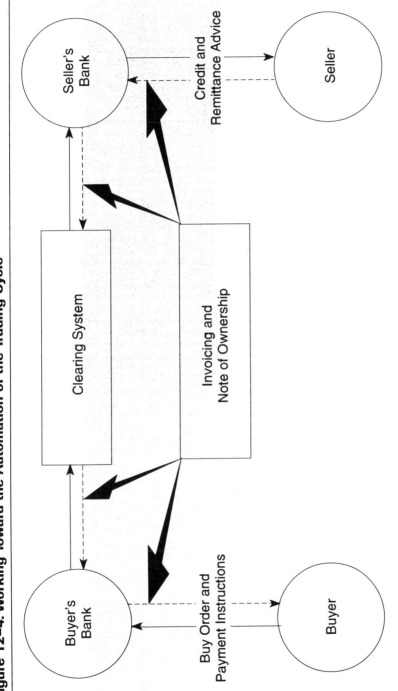

The bad news lies in the gearing effect of DVP, as documented by the securities lending cases we have seen in the preceding sections. Therefore, it is important that both legislators and regulators analyze DVP-generated exposure, both in a national and in a cross-border sense.

The need for paperless solutions in securities dealing, hence delivery versus payment, has been building up over the years. Several fairly practical goals underpin the drive for automating financial transactions in the capital markets:

❑ Necessary speed of action.

❑ Avoidance of massive paper transfers.

❑ Cost reduction.

❑ A drive toward the elimination of transaction errors.

Such goals can be fulfilled through an automated system able to simultaneously send and receive payments and associated remittance advice. This is the goal DVP aims to fulfill. Through the so-called affirming action, the seller of securities is guaranteed his money, and the buyer is guaranteed the financial paper due him.

This is done through delivery of the financial paper, not in physical terms, but by means of a computer-generated confirmation, which removes the need for expensive and time-consuming manual checking of remittance advises against bank statements. The payor is able to negotiate closer and better trading relationships with suppliers by guaranteeing payments.

Administrative savings are made by both the payor and payee, but without affirming action, guarantee sellers will be faced with uncertainties. In the long run, however, successful implementation requires users to be responsive to change. All new systems and procedures involve change in practices and a certain amount of organizational upheaval. Guaranteed security in the processing and transmission of payments and accompanying remittance advises is therefore most crucial.

The critical question is how far this "guaranty" should go. Is it enough to generate a change in debits and credits in the database and then to inform payor and payee accordingly? Or is it necessary to assure that the paperless, hence virtual, security will not be exposed to further manipulation in multiple places:

❑ Currently, through repos.

❑ In the future, by means of other processes, still to be invented.

No one would really argue that the system that provides this DVP service must be both efficient and secure. Both buyers and sellers can be nervous about making important payments electronically if there is no affirming action.

Though gearing and its consequences are central, there are other issues with which to cope in a DVP setting. To ally both perceived and real concerns, providers of databased services must assure effective security methods.

Physical and logical security are important aspects of any computer system. Banks are approaching this issue in different ways which, however, converge in the sense that they target an open payments environment.

Still another subject to be carefully studied in connection to DVP and regulated in a transborder sense is interchange agreements. These must clearly define the obligations, liabilities, and responsibilities of all the participants involved in an automated payment system. This is a basic requirement which presently, however, is not necessarily being fulfilled. For instance, the electronic document interchange (EDI) practice used with delivery versus payment has not been tested in a court of law, making eventual liability an unknown area.

Still another basic aspect of DVP is that virtual assets can be expanded rapidly and easily. We have seen the documentation for this statement through the examination of supergearing by means of repos. The cases we already studied help document that

❑ High leveraging through repos is, to a large extent, still uncharted territory for banks, brokers, and regulators.

❑ Much of the risk comes from the fact that even if the majority of banks are using low technology, the regulators are still further behind.

Changes in well-established business practices should always be scrutinized from a legal viewpoint. Even the most ardent advocates of new systems solutions—and I am among them—agree there are pitfalls to be avoided in implementing and operating totally new procedures. Making haste slowly is the best policy.

Change always needs to be managed. Different roles than those currently prevailing may be necessary when a largely manually based system is replaced by one based on networks, computers, and advanced software. This is written in a dual sense which should always be kept in perspective:

❑ Risk management.

❑ Cost control.

Today, risk management with DVP is substandard because many of the new business opportunities and their associated exposure have not yet been properly analyzed. As for cost control, banks have found to their dismay that costs of implementation are often higher than budgeted, due to inadequate systems planning that ignores or only pays lip service to high technology.

PART THREE

RIGOROUS MODELS AND STRATEGIES FOR DERIVATIVES-RISK MANAGEMENT

13

Using Return on Risk Capital to Control Exposure and Keep Ahead of Competition

1. Introduction

Over the years, the pace of economic development and of market activity quickened. The 19th century industrial revolution was a slow affair compared with the rate of development experienced today in post-industrial society. This acceleration has evident effects on finance at large and on the banking industry in particular.

Because of better integrated financial markets, greatly improved communications, and an increasingly sophisticated computer technology, it is now possible to move money much more quickly than in the past. Growth rates accelerate with leverage, but so do the risks.

Starting in about 1780, after the first developments that heralded the oncoming industrial revolution provided an impetus for change in structures, Britain took 58 years to double its real income per capita. But beginning in 1839, the United States required only 47 years to do the same thing. Starting in 1885, Germany took 40 years, and in the 20th century Japan took 34 years—a pattern shown in Figure 13–1.

After World War II, South Korea managed to industrialize in 11 years, beginning in 1966. More recently still, China has done the same job in less than 10 years. In other words, the pace of growth changes, as revealed by the trend lines in Figure 13–1.

Figure 13–1. Years of Transition in the Process of Industrialization—Compressed Timescales Lead to Growing Financial Stress

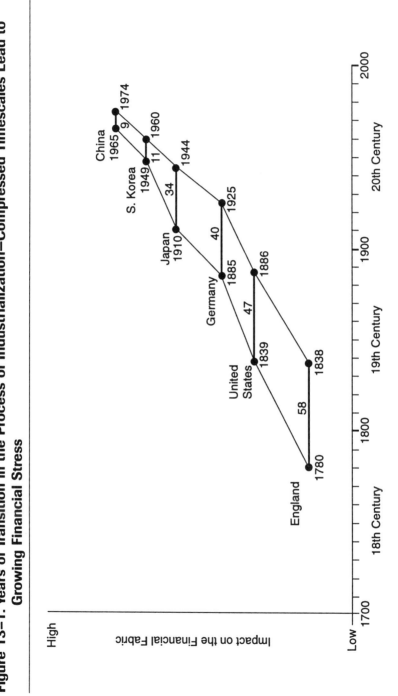

But there are risks assumed with rapid growth, and the financial fabric is under stress. A similar case to that concerning countries can be made about the banking industry as new financial instruments, their rapid spread in the markets, and the unknowns involved in the transition affect the prevailing level of confidence.

Etymologically, in the banking industry, *confidence level* is the degree of protection observed against price movements when setting capital requirements. The 1988 Basel Accord tackled this issue, and so did the proposed Market Risk Amendment of 1993. Both, however, seem to fail on at least two counts:

❏ They do not reflect appropriately on risk measurements.

❏ They do not target financial innovation, which steadily alters the risk types.

Fixed rates of capital requirements is a static approach in a dynamic marketplace, which could give false signals about the soundness of banks and create unwanted incentives for bankers, traders, and investors in cases inducing them to take on disproportioned or concentrated risks.

This chapter addresses the issue of risk management by setting up a system of incentives and disincentives, promoted through the support of high technology. Advanced technology is not only the networks, computers, and software we use, but also the sophisticated procedural solutions we deploy as well as the methodology and the tools we adopt for risk control reasons—all tooled to act in a dynamic environment such as off-balance-sheet financing.

2. The Billions of Dollars Lost with Derivatives

One of the paradoxes of the financial markets in the 1990s is that the instruments generating greatest risk are also among the best for managing risk; or at least that's what bankers say. Today, derivatives provide the common denominator in many trades and also in exploiting a number of new business opportunities. But are we taking due care with exposure?

As with every walk of industrial and financial life, the greatest exposures come from misunderstanding and miscalculation of risk and reward. Off-balance-sheet instruments offer the promise of high returns; however, many companies fail to realize that risk taking and risk control are highly interdependent activities. Both are aimed at raising rates of return by keeping under check the exposure being assumed. Derivatives are thought to be the way to limit treasury risk, yet they also carry a practically unlimited exposure with them.

Highly related to this statement is the fact that any virtue becomes a vice if taken to excess, particularly as with a great number of companies' derivatives trading strategies and, most particularly, risk-management strategies leave much to be wanted. There is also a bottleneck in the flow of information on derivatives, information which, for all practical purpose, should be treated in real time.

In 1992 a report by the Committee of Sponsoring Organizations (COSO), a group of leading accounting and auditing associations, concluded that risk control was not only the job of compliance and internal auditing departments, but also of line managers—from the board and the CEO down the line to lower supervision:

❑ *Risk management* is effective only when every responsible executive becomes convinced that it is *part of doing business*, not separate from it.

❑ *Risk identification* focuses on exposure limits and policies for metrics and measurements. These must be established in the context of a corporate control philosophy.

A valid risk control philosophy is enterprisewide, elaborated at board level, and disseminated to all employees. The biggest risk a company today has is someone in its employment messing up its reputation in the market. The CEO, and the board as a whole, should have no difficulty in following every minute the dictum of Harry Truman: "Tell the bastard to go to hell."[1]

The definition of a precise and rigorous mission for risk management is pressing, yet only very few derivatives dealers and users—from bankers to treasurers of manufacturing companies—have ordered top-to-bottom studies and associated organizational revamping. True enough, well-managed conservative financial institutions have implemented some controls and reforms, including

❑ Rewriting investment policies.

❑ Establishing exposure control procedures.

❑ Implementing advanced computer systems.

These, however, are exceptions. The majority continue to use 20-year-old software and slow-moving mainframes, which cost big money but help precious little, as they provide management with information that is too little and too late.

Shaken by the huge losses that hit the derivatives market in 1994,[2] some companies decided to restrict their hedging and associated expo-

---

[1] David McCullough, *Truman* (New York: Simon and Schuster, 1992).
[2] See also Chapter 1.

sure in the use of financial instruments to "plain vanilla" forwards, options, and futures. But this, too, is an exception. In a large number of cases, there are no top management directives.

Even more rare are radical solutions. As we have seen in Chapter 12, on October 20, 1994, Kodak sold its portfolio of derivatives and got out of the associated risks. For the time being, however, there is no board decision of a similar nature among manufacturing companies in the United States, Europe, or Japan.

Yet 1994 saw an explosive growth in losses. Figure 13–2 has a strong message. It shows that, counted in billions of dollars, losses with derivatives were rather insignificant in 1989 and 1990. They jumped to an estimated $0.5 billion in 1991 but were somewhat reduced in 1992, only to run out of control toward $2 billion in 1993.

Then, in 1994, came the shock wave. Losses with derivatives reached $10.42 billion. This is 521 percent higher than 1993 and about 3,000 percent higher than 1992.

The estimated $10.42 billion in losses with derivatives during one and only one year has five major components:

Figure 13–2. Publicly Announced Losses with Derivatives Financial Instruments in the United States

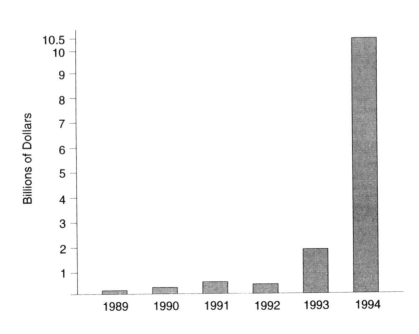

1. Some $6.8 billion reported in mid-October 1994, of which the bond debacle of February and March that same year constituted the lion's share.[3]

2. The $200 million in smaller accounts announced since then from various sources.

3. The whopping $1.5 billion written off by General Electric when it sold Kidder Peabody at a huge loss to Paine Webber after the manipulations done by its subsidiary with derivative financial instruments.

4. The $2 billion of red ink by Orange County in December 1994.

5. The $800 million in toxic waste absorbed by GE Capital and so on.

The estimated billions of losses with derivatives in the United States represents real money. What does this figure mean in terms of notional principal amounts? The answer evidently depends on the ratio we use to convert real money lost to the notional principal of original derivatives deals, in an inverse process to the one we followed in Chapter 2—going from notional principal to real money.

As it will be recalled, when it comes to a cumulative conversion, rather than following the path of instrument-by-instrument, some banks use a high-value demodulator of 50 to 60, which is very risky and irresponsible. Others apply a more conservative divisor of 30; in crisis cases, some banks divide by 25 or even 20.

Therefore, if we take 40 as an average ratio, which is quite evidently a guesstimate, we reach the conclusion that the $10.42 billion of real money lost in 1994 represents a notional principal of about $417 billion in different trades—in terms of order of magnitude.

Any serious financial analyst will take full notice of such huge losses, adjusting his estimates of the P&L of banks and other companies whose treasuries engage in off-balance-sheet trades. Top management should evidently do the same because there is now evidence that profits with derivatives are far from being what they are said to be—while the losses can be huge.

3. A Thorough Procedural Infrastructure for Efficient Risk Management

The statistics we have seen in section 2 must evidently be adequately analyzed through a fine-grain model that will sort out the losses by

---

[3] *Business Week*, October 31, 1994.

desk, instrument, currency, risk type, market, and counterparty. This however is not easily done because rare is the case of banks willing and able to keep their derivatives trades and other deals in real detail.

Yet every financial institution and every treasurer should know that risk management cannot be done in an average manner. "God is in the detail," as Mies van der Rohe once said. Risk management must be exercised book by book, for example:

- ❑ Foreign exchange.

- ❑ Interest rates.

- ❑ Equities and equity derivatives.

- ❑ Options written.

Each trading desk should look after the risks it takes, and the company should have a global risk manager who measures the bank's exposure interactively in real-time, along the frame of reference discussed in the first paragraph of this section.

Reports on the derivatives portfolio should be very analytical prior to being consolidated. They should be interactive, and visualize *past* and *new* risk areas, looking not only at the exposure on a marked-to-market basis, but also providing a *prognosis* of potential exposure

- ❑ By underlying reason.

- ❑ By function of highest likelihood.

Learning from the reporting requirements now being developed in the United States by the regulatory authorities, I have developed the four-way classification we saw in the last section of Chapter 1 and in Figure 5–1. It permits the sorting out of off-balance-sheet deals along a fairly consistent frame of reference.

In fact, now that losses from OBS trades approach the $10 billion mark in just one year, it would have been rewarding to see this pattern of risks in connection to the $9.5 billion lost in 1994 from derivatives. Management control can be enhanced if we sort the derivatives in each bank's or other institution's portfolio along the line of:

1. *Past Due.* Derivatives having a market risk similar to that of *bad loans* traded at huge discounts.

2. *Sour Derivatives.* Contracts in trouble because of credit risk.

Let's recall that *past due* and *sour derivatives* are off-balance-sheet exposures. At the same time, *sour derivatives* and *bad loans* are related because of counterparty troubles.

Institutions wanting to develop a more sophisticated model will also account for the fact that the risks involved in this frame of reference are *metastasizing* from bank to bank and company to company. They do so through single crossovers rather than simple mutations. Therefore, genetic algorithms can provide a good predictive platform.

As the losses mount in the years to come, it will be necessary to have interactively available knowledge artifacts (agents) that can answer queries such as the following:

❏ What might the snowball effect be if the derivatives losses were $10 billion? $15 billion? $20 billion?

❏ Which desks will be the hardest hit? Which banks? Which treasuries?

❏ How much metastasizing of exposure from bank to bank has there been?

A crucial query that must be immediately answered even with fragmented evidence is, What does the $9.5 billion in losses mean as a fraction of the ongoing exposure? It is evident that the answer to this query depends on whom to believe regarding the OBS risk-taking as a whole.

The Bank for International Settlements says that the worldwide exposure is today at the $15 trillion to $17 trillion level in terms of notional principal. My own research indicates that it is nearer to the $50 trillion level.[4]

❏ BIS counts the exposure figures only once, even if two parties are involved in each deal. Its estimate stands at the $16 trillion level as an average.

❏ I count these exposure amounts twice, because both counterparties take risks in each derivatives deal and I don't believe there is a magic netting formula. Either or both can fail.

In fact, taking the Orange County bankruptcy as an example, what Merrill Lynch sold to the county's treasury and CS First Boston has underwritten should have been counted more than twice, given the number of parties involved in the deal and the exposure taken by each one of them. In the last analysis it is not (yet) the bank that failed but the client.

Nevertheless, to be fair in the analytical estimates, Table 13–1 elaborates on both hypotheses: the $16 billion and the $50 billion. It also accounts for the fact that the reported losses are so far only in the

---

[4] See also D. N. Chorafas, *Derivative Financial Instruments* (London and Dublin: Lafferty, 1995).

Table 13–1. Estimate of 1994 Losses in the United States with Derivative Financial Instruments

	BIS Hypothesis	*My Hypothesis*
Total outstanding notional principal (worldwide)	$16 trillion	$50 trillion
Estimated total outstanding notional principal (USA)	$6.4 trillion	$20 trillion
Derivatives losses in 1994	$10.42 billion	$10.42 billion
Losses converted to notional principal by a factor of 40	$417 billion	$417 billion
Losses as percent of notional principal (worldwide)	2.6%	0.83%
Losses as percent of notional principal (only for the United States)	6.52%	2.09%

United States—whose banks and other companies roughly carry 40 percent of the reported risk.

The careful reader will appreciate that the worst-case scenario is, of course, under the BIS hypothesis. Counting only the U.S. companies' exposure to derivatives, from where the reported losses came in the first place, this scenario indicates a dramatically high rate of failure in 1994.

Even if it were a 2.09 percent rate of failure—which is the level featured in my hypothesis—it would have been too high. But 6.52 percent is scary. No serious bank executive, company treasurer, or financial analyst can take comfort in such a figure.

Let's not forget that the whole debacle with the popularization of junk bonds started with Michael Milken's thesis that fallen angels (which subsequently have been rebaptized high-interest bonds) carry with them "only" a 1–2 percent rate of failure. During the 1980s, we saw the results of gearing on junk bonds.

Because necessity is the mother of invention, there can be no better documentation than the one provided in Table 13–1 that a thorough procedural infrastructure is needed for efficient risk management. Figure

Figure 13–3. An Interactively Accessible Radar Chart for Off-Balance-Sheet Risk Management

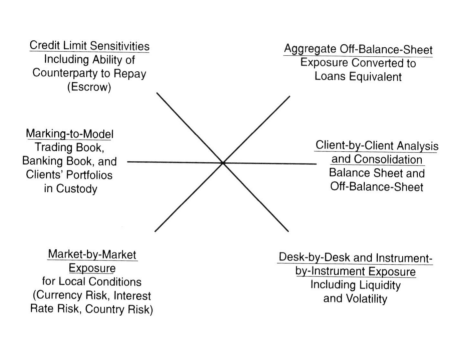

13–3 presents a radar chart developed for interactive reporting reasons. It is based on the results of the meeting with FASB and provides a framework on which a valid procedural infrastructure can be built.[5]

4.   Measuring Risks and Rewards Through Risk Capital

The exposure figures we have seen in section 3 suggest that a fairly significant investment in research and development is required to control risk effectively. Anything short of a thorough research effort will be insufficient, with the result that the blind will be leading the blind in the derivatives business.

That is part and parcel of a strategy of being at the forefront of the derivatives business without sustaining inordinate losses. The money to be invested in R&D is so significant that only a handful of players can

---

[5] See also D.N. Chorafas and H. Steinmann, *Off-balance-sheet Financial Instruments* (Chicago: Probus, 1994).

afford it. No wonder the large majority of the turnover in this business is controlled by a few money center banks. These banks typically have a strong presence in the world's financial markets, and their share in OBS trades is increasing. The others are "me too" players who never heard Winston Churchill's dictum: "One should not jump in the sea to fight the sharks."

Of course no one is immune to an eventual cataclysm, and all players in OBS deals have to be very careful about participating in a business where losses, theoretically at least, can be astronomical. Losses can be very substantial, as documented by the 1994 examples we have seen in sections 2 and 3—which run in the billions of dollars.

Every financial vehicle can turn belly-up. In the adjustable-rate mortgage (ARM) crisis of September 1992, some French banks were thought to have been extremely badly burned by the exposure of their derivatives teams to exchange rate movements because they had neither the technology nor the skills to follow up fluctuations in this exposure. This follow-up has many phases connected to risk management:

- ❑ Management analysis.
- ❑ Product planning.
- ❑ Market research.
- ❑ Choice of counterparties.
- ❑ Risk analysis.
- ❑ Costing of risks.
- ❑ Expert systems for steady follow-up.
- ❑ Real-time internal controls.
- ❑ Rapid corrective action.

Among the risk factors entering a rigorous risk-management model are credit equivalence, premium rate of counterparty, notional principal amount of the trade, market volatility, and time to maturity, to mention a few. The good news, however, is that the risk taken with any trade, evidently including derivatives, can be *costed*; with subsequent transactions and their P&L evaluation based on this costing principle.

Based on the appropriate infrastructure of risks and costs, a model similar to that of return on equity (ROE) can be developed, which rather than considering total equity—share capital, reserves, and other provisions—considers

- ❑ Risk capital.
- ❑ Entrepreneurial risk.

Risk capital set by and used within a financial institution or any other organization is capital put aside to cover *deliberate risks*. All off-balance-sheet operations fall under this heading. Let's face it,

Risk Capital = Acceptable Loss Potential

This acceptable loss potential must become a conscience at the board level and in all levels of management. For measurement purposes, it must be converted to *limits*[6] in a dual approach that addresses both qualification and quantification from market parameters to default probability.

It serves nothing to deny that the loss potential is real. When a couple of years back Salomon Brothers set aside $500 million for the creation of a AAA affiliate to deal in derivatives, this money had been risk capital. Other investment banks and brokers, such as Merrill Lynch, did the same. All of them therefore accepted the risk capital notion—with its associated entrepreneurial risk. A good solution rests on two factors:

1. The clear definition of business activity and of the potential risks it involves.

2. The willingness of the board to take risks, or, conversely, to follow a strategy of risk aversion.

Among the key variables that enter the entrepreneurial risk equation, we distinguish business policy at large—not just trading—as well as the recognition of existing risks, new risks to be undertaken, and their profit and loss potential.

The rationale for a rigorous approach to risk capital and the real-time management of exposure lies in the fact that the old systems that are almost universally used for risk evaluation are not responding to the challenges posed by derivative products. As financial transactions became more sophisticated, they resulted in reallocating various classes of risk among

❑ Lenders.

❑ Borrowers.

❑ Intermediaries.

This, in turn, made the financial institution a professional risk taker—a fact that has been magnified by the volatility that prevails in the markets as well as the proliferation of new financial instruments.

---

[6] See also Figure 1–3 and the Heisenberg principle, on which it is based.

Derivative financial instruments are not another sort of vanilla ice cream banking. It is a totally different ball game and is unorthodox by old standards. Every investor, every treasurer, and every banker must appreciate that tomorrow

❑   The *risk capital* he put on the balance may no longer be there.

❑   The best measure he can use to track exposure is the *return on risk capital* (RORC).

RORC constitutes a layered approach, one of its components resembling an insurance premium applicable to every transaction. We will see how this works in sections 5 and 6, after we first consider some background factors in fuzzy engineering.

In terms of metrics, the return on risk capital this text proposes can be a powerful tool that allows a link between the more traditional ROE and risk control. Its implementation requires advanced technology to simulate in real time the response of *different*

❑   Market scenarios.

❑   Financial products.

❑   Default(s) by counterparty(ies).

Such experimentation makes it feasible to find the best bet for optimizing returns on risk being taken, in connection to an expected reward. This is a feat that low-technology banks simply cannot accomplish.

As the preceding sections emphasized, detail is most important. To express risk and return in this frame of reference, it is necessary to break down the group target to the level of a single operating unit (for market scenarios) or atomic financial instrument (for products) and the individual counterparty with its default probability.

Since risk capital is expressed in financial terms, results must be integrated with the bank's planning and budgeting system, at a significant level of detail, not merely in a consolidated manner. In terms of technology, an object-oriented approach will permit the construction of ephemeral hierarchies for reporting reasons, as every new front-desk transaction, back-office operation, audit, or management control requires.[7]

---

[7] See also D. N. Chorafas and H. Steinmann, *Object-Oriented Databases* (Englewood Cliffs, NJ: Prentice Hall, 1993).

5. Using Fuzzy Engineering to Establish the Basis of an Insurance Premium

Market volatility, liquidity considerations, counterparty risk, and the proliferation of financial instruments make it difficult for any single individual to follow the market unassisted. A greater competition as well as global interactions between financial institutions see to it that managers and professionals must depend on technology to be ahead of the game.

Increasingly, more sophisticated customers see to it that we cannot handle our mission without breakthroughs in technology, hence the wisdom of classifying and identifying the type of risk we are taking in financial transactions well before we undertake specific commitments. There is a fundamental difference between

❑   Looking at a derivatives trade on its own.

❑   Examining what we get when a derivatives trade is seen as an integral part of a trading book or a portfolio.

In the latter case, we are interested in how the trade impacts the balance sheet and off-balance-sheet from a variety of viewpoints. Therefore, a global estimate on expected profit and loss is too summary to permit an informed decision and subsequent control. We must take into account—and in a detailed manner—different risks that may affect our transaction and its exposure.

Uncertainty is the bottom line of risk management. *Uncertainty* is the quality or state of not being certain about the subject we handle and its evolution. Many market conditions are characterized by doubt. The uncertainties associated with them are present because of factors

❑   Not exactly known.

❑   Not well determined.

❑   Possibly unsettled

❑   Involving contingencies.

Senior bankers will appreciate that these statements characterize an environment in which they have been operating for many years. The more sophisticated the products, the more their effects can be vague, undefined, not clearly stated, imprecise, or even unknown.

This constitutes an excellent domain for the implementation of *fuzzy engineering*.[8] The tools are available, but few banks know how to use them. Figure 13–4 presents a fuzzy engineering model for risk man-

---

[8] For practical applications of fuzzy engineering see D. N. Chorafas, *Chaos Theory in the Financial Markets* (Chicago: Probus, 1994).

Figure 13–4. A Fuzzy Engineering Model to Evaluate Return on Risk Capital

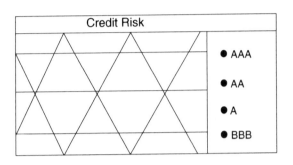

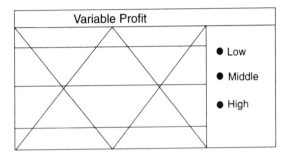

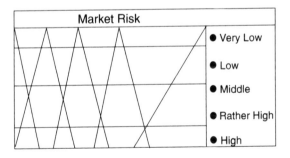

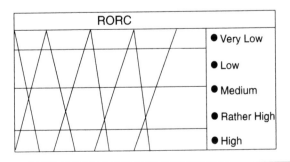

agement. The contents of each of these four quarter spaces force the financial analyst, the trader, and the investor to think in structured terms, though they use qualitative, not quantitative, responses. These quarter spaces represent

- ❏ Variable credit risk.
- ❏ Variable market risk.
- ❏ Variable profit.
- ❏ Return on risk capital (RORC)

Regarding credit risk, for instance, most banks follow the policy that *default risk* is taken as *losses*. What this new solution suggests is that it is better to use a *risk premium* that acts like an *insurance premium*. The goal of this approach is to

- ❏ Include default risk in product *pricing*.
- ❏ Assure that all derivative instruments address default risk.

It *looks* as though the system is geared to penalize the more risky transactions. It is in the sense of requiring the payment of an insurance premium commensurate with the risk being taken—the way the actuarians work. Every banker should feel at home with the idea of having insurance.

This dual concept of return on risk capital and of having an insurance on every derivatives transaction (in an accounting sense) can be instrumental in increasing the sensitivity of everyone about the exposure involved with derivatives. At the same time, it optimizes the bank's potential to enter risks.

The implementation of this solution is not difficult. But, apart from the fuzzy engineering model we have seen, it requires consistent board-level guidelines, coordination of activities worldwide, and both planned and actual control to make sure that

- ❏ Insurance premiums are always applied.
- ❏ Allocated limits are observed.
- ❏ Accurate and timely measurements are made.
- ❏ All operating units are able to control their actions.
- ❏ Centralized control activity is exercised on-line in real time.

There is also a significant amount of preparatory work that must be done, starting with the determination of the total risk capital. As has been already emphasized in this chapter, a good way to look at it from the board's and the CEO's viewpoint is as *the loss* the bank is willing and able to accept *in the worst case*.

Figure 13–5. A Three-Dimensional Framework Permitting the Visualization of RORC by Allocating It to Risk Classes

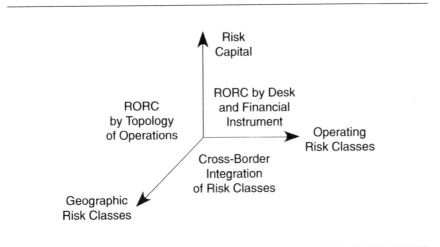

Once defined, this total risk capital has to be allocated to the different individual risk classes—which have to first be determined (both in terms of operating units and internationally). Then comes the evaluation of the worst-case-per-risk class. The limit for each risk category must be commensurate with the worst-case analysis.

6. Risk-Related Results and Return on Risk Capital

A frame of reference that suggests risk capital, operating risk classes, and geographical risk spread permits following RORC in three dimensions as well as keeping the bank's whole risk control system dynamic. Each one of these categories should be tested and reevaluated in real time, on the basis of worst-case scenarios.

Figure 13–5 explains this approach and identifies the target of each two-dimensional report definition. Notice that a three-dimensional approach, enriched with graphical presentation and color, can provide the best feedback possible for risk-management purposes. It can also lead to the implementation of fractals in n-dimensions to be viewed interactively in 3-D on a selective basis.

A number of risk factors can be examined in this way, flexibly arranged one by one and then grouped together to show compound events. As we will see in subsequent chapters, we have available today algorithms that aid in the analysis of

❑   Counterparty risk.

❑   Currency risk.

❑   Interest rate risk.

❑   Country risk.

❑   Equity price risk.

❑   Bond investment risk.

❑   Derivatives risk.

❑   Liquidity risk.

❑   Settlement risk.

❑   Operational risk.

Taken together, currency risk, interest rate risk, derivatives risk, bond investment risk, and equity risk give *position risk*. Counterparty risk, country risk, and liquidity risk contribute to the calculation of default risk. Position risk and default risk are *business risks*—whether on-balance-sheet or off-balance-sheet.

Each one of the risks in the list above can be broken down into smaller elements. For instance, liquidity risk can be divided into maturity, calling, and refinance exposure.

But while a finer breakdown is necessary to both qualify and quantify each type of risk by transaction, there is one more very important point not to be missed. The forementioned risks are not independent of one another. In a way they overlap, and it is also possible that two or more risks may be present in any one financial transaction, or all of them may apply to a long (complex) transaction by the same client.

This cumulation and superposition of risks has changed the rules of the game quite significantly. We no longer speak of the need to report the risk associated with a list of products by country of operation as the key to risk management, though undoubtedly this is important. Our grid must be much finer, permitting us to report interactively in a real-space sense, by

❑   Risk category and subclass.

❑   Operating department (or departments) reaching the limits of any one risk.

❑   Product or products entering the transaction(s).

❑   Creditworthiness of counterparty with whom the operation is done.

❑   Package deals that may involve many products in different currencies, countries, and conditions.

The growing need is one of minute detail and real-time integration, assessing on-line information at front desks and in back offices; including trading book, settlement area, banking book, treasury function(s), general accounting, and management accounting. The latter should include obtained price, incurred cost, expected margins, and above all, *assumed risk*.

To be in charge, management needs a model that can provide risk information affecting the bank as a whole: any time, for any product, in connection to any client, anywhere. It should operate separate from but in coordination with general accounting, and it should act in real time. The modules of the model should address well-defined goals:

❑ Optimize the bank's potential to enter risks.

❑ Assure consistency with top management's guidelines.

❑ Control the allocation of limits.

❑ Respond in real space to risk exposures.

❑ Provide the basis for worst-case scenarios and immediate reporting.

Default risk should be given particular attention, and the model must closely follow operations risk, including fraud and market breakdowns that cannot be easily quantified. Hence the model should serve to judge how much of the risk capital to keep in order to meet extraordinary conditions.

This last point brings another issue into perspective. Taking into account that banks today allocate about two-thirds of their credit lines to counterparties to off-balance-sheet deals, the analytics we establish should be able to follow a dual track:

1. *Risk capital* covering exposures that the bank deliberately enters, principally with off-balance-sheet deals.

2. *Classical equity* addressing the more traditional entrepreneurial risks that are on-balance-sheet.

As Figure 13–6 illustrates, these two lines should merge in a consolidated statement. But it is wise not to loose sight of the fact that while risk capital and classical equity complement one another in business activities, they don't perform the same functions; hence, they should retain their distinct identities.

In conclusion, the concept of *risk capital* is new and so is the metric of return on risk capital. The definition of risk capital identifies the willingness of the board of directors and of top management to take risks. It also helps to establish the domain of business activity in which the financial institution or any other company will concentrate.

Figure 13–6. Risk Capital and Classical Equity Are Distinct Entities, Though They Complement One Another

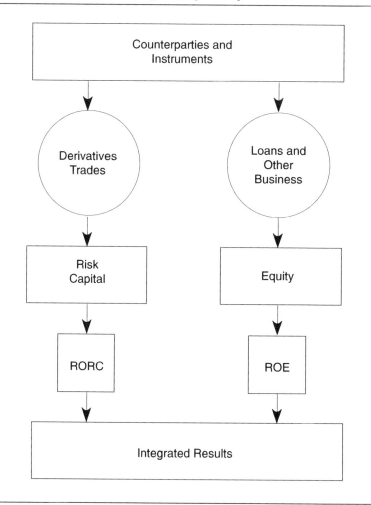

7. Using the Concepts of Margins and Insurance Premiums with Securities Lending

Chapter 12 outlined the risks involved with securities lending, or repo agreements. It also explained why the 5–10 percent margin that banks usually calculate is deadly inadequate—let alone the fact that it is taken as a classical static buffer rather than being steadily recalculated as a dynamic insurance premium, which changes with the market pattern.

My approach is different. First, I tune the risk percentage that constitutes the buffer to the potential price movement of the securities being borrowed or lent out. In so doing, I take as a basis the worst-case scenario of the last five years, in the closeout period between counterparty default and liquidation of collateral.

The liquidation of Orange County's collateral by Credit Swiss First Boston in early December 1994 may serve as an example. But while this is necessary, it is not enough. In principle, however, metrics and measures must be dynamic because there is always a case worse than the one before. Let's keep in view the fact of a two-layered approach that involves

1. A buffer risk margin, known as *haircut*.

2. An *insurance premium*, to be computed through risk-adjusted return on capital.[9]

The concept of an insurance premium was presented in Chapter 12. As it has been explained, it is a function of three variables:

❑ Credit risk.

❑ Market risk.

❑ Quality of loaned securities.

Not only is the actual quality important, but how diversified is the basket to be loaned. For any practical purpose, securities being borrowed by a counterparty are not confined solely to equities and bonds, even less to one type of these instruments. Similarly, chances are the collateral pledged will not be homogeneous, but that it will involve not only cash but also other forms.

Both haircuts and insurance premiums must be computed analytically, addressing every item in the lent-out or borrowed basket and its corresponding risk factor. Typically, risk percentages are statistically derived based on the assumption of collateralization in cash at 100 percent of market value of the securities in reference. This I find inadequate because computation is based on averages rather than detail by security in the basket and worst-case analysis regarding each security.

When banks engaging in repo agreements talk of detail, what they essentially mean is differentiating between bonds, exchange-traded equities, OTC equities, and warrants. This is a valid distinction, as each class carries its own risks, but it falls short of the detail needed.

Many banks lean toward applying a margin of 3–5 percent for bonds and 8–10 percent for exchange-traded equities, with convertible bonds falling in between these margins. By contrast, for over-the-counter equities a haircut of 13–15 percent is used, and for warrants the

---

[9] We will see an example in this section.

margin increases to a level of 20–25 percent on the principle that the risk being assumed is higher.

This practice is correct. Less commendable is the fact that the basket of lent/borrowed securities is not analyzed in detail item by item. Yet, with the appropriate fuzzy engineering models and databased price information, this would not have been a forbidding task. It is simple, and it is doable.

Because of lack of detail, there are miscalculations made in connection to repos, which can be partly corrected by applying the concept of an insurance premium. If, for instance, the risk equivalent of taking equities as collateral instead of cash is 8 percent, lending equities versus 105 percent cash would represent a risk of 3 percent; that is, 8 percent minus the 5 percent haircut. But borrowing equities versus 105 percent cash would represent a risk of 13 percent, which means 8 percent plus 5 percent the collateralization margin.

An insurance premium must address these risks, taking notice of the fact that, as can be appreciated, the relationship is asymmetrical. However, while attention to this subject is necessary, it is not enough. *Liquidity risk* must also be accounted for. The insurance premium should be kept dynamic by marking-to-market or marking-to-model. An extra credit risk premium must be added for less than AAA counterparties, and the use of another factor is advisable to reflect lack of basket diversification—which increases the risk.

Financial institutions engaged in repo agreements began paying attention to this last factor, using a multiplier k, which typically is in the range $1 < k < 2$. Still one more crucial factor is whether the securities are being lent or borrowed on an unsecured basis. The model reflecting the risk equation is not easy to develop, but it is feasible.

Finally, even if a financial institution follows the practice of netting with a counterparty with which it has both borrowing and lending agreements, the insurance premium should never be waived. Some banks think that offsetting can reduce the risk premium side. This practice has many dangers because in reality risks are never really netted.

8.   Applying Risk Premiums with Default Risk

In section 6 we said that default risk is composed of counterparty risk, country risk, and liquidity risk, among other factors. Classically, the default risk has been considered a loss, and it has been written postmortem in the P&L statement when it occurred. There is, however, a much better way to approach this issue as well as any other business risk:

❑   Calculate a risk premium, which should be integrated into product pricing.

❑   Use the risk premium as a basis for provision for risk capital.

❏ Treat the risk premium as an atomic element in connection to counterparty, country, and liquidity risk factors.[10]

This is a *new departure*, and, as it should be appreciated, new departures are necessary to face new risks—such as those arising with derivatives—or old risks in a new off-balance-sheet setting.

Charles Taylor, executive director of the Washington-based Group of Thirty think tank, argues that the model-based approach to market-risk management adopted by derivatives specialists should be extended

❏ To other areas of securities trading.

❏ To credit risk and other types of risk.[11]

This proposal has substance because the over-the-counter traded derivatives, which according to different estimates represent between one-third and one-half of all OBS trades, don't have an active market. This does not permit mark-to-market—as many central banks suggested, or commercial and investment banks pretend to do.

A similar argument is valid in regard to *default* risk. The issue of how best to police derivatives markets and their associated risks has been exercising the minds of regulators, bankers, and derivatives clients for years. No unique "best" solutions have been found so far. What this section proposes is a way out of this impasse.

Table 13–2 contrasts three concepts that are fairly distinct from one another yet often confused in people's minds: *Transaction* risk, *position* risk, and *default* risk. Each has its own characteristics as well as effects. Therefore, different models are necessary for their handling.

One of the added advantages of marking-to-model is that it serves the central idea that the amount of capital a bank needs is related to the riskiness of its business. The whole sense of risk capital and of RORC is based on this issue. For each class, the associated risk is measured by

❏ The volatility of market behavior.

❏ The volume and type of trades the bank undertakes.

❏ The accumulated past exposure in money terms.

❏ The chance of default inherent in transactions and investments.

Unlike the traditional approach of assessing credit exposure, the calculation of risk capital in connection to derivatives involves predict-

---

[10] As well as other risk factors, depending on the risk management policy followed by the bank.

[11] *Financial Times*, July 7, 1994.

Table 13–2. Comparison of Transaction, Position, and Default Risks

Transaction Risk	Position Risk	Default Risk
Consequence of give-and-take in a deal.	Consequence of market risk.	Consequence of credit risk, country insolvency, or illiquidity.
Taken as arbitrage or to fulfill a business strategy.	Taken for profits in the short, medium, or longer run.	Accompanying choice of counterparty, its grading and country.
Calculated at the time of the transaction.	Accumulated in the trading book and in the portfolio.	Considered as a loss at any time it comes.
Can be measured on a transaction and instrument basis.	Can be measured cross-transaction, cross-instrument, cross-counterparty.	Can be measured on a counterparty basis, and other factors.
Until now *not* subject to insurance. This should change.	Considered part of P&L.	Until now considered a dry hole. This should change.

ing future volatility, using tests of hypotheses regarding the future course of market events, and marking-to-model.

The whole trick in modeling counterparty risk lies in the ability to create a number that represents the position limit for default risk. Both fuzzy engineering and worst-case scenarios are applicable in this effort. The prerequisites are

❏ The development of *trading categories* for counterparties.

❏ The construction and steady update of counterparty, country, and liquidity watch lists.[12]

❏ The establishment and update of counterparty risk premium limit(s).

❏ The proper allocation of risk capital, as outlined in sections 3 and 4.

Genetic algorithms can be effectively used for risk capital allocation reasons,[13] taking into account risk premiums, component risks of default, derivatives instruments being used, loans equivalence of the notional principal amount, the types of risk in the transaction, and the time to maturity.

As we have seen in considerable detail in Chapter 2, loans equivalence is very important because loans is a subject every self-respecting banker understands. This is not yet true of derivatives. A snapshot on loans equivalence permits turning OBS deals toward a known landscape where it is possible to implement risk components related to

1. The counterparty, its rating, and collateral.

2. The instrument and market risk.

3. The time frame over which the transaction will mature.

The fuzzy engineering model outlined in Figure 13–4, can be used as the reference schema to which the above three characteristic risk factors are applied. A numerical example on the computation of risk capital is given in Table 13–3. Notice that the time to maturity has been purposely kept constant at one year to simplify this example.

As will be appreciated, the customer rating does not enter into the choice of a demodulator that is strictly instrument oriented. By contrast, counterparty rating influences the premium rate applied to loans equivalent. This is shown in Table 13–4.

---

12 The generally used "good customer watch list" is inadequate.

13 See also D. N. Chorafas, *Rocket Scientists in Banking* (London and Dublin: Lafferty Publications, 1995).

Table 13–3. Computation of Risk Capital for Different Trades

Customer	Rating	Transaction	Time to Maturity	Notional Amount	Demodulator	Loans Equivalent
I	AA	Binary option	1 year	$50 M	1	$50 M
II	AA	Oil futures	1 year	$200 M	25	$8 M
III	AA	Interest rate swap	1 year	$400 M	40	$10 M
IV	BBB	Interest rate swap	1 year	$160 M	40	$4 M
V	BBB	Loan	1 year	$20 M	1	$20 M
VI	BB	Gold futures	1 year	$100 M	30	$3.3 M

In both Table 13–3 and Table 13–4, Customer V has been taken as a control reference. His line of credit is used for a bread-and-butter loan. Hence, the demodulator in Table 13–3 is equal to one.

At an interest rate of 6 percent per year, the BBB grade of this client calls for a premium of 12 percent, which translates into interest of $1,344,000 for the loan—of which $144,000 is the risk premium. Similarly, all other counterparties who deal in derivatives pay a risk premium in function of their credit rating—which varies from 2 basis points for AAA to 20 basis points for BB, over and above the prevailing interest rate.

Notice that an interest rate risk is embedded in this approach. In the case of the straight loan customer V, if the loan has a fixed interest rate this is part of the risk the bank takes with its loan portfolio. In all other cases, however, should the interest rates significantly change, the risk premium can be overapplied or underapplied—depending on the direction of the change.

9. RORC and Necessary Organizational Decisions on Default Risk

The practical example we have followed in section 8 suggests a number of prerequisites in the application of return on risk capital. The quantification of RORC requires the able handling of default risk which, in turn, calls for the *credit classification* of the counterparties.

This should be done as a matter of course by any financial institution. Credit classification, however, can be carried to a higher level of sophistication through the application of sequential sampling techniques, known from mathematical statistics. Based on this concept, Bankers Trust has developed the successful risk-adjusted return on capital (RAROC) solution. The needed statistical tables are in MIL-STD-104[14] and therefore are in the public domain. These tables originated with the Manhattan Project and can be considered rocket science.

Risk-adjusted return on capital is a good example of the new metrics. Typically, when a borrower (company or individual) goes to a bank for a loan, a binary decision is made: Qualify/not qualify. Risk-adjusted approaches are not black or white:

❑ They stratify.

❑ They put a premium by risk ceiling.

This is another excellent example of risk insurance. *Risk assessment* aims to quantify dangers of exposure so that responsible officers can

---

[14]U.S. Government Printing Office, Washington, D.C.

Table 13–4. Application of Credit Risk Premium to the Counterparty

Customer	Rating	Loans Equivalent	Premium Rate	Time to Maturity	Applicable Rate	Applied Premium
I	AAA	$50 M	2 bp/IR*	1 year	0.12%	$60,000
II	AA	$8 M	6 bp/IR	1 year	0.36%	$28,800
III	AA	$10 M	6 bp/IR	1 year	0.36%	$36,000
IV	BBB	$4 M	12 bp/IR	1 year	0.72%	$28,800
V	BBB	$20 M	12 bp/IR	1 year	0.72%	$144,000
VI	BB	$3.3 M	20 bp/IR	1 year	1.20%	$39,600

* Basis points over the interest rate of 6% for 1 year

decide if a particular risk is worth running. Calculated risks should be covered by premiums. This *permits*

❏ Expanding money and securities trading.

❏ Further building up and market financial services.

This notion also fulfills the second prerequisite for the able handling of default risk: *instrument classification.* Very few banks have done their homework in this domain. The absence of instrument classification in a risk-oriented sense handicaps RORC by making impossible

❏ Determination of risk premium by instrument and desk.

❏ Computation of a demodulator by instrument to account for market risk.

❏ Separation of risk premiums in terms of customer-related and product-related factors.

As it has been seen in Table 13–3, the very risky *binary option,* which provides discontinuous payoffs in either an *all-or-nothing* or a *one-touch* mode,[15] has a demodulator equal to one. This has been chosen so because of the nature of the vehicle: If the option is in-the-money, the buyer will receive the whole notional principal amount of the contract. Therefore, it is quite normal that a high premium is asked even for a AAA client (see Table 13–4). This premium could exceed the price of the binary option, in which case the trade should not be done. If the premium is low, it will leave very little margin, which should not induce the trader in making the deal.

As this example helps document, failure to proceed with a rigorous classification of risks by instrument does not allow the dynamic utilization of risk capital or, for that matter, an approach that permits timely and effective risk management. It also makes very difficult, if not impossible, the frequent and close monitoring of:

❏ Transaction risk.

❏ Position risk.

❏ Default risk.

If bankers, investors, and treasurers followed this procedure, they would not have been stumbling on derivatives risks, which are unmanageable. The $2 billion would not have been lost by the Orange County fund, and we would not be talking today of so many other municipalities in the United States on the brink of bankruptcy, such as the City of

---

[15]See also Chapter 10 on exotic options.

San Jose in Silicon Valley, California's San Diego County and San Bernardino, or Cuyahola County in Ohio.

10. Maintaining and Enhancing the Quality of Banking Services

Maintaining and selectively enhancing the quality of banking services is inseparable from the risk identification and measurement procedure we examined in section 9. This, in turn, calls for the development of new information technology able to sustain product and market goals.

The careful reader will appreciate that the launching of new and sophisticated financial products is a dangerous task without the organizational work I have just emphasized. A sound risk-management policy must see to it that all players involved in OBS trades are able to decide, through interactive profit-and-loss evaluation, where to draw the line by

❑   Credit line.

❑   Capital exposure.

❑   Product specifications.

❑   Liquidity.

❑   Maturity level.

The solution we adopt should impose *no* geographic limitations and *no* time-zone constraints. The separation of product-related risk from counterparty rating, which we have seen in Tables 13–3 and 13–4, results in a sound as well as flexible financial accounting procedure.

There are additional prerequisites to fulfill that go beyond the determination of instrument risk and counterparty risk. They concern *responsibility units* for default risk. Every profit center in the bank should be endowed with means for quantitative and qualitative evaluation of risk and return—as well as a clearly defined accountability.

Some financial institutions say that decisions on default risk should be conditioned by a choice concerning whether the responsible unit is a profit center, a cost center, or a zero-income center—whatever the latter may mean. This is nonsense.

❑   Any *organizational unit* engaging in trading and relationship banking is a profit center and should be responsible for its P&L, hence for default risk.

❑   *Cost centers* are only internal service providers, who should always have in hand a sharp knife to cut their own fat.

❑   *Profit centers* should be required by policy to buy risk insurance from the bank's division responsible for risk management.

The added cost of such insurance should in no way negatively affect the quality of banking services because the profit center chooses to economize in other expense chapters. If risk insurance acts as a disincentive to certain trades, this is a goal rather than an accident.

In other words, contrarians might say that risk capital and RORC criteria would discourage certain trades and also siphon money out of one pocket to put it in another, within the same bank. This argument is for the birds and for those who wish to believe that irresponsibility is better than accountability.

Everything we do has *a cost*, and we better account for it earlier rather than later. *Risk* is no exception; let's never forget that. An example from a totally different domain helps to qualify this point.

As revealed after a giant oil spill destroyed tens of thousands of acres in north-central Siberia, Russian oil companies dedicate 1 percent of their revenue to investments versus the 15 percent that is the rule with Western oil companies.

As a result, 50 percent of all Russian pipelines are considered today to be in a very bad shape, ready to burst, and one out of 10 barrels being produced is lost through spills, costing the Russians much more than the prudent policy of Western oil companies would.

Setting up and maintaining a valid system for risk management is synonymous with keeping the financial institutions and any other organization—municipality or industrial company—as a going concern; preserving its goodwill in the market.

Goodwill is difficult to build up; it takes much time and effort. But it can be destroyed practically overnight. In the late 1990s, Deutsche Bank bought London's Morgan Grenfell for £950 million ($1.54 billion). The lion's share of this amount, a cool £500 million, was for goodwill.

14

Rocket Science and the New Metrics for the Control of Risk

1. Introduction

All around the world on-line terminals are collecting, storing, sharing, and reporting information on financial transactions. Even when the instruments used for data capture are not sophisticated, the data streams they produce are impressive—and so is the corresponding need for mathematical tools to analyze these data streams.

The experience from the engineering sciences suggests that a well-coordinated gathering and massaging of available information requires a lot of scientists in one place. But telecommunications now make possible a local execution of rigorous analytical studies and their subsequent integration.

It is no longer necessary to concentrate the brainpower in one place. We can capitalize on technology to support the nature of scientific inquiry.

Scientists in almost every field are producing, storing, and digesting data at higher rates than ever before. This acceleration has much to do with their belief that evolving analytical tools and the new generation of high-performance computers will be able to cope with the information torrent—whether in finance, engineering, or merchandising.

For decades, these three domains used to be separate from one another. Today they present a common frontier, whose foremost criteria

Figure 14–1. Three Criteria for a Valid Financial Solution

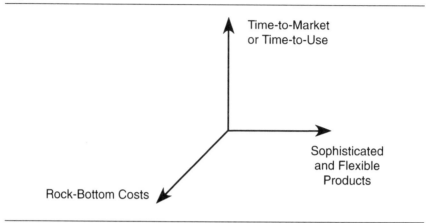

are shown in Figure 14–1. Paraphrasing Charles Wilson,[1] What is good for finance is good for engineering and manufacturing—and, I would add, vice versa.

Understanding how data is produced and what sort of meaning it conveys has always been fundamental to gaining competitive advantage. Financial analysts and rocket scientists should appreciate that it is part of their basic mission to avoid the dead end of a consensus built on partially understood information. Homogeneity of opinion and seamless convergence of thoughts is no friend to scientific creativity. This is precisely the reason why tier-one financial institutions comb the market for the best independent thinkers and give them free rein in their work.

A sound derivatives risk management favors new approaches over revamped ones. Able solutions are open to the interpretation of research findings which come not only from outlayers and externalities but also from the study of the mainstream course. These are the concepts this chapter discusses while presenting and elaborating the models necessary to the control of risk.

2.   Rocket Science Looks at Risk Management

Projects in high technology and in risk management have many things in common and therefore call for about the same skills. In one short sentence, what rocket science is all about is the golden rule of fighting: Make sure you have the advantage, not through brute force, but by means of rigorous analysis and well-studied prescription.

---

[1] Secretary of Defense in the Eisenhower Administration and former president of General Motors.

Rocket science and *rocket scientists* are terms that became popular in the mid-1980s, first in the United States and then in England. Physicists, engineers, and mathematicians who had worked in the aerospace and weapons industries, as well as in nuclear laboratories, brought their analytic skills into finance—from research to applications projects. There exist other similarities of which to take notice:

❑   In engineering and manufacturing, we are talking of Research and Development as being the *cost of staying in business.*

❑   The corresponding term in finance is Research, Development, and Implementation (RD&I) with very short time to market.

Since most financial products are logical rather than physical, implementation can proceed at a rapid pace. In fact, it has to do so because competition is ferocious, and delays can be deadly.

To understand why there has been so much interest in advanced financial analysis, one must appreciate the notion of *complementarity.* In the 1920s, Niels Bohr introduced the idea to physics and it is quite applicable in the expanding universe of financial transactions.

❑   Two seemingly contradictory ways of looking at the world can be equally valid.

❑   Complete understanding of a complex physical (or financial) process requires embracing both of them.

Two different ways of doing something are not necessarily in competition. Neither one is right; neither one is wrong. They are complementary, and both should be pursued because they can have a synergy. If nothing else, complementary ways broaden the base of discovery and of response. We will use this concept throughout this chapter.

Science and scientific investigation at large can be particularly helpful in derivatives, as evidenced by the sight of breakthroughs emerging from laboratories; they can contribute in a significant way to risk management. But while powerful tools are more important than ever, clear management objectives and policies are even more vital. Time and again long-term hedging strategies prove to be worthless if top management does not focus on risk. Because market conditions change, the board must always be ready to respond to the financial environment.

A permanent real-time watch on risks is a must. Clear management policies must account for the fact that derivatives are gaining importance in an investment world that is increasingly conscious of return enhancement but not conscious enough of exposure. No leveraged trades should be attempted without first-class risk control.

The role of rocket scientists is to investigate business opportunities and risks, provide the analytical support necessary to appreciate the rapid changes in the environment, and assure that models are available to keep exposure under control. The challenge is to

❑   Bring together a mass of disconnected threads.

❑   Make a pattern visible.

When used judiciously, derivatives can add significant flexibility to investment policies while providing excellent profit opportunities. But the risks should not be forgotten. Derivatives have an important part to play in fund management only if and when exposure is appropriately

❑   Identified.

❑   Computed.

❑   Tested.

❑   Embedded into the model.

All four functions require algebraic structures and heuristics approaches able to closely represent the risks we have analyzed in Chapter 13, leading to RORC yardsticks. The quantum mechanics notion that the order of observations is central to an accurate description applies in finance.

A crucial question when we approach risk from a control viewpoint is whether we can logically describe the role and participation of observers in the process of measurements. Every banker, every trader, and every investor is an observer of market behavior.

Another critical question the rocket scientist should ask is, With what rules of deduction and induction are physical (and financial) observations naturally manipulated to give revealing answers? "If you don't believe in induction," Dr. Betrand Russell once observed, "then you believe in nothing."

From the standpoint of the syntactical manipulation of observations, the answer to the foregoing question can be strengthened by responding to another query: What meaning, if any, can we derive from high-frequency financial data? We have come to appreciate that the time series, such as we have used so far, is a very coarse basis for analysis. There is a growing need for capturing and studying high-frequency financial data, tick-by-tick, at subsecond speed.[2]

Besides analyzing high-frequency observations, we must also take heed of their simultaneity. This can be done through the *exchange rule*,

---

[2] This concept is very new in finance. The change in culture is from *interday* to *intraday*, hence high-frequency data flows.

which permits the examination of finite sequences of formulas[3] and through the *contraction rule*, which states that the number of times we carry out an observation has no effect on the outcome.

The principle of a closed time loop is important in the study of the behavior of dynamically regular systems such as financial markets. The pattern is almost deterministic, as chaos theory teaches.[4] Researchers have discovered many cases where a sort of determinism holds, and this is important in developing models for risk management.

3. Risk Management, the Weibull Distribution and the Chorafas Algorithm

The drive behind high technology solutions in finance has its origin in the impossibility of working with day- or week-based time series for *predictive* reasons and for *risk management*. The same statement is valid regarding the search for higher level approaches in mathematical statistics.

Low-frequency market data and tools that are now classical in financial analysis don't make it possible to really understand the movements taking place, much less to exploit business opportunity and develop risk-control profiles. *High frequency financial data*[5] provides researchers with

❑ *10,000 times* more information than daily statistics, and

❑ *100,000 times* more than quarterly data, typically used in econometric studies.

The able exploitation of high-frequency data leads to new insights, drastically changing our view of how financial markets work. But the algorithms that we use should also be updated and made sharper. We should use the best available techniques rocket scientists can benefit from, such as the tools developed in the 1950s to face the major challenge of that decade: ballistic missiles and space research.

We can learn a great deal about how to calculate the risk involved in financial transactions by studying the algorithms applied in connection to *reliability* studies for missiles and other weapons systems. The mathematics for rigorous risk management are very similar. They rest

---

3 Mario Piazza, "Algebraic Structures and Observations. Quantates for Noncommutative Logic—Theoretic Approach to Quantum Mechanics," Ph.D. dissertation, University of Genova, Genova, Italy, 1992.

4 The concept of chaos theory and its application in finance are explained in D. N. Chorafas, *Chaos Theory in the Financial Markets* (Chicago: Probus, 1994).

5 See D. N. Chorafas *Rocket Scientists in Banking* (London and Dublin: Lafferty Publications, 1995).

on the Weibull distribution, which is a special case of the Poisson distribution.[6]

The Weibull distribution was proposed in 1951 for general statistical applications, or at least that was the intention of its developer, Wallodi Weibull. Recently it has been found, however, that

❑ Its contribution is quite significant in risk management studies, because

❑ Like reliability, risk management exploits the failures which occur.

In other terms, both risk control and reliability rest on the concept that there are *failures*—that is, incidents of first observation or conclusion regarding significant malfunctions.

Starting with the basic definition, reliability is the probability that a device will perform its intended function for a specific time under specified conditions.

$$\text{Reliability} \quad = \quad R(t) = p(0,t)$$
$$= \quad 1 - p(x \geq 1,t)$$

where

$$x \quad = \quad \text{number of failures at time } t$$
$$p(x \geq 1,t) \quad = \quad \text{probability of one or more failures at time } t$$

In the Poisson distribution, the fundamental equation of the population means is

$$\mu = \bar{\lambda} t$$

where

$$\mu \quad = \quad \text{expected number of failures, or universal mean number of failures}$$
$$\bar{\lambda} \quad = \quad \text{average failure rate, i.e., average number of expected failures per unit of time}$$

It is

$$\lambda \quad = \quad \lambda\,(t), \text{ and}$$
$$\bar{\lambda} \quad = \quad \lambda\,(t) = \frac{1}{t} \int_0^t \lambda\,(t)dt$$

---

[6] See D. N. Chorafas, *Statistical Processes and Reliability Engineering* (Princeton, NJ: D. Van Nostrand, 1960).

A helpful extension of the incidence described by the Poisson distribution is given by the Weibull distribution. The latter offers a variant of the reliability equation

$$R(t) = e^{-t^a/b}$$

where a and b are parameters. Reliability data conform to this expression if the range of *t* is great enough. The same is true about data concerning financial risk. It is

$$\lambda(t) = \frac{a}{b} t^{a-1}$$

If *n* is a shape parameter, x_0 a scale parameter, x_u a location parameter, and life test measurements start at t_0, then the Weibull *probability density function* is given by the algorithm

$$f(x) = \frac{m(x - x_u)^{m-1}}{x} e^{-(x - x_u)^{m/x_0}}$$

The corresponding cumulative function is

$$F(x) = \int_{x_u}^{x} f(x)dx$$

$$= 1 - e^{-(x - x_u)^{m/x_0}}$$

while

$$F(t) = 1 - e^{-t^{m/t_0}}$$

This cumulative distribution function can serve very well for *risk control* purposes. It can be used to indicate the total chance of failure by time *t*. Correspondingly, for reliability reasons the chance of no failure is

$$R = 1 - F(t) = e^{-t^{m/t_0}}$$

Let's now look into the use of the probability density function. During each time interval *t* between failures, a given device in a system—or financial vehicle in a market—survives to time *t* and then fails. The probability distribution between successive failures is given by

$$f(t) = \lambda e^{-\lambda t} = \frac{1}{T} e^{-t/T}$$

where in the case of reliability studies

$$\bar{T} = \text{mean time between failures (MTBF)}$$
$$= \frac{1}{\lambda}$$

Based on these two notions of time t and mean time $\bar{T}$, we can extend the use of the reliability equation

$$R = e^{-t/\bar{T}}$$

into other domains where systems behavior is characterized by failures, such as in finance and most particularly in regard to investments in derivative products.

This is a rewarding experience in technology transfer. After elaborating the precise meaning of T by application domain in the financial market, we can define the *risk factor* RF as equal to

$$RF = 1 - e^{-R_H/\bar{R}}$$

Write it down as the Chorafas algorithm. One fairly generalized implementation is to take R_H and $\bar{R}$ as

R_H = Highest return sought in an investment, basket of investments, or scenario

$\bar{R}$ = Average return available in the market

Or, alternatively, we can take $\bar{R}$ as equal to a standard return measured by economists—such as the 30-year Treasury bond. This is a domain that still requires significantly more research.

The implementation of the Chorafas algorithm is particularly important in the analysis of high-frequency financial data and most specifically in connection to *business time* ∂, and *intrinsic time* τ.[7]

❑ It can facilitate research on microseasonality in connection to failures, and

❑ It may effectively assist in the interactive visualization of analytical results.

There is much to be learned from the engineering of complex systems, just like there is a wealth of know-how to be transferred to finance from nuclear engineering and physics. In connection to the algorithm presented in this section, results can be rewarding: The Weibull distribution represents a powerful instrument for derivatives risk management.

---

[7] See D. N. Chorafas, *Rocket Scientists in Banking* (London and Dublin: Lafferty Publications, 1995). See also page 344 in this book.

4. Yield Curves Versus Missile Trajectory Curves

Whether the designer of new financial vehicles is an ingenious investor, an economics major, or a scientist, effective solutions rest on the designer's ingenuity in coming up with new ways to confront market challenges. This is true of many financial products and processes that are moving at a pace that only a few isolated cases previously enjoyed. The methods used in various branches of science are similar to those used in finance. The biologists of the human genome project catalog the contents of chromosomes in minute detail in a way no different than financial analysts do with high-frequency data. Ecologists ask for huge budgets to rigorously descend on certain ecosystems; similarly, interactive computational finance requires vast computing resources.

The basic message is that sophisticated analytical approaches, of the type we will see in this and the following chapters, have become crucial. Fast exchanges of information make it possible to construct distributed community intelligence systems with networked research facilities, and therefore first-rate skills are in great demand.

The work that scientists, engineers, and mathematicians do for the financial industry is not that different from what they were doing in the aerospace industry and in nuclear research. The analysis of yield curves is very similar to the analysis of missile trajectories. Rigorous mathematical studies can be instrumental in yield enhancement, as top researchers on Wall Street have found out.

The transition from stability to chaos and back to stability is one that complexity theory addresses. As shown in Figure 14–2, complexity is the domain that lies between stability and chaos. Complexity theory provides fundamental causality as well as *retrocausality*. The latter denotes causality from future to past.

The study of risk and its management requires both causality and retrocausality, which can be studied through a forward and backward exchange mechanism. Typically, this system operates within the environment, which will be discussed in sections 4 and 5.

Such analytical requirements are not too different from those encountered in quantum physics. Therefore, the physical sciences provide good examples that can open new horizons in financial analysis:

❏ Defining the path that advanced financial research will most likely take in the coming years.

❏ Helping to describe the kinds of technological skills that will be necessary in the banking industry.

Both the evolving goals of financial research and the technology are influenced by the nature of high-frequency financial data and the analytical requirements it poses. The fact that a growing number of nu-

Figure 14–2. Complexity Theory Addresses the Domain That Interfaces between Stability and Chaos

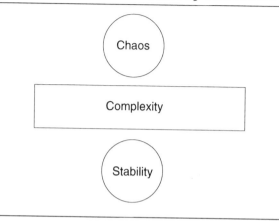

clear scientists now work for the financial industry is closely related to this fact.

Let's not forget that, in terms of investments, since World War II big money was spent on the two types of tools that physicists wanted most in order to bring forward their research on weapons systems:

❏   Nuclear reactors.

❏   Particle accelerators.

In the first, a supply of radioactive fuel produces a steady supply of energy and radiation. In the second, a beam of particles, usually electrons or protons, is pushed close to the speed of light by electromagnetic forces and thus attains high energies.

In nuclear engineering research, as in the financial markets, increasing size reflects increasing energy. Conversely, the more energy a particle carries, the shorter the distances that the analyst can probe.

By the 1970s, particle physicists were probing the world of quarks, subcomponents of the neutrons and protons in atomic nuclei. The energies needed were thousands of times those needed by the first atom smashers. Today, the most impressive beams are a million times more energetic than those with which Dr. Lawrence started splitting atoms; and researchers hope to reach energies six orders of magnitude higher still.

With these energies, particle physicists probe scales that are as small compared to the atom as the atom is compared to the objects of the everyday world. This approach distances present-day physics from its weapons systems origins, and indeed from almost everything else except the pursuit of *knowledge*—which is just as applicable in finance as in any other domain.

Serious readers will appreciate that the mutation of particle physicists in the financial world will have far-reaching consequences. While today it is difficult to forecast and estimate all the details, it is not far-fetched to suggest that the coming 10 to 20 years will see in finance a similar trajectory in research, development, and implementation to the one already experienced in physics.

5.   Handling Systematic and Specific or Unsystematic Risk

In which domains are the notions from quantum physics outlined in section 3 applicable? In Chapter 13, we defined risk capital and advanced the algorithm for return on risk capital (RORC). The two major factors that enter into this algorithm are

❑   Systematic or market risk.

❑   Specific or unsystematic risk.

These are the two basic types of risk associated with any transaction or investment, including the holding of equity. *Systematic risk* depends on market conditions, and therefore it is synonymous with *market risk*. *Unsystematic risk* is specific to a given counterparty. Hence, unsystematic risk is of a *credit* nature—whether we are talking about buying equities, giving a loan, or making a bilateral agreement with a counterparty. The fact is that *all* investments are exposed to market risks and credit risks—and many investments carry with them a horde of other risks that we need to analyze.

Both general and specific economic events can cause market values to fluctuate. As we will see in section 10, market volatility affects securities prices and may characterize the following:

❑   The market as a whole.

❑   A given industry within the market.

❑   A specific company within that industry.

❑   A security issue by that company.

Holding stock and giving a loan to a company are transactions exposed to risks, since both look to the future and have to do with the company's ability to repay the loan, provide dividends, or do other things that are contractually specified.

What can go wrong with an investment in a firm? The product line, a weak management succeeding a more successful administration, an explosion of costs while competitors make significant strides in re-structuring, and so on. These are specific factors behind systematic and unsystematic risk.

The more sophisticated the instruments we use, the more attentive we have to be to the effects of both systematic and unsystematic risk. Nor should we forget that, like the weather in the Alps, market senti-ment can change very rapidly. Therefore, banks and other companies have to have high asset quality and strong staying power to participate in the trading of new financial instruments:

❏ To maintain asset quality, they need traditional credit analysis of their own resources.

❏ To assure staying power, they need to monitor their credit posi-tions and that of their counterparties across the entire range of exposure.

Like every other company, every bank has its *credit quality*,[8] and the same is true of the financial system as a whole. In the developed nations, the credit quality of the banking system is measured by calcu-lating the spread between Treasury bills and time deposits in the banks.

The TED score measures the difference prevailing between U.S. Treasury bill futures and Eurodollar futures.

The results of this test have been used as proof that this relation-ship is not constant.

Beyond the $100,000 guaranteed to depositors in the banking sys-tem by FIDC in case of bank failure, investors would choose the greater security of the U.S. government rather than of commercial banks and other retail financial institutions.

This preference tends to drive down the yield on government se-curities relative to the yield on bank deposits. Just the same, banks with AAA ratings pay less interest than banks with AA or A ratings[9]—but the most important indicator is the TED spread. In other words, cash is also subject to unsystematic risk.

While diversification in a portfolio of stock holdings can mitigate unsystematic risk, it has little or no effect on market risk. Every stock in the portfolio will tend to move with the market, though some will be hit less than others. Therefore, diversification must also be done by invest-ment types—stocks, bonds, precious metals, and cash—all of which are subject to a risk component.

---

[8] Which is steadily assessed by the rating agencies.

[9] See also the examples on the effects of credit rating in Tables 13–3 and 13–4.

Rocket scientists have a lot of work to do in this connection because both systematic and unsystematic risk affect the computation of capital adequacy. Algorithmically, capital adequacy requires the calculation of capital needed to support the economic risk involved in a transaction or a portfolio of transactions.

An analytical approach typically uses the 99 percent confidence interval, including estimated volatility and historical correlation. It considers each disaggregated type of risk (market risk, credit risk, etc.) and computes for each risk element a worst-case scenario on the basis of largest potential loss.[10] It should also evaluate and assign to each transaction the cost of each risk, which permits buying risk insurance.

Figure 14–3 outlines the step-by-step procedure that should characterize the work of rocket scientists in connection to systematic and unsystematic risk as well as other types of exposure. This is a good example of RD&I, because it effectively shows the transition implementation based on analytical results.

6. Toward a Redefinition of Capital Requirements for Banks and Nonbanks

The job of rocket scientists is not to define capital requirements, but to assure that what is legally implied is observed in a factual and documented manner. This can be done by experimenting on real versus mandatory levels—from their calculation to their observance in an operating sense. The two levels do not necessarily need to be the same thing.

Defining capital requirements is the responsibility of central banks and of transnational regulatory bodies such as BIS. Such definitions, however, are static because it is not yet generally accepted that capital requirements have to be set in full appreciation of cross-border financial transactions and the increasing impact of derivatives.

Besides this, capital requirements should not only address the banking sector, but nonbanks and treasuries of industrial companies engaging in the derivatives trades. Hence, between the real level and the mandatory level, there are discrepancies on which an analytical study can capitalize. As was discussed in Chapter 13, risk insurance is a way of filling the gap between mandatory and real capital levels. Though this might be seen as a penalty to the bank, in reality it is a protection because it provides a dynamic buffer to absorb possible shocks.

Capital requirements, risk exposure, and cash flow should be studied in unison. As Figure 14–4 suggests, they form an integrative frame of reference. We have seen in Chapter 13, with risk capital, that the fun-

---

[10] Market value after tax, over a one-year holding period.

Figure 14–3. A Step-By-Step Description of the Rocket Scientist's Work in Connection to Systematic and Unsystematic Risk

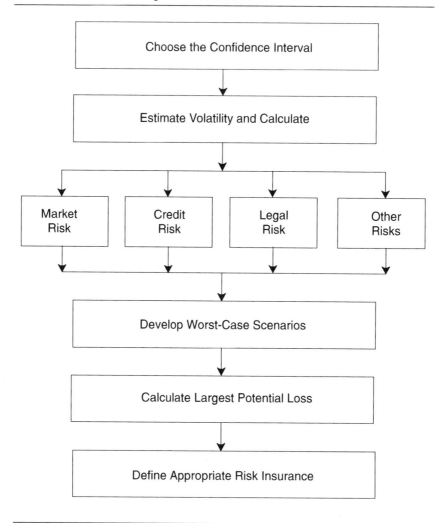

damental issue with capital requirements is that the amount of capital the bank needs is related to

❑ The financial riskiness of its business.

❑ The volatility of its *income* and *cash flow.*

A good way to measure income is to take *operating income* and the *gain or loss* in the value of assets and liabilities—including the bank's

Figure 14–4. The Solution Space for a Sound Trading and Investment Strategy Lies in This Framework

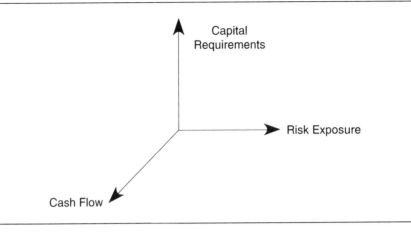

portfolio of derivatives. This means marking-to-market or marking-to-model and passing gains or losses into the income stream.

Cash flow is typically generated through business transactions, but the term does not have only one definition and method of computation.[11] To face the positive or negative impact of financial cash flows, rocket scientists have to improve the accuracy with which cash flows are estimated. Any asset or liability that has an expected future cash flow can be marked-to-market or marked-to-model by discounting that cash flow. Traditional loans meet this cash flow yardstick, and the same is true of many derivative financial instruments.

Therefore, capital adequacy standards should take cash flows into account when establishing minimum prudential levels of capital. In other words, the amount of capital a bank needs is related to the assets it has at risk, the project cash stream, and uncertainties about future asset and liability values. This creates a three-dimensional frame of reference, as indicated in Figure 14–4.

It is precisely within this complex view of capital standards and cash flows that the role of rocket science gains importance. A rigorous assessment of capital adequacy begins with measuring

❑ The probability of loss.

❑ The potential amount of loss.

---

[11] See also D. N. Chorafas, *Financial Models and Simulation* (London: Macmillian, 1995).

A valid approach sees to it that this is not done in a rough manner. It has to be analytical, and this is where a skillful usage of algorithms and heuristics can provide a significant contribution.

Whichever solution is taken must reflect recent risk measurements as well as account for innovations in financial instruments. It must use *risk types* as a basic unit of analysis and avoid all arbitrary assumptions.[12]

Most importantly, a valid analytical approach should never give false signals about the soundness of a trading book or portfolio or create perverse incentives to take on disproportionate and concentrated risks. Nevertheless, this is current practice.

Normalization of regulations as well as of auditing policies is necessary at the level of transnational organizations such as the Bank for International Settlements and the evolving European Reserve Institution. Evidently enough, normalization is no easy task because of the diversity in systems and procedures among central banks of the different countries.

Normalization is also handicapped by the fact that reserve institutions are not renouned for their use of rocket scientists in research, development, and implementation. Yet, they can hardly justify the financial risk of bringing forward unproven control concepts—or, even worse, of not providing risk-management guidelines and standards.

7. The Work Rocket Scientists Can Do with Central Banks

We have already spoken of the fact that the 1988 Basel Accord on capital requirements was essentially a compromise that produced a common denominator for all commercial banks. It was established by the Cooke Committee, which was composed of knowledgeable central bankers, but it neither followed a dynamic approach to defining capital requirements nor accounted for market risk.

Yet, rigorous analytical work, of the nature rocket scientists do for investment banks, could assist in thoroughly documenting capital levels and providing a platform for the customization of capital requirements according to each bank's trading book and portfolio. This is now being recognized as a need, hence the suggestion advanced by some central bankers that

---

[12]See also in D. N. Chorafas and H. Steinmann, *Off-Balance Sheet Financial Instruments* (Chicago: Probus Publishing Co., 1994), pp. 314–318.

❑ The proposed Market Risk Amendments to the Accord should address systematic risk.

❑ Other measures should be taken to account for exposures created by derivatives trades.

It is clear that norms and standards to be applied on a transnational level have to be based on compromises, since each central bank has its own ideas and culture as well as different local requirements to confront. What I personally deplore, however, is that no fine-grain model is currently advanced for systematic risk and unsystematic risk.

For instance, a fine-grain model focusing on unsystematic risk should fully cover transaction decisions, the trading book, and the portfolio. It should address the whole range of risk factors:

❑ The choice of counterparties.

❑ The type of instruments.

❑ The amount of money.

❑ The maturity of the deals being done.

The idea that risk can be controlled without thorough analytical studies and support from high technology is a pipe dream. There are intrinsic barriers to risk management, particularly in large organizations, which have to be overcome. This cannot be achieved without

❑ Clear directives from top management (discussed in Chapter 1).

❑ Innovative procedural solutions (outlined in Chapter 13).

❑ First-class technology (the need for which is presented in every chapter).

The algorithms, heuristics, and computer systems put in place must enable management to look at customers and at the bank itself, no matter where business is done. In a commercial banking sense, this is a corollary of 24-hour banking. From a central banking perspective, this is the only way to dynamically evaluate required reserves.

As it cannot be repeated too often, financial databases must be fully distributed and networked as well as mined by knowledge artifacts. Well-thought-out policies must assure open access for all qualified personnel, with flexibility in reporting procedures and ad hoc three-dimensional visualization in response to queries.

Both far-looking policies and high technology enable a bank to be a reliable player in the world market—both innovative and at the same time rooted in banking tradition. Admittedly, such a combination is difficult to obtain, but it is doable.

The current handicap does not result from lack of goodwill but rather from delays in cultural change. Every reserve institution has its auditors who have been, however, trained in old auditing procedures. Many banks try to recycle them in the new financial instruments, but this is a task that does not always meet with success—often for structural reasons.

For instance, in its role as the central bank of the central banks, the International Department of BIS has recently put together a supervision policy that reflects on both new financial products and new technological developments. The effects of this policy are, however, indirect. Its implementation cannot be dictated. It will only take place through the action of the national central banks.

Yet, the establishment, implementation, and follow-up of international standards is most urgent, precisely because of the explosive nature of off-balance-sheet trades and their impact on the portfolio of banks, nonbanks, and company treasuries. During our meeting in Frankfurt, German banks gave the following statistics on business growth in the 1990s:

1. On-balance-sheet business increased by 1.7 percent a year.

2. The usual currency and securities futures progressed by 4.9 percent a year.

3. The growth rate of other derivatives stood at 12.5 percent a year.

The careful reader will appreciate that number 3 is seven times higher than number 1 and that it also largely represents cross-border trades. Prudence therefore suggests paying attention to

- ❑ Credit risk.
- ❑ Market risk.
- ❑ Legal risk.
- ❑ Liquidity risk.

All of these risks impact OBS and are greatly influenced by over-the-counter traded derivatives. Recent estimates indicate that over-the-counter traded derivatives represent between one-third and one-half of all OBS trades. This represents a huge chunk of exposure in notional principal amounts in the trading book and banking book.

What is more, trades executed over-the-counter do not have an active market permitting marking-to-market. Therefore, they have to be marked-to-model for what they are worth, provided the models are approved and frequently reviewed by regulators. This, too, requires a significant amount of work in rocket science.

8.   Evaluating a Proposal on Capital Adequacy by the Group of Thirty

Charles Taylor, executive director of the Group of Thirty think tank, has published a paper in which he makes the point that the Market Risk Amendment could indeed allow banks to use better methods of risk measurement in limited circumstances.[13] But then he suggests that the cost of implementing it is out of proportion to any benefit the banks, or the system, might receive. Taylor further hammers on the proposed Amendment by adding that it would

❑   Engender inefficiency in the financial system.

❑   Encourage disintermediation by the banking sector.

These criticisms might be valid if there were a new formulation of capital standards, to account for market risk that applies only to the banking sectors. But as both governments and central banks should appreciate, this would be a mistake.

New capital standards and better methods for managing derivatives risk should not be seen as the exception, but rather encouraged as the rule applicable to all derivatives players, including

❑   Banks.

❑   Nonbanks.

❑   Treasuries of companies.

❑   Treasuries of government organizations.

Charles Taylor does not refer to this basic need, but he advances the following concepts regarding minimum prudential standards, emphasizing that these should be applied to banks.

Once again, this is an error because to my thinking these should be generalized to nonbanks as well as treasuries whose portfolios include derivatives. This means all of the multinationals, which today roughly account for 25 percent of the world's nonagricultural gross national product, as well as many other industrial firms and government outfits. Each and every player in the financial market should be supervised in terms of

❑   Capital sufficiency.

❑   Comprehensiveness.

❑   Recognition of portfolio effects.

___

13 Charles Taylor, *A New Approach to Capital Adequacy for Banks* CSFI (London: CSFI, 1994).

❑ Risk equivalence.

❑ Precision in risk measurement.

The wisdom of having a minimum regulatory burden and the need for sound supervision can coexist. The first reference in the foregoing list essentially calls for assuring that there is sufficient capital to cover most losses so that they can be absorbed by shareholders' equity and so that bank failures, and subsequent draws on public funds, are avoided.

Practically everyone agrees with this issue. The challenge is how to do it. The executive director of the Group of Thirty suggests that this value should be estimated by desegregating risks by type across all positions and activities:

❑ Evaluating those risks and reaggregating them.

❑ Taking into account reasonable estimates of correlations among them.

This proposal is not alien to that advanced in Chapter 13 about the separation of risk capital from other equity. But the parameters to be used for this separation, as well as the estimation of *value-at-risk*, should be provided by regulatory authorities after study of evolving market conditions and rigorous experimentation.

Rules must not only be tested experimentally but also be *comprehensive* and address all the financial risks that a bank, nonbank, or treasury may run. Otherwise, loopholes will exist in the system, and each one of the players will tend to take on more risk in areas not covered by regulations. For these reasons:

❑ Risk classification must be addressed in a rigorous and dynamic manner, identifying and treating equivalent risks.

❑ Portfolio effects should be recognized, requiring more capital for concentrated risks.

Models can help to interactively associate a given level of risk with a given amount of capital. The challenge of normalization is how to do it when practically every financial institution or treasury has a different concept of the same risk.

That's why precision in risk measurement and risk management is sound, provided that a solid definition of risks and their atomic elements precede measurement. Defining atomic risk elements is the job rocket scientists should be doing as well as defining metrics to accommodate financial innovation in an ever evolving market.

Much must also be done for the sake of efficiency and to minimize regulatory barriers to entry, but it should not be accomplished at the expense of supervision. The two goals—improved risk management and minimum burden—can be met only through the use of high-technology, real-time simulation; database mining; and graphics for the visualization of imaginative new solutions.

9.   Is There Substance in Netting and Offsetting?

One of the rather controversial proposals made by BIS regards netting and offsetting OBS positions. Since to be of any value, netting schemes must be polyvalent and therefore complex, currently under discussion among some central banks is the wisdom of separating:

❑   Exchange market netting, which is reasonably well organized.

❑   Netting in OTC markets, which is very diverse and not so well controlled.

The core of the matter is that the separation of these two issues or any other approach cannot be implemented without all major central banks agreeing to it. Nor can a local scheme be extended internationally *as is*, even if it works well in one country.

Another fundamental question is, Are the netting schemes *really* valid? Judging from the OBS catastrophes of 1994, the answer has to be negative. In the case of Metallgesellschaft, for example, the two legs of the derivatives transactions the company had undertaken for hedging did not balance themselves out when the oil prices crashed.

The $2 billion earthquake of the Orange County fund also seems to have netting imbalances at its roots. And there are plenty of other similar examples. Therefore, in the opinion of some leading banks, the netting proposal by BIS is not to be followed, as it is "junior high school stuff."

"The BIS proposal for vertical and horizontal netting," suggested Akira Watanabe, general manager of derivative products at Mitsubishi Bank, "is not wrong, but neither is it sophisticated enough for complex financial operations." Hence, it is *inadequate* for risk management reasons.

No major bank can manage its exposure based on smoke and mirrors. Therefore, some banks have chosen the alternative method recommended by BIS: the use of sensitivities.[14] Rocket scientists can play a significant role in this connection since sensitivities are first computed analytically.[15] Then, the evaluation of exposure proceeds by aggregation of sensitivities into meaningful groups.

---

[14] See also D. N. Chorafas, *Advanced Financial Analysis* (London: Euromoney, 1994).

[15] An example is given in section 10 with *duration*, which incorporates maturity and coupon into an algorithmic measure of a bond's sensitivity.

Whoever says sensitivities, says modeling but also implies the need for validation of models. In the years to come, a major job by national and supranational supervisory authorities will be validating the models banks use to do the following:

- ❑ Value positions.

- ❑ Project cash flow.

- ❑ Compute risk.

- ❑ Develop value-added instruments.

Even if netting and offsetting of positions is attempted, it will have to be done through formal rules that are effectively expressed in algorithms and heuristics, and their validity must be steadily reevaluated. It cannot be manual or based on rules of thumb. What is more, such formal rules will have to be universal. Derivatives is a global activity.

Beyond this, a valid netting scheme—if one is really possible—should cover not only bread-and-butter derivatives, but also exotics.[16] For instance, how should the bank and its supervisors classify a derivatives transaction in which two payment streams are linked to different interest rates, but are in different currencies?

The current BIS proposals do not address exotic derivatives, but without handling them effectively, offsetting will be impossible since such vehicles constitute an integral part of the trading book and of the portfolio.

It simply is not enough to say that financial institutions may take opposite positions in their cash book and in an index future or options. This is done as a matter of course either to hedge a cash position or to arbitrage between prices in the cash and futures or options market—a process known as equity index arbitrage. But it is *not* risk management.

Banks with experience in the control of exposure are able to appreciate that even if the example presented in the preceding paragraphs were perfectly handled—which is not often the case—there are still two risks that may arise:

- ❑ *Divergence risk,* which means an exposure due to imperfect portfolio tracking.

- ❑ *Execution risk* because of imperfect synchronization, which at its worst may involve an inability to deal.

Half-baked solutions can always be found. Partial offsetting for futures-related arbitrage strategies is usually done when an institution takes opposite positions in exactly the same index at different dates. In

---

[16]See also Chapter 10.

this case, the indices will move in price very closely. The difference between the prices will mainly be the cost of carry.

Partial offsetting is also attempted when an institution has opposite positions in different but similar indices on the same date. In this
case, supervisory oversight looks to ascertain that the two indices contain sufficient common components to justify offsetting. But this is essentially what more knowledgeable bankers call "junior high school
stuff."

10. Hedge Ratios, Duration, and Macaulay's Model

In order to determine the number of futures contracts for a hedge, it is
necessary to obtain an a priori estimate of a hedge ratio. Depending on
the type of hedge, different methods are used for its estimation. For instance, with interest rate futures the methods are

❑   Basis points.

❑   Duration.

Duration is also extensively used with bond pricing, providing a
useful measure of the bond's price sensitivity to interest rate changes.
The price of a high-duration bond is more sensitive to interest rate
changes than that of a lower-duration bond.

The way it is typically used in daily practice, duration incorporates
both the maturity and the coupon into a single numerical measure of a
bond's sensitivity. This algorithmic expression can be employed to compare price sensitivities of

❑   Different portfolios among themselves.

❑   Different bonds within the same portfolio.

In general, bonds with short maturities and high coupons have *low*
duration. By contrast, bonds with long maturities and low coupons have
high duration. The difference has a significant impact on pricing, as it is
instrumental in deciding whether the bond price goes up or down as
the market shifts.

A metric known as Macaulay's defines duration as the weighted
average of maturities of a bond's coupon and principal repayment cash
flow. The weights are fractions of the bond's price represented in each
time by the cash flow. The algorithm is

$$D \;=\; \frac{1}{TP} \sum_{t=1}^{n} \frac{t\, x_t}{(1+y)^i}$$

$$y \;=\; \frac{Y}{n}$$

where

$$D \quad = \quad \text{duration}$$
$$x_t \quad = \quad \text{interest payment of a bond in period } t^{17}$$
$$Y \quad = \quad \text{annual yield of the bond}$$
$$n \quad = \quad \text{number of payment periods in the year}$$
$$y \quad = \quad \text{annual yield of the bond divided by the number of payments in the year}$$
$$TP \quad = \quad \text{transaction price of the bond}$$

For instance, a two-year bond with a coupon of $x_t = 6$ percent paid every semester, purchased at TP = 96 and having an annual yield to maturity of 9 percent, will have a duration by semester equal to

$$D_s = \frac{1}{96} \left(\frac{1 \times 3}{(1 + 0.045)^1} + \frac{2 \times 3}{(1 + 0.045)^2} + \frac{3 \times 3}{(1 + 0.045)^3} + \frac{4 \times 4}{(1 + 0.045)^4} + \frac{4 \times 100}{(1 + 0.045)^4} \right)$$

But the annual duration will be

$$D_a \quad = \quad \frac{D_s}{2}$$

Since *n* is the number of periods, and *y* is a function of number of payments in the year, Macaulay's algorithm measures duration in periods, not years. To convert to a duration in years, MacCauley's formula must be multiplied by $1/f$, where *f* is the frequency of coupon payments per year.

In the context of risk analysis, Macaulay duration targets the weighted average time to return of a dollar of price. Alternatively (as we have seen in Chapter 4, section 6), the modified duration algorithm is used if cash flows are deterministic.

Macaulay duration of a 30-year Treasury bond is approximately 7 years, while it is 30 years for a 30-year principal STRIP—which stands for Separate Trading of Registered Interest and Principal Securities. STRIPs represent liabilities of the U.S. government. Pension funds are major investors in long-duration STRIPs.

Modified duration is a useful metric because it provides a percent measure of *price volatility*. The bond's modified duration measures the percent change in its price relative to a percent change in the bond's maturity.

An advantage of the duration approach is that it explicitly employs known information regarding coupon, maturity, and market price

---

[17] Can be either coupon interest or principal repayment.

of the bond. But it also has shortcomings. For instance, the estimation of the annual yield Y can be approached through different methods.

The alternative to this formula is regression analysis, which uses historical data to calculate hedge ratios. Its shortcoming lies in the hypothesis that historical market relationships will prevail in the future. This is a weak argument as the difference between historical and implied volatility in the credit markets helps document.

11. Calculating and Using the Volatility Factor *Beta*

Volatility is the typical measure of market risk. Its metric beta is the standard deviation of *historical volatility*; therefore, prior to proceeding with the algorithms we should define what each type of volatility means.

Reference to the historical volatility of a bond, stock, or derivatives contract is made in connection to its price fluctuations over some specific period in the past. For instance, we can talk about the volatility of gold or of IBM's stock over the last 90 days.

Historical volatility is important because it helps in making an educated guess about what the future volatility might be, but in reality what we target is the *future volatility*. This is what every option trader would like to know today.

In the derivatives business, future volatility expresses the extent to which, say, an underlying contract's price will fluctuate over some period in the future.

❑   *If* the trader knows the future volatility of a contract,

❑   *Then* he can evaluate options on the contract with increased confidence.

The problem is that no one *really* knows what the future volatility will be. Therefore, everyone uses guesstimates, which essentially amount to prognoses, or *forecast volatilities*.

Most services that forecast volatility do so for periods covering the life of options on that contract. Depending on his or her confidence in a forecast, the trader takes this volatility estimate into consideration in pricing, also keeping in mind that

❑   Exchange-traded options are more sensitive to changes in volatility in terms of dollars.

❑   Over-the-counter options are more sensitive to volatility changes in terms of percentages.

The incorporation of forecast volatility into a pricing model leads to the concept of *implied volatility*. Given the basic inputs required for option evaluation, such as volatility estimates, interest rates, time to expiration, exercise price, and underlying price, a mathematical model can run the factors in reference and their implied variation for pricing rea-sons, providing a theoretical value for an option. This is in essence what we mean by marking-to-model.

When we have evidence that this theoretical value is different from the price of the option in the marketplace, we can replace it with the market price of the option. Then we run our pricing model backwards to obtain a volatility that yields a theoretical value identical to the price of the option in the market.

In fact, this new volatility estimate is the volatility that the market-place is *implying* to the underlying contract through the pricing of the option, hence the term that is being used. Future, forecast, and implied volatility are estimates we make based on hard data and algorithms. Needed hard data can only be found in historical volatilities, which usu-ally are made in a coarse-grain manner.

If we change from this coarse-grain data collection to *high-frequency financial data*,[18] historical volatilities can become a much more reliable basis because both the time periods we use and those we forecast will be infinitesimal.

Another alternative is to implement better algorithms. One ap-proach uses beta as a metric of risk taken with equities, defined as the *covariance* between a stock's return and the general return on the mar-ket, divided by the variance s^2 of the return on the market

$$\beta = \frac{\text{covariance } (E_i, E_m)}{s^2 (E_m)}$$

where

$$E_i = \text{return on stock i}$$
$$E_m = \text{overall market return}$$

Using this algorithm, we can obtain a series of observed returns over time for stock *i* and for the overall market portfolio. A linear re-gression can be computed through the formula

$$E_{i,t} = a + \beta E_{m,t} + \varepsilon_{i,t}$$

where

$$a = \text{a constant}$$
$$\beta = \text{volatility of stock i}$$
$$E_{i,t} = \text{return of stock i over time t}$$
$$E_{m,t} = \text{overall market return over time t}$$
$$\varepsilon_{i,t} = \text{an error term}$$

---

[18]See D. N. Chorafas, *Rocket Scientists in Banking* (London and Dublin: Lafferty Publications, 1995).

The relevant rates of return $E_{i,t}$ are defined as the change in stock price in period *t* (which can be positive or negative) plus the dividends received over the same period, divided by the price of the stock at the end of the period t – 1. For this reason, stock betas are often estimated by

$$\frac{\Delta P_{i,t}}{P_{i,t-1}} = a + \beta \frac{\Delta P_{m,t}}{P_{m,t-1}} + e_{i,t}$$

$$\beta = \frac{\dfrac{\Delta P_{i,t}}{P_{i,t-1}} - a - \varepsilon_{i,t}}{\dfrac{\Delta P_{m,t}}{P_{m,t-1}}}$$

where

$\Delta P_{i,t}$ = difference in stock price

$P_{i,t-1}$ = price of stock i in period t – 1

This β is also known as the stock's *relative volatility*. If it is greater than one, the stock is more volatile than the market; if less than one, the stock is less volatile than the market. There are many estimates we can do with volatility, but it is always good to remember the difference between historical data and forecast or implied volatility.

15

Using Delta, Gamma, Theta, Kappa, and Rho for Better Risk Management

1. Introduction

The price of financial instruments, particularly those traded over-the-counter, is being increasingly determined by means of models. Similarly, the valuation of portfolios and computation of risks is being done by marking-to-model—not by marking-to-market—even if many bankers are shy about admitting it.

Though a great deal depends on the accuracy of the model, there is no denying that in a number of cases marking-to-market and marking-to-model do not correlate so well. But there is no alternative to algorithmic solutions, since for many derivatives, such as exotics and those in portfolio positions resulting from OTC trades, there is no active market.

The good news about the increasing use of mathematics in finance is that marking-to-model is less subjective than marking-to-market and can also ensure a common frame of reference—provided there is a lender of last resort, typically the central bank, who takes care of supporting the financial fabric in case of panics. Therefore, this approach has given invaluable assistance in financial analysis and in trading, even if trading is 20 percent analytical and 80 percent conceptual.

This uneven distribution reflects on the contents of both the trading book and the portfolio. The best traders are intuitive. They rely on their imagination, but can be assisted through real-time simulation.

The real-time market evidence acts as the engine. By contrast, financial analysis plays a crucial role in portfolio evaluation and management as well as the control of risk because portfolio handling is 80 percent analytical and 20 percent conceptual.

The examples we will see in this chapter can serve in both domains. The algorithmic and heuristic approaches that are used are kept at a fundamental level of reference, so that they are applicable to trading, the evaluation of the trading book, the banking book, a portfolio-oriented financial analysis, and the control of risk.

2.   Analytical Finance, Heuristics, and Technology

From option trading to exotics, complexities make derivatives products and markets an attractive domain for modeling. This is as true of real-time simulation as it is of knowledge engineering and its applications.[1] Workable solutions are welcome as new business opportunity plays a central role in modern financial practice, which is often characterized by

❏   Sophisticated trading strategies.

❏   A fairly complex portfolio management.

❏   Better methods for the control of exposure.

A characteristic of many deals in derivatives is that returns are contingent on future, uncertain market states with several possibilities as to how the market can turn. As a result, financial analysts, portfolio managers, and traders use *heuristic* and *ad hoc* techniques, basing their theory on a number of assumptions.

Evaluating the consequences of any policy or market move requires the use of a mathematical framework that ties together all actors and activities. The chosen frame of reference must simulate not just a snapshot of the product's behavior in the market, but the entire life cycle of the vehicle:

❏   From design to sales.

❏   From a static perspective to its dynamic role in a portfolio.

---

[1] See also D. N. Chorafas and H. Steinmann, *Virtual Reality: Practical Applications in Business and Industry* (Englewood Cliffs, NJ: Prentice Hall, 1995).

Financial research is no longer limited to statistical studies, but simulates both products and markets to perform *life-cycle analysis* of financial instruments. This is fundamental in developing strategies for minimizing risk while improving overall return from new products and ongoing investments.

A corollary to these axioms is that we must always be quick to implement new technology as soon as it becomes available and, in whatever we do, we should be open-minded and flexible. In terms of models, some of our projects may use genetic algorithms. Other projects may incorporate fuzzy engineering. Still others rest on the new risk metrics: delta, gamma, theta, kappa (beta prime, lambda), and rho—which we will study in this chapter.

But independently of the specific model we chose, our processes and procedures connected to financial analysis should be tuned to face ad hoc situations. Data collection, computation, and visualization must work in *real time*. Bankers who still use batch, mainframes, and COBOL for pricing and for risk analysis are idiots of all seasons, and they will pay the bill sooner rather than later.

Since response time is at a premium, market input has to be done on-line. For most trades, the same is true of the confirmation. A profit and loss statement used to be established on a daily basis; now it can be available on-line. Other items to be made available on-line are

❏ Interim control and commentary on strategies followed by market participants.

❏ Final control and accountability regarding the appropriate desk.

Interestingly enough, these principles apply both to trading and training. In the case of Nikko Securities in Tokyo, the Option Training and Trading (OTT) model has addressed both the area of training options dealers and of helping them in trading. In fact, there are two versions for training purposes: one for novices, the other for experienced options traders, who revamp their skill—which is the nearest thing to real-time trading.

The design and implementation of OTT highlights the right approach in terms of dealing with algorithmic and heuristic solutions. Not only is it necessary to allocate appropriate resources to lifelong training—hence to training simulators—but using models for training first permits them to be polished and brings them closer to reality.

Another sound policy Nikko Securities adopted with OTT is that its usage both for training and for trading focus not only on P&L but also on *risk management*. Database mining permits evaluation of performance, which again places attention on exposure and damage control.

As this example assists in documenting, a sound system solution would revolve around the fact that the professional entrusted with trading should be able to steadily evaluate his or her hypotheses and assumptions as the market moves, always being aware of the

❑   Business opportunities.

❑   Embedded risk.

❑   Cash flow.

❑   Profit and loss.

A financial professional's decisions involve all of these elements at the same time; therefore, he or she must be trained to think in that way. The development and use of simulators and expert systems helps in the sense that valuation techniques call for significant numerical calculation and require appropriate computational models. But beyond any doubt the final judgment has to be exercised by the trader.

3.   Training, Trading, Financial Analysts, and Rocket Scientists

Rigorous analytical studies done by rocket scientists go far beyond markets and products and into the realm of financial power, bargaining, and trust. This should be reflected in the development and use of simulators. What can be done through advanced mathematics is to analyze the interactions between actors such as investors, traders, bankers, and treasurers of corporations, while accounting in real time for an entire range of possible options and the most likely results.

"As long as I live, I learn," Socrates once said—and learning means cultural change. Rather than simply accepting the status quo or static solutions, the goal is to understand why existing financial, economic, and social arrangements are stable or unstable and what the alternatives might be.

Therefore, in the development of training and trading simulators, the best solutions are those residing in the space defined in Figure 15–1: low model complexity, but a high level of flexibility and sophistication. Good return on investment should also be a target. A valid model typically has high ROI as it is used time and again for training and trading reasons.

As a matter of principle, the more powerful the design instrument—examples being genetic algorithms, fuzzy engineering, and Monte Carlo—the simpler the model, even in connection to complex financial vehicles. When the product is complex, its pricing is nonlinear, its risk has unknowns, and the response of the market has still to be tested. Technology should be used in such a way that there is low complexity in product–market interaction but high experimental capabilities make feasible a significant return on risk capital (RORC).

Figure 15–1. High Technology Can Effectively Serve the Goals We Aim to Reach in Business Opportunity and the Control of Risk

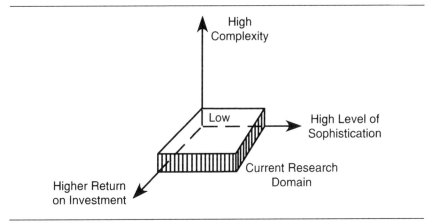

Superficially, the goals seem to be somewhat contradictory, but the job is doable if we know how to go about it. Simulators also present an excellent approach to global market valuation and the handling of larger portfolios.[2]

Generically simple cases are handled by investors and investment advisors through personal computers and spreadsheets. They typically seek answers to "what if?" questions involving constraints on limited option positions, as well as their risks and return. But the management of sophisticated vehicles and large portfolios is much more demanding. A design framework for a complete analysis must provide the following:

- ❑ A clear problem description with all crucial variables.

- ❑ Rule-based and/or heuristic models.

- ❑ A range of custom-made simulators.

- ❑ The ability to mine distributed deductive databases.

- ❑ Interactive facilities for three-dimensional graphical representation.

- ❑ Seamless networkwide access.

Rocket scientists and information technologists should address themselves to each and every one of these six factors. As we have seen

---

2 See also D. N. Chorafas, *Rocket Scientists in Banking* (London and Dublin: Lafferty Publications, 1995).

with the OTT example, a good way to start is with the *training* version of an artifact, which permits

❑   Establishing a position.

❑   Developing a trade.

❑   Proceeding with simulation proper.

❑   Visualizing the results.

Once this has been successful, a more thorough real-life model can be developed, converted into a *trading* tool, and put in production with support from high-performance computers. With the advanced model, the experienced dealer is able to sell or buy various call options, put options, and futures by setting up, evaluating on-line, and following the scenario of his or her choice.

Increasingly, the formulas utilized by the system for the calculation of risk-management parameters focus on premium pricing and exposure. In the case of Nikko Securities, the algorithms they use are delta, gamma, vega, and theta,[3] as well as the Black-Scholes model. During our meeting, it was said that a new version will use fuzzy engineering.

In spite of the higher-order mathematics it involves, the Nikko model is a user-friendly interactive system requiring a minimum amount of computer literacy. It is able to establish a position, simulate that position, and use visualization through graphics and icons for output.

The accuracy of the parameters has been thoroughly tested against real-life data. Parameter values were found to be fairly compatible with market data, which is hardly surprising since, at Nikko Securities, the rocket scientists have utilized the knowledge and expertise of several professionals in options trading.

Other financial institutions have used different approaches to gain competitive advantages from the investments they are making in technology. For instance, Sweden's Securum developed a graphic system to track its real estate properties in an interactive manner.

The first component is a scanning program to fetch the building drawings and register them in a database after vectorizing them. Then, a virtual reality artifact permits the user to walk through any one of the drawings he or she chooses, get information about the whole building— or a floor or section thereof—and make up to six layers of changes in the drawing.

This graphics system is integrated with real estate accounting for on-line updates as well as financial analysis. It is also connected with an

---

3 See section 5.

expert system that assists the user in selecting the changes or repairs to be done on the building and getting a complete specification of the job as well as a budget.

The management of Securum has achieved this and similar breakthroughs by instituting a new information technology culture. "If we have a chance to survive, we must keep costs rock-bottom and move very, very fast in a fluid market," Lars Thunell, the CEO, told his people. "We must have very sophisticated information technology tools at our disposal."

In a nutshell, the Securum strategy has focused on advanced solutions, rapid software development time frames, and low-cost information technology design and implementation. The software endowment was created from scratch exclusively on client servers in *five months with a small development team*, rather than in five years with a large development group, as demanded by the mainframers.

4. Using Mathematical Models for Optimization

Optimization involves the minimization or maximization of a given function subject to a number of constraints. The optimizer is an algorithm that describes the goal we search in minima or maxima, while the simulator represents the product we study or the system we experiment with.

Optimization goals may vary. For instance, an engineer may want to minimize the weight of a design, while a financial analyst may wish to maximize the return on risk capital *or* minimize the risk of a given instrument. Optimization should never try to reach two contradictory goals, such as simultaneously maximizing one variable and minimizing another. It should address only one goal at a time—either to maximize *or* minimize. Otherwise, the results will be inconclusive, and the effort will fail.

Since the development of the simplex method by Dr. George Danzig in the early 1950s, linear programming has been the most popular optimization technique.[4] In the 1960s, however, Dr. Richard Bellman developed dynamic programming, and in the early 1970s, Dr. Bellman and Dr. Lotfi Zadeh introduced the concepts underpinning fuzzy engineering.

Genetic algorithms were developed in the late 1970s by Dr. John Holland. Ten years later, they became the tool of choice in optimization studies. Successfully used for scheduling on the production floor and in offices, genetic algorithms have come into financial analysis and proved

---

4 See D. N. Chorafas, *Operations Research for Industrial Management* (New York: Reinhold Publishing, 1958).

to be a valuable means to locate minima and maxima with price functions and risk-control algorithms.

Optimization should not be confused with the broader scope of simulation. The simulator is mapping a real-life situation into the computer. As such, it formulates an object of interest, like a surface area, frequency of vibration, a financial instrument's diffusion in the market, market response, or profit and loss. No matter what the object of the exercise is, constraints define the set of rules or conditions when executing the optimization. With practically every application, a real-time approach is more rewarding, since the software interactively seeks the solution that best satisfies the constraints.

The word *mapping* used above is practically synonymous with representation. It means a representation of, say, a physical (or logical) system in a support such as computer memory. Some people say representations do not fully express the real-life function. This is only half true and failures can happen for two reasons:

❏ Either the system we map is too complex, and we purposely try to simplify it through idealization.

❏ Or we fully map the system according to our hypotheses, which—like all theories in science—are tentative statements that one day will be disproved.

Another basic concept of simulation and optimization is *boundary conditions*. The crucial role of boundary processes (and conditions) is fending off perils resulting from intruders and weeding out outliers due to excess stress and other reasons. There is, for instance, an information boundary that can have a number of effects, from sealing off what is included in the boundary envelope, to making the transmission process more complex or changing the coding scheme.

In principle, more information is transmitted between points within a system than across its boundary. If we assume that domestic and foreign letters have on average the same number of bits, then statistics on transmitted letters tell a story. The ratio of domestic to foreign mail tends to vary between 3 and 87 and is always significantly more than 1.[5]

An integral part of handling any model is its *instantiation*. This is a mathematical term whose root is the word *instant*: soon to happen, imminent, urgent, pressing, but also abbreviated. As a noun, *instantiation* denotes a point of very short space of time; a particular moment.

In general, optimization is not a process that comes naturally; it must be taught. It takes orientation, training, and experience to pose the

---

5 James Gried Miller, *Living Systems* (New York: McGraw-Hill, 1978).

problem properly, and no single optimization solution should be trusted without verification. This is also true of the different hedging metrics and algorithms we will examine in the following sections.

As in all real-life situations, misunderstanding a problem and/or misrepresenting our real objectives and constraints produces poor results. Lightly done, approaches to simulation and experimentation become increasingly unreliable as the number of design variables increases. Let's keep that in mind when we talk about the new generation of tools for risk management.

5. Delta and Delta Hedges

On several occasions, reference has been made to new and more powerful tools that are needed for pricing purposes as well as the control of risk. The most basic notions focus on metrics and measurements, and that's what we will study in the present and the following two sections—including how the new metrics can be used for hedging purposes. Say, then, that we have a pricing function for an option

$$F(x)$$

Delta is the first derivative of this function

$$\frac{df(x)}{dx}$$

or

$$F'(x).[6]$$

However, the slope of a curve $F(x)$ at any given point cannot be calculated by referring to the curve at that point alone. Instead, we must resort to a limiting process that is the basis of differential calculus. It might be helpful to think of delta as the speed with which an option moves with respect to its underlier. The maximum speed is 100 percent for very deeply in-the-money options, and the minimum speed is zero for very far out-of-the-money options.

The practical value of $\frac{dF(x)}{dx}$ is its polyvalence in terms of interpretation and therefore the range of applications to which it can be put. Basi-

---

6 For greater detail, see D. N. Chorafas, *Advanced Financial Analysis* (London: Euromoney, 1994).

cally, it expresses the rate of change in the theoretical value of an option with respect to the change in price of the underlying contract.

For example, an option with a delta of 33 (0.33) can be expected to change its value at 33 percent of the rate of change in the price of the underlier. If the underlier goes up (down) 1.00, the option's theoretical value can be expected to go up (down) 0.33.

Delta also approximately gives the probability that the option will finish in-the-money. Still another way to look at delta is that it represents the ratio of underlying contracts to option contracts required to establish a neutral hedge. If an option has a delta of 50 (0.50), a neutral hedge will require 1/2 (0.50) of an underlying contract for each option contract. If two option contracts are purchased, one underlying contract must be sold.

That's why delta is referred to as the hedge ratio. At the same time, delta expresses, at least in theory, the number of underlying contracts that the purchaser (seller) of a put is short (long) or the purchaser (seller) of a call is long (short).

If a trader buys (sells) a call with a delta of 25 (0.25), he or she is in theory long (short) 1/4 (0.25) of an underlying futures contract. Interpreted in this manner, the delta constitutes the *equivalent futures position.* Notice that these four definitions of deltas are different ways of saying the same thing. Figure 15–2 shows the payoff, the function of target option, and its delta slope.

For traders and investors, an interesting use of delta is to estimate the probability that the option will finish in-the-money. This rests on the hypothesis that an option with a delta of 75 can be expected to change its value at 75 percent of the rate of change in the price of the underlier. If the price of the underlying security changes by, say, 12, the option's theoretical value will tend to change by 9.

It could also be helpful to think of the delta as the speed with which an option moves with respect to its underlier, a concept already outlined in one of the definitions we have seen within this frame of reference.

❑ The maximum speed is 100 percent for very deeply in-the-money options.

❑ Speed of change can be at a standstill, or zero, for very far out-of-the-money options.

Delta hedging is based on these assumptions widely used in trading. Because it is fairly easy to comprehend the way it works, the delta hedge is the most common type of option replication.

For example, in terms of foreign-exchange markets, the delta of any financial instrument—be it an option, a forward rate agreement, or

Figure 15–2. Payoff Function of an Option and Delta Slope at 33 Percent and 50 Percent

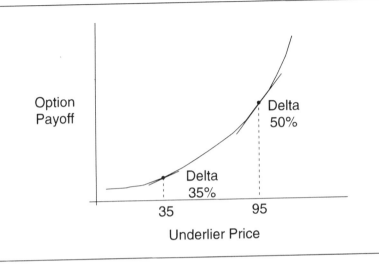

an interest rate swap—is the partial derivative of this instrument's market value with respect to the spot.

❏ Because delta is the change in the instrument's value given a unit change in the exchange rate.

❏ In a delta hedge position, contracts are constructed so as to match the delta of the target option.

Experts, however, contend that static delta hedges can be unreliable, especially in volatile markets. The delta of the hedge might drift from the delta of the target option, as the target option's delta changes with movements in the spot exchange rate, due to interest rates or simply as a result of the passage of time.

This is one of the reasons why delta hedges are implemented with instruments such as forward contracts and currency futures contracts that are not sensitive to changes because of movements in the spot exchange rate. Or, alternatively, improvements are sought beyond the simpler delta hedge.

An improvement to a static delta hedge is the *dynamic hedge* obtained by adding or subtracting to the forward or future position to track the changing delta of the target option. The algorithm aims to take into account factors affecting an option's delta, such as

❏ Time.

❏ Interest rates.

❏ Exchange rates.

Hedges require significant skill and if improperly done they can get financial analysts and traders into trouble. Not only must the calculation of hedges be analytical, factual, and documented, they must also be periodically adjusted for changes in operating conditions such as drift in the option's delta. This is one of the reasons I never tire of repeating the merits of real-time simulation.

6.   Gamma and Gamma Hedges

The metric *gamma* expresses the rate of change of an option's delta with respect to change in price of the underlying contract. If an option has a delta of 75 and a gamma of 10, the option's expected delta will be 85 if the underlier goes up one point and 65 if the underlier goes down one point.

Continuing with the analogy we have seen with delta, it might be helpful to think of gamma as the acceleration or deceleration of the option's price function; that is, how fast the option picks up or loses speed (speed meaning delta) as the price of the underlying contract rises or falls.

The measure of the acceleration of the option gamma provides tells how fast the option picks up or loses speed (hence delta) as the price of the underlying contract rises or falls.

A negative gamma can be the cost of entering into a certain trade, given the dealer's or investor's perception of price movements and the structure of the payoff function F(x).

The market can move in one direction or another, but the gamma may be behaving more negatively than the market. Among the reasons for such behavior are change in the interest rates or in the prevailing bid-and-ask patterns.

Gamma is often referred to as the option's curvature. Mathematically, it is the derivative of delta with respect to the price function

$$\frac{d^2\, F(x)}{dx^2} \quad \text{or} \quad F''\,(x)$$

Since delta is the first derivative of the option price with respect to the price of the underlying asset, gamma is the second derivative of the option price in regard to the underlier.

Gamma for options is analogous to convexity for bonds. A *convex* set is one in which the line connecting any two points belonging to it will not cross the set's boundaries. If it does, the set is concave.

These characteristics permit one to make a delta-gamma hedge, which uses options near to expiration for convexity. Traders take a position in forward and futures contracts to match the delta of the target option.

The effect of changes in the spot exchange rate on the option's delta are captured by gamma, which critically depends on the time remaining until expiration. Close-to-expiration options tend to be gamma neutral. Such options can be found easily in the marketplace; hence, they can be incorporated into a hedging strategy.

Three approaches are used to hedge gamma. The more evident way is to buy back options identical to the ones that have been sold. But such back-to-back deals are not profit making, and therefore they are very rare in the over-the-counter market.

The second method is to buy deep out-of-the-money options, known as *buying the tails*. This applies to portfolios with at-the-money or slightly out-of-the money options. The third approach is to do a horizontal spread. The computation of a gamma-neutral position is done through a formula reflecting change in future price

$$\frac{(\text{Change in Future Price})^2}{2} \times \text{Gamma}$$

In a delta-gamma hedge, for example, the analyst may take a position in a short-lived call to match the gamma of the targeted longer-life option. Given that short-lived calls have much larger gammas than long-lived calls, few of the former calls will be required.

7. Theta, Kappa, Rho, and Their Usage

Ten years ago, the computation of delta and gamma was the secret skill of rocket scientists. Not many dealers in the securities business knew what they stood for—much less how to use them. This, however, has changed.

As we have seen in sections 5 and 6, the first and second derivative of the price function can be of significant assistance in the valuation of options, futures, forwards, and swaps; for example, in connection to

❑ Stock options.

❑ Bond options.

❑ Index options written on the spot index.

❑ Index options written on index futures.

The instrument on which the option is written is used as the underlier. This is straightforward enough, but there are also certain practices to keep in perspective specific to the type of vehicle.

In the *shortest future* operation, the future with the shortest time to maturity is used as the underlying instrument. In a *closest future*, the underlier is the future with a maturity time closest to the expiration date of the option.

Other vehicles are the *following future*, where the first future to have its maturity following the expiration date of the option is employed as the underlying instrument; and the *preceding future*, where the last future to have its maturity preceding the expiration date of the option is the underlier.

Delta and gamma metrics can be effectively incorporated in a simulation. Simpler approaches use linear interpolation in time to derive the current underlying price. More complex software employs quadratic or higher-order nonlinear approximations. In many cases, however, the nature of the financial instrument sees to it that we need still other metrics than the first and second derivative of the price function. These are provided by

❑   Theta.

❑   Kappa, vega, or beta prime.

❑   Rho.

Theta measures the rate at which an option loses theoretical value for *each day* that passes with no movement in the price of the underlying instrument. For instance, an option with a theta of 0.02 can be expected to lose 0.02 in theoretical value for each day that passes with no movement in the price of the underlier. For this reason, theta is referred to as the option's *time decay*.

Kappa, also known as lambda, vega, and beta prime, expresses the sensitivity of an option's theoretical value to a change in *volatility*. An option with a kappa of 0.25 can be expected to gain (lose) 0.25 in theoretical value for each percentage point increase (decrease) in volatility. For this reason, *beta prime* is a better title since it connects to beta.

Finally, *rho* addresses the sensitivity of an option's theoretical value to a change in *interest rates*. There are traders who think that interest rates are relatively unimportant in the evaluation of options on futures and therefore consider rho as the least important of the option sensitivities. This is, however, absurd.

By knowing the delta, gamma, theta, beta prime, and rho of either a simple spread or a complex option, we are able to determine how the position is likely to react to changing market conditions. We can do so in terms of prognosis by following up on the derivative's behavior: The total position can be calculated by simply incorporating in our model the outlined metrics of each individual position. This is significant because the delta, gamma, theta, beta prime, and rho associated with each

Table 15–1. Message Conveyed by Delta, Gamma, Theta, and Beta Prime in Regard to the Trader's Position

Position Taken by Trader	Hedge Ratio Delta Position	Curvature Gamma Position	Time Decay Theta Position	Volatility Beta Prime Position
Long calls	Positive	Positive	Negative	Positive
Short calls	Negative	Negative	Positive	Negative
Long puts	Negative	Positive	Negative	Positive
Short puts	Positive	Negative	Positive	Negative
Long futures	Positive	0	0	0
Short futures	Negative	0	0	0

type of underlying and option position play a role in being long or short.

Table 15–1 outlines the messages being conveyed by the metrics we have examined in regard to the trader's position with certain derivatives deals. However, in addition to the delta, gamma, and so on, a trader is also interested in the position's profit potential, or total *theoretical edge.*

❑ The theoretical edge of an individual option is the difference between the option's price and its theoretical value.

❑ The theoretical edge of a portfolio is the sum of theoretical edges of each individual option position.

Both Table 15–1 and the preceding two bullets offer an idea of the theoretical edge gained by a trader using the new metrics. The bottom-line is that this edge derives from the results offered by a rigorous mathematical analysis, which helps to better appreciate risk and return with various option positions. The models we develop should be processed in real time and the results visualized interactively in color and three-dimensional graphics.

8. Learning to Use Differentiation and Integration

The new metrics we have studied in sections 5, 6, and 7 require applied mathematics beyond what is typically taught in business schools. Differentiation and integration is part of the armory of engineers and physicists, who now work with financial institutions as rocket scientists, but for the benefit of other financial analysts I will outline some basic notions.

The use of delta, gamma, and other metrics in financial analysis has prerequisites, the first of which is the *formulation of the problem*. Experience from systems engineering and other fields indicates that this is not always straightforward. When it is done, it must be followed by the definition of the price function, F(x), to be studied.

After F(x) has been defined, we use differentiation to calculate delta. Despite appearances, the definition of the price function and its differentiation is a challenge in finance rather than in mathematics. The following simple function provides an example. Say that the price function we develop is

$$F(x) = x^2 + 7x$$

This is one of the simplest nonlinear functions. It is *quadratic,* a polynomial in which each term is of no more than the second degree.

❑   F(x) stands for the value of the derivative.

❑   x stands for the value of the underlying financial instrument.

If we wish to calculate delta, the slope of the function, all we need to do is differentiate this function with respect to x. We have

$$\frac{dF(x)}{dx} = 2x + 7$$

The differential can be found by multiplying both sides by dx

$$\frac{dF(x)}{dx}\, dx = (2x + 7)\, dx$$

or

$$dF(x) = (2x + 7)dx \qquad (1)$$

Let's first consider the left side of the equation. The integral of the differential of the function F(x) is equal to the function itself. That's the definition of the integral sign. This means

$$\int dF(x) = F(x)$$

Subsequently, we integrate the right side of equation (1)

$$\int (2x + 7)dx = x^2 + 7x$$

In mathematics, and in science at large, a reverse operation can be most revealing. In finance, too, we often need the result of integration. One of the reasons is to test if it is equal to the original expression; another reason is to find the price function that might be unknown.

$F(x) = x^2 + 7x$ is an easy example of integration, since the function from which the derivative came is known. In real life, however, when an integration process must be performed, only the *derivative* is known, not the original price function, which must be found.

How can this help with the analysis of derivative instruments? The answer is that market data can provide us with the necessary informa-tion to plot the slope. Then, knowing the derivative $\frac{dF(x)}{dx}$ we proceed with integration to find the original function F(x).

Let's now look into the second derivative of the price function F(x), since we have already computed the first derivative

$$\frac{dF(x)}{dx} = 2x + 7$$

The second derivative of the price function—that is, gamma—is the derivative of delta. Hence,

$$\frac{d^2F(x)}{dx^2} = 2$$

Granted, the price function $F(x) = x^2 + 7x$ on which this example has been based is very simple, but the banker, the trader, and the inves-tor will never do by hand the computations we have seen. There is plenty of commodity software for this purpose.

By contrast, designers, dealers and users of derivative financial products must be able to calculate the price function. In relatively straightforward cases this can be done through existing relatively simple models like Black-Scholes, which we will discuss in Chapter 16. Sophis-ticated financial products, however, require special study of the payoff.

Lack of skill in computing price functions and in managing them is a major failure with most financial institutions today. They have entered in a big way into derivatives trades—which get increasingly sophisti-cated—without altering their culture, their analytics, and their technol-ogy. As cannot be repeated too often, this backwater is the main cause of derivatives risks.

9. Taking Care of Kurtosis in a Risk and Return Distribution

We can apply the concept of risk and expected return to specific trades and portfolio choices as well as to subsequent valuation of assets and liabilities. The most frequently used background notion is that, all things being equal, investors prefer portfolios with a higher expected rate of return. But at the same time, investors are risk averse. What they want is less risk with greater return.

There is a contradiction here in the sense that investors must be compensated to bear risk. This is the sense of profits. Therefore, high-risk assets must yield more than low-risk assets. But how do we measure risk and return?

A common but misguided assumption is that the variance existing in a portfolio is a sufficient measure of its riskiness. This hypothesis might hold if, and only if, the rates of return on financial assets and real assets are normally distributed, which is rarely if ever the case. Typically, risk and return distributions are not normal. They include issues that matter quite significantly and end in a *kurtosis*.

Kurtosis is the fourth moment of a statistical distribution and measures its fat tails. As a memory refresher, let's add that the first moment of a statistical distribution is the mean, the second moment is the variance (whose square root is the standard deviation), and the third moment is the skewness.

The normal distribution typically has zero skewness and zero kurtosis. The algorithm for the computation of kurtosis is fairly simple and consists of the expected value of

$$\frac{(x_i - \bar{x})^4 - 3}{s^4}$$

One line of thought in pricing financial products is that investors must be compensated for both the skewness and the kurtosis in their portfolio. Plotting a leptokurtotic curve, as in Figure 15–3, helps in understanding the trade-off between risk and return—but we must as well establish how much the investor should or could be compensated for bearing the risk.

To better appreciate how this process works we should return to the fundamentals. When and how was the kurtotic process studied in the first place?

In 1907, H. E. Hurst, a British hydrologist, analyzed the patterns of floods and droughts on the Nile. What he discovered was that two successive floods and two successive droughts came slightly more often than they should in a normal distribution, given the frequency of single floods or single droughts. This seems to suggest that the Nile had a memory of past events.

Such sequences are not reflected in the statistical theory of the normal (Gaussian) distribution that characterizes many random variations, such as those found in throwing honest dice. But because big floods and severe droughts are more common than expected, the tails of the graph are fatter, presenting a leptokurtotic pattern, as in Figure 15–3.

Figure 15–3. The Hypothesis of a Normal Distribution Does Not Always Hold with Financial Data

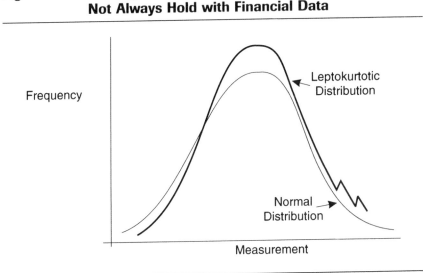

Hurst eventually came up with a way to measure the deviation of such graphs from the Gaussian, random shape. His method is now called *the Hurst exponent*, that is, the probability that one event will be followed by a similar event.

If the probability is 0.5, the graph is a normal distribution produced by a random process. If it is more than 0.5, the graph is kurtotic, produced by a process that tends to go in runs.

Wealth, for instance, follows a leptokurtotic shape because it is self-reinforcing. The fat tails of markets may imply a similar thing: The more they trend in one direction, the more that trend persists.

One of the reasons for fat tails is that many investors wait until they see a price established in an upward direction before they buy. They therefore tend to reinforce trends. But leptokurtotic models also affect the common means of measuring volatility because they depend on something other than the standard deviation as a measure of risk.

The more kurtotic a distribution curve is, the more misleading is the notion of standard deviation. The calculation of vital metrics is skewed by the largest price changes, which affect the beta factor.

At the same time, fat tails suggest that the stock market and other markets might be predictable; they might have memory. This seems to have been first suggested by Dr. Benoit Mandelbrot, who in the early 1960s advanced the hypothesis that financial markets would prove to be *fractal*.

A fractal object is one that occupies more than one certain dimension but not quite another. According to fractal geometry, a city's skyline is not one-dimensional because it is not an ordinary line, nor is it quite two-dimensional. A crumpled piece of paper is no longer two-dimensional, but it is not three-dimensional either. Both are said to have fractal dimensions.

A fractal dimension also exists with the behavior of capital markets and money markets. Each day's price depends to some extent on the previous day's price, and the market shows self-similarity at different scales. Fractal theory describes how a random process can reveal a pattern if we know how to look at it.

Based on these notions, chaos theory reflects the discovery that simple systems in which there are few causes can still show noisy, apparently random behavior.[7] Order and randomness can coexist, and as we have already seen, the transition from stability to chaos and vice versa is the domain of complexity theory.

10. Exploiting the Notion of Intrinsic Time

Evidence has been provided in the preceding sections not only that today we have available new metrics to gauge risk and return, but that some of the notions classically used with financial analysis need adjustment. They no longer fit the more rigorous exploitation of data streams that we need to do.

One of the new subjects in financial analysis is the change in the unit of measurement of time, which has to do with the time intervals themselves. Starting with 24-hour banking and trading, we tend to think that any hour is valid for any bank and any exchange. In reality, this is not so because of the limits imposed by *time windows*:

❑ One approach that has recently been adopted is to define a *business time* ∂, which characterizes the activities of financial markets: exchanges, banking institutions, and clearinghouses.

But even within a given time window, there are events, such as lunchtime, which see to it that in some markets time moves faster than in others. This introduces, so to speak, a concept of greater or less market productivity. The expression of the market productivity takes the form of *intrinsic time* τ, leading to the need of collecting high frequency financial data (HFFD) to assist in understanding market behavior.

Traditionally it has been thought that anywhere in the world market behavior is subject to the same standard units of time—be it the day,

---

[7] See also D. N. Chorafas, *Chaos Theory in the Financial Markets* (Chicago: Probus, 1994).

the hour, the minute or the second. But it is increasingly appreciated that this is not necessarily true. In financial analysis today, the concept of intrinsic time essentially means that minutes are shorter during the American lunch break than during the European or the Japanese lunch break because American traders eat lunch at their desks while continuing to deal in the market.

This observation brings up the concept of redefining *the width of time units* as well as the issue of tools to be used for management. In terms of tools, computer software draws graphs incorporating assumptions about how the different traders in different markets will react to a price movement in an intrinsic time sense.

❑   The first requirement is to understand the sense of intrinsic time.

❑   The second is to use it in an instrumental way for prognostication purposes.

Applications done in this domain tend to suggest that even if intrinsic time graphs present a similar overall shape, they have different slopes that can provide significant hints. These slopes are a function of each trader's time horizon.

In a similar manner, the study of kurtotic plots can help reveal the trader's risk profile.

Each trader is assumed to react in a nonlinear way to market movements: at first with a minor response to a price rising above its moving average, then with increasing interest, and finally with a major response as the trader thinks a clear trend has developed. In this process, the trader is exploiting the effects of kurtosis, but he also makes his behavior predictable.

The computer adds up these different measurements, indicating market profile and response and arriving at an estimate of how the market reacts to an event. Alternatively, the output can be a history of market behavior over the past day or hour.

Equipped with the appropriate analytical model, the computer forecasts what the market *might* do in the days or hours ahead, and it does so with an increasing width in confidence limits, to illustrate a growing margin of error.

A flashing point can signal the present moment. When the tolerance line goes below that point, the computer warns of an overbought opportunity, in which case one should go short. When the tolerance line goes above the present-moment point, the computer warns of an *oversold* opportunity, in which case one should go long. Both warnings are treated as advice.

The concept of intrinsic time changes the long-held beliefs regarding time behavior that have been based on standard units. The broadening or shrinking of time metrics—for example, the second—is also necessary in the exploitation of high-frequency financial data.

A recent project at MIT addresses tick-by-tick data in foreign exchange operations, which is inherently high frequency. Because subsecond-level data feeds do not conform to volatility levels, around which most models and tables have been constructed, the MIT researchers redefined time units of a variable width, the target being to observe a preset volatility level that, when reached, initiates further action.

This report has been promoted by the Morgan Bank, which seems to have put its results to good use. I expect that knock-in approaches of this type using kurtosis, intrinsic time, and business time, will multiply in the years to come as the results obtained from currently ongoing implementations start becoming known.

16

Creating a Culture for Risk Evaluation and Control

1. Introduction

Derivative financial products have been hailed by many as the hedger's paradise. Yet, because of the massive trading that goes on in OBS without a corresponding upgrading of the bankers' and investors' skills and technology, derivatives are not really risk-management tools. Rather, they have become the finance industry's equivalent to TNT. Metallgesellschaft and Orange County are two of the better-known failures.

On the other hand, properly managed derivatives can create a stream of profits, provided one keeps well in mind that they are liable to explode if not handled with extreme care. In the space created by these two statements, which seem to contradict one another, is where the skills of rocket scientists can flourish. Rocket science is a field that attracts a different type of thinker than traditional engineering or traditional business. The new generation of financial analysts thinks algorithmically and also comprehends that different rules apply in different cases.

Trading in derivatives and the management of a portfolio with off-balance-sheet instruments requires individuals who can rapidly change levels of abstraction, hence modeling, simultaneously seeing things *in the large* and *in the small*.

These two terms are borrowed from "programming in the large" and "programming in the small." The former means the *grand design*, with its broader perspective and overall impact—permitting us to judge not only how the solution we adopt fits in the current environment, but also what might be the most likely consequences.

By contrast, programming in the small looks at the nuts and bolts of a solution. In computer programming, it focuses on coding. In financial analysis, it concentrates on *detail*—whether the main theme is a product, a market, or the risk that results from active trading with a new financial instrument. This approach is very important with derivatives.

Used properly, derivatives could be effective. Companies of all sorts use them to hedge in ways that were not possible until recently. But proper risk management is a complex, four-stage process requiring companies to:

1. Identify where the company's risks really lie.

2. Design an appropriate strategy for managing them.

3. Select the right tools to execute the strategy.

4. Steadily follow up with sophisticated, often complex reevaluations.

Each of these steps is tough because finance has changed so much that hedging is often beyond the capabilities of many managers, while at the same time, the technological resources most companies have available from their legacy systems are substandard, and the same is true of their analytical skills.

Building on the concepts elaborated in Chapter 13 and 14 as well as the tools we have studied in Chapter 15, this chapter develops a framework for successful implementation. It suggests the type of studies to be done and advises procedural changes to make the management of risk more effective.

2.   Risk Policies and the Procedures to Support Them

Serious players in the banking industry have instituted intelligent information environments that integrate the voracious data-handling activities required during a product's life cycle. Tier-one organizations see to it that simulated output analyses are conducted off-line, often assisted through expert systems. The latter serve as advisors to financial analysts, traders, investment experts, or portfolio managers.

Simulation today is an iterative process in which end users establish the tolerances, rocket scientists design the model, end users decide the scenario, and rocket scientists run the experiment. Then, end users and rocket scientists

❏   Analyze the results.

❏   Decide on another scenario.

❏   Consult in real time with experts in other domains.

Tier-one banks are active in converting off-line models and activities into on-line interactive solutions. They see to it that their models and their computers are operating nonstop within an integrated financial environment—on any product, for any customer, anywhere in the world.

Real-time simulators are necessary for training and trading purposes[1] because many senior managers and traders of banks and nonbanks, as well as treasurers and senior staff of other companies, clearly do not understand OBS and its risks. Other bankers and financial advisors who understand them can on occasions miscalculate them, but not every error is a computing error.

❏   The greatest risk lies in superficial knowledge of the financial industry's hottest product.

❏   Any company can misuse derivative instruments, some of which are at the forefront of financial engineering.

Not only exotics, but many other financial derivatives demand complex mathematical studies. They need simulators and supercomputers both for opportunity analysis and for risk-management reasons. The control of exposure is in itself a difficult art.

It is not economical for a small firm to identify and solve all of its own hedging problems. But even big companies need help from outsiders in devising and executing their risk-management strategies. Therefore, it is not surprising that more and more firms are farming out all or some of their risk-control systems and procedures.

The skills of expert OBS advisors are not only expensive to maintain internally, but are beyond the day-to-day competence of most companies. Therefore, after establishing a strategy on OBS, a growing number of boards and CEOs subcontract its execution, including the final choice of instruments. However, the contracting company should:

❏   Learn from the experience of independent advisors.

❏   Ask for technology transfer.

❏   Revamp its system and procedures to get the best advantage from risk control.

---

[1] See also the discussion on OTT by Nikko Securities in Chapter 14.

The more exotic the financial instruments, the more they carry risks with them—as well as the threat of a global financial meltdown in a systemic sense. Bank regulators in the United States, Europe, Japan, and other countries are getting increasingly nervous about the lack of risk-management techniques to prevent a collapse in the capital markets. They are looking to algorithmic solutions, which can help to better focus.

In the United States, the Financial Accounting Standards Board has chosen the Black-Scholes algorithm for marking-to-model the contents of the trading book and banking book of financial institutions. While Black-Scholes is by now a low-technology algorithm, given other much more advanced developments in this field, it constitutes a model that a growing number of bankers and treasurers can comprehend. Hence, it is a common denominator.

Behind these analytical efforts is the notion that more orderly risk management will let business opportunity flourish but will decrease the odds of an international financial crash when the inevitable excesses occur. Better risk management, however, does not begin with models, but with thoroughly studied procedural solutions.

Even if the models being used are fairly accurate, an incoherent or unsystemic approach to exposure reporting carries in itself the seeds of bad management. Lack of sharp procedures simply does not make sense in the increasingly complex and perilous financial markets of the 1990s. Risk-control responsibility today

❑ Is too spotty and too narrowly focused to permit effective supervision by senior management.

❑ Is too fragmented in the different departments of the organization, both in a functional and a geographic sense.

❑ Is largely based on unwritten and imprecise policies, or on systems put together in a hurry.

❑ Rarely benefits from high-technology supports necessary for real-time control of exposure anywhere in the world.

Worse still is the fact that sound risk management is considered an impediment to the freewheeling of treasurers and traders. Therefore, monitoring is incomplete and largely relegated to the auditing and compliance departments—without having a precise mission.

I had two different experiences with financial institutions where the chief executive officer himself, while asking for a compass to assist in managing risk, impeded its development. He did so in order to keep his own hands and those of the traders free of controls and tighter supervision, hence, better positioned to generate profits, but also highly exposed to inordinate risk.

One of my professors at the University of California used to say that "Even human stupidity has limits, and where stupidity stops, conflict of interest starts." This is what is happening today, not only in banking but in many other lines of business. This trend should not be confused with corruption. Rather, the motor behind it is lust for inordinate profits and ever more inflated "results."

3.   Targeting the Entire Array of Risks

As any senior banker should appreciate, the lack of policies, systems, and procedures that permit the monitoring of exposure in real time and permit them to act on danger signals leads to huge risks. Top management has to realize that the only way to stem the tide of financial calamities, such as those that occurred with real estate and loans to developing countries in the 1980s and with derivatives in 1994, is by

❑   Instituting a deeply seated risk-control culture.

❑   Fundamentally overhauling the way the bank as a whole, and in particular the treasury department, deals with risk.

The chief executive officer and the members of the Board have to recognize that the effectiveness of their risk management can determine whether their company flourishes or withers away. But risk control requires comprehensive, companywide programs that

❑   Target the entire array of exposure factors, not just derivatives.

❑   Train all personnel in both new financial products and risk management.

What is good for the bank is also good for its clients since they are the most precious resource of the organization. Hence, the clients, also have to be trained in derivatives risk management, even if they have to do with OBS only remotely because the bank is doing the work for them.

Clear-eyed financial institutions and company treasurers know they have to find solutions for the problem of risk management connected to derivatives. Inordinate risks have become the daily practice of organizations without the appropriate cultural change, upgrading in know-how, and advanced technological supports.

The breadth of products offered, their complexity, and the global nature of markets make sophisticated risk management an absolute necessity, but the call that is now being heard for old-style centralized risk management is *wrong*.

The fact that this text calls for more rigorous risk policies and their supervision but at the same time speaks against centralization may seem contradictory. Careful study would demonstrate that this is not so. A hierarchical centralization is an aberration because it means stumbling backward into the future. It is simply not possible to centrally target the entire array of risks.

As we have seen on several occasions in the preceding chapters, the effective use of high technology can be instrumental in managing risk in a modern way. Intelligent networks, distributed deductive databases, and interactive visualization solutions can effectively create *real-space* environments with a very flexible reporting structure. This permits the control of risk

❏   At any time.

❏   For any instrument.

❏   Anywhere in the world.

A study on risk management by *Business Week*[2] brings into perspective the work that Judy Lewent is doing as Merck's chief financial officer. She uses Monte Carlo analysis, says the article, "as routinely as she used the slide-rule when she was a graduate student at Massachusetts Institute of Technology, in the early 1970s."

Analytical models can be successfully used in real time both to exploit business opportunity in the financial markets and to help manage risks. In the case of Merck, for instance, the company has operations in 140 countries. Hence, there is plenty of scope in experimentation and optimization.

Hedging with derivatives can be seen as part of an optimization process *if* the proper risk control policies, models, and computer systems are in place. Companies such as Merk need it to protect foreign currency earnings against fluctuations in the value of the dollar and to continue funding dividends as well as research costs. But as it cannot be too often stated, methods and tools alone will not effectively solve the risk-management problem. Organizational approaches must be rigorous and go to the heart of policy issues.

The creation of a board level risk-manager position is one of several organizational initiatives mandated by the control of exposure—particularly when a whole array of risks are targeted. This is important since, as stated on many occasions, there is a significant level of *illiteracy about derivatives* in most organizations—banks as well as nonbanks, and corporate finance or treasury units—who are transforming themselves into activist financial investors.

---

2 October 31, 1994.

Many boards look to OBS as a way to keep their companies out of trouble while boosting profits and competitive position. But without rigorous risk management, a company's vulnerability increases, rather than being brought under control. General statements and "soft" expressions of ethical standards don't solve the problems. They just increase the complacency quotient.

4. Reporting Practices for a Risk-Sensitive Culture

Every company has its own policies and practices concerning how to monitor risk. Perkin-Elmer, the instruments manufacturer, monitors foreign-exchange contracts by its finance officials in each country where it has operations. With help from a consulting firm, in 1994 the company initiated a pilot project to centralize foreign-exchange hedging. This project began with six countries, which represented half of the company's foreign currency exposure.

By offsetting positions in different currencies against each other, the management of Perkin-Elmer tries to optimize its treasury in regard to currency exchange risks but evidently takes on other risks.

"You take risks in whatever you do," said Dennis Weatherstone, chairman and CEO of J.P. Morgan. "But if you understand, measure, and account for them, that should keep you out of trouble."[3] At the Morgan Bank, every day its risk-management unit compiles a one-page report known as "4:15," so called because it gets handed to Morgan's top six executives by that time of day.

The idea of informing top management every day is good, but it would have been even better to have this report interactively available on the workstations of senior executives. It should have been handled through knowledge artifacts (agents) that gave an overview of the bank's exposure, including:

- ❑ Foreign exchange.
- ❑ Interest rate.
- ❑ Commodity trade.
- ❑ Bond investments.
- ❑ Equity positions.
- ❑ Exotic derivatives.
- ❑ All other exposures.

---

3 The system used by the Morgan Bank is RiskMetrics. I have serious reservations in regard to its sophistication.

The idea of using paper to daily present crucial information that may decide the survival of the financial institution comes out of the dark ages of organization and technology. This is true for all companies, most particularly the national and multinational firms engaging in derivatives trades. The technology for interactive on-line reporting is presently available.

By using heuristics and algorithms in connection with the trade book, the portfolio, and liquidity and volatility data, it is possible to calculate the daily earnings at risk as well as the key exposure measures that constitute salient problems for management. It is rumored that Morgan has set a maximum amount of 5 percent likelihood of losing per day. The metric is good. But batch reporting is dreadful.

In a way that complements the services provided by RAROC[4] of Bankers Trust, Morgan has its own risk-management program known as RiskMetrics. It offers daily risk information on different instruments and currencies through calculating exposures over one day or one month.

It must be that, as in so many other companies, one department does not know what another is doing because the same Morgan Bank sponsors a project at MIT that tracks market transactions tick-by-tick[5] and successfully manipulates this information until it confesses its secrets. In terms of a rigorous financial analysis,

❑   Subsecond data rates are far superior to hourly and daily, in terms of revealing patterns and background factors.

❑   Monthly rates are an aberration. They provide no insight or foresight, other than reflecting some events that are long past.

Morgan is not alone in this slow motion in a market that works at subsecond speed. Other banks have a daily risk report that tallies the exposure in their lines of business, but they also have doubts about the benefits to top management. Still other banks don't even have that service.

To make matters worse, in most cases, such reports are very confidential, circulated at the end of each day among half a dozen senior executives who simply don't have the time to take corrective action that late in the day—except when catastrophe has already hit.

Theoretically, this confidential approach to critical risk information is right. Practically, it has a major flaw because it does not permit corrective steps. Short-circuiting operating executives is the wrong policy. Nor is once a day a good pace in a highly dynamic market.

Not only should risk-management reporting be ad hoc, actuated on-line by the senior executives themselves rather than being given to

---

[4] Risk adjusted return on capital.
[5] See also the discussion on HFFD in Chapter 15.

Figure 16–1. Exposure Metrics Should Be Handled in Real Time with Reporting in a Three-Dimensional Frame of Reference

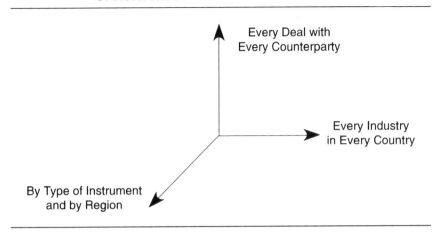

them in a dull format on a piece of paper, but it should also be possible to interactively take corrective action.

All senior executives should be able to experiment through their workstation by accessing distributed database resources. They should be able to use simulators and study how their bank would fare in the event of a *worst-case event*, such as a sharp and protracted rise in interest rates accompanied by a significant movement in foreign-exchange rates, a crash in the stock market index, a sustained movement in key commodities, and so on.

Then, when abnormalities occur, the top decision makers should be networked via teleconferencing in a circuit, the way Nynex's Shuttle works, not point to point. This will permit concerted action, no matter in which part of the world the senior executives are and without demanding an inordinate amount of their time.

Just as important is the ability to interactively follow a second layer of risk indicators, such as a buildup of loan concentrations in certain industries and/or in geographic regions—for instance, commercial real estate, the oil industry, selected major client accounts, countries in political or economic turbulence, and other windows on risk. As Figure 16–1 indicates

- ❑ Every deal and every counterparty must be risk-rated.

- ❑ Individual countries and industries must have their own limits and trip wires.

- ❑ Limits should also exist by type of financial instrument, by client, and by region.

Not just the corporate top, but all line managers must be account-able for the control of their positions. Networks, databases, and knowl-edge artifacts should be used to monitor risks in derivatives and all other products worldwide. Agents using simulators should be oversee-ing risk limits for particular issues, tracking the overall corporate risk limit, and informing the boss in real time.

5.   Choosing and Using Option Pricing Models

It is as important to support the real-time reporting policies outlined in section 4 through real-time simulation[6] as it is to institute a risk-sensi-tive culture in the entire organization in the first place. Both account-ability of staff and line, and advanced technology solutions are necessary to keep banks and other companies out of trouble.

As we have seen in section 3, real-time simulation is based on valuation models; therefore, the query, Which model? is legitimate. At an increasing pace, stock, index, and bond options as well as other de-rivative instruments are priced by computer. The system solution must be flexible:

❑   New option types and valuation models should be added as fast as rocket scientists develop them.

❑   Valuation models must be written for a range of instruments, their sophistication growing from simpler to more complex arti-facts.

A 23-year-old model that is rather simple but fast and efficient is the Black-Scholes[7] for option pricing. It is by far the most popular and is in the process of being adopted by FASB for marking-to-model.

Like all models, Black-Scholes is based on a number of hypotheses and therefore approximations. One of these approximations is that it has been designed for European-type options, but it is widely used for the valuation of U.S.-type options. With European-type options, value is cal-culated if the option is kept until expiry. But it might be more profitable to exercise the option prior to maturity, which is what the U.S.-type op-tion offers.

To check this possibility, for instance for equity options, Black-Scholes prices are calculated where time-to-expiration is equal to time-

---

[6] See also D. N. Chorafas and H. Steinmann, *Virtual Reality: Practical Applications in Business and Industry* (Englewood Cliffs, NJ: Prentice Hall, 1995).

[7] For the Black-Scholes model, in 1994 Fischer Black received the Dimitris N. Chorafas award, of the Swiss Academies of Sciences, for outstanding achievements in finance products.

to-dividend. Present value of dividends is escrowed from the underlying price, and the exercise price is properly adjusted.

When the model is used for U.S. put options, the extra premium is approximated and added to the European-type value because of the possibility of early exercise. A correction can be made with linear interpolation of Black-Scholes and quadratic approximation values.

While these solutions do not necessarily correlate one-to-one with market prices, they constitute one of the better available methods. The alternatives are binomial distribution[8] and Monte Carlo.[9] No doubt, new pricing models will be developed in the years ahead. For the most part, their results will not be perfect, but they will be much better than guesswork—which is how valuation, costing, and pricing are often done, particularly in socialist economies. Market economies have their imperfections, and some of them are in modeling, but the end result is much better than the lottery approach to prices.

The reason for the recent popularity of the Black-Scholes model is its remarkable acceptance by the financial markets. This, in turn, rests on the fact that over the years market prices of stock options and warrants on stock have exhibited a fairly close agreement with the algorithm:

$$F(x,y,T,r) = xN(d_1) - ye^{-rT} N(d_2)$$

where

$$
\begin{array}{rcl}
x &=& \text{stock price} \\
y &=& \text{strike price} \\
T &=& t^* - t = \text{time to maturity} \\
t^* &=& \text{maturity date} \\
t &=& \text{today's date} \\
r &=& \text{interest rate} \\
N &=& \text{cumulative normal density function[10]}
\end{array}
$$

This Black-Scholes option pricing formula, $F(x,y,T,r)$ estimates the value of an option (or warrant) on the stock, with d_1 and d_2 given by the following equations

$$d_1 = \frac{\ln(x/y) + (r + \tfrac{1}{2}s^2)T}{s\sqrt{T}}$$

---

8 See D. N. Chorafas, *Advanced Financial Analysis* (London: Euromoney, 1994).

9 See D. N. Chorafas, *Chaos Theory in the Financial Markets* (Chicago: Probus, 1994).

10 Which is tabulated in most statistical texts and can be approximated using a simple algebraic expression.

$$d_2 = \frac{\ln(x/y) + (r - \tfrac{1}{2}s^2)T}{s\sqrt{T}}$$

which can also be written

$$d_2 = d_1 - s\sqrt{T}$$

where

$$y = \text{strike price}$$
$$s = \text{standard deviation of the stock's return}$$
$$s^2 = \text{the variance}$$

$N(d_1)$ and $N(d_2)$ are lognormal distributions. The logarithm is not on base 10, but on base e. It is known as natural or Naperian, where e is Euler's number

$$e = 2.7182818 = 1 + \frac{1}{1!} + \frac{1}{2!} + \frac{1}{3!} + \ldots + \frac{1}{n!} + \ldots$$

Logarithms to the base e ($\log_e$ or ln) are called Neperian or *natural logarithms*. John Napier or Neper was a Scottish mathematician who invented logarithms in 1614. Their use leads to a significantly simple formula for differentiation

$$\frac{d}{dx}\ln x = \frac{1}{x}$$

There are practical reasons for the use of natural logarithms, which are a popular approach to option pricing. We will see further examples in section 6 and subsequent sections of this chapter.

6.   Lognormal Distributions and Transition Probabilities

A model for option pricing can use a lognormal process, a square-root process, or other processes. A lognormal distribution is shown in Figure 16–2. The approach employed by Black-Scholes is more general than others because it allows the local process to change over time:

❑   A lognormal distribution has a mean and a variance.

❑   Assuring a different lognormal short rate distribution for each future time allows both mean and variance to depend on time.

So long as the process for *log r* is linear in log r at each time, there is a lognormal distribution for the possible values of the short rate at a given future time. As we have seen in section 5, *r* is the local interest rate.

Figure 16–2. Typical Form of a Lognormal Distribution Used in Option Pricing

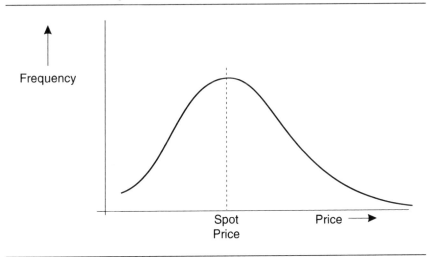

The first paragraph of this section made reference to the square root distribution as an alternative to the lognormal. The square root rule states that the standard deviation of the change in the independent variable is proportional to the square root of time.

This observation can have interesting practical applications in financial analysis. For instance, by incorporating the square root rule into the volatility estimate, we can account for the maturity of a given transaction.

If a given financial transaction is executed for final maturity in, say, three years, we must adjust the historical volatility estimate β_h to account for this change in time

$$\text{Adjusted } \beta_h = \beta_h \sqrt{t}$$

where t is the time to maturity of the financial transaction in fraction or multiples of one year. In this sense a three-year period will set t at 3; while for a six-month period the value of t will be 0.5. The annual historical volatility estimate β_a will be

$$\beta_a = s \sqrt{T}$$

where s is the standard deviation of the price volatility for a given instrument during the year, and T is the number of days in the year, usually taken to equal 250 workdays.

Another well-established mathematical tool most valuable in modeling derivatives pricing is *transition probabilities*, or Markov chains. Transition indicates the change of an operand into a transform, and transform is the final stage of the operand.[11] Transition probabilities lead to a process of transformation. This transformation is due to the change of one or several operands by an operator.

Named after the Russian mathematician who formalized them, Markov chains address the process of transition and associated probabilities. For instance, colonies of insects or of people are typically built out of migration phenomena. Finance is interested in such phenomena because this is the way capital markets and money markets act. The behavior of schools of fish and insect colonies provides good examples of interactions characterizing the *movement of capital.*

Research has documented that in situations outside their nests, ants get into *random walks.* But after an ant deposits chemicals to indicate it has found food, the system becomes a *tightly patterned* activity, controlling the speed of carrying food by keeping the procession steady. After the goal has been attained, the pattern again becomes random and deterministic.

Senior financial analysts who have experience with projects of similitudes between physical and logical systems suggest that survival patterns characterizing ant colonies can be found in financial markets:

❑ Applying an outside force can destroy the market's (colony's) structure.

❑ But with time comes recovery, and the market (colony) will be restructured.

A good real-life example of this is what happened in Eastern Europe and Latin America: Market destruction came as a result of high-handed forces, but then market regeneration took over. Interestingly enough both transitions have been:

❑ From stability to chaos and

❑ From chaos to stability.

One of the assumptions of transition probabilities is that the behavior of the key variables follows a lognormal stochastic process, such as that embedded in Black-Scholes, which can be assumed to be continuous. Behind this assumption is the belief that the movement of the independent variable is random in continuous time, and the change in

---

[11]See also D. N. Chorafas, *Statistical Processes and Reliability Engineering* (Princeton, NJ: D. Van Nostrand, 1960).

the price of the variable divided by the price of the variable (or instantaneous return) has constant *mean* and constant *variance*.

The resulting distribution of the independent variable is lognormal and is slightly skewed to the right, with its lower bound zero and its upper bound an asymptote to the abscissa.

The continuous type of stochastic distribution described above is also known as a *diffusion process* with a continuous probability density function. This is, of course, an approximation because most financial processes are discontinuous but can be taken as continuous within a reduced range.

7.   Applying the Diffusion Process to the Financial Markets

We said that there are always approximations in modeling real life. For instance, the diffusion process does not account for sudden discontinuities or jumps in behavior of variables. Rather, it rests on the hypothesis that these variables move smoothly in small increments. Hence, Black-Scholes, and most other models, do not fit the study of sudden market changes and panics.

Only within the range of the outlined assumptions can the independent variable under study take any value from *zero* to *infinity*, during the time *t* that we consider. Alternatively, we can reduce the range of its application to finite intervals under nonexceptional conditions. This is the usual assumption with economic and financial models.

Under these premises, and most particularly the assumption that normal conditions prevail, the price movement of a stock, index, currency rate, interest rate, or other instrument is

$$\frac{\Delta P}{P} = F(x)\Delta t + \beta S \Delta t$$

where

$$P \ = \ \text{the price of the instrument}$$
$$\Delta P \ = \ \text{the change in the price}$$
$$\frac{\Delta P}{P} \ = \ \text{the return of the instrument}$$
$$F(x) \ = \ \text{the function of expected return}$$
$$\beta \ = \ \text{the volatility of the instrument's price}$$
$$S \ = \ \text{a random sample from normal distribution with mean 0 and standard deviation 1}$$
$$\Delta t \ = \ \text{a very small time interval}$$

The return of the instrument is equal to the expected return over t, plus the volatility of the price adjusted for a small error, which could impact the end return at any point in time. It is

$$\frac{\Delta P}{P} = \frac{P_{t,\Delta t} - P_t}{P_t}$$

$$\frac{dP}{P} = \mu\, dt + \beta\, dz$$

Substituting the expected value of the parameter μ (where μ is the population mean) by the x statistic, and the volatility β (the parameter of standard deviation) by the s statistic

$$\frac{dP}{P} = \bar{x}\, dt + s\, dz$$

or

$$dp = \bar{x}\, P\, dt + s\, P\, dz$$

Both statistics $\bar{x}$ and s are functions of the instrument's price P and time t. The dz is known as the *Weiner process*.[12] This process is stochastic and normally distributed with mean 0 and standard deviation 1. The generic form is

$$dy = a\, dt + b\, dz \qquad (1)$$

The Weiner algorithm maps a process of transition probabilities, as discussed in section 6. The values of the instrument at times *t* and *t+1* are independent of one another. Hence, they have zero correlation.

In equation (1), *a* is an instantaneous rate of change in the independent variable and is called the *drift coefficient*. Correspondingly, *b* is the *diffusion coefficient*.

Neither *a* nor *b* are constant. They are functions of other variables and follow the so-called *Ito process*, where the functions of both variables are expressed in terms of *y* and *t*

$$y = f_a(y,t)dt + f_b(y,t)dt$$

The form of Ito's lemma, which is used for the solution of stochastic differential equations, is

$$df = \left(\frac{\partial f}{\partial y} a + \frac{\partial f}{\partial t} + \frac{b^2}{2} \frac{\partial^2 f}{\partial y^2} \right) + \frac{\partial f}{\partial y} b\, dz$$

This lemma helps in finding the differentials of functions of random variables. Interest rates, exchange rates, indexes, stock prices, bond

---

[12] Tables of z-scores can be found in R. Mills, *Statistics for Applied Economics and Business* (Tokyo: Kogakusha McGraw-Hill, 1977); W. Hines and D. Montgomery, *Probability and Statistics in Engineering and Management Science* (New York: John Wiley, 1990); and other statistical books.

prices, and other values of financial vehicles fit the characteristics of this algorithmic expression.

As can be seen from this presentation, there is a wealth of modeling structures that can be used to advantage in derivatives pricing. The fact that their usage is not yet widespread is mainly due to the illiteracy in real-time simulation prevailing in the financial sector. Most bankers, investors, and traders like to use the latest and most sophisticated financial instruments. But from mathematics to computers, their technology is paleolithic; hence, they end up taking inordinate risks.

For an orderly algorithmic procedure to risk management, together with the Weiner process and Ito's lemma, we need to consider the notion of *levels of confidence*. To appreciate the underlying concept, we should recall that the cumulative normal distribution function gives the relative frequency with which observations will fall lower than (to the left of) any given value, as shown in Figure 16–3.

This relative frequency is the area under the distribution curve from minus infinity to the given value. For normal distributions, the areas under the curve from minus infinity to

$$Z = \frac{x - \mu}{\sigma}$$

have been tabulated where x is the given value of the variable, μ is the population mean, and σ is the population standard deviation.[13] The table must be entered by way of the deviation of x measured in units. Z is often used for scoring. As expressed in equation

$$Z_i = \frac{x_i - \mu}{\sigma}$$

the distribution of scores will have a mean of 0 and standard deviation 1. By contrast, in equation

$$Z_i = 20 + 5 \frac{x_i - \mu}{\sigma}$$

the distribution will have a mean of 20 and standard deviation of 5.

Both μ and σ are constant and the same table can be used for any value of μ and σ. In Figure 16–3 the height h has been designed to correspond to the line that defines the shaded area of the normal distribution; h gives the frequency with which observations less than or equal to any given value of x will occur in the shaded area of the normal distribution.

---

[13] See W. J. Dixon and Frank J. Massey, *Introduction to Statistical Analysis* (New York: McGraw-Hill, 1951), Table 3, p. 305.

Figure 16–3. Cumulative Normal Distribution and the Area Under the Normal Distribution for a Given X

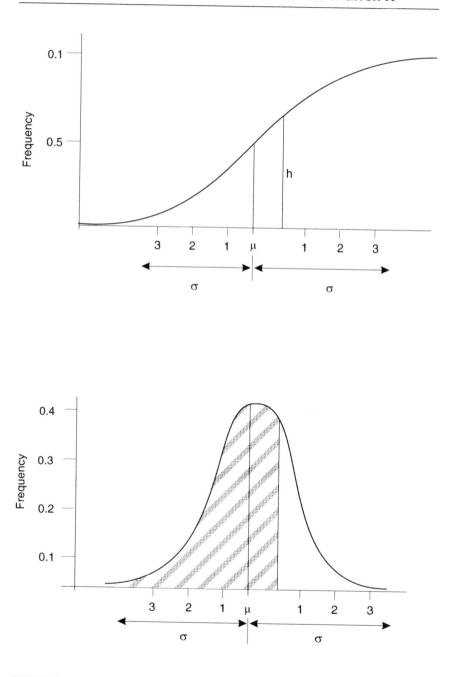

8.   What Is the Level of Confidence We Wish to Apply?

We can use the normal distribution tables to find the proportion of time we can expect to obtain a sample mean with a certain distance from the population μ. Say, for instance, that our choice is 95 percent of the time $\mu - x$ will be in the range

$$-1.96 \frac{\sigma}{\sqrt{n}} < \mu - \overline{x} < 1.96 \frac{\sigma}{\sqrt{n}}$$

where

$\overline{x}$ = the sample mean

n = the sample size

Notice that the multiplier 1.96 is used because 95.5 percent of the area under the normal distribution curve is within 2 δ of the mean, and 95 percent of the area is within 1.96 δ of the mean.

If we wish to use a level of confidence of 99 percent rather than 95 percent, the multiplier 1.96 δ must be replaced by 2.58. By contrast, if the chosen level of confidence is 90 percent, the multiplier of δ should be 1.64.

In the case of a level of confidence greater than 95 percent, the intervals must be longer in order to include μ a larger percent of the time. If the level of confidence is less than 95 percent, the intervals can be shorter, but the parameter μ will be included a smaller percent of the time.

The 99, 95, and 90 percent levels are the most used *confidence intervals*. The values at the end of the interval are called *confidence limits*. It should always be remembered that we are computing an interval based on the sample mean that has, say, a 99 percent chance of containing the population mean.

This notion is an integral part of the process of *statistical inference*, which bases itself on estimations in order to reach conclusions. Its counterpart is the concept of a *test of hypothesis*, when in essence we determine whether or not two samples have come from the same population with a mean equal to the μ parameter:

❏   The null hypothesis, H_0, states that there is no difference between the values of μ.

❏   The alternative hypothesis, H_1, states that there is a difference.

The procedure can be illustrated by the use of the sampling distribution of $\overline{x}$, a statistic computed for a sample of n observations. A sample mean far removed from μ will rarely occur if the null hypothesis is true.

By contrast, the null hypothesis will be rejected if a value $\bar{x}$ occurred that would be expected very rarely if the null hypothesis were valid. Just how rare this "rarely" is can be computed through the level of significance denoted through α.

As in the case of our discussion of z, the value of α may be chosen by the experimenter. Such a choice is instrumental in determining the acceptance or rejection of the hypothesis. Typically, we chose α at the 0.01, 0.05, and 0.1 *levels of confidence*, which corresponds to the 99, 95, and 90 percent confidence intervals. This choice must be made before testing begins.

However, in addition to the possible error of rejecting the null hypothesis when it is true—also known as Type I error, or producer's risk—there is also the possibility of the error β: accepting the null hypothesis when it is false. In this case the Type II error is β, or consumer's risk, and should not be confused with β, the volatility metric. Both α and β can be used to indicate the type of error. They also tell about the chance of making that error.

However, while for a given number of observations n (sample size) we can choose α as we please, the β is statistically determined. For a fixed n, a decrease in α will increase β; for a given α, a bigger sample will decrease β. On this simple notion rests the whole theory of operating characteristics (OC) curves.[14]

Let's now integrate what has been said about confidence intervals and tests of significance. Say that we believe the mean μ of a universe has a value μ_0 and that the universe variance is σ^2. Then it is usual practice to assume that the sampling distribution of

$$z = \frac{\bar{x} - \mu_0}{\sigma/\sqrt{n}}$$

is normal with mean 0 and standard deviation 1, which fits the z characteristics. μ_0, σ, n are constant. This, however, is true if $\mu = \mu_0$, i.e., the null hypothesis is true, and the universe has a normal distribution. The concept is approximately correct for large samples even if the universe of values is not normally distributed.

Notice also that the calculation of z is based on the population parameters μ and σ, which are not always known. In the sampling distribution of

---

[14]See D. N. Chorafas, *Statistical Processes and Reliability Engineering* (Princeton, NJ: D. Van Nostrand, 1960).

$$\frac{\overline{x} - \mu}{s / \sqrt{n}}$$

where σ is not known, we replace the population parameter σ by the sample standard deviation s and obtain the t distribution

$$t = \frac{\overline{x} - \mu}{s / \sqrt{n}}$$

To do so, we need to know the sample distribution of t, which was elaborated by W.A. Shewhart in the early 1930s. Dr. Shewhart published his papers under the pseudonym "Student", which is why this statistical algorithm is known as Student's t test.

If n is very large, the variance of the sample s^2 will tend to be quite close to the variance of the population σ^2. Otherwise, the sampling distribution of the statistic t will be somewhat more spread than a normal distribution.

If the standard deviation of the population is known, the confidence intervals will be

$$\overline{x} + \frac{(z_{\alpha/2})\,\sigma}{\sqrt{n}} \quad \text{and} \quad \overline{x} + \frac{(z_{1-\alpha/2})\,\sigma}{\sqrt{n}}$$

where x is the sample mean, n is the sample size, and $z_{\alpha/2}$ and $z_{1-\alpha/2}$ are the values from statistical tables. If we compute such limits from a sample, the chance of the interval covering μ is $1-\alpha$, where α typically takes the values 0.01, 0.05 or 0.1.

If the parameter σ is not known, we use its best estimate, the statistic s of the sample. Therefore, the confidence intervals are

$$\overline{x} + \frac{(t_{\alpha/2})\,s}{\sqrt{n}} \quad \text{and} \quad \overline{x} + \frac{(t_{1-\alpha/2})\,s}{\sqrt{n}}$$

If we have two samples, one from each of two populations, we might wish to know whether their means are equal. The *null hypothesis* H_0 states that there is no difference between μ_1 and μ_2, while the alternative hypothesis H_1 says there is a difference. It will be

$$H_0: \quad \mu_1 = \mu_2$$
$$H_1: \quad \mu_1 = \mu_2$$
$$\text{given } \sigma_1 = \sigma_2 = \sigma$$

To perform the test of hypothesis, we first decide on the level of significance α, then compute

$$z = \frac{\bar{x}_1 - \bar{x}_2}{\sigma \sqrt{(1/n_1) + (1/n_2)}}$$

If the universe is normally distributed, the sampling distribution of z is theoretically normal. If n_1 and n_2 are large, the distribution of z approximates the normal. The critical region will be

$$z_{1-1/2\alpha} < z < z_{1/2\alpha}$$

The confidence limits for the mean μ of a population in the case where the parameter variance σ is known are those we have seen in the preceding paragraphs.

These notions and algorithms lead to the concept of *tolerance limits*, which helps to obtain an interval that will cover a fixed portion of a population distribution with a certain confidence. Tolerance intervals defining the tolerance limits may be of the form

$$\bar{x} \pm ks$$

where k is a coefficient determined so that the interval will cover a proportion p of the population at a given level of confidence. This notion is behind quality control charts. Tolerance limits have a growing appeal in financial applications and most particularly in the control of risk.

9. Practical Use of Weiner's z Risk Factor in Connection to Notional Principal

In his book *Complex Derivatives*,[15] Erik Banks advances an algorithm that helps to estimate the market risk factor, RF, based on the adjusted historical volatility and z. Describing the practical use of the Weiner process, Banks denotes a transitional probability that helps to calculate RF

$$RF \quad = \quad \beta_h \sqrt{t} \, z \qquad\qquad (2)$$

where

$$\beta_h \quad = \quad \text{the historical volatility}$$
$$t \quad = \quad \text{the time to maturity of the financial transaction}$$

---

[15] Eric Banks, *Complex Derivatives* (Chicago: Probus, 1994).

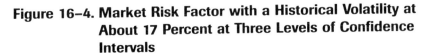

Figure 16–4. Market Risk Factor with a Historical Volatility at About 17 Percent at Three Levels of Confidence Intervals

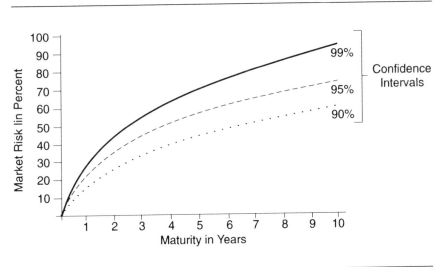

As we have already seen in sections 7 and 8, z is a parameter based on the population mean μ and population variance σ and the x values of the chosen variable.

Algorithm (2) permits the measurement of potential future market movements at a given level of confidence that can be incorporated into z and correspond, for that instance, to $\alpha = 0.01$, $\alpha = 0.05$, $\alpha = 0.1$, or any other choice.

The $\beta_h \sqrt{t}$ component in equation (2) permits the estimation of the annualized standard deviation of price movements. Among the contributions of the z score is the adjustment to the chosen level of confidence.

The inclusion of z permits us to say that we expect at, say, the 95 percent confidence level that the volatility measure will be "k" percent. For a specific financial instrument this constitutes the *market risk* (MR) at time of measurement and permits the development of worst-case scenarios.

As can be observed in Figure 16–4, the higher the level of confidence, the greater the market risk. Particularly at longer maturities, at 99 percent confidence level and 10 years to maturity MR is an asymptote to 100 percent. Not many financial institutions account for this fact. Yet, it is present in their transactions, their trading book, and their portfolio.

If, in general, case equation (2) provides a workable framework, there is no doubt that it can be improved in terms of precision by specifying exposure instrument-by-instrument, starting with the risk factor. It can also be made more sophisticated in a generalized sense through genetic algorithms and fuzzy engineering.

The careful reader will appreciate that the shape of the family of curves in Figure 16–4 reflects the function $y = \ln(x)$, which we have already studied in sections 5 and 6. They can be approximated by a parabola, and the whole structure can be expressed in 3-D, permitting the introduction of a third dimension—for instance, the price of the underlier.

Alternatively, equation (2) can be employed in a risk-equivalent computation involving the notional principal amount NP. This should be approached in a detailed manner and worked out derivative instrument by derivative instrument. A good approximation, however, is the more generalized algorithm

$$RE = RF \bullet NP$$

where

$$
\begin{aligned}
RE &= \text{risk equivalent exposure} \\
RF &= \text{market risk factor} \\
NP &= \text{notional principal of the transaction}
\end{aligned}
$$

This applies on a transaction-by-transaction basis and, therefore, on an instrument-by-instrument basis. If it were to calculate the risk equivalent exposure of the trading or of a portfolio, we whould use

$$RE = \sum_{i=1}^{n} RF_i \bullet NP_i$$

where RF_i and NP_i respectively represent market risk factors and notional principal amounts of the positions in the book, and n stands for the number of these positions.

We studied the concept of the notional principal amount in Chapter 2, including its conversion to loans equivalent. We have also treated the subject of notional principal amount and use it in the computation of risk equivalent exposure, including practical applications in Chapter 14. These concepts should by now be clear enough to the reader.

A numerical example of risk equivalence can be of further help. If the off-balance-sheet transaction is $1 billion in notional amount, and the market risk factor is 10 percent—over a six-month period at 90 percent confidence level[16]—the risk equivalent exposure, practically expressed in loans terms, will be

---

[16] See equation (2).

$$RE = 0.10 \bullet 1.000 = \$100 \text{ million}$$

This 10 percent is easily interpolated in Figure 16–4, taking a half-year maturity and 90 percent confidence level. Notice that again for six months to maturity but at the 99 percent level of confidence, the market risk will stand at 20 percent, therefore

$$RE = 0.20 \bullet 1.000 = \$200 \text{ million}$$

Two more numerical examples further aid in understanding the wide usage of this method as well as the risks the bank is taking. If the maturity were three years, at the 90 percent level of confidence, then the computation would be

$$RE = 0.34 \bullet 1.000 = \$340 \text{ million}$$

With the same three years maturity at the 99 percent level of confidence, the risk equivalent exposure becomes

$$RE = 0.53 \bullet 1.000 = \$530 \text{ million}$$

This example introduces a totally different dimension to the de-modulator from notional principal amounts to loans equivalent than the simpler divisor we have used so often because it creates a function $F(x,y)$ for the estimation of market risk, where

$$x = \text{ the maturity in years}$$
$$y = \text{ the chosen confidence interval}$$

The examples we have seen also help document that in the large majority of cases banks tend to apply a very low ratio in terms of risk equivalence because they fail to take into account both the *maturity* of the derivatives transaction and the *level of confidence* with which results are reported to top management and to supervisory authorities. In the example we have seen a six-month deal requires a demodulator of 10, and a three-year deal requires a demodulator of about 3. In both cases, the level of confidence in being right is 90 percent, while higher confidence levels have still smaller demodulators and hence higher levels of risk.

By calculating in real time that the risk of a $1 billion derivatives transaction is at the $100 million level or more, the trader will approach it cautiously. Most importantly, the bank will have a basis on which to evaluate the cost of the risk being taken as though it were buying reinsurance—adding this cost to the P&L of the transaction, as we have seen in Chapter 14.

Of course, this whole process is one based on hypotheses about risk exposure. Black-Scholes does the same thing but at a much lower level of sophistication. Each is a good method in its own domain and is currently used for quantifying derivatives prices and risks. However, the more complex the financial transaction, the more advanced the risk calculation method should be.

10. Integrating the Tools Provided by Analytical Computational Finance

We started this chapter by looking into risk policies and procedures because the reason for using models and computers is to support these policies effectively. This support is best provided through real-time reporting practices and visualization, as we saw in sections 3 and 4. An integral part of derivatives risk management is the choice and/or development of models—as sections 5 to 9 have explained.

We can now integrate these results with the solutions presented in the preceding chapters, most particularly in Chapter 14. As will be recalled, the strategy advanced in Chapter 14 is that

❑ *Risk* can be seen as a *cost.*

❑ Such cost needs to be qualified and quantified.

In conjunction with this strategy, we have spoken of the wisdom of correcting the insufficiency of worn-out tools through genetic algorithms and fuzzy engineering as well as overcoming the innumeracy problems in banking.

Financial decisions are made under uncertainty, and this is most true with derivatives vehicles. Therefore, the latter require a different set of rules and reasoning than the usual assumptions made in a world of certainty, which is a completely unrealistic hypothesis with off-balance-sheet financing.

We need to develop a measure of risk for financial assets and to describe the combination of risk and return available to the investor. Taken together, these two issues require a rigorous theory that explains what a financial asset with a certain level of risk should be earning.

Mathematical statistics provide the capability of massaging historical data, and extrapolating future patterns within a certain level of confidence. The so-called traditional business statistics offer no ideal measures, and though this process is well established, its results are substandard.

Precisely for this reason, the preceding sections presented and explained much more rigorous analytical tools for an examination based on financial data. We have seen examples from experimentation on market patterns and the control of risk. However, some of the algorithms available with business statistics should be retained as they can still be helpful in financial analysis.

An example of a useful statistic to which implicit if not explicit reference was made is the coefficient of correlation ρ. The symbol, a Greek rho, should not be confused with the *rho* metric we saw in Chapter 15, which signals effects of change in interest rate.

The operator ρ presents the degree of correlation between two independent variables that we measure. Since most studies in financial analysis deal with two or more independent variables, we need to study how they correlate two by two. This coefficient of correlation is a number varying between -1 and $+1$.

$$-1 \leq \rho \leq 1$$

When $\rho_{i,j} = +1$, the two independent variables perfectly correlate, but this happens very rarely. The algorithm to calculate the correlation coefficient reflects the fact that the regression curve of two variables x and y is not a straight line, in which case $\rho = 1$. The regression curve will be given by

$$y = a + bx + cx^2$$

where a, b, and c are parameters whose value is to be estimated by the sample, and x and y are the independent variables. Graphically, the regression curve is a parabola.

It has, however, been emphasized that as the financial instruments we develop get more complex, we need more sophisticated approaches than the tools of business statistics, which are at the lower end of the food chain of mathematics. We have spoken of t-test and Weiner's z. The x^2-test for the analysis of variance is also an important metric.[17]

One of the jobs of rocket scientists is to use available mathematical tools, even simple ones, to develop new and more powerful methods. Let's take the diversification formula and price of risk as an example.

Consider an investor with a net worth of Q dollars to invest and q_i dollars invested in asset i. The fraction x_i of the portfolio invested in asset i is given by the formula

$$x_i = \frac{q_i}{Q}$$

where

---

[17] See D. N. Chorafas, *Advanced Financial Analysis* (London: Euromoney, 1994).

$$\sum_{i=1}^{n} x_i = 1$$

n is the number of deals in the trading book or investments in the portfolio. The rate of return on the portfolio is

$$RR = \sum_{i=1}^{n} x_i r_i$$

where

RR = the total rate of return

r_i = the rate of return on each x_i

One time period down the line, the existing wealth in an investment portfolio will be

$$Q_t = Q_{t-1} (RR+1)$$

Notice, however, that in the $\sum_{i=1}^{n} x_i r_i$ formula, some of the x_i r_i may be negative.

The principle of a good diversification is that no x_i should be greater than 5 percent, no matter how solid the investment may look at the time the investment decision is made. This, too, can be expressed mathematically as a constraint

$$q_i \leq 0.05 Q$$

If N different portfolios are considered in a sample, the way to bet is that there will be a variance in their risk and return—often a significant one. This variance can be analytically formulated and an algorithm developed to demonstrate that diversification helps reduce the risk in a portfolio.

A mean variance efficient portfolio is said to be one that cannot be outperformed by another portfolio in both risk and return. This leads to the concept of the efficient combinations of two or more assets and their positive or negative correlation. There is plenty of opportunity for algorithmic expressions—and therefore for simulation.

17

Strategic Decisions in Technology for Greater Professional Clout

1. Introduction

Chapters 13 through 16 have explained the organizational and policy prerequisites underpinning an analytical approach, the thinking that goes into the development of a financial model, and the structure such a model could assume. They also made evident the need for algorithms and heuristics as well as for steady improvement of the artifacts we develop.

Once a risk-management model is successfully developed and implemented and experience is gained with it, the users ask for greater functionality. But the developers should also understand it is their duty to steadily improve upon their construct(s), in appreciation of the fact that models for the management of exposure have become a competitive weapon and that the market and the regulators depend on models because of the mounting amount of risk.

The state of the art in mathematical simulation as well as in the development of expert systems advances all the time. Competitors do more, and do it better, than they did before, and *we* have to move ahead in order to hold our own. But steady development requires

❑   Strategic decisions.

❑   The proper state of mind.

❑   Significant skill.

❑   The right infrastructure.

Therefore, implicitly if not explicitly, throughout our discussion on the use of mathematics with derivative financial products, and more generally in all branches of finance, several references have been made to the technological infrastructure necessary to effectively support the risk-control effort.

The sense of strategic decisions regarding the implementation of advanced technology is that unless top management sorts out its priorities and sets in motion a real-time financial analysis engine, nothing will really be done. Though many people know they need to come up with the best analytical solutions in order to remain competitive, there are a thousand excuses for inertia in prototyping financial and managerial problems and for upgrading one's own skills.

We have also spoken about technological illiteracy, as well as illiteracy in regard to the fast-evolving new financial vehicles. The steady development of human resources is the best way to break both illiteracy and inertia. Therefore, lifelong learning is a strategic priority.

2.   High Technology and Lifelong Learning

The making and use of mathematical models for derivatives risk management requires a significant amount of skill in the new technologies, not just in mathematics. The same is true of their use. No advanced solutions can be successful without the users being literate in computers and in analytical methods. Lifelong learning is necessary both for developers and for users. The users are the managers and professionals for whom the financial models are made.

The wheel of lifelong learning is difficult to start—and to stop. Those who know how it works appreciate that the theory of learning is at the heart of management and most particularly the *management of change*—which has become the number one issue in the survival of a financial institution.

Since we know that change comes, we should not waste effort protecting our turf and our past position. We should not hang on to past connections, nor should we spin our wheels in the vacuum by fighting the inevitable. There is a dual role in experimentation through computer-based mathematical models:

1.   Opening up research horizons and thus *learning how to learn*.

2.   Studying *the effects of change* before they happen so that we can prepare for them.

Leading-edge financial organizations appreciate that in the 1990s and beyond, understanding change is synonymous with survival. They also have enough experience to see that change is discontinuous. The new concepts that prevail, and the new structures coming into being, are in no way something which is slightly different or a little better than what it was in the past. Change can be—and often is—the negation of what we knew and what we did in the past. The process of change can even see to it that past patterns are turned upside down.

Therefore, learning how to study the financial world of the coming years, how to identify our own opportunities in this world, and how to control our exposure are some of the most critical tasks managers and professionals are faced with. Advanced financial analysis must be seen in this perspective.

We have to learn a great deal about the tools that both we and our competitors are and will be using. Artificial intelligence (AI) is one of them. An executive of Texas Instruments, one of the leaders in its implementation, said, "We don't talk about AI in our lab. We talk about modern computer science versus classical computer science."

People who have failed in their duty of lifelong learning see modern computer science and its analytical infrastructure as their enemy. With the advent of real-time simulation and practical knowledge engineering, classical data-processing executives and their computer "specialists" became concerned that they might be replaced through expert systems. But it is now clear that these "professionals" will not be replaced by knowledge artifacts, but by colleagues who know how to capitalize on the new technologies to achieve their bank's future success.

From the software developer's point of view, the most important single idea coming out of research in prototyping, simulation, and knowledge engineering is not a computer program per se, but *a new approach* to programming in general. As the processing requirements of the financial industry grow in sophistication, a steady development of our tools is certainly needed in order to stay in the business game.

It takes lifelong learning to appreciate that the tools we use become obsolete, and so do the methods. Seen in this way, and given that the user requirements continue to grow, centralized software development has long been a bottleneck. With conventional software engineering, it simply costs too much and takes too long to get the programs written and debugged.

This is especially true when it comes to projects in derivatives where development time should be counted in *hours* or *days*, not years. All the Wall Street firms that participated in the research that led to this book emphasized this fact.

Rapid development of software can easily be achieved when we establish a grand design and then analyze our problem module-by-module, putting each module to work as fast as it is written and tested. Figure 17–1 presents an example from a practical application in computer-supported financial analysis. The input parameters, the processing routines, and the required interactive output frames are modular.

By contrast, conventional software development tends to attack massive problems, and the thrust is to get all of the algorithms in place to guarantee a complete answer. So developers spend a year trying to nail down the detailed specifications for the problem, generating reams of paper and often producing a dead duck.

Bankers and treasurers will be well advised to learn that this is not automation, but the negation of it—even if it is done through computers. Besides, with that old and ossified approach, a seemingly simple alteration in the specifications can force a wholesale revision of the programming code, which leads to a whole new round of misconceptions, delays, and costs.

Few banks have the experience to appreciate the fundamental sense of these concepts and the fact that high technology and lifelong learning are inseparable. The number one advantage in finance, business, and industry can be found in the human mind. "The new empires are the empires of the mind," Winston Churchill said. Technology is necessary to assure that the assets represented by our knowledge get upgraded.

3.   Choosing What to Know Is an Act of Intelligence

The deeper reason for financial analysis—and most particularly for advanced analytical solutions—is competitiveness. Leadership in this domain, as outlined in Chapters 13 through 16, leads to a process that permits us to choose what to know. This is true all the way from the study of financial statements and of high-frequency market data to the way we program our computer, access our databases, and interact with the network.

What makes the knowledge engineering style of programming so different is the philosophy, which evolved out of years of experience, about what the software is really supposed to do. The goals are no longer the same as those of the 1950s and 1960s. But it takes lifelong learning to appreciate the change in values.

The most competitive goal now is to write programs that can cope with a financial world that finds itself in the middle of rapid change and to develop systems able to handle situations that cannot be predicted ahead of time, yet are sure to be found down the line. What we are talking about here is the foundation of the definition of *intelligence*. The practical implementation of such a concept is that instead of telling the computer precisely what to do at every point, as in a conventional pro-

Figure 17–1. A Comparison Scenario Through Computer-Supported Financial Analysis

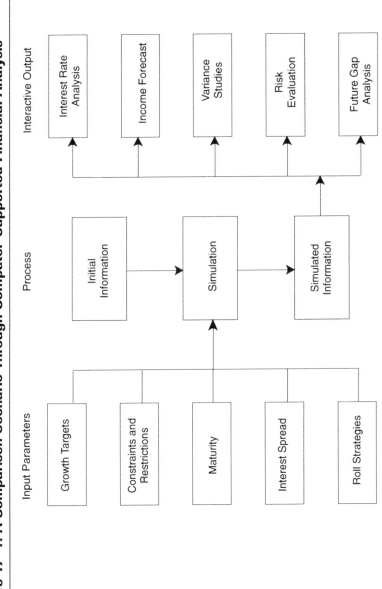

gram, the modern, efficiency-oriented approach tells the machine what to know.

In this simple statement can be found the roots of the development work now done with *agents,* the knowledge artifacts that will revolutionize financial vehicles, not just computer science. With agents, the computer uses embedded knowledge to reason about what to do, as new situations arise or past issues repeat themselves under different conditions.

Much of the advanced research going into AI artifacts, as well as financial modeling at large, revolves around how one actually represents the knowledge in a form the computer understands and processes. What to know is vital both to people and to intelligent machines. But it takes both learning and experience to sort things out and to choose.

Therefore, the foremost contribution of financial models is to promote the use of analytical thinking and provide the means for competitiveness. This also explains why it is practically impossible to dissociate learning from research.

It is not enough to be a nice fellow or to have good political connections in the bank. The chief information officer of the financial institution and his or her assistants must also strike a balance between

❑   Keeping an open mind to unorthodox arguments, because that's where future competitiveness and profits come from.

❑   Following well-established, sound policies that steadily improve the assistance provided to the bank's top professionals.

As cannot be repeated too often, competitiveness in banking and in any other business lies in moving ahead, not in hanging on to old connections. From financial products to software modules, what is already known and established is offered as a commodity. This happened with spreadsheets and other packages, and it continues to happen in new ways.

Software companies are aggressively entering into banking, but they offer commodities on which the financial institution should add value. There is no competitive advantage without value differentiation.

Capitalizing on networking experience, Microsoft might be offering everything from mutual funds to brokerage over its system, even without Intuit. There is a lot at stake in this world of *electronic commerce.* The companies that own the transaction infrastructure will be able to charge a fee, much as banks do today with their services. As a practice, this is very lucrative, since transaction-processing services now account for as much as 20–25 percent of noninterest income for banks.

If banks lose out in the development of new financial products (and their associated software) and fail to control the fast-moving networked solutions, they will end by paying for a service that they derive a good chunk of their income from. All this because of the inertia of their obsolete computer professionals, who can best be described by Winston Churchill's statement about Clement Attlee: "A modest man with much to be modest about."

4. The Pillars of Advanced Solutions Are Research and Learning

Lifelong learning can be instrumental in teaching people to *know what they want*. Simply saying *profit* is not good enough. Financial professionals and systems experts alike must learn how to set realistically ambitious targets—and how to experiment with means for reaching them.

Just as important as learning how to analyze each situation is developing and elaborating a list of factors influencing our own know-how and productivity. This is the sense of *learning how to learn*. Critical to this mission is the knowledge of how to best exploit the outcome of experimentation.

Section 3 made the point that it is practically impossible to dissociate learning from research. Not only do both constitute the pillars of advanced solutions in modern finance, but they are also interrelated: One helps promote the other. This statement is valid in a large spectrum of operations revolving around a kernel of competitiveness, from the acquisition of new knowledge and its fruitful implementation, to learning how to work with new tools—such as analytical models and computers.

The learned user should be free to add to or remove from the model elements he had previously contributed. But he must also be skilled in doing so without disruptive effects and without always depending on central resources for assistance.

A senior executive of the Dai-Ichi Kangyo Bank said in a recent meeting in Tokyo that, following the terminalization of practically everyone in the organization, the demand for new software development now amounts to 70,000 man-years. This is evidently unsustainable, and so Dai-Ichi is actively developing user-friendly computer languages profession-by-profession and seeks to enable the end users to satisfy their own programming requirements.

U.S. banks in New York have already moved in the direction of a layered structure in information technology, and have done so very successfully. The trend among tier-one financial institutions is to bring analysis and programming practically at desk level through rocket scientists and the appropriate training of traders and other professionals. This permits the integration of research, analysis, and learning where it counts, at the front desk, and the development of intelligence-enriched software in a few hours for simple programs and in a few days for complex programs.

This tremendously enhances competitiveness because it dramatically shortens time to market. It also sees to it that ingenious technical solutions make it feasible to integrate a number of facilities in a flexible and meaningful sense; for instance, to produce ad hoc graphics that represent movements of the market and expected changes in price levels as required at that very moment, not as might have been needed three years ago. Many visualization structures should be ephemeral, responding to the needs at hand. Managers and professionals must be provided with the appropriate road map for reaching further out into computer-integrated resources.

Part and parcel of software development, as well as of the training program, should be the appreciation of the fact that in a fast-moving financial environment interactive experimentation and rapid response are two of the best forms of lifelong learning. Experimentation leads to reframing of ideas and opinions, not only of data and trends. Reframing provides the ability to see concepts, situations, problems, and people, in a new way.

By using practical examples, research, development, and lifelong learning should instill the notion (as well as explain) why real-time simulators and expert systems help the professional. The domain expert whose knowledge is replicated through expert systems has been, in principle, a star performer in his line of business—whether in derivatives or anywhere else.

We must increasingly think of systems as something into which the ability to learn is integrated. This is done through the language of modeling, which is in essence a programming tool. What is essential is that the end user's training makes it easy to employ the facilities at his or her disposal. With the appropriate control language, models can be put together to prompt user input and then offer menus of options. An inexperienced user can be made more productive by means of icons, menus, and help screens.

These features of modeling software are especially helpful in end-user computing. Unless they themselves developed the artifact they employ, the users of financial models do not necessarily need to know how the construct works. What they need to know is what to put into it and what to get out. This is the so-called *black-box* approach.

As learning tools and as experimental structures, modeling languages—for instance visual programming—lend themselves well to personal computing environments. It is, however, essential that the user appreciates the basic fact that modeling does not offer crystal ball glimpses into the future. The role of modeling is to

❑ Permit a valid analysis of past events.

- ❏ Provide the possibility of making a prognosis.

- ❏ Encourage creative study of facts and figures.

Mathematical modeling is a language. The language we use forms our mind. When our language changes, behavior will not be far behind. This, too, is a concept that managers and professionals need to understand and appreciate, a goal that can be accomplished through lifelong learning.

5. Strategic Issues in Prototyping Managerial Problems

In an organizational sense, managerial-type problems may be a more difficult lot to handle than those of a strictly financial nature. The reason is that they are often poorly structured, involve a number of unknown parameters, and their successful solution relies to a large extent on an unclear structure of checks and balances.

From the simpler to the more complex cases, planning in the managerial domain brings up issues with characteristics involving more qualitative than quantitative aspects. These characteristics can be classified into four main categories, which are shown in a layered fashion in Figure 17–2, from the bottom up:

1. The simplest category is one for rather deterministic, well-structured, more operational types of problems.

2. The next category comprises stochastic models, involving probabilities, unknowns, and interdependencies—mainly of a quantitative nature.

3. More complex are possibilistic cases, which are qualitative, and where vagueness and uncertainty dominate.

4. Still tougher are political and organizational issues, requiring the understanding of behavior and the analysis of evolving patterns.

No single algorithmic approach or programming language can effectively address all of these problems. Those involving interpersonal interactions call for conflict resolution and complex negotiations and, therefore, for leadership that cannot be modeled.

The notion of *programming in the large* was explained in Chapter 16. Figure 17–2 offers a practical implementation example. The problems presented in class number 4 are political, and their possible solution lies in complex interpersonal communications. The issues involved are characteristic of an unstructured information environment; therefore, modeling is not of major assistance.

Figure 17–2. Managerial Problems Range from Simple to Complex and Can Be Classified into Four Categories

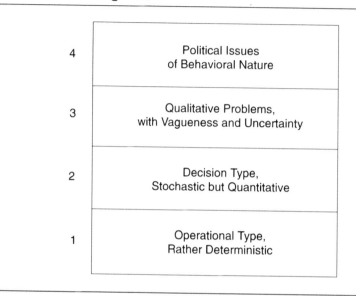

4	Political Issues of Behavioral Nature
3	Qualitative Problems, with Vagueness and Uncertainty
2	Decision Type, Stochastic but Quantitative
1	Operational Type, Rather Deterministic

Number 3 is rho characterized by a program in the large approach but it requires quantitative and qualitative methods for which the tools of fuzzy engineering exist, and they can be successfully applied. We have often spoken about this issue. Purely quantitative models have little to do with this class, though they may be of assistance.

Decision support systems (DSS) of the spreadsheet type, simulators for allocation and optimization, genetic algorithms, and rule-type expert systems make up layer number 2. Other tools are linear programming, plan versus actual evaluations, and other models addressing ratio analysis, as well as other acid tests.

Layers number two and number one are settled and their methods change very slowly. They also need a more detailed approach than that characterizing layers number three and number four. Therefore, they constitute good examples of *programming in the small* scenarios—to which reference has already been made in Chapter 16.

Layer number one represents a structured information environment and greatly contrasts to the top layer. It makes significant use of quantitative methods and models, getting commendable results out of them, but it addresses only those information environments that are well structured.

All quantitative approaches as well as qualitative solutions can be well served through *rapid prototyping*. The steps in the development of a model must be mapped into the computer in an interactive manner, permitting the domain expert to make an assessment on-line. How to use rapid prototyping methods and tools is one of the basic skills to be developed through lifelong learning. Many professionals in the financial industry have been prototyping part of their work with paper and pencil, perhaps without knowing what a prototype is. Competitiveness now requires that this job be done by means of interactive computer processing. Technology puts the necessary development tools at the disposal of managers and professionals.

The effective use of prototyping is much more important in today's finance and other sectors of industry, as many information management problems require tailor-made solutions that integrate the ability to

❑ Access the contents of large, diverse, and mostly heterogeneous databases.

❑ Extend the application to multimedia, with compound electronic document handling.

Prerequisites to state-of-the-art performance are the effective use of intelligent networks, distributed databases, and interactive workstations using three-dimensional graphics. Real-time visualization is important. The system must not only be at the user's disposition each minute but also assist the user in a user-friendly manner.

All this presents a number of challenges with which only advanced systems solutions can cope. Rules about the interrelationships among databases as well as user behavior can be developed that greatly simplify systems usage. They should also be instrumental in accelerating the data retrieval, screening, and display processes, even within heterogeneous environments. Let's always recall that heterogeneity increasingly dominates the implementation of information technology.[1]

6. The Need for Polyvalent Database Support

Different types of data are required as input to the financial models we have developed. Both users and knowledge engineers should understand that writing an expert system is far from being the most difficult part of interactive analytical finance. This honor belongs to the sophisticated, intelligent information network every competitive bank has to develop. Means must be provided for

---

1 See also the intelligent database assistant (IDA) in D. N. Chorafas, *Risk Management in Financial Institutions* (London: Butterworths, 1990); and D. N. Chorafas and H. Steinmann, *Solutions for Networked Databases* (San Diego: Academic Press, 1993).

❑ Accessing increasingly rich but heterogeneous databases in a seamless manner.

❑ Exploiting their contents through very flexible *database mining* operations.

New techniques to exploit large databases as well as to control information flows are required to match financial models with the available information resources. Review of successful projects in this field suggests that a significant step would be to individualize and automate information selection through intentional database approaches.[2]

This strategy is more important with derivatives because of the competitiveness and the complexity of new financial products. The goal of an integrative solution should be to allow each user to consistently obtain information that is both relevant and timely with regard to individual processing characteristics and requirements. Adaptive models knowing the profile of every one of their users must be actively employed. These are the agents able to evaluate critical functions of information selection and control.

The information elements coming to the database must be kept as raw data, using real-time computation for massaging and reporting. Such information elements must be accessible to all authorized personnel and should be provided with the means for seamless database access.

Any serious systems study will pay attention to the fact that the information requirements of end users can change. Flexibility is the key word, and it has to be built into the system, all the way from database architecture to the user's workstation.

One of the strategic prerequisites to business competitiveness is the development of a network of intelligent distributed databases with a seamless cross-database access. It should also be appreciated that in financial analysis, the model typically accounts for 20 percent of the solution. The other 80 percent is contributed by the information elements in our databases.

Contrarians would say that database mining solutions with seamless on-line access are not that simple. This is because of mismanagement that went on for years with databased information—as well as the lack of skill in database mining.[3]

---

[2] See also D. N. Chorafas, *Intelligent Multimedia Databases* (Englewood Cliffs, NJ: Prentice Hall, 1994).

[3] See also D. N. Chorafas and H. Steinmann, *Database Mining. Exploiting Marketing Databases in the Financial Industry* (London and Dublin: Lafferty, 1994).

Figure 17–3. Classically Split and Heterogenous Databases

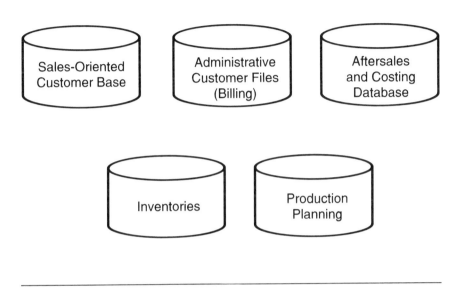

It is estimated that between 65 and 75 percent of corporate data held in computers is still in traditional, nonrelational, mainframe systems. Many of them are implemented on different platforms and serve distinct, unrelated, or loosely related parts of the company.

Figure 17–3 is based on the findings of a study I conducted not long ago with an industrial corporation, and it helps to explain the sense of database heterogeneity. It represents the traditional irrational split of vital company information into heterogeneous platforms that cannot easily be integrated. The figure shows five heterogeneous database platforms that should simultaneously be assessed by executive workstations to provide integrative reports.

This is not a worst-case scenario. In a study I conducted in three continents among money center banks, it was possible to identify between 15 and 25 heterogeneous databases that were used for operational reasons as well as for planning and control. Yet, every practitioner knows that the persistence of heterogeneity severely handicaps management planning and control operations.

Asset and liability management provides an example of why a financial institution must assure seamless database integration. At the beginning of the planning horizon, the bank's initial balance sheet must be categorized in detail with respect to type and maturity of assets and liabilities.

In theory, this presents no difficulty. In practice, however, it requires a collection of data that, as the preceding paragraphs have shown, is not routinely accessible. Not only must the bank's ordinary database operations be enriched, but the available databases must be made *virtually* homogeneous for real-time exploitation—which poses problems.

At the same time, interoperability between legacy systems and new applications is important because no bank can afford the resources that would be needed to abandon overnight existing setups and move everything immediately to a new environment. Efficient developments can be and should be undertaken using modern platforms and tools, and selected legacy applications must start to migrate to client-server environments with fully distributed resources.[4]

Migration requires skill, and it has to be accomplished over a chosen time frame. In the meantime, major financial institutions have few options other than to keep the majority of legacy systems providing for a virtual database integration, which should be done in a careful, well-planned manner.

The value of new and efficient solutions is increased when it unlocks legacy information resources and makes them available. Achieving the integration of client-server and legacy systems is an important task. There is a host of products on the market that claim to provide solutions, but selecting the right approach and the right tools involves both ingenuity and proper study.

Prudence in the transition to a client-server environment should not be seen as inertia, nor as a sign that old, inefficient database management systems such as DB2 and naive protocols such as 3270 or LU 6.2 should be kept in the circuit. Change is absolutely necessary, but it must be executed after proper planning and implemented through a rapid timetable without providing discontinuities and interruptions.

7.   Capitalizing on Hard Data and Soft Data

The argument is often being made, particularly among low-technology banks, that new developments will eventually see the light, as the data processors know their business. But cutting-edge financial institutions know that this is the wrong appreciation of the situation because it overlooks two basic facts:

1.   In the derivatives business, data is very dynamic, and the customers are sophisticated. No bank can afford to lose time.

---

[4] See also D. N. Chorafas, *Beyond LANs—Client-Server Computing* (New York: McGraw-Hill, 1994).

2. With their paleolithic concepts and tools, mainframe data processors don't know how to do the job that needs to be done in the first place.

One of the key reasons why so many chief information officers have fallen out of favor with their management, and some have lost their jobs, is precisely that they have no inkling of how to provide polyvalent support to traders and investors that capitalizes on new technology.

Inflexible people, naive protocols, substandard languages, and ossified databases go together. Typically, computer people who have lost their professionalism cocoon themselves into a mainframe database structure and forget about what the end user needs. Yet, the *product is for the consumer*, not just for the pleasure of its creator.

The new technology that advanced financial institutions are now implementing has many aspects that escape the classical data processors' attention because they are *nontraditional*. If we wish to put in a nutshell the different issues that the evolving branches of information science have in common, we must say that:

❏ The focal point of interest is *data-sharing*,

❏ As contrasted to the traditional *time-sharing*.

Time-sharing characterized computers, communications, and software for over 30 years. Its need rested on the fact that processor power was expensive. With one processor per mainframe, there were relatively few available processing cycles, and one process had to steal cycles from the other.

To a great extent, and for curious reasons, people of the old, mainframe-based mentality are unwilling or unable to understand that times have changed and obsolete concepts can be destructive. In an epoch of new financial products, rapid market evolution, and tremendous microprocessor power at minimal cost, it is silly to time-share one single processor no matter how powerful it may be. But we have to data-share our information resources among all users. Otherwise, we spoil our business opportunities, and we take inordinate risks.

In the asset-management case we saw in section 6, forecasts of future interest rates over the planning horizon offer a good example of required sharing of *input data*. Interest rate forecasts must be made for the various types and maturities of assets. Such predictions enter the model both

❏ *Directly*, as projected revenue inflows and expense outflows, and

❏ *Indirectly*, as the major determinant of capital gain and loss factors.

There are at least two ways of forecasting interest rates: One is based on subjective judgments on the part of management or designated experts; the other is based on the utilization of modeling techniques, along the lines we have discussed in Chapters 13 through 16.

Prognosis can be done through genetic algorithms and other microeconomic models. If we accept the validity of either the expectations hypothesis or the liquidity preference theory, the term structure of interest rates presently observed in the market can be used as a prognosis of future yield curves. Some financial institutions employ learning genetic algorithms for this purpose.

The message underlying these paragraphs is that in the financial industry we are increasingly handling two broad classes of information elements that reside in distributed databases and need to be shared:

1. *Hard data*, based on past values, historical facts, and statistics on the distribution of values that have already occurred.

2. *Soft data*, essentially projections, evaluations, and forecasts reflecting what we expect to happen, which are therefore sure to show deviations when the real-life values become available.

No financial analyst can work without soft data. The inputs to an assets and liabilities management model are forecasts of future loan demand, future interest rates, and other projections that have to be factored into the banker's decision model. Similar examples can be taken with derivative financial instruments.

Quite often, the natural tendency of the banking community is to conceive loan demand in terms of *stocks* rather than *flows*. In order to convert this stock-oriented thinking into the relevant flow form, it is necessary to understand the nature of the underlying market dynamics. This, too, leads to soft data.

An understanding of market dynamics cannot be obtained from information normally available through traditional sources, with low-frequency inputs and batch-type computations. Nontraditional financial research is necessary, and the same is true of real-time response. With mortgage-backed securities, for instance, projections must be done regarding the rates at which new house loans will be made, and existing loans will be repaid.

The forecasts of future loan demand that are used as input to a financial model should incorporate the implicit assumption that the bank's performance, in a given planning horizon, will exert a certain effect upon its market share.

Allowance for this market share should be altered by the loan-related feedback mechanisms. Other allowances should have been reflected in the model's constraints. This, too, is an issue that can be taught and appreciated through the proper lifelong learning mechanism.

Quite similar references are applicable to off-balance-sheet financing. Projections tend to assume forthcoming demand for new financial instruments as well as customization requirements. In fact, *derivative financial* products need a much higher level of technology than the loans examples we just saw.

8. Queries, Transaction, and Technical Prerequisites

One of the strategic decisions that needs to be reached by top management concerns ways and means for adopting new technology for rapid software development. Plenty of examples help document that this can have positive consequences in derivatives trading, but it requires supportive structures such as the interactive handling of queries.

Query processes supported by agents, or at least by rule-based expert systems, will be expected to perform a number of tasks that should be transparent to the banker, the trader, and the investor:

❑ One agent can open the log file and create appropriate user registration, whether the "user" is a person, program, or another database.

❑ Another agent may receive and immediately execute query requests, as well as security requests, from end user and dispatcher processes.

❑ Still another agent may initialize operations by accessing remote files, loading to local memory in a way that is secure but transparent to the user.

Knowledge robots can be instrumental in determining networked query process(es) that might be queuing up, evaluating their priorities, and executing them. In the past, these operations have been largely manual and must be automated.

Acting as dispatchers, database-oriented expert systems must initiate update processes through message passing. They should also keep a log and consult a data dictionary on the identification of every query process or update message, guaranteeing established security clauses.

To face high transaction rate requirements, other knowledge artifacts should support real-time capture and storage of multiple data feeds. A high database bandwidth network would feature significant data throughput and should provide polyvalent applications links.

Agents residing at the nodes of the bank's network should see to it that transaction handling in a distributed database environment preserves referential integrity at all times. Artifacts must be in place to guarantee

❏   Active data transfers.

❏   Remote procedure calls.

❏   Appropriate database locks.

❏   Two-phase commit operations.

❏   The avoidance of deadlocks.

Effective solutions to distributed database management should feature full-function query capability on all standard data types and structures. It must incorporate either an extended relational or an
object-oriented data model. Such solutions should include user-defined
abstract data types.

While these issues are technical, the establishment of the appropriate policies is not. It is a matter of top management decision, as is the
policy to utilize the parallelism embedded in client-server architectures.[5]
Management policy should indicate that systems solutions must include

❏   Efficient database-to-database communications.

❏   Sophisticated message exchange.

❏   A dynamic, real-time query execution.

As an example of dynamic query execution, Figure 17–4 shows an
application instituted by a leading bank for merits and demerits—which
means rewards and penalties—in connection to customer orders. Notice
how fully distributed on-line inputs and interactive outputs correlate
with one another. They should therefore be handled in a virtually homogeneous environment even if the databases themselves are heterogeneous.

Database solutions must be *fault-tolerant* and function well in demanding implementation environments. Backup, restore, and archival
functions—as well as commit, rollback, and integrity assurance—must
not only be present but also well developed. The same is true of advanced user interfaces.

All this is a far cry from the way databases were viewed until
quite recently. This change is no accidental development, but rather a
deeply rooted one, as financial analysis is moving away from traditional
mainframe toward networks of workstations and distributed file servers—also networked disk farms and high-performance computers,
which can handle jobs that are too cycle demanding for a workstation.

Architectural solutions worked out today must be able to fit this
new perspective and remain valid for some years. In an era when finan-

---

[5] See also D. N. Chorafas, *Beyond LANs—Client-Server Computing* (New York:
McGraw-Hill, 1994).

Figure 17–4. Objective Applications of Merits and Demerits Require a System Solution with the Financial Database at the Hub

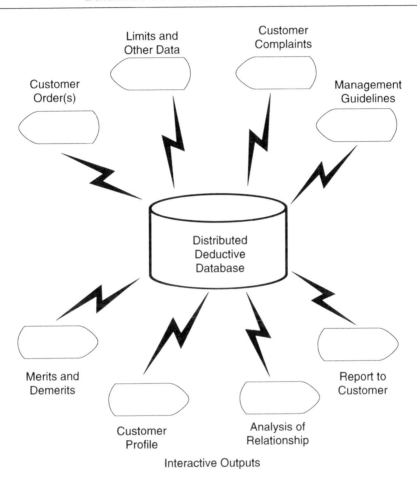

Interactive Outputs

cial leadership is largely influenced by intelligent networks and super-computer power, it is difficult for investment banks and commercial banks not to listen. Leading-edge users have discovered that competitive advantages are synonymous with new systems departures. This is true all the way from financial modeling to database structures.

The challenge starts with problem formulation made to fit developing requirements. The packaging of mortgage-backed securities, for instance, requires intense number crunching and has become a popular application for supercomputers on Wall Street. This in turn poses database challenges, ranging from structural issues to filtering and state selection operations.

Differences from past approaches include conceptual retrieve mechanisms (idea databases); new, flexible data structures; real-time updating and retrieval; time stamps; range scanning; the management of ad hoc requests; and dynamically maintained definitions. The latter are needed because of the demands posed by the system's most sophisticated users.

9.   Rethinking the Nature of Technological Support

Sections 6, 7, and 8 have demonstrated that both the content of and the way to manage financial databases have evolved tremendously over the years. Today there are many types of inputs and outputs that did not exist previously—some from transactions, others from models—which we can exploit. The effective use of our information resources will affect availability of funds, capital requirements, derivatives trades, risks, and profits.

In the process of revamping, restructuring, and rationalizing our technology, account should be taken not only of new media but also of omissions and gaps in the present system. *Nonevents* leave just as significant a footprint on the bank's performance as major events, but they are invisible to the untrained eye.[6] Nonevents are particularly important when the model's decision variables rest on some activities that have to take place or else, or, when the areas being left out of the model influence the capital and funds available in a significant way.

When certain critical events don't happen, economic considerations tend to indicate that either our assumptions are wrong or market behavior has changed. A valid system will include elements sensitive enough to capture such happenings.

We can protect our artifact from effects due to changed market behavior through cross-referencing. Typically, various types of input data are interdependent—in a way similar to the one we saw in Figure 17–4 in connection to outputs. Therefore, covariabilities inherent in economic factors and in the instruments themselves must be realistically embedded in the model to produce sensible results.[7]

Other refinements can also be made, such as having the input data seasonally adjusted or accounting for the effects of exogenous variables. To the extent that there are recurrent seasonal patterns, they should be

---

[6] For a discussion on nonevents, see D. N. Chorafas and H. Steinmann, *Database Mining, Exploiting Marketing Databases in the Financial Industry* (London and Dublin: Lafferty, 1994).

[7] See also the discussion at the end of Chapter 16 on correlation coefficient.

utilized in forecasting as well as in establishing constraints for control reasons.

Accounting for nonevents and reflecting seasonal patterns is simplified by the fact that professionals and managers are growing used to personal computers and databases. A computer-literate company controller, for instance, can build his own system on his workstation, get database access, and have a program up and running in a couple of hours. These professionals now want more.

What end users are increasingly demanding is the *full capacity* that high technology can offer and the *low costs* that come along with it as opposed to the trivialities of low technology. They want both results from advanced technology solutions and the same kind of flexibility and speed they are accustomed to getting from the stand-alone PC on their desk.

When a senior bank executive goes to data processing and expects instantaneous answers, it is useless for the DP manager to say, "Fine, but that will take at least a year, and it will cost $200,000." Yet, that is exactly the response the ossified data processors give to senior executives and other professionals, an answer that lacks business sense and deprives the end user of the tools he or she needs to remain competitive.

Financial software that does not follow a *knowledge-intense* course with object orientation is indeed out of contact with competitive business practices. In the future, nobody is going to accept noninteractive systems, and interactive systems have to have the outlined requirements. The same is true of multimedia solutions.

Still another of the prerequisites to the successful development of financial systems is attention to security—all the way from encryption of the lines in which this information travels to database encryption. Data encryption should be a policy in all locations of the distributed database structure.

As a matter of policy, security assurance requirements must include physical standards, multiple encipherment algorithms, and user-oriented security features to preclude unauthorized data flows. There should also be contextual reviews of database information in an auditing sense.

10. Conclusion

The use of derivative financial instruments places an extra burden on both front desks and back offices. Since the value of options is sensitive to a variety of market factors, such as underlying price, perceived volatility, interest rates, and the remaining life of the asset, a reliable real-time derivatives system is an essential part of the risk-control process.

By using high technology, it is both feasible and cost-effective to design and implement real-time risk management for OBS transactions, the trading book, and the portfolio. For instance, through a combination of a commercial real-time price feed and proprietary software, Lazard Investors has developed an in-house solution that tracks the exposure of portfolios of multicurrency derivatives on a real-time basis.[8]

Low technology such as that used today by a surprisingly large number of banks, to their misfortune and to the detriment of their customers, is just as lethal as inexperience in off-balance-sheet trades. Illiteracy in the intricate aspects of derivatives makes the front desk both dangerous and ineffectual. With low technology, the back office work is done in a manner that is costly, tedious, and difficult to control.

A bank is served precious little by statements made by some board members or even CEOs that their data processors must be doubly careful because the board has no experts in information technology. This is like giving carte blanche to the unable, who is being asked by the unwilling to do the unnecessary.

Derivatives risk management requires *deep knowledge* not only in financial trading, but also in new product development and the analysis of market behavior. The ability to use avant-garde technology is crucial to risk management—but by far the number one factor is *moral authority*. Similarly, amoral or immoral actions, obsolete systems make the control of derivative trades a daunting task. This can be said in conclusion:

❑ Low technology not only has high costs, but it is also incapable of tracking the movement of, say, variation margin on an hourly basis or tick-by-tick.

❑ High technology and the combination of a good cash flow system plus the synergy of local and global risk management can offer significant results in management visibility.

The systems solution we provide must reach all the way from deal capture to on-line database access, risk management, and settlement. This helps to make the administration of derivative accounts more effective, while also improving efficiency in a market more competitive than ever.

It is the responsibility of the board, the chief executive officer, and his or her immediate assistants not only to set a policy of change, but also to oversee its effective execution. And they have to be tough. It would be wise for the members of the board and the CEO to heed the advice of an Athenian senator in Shakespeare's *Timon of Athens*: "Nothing emboldens sin so much as mercy."

---

[8] International Bond Investor, *Euromoney*, London, January 1994.

Index